STEVEN GOLDSMITH

A Most Improper End

Marvellous Melbourne Murders - Book One

First edition

ISBN (paperback): 978-1-7642439-1-9
ISBN (hardcover): 978-1-7642439-2-6

This book was professionally typeset on Reedsy.
Find out more at reedsy.com

*To Mum and Dad – Thankfully, our gatherings involve less mystery!
With love and immense appreciation.*

Things are not always what they seem;
the first appearance deceives many.

- PHAEDRUS

Contents

Acknowledgments

First, my thanks to tea and biscuits, without which this book would have ended halfway through chapter four with a detective asleep on the chaise lounge. Caffeine and sugar are the true unsung heroes of literature.

To my family and friends: thank you for tolerating endless conversations about poison, Victorian gossip, and whether one can strangle a man politely. Your ability to nod and smile at the right moments deserves a medal.

To my proof readers: you have the patience of saints and the red pen of a surgeon. Thank you for pointing out that a corpse cannot attend afternoon tea twice in the same chapter-though I maintain it would have been a memorable plot twist.

To my critics-past, present, and inevitable-I offer a most improper toast. You keep me humble, sharp, and occasionally murderous (on the page, of course).

And finally, to you, dear reader. You could have been doing something respectable-gardening, dusting, or joining a croquet club-but instead you chose to tumble into murder, mischief, and Melbourne society with me. Should you be shocked, appalled, or faintly scandalised, remember: you were warned.

The end was always going to be *most improper.*

Prologue

The late spring Melbourne sun, already possessing a deceptive warmth for ten o'clock, cast long, sharp shadows across the immaculate lawns of the Toorak Croquet & Horticultural Society. Bartholomew Ainsworth stood near the edge of Lawn 1, hands clasped behind his back, surveying the scene. Perfection. Or, at least, the closest approximation achievable given the lamentable inadequacies of human effort. The grass, a precise blend of fescue and bentgrass, was cut to an exacting five millimetres – he'd measured it himself yesterday after young Barnaby's mowing. The hoops, gleaming white iron, were set at regulation width, though he'd need to double-check Number 3 hoop later; Smythe had been complaining about it again, the buffoon.

From here, one could almost forget the city sprawling just beyond the high, ivy-clad brick walls. The gentle *thwack* of mallet against ball, the distant murmur of polite, inconsequential chatter from the clubhouse verandah, the scent of roses mingling with freshly cut grass – it conspired to create an illusion of timeless, ordered tranquillity. An illusion Bartholomew had dedicated a significant portion of his retirement to maintaining, despite the constant frustrations posed by the Society's membership.

There, for instance, was Lord Harrington Smythe – 'Harry' to those who inexplicably tolerated his boorish familiarity – already gesturing emphatically near the aforementioned Number 3 hoop. His voice, carrying easily across the lawn, was raised in familiar indignation. Probably disputing a point of obscure etiquette no one else remembered, or cared about. Smythe, with his flashy blazers and inherited title, represented the kind of casual entitlement Bartholomew despised. All noise, no substance, and perpetually convinced of his own importance. Predictable.

And bustling near the tea pavilion, a floral print darting between tables, was Mildred Pettle, the Club Secretary. Efficient, certainly, in her own unobtrusive way. Always organising, always placating, always… there. Too eager to please, Bartholomew thought with faint distaste. A necessary cog in the machine, perhaps, but utterly lacking in vision or authority. He'd barely given her a second thought until recently. An oversight, he now knew, of monumental proportions.

He adjusted the set of his tie, the knot precise, the silk uncreased. A small, smug smile touched his lips, quickly suppressed. Soon, very soon, the carefully curated order of this little world would be disrupted. And it would be entirely thanks to him.

He turned and walked towards the small, slightly musty office allocated to the Treasurer, adjacent to the equipment shed. Inside, the familiar scent of old paper and furniture polish greeted him. He placed his polished briefcase on the desk and clicked it open, extracting a slim ledger and a sheaf of meticulously annotated bank statements. Here lay the proof. Not in dramatic, messy blotches of ink, but in the subtle, persistent trickle of discrepancies, expertly hidden within mundane columns of figures over years. Cash floats for garden fetes slightly rounded down. Anonymous donations slightly inflated before banking. Expenses for clubhouse refurbishment subtly padded. Each instance negligible on its own, but cumulative? Oh yes. Cumulative, substantial, and utterly damning.

He ran a finger down a column, savouring the cold, hard certainty of the numbers. It had taken him weeks of painstaking cross-referencing, fuelled initially by a vague dissatisfaction with Mrs Pettle's deferential explanations, then by a growing, thrilling suspicion. She, the mousy, helpful secretary, had been systematically bleeding the Society dry for years. The sheer, quiet audacity of it almost commanded respect. Almost.

What would she say when confronted? Would the meek facade crumble? Would there be tears? Denials? He pictured the scene with relish. He would be calm, precise, laying out the evidence piece by undeniable piece. There would be no room for obfuscation. Exposure was the only course. Not blackmail – that was messy, beneath him. No, simple, clean exposure before the Committee. Let them deal with the fallout, the embarrassment, the necessary restructuring. It would serve them right for their complacency.

He glanced at his watch. Nearly time for his mid-morning constitutional around the grounds. He carefully locked the ledger and papers back into his briefcase. From a small side pocket, he withdrew his personal thermos – gleaming stainless steel, always filled with precisely brewed Darjeeling, second flush. He poured a cup, the pale amber liquid steaming gently. Routine was essential. Quality was essential. He sipped it, the familiar warmth comforting.

Briefcase in hand, thermos safely stowed, he stepped back out into the brilliant sunshine. Perhaps he'd check the placement of the newly flowering foxgloves near Lawn 3. He suspected Chloe, the young gardener, had planted them slightly too close to the boundary line, a violation of Rule 47, subsection C. Details mattered. Standards must be upheld.

He surveyed his domain once more, the manicured lawns, the historic clubhouse, the members moving like predictable pieces on a chessboard. A wave of profound satisfaction washed over him. He, Bartholomew Ainsworth, was the guardian of this place, the one who truly understood its value, the one who would root out the hidden corruption and restore true order. He set off towards Lawn 3, entirely unaware that his meticulous schedule was about to be permanently, and most improperly, disrupted.

1

The Annual Tournament Commences

The Toorak Croquet & Horticultural Society wasn't merely a club; it was an institution, with its high brick walls like a carefully preserved Edwardian relic in the heart of modern Melbourne. On this late spring Tuesday, the opening day of the Annual Tournament, the air itself seemed to vibrate with a unique blend of manicured tranquillity and fiercely competitive tension. The Melbourne sun, already warm, promised a beautiful day for play, illuminating the impossibly green lawns and casting sharp shadows from the ancient oaks bordering the property.

From her customary wicker chair on the clubhouse verandah, Agnes Plummett surveyed the scene with the practised eye of a seasoned archivist cataloguing specimens. She observed the precise geometry of the lawns, the ordered flowerbeds Chloe Dubois tended with such quiet diligence, and the members themselves, moving across the landscape like familiar figures in a well-rehearsed play. Her gaze lingered on Mrs Weatherly adjusting a floral display – leaning slightly too far over the begonias, Agnes noted mentally, risking a Rule 14 infraction (Interference with Designated Horticultural Zones). A small notebook lay open on the table beside

5

her half-finished cup of Earl Grey, its pages already filling with her neat, precise script documenting the morning's minor triumphs and transgressions.

Down on Lawn 2, Ronald 'Rocket' Ronnie Peterson lined up a shot of improbable difficulty. His partner, a nervous young man named Cyril Postlethwaite, watched with unconcealed dismay. Ronnie, oblivious, was muttering about vectors and optimal angles of incidence, waggling his mallet as if taking complex measurements. "If I apply precisely 12.7 Newtons of force at an angle of 33 degrees relative to the longitudinal axis of the ball," he announced to the nearby hydrangeas, "allowing for the minor declination towards the southwest corner and the anticipated friction coefficient of the fescue… it *should* clear hoop five and cannon off Postlethwaite's ball into perfect position for a rover peel." He swung. The crack of mallet on ball echoed across the lawn, followed by the disheartening clunk of the ball striking the near wire of hoop four with considerable force and rebounding sideways into the petunias. Cyril sighed audibly. Ronnie frowned, already sketching frantic calculations in the small notebook he invariably carried. "Fascinating. The friction coefficient must be higher than anticipated this morning…"

Alistair Fitzwilliam sat at another verandah table, ostensibly reading the financial pages but mostly just trying to quell the familiar knot of anxiety in his stomach. He had drawn Bartholomew Ainsworth as his first-round opponent. Playing Ainsworth wasn't merely a game; it was an exercise in pedantic rule interpretation and thinly veiled condescension. Fitzwilliam took a nervous sip of his rapidly cooling coffee. He hated confrontation. He'd joined the Society hoping for gentle exercise and quiet contemplation, a refuge from the adversarial world of corporate law. Instead, he seemed to have stumbled into a different, albeit more politely attired, battlefield. He just hoped he could get through the match without

Ainsworth citing some obscure by-law he hadn't known existed.

Meanwhile, Chloe Dubois worked methodically along the border of Lawn 3, carefully deadheading the 'Peace' roses. The scent was heavenly, a sweet counterpoint to the smell of cut grass and the faint, expensive perfumes drifting from the clubhouse. She enjoyed these quiet moments of the tournament days before the main crowds arrived or after they dispersed. From her vantage point, partially screened by the large rhododendron bushes, she had an excellent view of the lawns and the members' interactions. She saw Mr. Peterson's wild shot go awry, heard the distant exasperation in young Cyril's sigh, noticed Miss Plummett making diligent notes on the verandah, and saw Mr. Fitzwilliam looking rather green around the gills. She liked the members, mostly, though their intricate social rules and unspoken rivalries often felt as complex and foreign as the botanical Latin Miss Plummett sometimes tried to teach her. Her focus was the earth, the plants, the rhythm of the seasons – things that made sense.

****

The polite murmur of the morning was abruptly punctuated by a familiar sound: the indignant, booming voice of Lord Harrington 'Harry' Smythe. He was standing near Number 3 hoop on Lawn 1, gesturing dramatically with his mallet – not the precious antique one, thankfully, but his modern playing mallet. His opponent, Bartholomew Ainsworth, stood opposite him, radiating smug composure.

"…utterly preposterous, Ainsworth!" Harry bellowed, his face already acquiring the reddish tinge that heralded a loss of temper. "The ball was clearly halfway through the hoop *before* your ball struck mine! Any fool could see that!"

Bartholomew Ainsworth adjusted his glasses, peering down his nose as if examining an unpleasant insect. "Rule 20, subsection 2, point 1, Smythe," he stated, his voice precise and carrying clearly. "Subject to Law 20.2.2, a ball completes running its hoop in order when it ceases to protrude out of the jaws of the hoop on the playing side while travelling forward through the hoop, Your ball was, by my estimation, approximately 4.8 centimetres short of achieving that status when struck by mine, which was, regrettably for you, the striking ball in that particular sequence. Therefore, hoop point denied, and play continues with my ball."

"4.8 centimetres?" Harry spluttered. "You measured it with your infernal eye?"

"My eye is quite sufficient for observing the rules, Smythe," Ainsworth replied coolly. "Unlike some members who rely on bluster rather than precision. Perhaps if you spent less time admiring your questionable choice of cravat and more time studying the regulations…"

"Now see here, Ainsworth!" Harry took a step forward, gripping his mallet tightly. Several nearby members paused their games, watching with varying degrees of amusement and apprehension. Agnes Plummett made a swift notation in her book. Ronnie Peterson looked up, briefly intrigued by the geometry of confrontation before returning to his friction coefficient problem. Mr Fitzwilliam winced, sinking lower behind his newspaper.

Before Harry could escalate further, a calming presence intervened. Mildred Pettle, the Club Secretary, appeared as if from nowhere, carrying a small tray with a teapot and cups. "Gentlemen, gentlemen," she said, her voice soft and placating. "Surely it's too fine a morning for disagreements? Lord Smythe, perhaps a calming cup of tea before your next shot? Mr Ainsworth, the committee minutes you requested are ready in the office."

She positioned herself deftly between the two men, offering a gentle smile that seemed to encompass them both. Ainsworth gave a curt nod, mollified perhaps by the mention of minutes he could critique. Harry, though still simmering, allowed himself to be momentarily distracted by the offer of tea. "Well… dashed unsporting of him, Mildred," he grumbled, but the immediate heat seemed to have dissipated, expertly diffused by Mrs Pettle's timely and unobtrusive intervention.

Chloe, watching from near the rhododendrons, marvelled silently at Mrs Pettle's skill. She always seemed to know just what to say, how to smooth ruffled feathers, how to keep the sometimes-volatile machinery of the club running without ever drawing attention to herself. She finished deadheading the last rose and gathered her tools, preparing to move towards the neglected ornamental bed near the back boundary – the one Mr Ainsworth had recently developed such a peculiar, critical interest in.

****

The afternoon wore on. Matches were won and lost, tea was consumed, polite congratulations and even more polite commiserations were exchanged. The fierce undercurrent of competition slowly eased as the tournament's first day wound towards its close. The long shadows Ainsworth had observed that morning now stretched fully across the lawns, painting stripes of gold and deep green. Most members had departed, their cars crunching softly on the gravel drive beyond the clubhouse.

Chloe appreciated this time of day. The air cooled, the scent of jasmine beginning to replace the roses on the evening breeze. She was working near Lawn 3 again, this time tackling the unruly ornamental bed tucked behind the large rhododendron bushes – the area Mr Ainsworth had been so critical of lately. He'd complained about the placement of the foxgloves, insisted the soil pH was incorrect for the azaleas, and questioned the lineage of the heritage hellebores. Chloe suspected he just liked finding fault, but she dutifully checked the soil and tidied the border as instructed.

She was reaching down to pull a stubborn weed near the base of a particularly dense rhododendron when she saw it. Not clearly at first. Just a shape, a patch of colour that didn't belong – a flash of polished brown leather against the mulch. An expensive brogue. Curious, she pushed aside a low-hanging branch covered in waxy green leaves.

The world tilted. Her breath caught in her throat. It wasn't just a shoe. It was attached to a leg, clad in the familiar pale grey trousers Mr Ainsworth always wore. And beyond that… the torso, face down, partially obscured by the foliage, but the vibrant blue of his club blazer was unmistakable. He was utterly still, lying at an unnatural, broken angle.

For a frozen moment, Chloe couldn't move, couldn't breathe. Her mind struggled to reconcile the peaceful garden setting with the horrifying tableau before her. Then, her gaze snagged on something else, lying on the grass just beyond the edge of the flowerbed, partially hidden by a clump of ornamental grass. Dark wood, gleaming slightly in the fading light, inlaid with silver. An antique croquet mallet. Lord Smythe's mallet.

A strangled gasp escaped her lips. She stumbled backwards, tripping slightly on an exposed tree root. Her heart hammered against her ribs, blood pounding in her ears. She turned, spurred by a sudden surge of adrenaline, and ran. Ran across the perfect, empty lawn towards the fading lights of the clubhouse, towards the lingering normality she desperately hoped still existed, her choked cries finally breaking the quiet hush of the evening.

2

Police Presence and Polite Panic

Chloe's choked cries, thin and reedy in the sudden stillness of the late afternoon, eventually coalesced into coherent shouts for help. They acted like a stone dropped into the placid, manicured pond of the Toorak Croquet & Horticultural Society, sending ripples of alarm outwards. First, old Colonel Abernathy, who had been practising his hoop shots with solitary determination on Lawn 4, cupped a hand to his ear and peered towards the rhododendrons bordering Lawn 3. Then Esme Weatherly, emerging from the clubhouse after reconciling the day's tea receipts, froze mid-step, her head tilted like a watchful bird. Within moments, it seemed the entire remaining population of the club – perhaps half a dozen members finishing late games or lingering conversations, plus the skeleton staff – was gravitating towards the source of the disturbance, their expressions ranging from vague irritation to dawning alarm.

The sight that greeted them cemented the alarm. Chloe Dubois, the quiet young gardener, usually so composed amidst the flowerbeds, was being awkwardly comforted by Colonel Abernathy near the edge of Lawn 3. She was pale, trembling, pointing with a shaking hand towards the dense, glossy leaves of the rhododendron bushes. Beyond her pointing finger, partially visible to those who dared edge closer, was the unmistakable, horrifyingly still form of Bartholomew Ainsworth, face down in the mulch, a splash of familiar blue blazer amidst the green. And lying nearby, horribly conspicuous on the otherwise perfect lawn, was the dark, polished wood and gleaming metal of an antique croquet mallet.

The initial reactions were a confused medley of polite Melbourne society grappling with visceral shock. Gasps, quickly stifled behind hands. Murmurs of "Good Lord!" and "Surely not!" A sudden, collective intake of breath that seemed to suck the remaining warmth from the air. Esme Weatherly, recovering first, took charge with practised efficiency honed by years of managing minor club crises (though none quite like this). "Colonel, bring Miss Dubois to the verandah chairs. Fetch some water. Someone else," her sharp gaze swept the stunned onlookers, landing on a perpetually flustered committee member, "call emergency services. Zero-zero-zero. Now. State there's been a… a serious incident. An accident, perhaps. No, best say… just request police and ambulance attendance. Urgently. And nobody," her voice firmed, cutting through the rising panic, "nobody is to go near Lawn 3. Understood?"

It was into this tableau of contained chaos, perhaps fifteen minutes later – fifteen minutes that stretched into an eternity of hushed speculation and anxious waiting – that the first police car arrived, its siren mercifully silent as it crunched to a halt on the gravel drive usually reserved for vintage Bentleys and sensible Volvos. Two uniformed officers emerged, young, crisp, their standard-issue blue suddenly looking stark and utilitarian against the soft greens and floral pastels of the Society grounds. They conferred briefly with a visibly shaken Esme, then proceeded briskly towards Lawn 3, their professionalism a stark contrast to the members' stunned inactivity. Blue and white tape appeared, unspooling like a garish, unwelcome party streamer, cordoning off the lawn and the surrounding flowerbeds.

Agnes Plummett watched their arrival from the verandah, having secured her preferred wicker chair and poured herself a fresh, steadying cup of tea. Her initial shock had quickly subsided, replaced by an intense, analytical focus. She observed the officers' movements, the way they carefully skirted the most obvious evidence, the slightly clumsy way Constable Whidden (she'd noted his name tag) nearly trampled on a prize-winning fuchsia while securing the tape to a decorative urn. She noted the members huddled near the clubhouse entrance, their reactions a fascinating study: Mrs Henderson dabbing her eyes with a lace handkerchief (performative grief, Agnes suspected; she'd loathed Ainsworth), young Cyril Postlethwaite looking utterly bewildered, and Lord Smythe, pacing near the putting green, his face a mask of thunderous disbelief. Agnes opened her notebook to a fresh page, her pen poised.

Alistair Fitzwilliam stood near Agnes, clutching his briefcase like a shield. The arrival of the police had done little to soothe the frantic knot in his stomach. If anything, it had made the situation feel terrifyingly real, irrevocably serious. Murder. Here. Amidst the cucumber sandwiches and gentle competition. His legal mind, usually a refuge of logic, felt swamped by the sheer incongruity. He found himself scanning the faces of the officers, the witnesses, looking for... what? Reassurance? Clarity? He didn't know. He felt horribly conspicuous, stranded between the need to maintain a facade of gentlemanly calm and the urge to retreat entirely. He caught Agnes's sharp, observant gaze and felt a flicker of absurd comfort. At least someone seemed equipped to process this nightmare.

Ronnie Peterson, however, seemed less horrified than utterly captivated. He'd retrieved his notebook and was now positioned as close to the police tape as he dared, sketching Lawn 3 from a different angle. His earlier calculations forgotten, he was now focused on the spatial relationship between the body's estimated position, the mallet, and a faint scuff mark he'd observed on the turf near the Number 5 hoop, some ten metres away. Could the mallet have been thrown? Or struck something else first? What were the physics of Lignum Vitae impacting bone versus turf? He mumbled equations under his breath, oblivious to the sideways glances he was attracting. He desperately wanted to get closer, to take measurements, to apply calipers to the situation. This was far more interesting than calculating the optimal trajectory for Cyril Postlethwaite's disastrously positioned ball.

Chloe, meanwhile, sat wrapped in a borrowed club blanket on the verandah, sipping the water Colonel Abernathy had procured. She felt numb, disconnected. The initial adrenaline rush had faded, leaving behind a hollow exhaustion. The young constable had been kind, but his repetitive questions only seemed to solidify the horror in her mind. The image of Mr Ainsworth, usually so upright and critical, lying broken amongst the plants she tended, refused to fade. She closed her eyes, focusing on the scent of crushed leaves and damp earth that seemed to cling to her clothes.

The decisive shift came with the arrival of the second police vehicle, an unmarked dark grey sedan. Detective Inspector Eleanor Davies stepped out, her movements brisk, her expression unreadable as her gaze swept the scene. She wore her authority not like a uniform, but like a well-tailored suit – understated but absolute. She took in the situation instantly: the body under the sheet, the isolated mallet gleaming faintly under the now-activated garden spotlights, the cluster of wealthy, anxious witnesses, the forensics van just pulling up behind her own car. She conferred quickly with the senior uniformed officer, Sergeant Henderson, her questions low and precise.

"Victim is Bartholomew Ainsworth, club treasurer," Henderson reported. "Found by the gardener, Chloe Dubois, around 5:15 PM. Apparent blunt force trauma to the back of the head. Mallet found nearby belongs to that gentleman over there – Lord Harrington Smythe. They had a very public altercation near this lawn earlier this afternoon."

Detective Inspector Davies nodded slowly, her eyes drifting towards Harry Smythe, who had stopped pacing and was now watching the police activity with ill-disguised apprehension. Then her gaze moved to the little group observing from the verandah – the sharp-eyed elderly woman with the notebook, the anxious man with the briefcase, the intense man still sketching. Interesting.

"Alright, Sergeant," Davies said, her voice calm but carrying authority. "Forensics takes priority. Full sweep. Bag the mallet, obviously. I want detailed shots of everything before they move him. Get uniformed personnel to start canvassing properly – anyone who saw Ainsworth or Smythe between, say, 3 PM and the time of discovery. Keep the witnesses separated for now. I'll speak to the gardener first, then his Lordship." She paused, her gaze briefly resting on Ronnie's sketchpad. "And find out what that gentleman thinks he's drawing." This wasn't just a murder; it was a murder in a gilded cage, and Detective Inspector Davies suspected unlocking it would require navigating a complex web of personalities as much as analysing physical evidence. The polite panic was just the beginning.

****

Detective Inspector Davies chose her interview location with care. Not the stuffy, slightly damp Treasurer's office, nor the main clubhouse lounge currently filled with the low hum of collective shock, but a relatively secluded corner of the wide, flagstone verandah. Two wicker chairs and a small matching table, recently vacated by anxious members fleeing the scene, offered a semblance of privacy while still being open to the cool evening air, now carrying the sweet scent of night-blooming jasmine overlaid with the faint, incongruous metallic tang from the forensic team's equipment. Floodlights cast long, distorted shadows from the verandah posts onto the lawns below, where uniformed officers moved with quiet purpose. It was a setting both intimate and exposed, perfect, Davies thought, for observing how a suspect handled pressure outside the sterile confines of an interview room.

Her first subject, Lord Harrington 'Harry' Smythe, sat opposite her, perched awkwardly on the edge of the floral cushion as if it might eject him at any moment. Detective Constable Miller, young and earnest, sat slightly to one side, pen poised over his notebook. Harry's earlier bluster had subsided into a restless, simmering indignation. He plucked imaginary lint from his expensive blazer, avoided Davies's direct gaze, and radiated an energy that vibrated between anger and sheer panic.

"Right, Lord Smythe," Davies began, her voice retaining its professional calm, a deliberate counterpoint to Harry's agitated state. She didn't consult her notes immediately, preferring to watch him. "Let's go over this again. You had an argument with Mr Ainsworth near Lawn 3 this afternoon. Can you tell me exactly what that was about?"

Harry bristled. "As I told that other fellow," he waved a dismissive hand towards the lawns, "it was about the game! Ainsworth... he was deliberately obtuse! Claimed my ball hadn't run the hoop when it was clear as day it had! Cost me the point, possibly the match!" His voice rose, colour flooding his cheeks again. "The man was an infuriating, rules-obsessed... pedant!"

Pedant. Fitzwilliam, standing near the verandah steps pretending to search for a dropped glove, winced. Not the word choice of an innocent man trying to downplay conflict. He could almost hear the prosecution cross-examining: *"So, Lord Smythe, you admit you found the deceased 'infuriating'? That you argued heatedly just before his death over a trivial point in a game?"* Harry was practically gift-wrapping motive for them. Fitzwilliam felt a bead of sweat trickle down his temple, despite the cool air. He intensely disliked being this close to raw emotion and official scrutiny.

Agnes Plummett, meanwhile, had strategically positioned herself near a large potted fern further down the verandah, ostensibly examining its fronds for blight. From this vantage point, she had a clear view of Harry's profile and could hear most of the exchange. She recalled a similar incident three years prior, during the President's Cup semi-final. Harry, convinced Ainsworth had deliberately misreported his score, had thrown his scorecard onto the lawn and called Ainsworth a "damned cheat" in front of half the membership. There had been talk of disciplinary action, smoothed over, inevitably, by Mildred Pettle. Harry's temper was a known quantity, volatile but usually short-lived, like a summer thunderstorm. But this… this felt different.

"He certainly seems to have inspired strong feelings," Davies commented mildly, making a brief note. "You described the argument as 'heated'. Were voices raised? Were there threats?"

"Raised? Of course they were raised! Have you ever tried arguing with Ainsworth? It was like reasoning with a brick wall wearing spectacles!" Harry huffed. "Threats? Good heavens, no! I might have said I'd… I don't know… wrap my mallet around his infernal neck if he didn't see sense, but it was just talk! Figure of speech! Everyone knew I didn't mean it literally!"

Figure of speech? Fitzwilliam felt a fresh wave of despair. *He actually mentioned his mallet? And violence? In the same sentence?* This was going from bad to worse. He risked a glance at Detective Inspector Davies. Her expression remained perfectly neutral, but he imagined the internal checklist ticking boxes: Motive – check. Opportunity – possible. Weapon connection – check. Expressed violent ideation – check.

"So, after this heated argument where you figuratively suggested strangling Mr Ainsworth with your mallet," Davies clarified, her tone utterly flat, making the statement sound even more damning, "you decided to take a walk to cool off?"

"Yes! Exactly!" Harry seized on the phrase. "Needed some air. Stormed off down towards the Yarra path, along the boundary fence."

"You often walk that way?"

"Sometimes. It's quieter down there. Less... people," Harry finished lamely.

"And you saw no one? No grounds staff, no other members, no one walking along the public path on the other side of the fence?"

Harry shifted uncomfortably. "Didn't notice anyone. My mind was... occupied. With the injustice of it all!"

Weak, Agnes thought, turning her attention back to the fern, though her ears remained sharply tuned. *A convenient lack of witnesses.* Ainsworth himself often complained about members using the boundary path for unauthorised cigarette breaks or private phone calls. It wasn't usually deserted.

"How long were you walking, Lord Smythe?" Davies asked.

"Oh, ages! Must have been... twenty minutes? Half an hour? Long enough to get my temper back under control." He attempted a reassuring smile that didn't reach his eyes.

"Twenty minutes or half an hour?" Davies pressed gently. "That's quite a difference. Can you be more precise?"

"Well, how should I know? I wasn't timing myself, was I?" Harry snapped, his irritation flaring again. "I walked until I felt calmer, then I came back up towards the clubhouse."

"And returned via…?"

"Past the tennis courts, then cut across Lawn 4."

Davies made another note. "And the mallet found near the body. The antique one. You confirmed it's yours?"

"Yes, yes, I told you! It's a Smythe family heirloom! Been in the family for generations."

"You usually keep it in your locker here at the club?"

"Yes. In its case. It's far too valuable…"

"And was the locker secured today, Lord Smythe?" Davies interrupted, her gaze steady on his face.

Harry's eyes flickered. He hesitated. "Secured? Well… yes. I mean, I always lock it. Habit."

"But did you check it was locked after you took your shoes out this morning?"

"I… I can't be absolutely certain," Harry admitted, looking flustered. "I was running late, dashed in, grabbed my shoes… I might have forgotten to properly twist the padlock. Sometimes it sticks a bit. But who would possibly…?" He trailed off, the implication hanging heavy in the air. Someone *had* possibly taken the mallet from his potentially unsecured locker.

Davies let the silence stretch for a moment, observing the way Harry fidgeted, avoiding her gaze, his earlier indignation now thoroughly replaced by a hunted look. *Too obvious?* she wondered briefly. *Or just guilty and incompetent?*

"Thank you, Lord Smythe," she said finally, her tone indicating the interview, for now, was over. "We appreciate your cooperation. As I said, please remain on the grounds. Detective Constable Miller here will take a formal written statement from you shortly."

Harry practically bolted from the chair, nodding jerkily before striding stiffly away down the verandah, pausing only to glare back towards Lawn 3 with a mixture of fear and resentment.

Fitzwilliam slowly pretended to find his 'lost' glove near the steps. He felt a profound sense of unease. Harry Smythe, for all his faults, didn't strike him as a cold-blooded killer. Hot-headed, certainly. Foolish, undeniably. But capable of this? Yet the evidence, circumstantial as it was, seemed to point directly at him, and Harry's own words were doing nothing to deflect the suspicion.

Agnes watched Harry retreat, her expression thoughtful. His panic felt genuine. But was it the panic of a guilty man caught out, or the panic of an innocent man realising he was trapped in a web of circumstance? Temperament, she reminded herself, was not causation. But it certainly made for a convenient narrative. And Detective Inspector Davies, Agnes suspected, was astute enough to recognise a convenient narrative when she saw one – whether she fully believed it or not was another question entirely. The investigation, Agnes felt with a certainty that settled deep in her bones, was only just beginning.

****

Dusk bled into evening over the Toorak Croquet & Horticultural Society grounds. The brilliant gold and pink hues of the sunset, usually a signal for a final, leisurely drink on the verandah, were now filtered through an atmosphere thick with shock and a cloying, morbid curiosity. Garden floodlights hummed to life, casting stark shadows that made the familiar lawns and flowerbeds seem alien and menacing. The air grew cooler, carrying the heavy perfume of night-scented stock and the underlying damp earth smell from the recently watered gardens – a scent Chloe now associated irrevocably with the image of Mr Ainsworth lying amongst the rhododendrons.

Most members had been allowed to leave after giving preliminary details, murmuring reassurances to each other about locking doors and the regrettable state of modern society as they retreated to their comfortable homes in nearby suburbs. A small, determined knot remained clustered near the tea pavilion, drawn together by a shared sense of disbelief and a reluctant need for company. Esme Weatherly moved among them, offering tea and hushed words, her usual cheerful energy subdued but her organisational instincts still functioning. The police tape gleamed under the lights surrounding Lawn 3, a stark boundary separating the mundane from the horrific, while the forensics team continued their methodical work within its perimeter.

The dominant narrative had already solidified, passed along in urgent whispers: poor Bartholomew, struck down in a fit of rage by Lord Smythe after their argument. The antique mallet, Harry's known temper, his flimsy alibi – it all fit together with a depressing neatness that seemed to satisfy the members' need for a quick, understandable explanation, however unpleasant.

"…heard Detective Inspector Davies practically had him confessing," Mrs Henderson confided in a stage whisper loud enough for several people to hear, dabbing her eyes again. "His lordship looked positively apoplectic when he came off the verandah. Guilt, plain as day."

Agnes Plummett, seated again with a fresh (and this time, untouched) cup of tea, pursed her lips but refrained from commenting on Mrs Henderson's interpretation or her crocodile tears. Nearby, Alistair Fitzwilliam shifted uncomfortably on another wicker chair, pretending to study the darkening sky but acutely aware of the circulating rumours. He felt a lawyer's instinctive rejection of trial-by-gossip, yet even he had to admit Harry Smythe had built a compelling circumstantial case against himself.

Ronnie Peterson had joined them, his notebook now filled with calculations and diagrams that looked more like orbital mechanics than a crime scene analysis. He stared intently towards the floodlit Lawn 3, occasionally tapping his pencil against his teeth. Chloe Dubois sat quietly beside Agnes, the borrowed blanket still around her shoulders, watching the others with wide, observant eyes. She seemed to have regained some composure, the initial shock replaced by a thoughtful stillness.

"It seems remarkably… conclusive," Fitzwilliam ventured, unable to remain silent any longer, his voice low. "The consensus appears to be that Lord Smythe simply lost his temper."

Agnes took a slow sip of her tea. "Consensus," she replied, her voice crisp, "is often another word for collective assumption based on incomplete data. Lord Smythe possesses a lamentable lack of self-control, that is undeniable. I have documented at least," she paused, mentally consulting her internal index, "seven instances in the past five years where his temper has led to public outbursts or minor property damage. However," she fixed Fitzwilliam with a sharp look, "none involved physical violence against a person, merely against inanimate objects or, regrettably, the English language."

Ronnie looked up from his notebook, his eyes bright with scientific dissent. "And the physics are still bothering me," he declared. "Assuming the mallet was the primary instrument – which seems probable given its proximity and the likely nature of the injury – the positioning is problematic. To achieve the likely impact point on the posterior cranium from a standing confrontation, the assailant – Smythe, hypothetically – would need to be positioned awkwardly, perhaps behind the victim, or the victim would need to be bending over significantly." He gestured vaguely. "Neither fits naturally with the scenario of a sudden flare-up during a face-to-face argument about hoop placement."

He tapped his sketch. "Furthermore, the mallet lying where it was… assuming it was dropped immediately post-impact, the trajectory doesn't quite align with the likely force vector. Unless," his eyes lit up again, "unless Smythe possesses an unusual follow-through involving significant counter-rotational torque, or the mallet struck something else *after* the primary impact, altering its final resting position!"

Fitzwilliam blinked. "Counter-rotational torque?"

Chloe spoke, her voice soft but carrying in the relative quiet. "He wasn't just bending over. He was face down. Properly face down, in the mulch under the rhododendrons. Not just fallen forward. It looked…" she hesitated, searching for the word, "…deliberate. And he was further into the garden bed than you'd expect if he just stumbled from the lawn." She looked at the others. "And Mr Ainsworth *hated* getting dirt on his trousers. He wouldn't have gone in there willingly unless he was…"

"Unless he was incapacitated *before* reaching that spot?" Agnes finished the thought, her gaze sharp. "Or placed there?"

A heavy silence fell upon the four of them. The circulating rumour – Harry's explosive temper, the argument, the mallet – suddenly felt thin, inadequate. Each observation, taken alone, was perhaps minor, easily dismissed. Agnes's historical perspective on Harry's (non-violent) temper. Ronnie's questioning of the physics and angles. Chloe's precise memory of the victim's unnatural position and location. Fitzwilliam's legal unease about convenient assumptions. But together? Together, they painted a picture riddled with inconsistencies.

"So," Fitzwilliam said slowly, rubbing his temples, the familiar thrum of anxiety now overlaid with a disconcerting pulse of intellectual curiosity. "We have Lord Smythe, who admittedly behaved abominably and has provided himself with the flimsiest of alibis. We have Mr Ainsworth, found in a location he likely wouldn't choose, in a position suggesting something other than a simple fall after being struck during an argument. And we have," he glanced at Ronnie, "questions about the physical mechanics of the presumed attack."

"And a missing tea thermos," Agnes added quietly, almost to herself, remembering the prologue of Ainsworth's morning routine she'd glimpsed. Had anyone found it? It seemed trivial, yet… Ainsworth was a creature of habit.

Ronnie leaned forward, suddenly animated. "Precisely! The data points don't converge neatly on the Smythe hypothesis! There are outliers! Variables unaccounted for!"

"It means," Chloe said simply, looking from one face to another, "that what everyone else is saying… it might not be what actually happened."

Fitzwilliam sighed, a long, weary exhalation that seemed to carry the weight of unwanted responsibility. He looked at Agnes, her posture radiating quiet certainty; at Ronnie, practically vibrating with equations; at Chloe, her initial shock now replaced by a focused, observant intensity. They were an improbable collection: a librarian, a physicist, a gardener, and an anxious lawyer. Yet, in the space of a few hours, bound by circumstance and a shared dissatisfaction with the obvious explanation, they had stumbled upon the edges of a deeper, more complex puzzle lying beneath the bloodstained gardens of Lawn 3.

He wasn't sure what came next. He wasn't sure he *wanted* to know what came next. But as he met Agnes's steady gaze across the wicker table, a silent acknowledgement passed between them, an unspoken agreement that extended, he somehow knew, to the other two. They would watch. They would listen. They would share what they observed. Because whatever had truly happened to Bartholomew

Ainsworth today, it was clearly, as Agnes might put it, significantly more complex than mere temper and a conveniently located antique mallet. It was, indeed, a most improper end, and the story was far from over.

25

3

The Weight of the Mallet

The following morning dawned bright and deceptively cheerful over Melbourne, the clear sky scrubbed clean by an overnight southerly breeze. But within the normally serene confines of the Toorak Croquet & Horticultural Society, the atmosphere remained thick with the previous day's events. Police tape still fluttered incongruously around Lawn 3, a stark blue wound on the perfect green. Small clusters of members spoke in hushed tones on the verandah, their usual conversations about handicaps and rose cultivars replaced by morbid speculation. The air hummed not with the usual gentle thwack of balls, but with unanswered questions.

Agnes Plummett, however, found a familiar refuge from the unsettling present in the meticulously ordered past. She had arrived at the clubhouse early, bypassing the subdued gathering on the verandah with a polite but firm nod, and retreated to the small, slightly cramped room tucked away behind the main lounge that served as the Society's official (and her unofficial) archive. It smelled faintly of dust, ageing paper, and furniture polish – a scent Agnes found infinitely more comforting than the cloying sweetness of the memorial lilies Esme Weatherly was already arranging in the foyer.

Sunlight streamed through the single window, illuminating dust motes dancing in the air and glinting off the spines of countless leather-bound minute books, ledgers, photo albums, and archival boxes that lined the shelves from floor to ceiling. This was Agnes's true domain. More than the lawns or the lounge, this room, with its carefully catalogued history of the Society's triumphs, controversies, and everyday life stretching back over eighty years, felt like its heart. And Agnes, its devoted custodian.

She bypassed the official Society Minute Books for now. While essential for recording formal decisions, they were often regrettably deficient in capturing the nuances of personality and conflict – nuances crucial for understanding the present predicament. Instead, she turned to a specific set of shelves holding her own supplementary records: cross-referenced index card files, folders of newspaper clippings related to club events, and, most importantly, the uniform series of navy blue, cloth-bound journals she herself had kept religiously for the past thirty-five years. *"Observations & Sundries,"* the spines read simply in gold lettering.

Selecting the volume marked '2020-2022', she carried it over to the small, sturdy oak table that served as her desk. She sat down, adjusting her spectacles, and opened the journal, its pages filled with her neat, slightly backward-slanting cursive. Her goal this morning was specific: to formally document and analyse the known history of conflict between Lord Harrington Smythe and the late Bartholomew Ainsworth. While Detective Inspector Davies might rely on recent witness statements regarding yesterday's argument, Agnes knew that context was everything. Patterns of behaviour, precedents, escalating tensions – these were the threads she sought in the tapestry of the past.

Her index card system first directed her to an entry dated October 17th, 2020. *"President's Cup Semi-Final. Smythe vs Ainsworth. Weather fine but blustery. Smythe appeared agitated from outset – suspect previous night's Port consumption. Disputed Ainsworth's scoring on Hoop 9. Accusation of 'deliberate miscounting' (unsubstantiated). Resulting outburst involved Smythe throwing scorecard onto lawn (minor infraction, Rule 11) and declaring Ainsworth a 'damned cheat' (significant breach of decorum, By-Law 6). Ainsworth remained impassive, merely cited relevant rules. Smythe conceded match default. Subsequent private apology by Smythe to Ainsworth noted by E. Weatherly (source reliable). No formal disciplinary action taken, intervention by M. Pettle cited."* Agnes nodded faintly. Yes, she remembered that day. Harry's face had been puce. But the key point: outburst followed by apology, and importantly, directed at the *scorecard*, not the person.

She flipped forward, consulting her index again. June 5th, 2021. *"Mid-Winter Social Tournament (Mixed Doubles). Smythe partnered with Mrs Henderson; Ainsworth with Miss Talbot (visiting member). Dispute arose regarding interpretation of 'Pegging Out' sequence (Rule 35). Ainsworth insisted Smythe's partner's ball was not eligible to be pegged out, citing obscure sub-clause. Smythe vehemently disagreed. Raised voices noted by several members. Smythe reportedly described Ainsworth's interpretation as 'malicious pedantry designed solely to obstruct play.' Incident diffused when Ainsworth conceded the point, stating it was 'simpler than arguing with ignorance.' Smythe remained disgruntled but completed the match."* Another instance of conflict, Agnes mused, but again, verbal. And Ainsworth, interestingly, had backed down that time, perhaps choosing smug superiority over prolonged argument.

Her pen tapped lightly on the page. These incidents confirmed Harry's short fuse and his particular animosity towards Ainsworth's rule-bound approach. They established a pattern of conflict, certainly providing a foundation for the police theory of simmering resentment boiling over. But where was the escalation? Where was the hint of physical violence?

She turned more pages, scanning entries about AGMs, garden fetes, committee meetings (often described with thinly veiled exasperation in her private journals). Then, an entry from earlier this year, February 12th, 2025. *"Greens Committee Meeting. Contentious discussion re. Lawn 3 refurbishment. Ainsworth (Treasurer) presented costing deemed excessive by Smythe. Smythe argued for alternative, less expensive turf supplier. Ainsworth questioned Smythe's expertise, implying favouritism towards proposed supplier. Exchange became heated. Smythe accused Ainsworth of 'deliberately obstructing progress for petty reasons' and 'knowing the cost of everything and the value of nothing.' Smythe struck the committee table with his fist (minor damage to veneer noted, later discreetly repaired). Meeting adjourned prematurely by Chair. Subsequent email from Smythe to committee apologised for outburst but reiterated objections to Ainsworth's figures."*

Agnes paused, rereading the entry. Striking the table. That was perhaps the closest Harry had come to physical violence in a club context. A loss of control, certainly. Directed at an inanimate object in frustration, not at Ainsworth himself. And again, followed by an apology, albeit a slightly grudging one. It fit the pattern: frustration, verbal explosion, perhaps a gesture of physical frustration towards an object, followed by regret or retraction. Did yesterday's argument, combined with the potential injustice of a wrongly denied hoop point, represent a significant deviation, a snapping point leading to lethal force? Or was it simply another iteration of the same pattern, tragically coinciding with Ainsworth's demise by other means?

She thought about the mallet. Harry cherished that mallet. Would he truly risk damaging such a valuable heirloom, let alone use it as a weapon in a fit of pique? It seemed almost… aesthetically wrong, inconsistent with his character, despite his temper. He might throw a modern mallet, yes, but the antique one?

Her gaze drifted towards a row of dusty archive boxes labelled

'Disciplinary Committee Records – Confidential'. Usually, she adhered strictly to access protocols. But these were unusual circumstances. Technically, as unofficial historian and compiler of club records, she had a *duty* to ensure all relevant information was considered. She glanced towards the closed door of the archive room. No one would disturb her here for hours.

With a decisive nod, Agnes rose and retrieved the box labelled '1995-2005'. She carefully untied the ribbon and lifted the lid. Inside lay folders filled with correspondence, hearing minutes, formal warnings. She quickly located the file pertaining to Lord Smythe. There wasn't much. A formal warning regarding "language unbecoming a member" following the 2001 scorecard incident. A note about mediating a dispute between Smythe and another member over parking etiquette in 2003. Nothing involving physical altercations.

She then located the file for Bartholomew Ainsworth. It was considerably thicker. Not disciplinary actions against *him*, but records of complaints *he* had lodged against other members for minor infractions: incorrect attire, improper hoop running technique, unauthorised pruning of club roses, failure to pay subscriptions by the precise due date. Page after page of petty grievances, meticulously documented. Ainsworth hadn't just been unpopular; he seemed to have actively cultivated animosity through his rigid application of rules. The list of people who might have felt intense irritation, even hatred, towards him was potentially far longer than just Lord Smythe.

Agnes closed the file, a thoughtful frown creasing her brow. Harry Smythe certainly had the temper, the history of conflict with the victim, and apparently, the opportunity and weapon. The police narrative was strong, logical even. Yet, her carefully compiled history suggested a pattern that stopped short of lethal violence.

And Ainsworth himself had created a fertile ground for resentment from numerous quarters.

The weight of the mallet seemed, in the context of Harry's documented history, perhaps less significant than the weight of Ainsworth's own pedantry. She made another note in her journal: *"While Smythe presents as the most obvious suspect due to temperament and recent altercation, historical pattern analysis suggests outbursts are primarily verbal/symbolic, not physically targeted at persons. Consider alternative motives arising from Ainsworth's documented history of antagonism towards multiple members re: rules enforcement & financial matters."*

Satisfied for the moment, she carefully replaced the files and her journals. The archive had provided context, reinforced the obvious case against Harry, but also subtly undermined it. Her work here was done for now. It was time, perhaps, to see what Mr Peterson had made of the physics of the situation. The simplest explanation was rarely the whole story, especially within the deceptively placid walls of the Toorak Croquet & Horticultural Society.

****

While Agnes Plummett immersed herself in the documented history of club conflicts, Ronnie Peterson was wrestling with the immutable laws of physics as applied to the brutal present. He stood on the edge of Lawn 2, the site of his disastrous match attempt the previous day, though his mind was far from croquet strategy now. The bright Melbourne morning sun felt almost offensively cheerful, highlighting the dew sparkling on the pristine grass, a stark contrast to the grim activity still visible under floodlights just one lawn over. The forensics team, methodical in their white suits, continued their painstaking work on Lawn 3, occasionally pausing to confer or place small numbered markers.

Ronnie held his own, standard-issue croquet mallet, not swinging it, but using it almost as a pointer, a prop for his thoughts. His notebook lay open on a nearby bench, covered in a dizzying array of equations, force diagrams, and hastily sketched trajectories that would have baffled anyone but him. He paced a small area, muttering calculations involving estimated mass, velocity, impact duration, and material stress tolerances. He'd managed to glean some basic information – the approximate weight and material of Harry Smythe's antique mallet (Lignum Vitae head, likely around 3 lbs total, significantly denser than standard boxwood), and the reported nature of the injury (a single, severe blow to the occipital region, though details were scarce, based mostly on overheard police radio snippets and informed speculation filtering through the clubhouse).

Alistair Fitzwilliam, having escaped the hushed, speculative atmosphere of the verandah, spotted Ronnie and felt an odd pull. He didn't understand Ronnie's obsession with physics, found his explanations often impenetrable, but there was a certainty in Ronnie's focus, a reliance on quantifiable facts, that felt strangely grounding amidst the swirling rumours and messy human emotions surrounding Ainsworth's death. He approached cautiously, briefcase still in hand.

"Ronnie?" Fitzwilliam began tentatively. "Everything alright?" An absurd question, given the circumstances, but it was the only opening he could think of.

Ronnie looked up, his eyes bright with intellectual fervour rather than any discernible grief or shock. "Alright? No, Alistair, it's not 'alright' at all! It's fundamentally… perplexing!" He gestured emphatically with his mallet towards the scene on Lawn 3. "From a purely mechanical standpoint, the official narrative presents significant inconsistencies!"

Fitzwilliam stepped closer, intrigued despite his apprehension. "Inconsistencies? The police seem rather convinced it was Lord Smythe."

"Police!" Ronnie scoffed, not unkindly, but with the exasperation of a cosmologist dealing with flat-earthers. "They're looking at motive, opportunity – the human factors. Important, yes, but they ignore the physics! Look," he grabbed his notebook, flipping to a page covered in diagrams. "Assume Smythe, average male, approximate height 1.8 metres, confronts Ainsworth, slightly shorter, say 1.75 metres. Argument ensues. Smythe, enraged, swings the mallet." Ronnie demonstrated a hypothetical overhand swing with his own mallet. "To strike the back of Ainsworth's head with significant force *from the front or side* in that scenario requires either Ainsworth turning away completely and conveniently lowering his head, or Smythe executing an extremely awkward, inefficient looping blow."

He pointed to another diagram. "Consider the mallet – Lignum Vitae head, estimated mass around 1.2 kilograms, handle perhaps 0.15 kg. Total mass approximately 1.35 kg. Length roughly 0.9 metres. To generate instantly fatal force with a single blow to the occiput, assuming minimal skull fracture reported – which seems implied by the relative lack of visible… well, *mess* – you'd need considerable velocity. Smythe's enraged, yes, but is he capable of generating, say, 15 metres per second velocity in a spontaneous, awkwardly angled swing? Possible, but metabolically demanding and bio mechanically inefficient."

Fitzwilliam tried to follow, his legal mind attempting to translate physics into courtroom plausibility. "So you're saying… it would have been difficult for Harry to land such a blow effectively during that argument?"

"Difficult to land it *in the manner implied*," Ronnie corrected passionately. "A blow from directly behind? Much easier bio mechanically. Or if the victim," he lowered his voice slightly, "was already significantly lower – kneeling, perhaps, or already falling?" He looked at Fitzwilliam expectantly.

Fitzwilliam felt a chill despite the morning sun. Chloe's words echoed in his mind: *He wasn't just fallen forward... deliberate... further into the garden bed...* "The gardener, Miss Dubois," he said carefully, "did mention Mr Ainsworth was found face down, quite far into the shrubbery."

Ronnie's eyes lit up. "Exactly! If he was already low, perhaps disoriented or incapacitated by other means," – he shot Fitzwilliam a significant look – "then a subsequent blow, even with less force or from an unusual angle, could appear causative! It could even be designed to *simulate* death by blunt force trauma, masking the primary cause!"

"Other means?" Fitzwilliam felt his anxiety spike again. "You mean… poison?

"Poison, drugs, a medical event precipitated by stress… the physics don't dictate the primary cause, only the mechanics of the *final* impact!" Ronnie was pacing again. "And then there's the mallet's resting position! I only saw it briefly before they covered everything, but it seemed too… neat. Too close to the body, perhaps, but not quite where you'd expect it to fall or be dropped after a violent, uncontrolled swing. Unless," he paused dramatically, "it was *placed* there."

Fitzwilliam stared at him. Placed there? The idea was chilling. Staging. It suggested premeditation, cold calculation, not the hot-blooded, clumsy rage attributed to Harry Smythe. "But Ronnie," Fitzwilliam argued, clutching at the official narrative, "the police have the weapon, they have Smythe's argument, his terrible alibi…

Surely that's compelling?"

"Compelling narrative!" Ronnie conceded. "But potentially flawed physics! Think about it, Alistair. Lignum Vitae is incredibly dense – around 1250 kg per cubic meter. Impacting the human skull… the energy transfer would be significant. You'd expect… well, without precise forensic data, it's speculation, but my preliminary calculations suggest either *less* apparent damage than reported for a fatal blow, implying a pre-existing condition or incapacitation, or *more* damage than seems evident from distance if it were a truly unrestrained, fatal assault from standing. The force required sits in an awkward zone if we assume the simple argument-turned-violent scenario."

He looked earnestly at Fitzwilliam. "I'm not saying Smythe is innocent. I deal in probabilities, not guilt. But the *probability* of the event occurring exactly as assumed by the prevailing narrative seems… lower than optimal. The physical evidence, as far as observable, presents anomalies demanding further investigation!"

Fitzwilliam rubbed his forehead. Ronnie's certainty, grounded in numbers and forces Fitzwilliam barely understood, felt strangely convincing despite its esoteric nature. Combined with Agnes's historical analysis of Harry's behaviour, and Chloe's disturbing description of the body's position… the neat police theory was looking increasingly frayed around the edges. If Harry hadn't done it, or at least not in the way everyone assumed, then who had? And how? The thought sent a fresh wave of unease through him. This wasn't just a tragic loss of temper; this was potentially something far more complex, far more calculated. And they, an unlikely quartet bound by little more than proximity and curiosity, seemed to be the only ones noticing the equations didn't quite add up. He looked towards the taped-off area of Lawn 3, no longer seeing just a crime scene, but the centre of a deeply perplexing, and potentially dangerous, problem.

****

By lunchtime, a semblance of strained normality had returned to the Toorak Croquet & Horticultural Society, but it was a thin veneer stretched taut over a deep well of unease. The main police presence had withdrawn from Lawn 3, leaving only a single uniformed officer stationed near the fluttering blue tape, a stark reminder of the morning's grim proceedings. The forensics team had packed their mysterious cases and departed. Yet, the incident lingered. It clung to the hushed conversations on the verandah, echoed in the unnatural quiet from the usually busy lawns, and manifested most acutely in the collective gaze directed towards Lord Harrington 'Harry' Smythe.

Harry had become the unwilling focal point of the club's simmering anxiety and morbid curiosity. He seemed unable to settle, pacing the verandah like a caged, rather flamboyant tiger, occasionally venturing out onto the edge of Lawn 1 only to retreat abruptly when he noticed eyes upon him. He made several attempts to engage other members in conversation, perhaps seeking reassurance or attempting to project normalcy, but these efforts invariably faltered. Conversations would wither under the weight of unspoken questions; members would suddenly remember urgent appointments elsewhere or become intensely interested in the distant Melbourne skyline. He was, Fitzwilliam observed with a grimace from the relative anonymity of a corner table where he pretended to read club newsletters, effectively being socially quarantined.

His behaviour did little to help his cause. Twice, Harry retreated to the far end of the rose garden, near where Chloe Dubois was now quietly but diligently working on staking some delphiniums, to take urgent, low-voiced phone calls on his mobile. His back was turned to the clubhouse, but his agitated posture and fragments of conversation carried on the breeze were easily (and eagerly) interpreted by onlookers.

"...no, absolutely not! I told you, I just need more *time!*" His voice, though low, was tight with stress. A pause, then, "Don't be ridiculous, it has nothing to do with... *that.* This is entirely separate... Look, later. Not here." He glanced around furtively before snapping the phone shut and shoving it back into his blazer pocket, his face flushed.

"Trying to arrange an alibi, no doubt," murmured Mrs Henderson to her companion, loud enough for several people, including Agnes Plummett, to hear. "Or perhaps trying to silence someone else who knows something."

Agnes, sipping her tea (she was now on her third cup, finding the ritual soothing even if the tea itself remained largely untouched), made a small, noncommittal sound. She watched Harry stride back towards the clubhouse, his movements jerky, his eyes darting around as if seeking both connection and escape. The anxiety radiating from him was undeniable. But Agnes, recalling the meticulous documentation of his past behaviour, found herself questioning its source. This wasn't the explosive, righteous indignation she'd seen before when he felt wronged in a game or slighted socially. This felt different. More contained, more... hunted. Was it the fear of a murderer about to be exposed? Or the desperate, cornered fear of something else entirely?

Ronnie Peterson, having temporarily exhausted the possibilities of remote analysis of Lawn 3, had cornered Barnaby Thornton near the equipment shed, bombarding the young apprentice with highly technical questions about the tensile strength of mallet handles and the potential for vibrational energy transfer through Lignum Vitae

– questions Barnaby seemed both flattered and utterly baffled by. Ronnie appeared oblivious to the social drama swirling around Harry Smythe, his focus narrowed to the mechanical puzzle. Yet, even he couldn't entirely miss the pervasive tension.

Fitzwilliam felt a growing sense of professional and personal discomfort. Watching Harry Smythe self-destruct was agonising. Every furtive glance, every agitated gesture, every tense phone call was building the circumstantial case against him brick by brick in the minds of the members, and likely, the police. *He needs legal counsel,* Fitzwilliam thought despairingly. *He needs to stop talking, stop pacing, stop looking like a man with the world closing in on him.* But offering unsolicited legal advice, especially in this environment, was unthinkable. He could only watch, his stomach churning, as Harry inadvertently tightened the noose of suspicion around his own neck.

Adding fuel to the fire was Harry's peculiar interaction with a sleek, dark grey Jaguar that pulled up briefly just outside the main gates around 1 PM. Harry, seeing the car arrive, almost ran down the gravel drive. He spoke intensely with the driver – a burly man in a sharp suit whose face remained impassive – through the tinted window for less than a minute. No handshake, no pleasantries. Harry seemed to be pleading or arguing, his gestures sharp, before the driver simply shook his head and the Jaguar pulled away smoothly, leaving Harry standing there looking utterly defeated, his shoulders slumped.

This brief, tense meeting did not go unobserved. "Bookie, I'd wager," Colonel Abernathy opined gruffly to a small group by the entrance. "Smythe's always had expensive tastes. Wouldn't surprise me if he owed money all over town. Perhaps Ainsworth found out? Threatened to expose him to the committee?"

"Or perhaps," countered Mrs Henderson with relish, "he

needed money *because* he planned to flee after dealing with poor Bartholomew!"

The speculation spiralled, each theory feeding the next, painting Harry as financially desperate, temperamentally explosive, and now, demonstrably acting suspiciously.

Chloe, from her vantage point near the delphiniums, had seen the Jaguar arrive and depart. She didn't recognise the car or the driver, but she noted Harry's desperation during the brief exchange. It hadn't looked like the relief of someone arranging an escape, she thought. It looked more like someone being refused help. She carefully loosened the soil around a root-bound plant, her thoughts troubled. People saw what they expected to see. Right now, everyone expected to see a guilty man in Lord Smythe. But the image of Mr Ainsworth, face down in the mulch, felt wrong, discordant, not like the result of a sudden, messy argument.

Later, as the few remaining members began gathering their belongings, preparing to leave the troubled sanctuary of the club for the day, Harry made another abrupt move. He'd been cornered by Esme Weatherly, who was likely attempting to offer some form of practical support or perhaps gently probe for information herself. Mid-conversation, Harry glanced at his watch, muttered something about a forgotten, urgent appointment, and practically bolted towards the car park, nearly colliding with Ronnie who was demonstrating mallet impact dynamics using a discarded croquet ball and a patch of unsuspecting lawn. Harry didn't apologise, just jumped into his own expensive but slightly dated sports car and roared down the drive, gravel spitting behind him.

"Well!" Esme exclaimed, flustered but also slightly indignant. "Talk about adding fuel to the fire! Running off like the devil himself is on his heels!"

The remaining members exchanged significant glances. Harry

Smythe's performance throughout the day had been, from the perspective of anyone assuming his guilt, utterly damning.

Agnes watched his car disappear down the leafy Toorak street. Running *from* something, certainly, she mused. But was it from the law? Or towards a creditor? The weight of the mallet, the physical evidence, seemed less compelling to her now than the weight of Harry Smythe's other, hidden burdens. And the crucial question remained unanswered: if Harry's panic wasn't about the murder, then whose was? Somewhere within this manicured garden, beneath the veneer of polite society, the real story – and the real killer – remained hidden. And the suspicion directed so squarely at Harry Smythe was providing the perfect shade for them to hide in.

4

Seeds of Doubt

The following morning, the relentless Melbourne sunshine seemed almost indecently cheerful, mocking the sombre mood that still clung to the members of the Toorak Croquet & Horticultural Society like damp tweed. Lawn 3 remained cordoned off, a stark blue and white scar on the otherwise immaculate grounds, though the police presence had dwindled further. The official narrative – Lord Smythe's fatal loss of temper – had taken root firmly in the fertile ground of club gossip, nurtured by the previous day's observations of his agitation and flight. Yet, for four members, that narrative felt increasingly ill-fitting, like a borrowed suit cut for a different man entirely.

By unspoken agreement, precipitated perhaps by a shared glance of profound unease as they'd separately departed the club the previous evening, they convened not amidst the charged atmosphere of the clubhouse, but in the quiet, comforting order of Agnes Plummett's South Yarra apartment. It was a space that reflected its owner precisely: impeccably tidy, shelves filled not just with books but with neatly labelled archival boxes, walls adorned with framed botanical prints and historical maps of Melbourne, the air

41

smelling faintly of beeswax polish and Earl Grey tea. Sunlight streamed through the large bay window, illuminating a room where knowledge felt curated and chaos was kept firmly at bay – a stark contrast to the events consuming their thoughts.

Agnes had served tea in her best china cups, accompanied by a plate of surprisingly delicate lemon shortbread. Ronnie Peterson perched on the edge of an antique armchair, his notebook already open on his lap, seemingly oblivious to the potential for crumbs on the upholstery. Chloe Dubois sat quietly on the sofa, clutching her teacup, looking less pale than the day before but still carrying a shadow of shock in her wide, observant eyes. Alistair Fitzwilliam occupied the other end of the sofa, sipping his tea with a practised formality that didn't quite conceal the nervous tension in his shoulders. An air of slight awkwardness hung between them – they were acquaintances through the club, certainly, but not necessarily intimates. This gathering felt purposeful, almost conspiratorial.

Agnes, naturally assuming the role of chair for this impromptu committee of inquiry, cleared her throat. "I trust everyone slept adequately?" she began, her tone practical. "Though I imagine recent events have been somewhat… disruptive to routine."

"Sleep?" Ronnie scoffed lightly, looking up from a complex equation involving torque and bone density. "Biological necessity, but vastly overrated when there are intriguing physical anomalies to consider! The coefficient of restitution between lignum vitae and the human cranium presents a fascinating challenge, especially given the reported…"

"Yes, thank you, Ronnie," Agnes interjected smoothly, cutting off a likely impenetrable physics lecture before it could begin. "Perhaps we could start by pooling our observations from yesterday? Alistair, you witnessed Lord Smythe's interview with Detective Inspector Davies, I believe?"

Fitzwilliam nodded, grateful for a structured starting point. He recounted the interview in detail, focusing on Harry's blustering denials, his disastrously weak alibi, his admissions regarding the argument and the mallet, and the unfortunate turn of phrase involving hypothetical strangulation. "Objectively," he concluded, polishing his spectacles, "he presented as evasive, agitated, and entirely lacking credibility. From a purely circumstantial standpoint, if I were advising the prosecution, I'd feel rather confident. He practically gift-wrapped motive and opportunity, however inadvertently." He sighed. "Yet… watching him, I couldn't shake the feeling his panic felt… misdirected. As if he were terrified, yes, but perhaps not specifically of a murder charge."

Agnes nodded slowly. "My own research corroborates that impression, to a degree." She opened one of her navy journals. "I spent the morning reviewing my records of Lord Smythe's past… incidents." She detailed the previous altercations with Ainsworth – the scorecard incident, the pegging-out dispute, the outburst at the Greens Committee meeting where he'd struck the table. "You see the pattern?" she asked, looking at the others. "Frustration, verbal explosion, occasionally misdirected physical force against *objects*, inevitably followed by retraction or apology. There is no documented precedent for physical violence against a person. While not conclusive, it suggests yesterday's tragic outcome would represent a significant, almost aberrant, escalation if he were indeed responsible in the heat of the moment."

Ronnie tapped his pen. "Consistent with inefficient energy transfer in a spontaneous rage scenario," he murmured, scribbling a note.

"There's something else," Chloe spoke up, her voice quiet but firm, drawing their attention. They all turned to her. She had barely spoken since they arrived, seeming content to listen, absorbing the information. "It's about Mr Ainsworth. And that spot where he was found."

"Yes, Miss Dubois?" Agnes prompted gently. "You mentioned yesterday it was an unusual location for him."

"More than unusual," Chloe confirmed. "He *disliked* that area behind Lawn 3. Complained the soil wasn't right for the rhododendrons, though they grow perfectly well. Said the heritage hellebores were probably misidentified fakes." She paused, gathering her thoughts. "But in the last couple of weeks, he kept going back there. Not just glancing at it, but *looking*."

"Looking?" Fitzwilliam queried. "Looking for what?"

"I don't know," Chloe admitted. "The first time, I thought he was just finding fault with my weeding again. He came over while I was working near there and asked about the drainage, about whether the ground ever got waterlogged after heavy rain. Seemed odd, because it drains perfectly well. Then, maybe a week ago, I saw him there again, poking around near the base of the big rhododendron – the one closest to where…" she swallowed, "…where I found him. He had one of the old planting ledgers from the archive with him."

Agnes sat up straighter. "Which ledger, Chloe? Do you recall?"

"One of the very old ones," Chloe said, frowning in concentration. "Dark green cover, from maybe the 1930s or 40s? He was comparing something in the ledger to the ground, almost like he was measuring or searching for a specific spot referenced in the old plan."

"Fascinating," Agnes breathed. "Those early ledgers contain detailed planting diagrams, notes on soil amendments, even locations of original irrigation lines long since disused." She looked sharply at the others. "Why would Bartholomew Ainsworth, a man primarily concerned with financial accounts and rule enforcement, suddenly develop such a keen interest in decades-old planting schemes and soil composition in that specific, previously ignored, corner of the garden?"

"Unless he wasn't interested in the *plants* at all," Fitzwilliam suggested slowly, the legal part of his brain shifting gears. "Unless he believed something was *hidden* there? Something referenced in that old ledger?"

"Hidden?" Ronnie looked up, intrigued. "What sort of hidden? Buried treasure? A body? Kinetically interesting, but statistically improbable in Toorak."

"Perhaps not treasure," Agnes mused, tapping her finger against her teacup. "But Ainsworth, for all his pedantry, was meticulous. If he was investigating the club's finances, as his recent review of accounts suggests…" – she briefly explained her findings from the previous day regarding Ainsworth's coded notes hinting at embezzlement – "…perhaps he suspected illicit funds were somehow connected to the grounds themselves? Or perhaps he found reference to an old, forgotten club asset documented only in those early records, something someone else might have an interest in keeping hidden?"

Chloe nodded. "He definitely seemed like he was searching for something specific. He looked frustrated when I saw him that second time, like he couldn't find what he was expecting based on the ledger."

The room was silent for a moment as they absorbed this new information. Ainsworth, the victim, hadn't just been randomly attacked near Lawn 3. He had been actively investigating something *in that specific location* shortly before his death, using old club records as his guide. It cast the entire scene in a new light. His presence there wasn't anomalous; it was purposeful. And his death, therefore, might not have been a random consequence of Harry Smythe's temper, but a direct result of whatever he was looking for – or perhaps, what he had found.

"This," Fitzwilliam said, his voice hushed with the dawning

implications, "changes the complexion of things considerably. If Ainsworth was searching for something specific, something potentially valuable or incriminating hidden on the grounds, based on old records…"

"…then his murder might have been premeditated," Agnes finished grimly. "Designed to silence him before he uncovered it, or perhaps *after* he had. Which would make Lord Smythe's very public, very convenient argument look less like a motive and more like… a smokescreen."

The seeds of doubt, already sown by their individual observations, were beginning to sprout, twisting together into a narrative far more complex, and potentially far more dangerous, than simple, hot-blooded murder on the croquet lawn.

****

The implications of Chloe's revelation settled over the small group in Agnes Plummett's sunlit living room. The scent of lemon shortbread mingled with the faint, dusty aroma of old books and pianola rolls, a strangely domestic backdrop for the increasingly sinister picture they were piecing together. Bartholomew Ainsworth hadn't just been murdered; he might have been murdered *because* he was on the verge of uncovering a secret hidden within the very grounds of the Society, a secret possibly documented in eighty-year-old planting ledgers.

Alistair Fitzwilliam felt a familiar tightening in his chest, but this time it wasn't just anxiety; it was overlaid with a lawyer's indignation. "This changes everything," he repeated softly, placing his delicate teacup back onto its saucer with a hand that trembled slightly. "And it makes the police's apparent focus on Lord Smythe seem… well, dangerously premature."

He leaned forward, unconsciously adopting the posture he used when explaining a complex point of law to a particularly obtuse junior counsel. "There's a well-documented phenomenon in investigations," he explained, looking earnestly at the others, "known as 'confirmation bias'. Investigators identify a likely suspect early on – often the most obvious one – and then they subconsciously tend to seek out or interpret evidence in a way that confirms that initial suspicion, while downplaying or ignoring evidence that contradicts it."

He gestured vaguely towards the window, in the direction of Toorak and the club grounds. "Think about it. You have Lord Smythe: loud argument with the victim shortly before discovery, known history of conflict, documented temper, owns the apparent murder weapon, provides a disastrously weak alibi, and behaves shiftily afterwards. From Detective Inspector Davies's perspective, arriving cold onto that scene, Smythe must have looked like a textbook prime suspect. It's the simplest, most direct narrative."

"And yesterday," Fitzwilliam continued, warming to his theme despite his nervousness, "everything Smythe did only served to reinforce that narrative. His defensiveness, his agitation – which we now suspect," he glanced at Agnes, "might stem from other financial pressures – looks exactly like guilt to an investigator predisposed to see it. They might spend valuable time trying to break his (possibly truthful) alibi or finding forensic links between him and the mallet, while potentially ignoring other avenues of enquiry entirely."

"Such as Mr Ainsworth's peculiar horticultural research?" Agnes supplied drily.

"Precisely! Or the possibility the mallet wasn't the primary cause of death. Or the inconsistencies Ronnie has noted." Fitzwilliam paused, considering the procedural implications. "Standard procedure should involve thoroughly investigating the victim's recent activities, his known associates *and* enemies – and poor Bartholomew seems to have cultivated quite a few of the latter, judging by Agnes's research. They should be looking into his finances, his communications… not just focusing on the man with the loud voice and the convenient mallet." He sighed. "But confirmation bias can be insidious. Once a narrative takes hold, it's very difficult to dislodge."

Ronnie, who had been listening with surprising stillness, nodded vigorously, setting down his teacup with a decisive click. "Exactly! And the physical evidence, as currently understood, actively *contradicts* the simple narrative! Which brings me back to the impact dynamics." He leaned forward, his earlier excitement returning, his hands sketching shapes in the air. "Alistair, you grasped the core issue: the difficulty of inflicting that specific injury, in that specific location on the body, during a spontaneous face-to-face altercation without significant bio mechanical inefficiency or leaving more obvious signs of a struggle or differently angled impact."

"But," Ronnie continued, his gaze sweeping over them, "consider the alternative hypothesis prompted by Chloe's observation of the body's position – face down, well into the shrubbery. What if Mr Ainsworth was already incapacitated *before* the blow was struck?"

The air in the room seemed to still. Even the grandfather clock in the corner seemed to hold its breath between ticks.

"Incapacitated?" Chloe whispered.

"Think about it," Ronnie urged, his voice low but intense. "Poison. A drug. A medically induced collapse – perhaps from a pre-existing condition exacerbated by stress, though less likely to be relied upon by a killer. Something that rendered him unconscious or immobile *first*. He falls, or is pushed, into the flowerbed. Then," Ronnie paused for effect, "the assailant delivers the blow with the mallet. Not in rage, necessarily, but as a calculated act."

"To... to ensure death?" Fitzwilliam asked, horrified.

"Possibly. Or, more cunningly," Ronnie suggested, "to *obscure* the true cause of death. To create a violent, obvious injury that directs all attention away from the subtle work of a poison, which might otherwise be detected in a thorough autopsy if the coroner were looking for it specifically." He tapped his notebook. "A significant blow to the head *postmortem*, or even *peri-mortem* while the victim is unconscious, might present differently in autopsy than one delivered during a violent struggle to a fully conscious individual. Less bruising at the impact site relative to the skull fracture, perhaps? Different blood spatter patterns – or lack thereof? I'd need precise forensic data, of course, but the *possibility* is physically plausible!"

He looked directly at Chloe. "You said he looked 'arranged', Chloe. Not just fallen. Could that be consistent with someone positioning an already unconscious body before delivering a final, staged blow?"

Chloe closed her eyes briefly, recalling the awful stillness, the unnatural angle. "Maybe," she said hesitantly. "He looked... wrong. Not like someone who just tripped and hit their head. Stiffer, somehow."

Agnes nodded slowly, her mind already racing through possibilities. "Poison administered how, though? In his tea?" She recalled Ainsworth with his thermos, a constant fixture. "Mildred Pettle often prepared tea for volunteers working late..." She trailed off, aware of the implication but lacking any evidence. "Or perhaps something ingested earlier? Bartholomew was notoriously fussy about his food and drink."

"And some poisons mimic natural causes," Fitzwilliam added, his legal mind recalling infamous cases. "Heart attack, stroke... easily missed unless specifically tested for, especially if there's an obvious alternative cause of death like blunt force trauma staring you in the face."

The pieces hung in the air, coalescing into a disturbing but increasingly coherent alternative picture. Ainsworth wasn't killed in a fit of rage by Harry Smythe. He was potentially poisoned or otherwise incapacitated, likely because of his investigation into the club's secrets (*financial or otherwise, possibly linked to the spot near Lawn 3*). The body was moved or positioned deliberately. The blow with the mallet was delivered afterwards, a calculated misdirection, possibly using Harry's conveniently located (*and perhaps unsecured*) antique mallet specifically to frame the club's most obvious hothead.

"It makes a horrible kind of sense," Fitzwilliam admitted reluctantly. "It explains the victim's position, the potential awkwardness of the blow Ronnie described… and it provides a motive far stronger than a disputed hoop point – the silencing of someone about to expose long-hidden secrets or theft."

"But," Agnes cautioned, bringing them back to practicalities, "it remains pure speculation without evidence. Convincing Detective Inspector Davies to look beyond Lord Smythe, especially when he seems determined to incriminate himself, will require more than theoretical calculations and historical patterns."

Ronnie frowned, already pondering how to quantify the probability of poison versus mallet as primary cause. Chloe looked thoughtful, perhaps recalling other details about Ainsworth's recent behaviour – had he seemed unwell? Complained of anything unusual? Fitzwilliam felt the weight of the situation settle upon him more heavily than ever. If they were right, then not only was an innocent man (*however foolishly he behaved*) the prime suspect, but a calculating killer was still walking among them, hidden behind a facade of clubhouse civility. And they, it seemed, were the only ones beginning to look in the right direction. The question was, what could they possibly do about it?

****

The grandfather clock in the corner of Agnes Plummett's meticulously ordered living room chimed midday, each resonant strike seeming to deepen the sudden, heavy silence that had fallen over the four occupants. Ronnie's hypothesis – poison, incapacitation, a staged blow – hung in the air, stark and chilling against the backdrop of sunlit bookshelves and floral china. It was a theory born from physics and observation, yet it felt intuitively right in a way the simple narrative of Harry Smythe's explosive rage no longer did. It accounted for the inconsistencies that had snagged at each of their minds: Harry's historical pattern stopping short of actual violence, the victim's strangely deliberate position amongst the rhododendrons, the questionable mechanics of the mallet blow itself, and Bartholomew Ainsworth's own recently documented, peculiar interest in that specific, neglected corner of the Society grounds.

Alistair Fitzwilliam broke the silence, voicing the conclusion that had settled upon them all. "So," he began, his voice hushed, as if speaking too loudly might solidify the terrifying possibility, "we are seriously suggesting that the police's prime suspect, Lord Smythe, is likely innocent? That Mr Ainsworth was, in fact, deliberately incapacitated – probably poisoned – *before* being struck with the mallet, and that the entire scene was staged to implicate Smythe?" He ran a hand through his already slightly rumpled hair. "It sounds like something out of… well, out of one of those convoluted mystery novels Agnes occasionally recommends."

Agnes, however, showed no sign of finding the situation fictional. "Truth," she stated, her gaze steady, "is frequently more convoluted than fiction, Alistair. Especially when human greed and self-preservation are involved. If Bartholomew had indeed uncovered significant financial irregularities, as his notes suggest, or stumbled upon some other long-buried secret connected to that specific location…" She let the sentence hang, the implication clear. Motive. A motive far more compelling than a disputed point in a game of croquet.

"The poison hypothesis elegantly resolves the physical anomalies," Ronnie declared, already sketching again, perhaps trying to model diffusion rates or calculate lethal dosages based on sheer speculation. "It accounts for the victim potentially being moved or positioned *after* collapse. It explains why a single, perhaps even awkwardly delivered, blow could appear fatal if the victim's system was already compromised or shut down. It fits the 'arranged' appearance Chloe noted. And," he tapped his pencil decisively, "it allows for a premeditated crime, where the choice of weapon – Smythe's highly recognisable, historically significant mallet, left conveniently near the scene – becomes not an impulsive act of rage, but a calculated piece of misdirection." He looked up, momentarily abandoning his equations. "The crucial variable becomes the *method* of incapacitation, not just the final impact."

Chloe nodded slowly, absorbing the technicalities. "He did seem… a bit off, the last week or so," she offered hesitantly, dredging her memory for details that hadn't seemed significant until now. "More irritable than usual, which is saying something for Mr Ainsworth. And I think he complained to Esme about indigestion once or twice? And maybe looked a bit… pale?" She frowned, unsure if she was projecting or recalling accurately. "I just thought he was stressed about the tournament finances."

"Indigestion? Pallor? Irritability?" Agnes's eyes sharpened. "Symptoms consistent with any number of minor ailments, of course. But also potentially consistent with the cumulative effects of certain slow-acting toxins, depending on dosage and frequency." Her mind, a repository of information gleaned from decades of reading everything from horticultural journals to forensic pathology textbooks (*"for research," she always maintained*), began sifting through possibilities. Arsenic? Antimony? Something more exotic, derived perhaps from the very horticultural specimens the Society cultivated? The irony would be… appropriate.

Fitzwilliam felt a wave of nausea. This was spiralling far beyond a simple case of tempers frayed on the playing field. Poison, embezzlement, historical secrets buried in the garden, a calculating killer hiding amongst their own club members… it felt overwhelming, dangerous. "But," he argued, clinging to a raft of pragmatism in a sea of speculation, "this is all theory. Highly plausible theory, I grant you, based on our combined observations, but theory nonetheless. We have no concrete proof of poison. No evidence linking anyone *else* to the crime besides the circumstantial net tightening around Smythe. What can we possibly *do*? We can hardly march up to Detective Inspector Davies and present her with Ronnie's equations and Agnes's historical character analysis!"

"No," Agnes agreed calmly. "We cannot. As you rightly pointed out, Alistair, confirmation bias is likely already influencing the official investigation. Presenting speculative alternatives without concrete evidence would likely see us dismissed as interfering amateurs, possibly even obstructing justice." Her gaze was firm. "If the police are indeed focused solely on Lord Smythe, then any investigation into alternative possibilities must, initially at least, be undertaken by ourselves. Discreetly, of course."

"Investigate? Ourselves?" Fitzwilliam felt a fresh surge of anxiety. "Agnes, we're talking about murder! And potentially, financial crimes, artefact theft… things that are well outside our purview or expertise! It could be dangerous. What if the killer realises we're looking beyond Lord Smythe?" He recalled the subtle sense of unease Chloe had mentioned, the feeling of being watched. What if it wasn't just paranoia?

"Precisely why discretion is paramount," Agnes stated. "But consider the alternative. Allowing an innocent man – however foolishly he has behaved – to potentially face ruin or wrongful conviction, while a calculating killer remains free within our community? Is that acceptable?" She looked pointedly at Fitzwilliam, whose professional life was dedicated, in theory at least, to the pursuit of justice.

Fitzwilliam squirmed internally. She was right, of course. Ethically, morally… allowing the likely course of events to proceed unchallenged felt deeply wrong, especially now they collectively believed it *was* wrong. His anxiety warred with his sense of duty. He thought of Harry Smythe, blustering and terrified, digging himself deeper with every word. He thought of the calm, efficient killer potentially watching them all, hidden behind a mask of normalcy.

Ronnie seemed unfazed by the danger. "Data," he said simply. "We need more data. Precise forensic details – were toxicology tests performed? What was the *exact* nature of the head wound? What was the estimated time of death versus Smythe's corroborated movements, even allowing for his vague alibi? Can we obtain the mallet's exact weight and dimensions? Access to reliable data is key to refining the hypotheses." He was already formulating a list, treating it like preparing for an astronomical observation run.

"And we need to know what Mr Ainsworth found, or what he was looking for," Chloe added quietly but firmly. "That ledger he had, the old green one. If it pointed him to that spot, maybe it holds the answer." Her earlier shock seemed to have been replaced by a quiet determination, a need to understand the 'why' behind the horror she had discovered.

Agnes nodded, bringing her organisational skills to bear. "Excellent points. Our course, therefore, seems clear, if undertaken with extreme caution. We must pursue parallel lines of inquiry, sharing our findings only amongst ourselves for now." She looked at each of them in turn, assigning roles as naturally as if organising a library cataloguing project.

"Ronnie," she began, "your pursuit of precise physical data is crucial. Perhaps you could engage Barnaby Thornton further? Young apprentices often have access to technical specifications or workshop areas. And Doug Peterson's practical experience might yield insights into operational routines or security lapses that could be relevant."

Ronnie nodded eagerly, already planning his approach angles for information extraction.

"Chloe," Agnes continued, her tone softening slightly, "your knowledge of the grounds and your access as staff are invaluable. That ledger Mr Ainsworth was using – can you ascertain its current location? Is it back in the archive? Still logged out to him? Finding it could be pivotal. And continue observing the area near Lawn 3. Any further disturbances, unusual activity, anything out of place, no matter how small."

Chloe nodded, her expression serious. She understood the importance of small details.

"Alistair," Agnes turned to Fitzwilliam, "your understanding of legal procedure and your professional standing could be useful. Perhaps you could discreetly inquire about the *scope* of the police investigation? Are they considering toxicology as a matter of course? Are they looking into the club's finances beyond a superficial level? Without appearing to interfere, of course," she added, acknowledging his earlier concerns. "And perhaps," her eyes held a glint of steely purpose, "you could ascertain Lord Smythe's legal representation status? He desperately needs competent advice, whether guilty or innocent."

Fitzwilliam swallowed. It felt like crossing a line, moving from passive observation to active, albeit discreet, intervention. But looking at the determined faces around him, and thinking of the smug certainty on Mrs Henderson's face as she'd condemned Harry Smythe earlier, he knew he couldn't stand by. "I… I can make some discreet inquiries," he conceded, feeling his pulse quicken. "Gauge the direction Inspector Davies seems to be taking. And perhaps find a way to suggest to Smythe, through a neutral third party, that he consult a solicitor immediately."

"And I," Agnes concluded, closing her journal with a soft snap, "will delve deeper into Bartholomew Ainsworth's recent activities. His appointments, his communications – if any records exist. I will also continue my analysis of potential financial motives, focusing particularly on discrepancies related to club events or assets documented in the older records. And," she added, a thoughtful look in her eyes, "I believe a thorough review of the membership list, cross-referenced with known grievances against Mr Ainsworth, might prove illuminating."

They sat for another moment in silence, the plan laid out, the commitment made, tacitly or explicitly. The initial shock of the murder was giving way to a shared sense of purpose, a quiet determination to look beyond the obvious, to follow the data, the history, the subtle inconsistencies. It was a dangerous path they were setting out on, armed with little more than observation, deduction, and a shared sense of unease. They were four disparate individuals, brought together by chance and violence, now united, however informally, in the pursuit of a truth hidden beneath layers of garden mulch, financial ledgers, and polite deception. The real investigation, Fitzwilliam thought with a mixture of dread and undeniable anticipation, had just begun.

5

The Treasurer's Ledger

The day following the quartet's impromptu meeting at Agnes Plummett's apartment found the Toorak Croquet & Horticultural Society operating under a cloud so thick it seemed to absorb the very sunlight slanting across its famous lawns. The police tape remained, a garish blue and white slash against the emerald green of Lawn 3, but the overt presence of law enforcement had vanished, leaving behind a vacuum filled with swirling currents of speculation, fear, and a peculiarly Melbourne brand of morbid social analysis. It was clear, from the way conversations ceased abruptly when one approached and the intense, sidelong glances exchanged across the tea tables, that Lord Smythe had been tried and found guilty in the court of clubhouse opinion. His continued absence – rumour had it he'd retreated to his Portsea beach house under doctor's orders (or perhaps solicitor's advice) – only served to cement this verdict.

Alistair Fitzwilliam found the atmosphere almost unbearable. He'd come to the club ostensibly to retrieve a file left in his locker, but truly, he felt a reluctant pull, a need to gauge the prevailing mood and perhaps, discreetly, test the waters regarding Ainsworth's other potential enemies, as agreed upon in Agnes's quiet living room.

He nursed a lukewarm coffee on the verandah, the familiar wicker chair feeling less comfortable than usual. He tried to focus on a ridiculously complex VCAT ruling summary in *The Age*, but the hushed, insistent buzz of conversation from nearby tables kept snagging his attention.

"…always knew Ainsworth would come to a sticky end," Colonel Abernathy declared, his voice a low rumble meant to convey authority but primarily carrying pomposity. He leaned conspiratorially towards Mrs Henderson and a younger, wide-eyed member named Penelope Cartwright. "Man collected enemies like stamps. Remember that business with the Country Womens Association bake sale funds? Accused poor Mrs Fitzherbert – bless her soul – of misallocating threepence! Pursued it for years!"

Mrs Henderson sniffed, adjusting her pearls. "And the time he tried to have Major Dawson suspended for wearing non-regulation socks during a friendly match? The *impertinence*! Bartholomew had no sense of proportion, none at all. Quite frankly," she lowered her voice dramatically, "while one deplores violence, one can almost *understand* poor Harry Smythe finally snapping."

Fitzwilliam felt a familiar surge of despair mixed with irritation. This was precisely the problem. Everyone focused on Ainsworth's petty tyrannies, his talent for causing offence over trivialities. It made him universally disliked, yes, but did it make him murderable? And did it conveniently excuse everyone from looking further? He forced himself to catch Colonel Abernathy's eye as the older man turned from his gossip circle.

"Colonel," Fitzwilliam began, trying to sound casual, "a dreadful business yesterday. Truly dreadful."

"Indeed, Fitzwilliam, indeed," the Colonel boomed, turning his full attention, sensing a fresh audience. "Shakes one to the core. Standards just aren't what they were. Man like Smythe, good family, letting temper get the better of him..."

"Quite," Fitzwilliam interjected smoothly, before the Colonel could gain momentum. "Though, I was wondering... beyond the well-known... friction... with Lord Smythe, had Mr Ainsworth seemed particularly preoccupied recently? Or mentioned any specific worries? As Treasurer, he must have carried significant responsibility." Fitzwilliam felt a pang of anxiety at his own clumsy attempt at interrogation, hoping it sounded like idle curiosity.

The Colonel stroked his moustache thoughtfully. "Preoccupied? Ainsworth was *always* preoccupied! Usually with finding fault. But now you mention it..." He paused. "He *did* seem unusually agitated at the last Finance Committee meeting. Kept going on about needing full historical audits for some of the capital expenditure accounts. Something about inconsistencies in the records for the 1980s clubhouse extension. Seemed excessive even for him. Old Henderson Minor," he nodded towards Mrs Henderson's husband, currently engrossed in the crossword, "tried to tell him it was water under the bridge, but Ainsworth wouldn't let it go. Said something about 'fiduciary duty' and 'unaccounted contingencies.'"

Unaccounted contingencies? 1980s extension? Fitzwilliam filed the information away mentally. Decades-old finances? Could that possibly connect to a murder *now*? It seemed unlikely, yet Ainsworth's recent interest in old planting ledgers suggested he *was* digging into the past for some reason.

Just then, Agnes Plummett arrived, navigating the verandah with her usual quiet determination, nodding politely to acquaintances but making a clear trajectory towards Fitzwilliam's table. She carried a small, leather-bound notebook. Her presence seemed to subtly shift the dynamic; gossip felt less appropriate under her steady, observant gaze.

"Alistair," she greeted him, pulling up a chair. "Colonel. Mrs

Henderson. Miss Cartwright." She acknowledged the others with a precise nod. "A trying time for the Society."

"Indeed, Miss Plummett," Mrs Henderson said, adjusting her pearls again. "We were just discussing poor Bartholomew. Such a… meticulous man."

"Meticulous, certainly," Agnes agreed, her tone neutral but carrying an edge Fitzwilliam recognised. "He applied that meticulousness to many areas. I understand from Esme Weatherly," she continued, addressing Fitzwilliam but ensuring the others could overhear, "that Mr Ainsworth had recently requested access to *all* archived receipts pertaining to major grounds maintenance contracts from the last twenty years. Esme found the request rather broad and time-consuming, especially given his focus seemed to be on minor discrepancies in invoicing from over a decade ago."

Fitzwilliam's internal alarms rang again. The 80s extension, twenty years of grounds maintenance receipts… Ainsworth hadn't just been looking into current accounts or the old planting ledger Chloe mentioned. He seemed to have been undertaking a wide-ranging, potentially explosive, historical audit of the club's entire financial and operational past. Why? What could have triggered such an extensive, and likely highly unpopular, investigation?

"Sounds like Bartholomew, alright," Colonel Abernathy grumbled. "Digging up dirt just for the sake of it, probably. Man loved finding fault more than he loved croquet."

"Perhaps," Agnes allowed, her gaze calm. "Or perhaps he had reason to believe significant discrepancies existed, warranting such a thorough review. His fiduciary duty, as he apparently mentioned." She subtly emphasised the phrase the Colonel had used earlier, linking the two pieces of information.

Fitzwilliam watched the others process this. Mrs Henderson looked vaguely scandalised at the thought of financial impropriety within *their* club. Miss Cartwright looked simply bewildered. Colonel Abernathy harrumphed, perhaps uncomfortable with the idea that Ainsworth's pedantry might have had a genuine, serious purpose after all.

This was crucial, Fitzwilliam realised. Ainsworth wasn't just a universally disliked pedant who tragically crossed paths with Harry Smythe's temper. He was actively, perhaps obsessively, investigating the club's past, focusing on areas involving significant expenditure and historical records. This provided a fertile ground for motives far more complex and dangerous than a simple argument over a hoop point. Who might have been threatened by such an investigation? Someone involved in the 80s extension? A contractor from years ago? A current or former committee member who had overseen those accounts? Mildred Pettle, whose long tenure as Secretary would have given her intimate knowledge of, and potential influence over, those very records?

He felt a renewed sense of urgency, mixed with dread. Their theory – that Ainsworth was silenced because of what he was uncovering – felt increasingly plausible. And the number of people who might have wished him silenced was potentially far larger than just the obvious suspect currently hiding out in Portsea. He needed to find out more about Ainsworth's specific lines of inquiry, and, perhaps more importantly, who else knew about them. He caught Agnes's eye again. Her slight nod confirmed they were thinking along the same lines. The polite panic and easy assumptions of the general membership were a dangerous distraction from the real work that needed doing. Their discreet investigation felt less like meddling now, and more like a necessity. He took a deep breath, steeling himself. Time to subtly inquire about Ainsworth's locker.

****

Later that same afternoon, as the initial wave of morbid discussion began to subside, replaced by the quieter, more persistent hum of ingrained club routine, Agnes Plummett decided it was time. The conversations on the verandah had confirmed her suspicions: Bartholomew Ainsworth hadn't just been unpopular; he'd been actively, and recently, digging into the Society's past financial dealings with a potentially dangerous single-mindedness. If he had indeed found something incriminating, proof might still exist amongst his immediate papers, assuming the killer hadn't been as meticulous in sanitising the scene as Ainsworth himself had been in life. Accessing the small, slightly imposing room designated as the Treasurer's Office, however, presented a challenge. Since the discovery, it had been briefly examined by police but, not being the primary crime scene, was now simply locked, awaiting some future, undetermined administrative process.

Agnes needed a plausible pretext. Rummaging through a murdered man's office, even one she technically shared responsibility for overseeing aspects of via her archival work, felt uncomfortably close to the kind of interference Fitzwilliam had cautioned against. But the potential for vital clues, perhaps missed by an official investigation focused elsewhere, gnawed at her sense of order and her burgeoning need for answers. She formulated a plan, based, as always, on established procedure and verifiable fact.

She found Esme Weatherly in the main lounge, looking harassed as she attempted to field phone calls from concerned (or merely nosy) members and coordinate with the catering staff for the hastily arranged memorial tea planned for the following day. Esme's usual cheerful efficiency was strained, her smile tight around the edges.

"Esme, my dear," Agnes began, her tone carefully pitched between sympathy and practicality. "A moment, if you are not too overwhelmed?"

Esme looked up, pushing a stray lock of hair from her forehead. "Miss Plummett. Of course. Though it's all rather dreadful, isn't it? Poor Bartholomew... and Lord Smythe, well, one hardly knows what to think." She lowered her voice. "The police seemed quite... definite... when they spoke to me earlier."

"Indeed," Agnes acknowledged gravely. "Which brings me, indirectly, to my query. I was assisting Mr Ainsworth last week with sourcing historical donation records for the upcoming Centenary Appeal brochure. Specifically, details regarding the initial endowment for the Abernathy Rose Garden – Colonel Abernathy's grandfather, you know. Bartholomew mentioned he had the relevant accession file from the archive in his office for cross-referencing with early financial ledgers." Agnes allowed a small frown of concern to crease her brow. "With the brochure deadline looming, and poor Bartholomew... indisposed... I was hoping I might retrieve that specific file. It's likely in a plain manilla folder, labelled perhaps 'Abernathy Endowment' or similar."

It was a fabrication, of course, but a plausible one. Ainsworth *had* been interested in historical finances, and Agnes *was* peripherally involved with the Centenary committee. Esme hesitated, clearly uncomfortable.

"His office? Oh, I don't know, Miss Plummett. The police said not to disturb anything unnecessarily..."

"Quite right," Agnes agreed smoothly. "But this is a specific, documented item related to ongoing Society business. Not personal effects. I would merely retrieve the single file and depart immediately. It would save considerable difficulty later, trying to reconstruct the donation records from scratch." She paused, adding gently, "And I believe Bartholomew himself, meticulous as he was about Society affairs continuing uninterrupted, would have wished it."

Esme wavered, caught between protocol and Agnes's undeniable authority within the club's historical sphere, combined with the appeal to Ainsworth's known character. "Well… I suppose… if it's just the one file, and you're certain you know where it might be?" She glanced around the lounge nervously. "Perhaps if you were very quick? I have the master key here." She fumbled in her pocket, producing a small ring of keys, her hand trembling slightly. "Let me just check no one official is still about…"

Agnes had anticipated this and enlisted Chloe Dubois, who happened to be quietly tidying the magazine rack nearby – a task Esme had given her earlier, perhaps just to keep her occupied and away from the more morbid gossip circles. "Chloe, dear," Agnes said, turning to her, "perhaps you could accompany me? Just to hold the door? My hands might be full with the file." It provided Chloe with a legitimate reason to be there, acting as both assistant and subtle lookout.

Chloe nodded, her expression serious. She understood, without needing explicit instruction, her secondary role.

Esme, somewhat reassured by the pragmatism of the request and Agnes's inclusion of Chloe, finally acquiesced. "Alright then. But please, Miss Plummett, be as quick and discreet as possible. This whole situation is… unsettling." She led the way down the quiet corridor towards the Treasurer's office, unlocked the door with a soft click, and pushed it open, hovering anxiously in the doorway as Agnes and Chloe stepped inside.

The office was small, dominated by a large, dark wood desk and several tall, grey filing cabinets. A single window looked out onto the less-frequented western side of the grounds, where the compost heaps and potting sheds were located. The room smelled strongly of lemon-scented furniture polish and slightly stale paper. And it was, as expected, impeccably, almost unnaturally, tidy.

Unlike the controlled chaos of her own archive, filled with overflowing boxes and stacks of research materials, Ainsworth's office was a monument to minimalist order. The desk surface was clear except for a neat blotter, a pen set, an old-fashioned Rolodex, and a single, slim folder labelled "Tournament Expenses – Current". No stray papers, no works-in-progress, no piles awaiting filing. The 'In' tray was empty; the 'Out' tray contained only two stamped letters addressed to banking institutions. The bookshelves held rows of financial ledgers, arranged by year, spines perfectly aligned. Even the wastepaper bin was empty.

Agnes felt a prickle of profound unease that had nothing to do with being in a dead man's office. This wasn't just tidy; it felt… sterile. Sanitised. Where were the files related to the extensive historical investigations members had mentioned Ainsworth undertaking? The grounds maintenance receipts? The 1980s extension audit papers? The old green planting ledger Chloe had seen him with? There was no sign of any active research, no hint of the obsessive digging people had described. It was as if his recent, potentially controversial work had simply evaporated. Had the police taken everything? Unlikely, given this wasn't the primary crime scene and their focus seemed fixed on Harry Smythe. Had Ainsworth himself, in a fit of supreme organisation, filed everything away perfectly before his demise? Possible, given his nature, but it felt improbable for multiple active investigations. Or had someone else been in here *after* his death but *before* the office was officially secured? Someone who knew exactly what potentially incriminating papers to remove?

"See anything resembling the Abernathy file, Miss Plummett?" Esme whispered anxiously from the doorway.

"Not immediately, Esme," Agnes replied calmly, masking her disquiet. "Allow me a moment to check the main filing cabinet under 'Donations'." She moved towards the grey metal cabinets, her movements deliberate. Chloe stood quietly near the desk, her eyes scanning the room, noticing the almost aggressive lack of personal touches – no photographs, no decorative items, just functional office equipment. It felt less like an office, more like a holding cell for numbers.

Agnes opened the drawer labelled 'C-F'. The files within were perfectly ordered, tabs aligned. She located 'Donations – Historical' and pulled it out. Inside, various endowments were neatly sectioned. She quickly found the 'Abernathy Rose Garden' sub-folder. It contained copies of original correspondence and bank statements from the 1920s, meticulously preserved. But it was thin. No sign of recent notes, no indication Ainsworth had been actively working on it. Her stated reason for being here yielded nothing, confirming her internal suspicion.

"Ah, here seems to be the core Abernathy material," Agnes announced, keeping her voice neutral for Esme's benefit. "Though perhaps Bartholomew kept his working notes separately." A plausible excuse to continue looking.

She replaced the file and moved towards the desk, her gaze sweeping across its clean surface. Nothing. She gently lifted the desk blotter. Beneath it lay only a pristine sheet of blotting paper, unnaturally blank. No indentations from recent writing, no stray ink marks. It was almost *too* clean. Had it been recently replaced?

Her eyes scanned the desk again. The Rolodex – filled with business contacts, committee members, suppliers. The pen set – standard, functional. The single folder – "Tournament Expenses". Almost dismissively, she opened it. Inside were receipts for tennis ball orders, line marking paint, trophy engraving – all neatly clipped together, awaiting Ainsworth's final sign-off. Mundane. Except… tucked right at the back, almost hidden behind the last receipt, was something that didn't belong.

It wasn't a receipt. It was a small, stiff card, the type used for library catalogue systems in decades past, slightly yellowed with age. It looked like a call slip from a major research library – perhaps the State Library of Victoria. Typed neatly on the slip was a call number – alphanumeric, specific to a library classification system – and beneath it, handwritten in Ainsworth's spiky, precise script, were two words: *"Pyrus Malus."* Below that, another annotation: *"Cf. Sect. IV, Para 12."*

Agnes felt a jolt, a spark of connection in the sterile room. *Pyrus Malus*. The botanical name for the common apple tree. Why would Ainsworth, Treasurer of the Society, make a note of a library call number for a book presumably about apples, especially using its Latin name? And what did "Cf. Sect. IV, Para 12" refer to? Section IV of what? The apple book? Or something else entirely?

She glanced towards the doorway. Esme was fidgeting nervously. Chloe met Agnes's eyes briefly, sensing a shift in her focus. Quickly, heart thudding almost guiltily, Agnes slipped the call slip into the pocket of her cardigan. It was improper, potentially interfering with evidence, but her instinct screamed that this small, anomalous card, overlooked perhaps by police focusing on obvious financial documents, was important. It felt like the first tangible thread leading away from the convenient narrative surrounding Harry Smythe.

"No, nothing further here, Esme," Agnes said, turning back towards the door, her expression calm, betraying none of her internal excitement or unease. "Thank you for allowing me access. Bartholomew must have filed his working notes elsewhere. No matter, I shall manage."

She ushered Chloe out, allowing Esme to lock the door securely behind them. As they walked back down the corridor, the scent of lemon polish replaced by Esme's nervous lavender perfume, Agnes's mind raced. *Pyrus Malus*. An apple tree. Section IV, Paragraph 12. A library call slip hidden in the tournament expenses. It made no logical sense in the context of croquet club finances. Which meant, Agnes suspected with growing certainty, it probably made perfect sense in the context of whatever secret Bartholomew Ainsworth had been digging for – the secret that had ultimately led to his most improper end. The sterile office hadn't yielded Ainsworth's research, but it had offered something potentially more valuable: the first cryptic clue pointing towards its hidden subject.

****

The rhythmic clink of silver spoons against fine bone china, the gentle murmur of subdued conversation, the comforting aroma of freshly brewed tea and warm scones – the rituals of afternoon tea at the Toorak Croquet & Horticultural Society continued, albeit under the long shadow cast by murder. It was as if the members, adrift on a sea of shock and uncertainty, clung fiercely to these familiar customs, seeking reassurance in the established order of things. And at the centre of this carefully reconstructed normality, moving with quiet grace and seemingly infinite empathy, was Mildred Pettle.

Agnes Plummett, seated once more on the verandah, observed the Club Secretary with an intensity that belied her placid expression. Having secured the cryptic library call slip from Ainsworth's sterile office, Agnes felt a renewed, sharper focus. Mildred, who had appeared merely efficient and perhaps slightly obsequious before, now seemed transformed in Agnes's perception into a figure of profound, unsettling ambiguity. Every gesture, every carefully chosen word, demanded scrutiny.

Mildred was currently consoling Mrs Henderson, who seemed to have appointed herself chief mourner despite her well-known antipathy towards the deceased. "Such a dreadful shock, Mildred," Mrs Henderson was saying, dabbing her eyes with a predictably pristine handkerchief. "Poor Bartholomew... to think, just yesterday he was arguing about the petunia placement."

"It is indeed tragic, Sybil," Mildred murmured, placing a comforting hand briefly on Mrs Henderson's arm. Her voice was pitched perfectly – soft, sympathetic, yet carrying just enough to be overheard by those nearby, including Agnes and Fitzwilliam, who had joined her at the table. "He seemed terribly stressed lately, did you notice? The pressures of the Treasurer role, the upcoming tournament... I did urge him to perhaps delegate more, but he was always so very conscientious."

Agnes mentally filed away the carefully chosen words. *Stressed.* A general, non-specific term. It subtly countered the narrative that Ainsworth might have been stressed about a *specific* investigation. It painted a picture of a man already overburdened, perhaps prone to collapsing under pressure, lending a shred of plausibility to an accident theory, even though the mallet blow complicated that. And the compliment – *conscientious* – sounded genuine, a respectful nod to the deceased that simultaneously masked any deeper knowledge of his recent, potentially troublesome activities. It was, Agnes admitted with grudging admiration, a masterful performance of compassionate deflection.

Fitzwilliam, seated opposite Agnes, shifted uncomfortably. He found Mildred Pettle's solicitousness almost suffocating. He remembered her smooth explanations regarding the minor financial anomaly he'd queried earlier – plausible, slightly flustered, making *him* feel like the one being intrusive. Now, watching her manage the collective grief and speculation, he saw not just efficiency, but a formidable level of social control. She was subtly shaping the narrative, reinforcing the acceptable versions of events while quietly discouraging uncomfortable lines of inquiry.

Colonel Abernathy approached the table, accepting a cup of tea from Mildred. "Any further word from the police, Mildred?" he rumbled. "Heard they let young Smythe go back to Portsea? Seems dashed premature if you ask me."

Mildred sighed softly, a picture of concerned propriety. "The Detective Inspector was very… thorough, Colonel. Very professional. One must trust they know what they are doing. She assured me they are pursuing all lines of inquiry." Another carefully neutral statement, designed to reassure while revealing nothing. She then added, almost as an afterthought, "Though one does feel for Lord Smythe. That dreadful temper… but to imagine it could lead to *this*… it's simply unthinkable, isn't it?"

Unthinkable. The perfect word, Fitzwilliam noted grimly. It validated the members' shock while subtly reinforcing the idea that while Harry's temper was known, *murder* was beyond the pale, thus paradoxically making the leap to believing he *did* snap seem even larger, yet simultaneously implying that if *he* didn't do it, who else possibly could? It cleverly shut down further speculation by appealing to the members' sense of social boundaries.

He decided to test the waters himself, seizing a brief pause in the conversation. "Mildred," he began, attempting a tone of casual concern, "Agnes mentioned Mr Ainsworth had been looking into some historical club records recently – finances, maintenance, that sort of thing. Did he seem particularly concerned about anything he found? Mention any specific discrepancies?"

Mildred turned her gaze towards Fitzwilliam, her expression one of mild, sympathetic confusion. There was no flicker of alarm, no hesitation. "Historical records? Oh, Bartholomew was always interested in the details, wasn't he?" she said with a small, sad smile. "Especially leading up to the Centenary – ensuring everything was perfectly documented. He did ask me for access to the older account ledgers a few weeks ago, yes. Said something about wanting to verify donation sources for the Appeal brochure Agnes is working on." She glanced at Agnes, seamlessly weaving Agnes's own fabricated pretext into her narrative. "I believe he also mentioned cross-referencing some grounds-keeping invoices from years back, possibly related to warranty claims on old equipment? He didn't mention any specific *worries*, Alistair. Just his usual meticulous attention to detail. Perhaps," she added softly, "he was simply overworking himself. He seemed quite tired."

Tired. Stressed. Overworked. Fitzwilliam felt a profound frustration. Mildred was expertly painting a picture of Ainsworth as a man burdened by general pressures, his historical research framed as benign administrative tidying or routine Centenary preparations. She acknowledged his actions but stripped them of any potentially sinister context. She confirmed he accessed records she controlled, yet portrayed it as utterly unremarkable. Every avenue Fitzwilliam had hoped to explore, she gently blocked with a plausible, harmless explanation, all while maintaining an air of gentle concern. It was like wrestling with smoke.

Agnes, meanwhile, observed Mildred's hands as she poured more tea for the Colonel. Perfectly steady. Her gaze, when it met Agnes's, was clear, perhaps a little sad, but revealed nothing. Yet Agnes couldn't shake the image of the sterile office, the missing research papers, the almost aggressively clean desk blotter. Someone had likely been in that office after Ainsworth's death. Someone who knew what to look for. Mildred, with her master key and her intimate knowledge of Ainsworth's work habits, would have had both opportunity and, if she were the embezzler Ainsworth had potentially uncovered, overwhelming motive. But proving it? That seemed, at this moment, almost impossible. The woman was a fortress of polite deflection.

Chloe arrived then, carrying a tray of fresh scones from the kitchen. She placed them on the table, avoiding meeting anyone's eye directly, still uncomfortable being near the centre of the club's attention. Mildred gave her a warm, encouraging smile. "Thank you, Chloe dear. You've been such a help today, especially after your dreadful ordeal yesterday. We do appreciate it."

Chloe mumbled something noncommittal and quickly retreated towards the relative anonymity of the doorway. Agnes watched her go, then looked back at Mildred. Had Mildred noticed Chloe assisting Agnes in accessing the office earlier? Unlikely, perhaps, but Mildred seemed to notice everything. Was that warm smile genuine appreciation, or a subtle reminder of Chloe's junior status, a warning not to step outside her designated role? With Mildred, it was impossible to be sure. Every interaction felt layered, potentially coded.

Ronnie Peterson wandered over, looking vaguely dissatisfied. "No useful data," he announced to the table at large, apparently having failed to extract meaningful forensic details from Barnaby or any lingering police contacts. "Plenty of speculation about mallet velocity based on televised cricket swings, utterly irrelevant. Need mass, impact angle, tissue displacement metrics…"

"Ronnie," Agnes said quietly but firmly, "perhaps we could discuss coefficients later? We were just reflecting on poor Bartholomew."

Ronnie blinked, momentarily pulled from his calculations. "Ah. Yes. Unfortunate termination. Though," he added, unable to resist, "the mechanics remain sub-optimal for the Smythe hypothesis."

Mildred gave Ronnie a look of gentle pity, as one might regard a clever but socially inept child. "Science is wonderful, Mr Peterson, but sometimes… things are just tragically simple, aren't they? A moment's anger, a dreadful mistake…" She sighed again, letting the implication hang. *Tragically simple.* The phrase seemed designed to shut down further complex analysis, reinforcing the easy answer.

As Mildred turned to offer scones to Colonel Abernathy, expertly drawing him into a discussion about the need for enhanced security lighting near the boundary fence (a practical, forward-looking suggestion that subtly shifted focus away from internal matters), Agnes felt a grudging respect for her adversary, assuming her suspicions were correct. Mildred Pettle was playing a masterful game, using the club's inherent inertia, its reliance on social codes, and its members' willingness to accept the obvious narrative as her shield. She was hiding in plain sight, protected by decades of perceived harmlessness and her current performance of unimpeachable competence and sympathy.

Fitzwilliam caught Agnes's eye. His expression was glum, mirroring her own internal frustration. They had their doubts, their theories, their tiny, cryptic clue from the library slip burning a hole in Agnes's pocket. But Mildred Pettle, surrounded by tea, sympathy, and a smokescreen of perfectly plausible explanations, seemed utterly untouchable. Breaking through that facade would require more than just observation and deduction. It would require concrete evidence, a lever strong enough to dislodge the carefully constructed narrative she was so expertly maintaining. And finding that lever, Fitzwilliam suspected, would be very difficult – and potentially very dangerous – indeed. The polite surface of the Toorak Croquet & Horticultural Society felt thinner, more brittle than ever before, barely concealing the darkness they were now certain lay beneath.

6

Following the Money (or Lack Thereof)

The Treasurer's office, when Alistair Fitzwilliam entered it for the second time in two days, felt different. Yesterday, under the guise of retrieving a non-existent file with Agnes, the space had felt sterile, unnervingly tidy, hinting at secrets removed. Today, armed with reluctant but official permission from the Club Committee (facilitated by a carefully worded request from Fitzwilliam emphasising the need for continuity in managing essential payments, and likely swayed by Esme Weatherly's discreet support), the room felt less sterile and more like a meticulously constructed illusion beginning to fray at the edges under close scrutiny.

He wasn't granted unsupervised access, naturally. Esme Weatherly herself sat in the only other chair, ostensibly catching up on correspondence but casting frequent, anxious glances towards Fitzwilliam and the large, leather-bound cash books and weighty box files she had retrieved for him from the main safe. Her presence was both a procedural necessity and, Fitzwilliam suspected, a subtle form of oversight encouraged by a committee deeply uncomfortable with the idea of *anyone* – let alone a lawyer known for his anxious precision – scrutinising finances in the wake of the Treasurer's murder.

"The main cash book for the last financial year, Mr Fitzwilliam," Esme said, her voice strained. "And the reconciled bank statements. Mildred usually prepares the quarterly reports from these… she's offered to assist, of course, but the Committee felt… well, perhaps an external eye initially…" She trailed off, clearly uncomfortable with the implications.

"Quite understandable, Esme," Fitzwilliam replied soothingly, though his own nerves were taut. "Just ensuring upcoming supplier payments can be processed smoothly. Wouldn't want the caterers or the lawn care service going unpaid in all this… disruption." He opened the heavy cash book, the pages thick and smelling faintly of quality paper and old ink. The columns were filled with Bartholomew Ainsworth's spiky, precise handwriting documenting receipts and payments, each entry meticulously dated and referenced. At the bottom of each page, however, the reconciliation calculations and summary notes were in a different hand – a neat, rounded, almost self-effacing script that Fitzwilliam recognised instantly as Mildred Pettle's. Ainsworth recorded; Mildred reconciled and reported.

Fitzwilliam began his review, forcing himself into the methodical mindset he used when auditing discovery documents in complex litigation. He started with the basics: checking that opening balances carried forward correctly, ensuring page totals added up (a task Ainsworth, of all people, was unlikely to have erred on, but thoroughness was key), comparing logged receipts against bank deposit statements, cross-referencing major payment entries against supplier invoices requested from the corresponding box file.

Hours seemed to pass. The grandfather clock in the main lounge chimed three, then four. Sunlight slanted lower through the window, illuminating dust motes stirred by the turning pages. Esme shifted occasionally, wrote a few letters, sighed softly. Outside, the muffled sounds of a croquet match starting on Lawn 1 – the club attempting, however tentatively, to reclaim normalcy – provided a surreal counterpoint to Fitzwilliam's grim task.

And he found… nothing. Absolutely nothing amiss. Every deposit slip matched the banked total. Every payment entry corresponded precisely to an approved invoice, signed off by Ainsworth and often a committee head. Petty cash withdrawals were documented, reconciled, and signed for. Even notoriously tricky areas like bar takings versus stock levels, or income from social event ticket sales versus attendance numbers (areas where minor 'leakage' often occurred in club accounts), seemed impeccably aligned. The reconciliations prepared by Mildred were flawless, explaining every minor variance, cross-referencing every adjustment, presenting a picture of absolute financial probity.

It was this very perfection that gnawed at Fitzwilliam, amplifying the unease he'd felt the previous day. He'd spent twenty years re-viewing corporate accounts, from small businesses to multinational subsidiaries. He knew the natural ebb and flow of finances, the inevitable small discrepancies, the occasional transposition errors, the slightly late reconciliations, the minor disputes with suppliers, the odd unexplained variance that required investigation. Accounts, like life, were rarely perfectly neat. They had texture, friction, loose ends.

These accounts, however, were smooth as polished glass. Too smooth. There were no loose ends. Refunds from suppliers seemed to be processed instantly, without the usual lag. 'Miscellaneous Expenses', often a dumping ground for minor, hard-to-categorise items, were remarkably infrequent and always seemed to involve suspiciously round numbers. Reports generated from these books – presumably by Mildred – were formatted with unnerving consistency, lacking the usual annotations or corrections one might expect, especially from someone as notoriously critical as Ainsworth.

Fitzwilliam paused, leaning back in the hard wooden chair, rubbing his eyes. Was he projecting suspicion where none was warranted? Was this simply the result of two meticulous individuals – Ainsworth in recording, Mildred in reconciling – achieving a level of accounting perfection rarely seen in the volunteer-run world of social clubs? Perhaps. Ainsworth *was* obsessive about detail. And Mildred *was* universally acknowledged as supremely efficient, the quiet engine that kept the Society running smoothly behind the scenes.

Yet… his conversation with Agnes and the Colonel resonated. Ainsworth hadn't just been reviewing current accounts. He'd been digging into *historical* expenditure. The 80s extension. Twenty years of grounds maintenance contracts. Why? If the current books were this perfect, what had driven him to look backwards with such intensity? Unless… unless the perfection *itself* was the camouflage.

He thought about sophisticated embezzlement techniques he'd encountered professionally, usually in far larger organisations. Lapping schemes, where incoming payments were diverted and covered by subsequent receipts – difficult to sustain long-term and requiring constant manipulation. Ghost employees or suppliers – unlikely in a club where most people knew each other. Fraudulent expense reimbursements – possible, but Ainsworth likely scrutinised those closely. Misclassification of expenses – hiding illicit spending within legitimate budget categories? That felt more plausible here. Large, opaque categories like 'Clubhouse Maintenance' or 'Centenary Preparations' could potentially conceal significant diversions if not properly audited with supporting documentation.

And who prepared the summaries? Who allocated expenses to categories for reporting purposes? Mildred. Ainsworth signed off, yes, but did he merely check the totals? Did he rely on Mildred's summaries rather than auditing the underlying transactions himself? Fitzwilliam recalled the sheer volume of invoices in the box files. It would take days, possibly weeks, to audit even one year thoroughly. Had Ainsworth, despite his pedantry, simply trusted Mildred's summaries, his signature becoming a rubber stamp on her carefully constructed financial narratives?

Then Fitzwilliam remembered something else – Ainsworth's supposed recent agitation about needing *full historical audits*. His comments about 'fiduciary duty' and 'unaccounted contingencies'. This wasn't the behaviour of a man satisfied with the current state of perfectly reconciled books. This was the behaviour of a man who suspected the perfection was a lie, who had perhaps found a thread in the past – maybe related to that 80s extension or an old contract – that, if pulled, might unravel the entire tapestry. He had likely started digging backwards to find the *origin* of a discrepancy he suspected was still ongoing, cleverly hidden beneath the flawless surface of the current accounts.

Fitzwilliam felt a surge of adrenaline that quickly morphed back into anxiety. If this were true, then Mildred Pettle wasn't just an efficient secretary; she was potentially a highly skilled, long-term embezzler who had expertly managed the accounts – and perhaps Ainsworth's scrutiny – for years. Until now. Until Ainsworth started pulling on that historical thread.

He needed to look closer, not just at the totals, but at the *nature* of the expenditures, especially in those broad categories. He pulled one of the box files towards him: 'Grounds Maintenance Invoices, 2023-2024'. He started going through them, not just checking the amounts against the cash book entry, but looking at the suppliers, the descriptions of work done. Fertilisers, lawnmower repairs, tree surgery, line marking… it all seemed plausible. He compared invoices month by month. Mostly consistent suppliers, amounts varying seasonally as expected. Nothing immediately jumped out.

He moved to the 'Clubhouse Maintenance' file. Plumbing repairs, electrical checks, painting, new carpet for the lounge last year... again, seemingly legitimate invoices from known local firms. He paused at a series of invoices from late last year labelled "Urgent Roof Repairs – West Wing". The amounts were significant. He vaguely recalled discussions about leaks over the billiards room. He checked the cash book – payments duly recorded, signed off by Ainsworth. He looked back at the invoices. 'WeatherTech Roofing Solutions'. He didn't recognise the name. Most other repairs used 'Henderson & Sons Plumbing' or 'Toorak Electrical'. He made a small, discreet pencil mark next to the entry in his notepad. Probably nothing, just a specialist contractor. But still... an unfamiliar name for a major expense.

He spent another hour trawling through invoices, his initial frustration replaced by a grim determination. He found two more unfamiliar supplier names under 'Centenary Event Deposits' – 'Vintage Marquee Hire Pty Ltd' and 'Bespoke Botanical Displays'. Again, plausible expenses, properly recorded and signed off. But unfamiliar. He noted them down.

Esme cleared her throat pointedly. "Getting late, Mr Fitzwilliam. Will you be needing these records much longer?"

Fitzwilliam started, realising the office was now deep in shadow, the sun having dipped below the clubhouse roof line. "Ah, no, Esme. Thank you. I believe I have what I need for now to ensure the immediate payments are in order." He carefully closed the ledgers and stacked the files, his mind racing. He hadn't found a smoking gun, no obvious fraud leaping off the page. But he had found... perfection. A suspicious, unnerving perfection in the current books, coupled with hints of Ainsworth's deep dive into historical accounts and a few unfamiliar supplier names tucked away in recent major expenses. It wasn't proof. But it was enough. Enough to confirm that the smooth surface of the Society's finances, so expertly maintained by Mildred Pettle, likely concealed something deep, complex, and worth killing to protect. His role, he now saw, wasn't just about verifying payments. It was about finding the single flaw in that perfect facade. And he had a dreadful feeling it would be like searching for a single grain of sand on a vast, deceptive beach.

****

The following morning found Agnes Plummett ensconced within her own personal archive, a small study off the main living room of her South Yarra apartment. If the Society's archive felt like a repository of official history, this room felt like its annotated, cross-referenced, and occasionally opinionated companion volume. Floor-to-ceiling bookshelves lined three walls, housing not just literature but rows upon rows of archival boxes, meticulously labelled binders, and decades of her personal journals. The fourth wall was dominated by a large antique partner's desk, its surface currently occupied by several open folders, a magnifying glass, a fresh pot of Darjeeling tea, and Agnes herself, posture upright, spectacles perched precisely on her nose.

Sunlight, filtered through the leaves of the plane tree outside her window, cast dappled patterns across the room, illuminating the faint scent of ageing paper, beeswax polish, and brewing tea. A grandfather clock ticked rhythmically in the hallway, a sound that usually provided Agnes with a sense of comforting order, but today seemed to mark the passing of precious time in a race against… what, precisely? Against Detective Inspector Davies potentially closing the case on Harry Smythe? Against the killer realising their carefully constructed facade was being subtly probed? Agnes wasn't entirely sure, but a sense of quiet urgency propelled her work.

Alistair Fitzwilliam's findings from the Treasurer's office the previous afternoon had been profoundly unsettling. His description of the club's current accounts as *too* perfect, suspiciously devoid of the minor variances and scuffs of everyday financial life, resonated deeply with Agnes's own observations of Mildred Pettle's smooth, almost invisible, control over administrative matters. It suggested a level of sophisticated, long-term manipulation that was deeply alarming. But it was Fitzwilliam's confirmation that Ainsworth *had* been digging into historical accounts – specifically the 1980s clubhouse extension and decades of grounds keeping contracts – that had crystallised Agnes's own research objective this morning.

If Ainsworth suspected present-day perfection was masking past sins, Agnes needed to understand that past. More specifically, she needed to understand Ainsworth's *own* relationship with the club's financial history. Had he always been the inflexible stickler for rules everyone knew (and mostly disliked)? Or was his recent crusade against historical discrepancies a new development? And if so, why? Was it truly just fiduciary duty, as the Colonel had scoffed? Or was there something more personal driving him? Had he, perhaps, encountered financial irregularities in the past and reacted… differently?

Her starting point was the 1980s – specifically, the period covering the major West Wing extension to the clubhouse, a project known to have run significantly over budget and caused considerable controversy at the time. She had retrieved the relevant Society Minute Books, the Treasurer's Reports from that era (prepared by Ainsworth's predecessor, a notoriously laissez-faire gentleman named Humphrey Carmichael, Vivienne's late husband), and, crucially, her own journals from the period. Agnes, even then in her late thirties and already a respected librarian and meticulous observer, had been on the House Committee during the extension planning.

She opened her journal, Volume XII, labelled '1985-1987'. Her handwriting then was slightly rounder, less angular than now, but just as precise. She scanned the entries, bypassing notes on tournament results and horticultural society lectures, searching for references to the extension project. Ah, here. *"July 10th, 1986. House Committee Meeting. Heated discussion re: West Wing budget overrun. Contractor (Modern Build Pty Ltd) claims unforeseen foundation issues. Humphrey Carmichael (Treasurer) presents revised forecast – 35% above original estimate. Considerable consternation. B. Ainsworth (newly elected committee member, ex-auditor background noted) questions lack of contingency planning in initial budget. Raises point re: contractual penalties for delays. Appears well-informed but excessively critical for a newcomer. Motion to approve revised budget passed, majority reluctant."*

Agnes paused, remembering that meeting. Young Bartholomew, barely forty then, already displaying the rigidity and critical eye that would become his hallmark. He'd been right about the lack of contingency, of course, but his manner had ruffled feathers immediately.

She cross-referenced the official Minute Book for the same date. It recorded the discussion far more blandly: *"Treasurer presented revised budget forecast for West Wing Extension due to unforeseen site complications. After discussion, motion to approve revised forecast proposed by Mr Henderson Sr, seconded by Mrs Albright, carried."* No mention of heated debate, Ainsworth's specific objections, or the committee's reluctance. The official record, as so often, smoothed over the uncomfortable realities.

Agnes continued reading through her journal entries for late 1986 and early 1987. More budget blowouts. Delays attributed to supplier issues. Arguments about the quality of fixtures. Ainsworth consistently raising objections, demanding stricter oversight, often clashing with Humphrey Carmichael, who favoured a more 'gentlemanly agreement' approach with contractors. Then, a significant entry: "*March 4th, 1987. Special Finance Subcommittee meeting (attended: H. Carmichael, B. Ainsworth, G. Henderson Sr.). Purpose: Address final $50,000 shortfall for West Wing completion. Mood tense. Carmichael reveals unexpected anonymous donation of $50,000 received via solicitor's trust account, specifically earmarked for West Wing completion. Source strictly confidential per donor's request. Ainsworth questions provenance & timing intensely. Argues for rejection pending clarification. Henderson Sr argues pragmatic need – accept donation, complete project, avoid further member levies. Ainsworth eventually withdraws objection, citing lack of concrete grounds for refusal, but voices 'profound reservations regarding anonymous contributions lacking transparency'. Minutes likely to record only 'Generous anonymous donation gratefully received, enabling project completion'.*"

Agnes sat back, her teacup halfway to her lips. An anonymous $50,000 donation, appearing precisely when needed to cover a controversial budget shortfall? That was highly irregular, even back in the more relaxed financial climate of the 80s. And Ainsworth, despite his reservations, had ultimately acquiesced. He hadn't pursued the issue, hadn't demanded transparency, hadn't resigned in protest. He had, it seemed, allowed the matter to be swept under the carpet in the name of expediency.

Why? Was it pressure from senior committee members like Henderson Sr (father of the current member who disliked Ainsworth)? Was it deference to Humphrey Carmichael, the well-liked, easygoing Treasurer? Or was it simply that, despite his critical nature, the younger Ainsworth lacked the political capital or perhaps the unwavering conviction to force the issue against the prevailing desire to simply get the problematic project finished?

She cross-referenced the official Finance Subcommittee minutes for that date. Just as she'd predicted in her journal: *"Discussion held regarding final project funding. Treasurer reported receipt of a significant anonymous donation sufficient to cover outstanding costs. Donation accepted with gratitude. Motion to proceed with final payments carried unanimously."* Unanimous. Ainsworth's "profound reservations" had vanished entirely from the official record.

This discovery fundamentally shifted Agnes's perception of the victim. Bartholomew Ainsworth wasn't an unwavering monolith of probity throughout his club tenure. He had, at least once, compromised. He had been aware of a significant financial irregularity – a highly suspicious, anonymous donation potentially masking something else entirely (a loan? funds diverted from elsewhere? payoff?) – and had chosen not to pursue it rigorously.

Now, decades later, he embarks on a relentless historical audit, demanding transparency, digging into old accounts, focusing on precisely the kinds of areas where past issues might have been buried. Was his recent crusade driven by a belated attack of conscience? Was he trying to rectify his own past complicity? Or had he stumbled upon *new* evidence related to that old $50,000 donation, perhaps realising its true source or discovering that the pattern of financial manipulation hadn't stopped in 1987?

And who else remembered that anonymous donation? Henderson Sr was long gone. Humphrey Carmichael had passed away years ago. But others on the main committee at that time might still be members, or have close ties. Could Ainsworth's digging have threatened to expose not just historical irregularities, but individuals who had benefited from, or been complicit in, that long-ago arrangement?

Agnes felt a familiar thrill of intellectual discovery mingled with a growing sense of dread. This wasn't just about recent embezzlement potentially committed by Mildred Pettle, skilfully hidden within flawless current accounts. It might also be about secrets buried decades ago, secrets involving people beyond Mildred, secrets that Ainsworth, in his final, obsessive investigation, had unwittingly threatened to unearth.

She carefully marked the relevant pages in her journal and the minute books. She needed to research 'Modern Build Pty Ltd', the contractor for the extension. She needed to review membership lists from the late 80s, identifying committee members from that era who were still involved with the Society. The pool of individuals who might have wished Bartholomew Ainsworth silenced was widening, stretching back through the seemingly placid history of the club.

Her gaze fell upon the small library call slip still tucked safely in her pocket. *Pyrus Malus. Cf. Sect. IV, Para 12.* An apple tree. It seemed completely disconnected from clubhouse extensions and anonymous donations. Yet… Ainsworth had hidden it. It felt important. Could it be a code? A reference completely outside the club's context? Or was there, somehow, a link between apples, eighty-year-old planting ledgers, thirty-five-year-old financial secrets, and a murder committed two days ago? The complexity was daunting, but for Agnes, the disparate threads only strengthened her resolve. Somewhere within this tangle of history, finance, botany, and human failing lay the truth. And she would, with her characteristic meticulousness, unravel it. She reached for a fresh index card, her pen poised. The investigation into the past had just become critical to understanding the present.

****

While Agnes delved into the sedimentary layers of past financial dealings and Fitzwilliam chipped away at the polished facade of the current accounts, Ronnie Peterson applied himself to the more dynamic, if equally complex, problem of spacetime – specifically, Bartholomew Ainsworth's trajectory through it on the day of his death. For Ronnie, human testimony was merely data, often frustratingly imprecise data, but data nonetheless. If plotted correctly, accounting for variables like walking speed, duration of known interactions, and spatial constraints, it should reveal patterns, anomalies, and, most crucially, periods of unaccountability. Opportunities.

He'd commandeered a table in the club's small, underused library – a room lined with dusty volumes on croquet history and horticultural encyclopedias, offering quiet and a large surface. Spread across the polished mahogany was a detailed architect's plan of the Society grounds and clubhouse he'd requested from Esme (under the pretext of analysing sight lines for optimal spectator viewing positions – a justification Esme had accepted with weary resignation). Beside it lay his notebook, now bristling with lists of timings, witness statements (relayed with varying degrees of precision by Agnes and Fitzwilliam from their own inquiries), and calculations involving average human locomotion. A stopwatch lay nearby, which he occasionally clicked, pacing imaginary distances across the Axminster carpet.

The Melbourne afternoon sun, now lower in the sky, slanted through the lead light windows, casting long rhomboids of light across the room. Outside, the sounds of the club seemed muffled, distant – the occasional *thwack* of a mallet, the murmur of voices from the clubhouse. Inside, the only sounds were the rustle of Ronnie's papers, the furious scratching of his pencil, and his own muttered calculations.

"Right," he muttered, consulting his notes. "Subject: B. Ainsworth. Tuesday. Start point: Arrival at club, approx. 9:15 AM, noted by groundskeeper Henderson Jr. Proceeded directly to Treasurer's office." Ronnie drew a neat vector on the map from the entrance gate to the office wing. "Duration in office: Unknown initially. First confirmed sighting *outside* office: approx. 10:00 AM by Agnes Plummett, observing argument between Smythe and Ainsworth near Lawn 1 regarding hoop placement during their match warm-up. Ergo, Ainsworth was on Lawn 1 by 10:00 AM." He calculated the minimum walking time from office to Lawn 1 – perhaps 90 seconds at Ainsworth's usual deliberate pace. "Allows for considerable time in office, 9:15 to ~9:58."

He continued plotting. "Match: Ainsworth vs Fitzwilliam, Lawn 1, scheduled 10:30 AM. Fitzwilliam confirms match started on time. Duration approx. 75 minutes (Ainsworth won, naturally, likely extending duration via pedantic rule clarifications)." Ronnie added a time block annotation to Lawn 1. "Match concludes approx. 11:45 AM."

"Post-match: Fitzwilliam retreated directly to clubhouse for strong coffee. Ainsworth seen by Mrs Henderson proceeding towards the clubhouse main entrance, presumably for refreshments or ablutions. Approx. 11:50 AM." Another vector.

"Lunch period: Unclear. Ainsworth often took a solitary sandwich *in his office* while reviewing papers. Esme Weatherly confirms seeing him enter the office around 12:05 PM. No confirmed sightings between 12:05 PM and..." Ronnie scanned his notes, frowning at the imprecision. "...'sometime after 1:30 PM.'" This fuzzy data point came from Colonel Abernathy, who thought he'd seen Ainsworth heading towards the archives wing 'after lunch'. Highly unreliable.

"Okay, let's bracket that," Ronnie decided. "Known location: Office, 12:05 PM. Potential next location: Archives. Minimum walk time: 60 seconds. Maximum time in office before heading to archives, assuming Abernathy's sighting is even remotely accurate?

Could be over an hour." He tapped the office location on the map. "Ample time for solitary lunch. Ample time to consult research materials. Ample time," his voice lowered slightly, "for someone to potentially access his office, or for him to consume something prepared earlier… like tea from his thermos."

He moved on. "Archives visit: If Abernathy is correct (low probability assigned), duration unknown. Let's assume 15-30 minutes based on Agnes's estimate of likely research tasks Ainsworth might undertake there related to old ledgers. Exit archives approx. 2:00 PM - 2:30 PM?" He drew a dotted line to the small archive room adjacent to the library where he now sat.

"Next sighting: The crucial one. The argument with Smythe near Lawn 3." Ronnie consulted Fitzwilliam's and Agnes's combined notes on witness accounts. "Timing is contested. Some say 'around 3 PM', others 'mid-afternoon'. Smythe himself was vague. Let's assume a window: 2:45 PM - 3:15 PM." He marked this interaction near Lawn 3. "Duration of argument: witnesses suggest brief but heated, perhaps 2-3 minutes."

"Post-argument: Smythe storms off towards river path (approx. 3:00 PM - 3:18 PM). Where does Ainsworth go?" Ronnie scanned his notes again. "No confirmed sightings. This is a critical gap."

He stood up and began pacing the library, tracing potential routes on the air with his finger. "From Lawn 3… back to the office? Possible. To the clubhouse for tea? Plausible. To continue his research in the archives? Also possible. To investigate the specific spot near the rhododendrons Chloe mentioned?" He stopped pacing. "That spot is *adjacent* to Lawn 3. If he went there directly after the argument with Smythe…"

He walked back to the map. The shrubbery bordered the eastern edge of Lawn 3. It wasn't on a direct path back to the clubhouse or the office from where the argument likely occurred near hoop

5 or 6. Ainsworth would have had to deliberately walk *towards* the boundary, *towards* the spot Chloe had seen him investigating previously.

"Okay," Ronnie theorised, "Scenario A: Argument ends ~3:15 PM. Ainsworth, perhaps agitated or wanting to continue his earlier research, proceeds directly to the rhododendron bed. Spends time searching (5 min? 10 min?). Killer confronts/incapacitates him there. Time of incapacitation/death: ~3:20 PM - 3:30 PM?"

"Scenario B: Argument ends ~3:15 PM. Ainsworth returns to his office first." Ronnie traced the path. "Walk time: ~2 minutes. Spends time in office (accessing files? drinking poisoned tea?). Killer confronts/incapacitates him *in the office*? Or poison takes effect there. Killer then moves body?" He frowned. "Moving an unconscious or deceased adult male across lawns, even discreetly... high risk of observation, significant physical exertion required. Lower probability, unless killer had assistance or exceptional timing/opportunity."

"Scenario C: Argument ends ~3:15 PM. Ainsworth goes elsewhere – clubhouse, library, changing room? Encounters killer there? Less likely locations for premeditated incapacitation compared to the privacy of his office or the seclusion of the shrubbery."

He focused back on the timeline gap. "Ainsworth last definitively seen arguing with Smythe around, let's say, 3:15 PM at the latest. Body discovered by Chloe Dubois at approximately 5:15 PM. That leaves a two-hour window." He drew a large bracket around this period on his timeline chart. "Smythe's alibi walk: claims 20-30 minutes, starting ~3:15 PM. Even if true, he returns ~3:45 PM. Still leaves a 90-minute window *after* Smythe's return when the murder could have occurred, or when the scene could have been staged if incapacitation happened earlier."

But Ronnie's focus wasn't just on when the murder *could* have happened; it was on optimising the opportunity for the *poisoning* hypothesis. If poison were administered via the thermos, the optimal window was when Ainsworth was likely alone with it – primarily during his solitary lunch in his office between roughly 12:05 PM and, say, 1:45 PM (allowing time to reach archives if Abernathy was right).

"Hypothesis P," Ronnie murmured, starting a new page labelled 'Poisoning Timelines'. "Agent introduced into thermos flask, likely during morning (killer needs access to office/thermos before Ainsworth uses it extensively). Ainsworth consumes agent during lunch period (12:00 PM - 1:45 PM). Agent is slow-acting, designed to cause disorientation/collapse within, say, 60-90 minutes?" He scribbled calculations. "Onset of symptoms: approx. 1:45 PM - 3:15 PM."

His eyes widened slightly. "The argument with Smythe occurred *within* this potential symptom onset window!"

He paced again, faster this time. "What if Ainsworth was already feeling unwell during the argument? Disoriented? Irritable beyond his usual baseline? Could that have *contributed* to the argument's severity? Could his subsequent actions – walking towards the shrubbery instead of directly back to the clubhouse – be due to confusion or feeling faint?"

This felt... elegant. It integrated the known events with the poisoning hypothesis seamlessly. Ainsworth consumes poison at lunch. Feels increasingly unwell mid-afternoon. Has argument with Smythe, perhaps exacerbated by his condition. Stumbles towards the secluded shrubbery feeling faint or confused, possibly intending to sit down or even recalling his earlier research there vaguely. Collapses. Killer, having administered poison earlier and perhaps monitoring Ainsworth, follows him. Finds him incapacitated. Delivers the blow with the conveniently available (or previously planted?) mallet to simulate death by violence and mask the poisoning. Killer then departs, leaving the scene for Chloe to discover later.

"Yes," Ronnie breathed, excitement replacing his earlier frustration. "This timeline accommodates all known data points *and* the physical inconsistencies! The crucial window isn't just the two hours before discovery; it's the period *before* the argument, allowing for poison administration, and the period *during and immediately after* the argument, allowing for symptom onset and the staged final blow!"

He grabbed his mobile phone, fingers flying across the keypad to call Fitzwilliam. He needed to share this. The timeline wasn't just missing minutes; it held the key coordinates for a completely different crime. "Alistair," he began without preamble when Fitzwilliam answered, his voice buzzing with energy, "Forget Smythe's alibi walk! The critical temporal anomaly isn't *after* the argument; it's *before* and *during*! I've mapped Ainsworth's probability distribution across spacetime, and there's a distinct locus of opportunity between 12:05 PM and approximately 1:45 PM in the Treasurer's office, perfectly correlating with potential ingestion of a slow-acting agent via his personal thermos, leading to symptom onset coinciding with the Smythe altercation!" He paused, realising Fitzwilliam might need a translation. "What I mean is, Alistair, I think I know *when* the murder really began. And it wasn't with the swing of a mallet."

7

The Gardener's Scrutiny

The morning sun, climbing higher in the Melbourne sky, did little to dispel the chill that clung stubbornly to the cordoned-off area bordering Lawn 3. It wasn't just the lingering dampness from the overnight dew evaporating slowly from the shaded rhododendron leaves; it was a deeper cold, an invisible miasma of tragedy that seemed to emanate from the disturbed earth itself. Blue police tape, already looking slightly weathered, formed a stark, intrusive perimeter, guarding the space where Bartholomew Ainsworth had met his end. Inside the tape, small numbered plastic markers dotted the ground, testament to the forensic team's methodical harvest of potential evidence. Outside, the rest of the Society grounds were stirring back to a semblance of life – the distant *thwack* of a practice shot, the drone of a mower starting up near the entrance – sounds that felt both normal and jarringly inappropriate.

Chloe Dubois stood just outside the tape, hesitating. She had official sanction to be here – sort of. Detective Inspector Davies, during a brief follow-up conversation yesterday, had asked her to identify the specific rare plants near the body's location, seemingly as a routine part of documenting the scene. Agnes Plummett, with characteristic foresight, had suggested Chloe offer to check the plants for any damage caused during the incident or subsequent police activity, providing a legitimate horticultural reason to examine the area closely. It felt like a flimsy pretext, a necessary fiction allowing her access she wouldn't otherwise have, and her stomach churned with a mixture of grim determination and nervous apprehension. This wasn't just another flowerbed; it was the place where she had found him.

A uniformed constable, looking bored and faintly uncomfortable, stood guard nearby. "Just identifying the plants, miss?" he asked, his tone polite but weary. He'd likely been briefed about the 'gardener needing to check damage'.

"Yes, Constable," Chloe replied, keeping her voice steady. "And checking for any… disturbance to the root systems near where… near where he was." She gestured vaguely towards the rhododendrons. "Some of these are quite delicate specimens."

He nodded, seemingly satisfied. "Righto. Just… stay within the area immediately adjacent to the shrubs, if you would. Forensics are done here, but the Detective Inspector wants it kept clear for now." He returned his attention to scanning the peaceful expanse of Lawn 4, clearly wishing he were anywhere else.

Taking a deep breath, Chloe ducked under the tape. The simple action felt like crossing a significant threshold, stepping from the world of polite avoidance into the raw centre of the mystery. The air here felt different – heavy, still. The scent of damp earth and crushed vegetation was stronger, mingled with a faint, almost metallic odour she couldn't quite place – perhaps residue from the forensic powders. She forced herself to look, *really* look, not just at the plants she knew so well, but at the ground beneath them, the context, the small details the police might have overlooked or misinterpreted.

Her eyes, trained by years of observing subtle changes in leaf colour, soil texture, and growth patterns, began a systematic sweep. She started with the outer edge of the bed, near where the constable stood. Here, the grass showed signs of trampling from the initial discovery and police movements – unavoidable, expected. But as she moved deeper, towards the dense cluster of rhododendrons where Mr Ainsworth's body had lain, the ground beneath the foliage told a different story.

She knelt down, ignoring the damp chill seeping through her work trousers. The layer of dark mulch, usually kept loose and even by her own raking, was disturbed in several places *within* the cordoned area, near the base of the largest rhododendron – the one whose lower branches partially obscured the spot where Ainsworth's head had rested. These weren't the broad scuffs of police boots; these looked different. Smaller, more localised areas where the mulch seemed pushed aside, compressed, as if someone had knelt or placed significant weight there. Was this from Ainsworth falling? Or from someone else... tending to him? Positioning him?

Her gaze tracked meticulously across the ground. She noted the precise locations of the remaining forensic markers – mostly clustered in the area immediately around where the body had been, with a few trailing towards where the mallet lay on the grass just outside the bed. Then, slightly further under the low-hanging leaves, almost hidden against the dark soil, she saw it. An indentation. Not deep, but clearer than the surrounding mulch compressions. It was partial, obscured by fallen leaves she carefully brushed aside, but it had definite edges, suggesting the heel and part of the sole of a shoe.

Her heart gave a small jump. She leaned closer, examining it with the same focused intensity she'd use to diagnose a plant disease. It wasn't a large print, definitely not from a heavy work boot like the groundskeeper's, nor did it look like the standard police-issue footwear she'd seen yesterday. The impression suggested a relatively smooth sole, perhaps leather or a fine rubber composite, with a distinct, fairly narrow heel. A town shoe? Maybe a loafer or a dress shoe? It seemed incongruous for this damp, mulch-filled flowerbed. And crucially, it seemed pressed *into* the soil with significant weight, not the glancing scuff of a fall. Whose shoe? Ainsworth's own brogues wouldn't have made this mark. Harry Smythe favoured sturdy golfing shoes or country brogues, neither likely to match this finer print. Could it have been left by the killer? Someone kneeling beside the body?

She resisted the urge to touch it, knowing its evidentiary value. Instead, she took out her phone, her fingers slightly clumsy with adrenaline, and took several photos from different angles, making sure to include a nearby fallen leaf for scale. She'd show these to Agnes and the others later.

Her attention shifted to the plants themselves. The heritage hellebores Ainsworth had been so critical of seemed undisturbed. The azaleas looked fine. But near the base of the main rhododendron, close to the mysterious footprint, she noticed several small, freshly broken twigs on the lower branches, the breaks looking clean, recent. And the soil right at the base of the trunk… it looked different. More disturbed than the surrounding mulch compressions. Looser. As if someone had been… digging? Or probing?

Chloe frowned. She gently probed the area with her fingers, feeling the difference in texture. It wasn't deep digging, not like planting a new shrub. More like someone had pushed something – a thin trowel? A stake? Even just fingers? – into the ground several times around the base of the plant. Why? Was Ainsworth looking for something buried there, using the old ledger? Or had the killer been searching for something? Or hiding something small? The disturbed soil felt recent, the edges of the small holes still sharp, not weathered. It was another anomaly, subtle but definite.

She meticulously photographed this area too, trying to capture the texture difference, the broken twigs. As she worked, her mind replayed Ainsworth's questions about this specific area – the drainage, the old ledger, his frustration. He *had* been searching for something here. Something important enough to draw him back repeatedly, important enough, perhaps, to die for.

Then, tucked slightly under a broad rhododendron leaf, almost missed, lay something else. Not natural. A small object, muted in colour against the dark mulch. Chloe reached for it carefully, using a twig to lift the edge of the leaf. It was a glove. A single, expensive-looking gardening glove. Not the heavy-duty canvas type the club provided for staff, nor the worn leather ones favoured by some members. This was finer, made of soft, supple grey suede or nu-buck, with reinforced fingertips and an adjustable wrist strap. It looked like something one might buy at a high-end nursery or boutique garden store. It was relatively clean, showing little sign of heavy work, but had a distinct smudge of darker, damp soil near the palm, consistent with the earth around the rhododendron base.

Chloe's breath hitched. She picked it up carefully, holding it by the cuff. It felt… expensive. Well-made. Definitely not standard club issue. Whose was it? Had Ainsworth dropped it during his search? Unlikely; he rarely did any physical gardening himself and preferred leather driving gloves if he handled anything outdoors. Had the killer dropped it? Perhaps while kneeling near the body, while delivering the blow, or while disturbing the soil? It felt significant, tangible. A direct link, potentially, to someone present at the scene besides the victim. She photographed it carefully from all angles before tucking it meticulously into a clean specimen bag she carried in her gardening apron for collecting interesting seeds or diseased leaves. This felt far more significant than a diseased leaf.

She spent another twenty minutes conducting her careful survey, moving slowly, missing nothing. She checked the *Digitalis* bed Ainsworth had complained about – nothing amiss there. She examined the grass edge where the mallet had lain – just the indentation noted by police. She looked for any other foreign objects, any other signs of disturbance. Finding nothing further, she finally straightened up, brushing damp earth from her knees.

The sun felt warmer now, the normality of the club reasserting itself just beyond the tape. But Chloe felt colder than before. She hadn't found what Ainsworth was looking for, but she had found clues suggesting his search was real, and evidence – the footprint, the disturbed soil, the glove – hinting that someone else had been here, someone who didn't belong, someone who had perhaps silenced Ainsworth before he could unearth the secret buried beneath the rhododendrons. The weight of the mallet might be misleading, but the weight of these small, tangible discoveries felt heavy indeed. She ducked back under the police tape, giving the constable a brief, composed nod, her mind already racing ahead, planning how to share these crucial findings with Agnes, Fitzwilliam, and Ronnie. The polite surface had been scratched, and the darkness underneath was starting to show through.

****

While Chloe Dubois meticulously catalogued the physical anomalies near Lawn 3, Alistair Fitzwilliam embarked on a far more delicate, and potentially hazardous, form of excavation: probing the layers of club politics and personal history surrounding Bartholomew Ainsworth's final, fatal investigations. His target was Mr Charles Abercrombie, the long-serving Chairman of the House Committee, a man generally respected for his pragmatism and discretion – qualities Fitzwilliam hoped would make him both knowledgeable and, perhaps, cautiously candid if approached correctly. Abercrombie represented the 'old guard' of the Society; he had seen treasurers come and go, weathered past controversies, and possessed an encyclopedic knowledge of not just the club's rules, but its unwritten codes and buried tensions. He also, Fitzwilliam recalled, occasionally expressed a weary exasperation with Ainsworth's more extreme forms of pedantry, suggesting a degree of objectivity lacking in many other members.

Fitzwilliam engineered the encounter with careful precision, choosing a time in the early afternoon when he knew Abercrombie often enjoyed a quiet pipe in the club's seldom-used billiards room after lunch. The room itself felt like a step back in time – dark wood panelling, walls lined with faded photographs of past club presidents and triumphant croquet teams, leather armchairs slightly cracked with age, the faint, pleasant smell of beeswax, old books, and the lingering aroma of Abercrombie's preferred pipe tobacco. Sunlight struggled to penetrate the heavy velvet curtains, creating a hushed, confidential atmosphere far removed from the bright anxieties of the verandah.

Abercrombie was seated in one of the armchairs, contemplating the intricate patterns of the Persian rug, his pipe emitting gentle puffs of smoke. He looked up as Fitzwilliam entered, his expression one of mild surprise but not displeasure. "Ah, Fitzwilliam," he greeted, his voice a low, calm baritone. "Taking refuge from the madding crowd?"

"Something like that, Charles," Fitzwilliam replied, attempting a relaxed air that felt entirely fraudulent. His heart hammered against his ribs. This felt dangerously close to tampering with potential witnesses, skirting the edges of professional ethics. But Agnes's words about letting an innocent man potentially suffer while a killer walked free echoed in his mind. "Just needed a quiet moment to gather my thoughts. This whole business with poor Bartholomew… utterly dreadful."

Abercrombie nodded slowly, tamping down the tobacco in his pipe bowl with a practised thumb. "Dreadful," he agreed. "A black mark on the Society. Haven't seen anything like it in my forty years here. Shakes the foundations, you know."

Fitzwilliam saw his opening, a way to frame his inquiry within the context of the club's well-being. "Precisely," he said, sinking into the opposite armchair, grateful for its solid embrace. "And as a member of the Governance subcommittee, I feel a certain… responsibility… to ensure we understand any underlying issues that might have contributed. Not," he added hastily, "to interfere with the police investigation, of course. But purely from a procedural standpoint, ensuring the smooth continuation of the club's affairs requires understanding any… significant matters Bartholomew might have had pending." He paused, hoping he sounded concernedly administrative rather than suspiciously inquisitive.

Abercrombie drew on his pipe, regarding Fitzwilliam through a haze of smoke, his eyes shrewd. "Significant matters?" he repeated slowly. "Bartholomew always had 'significant matters' pending, Fitzwilliam. Usually involving the precise angle of a hoop or the unacceptable provenance of the coffee beans." A faint smile touched his lips, quickly fading. "But I take your point. Continuity is important." He seemed to be considering how much to say.

"Was there anything… specific?" Fitzwilliam pressed gently, emboldened slightly by Abercrombie's lack of outright dismissal. "Anything beyond the usual day-to-day treasury functions? I overheard Colonel Abernathy mentioning Bartholomew seemed agitated about historical accounts recently? Something about the West Wing extension from the… eighties, was it?"

Abercrombie sighed, a plume of smoke escaping with the sound.

He took the pipe from his mouth and examined the bowl, seeming to weigh his words. "Ah, yes. The West Wing. Bartholomew had developed something of an obsession with it these past few months. Stirring up a hornet's nest, frankly."

"An obsession?" Fitzwilliam kept his tone neutral, merely seeking clarification. Inside, his pulse quickened.

"He acquired some notion," Abercrombie continued, choosing his words with care, "that the final accounting back in… '87, was it?… wasn't entirely… transparent. Specifically," he lowered his voice slightly, "that rather convenient anonymous donation that appeared out of the blue to cover the final shortfall."

Fitzwilliam nodded, recalling Agnes's discovery in the archives. "I vaguely recall hearing something about that era. Before my time on the committee, of course."

"Indeed. Most people have forgotten, or chosen to forget," Abercrombie said drily. "It was a difficult period. Costs spiralling, members grumbling about levies… the donation saved the committee significant embarrassment, mine included, I was junior then. Humphrey Carmichael, bless his easy-going soul, was relieved to accept it and close the books. Bartholomew, even back then as a new committee member, made noises about transparency, but…" he shrugged, "…the prevailing mood was 'problem solved, let's move on'. And so we did."

"Until now?" Fitzwilliam prompted.

"Until Bartholomew, yes," Abercrombie confirmed, tapping his pipe gently against the heavy glass ashtray on the side table. "For reasons known only to himself, he decided, nearly forty years later, to rake over those particular coals. Started demanding access to all the original contractor invoices, bank transfer records related to the donation – documents buried deep in the off-site storage, mind you. Caused Mildred Pettle no end of trouble trying to locate them."

He paused. "Made himself rather unpopular with the few of us who remembered that period."

Mildred again, Fitzwilliam noted. *Controlling access to the very documents Ainsworth needed.* "Unpopular with whom, specifically, Charles?" Fitzwilliam asked, trying to sound merely curious about club history.

Abercrombie hesitated, clearly reluctant to name names or fuel gossip, especially now. "Oh, you know," he said vaguely. "People who were on the committee back then, people involved with managing the project... Old Henderson Senior was chairing, he pushed hard to accept the donation. And young Ainsworth, despite his initial objections, eventually fell in line. Perhaps," Abercrombie added thoughtfully, "that old compromise always rankled him? Perhaps his recent... zeal... was a way of making amends for what he saw as a past failure of scrutiny?"

It was plausible. It fit with Agnes's findings. Ainsworth, perhaps embarrassed by his youthful compromise, now trying to belatedly enforce the standards he felt he should have upheld decades earlier. But it also meant he was directly challenging decisions made by powerful figures from the club's past, some of whom might still hold influence or have vested interests in keeping that history buried.

"Did he voice specific accusations?" Fitzwilliam asked. "Did he suggest what might have been improper about the donation or the accounting?"

Abercrombie shook his head slowly. "Not directly to the House Committee, no. Not in formal terms. It was more... insinuations. Demands for documentation. Mutterings about 'undisclosed interests' and 'irregular procedures'. He cornered me after the last meeting, wanting my recollections of the final payment authorisations back in '87. Frankly, Alistair, my memory isn't what it was, and I found his persistence rather tiresome." He sighed again. "I told him, perhaps rather curtly, that some matters were best left undisturbed, especially when all the key players like poor Humphrey were long gone."

Undisclosed interests. Irregular procedures. Ainsworth *had* been specific, just not formally. And Abercrombie, representing the established order, had effectively told him to drop it. Had Ainsworth ignored that advice? And who else might have delivered similar warnings, perhaps less politely?

"Besides the West Wing," Fitzwilliam probed further, sensing Abercrombie was willing to talk, perhaps needing to unburden himself slightly, "were there other historical matters he was pursuing? Agnes mentioned something about grounds maintenance contracts?"

Abercrombie grimaced. "Oh, heavens, yes. That was another bee in his bonnet. Dug out contracts from fifteen, twenty years ago. Questioning invoices from Henderson & Sons Plumbing – old man Henderson's firm, naturally. Questioning the tendering process for the irrigation system upgrade back in '05. Claimed the specifications were written to favour one supplier." He puffed on his pipe again. "He accused half the long-serving members of cronyism or incompetence, indirectly if not directly. Ruffled some very established feathers, believe me. People who pride themselves on their service to this club."

Fitzwilliam absorbed this, his mind racing. Henderson & Sons Plumbing – the firm used for most repairs, unlike the unfamiliar 'WeatherTech Roofing Solutions' he'd noted on the recent roof repair invoices. Had Ainsworth compared historical Henderson invoices with recent ones? Or with the WeatherTech ones? And the irrigation system – another major capital expense. Ainsworth's investigation wasn't just about one potentially dodgy donation forty years ago; it was a broad sweep, challenging decisions and expenditures across decades, potentially implicating multiple long-standing members or their associates.

"Did he mention *who* he suspected of… impropriety?" Fitzwilliam asked, keeping his voice carefully neutral.

Abercrombie hesitated again, swirling the smoke in his mouth before exhaling slowly. "He never named names to me directly in accusation. Bartholomew, for all his faults, usually liked to have incontrovertible proof before making a formal charge. But his *questions*… they certainly seemed directed towards certain individuals who had overseen those projects or budgets." He looked uncomfortable. "People who are still very much involved in the Society. People who would not take kindly to having their past decisions, or potential conflicts of interest, dragged into the light." He met Fitzwilliam's gaze. "Frankly, Alistair, while I find the notion of Smythe resorting to murder hard to swallow, I can well believe that Bartholomew Ainsworth had recently made himself enemies far more dangerous, and perhaps far more subtle, than poor Harry."

The implication hung in the quiet, smoke-filled room. Ainsworth hadn't just stumbled into danger; he had, it seemed, marched directly towards it, armed with ledgers and invoices, potentially threatening to expose secrets held by powerful, established figures within the club's seemingly placid hierarchy. The conversation had yielded no smoking gun, no direct accusation Fitzwilliam could take to the police. But it had confirmed, beyond doubt, that the placid surface Fitzwilliam had sought refuge in was illusory. Beneath it lay decades of potential motives – financial irregularities, old compromises, wounded pride, hidden interests – all stirred up by one inconveniently meticulous Treasurer. And the list of people who might have wished him silenced, Fitzwilliam now realised with a deepening sense of dread, was growing disturbingly long. He thanked Abercrombie for his time, his mind already preoccupied with the daunting task of figuring out which specific 'ruffled feather' might have belonged to a killer.

****

As the late afternoon sun cast long, dramatic shadows across the now mostly deserted croquet lawns, Ronnie Peterson remained sequestered in the quiet sanctuary of the Society's library. The faint scent of old paper and Abercrombie's lingering pipe smoke provided a strangely academic backdrop to the violent equations and trajectory analyses sprawling across his notebook pages. He had received brief, coded updates via text message from Fitzwilliam and Agnes earlier – Fitzwilliam confirming Ainsworth *had* indeed been aggressively pursuing sensitive historical financial matters, causing significant friction; Agnes relaying Chloe's crucial findings from the garden bed near Lawn 3: the distinct footprint, the disturbed soil suggesting kneeling or probing, the out-of-place, high-quality glove.

While the glove itself was, from a purely physics standpoint, largely irrelevant (unless its material offered clues about friction coefficients during a hypothetical struggle, which seemed unlikely), Chloe's precise description of the body's location *within* the flowerbed and the disturbed soil *around* the rhododendron base was pure gold. It provided critical spatial data and strongly supported the hypothesis that Ainsworth hadn't simply fallen where he was struck during the argument, but had ended up there through other means, potentially already incapacitated.

Ronnie retrieved the architect's plan of the grounds again, smoothing it out on the large mahogany table. Using a ruler and protractor, he meticulously marked Chloe's estimated location for the footprint relative to the rhododendron trunk and the likely position of Ainsworth's body. He then added vectors representing the possible positions and orientations of someone kneeling or digging in that confined space. The geometry immediately became more complex, but also more revealing.

"Right," he murmured, tapping the diagram. "If Ainsworth was *here*," pointing to the spot deep within the mulch, "and potentially already kneeling or prone due to incapacitation (Hypothesis P), then the dynamics of the mallet impact change fundamentally." His previous calculations had focused on the difficulty of delivering the observed blow during a standing argument. Now, he modelled the impact on a stationary or slow-moving target already low to the ground.

"Target altitude significantly reduced," he scribbled. "Angle of impact becomes less constrained. Assailant could stand adjacent or slightly behind the victim. Required swing arc potentially shorter, requiring less wind-up, less obvious telegraphing of intent." He began calculating impact forces again, incorporating assumptions about a less resistant target (already unconscious or collapsing) versus a potentially bracing or moving one. "Energy transfer… still significant due to mallet mass and density. Lignum Vitae – approx. $1.25\ \text{g/cm}^3$. Skull bone density variable, but let's use average values… Force required for fracture depends heavily on impact point and angle."

He paused, frustrated by the lack of concrete data. "Need mallet specifics!" He briefly considered marching over to Detective Inspector Davies and demanding the exhibit details but dismissed the idea; civilian interference with ongoing investigations rarely yielded optimal results. Instead, he recalled Barnaby Thornton, the engineering apprentice. Barnaby wouldn't know about the antique mallet, but he *would* know about standard club mallets and workshop materials.

Ronnie found Barnaby in the equipment shed, carefully cleaning and oiling modern mallets from the club's general stock. The young man looked up, slightly surprised to see Ronnie, whose usual habitat was the lawns or the library, not the practical hub of the shed.

"Barnaby," Ronnie began directly, dispensing with pleasantries, "quick questions, if you have a moment. Purely hypothetical, you understand. Standard club mallet head – typically Boxwood, yes? Approximate mass?"

Barnaby, though slightly taken aback, brightened at the technical query. "Usually English Boxwood, sir, yes. Or sometimes lignum vitae for older practice mallets, though they're heavier. Standard head... maybe 0.9 to 1 kilogram?"

"And the handles? Ash? Hickory?"

"Mostly ash these days, sir. Good strength-to-weight ratio."

"Excellent. And by any chance, do you have access to precision scales here? For weighing components?" Ronnie asked hopefully.

Barnaby looked apologetic. "Just the old parcel scales in the office, sir. Not really precise enough for fine measurements, I wouldn't think."

Ronnie sighed inwardly. Insufficient data precision. "No matter. One more thing – Lignum Vitae. You said it's heavier. Significantly denser than Boxwood?"

"Oh, much denser, sir," Barnaby confirmed enthusiastically. "And harder. Self-lubricating too, which is why they used it for bearings and propeller shafts back in the day. A Lignum Vitae head of the same size as a Boxwood one would be noticeably heavier, maybe 20-30% more?"

"Fascinating. Thank you, Barnaby. Most helpful." Ronnie retreated, his mind already incorporating the estimated density increase into his calculations. A heavier mallet meant greater potential impact force for the same velocity, or the same force could be achieved with a slower, perhaps more controlled, less obvious swing. This further supported the possibility of a calculated blow rather than a wild, enraged one.

Back in the library, Ronnie integrated the new estimates. He modelled scenarios: a controlled, precise blow delivered downwards onto a kneeling or prone victim using the heavier antique mallet. The required force and swing mechanics seemed far more plausible, less 'inefficient' than the standing argument scenario. It fit the limited visual evidence (relative tidiness) and Chloe's description.

He then considered the footprint Chloe described – narrow heel, smooth sole, pressed firmly down. Likely left by someone kneeling or putting significant weight on one foot while bending low. Consistent with someone tending to, searching near, or delivering a final blow to someone already on the ground. It wasn't *proof* of the killer's identity, but it was another data point contradicting the image of Harry Smythe wildly swinging his mallet during a standing argument.

His timeline chart also gained clarity with Chloe's confirmation of Ainsworth actively *searching* near the rhododendrons. This provided a strong reason for Ainsworth to *be* in that secluded spot after the argument, separate from simply feeling faint. He went there deliberately. Did he find what he was looking for? Was he interrupted during the search? Or did the killer lure him there? Ronnie couldn't answer those questions with physics, but they opened up new avenues beyond simple opportunity.

He reviewed his 'Hypothesis P' timeline: Poison ingested during lunch (12:00-1:45 PM in office). Symptoms onset (1:45 PM - 3:15 PM). Argument with Smythe (~3:00-3:15 PM, potentially exacerbated by symptoms). Ainsworth proceeds to rhododendron bed (~3:15-3:20 PM, driven by research goal, possibly feeling unwell). Confrontation/Incapacitation/Staged Blow in shrubbery (~3:20-3:45 PM? – allowing for killer's arrival/action). Body discovered

5:15 PM.

This timeline felt robust. It incorporated the known sightings, accounted for the physical anomalies of the crime scene, provided a window for poison administration and onset, and linked Ainsworth's own actions (his research) directly to the location of his death. The public argument with Smythe became almost incidental – perhaps the trigger for Ainsworth retreating to the garden bed, or merely a coincidental event during the poison's onset phase, later exploited by the killer.

The conviction settled in Ronnie's mind, not as emotional belief, but as the logical conclusion derived from the available physical and temporal data. The probability of the official narrative being correct had significantly decreased based on his analysis. The probability of Hypothesis P – poisoning followed by a staged blow – was now, in his assessment, markedly higher. It was the more elegant solution, fitting the disparate data points with fewer contradictions.

He needed to communicate this effectively. Simply stating the physics were 'wrong' wasn't enough. He needed to convey the *implications*. He pulled out his phone, dialling Fitzwilliam first – the lawyer seemed better equipped to handle probabilistic arguments and potential legal ramifications than Agnes, whose focus was more historical and factual.

"Alistair? Ronnie here." He didn't wait for a reply. "Further analysis confirms significant deviations from the expected physical parameters under the Smythe-Rage hypothesis. Incorporating Chloe's spatial data regarding victim position and localised soil disturbance strengthens the Incapacitation-Precedes-Impact model exponentially."

He took a breath, picturing Fitzwilliam's likely bewildered expression. "What I mean, Alistair, is that the physics strongly indicate Ainsworth was likely already down, possibly kneeling or prone, perhaps due to prior incapacitation via poison ingested during his lunch period – the timeline fits perfectly – when the blow was delivered. The blow itself appears increasingly likely to be a secondary event, possibly staged. The probability of the official narrative being the primary cause is now, in my estimation, below 0.15, while Hypothesis P exceeds 0.75."

He paused, letting the numbers sink in, though he knew Fitzwilliam dealt in reasonable doubt, not decimal points. "The salient point, Alistair, is this: based purely on the physical and temporal evidence as we understand it, it is significantly more probable that Bartholomew Ainsworth was poisoned sometime between midday and 2 PM, collapsed near the rhododendrons shortly after 3:15 PM, and was then struck with the mallet by a killer capitalising on the situation and likely framing Lord Smythe. The physics simply do not support a spontaneous, fatal altercation with Smythe as the primary event." He waited, the receiver silent for a beat before Fitzwilliam's hesitant, slightly breathless voice came back down the line. Ronnie felt a surge of satisfaction. The data was speaking. Now, they just needed to find the evidence to make everyone else listen.

8

The Autopsy Report

Two days had passed since Bartholomew Ainsworth's body had been discovered amongst the rhododendrons. Two days in which the Toorak Croquet & Horticultural Society had existed in a state of suspended animation, performing the outward rituals of normality – tea service continuing, practice sessions resuming on the farther lawns, committee meetings conducted with strained formality – while underneath, the currents of speculation and unease ran deep and cold. The police presence had become less visible, the blue tape around Lawn 3 now seeming less like an active barrier and more like a grim memorial. Yet, for Alistair Fitzwilliam, the lack of overt police activity only amplified his anxiety. He knew major investigations moved at their own pace, often slowly, but the apparent consensus solidified around Harry Smythe felt dangerously premature, especially given the inconsistencies he and his unlikely collaborators had unearthed.

He sat in his own office now, a world away from the manicured lawns and hushed gossip of the Society. Here, high above Collins Street in the heart of Melbourne's bustling legal precinct, the dominant sounds were the distant rumble of trams, the hum of conditioned air, and the rhythmic clicking of keyboards from adjacent offices. His desk was piled high with briefs related to complex commercial litigation – disputes over contractual clauses, shareholder disagreements, breaches of fiduciary duty ironically mirroring, in a sanitised corporate fashion, the potentially lethal breaches being investigated back in Toorak. Sunlight streamed through the floor-to-ceiling windows, illuminating the cityscape, a panorama of architectural styles from ornate Victorian facades to sleek, modern glass towers. Normally, Fitzwilliam found a certain detached comfort in this ordered, professional environment, a refuge from the often-illogical demands of personal life (and croquet club politics). Today, however, the legal complexities felt trivial, the cityscape view remote and irrelevant compared to the tangled human drama unfolding just a few kilometres away.

He'd spent the morning ostensibly reviewing a particularly dense affidavit regarding derivatives trading, but his mind kept drifting back to Lawn 3, to Ronnie's equations, Agnes's historical context, Chloe's description of the scene, and his own unsettling conversation with Charles Abercrombie. Ainsworth hadn't just been difficult; he'd been actively investigating potentially explosive historical issues. He hadn't just fallen during an argument; the physical evidence suggested something far more calculated. And Harry Smythe, despite his behaviour, seemed increasingly like a convenient, if unwitting, scapegoat.

The critical missing piece, Fitzwilliam knew, was the official autopsy report from the Victorian Institute of Forensic Medicine (VIFM). That document held the objective, scientific truth – or at least, as close as pathology could get. Was there definitive evidence of poison? Were the details of the head wound truly consistent with a spontaneous mallet blow? Did the lividity patterns confirm or contradict Chloe's sense that the body had been 'arranged'?

Accessing that report directly was impossible for him, a civilian, an amateur investigator meddling on the fringes. But perhaps… perhaps he could glean *something*.

He'd placed a carefully worded call earlier that morning to a contact within Melbourne Homicide – Detective Sergeant Colin Riley, a man with whom Fitzwilliam had occasionally liaised on peripheral matters during complex corporate fraud cases that sometimes intersected with criminal investigations. Their relationship was professional, built on mutual respect, but certainly not close enough for Riley to casually divulge confidential autopsy details. Fitzwilliam had framed his call purely around offering any assistance his knowledge of the Society's internal structures might provide Detective Inspector Davies, subtly mentioning the victim's known meticulousness and recent workload, hoping Riley might let something slip in return. It was a long shot, ethically dubious, perhaps, but Fitzwilliam felt the potential injustice surrounding Harry Smythe warranted the slight bending of professional boundaries.

His desk phone emitted a discreet chime, startling him. The internal display showed Riley's extension. Fitzwilliam took a steadying breath, smoothed his tie, and picked up the receiver, adopting his most professional, collegial tone.

"Alistair Fitzwilliam speaking."

"Alistair, Colin Riley here," the detective sergeant's familiar, slightly weary voice came down the line. "Returning your call regarding the Toorak Croquet Club matter."

"Colin, thank you for calling back. Much appreciated," Fitzwilliam said, keeping his voice even. "As I mentioned, just wanted to reiterate my willingness to assist Detective Inspector Davies should any questions arise regarding club governance or Mr Ainsworth's role. It's a rather… opaque little world, the Society."

"Tell me about it," Riley grunted. "Dealing with that lot… makes interviewing hardened criminals seem straightforward sometimes. Anyway, the Detective Inspector appreciates the offer. Things seem fairly clear-cut at this stage, though."

Fitzwilliam's heart sank slightly. *Clear-cut.* That meant the focus was still squarely on Harry Smythe. "Ah, yes," he said carefully. "Lord Smythe's rather public disagreement with Mr Ainsworth certainly provides an obvious… starting point."

"Starting point? More like the whole damn story," Riley said, a note of cynical certainty in his voice. "Argument, history of bad blood, suspect has known temper, weapon belongs to suspect, suspect has flimsy alibi… doesn't take Sherlock Holmes, mate. The preliminary findings from VIFM back it up."

"Ah," Fitzwilliam felt a knot tighten in his stomach. This was it. "The autopsy results are in, then?"

"Prelim report, yeah. Came through late yesterday. Look, Alistair, this is strictly unofficial, just between us, alright? Wouldn't want the Detective Inspector thinking I'm briefing club members."

"Absolutely, Colin. Completely understood. Professional discretion," Fitzwilliam assured him, gripping the receiver tightly.

"Right. Well, VIFM confirms cause of death as blunt force trauma to the posterior cranium, consistent with a significant impact from an object matching the dimensions and likely mass of that antique croquet mallet. Single blow, apparently sufficient force to cause fatal skull fracture and associated intracranial haemorrhage." Riley relayed the information matter-of-factually, the detached language of official reports.

Fitzwilliam felt a wave of disappointment wash over him, so strong it almost made him dizzy. Blunt force trauma. Consistent with the mallet. Single blow. It directly contradicted Ronnie's theories about insufficient force or multiple, messier impacts. Had Ronnie been wrong? Had their entire alternative hypothesis been built on flawed assumptions? Was it really just Harry Smythe's temper after all? The simplicity was crushing.

"I see," Fitzwilliam managed, keeping his voice level despite the sudden collapse of their carefully constructed theory. "So, fairly conclusive then."

"Looks that way," Riley agreed. "Ties things up neatly. Saves a lot of digging around in boring club finances, eh?" He chuckled humorlessly.

Fitzwilliam's mind raced. If it was just the mallet blow, why Ainsworth's position? Why his recent investigations? It didn't make sense. Unless… "Was there… anything else?" he asked, grasping at straws. "Anything unusual noted in the report?"

There was a slight pause on the other end of the line. Fitzwilliam could almost hear Riley mentally debating how much to say, weighing professional caution against perhaps a hint of bureaucratic frustration with overly thorough pathologists.

"Well," Riley said eventually, his tone shifting slightly, becoming more conspiratorial, less official. "There's always *something* unusual with VIFM reports, isn't there? They note every damn detail. Look, there *was* a mention… probably nothing."

Fitzwilliam held his breath.

"Firstly, the lividity," Riley continued, sounding slightly bored by the technicality. "You know, the blood pooling after death. The pathologist noted the pattern was *slightly* inconsistent with someone simply falling face down and remaining in that position. Suggested the body *might* have been lying differently for a period – maybe supine or on its side – before settling in the final face-down position where it was found. But," he added quickly, "that could easily be postmortem shifting, movement during the initial fall, animal disturbance, anything. Pathologist noted it as 'inconclusive but observed'. Detective Inspector reckons it's irrelevant given the clear

COD."

Lividity inconsistent with final position. Fitzwilliam's mind seized on the phrase. It wasn't proof of staging, but it was *exactly* what Ronnie had theorised would occur if the body was moved after death had occurred in a different position – perhaps after collapsing from poison. Detective Inspector Davies might dismiss it, but to Fitzwilliam, it felt like a crucial crack appearing in the "clear-cut" official story.

"And secondly," Riley went on, clearly deciding to share the other minor point now he'd started, "standard toxicology screening came back negative for common drugs, alcohol, etc. But the lab did find trace amounts of an… unidentified organic alkaloid compound in the stomach contents. Very low concentration. Doesn't match anything on their standard toxicology panels. They've sent it for further analysis, mass spectrometry, the whole works, but the pathologist reckons it's almost certainly an artefact, maybe something from an unusual herb tea Ainsworth drank, or even contamination from the garden soil. Definitely not considered contributory to death. The report explicitly states COD remains blunt force trauma."

Unidentified organic alkaloid compound. Fitzwilliam scribbled the words down, his hand shaking slightly. *Alkaloid.* Many potent plant-based poisons were alkaloids. Nicotine, atropine, strychnine… and countless others derived from common or obscure plants. *Something from an unusual herb tea? Contamination from garden soil?* Or something deliberately administered? Something slow-acting, perhaps, designed to incapacitate rather than kill directly, leaving the mallet blow to finish the job and provide the obvious cause of death?

"An alkaloid?" Fitzwilliam repeated, trying to keep the excitement – and dread – out of his voice. "Did they hazard a guess as to its source?"

"Nah," Riley said dismissively. "Like I said, probably nothing significant. Background noise. Happens all the time with trace analysis these days. They have to note it down, but it's ninety-nine percent likely to be irrelevant. The main finding is clear: guy got whacked on the head with a croquet mallet. End of story."

End of story for you, perhaps, Fitzwilliam thought, his mind racing with the implications. *But for us... this might be the beginning.* He thanked Riley profusely for the 'unofficial heads-up', assured him again of his discretion, and ended the call, his hand trembling as he replaced the receiver.

He stared out at the Melbourne skyline, the familiar buildings seeming distant and unreal. The official cause of death stood: blunt force trauma. Yet, beneath that stark finding lay two crucial anomalies the police were seemingly dismissing: lividity suggesting the body was moved after death, and an unidentified alkaloid in the victim's system. These weren't just minor discrepancies; they were potential bombshells, perfectly aligning with the alternative theory the quartet had been building. Ronnie's physics, Agnes's history, Chloe's observations, and now, faint but distinct echoes from the VIFM itself.

The police might be satisfied with their simple narrative, focusing all their resources on breaking Harry Smythe. But Fitzwilliam knew, with a certainty that settled deep in his anxious gut, that they were wrong. The real story was far darker, far more complex. And the trace alkaloid… could it be linked to the specific rare plants Chloe had identified near the body? The plants Ainsworth himself had shown such a strange interest in? The pieces were starting to connect, forming a picture far more alarming than he could have imagined. He needed to convene the others immediately. This changed everything. Again.

****

Evening had drawn in across Melbourne by the time Alistair Fitzwilliam arrived back at Agnes Plummett's South Yarra apartment. The sky outside the bay window had changed from the clear blue of the afternoon into shades of deep violet and bruised grey, and the first heavy drops of a forecasted southerly change had begun to spatter against the glass, bringing with them a distinct chill that seemed to seep into the very bones of the city. Inside, the lamps cast warm pools of light, illuminating the familiar, comforting order of Agnes's study, but the atmosphere was anything but relaxed. Agnes, Ronnie, and Chloe were already waiting, their expressions varying degrees of tense anticipation. The remnants of an earlier tea service sat largely untouched on a side table – the social ritual having clearly given way to nervous expectation.

Fitzwilliam paused in the doorway, shedding his damp coat, the weight of the information he carried feeling almost physical. He saw the question in their eyes. Had the autopsy confirmed their suspicions? Or had it validated the simple, official narrative and rendered their amateur deductions obsolete? He knew his news was a confusing, potentially dangerous mix of both.

"You spoke to your contact?" Agnes asked immediately, her usual calm laced with an uncharacteristic edge of impatience. She put down the volume of *Famous Australian Poison Trials* she had been consulting, her finger marking a specific page.

"I did," Fitzwilliam confirmed, walking further into the room, feeling the familiar anxiety churn within him, now mixed with a strange, nervous energy. He sank into an armchair, loosening his tie. "It was… informative. Though perhaps not in the way we might have hoped, initially."

Three pairs of eyes were fixed on him. Ronnie had stopped

doodling complex molecular diagrams in his notebook and was leaning forward, practically vibrating. Chloe sat very still, her hands clasped tightly in her lap.

"The preliminary report from VIFM is in," Fitzwilliam began, choosing his words with legal precision. "And the official, primary finding is… conclusive." He saw Ronnie deflate slightly, Agnes's lips thin. "Cause of death is listed as blunt force trauma to the posterior cranium. The pathologist confirms the injury is consistent with a significant impact from an object like Lord Smythe's mallet. Apparently, a single blow was deemed sufficient."

A heavy silence descended, broken only by the ticking grandfather clock and the increasing tattoo of rain against the window. It felt like a definitive end to their speculation. Harry did it. The police were right. Their intricate theories about poison and staging were just that – theories, unsupported by the hard science of the autopsy.

Ronnie slumped back in his chair, looking genuinely disappointed. "Consistent?" he muttered, flipping his notebook shut with a snap. "Physics allows for consistency with multiple scenarios! 'Consistent' is not the same as 'exclusively caused by'! Did they even calculate the energy transfer required versus…"

"However," Fitzwilliam interrupted, holding up a hand, feeling a reluctant surge of dramatic timing, "that wasn't *all* the report contained. My contact," he stressed the unofficial nature, "mentioned two… anomalies… noted by the pathologist, though apparently dismissed by the investigating team as likely insignificant."

Ronnie sat bolt upright again, his eyes gleaming. Agnes leaned forward, her earlier disappointment vanishing, replaced by sharp focus. Chloe watched Fitzwilliam intently.

"Firstly," Fitzwilliam continued, relaying Sergeant Riley's words as accurately as possible, "the lividity. The postmortem blood pooling. The pathologist observed that the pattern of fixation was, quote, 'slightly inconsistent' with the final face-down position in which the body was found. It suggested the body *might* have been lying in a different position – perhaps supine or on its side – for a period *after* death, before settling into that final position."

"Lividity!" Ronnie almost shouted, jumping up from his chair to pace the small space in front of the fireplace. "Exactly! Fixed lividity takes hours to establish – typically starting within 30 minutes, becoming fixed in maybe 8 to 12 hours! If the pattern doesn't match the final body position, it's almost definitive proof the body was moved *well after* death had occurred! 'Slightly inconsistent' is pathologist-speak for 'this doesn't add up'! How long after death? Did they estimate? What was the ambient temperature? That affects fixation time!" He peppered Fitzwilliam with questions the lawyer couldn't possibly answer.

"My contact didn't elaborate," Fitzwilliam said, feeling slightly overwhelmed by Ronnie's intensity. "He said Detective Inspector Davies considered it inconclusive, possibly due to postmortem shifting or even animal interference, though that seems unlikely in that location."

"Inconclusive?" Ronnie scoffed. "It's a fundamental contradiction! If he died instantly from the blow while face down, the lividity should match! If he died while lying differently, *then* was moved and potentially struck again… it fits Hypothesis P perfectly!"

Agnes nodded slowly, her mind already working through the implications. "If the body was moved significantly after death, it strongly suggests staging. It supports the idea that the location near the rhododendrons wasn't where the primary event – or death itself – occurred. He could have collapsed elsewhere – perhaps near his office, after consuming tea – died there, and then been moved later under cover of darkness or confusion, with the scene near Lawn 3 arranged to frame Lord Smythe." She looked thoughtful. "It would require careful timing, knowledge of the grounds, and considerable nerve."

"And the second anomaly?" Chloe asked quietly, her voice cutting through Ronnie's continued muttering about gravitational pooling vectors.

Fitzwilliam took another breath. "Toxicology. Standard screens were negative for alcohol, common drugs of abuse, prescription medications etcetera. However," he paused, ensuring he had their full attention, "the lab detected trace amounts of an 'unidentified organic alkaloid compound' in the stomach contents."

The effect was electric. Ronnie stopped pacing mid-stride. Agnes's hand tightened on her book. Chloe's eyes widened, her mind immediately flashing to the plants near Lawn 3.

"An alkaloid?" Agnes breathed, her voice sharp with significance. "Unidentified? Did they specify anything further? Potential class? Origin?"

"No," Fitzwilliam admitted. "Apparently it didn't match standard tox panels. They've sent it for further, more detailed analysis – mass spectrometry was mentioned – but the pathologist suggested it was likely an 'artefact'. Possibly environmental contamination from the soil," he glanced at Chloe, "or residue from an unusual herbal tea. It was explicitly noted as 'not considered contributory to death' in the preliminary report."

"Not contributory because they already *had* a cause of death!" Ronnie exploded, abandoning scientific detachment for pure frustration. "Confirmation bias again! They see the head wound, they stop looking! Alkaloids! That's huge! Countless potent plant toxins are alkaloids! Digitalis from foxgloves – cardio-toxic! Aconitine from monkshood – neurological and cardio-toxic! Even simple things like nicotine in high concentration, or coniine from hemlock! What about colchicine? Atropine? Hyoscyamine?" He fired off names like ammunition.

Agnes was already pulling other books from her shelves – a hefty volume on poisonous plants, another on historical poisons. "The symptoms are key," she murmured, flipping pages rapidly. "Nausea, confusion, cardiac arrhythmia, respiratory distress… many can mimic natural causes or general malaise initially, especially in low or cumulative doses. If Ainsworth ingested something hours earlier…"

"He *did* seem unwell," Chloe insisted, finding her voice again, stronger this time. "More than just stressed. I told you he looked pale, and complained about indigestion. Maybe… maybe he tasted something wrong? I remember now, a few days before… he was drinking his tea in the office and made a face, muttered something about Mildred needing to clean the thermos properly. I thought he was just being fussy, but what if…?"

The implication hung in the air. Had the killer made an earlier attempt? Or was the poison administered subtly over days? Or was the thermos the delivery method on the final day?

"And the plants near where he was found…" Chloe continued, thinking aloud. "The main ones are rhododendrons – toxic if ingested, but usually cause gastrointestinal upset, less likely rapid incapacitation unless a huge amount was eaten, which seems absurd. The hellebores – also toxic, cardio-toxins mostly. But the foxgloves (*Digitalis purpurea*)…" her voice dropped slightly. "Ainsworth complained about them, but they *are* beautiful. And they contain digitoxin and other cardiac glycosides. Highly toxic. Affects the heart. Could cause collapse, arrhythmia… confusion?"

"Digitalis poisoning," Agnes murmured, finding the relevant page. "Symptoms can include nausea, vomiting, visual disturbances – seeing yellow halos, interestingly – confusion, irregular heartbeat, potentially leading to cardiac arrest. Onset time varies with dosage and preparation." She looked up. "Difficult to detect without specific tests, especially if death is attributed to another cause."

"It fits," Ronnie declared, sketching frantically again. "Slow onset after ingestion, maybe feeling unwell, wanders to secluded spot feeling faint or confused by visual disturbances, collapses. Killer follows, delivers blow, arranges scene. Perfect."

Fitzwilliam felt a dizzying sense of vertigo. The pieces were falling into place with terrifying speed. The historical financial irregularities Ainsworth was chasing, providing motive for someone like Mildred or others connected to the past. Ainsworth's recent ill-health and peculiar interest in the garden bed. Chloe's discovery of the footprint, the disturbed soil, the glove. Ronnie's calculations showing the mallet blow was likely staged. And now, the autopsy revealing lividity patterns indicating the body was moved, and the presence of an unidentified alkaloid, a potential poison, explicitly dismissed by the police but perfectly fitting their alternative theory, potentially even linking to the specific flora at the scene.

"We have to tell Detective Inspector Davies," Chloe said, looking anxiously at Fitzwilliam. "Surely *now* she has to listen?"

Fitzwilliam sighed, running a hand over his face. "Chloe, I understand. And ethically, perhaps we should. But consider it from her perspective. We approach her, a group of amateur sleuths from the club, armed with unofficial, potentially leaked autopsy details that her own pathologist deemed insignificant. We present theories based on physics, historical gossip, and vague recollections of indigestion. We suggest the real killer is the seemingly harmless Club Secretary or some other respected member, based on complex theories about decades-old finances or poisonous flowers, while they have a prime suspect with motive, opportunity, weapon, and terrible behaviour already gift-wrapped." He shook his head. "Best case scenario, she dismisses us as well-meaning but interfering busybodies. Worst case? She suspects *us* of trying to deliberately muddy the waters or obstruct her investigation, perhaps to protect Smythe or someone else."

"So we do nothing?" Chloe asked, dismayed.

"No," Agnes said firmly, closing her toxicology textbook with a decisive thud. "We do not do nothing. Alistair is correct; we cannot rely on the official investigation at this stage. Our path remains the same, but with increased urgency and focus." She looked at each of them, her gaze sharp and resolute. "The autopsy findings, however preliminary and downplayed, validate our core hypothesis. Poisoning, followed by staging, is now the most probable scenario. Our task is to find the evidence the police are not looking for."

She stood up, moving towards her desk where she kept her index cards. "Ronnie, continue refining your models, but perhaps focus now on lividity fixation times – could you estimate *when* the body might have been moved based on likely ambient temperature? Fitzwilliam, can your contact provide *any* further detail, however minute, on that alkaloid analysis when it comes through? Even a potential chemical class? Chloe, the *Digitalis*. You know plants. How might it be prepared? Could traces be found on site, perhaps discarded during preparation? And I," she picked up a fresh index card, "will focus my research intensely. Trace alkaloid. *Pyrus Malus*. Section IV, Paragraph 12. And Mildred Pettle."

The room was quiet again, save for the rain drumming against the windows and the determined ticking of the clock. The initial excitement had sharpened into a focused, almost grim, determination. They had crossed a threshold. They weren't just doubting the official narrative anymore; they were actively building a counter-narrative, one supported by fragmented science, whispered history, careful observation, and now, two crucial anomalies buried in an official report. The game had become far more serious, the stakes infinitely higher. And the killer, whoever they were, was still out there, perhaps watching, believing themselves safe behind the convenient shield of Harry Smythe's guilt.

****

The rhythmic drumming of rain against the bay window of Agnes Plummett's study provided a sombre soundtrack to the thoughts swirling within the small room. Outside, the Melbourne evening had descended into a full, gusty downpour, washing the South Yarra streets clean but doing little to clear the muddied, dangerous waters the four individuals inside now found themselves navigating. The initial, almost feverish excitement sparked by Fitzwilliam's news – the validation of the lividity inconsistency, the tantalising mystery of the unidentified alkaloid – had subsided, replaced by a heavier, more sobering understanding of their predicament.

Fitzwilliam articulated it first, voicing the pragmatic concerns that tempered their theoretical breakthroughs. He leaned back in his armchair, the lamplight catching the weary lines around his eyes. "So," he began, his tone devoid of its earlier nervous energy, replaced by a lawyer's measured assessment, "we find ourselves in a… highly irregular position. We possess unofficial information suggesting significant anomalies in the official findings – anomalies that strongly support our alternative hypothesis of poisoning and staging. However," he held up a cautionary hand as Ronnie opened his mouth to interject, "we must be realistic about how the authorities will view this."

He took a slow sip from a glass of water – the tea had long gone cold. "Detective Inspector Davies has a victim, a plausible suspect with motive and opportunity, a readily available weapon belonging to that suspect, and a preliminary autopsy report officially citing blunt force trauma consistent with that weapon as the cause of death.

That," he stated flatly, "is a prosecutable case, circumstantial perhaps, but compelling enough for charges to likely be laid against Lord Smythe in due course, especially given his lamentable performance under initial questioning and his subsequent flight – however temporary – to Portsea."

"But the lividity! The alkaloid!" Ronnie protested, unable to contain himself. "That's not just 'circumstantial'! That's contradictory physical evidence! It demands investigation!"

"It *should* demand investigation, Ronnie," Fitzwilliam agreed patiently. "But police resources are finite. Detectives, like all humans, are susceptible to confirmation bias, as we discussed. They have a strong narrative; these anomalies, dismissed by the pathologist herself as inconclusive or irrelevant background noise, are unlikely to derail that narrative unless we can provide *irrefutable proof* to the contrary. And 'irrefutable proof' in a legal sense," he fixed Ronnie with a meaningful look, "requires more than probability calculations, however elegant."

He continued, his gaze sweeping across the others. "We cannot march into Russell Street," he gestured vaguely towards the city centre, location of police headquarters, "and demand they reopen the investigation based on our theories and Sergeant Riley's potentially career-limiting indiscretion. We have no standing. Our 'evidence' – historical analysis, botanical knowledge, timeline gaps, interpretations of physics – would be dismissed as amateur speculation. The only pieces of potentially hard evidence – the lividity and the alkaloid – are already known to the police and officially deemed insignificant. They hold the VIFM report, not us. They control the samples, the exhibits, the official lines of inquiry."

Agnes nodded slowly, her expression grim but accepting. "Alistair is correct. While morally and intellectually unsatisfying, the practical reality is that the official investigation will likely proceed down the path of least resistance towards Lord Smythe unless, or until, something fundamentally contradicts that narrative *in a way they cannot ignore.*" She paused, her gaze sharp. "Which means the onus falls entirely upon us to uncover such evidence."

The weight of that statement settled upon them. They weren't just supplementing the official investigation anymore; they were effectively conducting a parallel, secret one, working against the tide of official opinion with minimal resources and considerable personal risk.

"But how?" Chloe asked, her voice barely above a whisper, echoing Fitzwilliam's earlier anxiety but now imbued with a sense of shared responsibility. "What can we actually *do*? We can't get the full autopsy report. We can't force them to test the *Digitalis* specifically. We can't demand access to Mildred's bank accounts or search her home for hidden thermos flasks."

"No," Agnes conceded. "We cannot use official channels. Therefore, we must rely on our own strengths: observation, deduction, research, and discretion. We must look where the police are likely *not* looking." She picked up her pen and drew her notepad closer, her earlier methodical energy returning, now channelled into strategic planning.

"Our immediate objectives remain, but with sharper focus," she declared. "Firstly, the poison vector. The unidentified alkaloid is key. While we await any further potential – though unlikely – leaks via Alistair's contact, our best hypothesis remains botanical, given Chloe's observations and Ainsworth's location." She looked at Chloe. "You mentioned the *Digitalis purpurea*. Can you ascertain, discreetly of course, if any plants show signs of recent harvesting? Missing leaves, cut stems? And are there *other* potentially toxic plants in that specific bed or nearby that contain notable alkaloids?"

Chloe nodded, already thinking. "The foxgloves are distinctive.

I can check them carefully when I'm next working near there – ostensibly tidying up after the police. There are other plants nearby – Daphne, Yew slightly further off – both toxic, but less likely alkaloid sources in the way Digitalis is. I can make a list, check their properties." Her mind was already working, translating the abstract threat of poison into tangible botanical possibilities.

"Excellent," Agnes approved. "Secondly, the opportunity. Ronnie, your timeline analysis identifying the potential poisoning window during Ainsworth's lunch break in his office is crucial." She turned to Ronnie. "While precise lividity calculations might be difficult without exact timings and temperature data, can you refine the window for *body movement*? If death occurred, say, between 1 PM and 3 PM, and the lividity suggests movement *after* fixation began, could you estimate the earliest time the body might have been re-positioned?"

Ronnie frowned, tapping his pencil. "Difficult without knowing the *exact* fixation state noted by the pathologist. But assuming fixation began within, say, one to two hours postmortem… significant movement *after* that point would indeed leave inconsistent patterns. So, if death occurred around 2 PM, noticeable lividity inconsistency might imply movement occurring perhaps 4 PM or later? Plausible if the killer waited until the initial commotion subsided or dusk approached before staging the scene near Lawn 3." He made a note. "I can model scenarios based on average cooling rates and lividity progression tables. It won't be definitive, but it could narrow the window for the staging activity."

"Helpful," Agnes acknowledged. "Thirdly, motive and means beyond Smythe. Alistair," she looked at Fitzwilliam, "your conversation with Mr Abercrombie confirmed Ainsworth was ruffling feathers regarding historical finances, particularly the 80s extension and old contracts. We need to identify *who* specifically felt most threatened. This requires delving into records related to those periods – committee memberships, contractors involved, anyone potentially implicated in that anonymous donation or subsequent costings." She paused. "This falls largely to me, given my access to the archives. I will cross-reference membership lists from the 80s and 90s with current members and committee positions. I will also attempt to trace the contractors involved, particularly 'Modern Build Pty Ltd' from the extension."

"And Mildred Pettle," Fitzwilliam added quietly but firmly. "Her control over the accounts, her presence, her deflection… she remains central, even if that anonymous donation predates her longest likely tenure as Secretary. We need to understand her role, past and present."

"Agreed," Agnes nodded. "My research will include scrutinising any records pertaining to her appointment and her handling of accounts over the years, looking for any anomalies *before* Ainsworth's recent deep dive." She then looked back at Fitzwilliam. "And your role, Alistair, remains critical in monitoring the official investigation. Any hint that Detective Inspector Davies is wavering, any further detail, however small, on that alkaloid analysis when or if it becomes available… that could be vital. And," she added, "continue discreet inquiries regarding legal representation for Lord Smythe. An undefended Smythe only makes the path easier for the true culprit."

Fitzwilliam nodded grimly, accepting the necessity despite his reservations.

Finally, Agnes looked around the table, her gaze resting on each of them. "We must acknowledge the increased risk. We are no longer merely curious observers. We are actively seeking evidence that contradicts the official findings and potentially points towards a calculating killer who has already murdered once to protect their secrets. This individual may be aware of our interest, particularly if they observed our interactions or if Ainsworth mentioned his suspicions to anyone before his death. We must exercise extreme caution in our inquiries, be mindful of who we speak to, and above all, continue to share information only amongst ourselves."

Her words hung in the air, heavy as the rain still falling outside. The initial intellectual excitement of solving the puzzle was now tempered by the cold reality of potential danger. They were four very different people, united by chance and a shared sense of justice, embarking on a course that set them against both the official investigation and an unknown, ruthless killer.

Ronnie, typically, broke the tension. "Risk is merely a variable to be quantified and mitigated," he stated, already sketching potential risk assessment matrices in his notebook. "Optimal strategy involves maximising data acquisition while minimising detection probability."

Chloe managed a small, determined smile. "I'll be careful when I'm checking the plants."

Fitzwilliam sighed, but his expression held a new resolve. "Discretion is second nature in my profession. I'll do what I can."

Agnes gave a single, decisive nod. "Then we have our tasks. Let us proceed. Methodically. Carefully. And find the truth that lies buried beneath the Society's carefully manicured surface." The grandfather clock chimed again, marking not just the passage of time, but the moment their informal collaboration solidified into a shared, dangerous mission.

9

Tea, Sympathy, and Subtle Manipulation

Two days after the discovery that had shattered the genteel calm of the Toorak Croquet & Horticultural Society, the main clubhouse lounge hosted an event both necessary and profoundly awkward: the memorial afternoon tea for Bartholomew Ainsworth. The weather, with typical Melbourne capriciousness, had decided to follow the previous day's dramatic downpour with brilliant, almost brittle sunshine, making the sombre occasion feel even more incongruous. Light streamed through the tall windows, illuminating the room's traditional comforts – the plush armchairs, the display cabinets filled with silver trophies, the slightly faded portrait of the club's founding president – but it couldn't dispel the heavy pall of shock, suspicion, and hushed speculation that clung to the air like the scent of beeswax and old money.

The event was, by unspoken consensus, deemed essential. Not necessarily out of affection for the deceased – affection for Bartholomew Ainsworth had always been a scarce commodity – but out of adherence to propriety, a collective need to perform the rituals of mourning and attempt to smooth over the jagged edges of the preceding forty-eight hours. It was an exercise in maintaining appearances, a core tenet of Society life, now performed under the most trying of circumstances.

And orchestrating this delicate performance, moving through the subdued gathering with an air of quiet competence and almost saintly compassion, was Mildred Pettle.

To observe her, as Agnes Plummett was doing with forensic intensity from a strategically chosen armchair near the fireplace, was to witness a masterclass in unobtrusive control. Dressed in a simple, dove-grey dress that managed to look both respectful and self-effacing, Mildred seemed to be everywhere at once, yet never drawing undue attention to herself. Her expression was one of gentle sadness, perfectly modulated – not overly distraught, which might seem performative given Ainsworth's unpopularity, but conveying a genuine sorrow for the *tragedy* itself, for the violation of the club's sanctuary.

She greeted arriving members near the entrance, her voice a low murmur of sympathy. "Colonel Abernathy, so good of you to come... such a shock for us all..." "Sybil dear," addressing Mrs Henderson with a brief, comforting touch on the arm, "do find a seat near the window, the light is lovely today, perhaps it will help..." She seemed to remember every member's preference, their minor ailments, their social connections, weaving these details seamlessly into her condolences, creating an atmosphere not just of shared grief, but of shared *community*, implicitly reinforcing her own role as its quiet, nurturing centre.

She conferred briefly, almost silently, with the two catering staff borrowed from a local Toorak establishment (renowned for its discretion and cucumber sandwiches), ensuring the three-tiered platters of sandwiches (crusts meticulously removed), miniature scones, and dainty lamingtons remained replenished. Her gestures were minimal, efficient – a slight nod towards an empty milk jug, a subtle glance indicating the need for more Earl Grey in the main urn. She moved with a practised fluidity, her steps nearly silent on the thick Persian carpet, refilling teacups, offering napkins, adjusting a slightly askew floral arrangement of white lilies and baby's breath whose cloying scent seemed to Agnes almost offensively funereal.

Ronnie Peterson, dragged along by Fitzwilliam under the rationale that their collective presence was necessary to observe reactions, stood awkwardly near the trophy cabinet, looking utterly lost. He'd attempted to engage Barnaby Thornton (also present, looking young and miserable) in a discussion about the potential energy stored in the tightly wound springs of antique clocks, but Barnaby seemed incapable of focusing. Ronnie's gaze kept drifting towards the tea service, possibly contemplating the thermodynamics of the urn or the optimal pouring velocity to minimise spillage – the human drama seemed to register primarily as inefficient data points. He accepted a cup of tea from Mildred when offered, blinking in surprise as if suddenly remembering where he was, and took an absent-minded bite of a scone, likely unaware of its buttery perfection.

Fitzwilliam, meanwhile, felt trapped in a social minefield. He nursed a cup of tea he didn't want, nodding gravely to members expressing predictable sentiments ("Dreadful business… poor Bartholomew… police seem certain about Smythe, though?"). He watched Mildred with a mixture of suspicion and grudging admiration. Her performance was flawless. She was the picture of selfless service, the calm eye in the storm, anticipating needs, soothing anxieties, ensuring the delicate machinery of Society ritual continued to function despite the grit of murder that had jammed its gears. Yet Fitzwilliam, armed with the knowledge of Ainsworth's investigations and the autopsy anomalies, couldn't see her simply as a competent secretary anymore. He saw the potential architect of the "too perfect" accounts, the possible manipulator of past records, the individual with perhaps the strongest motive if Ainsworth had indeed uncovered embezzlement tied to her long tenure. Every gentle smile seemed like a mask, every sympathetic murmur a potential deflection. His legal training screamed caution – *no proof, only speculation* – but his gut, increasingly attuned to the dissonances beneath the club's polite surface, felt a profound disquiet whenever Mildred drew near.

Chloe Dubois had positioned herself near the edge of the room, by the French doors leading out to the verandah, ostensibly examining the potted ferns. She felt out of place, a staff member lingering at a members' function, but Agnes had insisted she attend, to observe. Chloe watched Mildred too, but from a different perspective. She saw the practical efficiency Agnes had noted, but also something else – a meticulous attention to *detail* in her social interactions that mirrored Ainsworth's own obsession, albeit applied to people rather than rules or numbers. Mildred seemed to know exactly how long to linger with one group, precisely what tone to adopt with another, whose cup needed refilling, whose ego needed stroking. It was a constant, subtle calibration, an exercise in social engineering disguised as simple helpfulness. Chloe remembered Mildred's warm smile towards her yesterday, after the discovery in the Treasurer's office, and felt a sudden, unexpected chill despite the warm room. Was that warmth genuine, or just another part of the perfectly managed facade?

Mildred paused near Agnes and Fitzwilliam's table. "Miss Plummett, Mr Fitzwilliam," she murmured, her expression one of weary concern. "Can I refresh your tea? Such a difficult day for everyone. Poor Bartholomew... whatever his... meticulous ways... he was part of the Society for so long. It feels quite... empty... without his critiques of the minutes, doesn't it?" She managed a small, watery smile.

It was perfectly pitched. Acknowledging Ainsworth's difficult personality ("meticulous ways" being a generous euphemism) while simultaneously expressing loss and emphasising his long connection to the club. It subtly normalised his unpleasantness, making extreme reactions like Harry Smythe's seem even more aberrant, while positioning herself as someone who understood and tolerated him, warts and all.

"Indeed, Mildred," Agnes replied, her voice steady. "His attention to detail was certainly… unique. He seemed particularly focused on historical details recently, I gather?" It was a gentle probe, dropped into the conversation like a pebble into a still pond.

Mildred didn't react, merely sighed softly. "The Centenary preparations, I suppose," she said vaguely, echoing her previous deflections. "He did feel the weight of responsibility keenly. Perhaps too keenly, in retrospect. One worries he simply worked himself into a state." She deftly changed the subject. "Alistair, I trust you found everything you needed yesterday to ensure the club's payments remain on schedule? Please don't hesitate to ask if there is any documentation you require. Continuity is so important at a time like this." Again, helpful, competent, steering the conversation back to safe, administrative ground, while subtly reminding Fitzwilliam of the official, limited scope of his access to the accounts.

Fitzwilliam murmured his thanks, feeling outmanoeuvred yet again. Before he could formulate a follow-up question, Mildred had spotted an empty cup across the room and glided away, a figure of quiet solicitude, leaving Agnes and Fitzwilliam to exchange another look of shared frustration.

Agnes watched Mildred's retreating back. The dove-grey dress, the neat hair, the quiet efficiency – it was all a carefully constructed uniform, she suspected, designed to render the wearer almost invisible, unremarkable. Yet, like a master spy hiding in plain sight, Mildred Pettle seemed to operate at the very centre of the club's network, managing information, subtly influencing opinions, all while seeming to do nothing more than pour tea and offer sympathy. Her performance was, in its own way, as meticulous and controlling as Ainsworth's approach to finance had ever been. And far, far more dangerous. Agnes picked up her teacup, the lukewarm liquid suddenly tasting bitter. The memorial tea wasn't just about remembering Bartholomew Ainsworth; it was about watching his potential killer command the stage with unnerving, invisible skill.

****

The memorial tea progressed with the muted, solemn rhythm of uncomfortable obligation. China clinked softly, polite murmurs filled the spaces between silences, and the scent of Earl Grey mingled with the funereal sweetness of lilies and the comforting aroma of baking from the replenished scone platters. Yet beneath this veneer of civilised mourning, an invisible current flowed – the current of speculation, fear, and nascent judgment, and Mildred Pettle navigated it like an expert pilot steering a vessel through treacherous waters.

Agnes Plummett, maintaining her position near the fireplace, had abandoned all pretence of engaging with the book she held open in her lap (a slim volume on Victorian garden design). Her focus was entirely on the Club Secretary. She watched Mildred move from group to group, a study in perfectly calibrated empathy, her voice rarely rising above a sympathetic murmur, yet somehow always subtly directing the flow and framing the narrative.

Mildred paused beside a small cluster near the window, where Mrs Henderson held court with Penelope Cartwright and another middle-aged member, Mrs Albright. They were discussing Bartholomew Ainsworth's recent demeanour.

"…seemed almost *driven*, Mildred," Mrs Albright was saying, shaking her head. "Positively obsessed. Not just with the tournament finances, but digging up all sorts of ancient history. Frankly, it seemed unhealthy."

Mildred sighed, placing a hand gently on the back of Mrs Albright's chair, instantly making herself part of their intimate circle. "He *was* under immense strain, wasn't he, Eleanor?" she agreed, using Mrs Albright's first name with practised familiarity. "I did worry. He took his responsibilities so very seriously – perhaps too seriously towards the end." She lowered her voice confidentially. "The Centenary preparations, on top of the regular accounts, *and* his self-imposed task of reviewing all those historical records… he mentioned to me only last week how the sheer volume was giving him dreadful headaches. Poor man."

Agnes mentally dissected the intervention. Masterful. Mildred acknowledged Ainsworth's obsessive digging ("driven") but immediately re-framed it not as potentially uncovering wrongdoing, but as self-inflicted "immense strain" and "overwork". She lumped the potentially dangerous historical research in with the mundane Centenary preparations, diluting its significance. She introduced physical symptoms – "dreadful headaches" – subtly suggesting Ainsworth might have been physically unwell, perhaps prone to collapse or poor judgment, entirely separate from any external threat. And the concluding sigh – "poor man" – positioned Mildred firmly on the side of sympathy, making her interpretation seem compassionate rather than manipulative. Mrs Henderson and Mrs Albright nodded sadly, absorbing Mildred's version without question. The possibility that Ainsworth's "stress" stemmed from discovering decades of embezzlement, possibly orchestrated by the very woman offering sympathy, didn't even seem to register.

Fitzwilliam, hovering near the edge of this group while pretending to examine a framed photograph of the 1956 Pennant-winning croquet team, felt a chill. Mildred wasn't merely deflecting; she was actively constructing an alternative narrative for Ainsworth's recent state of mind, one that conveniently pathologised his investigations as symptoms of stress rather than purposeful inquiry. It was subtle, almost impossible to challenge without sounding accusatory or revealing their own suspicions. He noted how she used vague terms – "immense strain," "historical records" – avoiding any specifics that might connect to the 80s extension or grounds contracts they now suspected were key.

Mildred soon glided away, pausing to straighten a slightly crooked trophy in a display cabinet before approaching Colonel Abernathy, who was pontificating near the doorway about declining standards of sportsmanship. Fitzwilliam subtly shifted his position, straining to hear.

"…and young Smythe," the Colonel was grumbling, "always had more money than sense, and a temper like a faulty kettle. Still, murder… seems a bit much, even for him. Are the police absolutely certain?"

Mildred placed a calming hand on the Colonel's arm. "Oh, Colonel, it's not for us to question the police, is it? Inspector Davies seemed very capable. And one must admit," she sighed again, that same carefully deployed sound of weary resignation, "poor Harry *has* been under considerable pressure lately."

"Pressure?" the Colonel asked, intrigued.

"Well," Mildred lowered her voice, creating an instant pocket of confidentiality, "it's hardly a secret around the club, is it? His… unfortunate reverses at the track? The string of bad investments? One heard whispers… quite significant sums involved. It does prey on a man's mind, financial worry. Makes one… volatile, perhaps? Less able to control one's impulses?"

Fitzwilliam's eyes widened slightly behind his spectacles. This was brilliant, in a horrifying way. Mildred wasn't just relying on Harry's known temper. She was subtly weaving in his *other*, unrelated secret – the gambling debts Agnes suspected and Fitzwilliam had confirmed Smythe was agitated about – and presenting it as a contributing factor, a pressure cooker environment that made his (alleged) violent outburst almost understandable, tragically inevitable even. It provided a secondary, reinforcing motive – perhaps Ainsworth had discovered the debts too? Threatened exposure? – muddying the waters while keeping the spotlight firmly fixed on Harry. She wasn't lying, necessarily – Harry *was* likely under financial pressure – but she was twisting that truth, using it to bolster the case against him for a crime he likely didn't commit.

Agnes, observing from her chair, felt a cold knot tighten in her stomach. She had suspected Harry's financial woes were a separate issue, the cause of his suspicious behaviour *after* the murder. Mildred was now expertly re-purposing that behaviour, retroactively painting it as part of the build-up *to* the murder. It was a chillingly effective manipulation, playing on the members' existing knowledge and prejudices. The Colonel was already nodding slowly, his expression shifting from slight doubt to grim understanding. "Debts, you say? Hmm. Yes, pressure can do terrible things to a chap's nerves. Terrible." Mildred had successfully shored up the primary narrative by introducing a supporting beam constructed from unrelated truths.

Having planted that seed, Mildred excused herself – "More tea, Colonel?" – and moved towards a quieter corner where Miss Penelope Cartwright sat alone, looking rather overwhelmed by the whole affair. Agnes watched Mildred sit down beside the younger woman, adopting an almost maternal air. Fitzwilliam found himself drifting slightly closer, ostensibly to examine a watercolour painting of the clubhouse from the 1920s.

"...such a private man, really," Mildred was saying softly to Penelope, apparently continuing a conversation. "Bartholomew, I mean. So focused on the club, one sometimes wondered if he had any life outside these walls. Any other... pressures." She paused, as if a thought had just occurred to her. "He did mention something vaguely, a few months ago, about a property dispute he was involved in. Something down the coast? Sounded rather contentious. He waved it away when I asked, of course, in his usual fashion." She sighed. "One does hope he didn't have enemies we knew nothing about. It would be dreadful to think poor Harry is taking the blame if..." She let the sentence trail off, leaving the implication hanging.

Fitzwilliam almost stopped breathing. A property dispute? Down the coast? Completely unrelated to the club? This was a classic red herring, expertly deployed. Mildred was now introducing the possibility of an unknown, external antagonist, someone entirely outside the Society's orbit. It served multiple purposes: it offered a potential alternative to Harry Smythe *without* implicating anyone within the club (especially not herself), it made Ainsworth seem even more complex and secretive (justifying why no one knew his 'real' worries), and it subtly shifted the focus away from any *internal* club matters, such as potentially embarrassing financial investigations. It was another layer of obfuscation, beautifully delivered under the guise of worried speculation. Penelope Cartwright looked wide-eyed, clearly absorbing this new possibility with fascinated horror.

Agnes felt a chill despite the warm room. Mildred wasn't just defending; she was actively creating alternative narratives, smoke screens designed to obscure the truth she potentially represented. The mention of a "property dispute" was so vague as to be untraceable, yet planted just enough doubt to make the internal club motives seem less certain, less pressing. Mildred was not merely reacting; she was proactively managing the information landscape.

Throughout these interactions, Mildred's composure remained flawless. Her hands were steady as she poured tea, her expression consistently registered gentle sorrow and concern, her voice never wavered from its soft, sympathetic cadence. Only Agnes, watching with unwavering focus, thought she detected something – a momentary hardness in the eyes when mentioning Harry's debts, a fleeting coolness when Fitzwilliam had probed about the historical accounts, a slight, almost imperceptible tension in her shoulders beneath the dove-grey dress. These were minuscule tells, easily missed, possibly imagined. But Agnes, trained in the meticulous observation of details, filed them away alongside the library call slip and the inconsistencies in the official narrative.

The memorial tea eventually wound down. Members began to depart, offering final condolences to Esme or Mildred, their conversations now likely peppered with Mildred's carefully planted seeds of thought regarding Ainsworth's stress, Harry's financial woes, and potential unknown external enemies. Mildred oversaw the clearing of the tables, assisting the catering staff, ensuring everything was left tidy, restoring order.

As Fitzwilliam collected his briefcase, preparing to leave, Mildred approached him one last time. "Alistair," she said quietly, "thank you for your support today. And for your diligence regarding the accounts. Do let me know if any... significant queries arise from Bartholomew's recent work. I would, naturally, wish to assist the Committee in resolving any outstanding matters promptly and discreetly."

It was perfectly phrased. An offer of help that simultaneously asserted her control over the information ("let *me* know"), implied any issues were merely routine ("outstanding matters"), and stressed discretion, subtly warning against broader discussion. Fitzwilliam merely nodded, murmuring something noncommittal about procedure, unable to meet her calm, clear gaze directly. He felt, quite distinctly, like a fly being invited courteously into a spider's web. He retreated from the clubhouse into the now rain-washed, late afternoon air, feeling more certain, and more apprehensive, than ever. Mildred Pettle was not just hiding something; she was actively, brilliantly, terrifyingly in control.

****

The memorial tea was drawing to its inevitable close. The initial flurry of arrivals had long passed, and the subdued murmur of conversation had dwindled as members began, one by one, to make their excuses and drift away, perhaps eager to escape the oppressive atmosphere or simply return to the routines momentarily disrupted by death and suspicion. The catering staff moved with quiet efficiency, discreetly clearing away plates bearing the remnants of cucumber sandwiches and half-eaten scones. The scent of lilies hung heavy in the air, almost cloying now, competing with the fading aroma of brewed tea. Outside, the rain had stopped, leaving the gardens glistening under a weak, late-afternoon sun that struggled to break through the lingering cloud cover.

Alistair Fitzwilliam knew it was now or likely never, at least not in this semi-formal context. He had watched Mildred Pettle all afternoon, observed her masterful handling of grief-stricken members and rumour-mongers alike, her subtle reinforcement of the narrative that painted Harry Smythe as the tragic, if culpable, figure in this drama. He had listened to her deftly re-frame Ainsworth's obsessive investigations as mere symptoms of overwork and stress. Every instinct, both personal and professional, screamed that this woman was hiding something significant beneath her veneer of gentle competence. But suspicion, however strong, was not evidence. He needed something more, some crack in the facade, some inconsistency he could pursue. Linking his official task of ensuring financial continuity to Ainsworth's recent activities seemed the only legitimate avenue open to him for a direct approach.

He saw Mildred near the large mahogany sideboard where condolence cards were accumulating beside a rapidly emptying tea urn. She was speaking quietly with Esme Weatherly, likely coordinating the final clearing up. Taking a deep breath, Fitzwilliam straightened his tie – a nervous habit he couldn't seem to break – and walked over, aiming for an air of casual professionalism he was far from feeling. His stomach churned; confronting anyone, let alone someone as potentially formidable as Mildred Pettle seemed to be, went entirely against his nature.

"Mildred? Esme?" he began, pausing beside them. "Just before I head off, I wonder if I might have a brief word, Mildred? Purely about ensuring a smooth handover of Bartholomew's treasury responsibilities."

Esme looked relieved to have an excuse to escape. "Of course, Mr Fitzwilliam. I need to check on the caterers anyway." She gave Mildred a quick, anxious smile and bustled away, leaving Fitzwilliam alone with the Club Secretary.

Mildred turned towards him, her expression one of polite, slightly weary helpfulness. "Alistair. Of course. Anything I can assist with? Although I imagine the Committee will need to formally appoint an interim Treasurer soon. Until then, any urgent payments…"

"Quite, quite," Fitzwilliam interrupted gently, wanting to get to his point before his nerve failed. "But as I mentioned when I reviewed the immediate payables yesterday, understanding the context of any outstanding queries Bartholomew might have had is rather crucial for ensuring continuity. Prevent suppliers getting anxious, you understand." He paused, gathering his thoughts, trying to frame the question carefully. "Agnes Plummett happened to mention – and Colonel Abernathy too, I believe – that Bartholomew had seemed particularly focused on certain historical accounts lately? The West Wing extension funds from the eighties, and some older grounds maintenance contracts?"

He watched her face intently for any reaction. There was none. Or rather, none that was obvious. Perhaps a flicker behind the eyes, instantly suppressed? A fractional tightening around the mouth, immediately smoothed into her default expression of gentle concern? He couldn't be sure. Her composure was remarkable.

"Oh, dear," Mildred sighed, her tone perfectly pitched between mild confusion and sympathy for Ainsworth's perceived eccentricities. "Bartholomew did have rather… wide-ranging interests when it came to the club's history, didn't he? Especially with the Centenary approaching, he felt very strongly that every detail should be absolutely correct." She picked up a stray teaspoon from the sideboard and began polishing it absently with a napkin – a small, domestic action that somehow made her seem less like a potential suspect and more like the efficient homemaker of the club.

"He *did* ask me to retrieve quite a number of older files from storage recently," she continued thoughtfully, her gaze distant as if genuinely trying to recall. "Ledgers from the Carmichael era, building plans… even some rather dusty personnel files related to past groundskeepers, I believe. He was cross-referencing something regarding original planting grants, I think he said?" She offered this detail freely, a seemingly helpful piece of information that cleverly misdirected from the core financial issues Fitzwilliam had raised – the extension funding, the contracts.

Fitzwilliam felt a familiar wave of frustration but pressed on, trying a slightly different tack. "Yes, I'm sure the Centenary was a factor," he conceded. "But did he express any specific *concerns* to you regarding those older accounts he was reviewing? Any discrepancies he'd found? Any particular contractors or budget lines he seemed worried about? As the person who prepares the current reports and reconciliations, you might have been the natural person for him to confide in if he found something amiss." He tried to make it sound like a logical procedural query.

Mildred stopped polishing the spoon and looked directly at him. Her eyes, a pale, indeterminate blue, held an expression of faint surprise, perhaps even mild hurt, as if he were suggesting something improper. "Concerns, Alistair? Bartholomew rarely confided his *concerns* in that sense. He stated facts, cited rules, pointed out errors – usually mine, I must confess," she added with a small, self-deprecating smile that didn't quite reach her eyes. "If he had found a concrete discrepancy in those historical records, I feel certain he would have raised it formally at the next Finance Committee meeting, with precise documentation. That was always his way. Direct. Methodical."

She placed the polished spoon carefully back on the sideboard. "He didn't mention any specific *worries* to *me*, no. Only, as I said, that he seemed rather burdened by the sheer volume of historical detail he was trying to sift through. He complained about the poor state of some of the older records, the difficulty in tracing specific payment authorisations from decades ago." She sighed again. "Frankly, between you and me, I did wonder if perhaps he was getting slightly… lost… in the past? Fixated, perhaps? It can happen, when one delves too deeply into history." Again, the subtle pathologising of his investigation. Framing it as an old man's obsessive fixation rather than a potentially dangerous discovery.

Fitzwilliam felt like he was trying to grasp smoke. Every direct question was met with a plausible, reasonable-sounding answer that acknowledged the premise but denied any incriminating substance. She admitted Ainsworth accessed the files, admitted he was focused on history, but framed it all as either routine Centenary work or harmless eccentricity. She used phrases like "concrete discrepancy" and "formal charge" – terms Ainsworth himself might use – implying that anything less wasn't worth discussing, effectively dismissing any tentative suspicions he might have been harbouring.

"So," Fitzwilliam persisted, feeling clumsy but unwilling to retreat entirely, "regarding, for instance, the '87 extension finances, or those large grounds contracts from the early 2000s… you weren't aware of him finding anything he considered… problematic?"

Mildred's expression became slightly cooler, though her voice remained soft. "Alistair," she said gently, almost chidingly, "Bartholomew considered many things 'problematic'. The alignment of the spoons in the cutlery drawer was 'problematic' to him last week." A faint smile touched her lips again, inviting him to share the perceived absurdity. "As I said, he didn't bring any *formal* financial irregularities from those periods to my attention. My role primarily involves the current accounts and assisting with record retrieval when requested by the Treasurer or Committee. Interpreting or investigating decades-old transactions…" she gave a small, helpless shrug, "…that was Bartholomew's self-appointed task. One sadly left unfinished."

She paused, then added, her tone shifting back to one of gentle concern, "One hates to speculate, especially now, when poor Bartholomew isn't here to clarify his intentions or findings. It feels rather… unfair to him, doesn't it? Perhaps it's best to let the police conduct their investigation and focus ourselves on supporting the club through this difficult time?"

It was a masterstroke of conversational closure. She had validated Fitzwilliam's query by acknowledging Ainsworth's activities, provided plausible but non-incriminating explanations, subtly questioned the legitimacy of Ainsworth's concerns by framing them as potentially obsessive, asserted her own limited (official) role, appealed to propriety and respect for the dead, and gently steered him back towards focusing on the present and trusting the authorities. She had done all this without seeming defensive, unhelpful, or overtly suspicious.

Fitzwilliam felt utterly defeated. He had tried a direct probe, and the fortress walls had held firm, indeed, had seemed to gently push him back with polite, unyielding pressure. He murmured something about understanding, about the need for discretion, gathered his briefcase, and made his retreat.

Agnes caught his eye as he passed her chair near the fireplace. She had likely overheard much of the exchange. Her expression was unreadable, but Fitzwilliam suspected she understood perfectly. He gave a barely perceptible shake of his head.

As he walked out of the clubhouse into the damp, cool air of the late afternoon, the scent of wet earth and lingering jasmine filling his lungs, Fitzwilliam felt a profound sense of frustration mixed with a cold certainty. Mildred Pettle knew far more than she was letting on. Her deflections were too smooth, her narrative too convenient. She was hiding something, protecting something – or someone. His attempt to glean information directly had failed, stonewalled by her impeccable facade. But the very smoothness of her denial, the calculated way she controlled the conversation, served only to deepen his conviction. She wasn't just an efficient secretary caught up in tragic events. She was, he felt increasingly sure, a central player, perhaps *the* central player, in the entire deadly game. And proving it, he now realised with daunting clarity, would require bypassing her defences entirely. They needed evidence she couldn't explain away with a sympathetic sigh and a carefully chosen anecdote.

10

A Coded Clue

The day after the strained civility of the memorial tea dawned over Melbourne with a deceptive calmness. The rain had passed, leaving behind washed streets and a sky of pale, watery blue. Inside her South Yarra apartment study, however, Agnes Plummett felt a gathering storm of intellectual energy. The previous day's observations of Mildred Pettle's masterful performance had solidified her suspicions, transforming them from uneasy intuition into near certainty. Mildred's careful deflections, her subtle manipulation of the narrative surrounding both Ainsworth's stress and Harry Smythe's culpability, her very *presence* at the centre of the club's administrative web – it all pointed towards someone with a great deal to hide, someone adept at controlling information. But certainty in one's own mind was a far cry from proof. What Agnes needed was a key, something tangible to unlock the secrets Mildred guarded so well.

Her attention returned to the small, stiff, slightly yellowed library call slip she had retrieved from Bartholomew Ainsworth's meticulously – perhaps *too* meticulously – tidy office. She had placed it carefully beneath a glass paperweight on her desk, treating it with the reverence usually reserved for fragile historical documents. It felt incongruous, this small piece of library ephemera amidst the unfolding drama of embezzlement and murder, yet her instincts, honed by decades of archival research where significance often lay hidden in the seemingly trivial, told her it was important. Ainsworth had hidden it deliberately, tucked away in a file utterly unrelated to its apparent subject matter. Why?

She picked it up again, examining it under the bright light of her desk lamp. The paper was thick defences, the typed call number precise, professional. Below it, Ainsworth's familiar, spiky handwriting: *"Pyrus Malus."* And beneath that, the cryptic reference: *"Cf. Sect. IV, Para 12."*

Pyrus Malus. The common apple. Why would Ainsworth, a man obsessed with finance, rules, and recently, historical club records, be consulting library resources on apples? It seemed absurdly out of character. Unless… unless it wasn't about apples at all. Unless it was code. Ainsworth, she suspected, possessed a mind that appreciated intricate systems – financial, regulatory, perhaps even cryptographic.

Her first step was purely logistical: identify the book associated with the call number. The format looked like Dewey Decimal Classification, but with institutional prefixes common in large research libraries. She turned to her laptop, navigating first to the State Library of Victoria's online catalogue, then the University of Melbourne's Baillieu Library catalogue. She carefully typed in the alphanumeric sequence.

No exact match in the University library. But the State Library… Bingo. The system returned a single hit. Her breath caught slightly as she read the title. It wasn't a simple horticultural text. The book was titled: ***"Orchards of Progress: A History of Land Use and Horticultural Development in the Port Phillip District, 1835-***

1910," by an obscure historian named Alistair P. Fincham, published in 1912.

Agnes felt a familiar thrill – the jolt of discovery that came when disparate pieces began to align. *Pyrus Malus* wasn't just 'apple'; it was likely Ainsworth's shorthand reference to this specific, rather academic, volume focusing on historical land use, including orchards, in the very region where the Toorak Croquet & Horticultural Society now stood. This immediately felt more relevant than pomology. Ainsworth, digging into the club's past, was consulting external historical sources about the land itself or its early development. Why?

The reference – *"Cf. Sect. IV, Para 12."* – now demanded attention. *Cf. – confer,* meaning 'compare'. Compare with Section IV, Paragraph 12 *of what?* The logical assumption was Section IV, Paragraph 12 of Fincham's *Orchards of Progress.* Agnes immediately checked the State Library catalogue entry for the book. It was available, though held in their closed-access heritage collection, requiring special request. Annoying, but not insurmountable. She could visit the library later today or tomorrow.

But first, was there another possibility? Could the reference point elsewhere? Section IV, Paragraph 12... of the club's constitution? Unlikely; constitutional references were usually by Article number. Section IV, Paragraph 12 of a specific *financial report?* That felt more promising, given Ainsworth's role and recent focus. He had access to decades of those. Could *Pyrus Malus* be a keyword or code linked to a specific *type* of report or event?

She pulled out the Society's annual reports from the last ten years – copies she kept as part of her unofficial archive. She began checking the fourth section of each report. Section IV varied slightly year by year, but often dealt with 'Membership Activities' or 'Social Events'. She looked for Paragraph 12 within that section.

In some years, it didn't exist or referred to something mundane like lawn maintenance schedules. But in the reports for years where the Annual Garden Fete was held (a major biennial fundraising event), Section IV often detailed the Fete's subcommittee report, and Paragraph 12… consistently seemed to fall within the summary of *income and expenditure* for the Fete stalls or the overall Fete reconciliation.

Her pulse quickened again. The Annual Garden Fete. A large, sprawling event, often involving significant cash handling from plant stalls, cake stands, white elephant sales, and entry donations. An event where meticulous accounting could easily be blurred by the sheer volume of small transactions, volunteer involvement, and temporary setups. An event whose overall financial reconciliation, Agnes recalled, was often presented as a single summary figure in the main reports, prepared and signed off by… Mildred Pettle, in her capacity as Secretary overseeing volunteer coordination and event logistics support.

Could *Pyrus Malus* be Ainsworth's code for the Annual Garden Fete? It seemed cryptic, almost whimsical, but perhaps there was a connection. She vaguely remembered reading somewhere that the land the Society now occupied had included a small, remnant apple orchard when it was first acquired in the 1920s. The oldest members sometimes referred to the western boundary near the compost heaps as the 'old orchard end'. Perhaps Ainsworth, delving into the Fincham book about local land use, had found a reference to this original orchard and adopted *Pyrus Malus* as his private shorthand for activities or accounts related to that physical area or, more metaphorically, to the 'fruits' or proceeds of major club fundraising events like the Fete often held near there?

It was a leap, but it felt plausible for Ainsworth's precise, slightly eccentric mind. Compare the historical land use detail (from

Fincham's book?) with the financial summary (Section IV, Paragraph 12) of the Fete accounts year after year. Why? What was he comparing?

Agnes pulled out her copies of the detailed Fete reconciliation summaries she had insisted the committee archive separately years ago, much to Humphrey Carmichael's initial bemusement and Ainsworth's later (probable) gratitude. These were the working papers, not just the final summary line presented in the Annual Report. She found the reports for the last five Fetes – 2023, 2021, 2019, 2017, 2015. She turned to Section IV (or its equivalent section detailing income/expenditure) and located Paragraph 12 (or the relevant summary line item for cash reconciliation).

At first glance, nothing seemed amiss. Income from stalls listed, expenses detailed (marquee hire, supplies, volunteer refreshments), net profit calculated. All signed off by Mildred Pettle and the relevant Fete convenor for that year. But Agnes, prompted by Fitzwilliam's findings of 'too perfect' accounts, looked closer. She compared the figures year on year.

There *was* a pattern. The figure listed under 'Sundry Cash Donations (Gate & On-Site)' was always a remarkably round number – $2500 in 2015, $2750 in 2017, $3000 in 2019, $3250 in 2021, $3500 in 2023. Always ending in 00 or 50. Highly improbable for genuine cash collections involving thousands of small coin and note transactions. And the expense line item for 'Volunteer Refreshments & Sundries' seemed consistently high relative to the number of volunteers listed, and always vaguely documented – just a bulk figure, no detailed receipts required in the summary apparently.

Could this be it? Was Ainsworth comparing something he found in the Fincham book – perhaps details about expected yields from an orchard, or historical land values – to these Fete accounts? No, that seemed too obscure. More likely, Agnes realised, the *Pyrus Malus* reference and the Fincham book were part of his *historical* research track, while the "Cf. Sect. IV, Para 12" was his instruction to himself to compare *that historical context* (whatever it was) with the *modern financial practice* represented by the Fete accounts.

But what was the link? She stared at the call slip again. What if *Pyrus Malus* wasn't just about the Fete? What if it related to the *land itself*, specifically the 'old orchard end'? What if Ainsworth suspected something related to *that land* – its historical value, its use, perhaps something buried there literally or figuratively – was being referenced or funded, illicitly, through discrepancies in the Fete accounts year after year? A recurring 'skimming' operation, perhaps, masked by the cash-heavy nature of the event, with funds potentially diverted towards something related to that specific piece of Society property? Perhaps linked to the 1980s extension costs, or ongoing 'maintenance' in that area?

It was still speculative, but it provided a potential bridge between Ainsworth's historical digging (Fincham book, 80s extension) and his scrutiny of current event finances managed by Mildred. He suspected a long-term pattern, rooted in the past, continuing into the present, and potentially connected physically to the 'old orchard end' – which was adjacent to the compost heaps, the potting sheds, and, Agnes realised with a jolt, not far from the dense rhododendron bed bordering Lawn 3 where his body was found. The location he was investigating, the potential financial irregularities, and the historical context might all be intertwined.

She needed that Fincham book. She needed to see what was in Section IV, Paragraph 12 of *Orchards of Progress*. What specific detail about apples, or orchards, or land use near Toorak in the early 1900s had Ainsworth deemed relevant enough to compare against Mildred Pettle's meticulously rounded Fete donation figures?

Agnes carefully placed the call slip back under the paperweight.

She felt the familiar thrill of the chase, the satisfying click of disparate facts beginning to align into a coherent hypothesis. She glanced at the clock. Still time before lunch. The State Library awaited. She gathered her handbag, her notebook, and her formidable intellect. The trail might be cryptic, coded in botanical Latin and obscure historical references, but Agnes Plummett was nothing if not persistent. Bartholomew Ainsworth had left them a puzzle, hidden in plain sight. And she intended to solve it.

****

The sterile blue light of early morning in Melbourne's CBD filtered through the blinds of Alistair Fitzwilliam's law office. He'd arrived well before his usual time, foregoing his customary nervous perusal of the *Australian Financial Review* at his favourite Flinders Lane cafe. Instead, a large takeaway coffee steamed beside him on his otherwise cleared desk, its strong aroma doing little to cut through the fatigue from a mostly sleepless night spent pondering alkaloids, lividity, and coded references to apple trees. Spread out before him, stark against the polished mahogany, were not the complex prospectuses and shareholder agreements that usually occupied his attention, but photocopies of the Toorak Croquet & Horticultural Society's Annual Garden Fete reconciliation summaries for the past ten years – specifically, the detailed working papers Agnes had directed him towards following her deciphering of Ainsworth's cryptic note.

Agnes had called him late the previous evening, her voice crackling with suppressed excitement as she explained her hypothesis: *Pyrus Malus* likely Ainsworth's code for the Fete (perhaps linked to the old orchard location), and "Section IV, Paragraph 12" pointing directly to the cash reconciliation summaries within the Fete reports, an area consistently managed by Mildred Pettle and exhibiting suspicious rounding patterns in the final figures. It felt like a significant leap based on a single, obscure clue, yet it resonated powerfully with Fitzwilliam's own deeply ingrained suspicion of the club's 'too perfect' accounts and Mildred's seamless control over them. Agnes had discreetly provided him with copies of the detailed reconciliation breakdowns she had archived – documents showing the raw inputs before they were consolidated into the neat summaries presented in the official Annual Reports. Now, under the harsh fluorescent lights of his office, away from the emotionally charged atmosphere of the club, Fitzwilliam intended to apply cold, legal scrutiny to these seemingly innocuous records.

He started, as was his habit, with procedure. According to the Society's own financial guidelines (a document Agnes had thoughtfully included), the reconciliation of cash takings from major events like the Fete required a clear process. Cash from various stalls (plants, cakes, white elephant, gate donations) was to be counted by at least two designated volunteers, recorded on standardised tally sheets, consolidated by the Fete Treasurer (a temporary role usually filled by a committee volunteer), verified against ticket sales or other metrics where possible, and then summarised on a final reconciliation form. This form, detailing gross receipts, itemised cash expenses paid out on the day (e.g., float returns, minor supplier payments), and the final net cash amount for banking, required the signatures of both the Fete Treasurer *and* the Club Treasurer (Ainsworth) or Secretary (Mildred) before the deposit was made. A copy of this signed form, along with the underlying tally sheets, was then to be archived.

Fitzwilliam began with the most recent Fete, held the previous spring (2024, as it was biennial). He found the reconciliation summary easily within Agnes's copied file. A single page, neatly typed, detailing income sources, cash expenses (including a vague but substantial line for 'Volunteer Refreshments & Sundries'), and the final net cash deposit figure. At the bottom, two signatures: Mildred Pettle's neat, rounded script, and Bartholomew Ainsworth's spiky, impatient scrawl. Everything appeared to be in order, matching the final figure presented in the subsequent Annual Report. He then looked for the underlying tally sheets, the raw counts from the stalls. They weren't attached. Odd, but perhaps filed separately.

He moved back to the 2022 Fete reconciliation summary. Same format, different figures. Again, signed by Mildred Pettle and Bartholomew Ainsworth. Again, no attached tally sheets.

Then 2020. Signed by Mildred Pettle and... Bartholomew Ainsworth. Fitzwilliam paused. Hadn't Mildred only taken over full reconciliation duties more recently? He quickly cross-referenced with the Annual Report for that year. Yes, the Fete report explicitly thanked "Mrs Henderson for her tireless work as Fete Treasurer". Why hadn't Mrs Henderson co-signed the final cash reconciliation summary? Why Mildred and Ainsworth? It broke the club's own stated procedure requiring the Fete Treasurer's sign-off.

His focus sharpened. He went back further: 2018, 2016, 2014. Each Fete reconciliation summary told the same story. Neatly typed, plausible figures (though Agnes's point about the suspiciously round numbers for 'Gate & On-Site Donations' now seemed glaringly obvious), and always, *always*, signed off only by Mildred Pettle and the Club Treasurer (Ainsworth in recent years, Humphrey Carmichael before him). The designated Fete Treasurer for each event, despite being thanked profusely in the main report, seemingly had no role in signing off on the final, crucial cash reconciliation deposited to the club's bank account.

Fitzwilliam felt a cold prickle of understanding. This wasn't just sloppy procedure; this was a systemic control failure, consistently occurring for at least a decade, possibly longer. The crucial step of having the person directly responsible for managing the Fete's day-to-day finances (the Fete Treasurer) verify the final cash amount before banking and reporting had been bypassed, every single time. Instead, the reconciliation was handled internally by the Club Secretary (Mildred) and signed off by the Club Treasurer (Ainsworth or his predecessor).

How could this happen? Was it deliberate? Or just administrative drift? Fitzwilliam considered the club dynamics. Fete Treasurers were temporary volunteers, often stressed and exhausted after the event, likely grateful to hand over boxes of unsorted cash and tally sheets to the calm, efficient Club Secretary to handle the final count and banking. Mildred, ever helpful, would have taken charge, produced a neat summary for the Club Treasurer to sign – who, whether the easy-going Humphrey Carmichael or the detail-obsessed Ainsworth, might simply have checked the arithmetic on the summary sheet against the bank deposit slip Mildred provided, without demanding the underlying messy tally sheets for a full audit. It was plausible, especially in a volunteer organisation built on trust (or the appearance of it).

But this procedural loophole provided the perfect opportunity for manipulation. Mildred, as the sole person consolidating the raw cash and preparing the final summary before it reached the Treasurer, was perfectly positioned to under-report the true cash takings. She could skim a certain amount off the top, adjust the summary figures accordingly (perhaps creating those suspiciously round donation numbers), and ensure the final deposit slip matched her neat summary report. As long as the overall profit seemed reasonable for the event's scale, and the final summary was signed off by the Club Treasurer, who would question it? The volunteer Fete Treasurer likely never saw the final reconciliation sheet bearing Mildred's and the Club Treasurer's signatures. The underlying tally sheets? Probably bundled away into deep storage by Mildred herself, unlikely ever to be scrutinised unless a major discrepancy was flagged – which it never was, because Mildred ensured the books balanced perfectly *on the surface*.

Fitzwilliam felt a surge of adrenaline, quickly tempered by legal caution. He had identified a significant, long-standing internal control weakness directly involving Mildred Pettle's handling of substantial cash amounts. He had identified a plausible *mechanism* for embezzlement. Agnes had identified suspicious patterns (the rounded numbers) in the figures Mildred produced. Ainsworth himself had apparently become suspicious enough to start digging, prompted perhaps by his coded *Pyrus Malus* clue linking history to these specific event accounts. It all fitted together.

But, damn it, it still wasn't *proof* of fraud. It was proof of poor procedure, opportunity, and suspicious circumstances. Proving *intent*, proving that Mildred *deliberately* exploited this loophole to steal money, required more. It required tracing the missing funds, finding evidence of unexplained wealth or hidden expenditure on Mildred's part. Without that, her defence would be simple: administrative oversight, perhaps, maybe some confusion in procedures inherited from Mr Carmichael's time, but certainly no intentional wrongdoing. She could claim the rounding was merely for ease of reporting, the high refreshment costs due to generous volunteer support, the lack of tally sheets an unfortunate archival oversight. Her impeccable reputation, her years of service, her performance of gentle competence would all weigh heavily against Fitzwilliam's complex theory based on unsigned forms and suspiciously round numbers.

He leaned back, staring at the neat columns of figures that now seemed to mock him with their superficial perfection. He understood Ainsworth's frustration now, the almost obsessive need to dig deeper, to find the irrefutable evidence. Ainsworth must have spotted this same procedural anomaly. Perhaps he'd tried to find the missing tally sheets himself. Perhaps he'd started cross-referencing historical land values or yields (the *Pyrus Malus* connection?) trying to establish a baseline for expected Fete income, revealing a consistent shortfall. Perhaps he'd even confronted Mildred directly, triggering her desperate act.

Fitzwilliam looked again at the signature section on the 2022 reconciliation. Mildred Pettle. Bartholomew Ainsworth. Ainsworth's signature… was it slightly more hurried than usual? Did it press less firmly on the page? Probably just his imagination. Yet, knowing what he now suspected, the image of Ainsworth signing off on these summaries, potentially unaware for years that they might be masking a slow, steady drain on the Society's funds by the very person presenting them for approval, felt deeply unsettling. Had he finally realised? And was that realisation, documented perhaps in notes now missing from his office, the true reason for his death?

Fitzwilliam meticulously gathered the photocopied reconciliation summaries. He hadn't found direct proof of embezzlement, but he had found the fertile ground in which it could flourish, tended carefully for years by the Club Secretary. He knew, with a certainty that chilled him far more than the air conditioning humming through his office, that their investigation had moved beyond mere suspicion. They had identified the likely method. Now, they just needed to find the money, or the poison. He reached for his phone to update Agnes. The paper trail was faint, deliberately obscured, but it was starting to lead directly towards Mildred Pettle.

****

Evening had once again settled over Agnes Plummett's South Yarra

159

apartment, but tonight, the atmosphere was starkly different from the anxious uncertainty that had pervaded their previous gatherings. The rain had ceased, leaving behind a rain-washed clarity in the Melbourne air outside, mirroring, perhaps, the sharp, almost alarming clarity emerging within the study itself. The remnants of hastily consumed sandwiches and multiple empty teacups littered the large partner's desk, pushed aside to make room for a chaotic but purposeful spread of documents: Agnes's annotated club reports, Fitzwilliam's highlighted financial summaries, Ronnie's sprawling timeline charts and diagrams, Chloe's photographs of the footprint and the glove, and, sitting ominously under the glass paperweight, the small, yellowed library call slip that had proven to be the key.

An electric current of shared discovery hummed in the room, a volatile mixture of intellectual excitement, vindication, and a chilling awareness of the implications. They had been circling the truth, collecting disparate, puzzling pieces, but now, following Agnes's deciphering of the *Pyrus Malus* clue and Fitzwilliam's identification of the procedural loophole in the Fete accounts, the fragments had suddenly, shockingly, clicked into place.

"So," Fitzwilliam began, his voice low but resonating with new-found conviction, summarising their combined findings as much for his own benefit as for the others. He stood near the desk, looking down at the scattered papers as if piecing together a complex legal argument. "Let's consolidate what we believe we now know. Agnes establishes that Ainsworth wasn't just generally stressed; he was actively, possibly obsessively, investigating specific historical financial matters – the '87 West Wing funding, old grounds contracts – potentially linked to a past compromise *he himself* was party to." He looked at Agnes, who nodded gravely.

"Furthermore," Fitzwilliam continued, picking up one of his own annotated Fete summaries, "Agnes deciphers Ainsworth's cryptic note – *Pyrus Malus*, the library call slip – connecting his historical research not just to apples, but likely to the Annual Garden Fete accounts via the 'Sect. IV, Para 12' reference, suggesting he suspected a *pattern* linking past irregularities to present ones."

"A pattern I subsequently confirmed," Agnes interjected, tapping her own neat notes. "Suspiciously rounded cash donation figures reported from the Fete year after year, coinciding precisely with the period Mildred Pettle assumed responsibility for consolidating those specific funds."

"And," Fitzwilliam pressed on, the pieces falling into place in his own mind as he spoke, "my review of the detailed reconciliation procedures for those Fetes reveals a critical, consistent control failure. The volunteer Fete Treasurer *never* co-signed the final cash summary presented to the Club Treasurer. That summary, detailing the crucial net cash for banking, was prepared and presented solely by Mildred, requiring only the Club Treasurer's signature – Ainsworth's in recent years, Carmichael's before him. A procedure," he added with emphasis, "that provided Mildred with the perfect, recurring opportunity to potentially under-report cash takings and skim funds before the official deposit was made and the neat summary report generated."

Ronnie Peterson, who had been adding arrows and probability ratios to his own master timeline chart spread across half the desk, looked up, his eyes bright. "The mechanism! Precisely! Fitzwilliam identifies the exploitable systemic weakness! And my timeline analysis confirms opportunity. The period immediately following the Fete closure, when cash is counted and reconciled, often involves late-night work, fewer people around. Mildred, as Secretary overseeing logistics, would have had justifiable access and control during this critical window." He drew a thick red circle around several points on his timeline. "High probability windows for fund diversion align perfectly with post-Fete reconciliation periods across multiple years."

"And Ainsworth must have spotted it," Chloe said quietly, looking at the complex charts with dawning understanding. "The rounding, the missing signature, maybe he finally decided to check the old tally sheets himself? Or maybe," she added, thinking back to Agnes's earlier finding, "he connected it somehow to that dodgy anonymous donation for the West Wing back in the 80s? Like it was the start of a pattern?"

"Entirely possible," Agnes agreed. "He might have suspected the Fete skimming wasn't isolated, but part of a longer-term strategy, perhaps originating from, or inspired by, that earlier, larger irregularity involving the West Wing funding. His investigation wasn't just about correcting the record; it was about uncovering a potentially decades-long deception." She paused, her expression grim. "A deception Mildred Pettle was perfectly positioned to orchestrate and conceal."

Fitzwilliam nodded. "So, Motive established: Ainsworth discovers, or is close to discovering, long-term embezzlement potentially orchestrated by Mildred, threatening her position, her reputation, and possibly involving others connected to past financial irregularities."

"Means?" Agnes prompted, looking towards Ronnie and Chloe.

"The autopsy anomalies point strongly towards poisoning or prior incapacitation," Ronnie stated firmly, tapping his calculations regarding lividity and impact dynamics. "Consistent with Hypothesis P. The blow with the mallet appears increasingly likely to be a secondary event, a staging."

"And the *Digitalis purpurea*," Chloe added, her voice gaining confidence, "the foxgloves near where he was found, contain potent cardiac glycosides. They are accessible – Mildred sometimes assists the gardening committee with light duties, deadheading mostly, she knows the grounds intimately. Processing them to extract a toxin wouldn't necessarily require specialist knowledge, just care and perhaps reference to older herbalist texts Agnes might even have here." She gestured towards Agnes's overflowing bookshelves. "It's plausible as the 'unidentified organic alkaloid compound' found in trace amounts, especially if administered subtly over time or in a single dose designed to incapacitate rather than kill instantly."

"Motive, Means, *and* Opportunity," Fitzwilliam concluded, the legal triad falling into place with chilling certainty. "Mildred had the motive – protecting her long-running embezzlement and reputation. She had the potential means – access to Ainsworth's routine (his thermos?), knowledge of potentially poisonous plants on site. And she had opportunity – both for administering something beforehand and potentially for staging the scene during the two-hour window Ronnie identified, using her ubiquitous, almost invisible presence at the club as cover."

They looked at each other, the enormity of their conclusion settling upon them. It wasn't Harry Smythe, the obvious, blustering suspect. It was Mildred Pettle, the quiet, efficient, helpful Club Secretary, the woman currently managing condolence cards and organising memorial catering with seamless competence. The killer wasn't just hiding in plain sight; she was practically directing the stage play designed to conceal her own crime.

"But proof," Fitzwilliam stated, the lawyer in him immediately throwing cold water on their collective certainty. "We have a strong, coherent theory supported by numerous circumstantial pieces. But we have no *direct* proof linking Mildred to the poison, or to the financial discrepancies beyond opportunity and suspicion. No confession, no witness seeing her administer anything, no bank records showing unexplained wealth – yet."

"The Fincham book," Agnes said suddenly, remembering the library slip. "*Orchards of Progress*. And the reference: Section IV, Paragraph 12. Ainsworth linked it to the Fete accounts via *Pyrus Malus*. I need to see what that paragraph contains. It might be the piece that connects the historical land context directly to the financial manipulation, the piece Ainsworth found so crucial."

"And the unfamiliar suppliers on the recent invoices," Fitzwilliam recalled his own finding. "'WeatherTech Roofing Solutions', 'Vintage Marquee Hire', 'Bespoke Botanical Displays'. Plausible expenses, yes, but unfamiliar names. Could these be phantom suppliers? A way for Mildred to extract larger sums more recently, beyond just skimming Fete cash?"

"We need to trace those companies," Agnes agreed immediately. "Check their registration, their directors, see if they genuinely exist and performed the work invoiced."

"And the glove?" Chloe asked, holding up the evidence bag containing the grey suede glove she'd found. "It felt expensive. Not like something Mildred usually wears, but maybe for gardening?"

"We need to identify its owner," Agnes said. "Perhaps discreet inquiries among members known for their expensive gardening attire? Or," her eyes narrowed slightly, "perhaps we could find an opportunity to compare it to gloves Mildred herself might own or use?"

Ronnie, meanwhile, was focused on the physical evidence, or lack thereof. "The poison itself," he mused. "If it was *Digitalis*, extracting it crudely might leave traces. Chloe, you mentioned checking the plants for harvesting – that's critical. Also, disposal – where would someone dispose of preparation materials or the thermos afterwards? The club compost heaps? Incinerator? Off-site?"

Their minds were racing, firing off possibilities, potential leads blossoming from the central stem of their hypothesis. The task ahead seemed immense, a web of interconnected threads spanning decades, finances, botany, and human deception.

"Alright," Agnes said, bringing order to the burgeoning chaos of ideas. "Let's refine our next steps, focusing on finding that crucial direct evidence." She picked up her pen and a fresh index card.

"Priority One: The Fincham Book. I will go to the State Library tomorrow morning and examine Section IV, Paragraph 12 of *Orchards of Progress*. We need to understand the significance Ainsworth attached to it."

"Priority Two: The Suppliers," Fitzwilliam took charge of this. "I can use legal search databases to check the registration and directorships of 'WeatherTech Roofing', 'Vintage Marquee Hire', and 'Bespoke Botanical Displays'. See if they are legitimate entities or potentially shell companies."

"Priority Three: The Poison Source," Agnes continued, looking at Chloe. "Chloe, your examination of the *Digitalis* plants for signs of harvesting is vital. And perhaps a general survey of other accessible toxic plants on the grounds? Also, consider disposal sites – any unusual activity near compost heaps or incinerators recently?"

Chloe nodded, her expression determined. "I can check the foxgloves during my regular rounds tomorrow. And I know where the main compost area is behind the sheds."

"Priority Four: The Glove," Agnes went on. "Difficult without drawing attention. Perhaps initially, simply observe members' gardening attire? See if anyone favours that particular style or brand?"

"Priority Five: Mildred's Finances," Fitzwilliam added grimly. "The hardest part. We have no legal means to access her bank accounts. Our only hope here is indirect – if tracing the suppliers reveals payments going to unexpected places, or if Agnes uncovers historical evidence strong enough to finally convince Detective Inspector Davies to seek warrants."

"And Priority Six," Ronnie piped up, "Quantifiable Data. I will refine the lividity timing models. I will also research detection methods for common *Digitalis* glycosides – could trace amounts linger on clothing, gloves, or the hypothetical preparation site?"

Agnes finished writing, reviewing the list. It was ambitious, fraught with potential difficulties and risks. They were stepping firmly into the realm of active, covert investigation, driven by the conviction that the official inquiry was heading towards a grave injustice. She looked around at her unlikely collaborators – the anxious but principled lawyer, the brilliant but eccentric physicist, the quiet but sharply observant gardener. None of them had sought this role, yet none of them, it seemed, was willing to turn away from it now.

"We proceed with extreme caution," Agnes reminded them, her voice low and serious. "We share findings only amongst ourselves. We avoid direct confrontation. We trust no one outside this room implicitly, especially," her gaze hardened slightly, "our efficient Club Secretary."

The grandfather clock chimed again, marking the late hour. The rain had stopped outside, leaving behind the clean scent of wet earth and the glistening reflection of streetlights on the damp pavement. Inside the small study, the four companions looked at each other, a silent acknowledgement passing between them – they were in this together, for better or worse, until the truth behind Bartholomew Ainsworth's most improper end was finally brought into the light.

11

Unlocking Ainsworth's Investigation

Several days had passed since the discovery on Lawn 3, and a fragile, brittle layer of normality had begun to crystallise over the raw edges of the event at the Toorak Croquet & Horticultural Society. The police tape remained, a persistent blue accusation against the manicured green, but the officers themselves were less frequently seen. Forensics had long since departed. Members, initially hesitant, were starting to reclaim the lawns further from the scene, the familiar *thwack* of mallet on ball sounding almost defiant in the clear, crisp air. Yet, it was a performance of normalcy rather than its true restoration. Beneath the surface, the current of unease ran strong and deep, swirling with speculation, and nowhere was this more evident than on the sun-dappled clubhouse verandah during the mid-morning lull.

Agnes Plummett sat at her preferred table, ostensibly reviewing printouts from the State Library's catalogue related to Alistair P. Fincham's *Orchards of Progress* – the *Pyrus Malus* clue from Ainsworth's office. She hadn't yet had a chance to visit the library itself, her time consumed by analysing club records and conferring with Fitzwilliam and Ronnie. The library slip felt warm and significant in her pocket, a tangible link to Ainsworth's hidden research, but deciphering its precise meaning still felt just beyond her grasp. She tried to focus on the catalogue description, noting the book's focus on early land grants and horticultural experiments in the Port Phillip district, her mind automatically cross-referencing keywords with Society history, but the persistent buzz of conversation from a nearby table made concentration difficult.

Alistair Fitzwilliam sat a short distance away, nursing a rapidly cooling flat white, a thick legal brief open but unread before him. He felt physically present on the verandah, observing the play of sunlight on the polished floorboards, the meticulous arrangement of potted geraniums, the distant figures in pristine white moving across Lawn 1, but mentally, he was still parsing Sergeant Riley's reluctant admissions about the autopsy and Charles Abercrombie's confirmation of Ainsworth's historical digging. The inconsistencies – the lividity, the alkaloid – felt like boulders dropped into the seemingly clear waters of the investigation, sending out ripples that complicated everything. His anxiety, never far beneath the surface, was now tinged with a new urgency, a fear that the official investigation, blinded by confirmation bias towards Harry Smythe, would entirely miss the deeper, colder current flowing beneath.

The source of the distracting buzz was a table occupied by Mrs Henderson, Colonel Abernathy, and Penelope Cartwright, who seemed to have attached herself to the older members, perhaps seeking safety in established social structures amidst the unsettling events. Their voices, initially low and conspiratorial, gradually rose in pitch and intensity, fuelled by shared indignation and the undeniable pleasure of dissecting a fresh piece of club drama.

"...absolutely beside himself, apparently!" Mrs Henderson declared, leaning forward, her pearl necklace gleaming against her floral print dress. "Esme told me Ferguson was practically foaming at the mouth in the equipment shed yesterday. Said Bartholomew had finally gone too far!"

"Ferguson?" the Colonel queried, adjusting his regimental tie. "Major Ferguson? Thought he kept himself to himself mostly, fussing over those blasted dahlias of his."

"Precisely!" Mrs Henderson seized on the point. "His dahlias! That's the heart of it! You know that allotment patch he has down near the western boundary? The one that gets all the morning sun, near the old compost heaps?"

Agnes's attention sharpened, tuning out the library catalogue description. The western boundary – the 'old orchard end', as some called it. Adjacent to the area where Ainsworth's body was found, and potentially linked to the historical land use research suggested by the *Pyrus Malus* clue.

"Finest dahlia display in Melbourne, Ferguson reckons," the Colonel grunted. "Wins prizes year after year. Bit obsessive, mind you."

"Obsessive is putting it mildly, Colonel," Mrs Henderson corrected. "Devoted. He treats those tubers like children. And Bartholomew," she lowered her voice dramatically, "apparently decided, just last week, that half of Ferguson's prize plot wasn't actually his!"

Penelope Cartwright gasped audibly. "No! But he's had that plot for ages, hasn't he?"

"Decades!" Mrs Henderson confirmed, clearly relishing the unfolding narrative. "Since old Mr Carmichael allocated it to him back in the nineties. But Bartholomew, armed with some dusty old map he'd apparently dug up," – Agnes's ears pricked up again; *a map? Linked to his historical research?* – "marched down there and told Ferguson that the original boundary markers indicated half the plot was designated 'utility access' or some such nonsense, and that the Society needed the space back for... wait for it... installing a new three-bay composting system!"

"Composting system?" the Colonel scoffed. "Good Lord, what's wrong with the perfectly adequate heaps we have already? Sounds like Ainsworth stirring up trouble for the sake of it, as usual."

"Exactly!" Mrs Henderson agreed eagerly. "Ferguson apparently told him, in no uncertain terms, that he'd install a composting system over his dead body – rather unfortunate turn of phrase, in hindsight! He accused Bartholomew of deliberately targeting him, of trying to sabotage his chances for the upcoming Dahlia Society championships. Said Ainsworth was just jealous because his own attempts at gardening were universally pitiful."

Fitzwilliam listened, his legal mind automatically categorising the dispute. Boundary disagreement, potential breach of club rules regarding land allocation, slanderous accusations... messy, certainly, but motive for murder? It seemed disproportionate, almost farcical. Yet, he recalled cases where seemingly minor neighbourhood disputes over fences or barking dogs had escalated tragically. Passions could run unexpectedly deep when it came to cherished territory, whether a suburban backyard or a prize-winning dahlia plot. Could Major Ferguson, known for his military background and obsessive horticultural pride, truly have been pushed to violence over his tubers?

Agnes, however, was processing the information differently. Ainsworth invoking historical boundary markers based on an old map? This sounded less like petty trouble making and more like a direct extension of the historical research suggested by the Fincham book clue. Was the composting system just a pretext? Was Ainsworth *really* interested in that specific piece of land for another reason, perhaps related to the old orchard, or something buried there referenced in the Fincham book or the planting ledgers? And Ferguson's plot, being adjacent to the 'old orchard end', was also worryingly close to the rhododendron bed where Ainsworth was ultimately found. Could the dispute have drawn Ainsworth to that specific area on the fatal afternoon, entirely separate from his argument with Harry Smythe?

"…and that's not the worst of it!" Mrs Henderson continued, leaning in further, her voice dropping to a conspiratorial whisper. "Just two days before… before *it* happened… Ferguson apparently found several of his most prized dahlia tubers dug up and sliced in half! Sabotage! He was apoplectic! Marched straight into the Treasurer's office and accused Bartholomew to his face! Said he knew Bartholomew was behind it, trying to drive him off the plot!"

"Good heavens!" Penelope breathed. "Did he?"

"Did Bartholomew do it? Who knows?" Mrs Henderson shrugged theatrically. "He certainly denied it, apparently just cited some rule about members not making unsubstantiated accusations. But Ferguson wouldn't let it go. Esme said the shouting was audible all the way down the corridor. Ferguson swore he'd get proof, swore Ainsworth wouldn't get away with it…" She let the implication hang, dark and suggestive.

Fitzwilliam felt a growing sense of alarm. Sabotage, public accusations, furious arguments, threats… This wasn't just a minor tiff over garden boundaries. This had escalated. If Ferguson genuinely believed Ainsworth had destroyed his prized dahlias – the culmination of years of work – his rage might indeed have reached dangerous levels. And unlike Harry Smythe's hot-blooded but ultimately harmless outbursts, Ferguson's military background might imply a capacity for more controlled, decisive action. Could this be the answer? A crime of passion, but committed by Ferguson, not Smythe? It was plausible enough to seriously muddy the waters, potentially derailing the police focus on Harry entirely. Which might, Fitzwilliam realised with a sickening lurch, be exactly what the *real* killer – Mildred? – wanted.

Agnes considered the sabotage angle. It felt... theatrical. Too convenient. Would Ainsworth, meticulous and rule-bound, resort to such petty vandalism? It seemed out of character, even for him. More likely, perhaps, that someone *else* had damaged the dahlias, knowing it would inflame the conflict between Ferguson and Ainsworth, creating noise and misdirection? Someone who knew Ferguson's obsessive nature and Ainsworth's provocative one? Someone like Mildred Pettle, perhaps, wanting to create alternative suspects or simply general chaos to obscure her own activities?

"So," Colonel Abernathy concluded, stroking his moustache thoughtfully, "we have Ferguson, driven half-mad about his flowers, threatening Ainsworth just days before he turns up dead practically on Ferguson's doorstep. Sounds dashed suspicious if you ask me. More suspicious than young Smythe losing his rag over a hoop point, perhaps."

"Exactly!" Mrs Henderson agreed triumphantly. "I always thought there was more to it than poor Harry. Major Ferguson... he's a quiet one mostly, but still waters run deep, they say. And that military training..."

Agnes decided it was time to subtly intervene, before this narrative gained unstoppable momentum. "Major Ferguson certainly values his dahlias," she commented mildly, turning towards their table as if just noticing their conversation. "Though I believe his service was primarily in logistics and quarter mastering, Colonel, rather than front-line combat." A gentle correction, subtly downplaying the 'military training implies capacity for violence' trope. "And regarding the boundary," she continued smoothly, "Mr Ainsworth *was* consulting several very old survey maps from the Society's earliest days recently. His interest seemed genuinely focused on clarifying original land usage demarcations for the Centenary records. Sometimes," she added with a sigh, "historical accuracy can unfortunately clash with long-standing practice. A regrettable, but perhaps unavoidable, friction." She framed Ainsworth's actions as academic and procedural, not malicious, subtly undermining the 'deliberate provocation' angle.

Mrs Henderson looked slightly deflated, her dramatic narrative punctured by Agnes's calm historical context. The Colonel harrumphed noncommittally. Fitzwilliam shot Agnes a look of immense gratitude. She had, with a few carefully chosen sentences, introduced doubt and perspective without revealing their own deeper suspicions or directly contradicting the gossipers.

But the seed had been sown. The Ferguson-Ainsworth dispute was now officially part of the club's speculative narrative. Fitzwilliam felt certain it would reach Detective Inspector Davies's ears soon enough, if it hadn't already. It *was* a convenient distraction. Plausible enough to warrant investigation, emotional enough to capture the imagination, and importantly, it shifted focus away from internal financial matters, away from historical accounts, away from Mildred Pettle. Whether it arose organically from Ainsworth's clumsy historical digging colliding with Ferguson's obsession, or whether it was subtly encouraged, perhaps even physically instigated, by a third party... its effect was the same. It complicated everything. It provided cover.

Agnes returned to her library printouts, but her mind was no longer on Fincham's orchards. It was considering the complex, intersecting lines of conflict radiating from Bartholomew Ainsworth. The simmering resentment over petty rules. The fury over the dahlia plot. The potentially explosive secrets buried in decades-old finances. And perhaps, other hidden conflicts they hadn't even uncovered yet. Ainsworth hadn't just collected enemies like stamps, as the Colonel suggested. He seemed to have curated a veritable exhibition of potential motives for murder, leaving behind a puzzle so tangled it threatened to obscure the very truth they sought. Disentangling deliberate misdirection from genuine conflict, Agnes realised, would be their greatest challenge yet.

****

Like dry tinder catching a spark, the story of Major Ferguson's dahlia dispute with Bartholomew Ainsworth ignited the subdued atmosphere of the Toorak Croquet & Horticultural Society. By mid-afternoon, the narrative shared with such relish by Mrs Henderson and Colonel Abernathy on the verandah had spread through the clubhouse and grounds with astonishing speed, passed along in hushed tones over half-finished games, whispered across tables in the lounge, and debated with renewed vigour near the steadily depleting memorial tea urn. The effect was immediate: a collective, almost audible sigh of relief seemed to ripple through the member-ship.

Finally, there was an alternative. An explanation that didn't involve one of their own titled members completely losing control over a mere hoop point. Major Ferguson, while respected for his horticultural prowess, was known to be somewhat... eccentric. A retired military man, fiercely proud, obsessively devoted to his prize-winning dahlias – it wasn't difficult for the members to picture him, perhaps pushed too far by Ainsworth's alleged provocation and sabotage, reacting with disproportionate, even violent, anger. It felt, to many, like a more fittingly dramatic, if equally tragic, narrative than poor Harry Smythe simply snapping.

Alistair Fitzwilliam, nursing a lukewarm mineral water near the bar (he felt incapable of facing more tea or coffee), observed the shift with deep misgiving. He watched as groups formed and reformed, the Ferguson theory dissected with the enthusiasm usually reserved for debating controversial umpiring decisions or critiquing the quality of the cucumber sandwiches.

"…always said Ferguson had a screw loose about those flowers," declared Mr Henderson Minor, polishing his spectacles vigorously. "Remember when young Barnaby accidentally deadheaded the wrong bloom last year? Ferguson practically had him court-martialled! If Ainsworth really did damage those tubers…"

"And digging them up! Slicing them!" added Penelope Cartwright, her eyes wide with horrified fascination, the details clearly having gained potency in the retelling. "That's just… vicious! No wonder the Major was furious."

"Military men, you know," offered Colonel Abernathy sagely to anyone within earshot, conveniently forgetting Agnes's earlier correction about Ferguson's logistical background. "Trained for action. Pushed too far… well, old instincts might just take over. Dashed unfortunate."

Fitzwilliam felt a familiar wave of anxiety wash over him. It was happening exactly as he'd feared. The membership, uncomfortable with the idea of one of their prominent figures being a murderer, was eagerly embracing a narrative that shifted the blame onto someone perceived as slightly outside the core social hierarchy, someone whose known obsession provided a seemingly understandable (if extreme) motive. The nuances – Ainsworth's historical digging possibly *provoking* the boundary dispute, the lack of any history of *physical* violence from Ferguson, the sheer improbability of dahlia-rage escalating to murder with an antique mallet – were being swept aside in the collective rush towards a more palatable suspect.

He glanced across the lounge towards Agnes Plummett, who was seated near the window, ostensibly reading *The Age* but clearly absorbing the surrounding conversations with her usual quiet intensity. Her expression was, as always, difficult to read, but Fitzwilliam thought he detected a faint tightening around her lips, a subtle disapproval of the speculative frenzy. Ronnie Peterson seemed largely oblivious, deeply engrossed in trying to explain fluid dynamics to a bewildered-looking Esme Weatherly near the noticeboard, likely using the tea urn's flow rate as an example. Chloe Dubois, thankfully, had finished her work for the day and retreated, sparing her from this latest round of morbid gossip.

The lounge door opened, causing a momentary lull in the chatter. Detective Inspector Davies stood there, accompanied by the young, note-taking Detective Constable Miller. Her presence instantly cooled the atmosphere, the members' expressions shifting from animated speculation to studied neutrality. Detective Inspector Davies's gaze swept the room – calm, assessing, missing nothing. She hadn't come to make an arrest, Fitzwilliam guessed; more likely a follow-up query for Esme or another committee member.

As she spoke quietly with Esme near the entrance, Colonel Abernathy, clearly unable to resist sharing the exciting new development, cleared his throat importantly and approached the detective. Fitzwilliam strained to hear, positioning himself nearer the potted palm.

"Inspector," the Colonel began, puffing himself up slightly, "thought you ought to know. Information has come to light… another avenue, perhaps. Regarding poor Ainsworth."

Detective Inspector Davies turned towards him, her expression polite but non-committal. "Oh? And what information is that, Colonel?"

"Major Ferguson," the Colonel announced, lowering his voice conspiratorially. "Had a devil of a row with Ainsworth just days before the… incident. Over his dahlia patch. Ainsworth trying to pinch his land, Ferguson accusing him of sabotage – dug up his prize tubers, apparently! Ferguson swore he wouldn't stand for it. Made threats, by all accounts. Worth looking into, wouldn't you say? Man's got a military background, after all."

Fitzwilliam watched Detective Inspector Davies closely. She listened patiently, her gaze steady on the Colonel's face. There was no flicker of surprise, no visible reaction to this potentially significant new lead. When the Colonel had finished, puffing slightly with self-importance, Davies simply nodded.

"Thank you for the information, Colonel Abernathy," she said, her tone professionally neutral. "We consider all possibilities during an investigation. Rest assured, we follow the evidence wherever it leads." She gave him a brief, dismissive nod, then turned back to conclude her quiet conversation with Esme before she and Detective Constable Miller departed as unobtrusively as they had arrived.

The members who had witnessed the exchange immediately began buzzing again. "She took notes!" someone whispered excitedly. "She seemed very interested!" "Definitely going to question Ferguson now!"

Fitzwilliam, however, felt a deep unease. Davies hadn't seemed particularly interested at all. Her reaction had been textbook professional neutrality, giving nothing away. Had she already known about the Ferguson dispute? Possibly; police canvassing likely would have picked it up. Was she taking it seriously? Impossible to tell. But Fitzwilliam suspected she might view it exactly as Agnes likely did: a potentially convenient distraction, perhaps even deliberately amplified by club gossip, but lacking the immediate confluence of factors surrounding Harry Smythe (the weapon, the timing of the argument, the weak alibi). She might assign an officer to follow it up as a matter of due diligence, but would it fundamentally shift her focus from Smythe? Fitzwilliam doubted it, not without stronger evidence.

Yet, the *effect* on the club membership was undeniable. The intense pressure of suspicion was momentarily lifted from Harry Smythe, diffused onto Major Ferguson. It created breathing room, perhaps, but Fitzwilliam feared it was dangerous breathing room. It allowed the members to relax back into comfortable assumptions, to stop questioning, to potentially overlook other inconsistencies. It allowed the *real* killer – the calculating figure he and Agnes suspected was hiding behind a mask of normalcy – to operate more freely, perhaps even subtly encouraging the Ferguson rumour while pursuing their own agenda.

He caught Agnes's eye across the room. She gave a minuscule shake of her head, confirming his own assessment. This new scandal, however dramatic, felt like noise, not signal. It was a subplot, potentially a tragic one for Major Ferguson if the police took it too seriously, but likely irrelevant to the core mystery they were trying to unravel – the mystery hinted at by cryptic library slips, perfectly balanced accounts, inconsistent lividity, and unidentified alkaloids. This convenient distraction, Agnes's slight frown seemed to say, must not be allowed to divert *their* attention from the main thread. Their investigation needed to remain focused, methodical, and deeply suspicious of anything that seemed too easy an answer.

****

That evening, the familiar sanctuary of Agnes Plummett's study felt less like a quiet repository of history and more like an operations centre bracing against incoming interference. The day's prevailing gossip from the club – the dramatic tale of Major Ferguson, his savaged dahlias, and his furious confrontation with Bartholomew Ainsworth – hung heavy in the air, an unwelcome static disrupting the clearer signal they thought they had begun to receive. Outside, the brief respite from the rain had ended; a persistent drizzle, typical of a Melbourne spring evening turning cool, whispered against the window panes, mirroring the subdued but focused intensity within the room.

Maps, timelines, photocopied accounts, and Agnes's notebooks were spread across the large desk under the warm glow of a green-shaded banker's lamp. Fitzwilliam, looking drained but resolute, recounted Detective Inspector Davies's noncommittal reaction to Colonel Abernathy's eager presentation of the Ferguson theory.

"She gave nothing away," he concluded, swirling the amber liquid in the small glass Agnes had pressed upon him – a decent single malt, offered with the quiet understanding that tea might no longer suffice. "Professionally neutral. Which could mean anything. She could be taking it seriously, assigning resources, checking Ferguson's alibi... or she could have mentally filed it under 'irate members grasping at straws' and remained entirely focused on Smythe. We simply don't know."

"What we *do* know," Agnes stated, tapping a neatly written list summarising the Ferguson narrative as reported by various members, "is that this story provides a convenient, emotionally resonant alternative suspect precisely when scrutiny might otherwise have begun to shift. The timing is... noteworthy."

"And the *enthusiasm* with which it's been embraced," Fitzwilliam added grimly. "People *want* to believe it wasn't Harry. Ferguson, being slightly eccentric, slightly peripheral, makes for a much more comfortable villain in their narrative."

Ronnie, who had been attempting to overlay thermal decay curves onto his timeline chart, looked up, frowning. "From a motivational standpoint, it seems... disproportionate. Homicide triggered by horticultural sabotage? While intense passion for specialised subjects is well-documented, the escalation pathway from tuber-tampering to fatal blunt force trauma seems statistically improbable without significant underlying psychological instability." He paused. "Has anyone profiled Major Ferguson for psychopathic tendencies correlated with dahlia obsession?"

"Ronnie," Agnes said patiently, "while Major Ferguson is undoubtedly devoted to his flowers, and possesses a temperament perhaps best described as 'brusque,' attributing psychopathy based on horticultural passion seems premature. Let us analyse the known factors logically."

"Okay, logically," Fitzwilliam picked up the thread, grateful to move away from psychopathy profiling. "Motive: Ferguson was clearly furious with Ainsworth over both the boundary dispute – threatening his long-held territory – and the alleged sabotage of his prize dahlias. Emotionally potent? Yes. Sufficient for murder? Questionable, compared to the potential exposure of long-term financial fraud."

"Means?" Agnes prompted. "Ferguson certainly had access to the grounds. As for a weapon, numerous heavy gardening implements exist – spades, forks. Though none were apparently found near the scene, unlike Smythe's mallet. Does his profile suggest poisoning?"

"Unlikely," Chloe offered quietly. She'd been studying her photos of the footprint and the glove, comparing them mentally to Ferguson. "The Major uses standard heavy-duty tools and well-worn boots. That footprint didn't look like his usual gardening wear. And while he uses fertilisers and pesticides, knowledge of extracting something like *Digitalis* toxin feels... out of character. He's about soil composition and bloom size, not arcane botany."

"Opportunity?" Ronnie consulted his timeline. "Ferguson was present at the club on Tuesday, participated in the morning rounds. His known movements seem... average. No glaring inconsistencies noted by witnesses *I've* collated data from, anyway. He claims he went home for lunch around 1 PM and didn't return until later for a committee meeting – which *was* cancelled due to the... event. Crucially, this means he was likely *off-site* during the probable poisoning window (12:00-1:45 PM) if Hypothesis P holds true."

"Unless he returned unnoticed? Or the poisoning occurred differently?" Fitzwilliam queried, playing devil's advocate.

"Possible, but lowers probability," Ronnie countered immediately. "Requires additional assumptions – stealthy re-entry, alternative poison vector – whereas Mildred Pettle's known presence and access provide a more parsimonious fit with the optimal poisoning window via the thermos."

Agnes summarised their analysis. "So, Ferguson possesses a possible, albeit emotionally driven and perhaps disproportionate, motive. His means seem ill-suited to the suspected method (poisoning) or the apparent method (mallet use is unsubstantiated). And his opportunity, particularly for administering poison during the optimal window Ronnie identified, appears limited compared to Mildred's."

"Conclusion?" Fitzwilliam asked.

"Conclusion," Agnes stated firmly, "Major Ferguson is almost certainly a red herring. A convenient distraction, diverting attention from more probable, more complex lines of inquiry."

"But," Fitzwilliam cautioned, swirling the whisky in his glass, "a red herring the police *might* pursue, even briefly. And one we probably need to definitively eliminate for our own peace of mind before focusing exclusively on Mildred." He didn't like loose ends, even unlikely ones.

"Agreed," Agnes nodded. "Due diligence requires we formally exclude him, however low Ronnie's probability assessment." She made a note. "A quick verification seems sufficient. Alistair, perhaps you could discreetly ascertain if Ferguson's alibi for the lunchtime period holds? Did anyone see him leave? Did he receive any calls or visitors at home? Without alerting him directly, of course."

"I could perhaps have a quiet word with Mrs Ferguson?" Fitzwilliam suggested hesitantly. "She sometimes volunteers at the local library where I occasionally do pro bono work. Frame it as general concern?"

"Excellent," Agnes approved. "Subtle, low-risk. Meanwhile," she continued, "we must not allow this distraction, however convenient for the real killer, to derail our primary investigation." She turned back to the papers spread across the desk. "Mildred Pettle remains the focal point."

"Could *she* have started the rumour about Ferguson?" Chloe wondered aloud. "Or even… damaged the dahlias herself?"

"It's certainly possible," Fitzwilliam mused, horrified by the implication. "Creating a secondary suspect, fanning the flames of an existing conflict to provide cover… it demonstrates a certain ruthless cunning entirely consistent with the person who could embezzle funds for years and stage a murder."

"Mildred possesses an intimate understanding of the club's social dynamics and personal sensitivities," Agnes added, her expression grim. "She would know precisely how to amplify the Ferguson narrative, perhaps through a carefully placed 'sympathetic' comment to Mrs Henderson or Colonel Abernathy, knowing it would spread like wildfire. Proving it, however…" she left the sentence unfinished.

"Regardless of its origin," Fitzwilliam stated, feeling a renewed sense of purpose, "our path remains clear. We focus on Mildred. We need concrete evidence."

"The Fincham book," Agnes tapped the library printout. "I *must* examine that Section IV, Paragraph 12. It felt important to Ainsworth; it may provide the missing link between the historical land issue and the ongoing financial discrepancies."

"The suppliers," Fitzwilliam confirmed. "I'll run those corporate registry searches tomorrow morning first thing – WeatherTech Roofing, Vintage Marquee Hire, Bespoke Botanical Displays. See who is behind them."

"The *Digitalis*," Chloe affirmed. "I'll check the plants near Lawn 3 tomorrow during my rounds, looking for any signs of harvesting. And I'll survey the compost area and incinerator, just in case."

"And I," Ronnie declared, already sketching new diagrams, "will refine the lividity fixation probability curves based on Melbourne meteorological data for Tuesday afternoon, and research detectability thresholds for cardiac glycosides in postmortem tissue, assuming sub optimal sample preservation!"

They looked at each other, a silent pact renewed in the quiet, lamp-lit room. The Ferguson rumour was a nuisance, a potentially dangerous distraction, but they wouldn't let it divert them. The real quarry, they felt increasingly certain, was the quiet, efficient woman who served tea and sympathy while potentially harbouring decades of secrets and the capacity for calculated, lethal action. The path forward was fraught with difficulty and uncertainty, requiring them to operate in the shadows while the official investigation chased phantoms, but the conviction that they were on the right track burned brighter now, fuelled by the very attempts to obscure it. The hunt for proof against Mildred Pettle was on.

****

The following afternoon, Alistair Fitzwilliam found himself navigating the hushed aisles of the Toorak Public Library, a low-slung, strangely comforting brick building nestled just off the main village strip. It wasn't part of his usual routine – his legal research typically demanded the vast resources of the Supreme Court Library or online databases – but today's visit had a specific, discreet purpose. Agnes's methodical approach was infectious; before focusing entirely on Mildred Pettle, they needed to definitively, if only for their own satisfaction, eliminate the distraction of Major Ferguson. Fitzwilliam had taken upon himself the task of verifying the Major's alibi for the crucial lunchtime period on the day of the murder – the window Ronnie's calculations pinpointed as the most probable time for poison administration. His chosen method: a seemingly casual conversation with Marjorie Ferguson, the Major's wife, who volunteered at the library issuing desk every Friday afternoon.

He located her easily – a small, bird-like woman with kind, anxious eyes behind spectacles, diligently scanning bar codes and stamping due dates with practised efficiency. She looked tired, Fitzwilliam noted, her usual gentle smile strained. The cloud hanging over the Croquet Club extended even here, into this quiet sanctuary of books and suburban tranquillity. He waited patiently until there was a lull in borrowers, then approached the polished oak counter.

"Marjorie," he began, offering what he hoped was a reassuring smile. "Alistair Fitzwilliam. Just returning these." He placed two uncontroversial legal history books he'd borrowed weeks ago onto the counter.

Marjorie Ferguson looked up, her eyes widening slightly in recognition, perhaps tinged with apprehension. "Oh! Mr Fitzwilliam. Hello." Her hands fluttered nervously over the date stamp. "Thank you. Are you… finding everything you need?"

"Yes, thank you," Fitzwilliam said, keeping his tone light. He leaned slightly closer, lowering his voice. "I was so sorry to hear about the dreadful business at the club. Utterly shocking. And," he added, injecting a note of sympathetic concern, "I gather Charles – the Major – has been rather caught up in the… the speculation surrounding it all? Particularly concerning his dispute with poor Mr Ainsworth over the dahlia plot?"

Marjorie's face crumpled slightly. "Oh, it's been dreadful, Mr Fitzwilliam, simply dreadful!" she whispered, glancing around to ensure no one else was within earshot. "Charles is beside himself. First, that awful man threatening his garden, then the sabotage – those prize tubers, utterly ruined! – and then... *this*! And now people are whispering... The police haven't spoken to him directly yet, but Esme Weatherly called this morning, very discreetly of course, just to say... well, that his name had come up." Her eyes welled up momentarily. "Charles wouldn't hurt a fly! He shouts about the dahlias, yes, he gets obsessed, but he's not... not *violent*."

Fitzwilliam nodded sympathetically. "Of course not. Charles is a pillar of the club, everyone knows that. But Ainsworth could be... provocative. I imagine the Major was extremely upset, especially after the sabotage incident." This was the crucial opening.

"Upset?" Marjorie gave a short, watery laugh that held little humour. "He was incandescent! When he came home for lunch on Tuesday," – Fitzwilliam's internal antennae twitched; *Tuesday lunch* – "after discovering the damage that morning, he could barely speak for rage. Didn't eat a bite. Spent the entire time between," she paused, thinking, "oh, must have been just after midday when he got back, and well after three when he finally calmed down enough to even consider going back to the club for his cancelled committee meeting... spent the *entire* time in the back garden, trying to salvage what he could of those poor dahlias, ranting and raving to himself about Ainsworth and 'petty tyrants' and 'vandals'."

Fitzwilliam kept his expression carefully neutral, empathetic, while his mind processed the information rapidly. Home for lunch. Between midday and well after three PM. Ranting and tending dahlias. It placed Major Ferguson squarely at home, miles away from the Croquet Club and Ainsworth's thermos, during the entire probable poisoning window (12:00 PM - 1:45 PM) identified by Ronnie. Unless Marjorie was lying to protect her husband – which Fitzwilliam intuitively doubted, given her genuine distress and the plausible detail – Ferguson simply couldn't have administered poison at the club during that critical period.

"So he was home all through lunchtime then?" Fitzwilliam confirmed gently, as if merely clarifying the extent of his understandable distress. "Didn't pop back to the club at all between, say, twelve and two?"

"Good heavens, no!" Marjorie looked aghast at the suggestion. "He wouldn't leave the garden. Said he couldn't trust 'that man' not to come back and finish the job. He was out there with his trowel and his special bone meal mix, trying to perform surgery on the tubers, muttering about boundary lines and historical injustices. I took him out a cup of tea around two-thirty, just before he finally came inside to change for his meeting. He certainly didn't go anywhere near the club during that time, I can assure you."

The alibi felt solid. Specific, detailed, anchored by the very dahlia obsession that made him a suspect in the first place. His rage had kept him home, tending his wounded horticultural charges, inadvertently providing him cover for the time the murder was most likely set in motion. Fitzwilliam felt a wave of relief, tinged with pity for the Ferguson's being dragged into this through gossip and circumstance.

"That must have been incredibly stressful for you both," Fitzwilliam said sincerely. "Please, Marjorie, try not to worry too much about the whispers. These things have a way of resolving themselves once the facts come out. Charles's dedication to his garden is well known; people understand passions can run high." He offered another brief, reassuring smile.

"Thank you, Mr Fitzwilliam," she whispered, looking slightly comforted. "It's just… horrible."

He collected his library card and retreated, leaving Marjorie to her duties. Outside the quiet library, the Toorak village street seemed bustling and normal, shoppers Browse boutiques, people sipping coffee at sidewalk cafes. It felt jarringly disconnected from the dark undercurrents swirling just blocks away at the Croquet Club.

Fitzwilliam found a quiet bench under a plane tree and quickly dialled Agnes. "Agnes? Alistair here," he said when she answered. "Update on the Ferguson angle. I spoke with Mrs Ferguson. Quite distraught, poor woman. But she confirms, quite definitively I believe, that the Major was at home tending his damaged dahlias between approximately midday and well after three PM on Tuesday. He was incandescent with rage about the sabotage, apparently, but firmly planted in his own garden during the entire likely time frame for any poison administration at the club."

He could almost hear Agnes's sharp nod of satisfaction down the line. "Excellent, Alistair. Corroborates our assessment. A red herring, almost certainly fuelled by gossip, perhaps even deliberately. We can formally discount Major Ferguson."

"My thoughts exactly," Fitzwilliam agreed, feeling a weight lift. "It clears the path. Allows us to focus all our attention where it belongs."

"Precisely," Agnes's voice was crisp. "On Mildred Pettle. And on the secrets Bartholomew Ainsworth died trying to uncover. I am heading to the State Library now to pursue the *Pyrus Malus* connection. Keep your phone close."

Fitzwilliam ended the call, feeling a renewed sense of clarity, despite the inherent dangers. The distraction, however plausible it had seemed to the gossiping members, had been swiftly investigated and dismissed. Their instincts, backed by Agnes's archival research, Ronnie's physics, Chloe's observations, and now his own verification, were proving sound. Major Ferguson was a victim of circumstance and Ainsworth's provocative actions, not a killer. The real investigation – the one focused on the quiet secretary, the historical finances, the cryptic clue, and the unidentified alkaloid – could now proceed without diversion. The path ahead remained complex and fraught, but at least, Fitzwilliam thought, it felt like the *right* path. He tucked his phone away and headed back towards his office, his mind already turning to corporate registry searches and unfamiliar supplier names.

<h1 style="text-align:center">12</h1>

Botanical Shadows

The following morning broke clear and cool over Melbourne, the kind of crisp, bright day that usually invigorated Chloe Dubois, making the prospect of tending the Society's extensive gardens a pleasure rather than just a job. Today, however, as she approached the still-cordoned area bordering Lawn 3, her usual enthusiasm was replaced by a cold knot of apprehension. Armed with secateurs, twine, and the official pretext of 'checking for damage and performing necessary tidying' negotiated by Agnes, she felt less like a gardener and more like a forensic botanist venturing into contaminated territory. Her task, agreed upon during the intense discussion in Agnes's study, was crucial: to examine the *Digitalis purpurea* – the elegant, bell-flowered foxgloves growing in the shaded, slightly damp soil near where Ainsworth's body had lain – for any signs of recent, illicit harvesting.

The single constable stationed nearby nodded almost gratefully as she approached, clearly bored with his solitary vigil. "Morning, miss. Just the plants again?"

"Yes, Constable," Chloe replied, keeping her voice even. "Need to check if any roots were disturbed when... before. And trim any damaged stems." She ducked under the blue and white tape, the familiar scent of damp earth and decaying leaves instantly transporting her back to the moment of discovery, a sensation she had to consciously push aside. Focus, she told herself. Observe.

She deliberately started away from the foxgloves, busying herself first with staking some delphiniums that hadn't been involved, making a show of examining leaves and checking ties, allowing herself to acclimatise to being back inside the taped area. The forensic markers were still there, small plastic flags standing like alien growths amongst the familiar foliage. The ground bore faint traces of the investigators' presence – slightly compressed soil, a few stray fibres snagged on thorns – but nature was already beginning to reclaim the space, blurring the sharp edges of human intrusion.

From the corner of her eye, she saw Barnaby Thornton wrestling with a recalcitrant lawnmower near the equipment shed on the far side of Lawn 4. He paused, wiping his brow, and caught her eye, offering a brief, sympathetic wave. Chloe waved back, a small gesture of normalcy in the midst of the pervasive strangeness. His presence, focused on mundane mechanics, was oddly comforting, a reminder that not everything at the club revolved around the grim events of the past few days. Yet, it also subtly underscored the ease with which staff and dedicated volunteers could move around the grounds, often unnoticed, accessing sheds, workshops, and secluded garden beds. Opportunity, as Ronnie would say, was a variable dependent on routine and access.

Taking another steadying breath, Chloe moved towards the stand of foxgloves. They were beautiful plants, really, despite their sinister potential. Tall spires of nodding, bell-shaped flowers in shades of purple and pink, speckled within their throats. Their leaves were large, downy, forming lush basal rosettes. They thrived in this slightly shaded, moist corner, providing vertical interest against the dark green backdrop of the rhododendrons. Mr Ainsworth had often complained they were too vigorous, threatening to self-seed excessively (a violation, no doubt, of some imagined rule of horticultural tidiness), but Chloe secretly admired their resilient charm. Now, however, she looked at them with new, suspicious eyes.

She knelt beside the first clump, her gaze scanning not the showy flower spikes, but the lower leaves and stems. *Digitalis* leaves, particularly the larger basal ones from first-year plants or the lower stem leaves of flowering plants, were known to be rich in the potent cardiac glycosides – digitoxin, digoxin. Someone wanting to extract the poison wouldn't need the flowers; they'd target the leaves.

Methodically, she began examining each plant. Most looked untouched, their rosettes full, their stems intact. But then, on the third clump, partially hidden behind a larger rhododendron branch, she saw it. Several of the large, lower leaves were missing. Not yellowed and fallen, not nibbled by pests, but cleanly removed. Looking closer, she could see tiny, neat stubs where the leaf stalks had been cut, close to the main stem. The cuts looked clean, sharp, not torn or broken. And they looked recent – the exposed tissue hadn't fully dried or calloused over.

Her heart beat a little faster. This wasn't natural leaf drop. This looked deliberate. Careful. Someone had selectively harvested leaves from this specific plant. How many leaves? She counted the stubs – four, maybe five, from this one clump. She moved to the next clump, slightly further back, even more screened from view from the main lawns. Here too, several lower leaves were gone, snipped off with similar neatness.

This wasn't random damage. It wasn't an animal. It felt purposeful, knowledgeable. Someone knew which leaves to take – the larger, more mature ones likely containing higher concentrations of the toxins. Someone had taken care not to damage the main flowering stem, perhaps to avoid drawing immediate attention. Someone had been here, likely within the last few days or week, carefully harvesting poison.

Who had access? Technically, any member could wander through this part of the garden, though it wasn't on a main path. Staff like herself and the groundskeeper, obviously. Volunteers working on garden maintenance. And Mildred Pettle... Chloe recalled Agnes mentioning Mildred sometimes did 'light duties' with the gardening committee, mostly deadheading or weeding. Did 'light duties' ever extend to this secluded corner? Did Mildred possess the botanical knowledge to identify foxglove and understand its properties? It seemed unlikely for the efficient, seemingly indoors-focused secretary, yet Ainsworth's research had apparently led *him* to obscure botanical texts. Perhaps Mildred shared a hidden interest? Or perhaps she had simply researched the most effective, accessible poison available on the grounds once she knew Ainsworth needed silencing.

Chloe continued her examination, moving along the stand of *Digitalis*. She found similar signs on two other clumps, always the lower, larger leaves, always removed cleanly. In total, perhaps a dozen or more leaves seemed to have been harvested recently. Enough for multiple doses? Enough to cause serious illness or death? Her horticultural knowledge extended to identifying poisonous plants, but not to calculating lethal dosages of extracted alkaloids. Ronnie or Agnes would need to research that.

She thought about processing. How would one extract the toxin? Traditional methods involved drying the leaves, then infusing them, often in alcohol or hot water. Drying could be done discreetly indoors. Infusion... heating might be required. Where could that be done unnoticed at the club? The staff kitchen? Unlikely, too public.

The equipment shed? Possible, if one had access and privacy. The potting sheds near the compost heaps? More secluded, certainly. She made a mental note to check those areas later for any unusual residues or equipment.

As she finished examining the last foxglove plant, she noticed something else nearby, almost buried under fallen rhododendron leaves – a few discarded *Digitalis* leaf fragments, slightly wilted, that didn't seem to have fallen naturally. Had the harvester dropped them accidentally? Or perhaps discarded leaves deemed unsuitable? She carefully collected these fragments into another specimen bag. They might contain traces of something, or at least confirm the harvesting occurred very recently.

She stood up slowly, brushing mulch from her knees, her mind racing. She had found what she feared she might. Clear evidence that someone had recently harvested leaves from the poisonous foxgloves growing just metres from where Bartholomew Ainsworth's body was found. It wasn't absolute proof of poisoning, let alone proof linking it to Mildred Pettle. But combined with the autopsy anomalies – the lividity, the unidentified alkaloid – it transformed the poisoning hypothesis from plausible speculation into a terrifyingly concrete possibility. The means for murder were right here, growing silently amidst the manicured beauty of the Society gardens. And someone, it appeared, knew exactly how to use them. The cool morning air suddenly felt much colder. She needed to report this to Agnes, immediately. The botanical shadows around Ainsworth's death were beginning to take tangible, poisonous shape.

****

Evening had descended fully by the time Chloe Dubois let herself into her small apartment in Richmond. The familiar click of the lock behind her felt like sealing off the unsettling world of the Toorak Croquet & Horticultural Society, at least physically. Mentally, however, the images and implications of the day crowded in on her: the neat, clinical cuts on the foxglove leaves, the indistinct footprint beneath the rhododendrons, the heavy weight of the expensive suede glove tucked away in her work bag. The discovery in the garden hadn't brought clarity, only a deeper, more specific kind of dread.

Her apartment, a third-floor walk-up overlooking a typically narrow Melbourne lane way vibrant with street art, was her sanctuary. Usually. Tonight, the familiar clutter – stacks of gardening magazines, pots overflowing with indoor plants jostling for space on the windowsill, half-finished sketches pinned to a cork board – felt less like cosy creative chaos and more like a fragile defence against the complexities she'd stumbled into. The rhythmic sigh of tyres on wet asphalt drifted up from the lane way below; the southerly change had brought more rain, a persistent drizzle blurring the city lights. It was Thursday, April 10th, 2025 – a date now indelibly linked in her mind with poisonous plants and unpleasant truths.

After shedding her damp jacket and work boots, Chloe made herself a strong cup of peppermint tea – deliberately avoiding anything resembling Ainsworth's preferred Darjeeling – and cleared a space on her small kitchen table. She'd called Agnes briefly on her walk back to the tram stop, relaying her findings about the harvested foxglove leaves in clipped, factual tones. Agnes had listened intently, confirmed the significance, and promised to drop off some relevant reference books later that evening or tomorrow. But Chloe couldn't wait. The need to *understand* the practicalities, the effects, the sheer *feasibility* of using *Digitalis* as a weapon, felt urgent.

She opened her laptop, the screen casting a cool blue light in the otherwise dimly lit room. Beside it, she placed her own well-thumbed copy of *Toxic Plants of Victoria* and a notebook. Her initial searches were broad: "Digitalis purpurea toxicity," "cardiac glycoside poisoning," "digitoxin symptoms." Link after link pulled her deeper into the world of medical toxicology and pharmacognosy – worlds far removed from soil pH and pruning techniques.

She learned the specifics quickly. The primary active compounds: digitoxin and digoxin. Their mechanism: inhibiting the sodium-potassium pump in heart muscle cells, leading to increased intracellular calcium, stronger but potentially dangerously irregular contractions. The historical context: *Digitalis* had been used medicinally for centuries to treat 'dropsy' (heart failure), famously studied by William Withering, but the therapeutic dose was perilously close to the toxic dose. It was a plant demanding respect, capable of both healing and killing with subtle shifts in concentration.

Then came the symptoms. Nausea, vomiting, diarrhoea – common enough, easily dismissed as indigestion or a stomach bug. Headache, fatigue, confusion, disorientation – again, attributable to stress, overwork, myriad minor ailments. But then, the more specific, more sinister signs: visual disturbances, particularly xanthopsia – seeing objects tinged with yellow or green, or seeing halos around lights. And the cardiac effects: bradycardia (slow heart rate), tachycardia (fast heart rate), palpitations, potentially fatal arrhythmias like ventricular fibrillation.

Chloe stared at the list, a cold knot forming in her stomach. *Irritability. Pallor. Indigestion.* Her own recollections of Ainsworth's recent behaviour, previously dismissed as mere extensions of his unpleasant personality or signs of general stress (as Mildred Pettle had so smoothly suggested), now seemed to align with the early or cumulative symptoms of glycoside toxicity with frightening precision. Had his 'fussiness' hidden genuine confusion? Had his complaints about the lighting in the office been literal, related to visual disturbances? Had his general cantankerousness been exacerbated by persistent nausea or headache? She remembered him rubbing his temples frequently during a committee meeting about two weeks ago. At the time, she assumed it was due to the tedious debate about resurfacing the tennis courts. Now, she wondered.

How much would it take? The articles and texts were cautious, emphasising variability based on plant part, harvest time, individual sensitivity, and preparation method. But they generally agreed that ingesting even a few leaves, especially the mature basal ones she'd seen harvested, could cause serious poisoning in an adult, and a concentrated extract or infusion could easily be lethal.

Her next search focused on administration. Could it be hidden in food or drink? The bitter taste of the glycosides was mentioned frequently. However, several sources noted that in strong-tasting infusions, like dark tea or coffee, or mixed with sugary foods, the bitterness could potentially be masked, especially if administered in smaller, repeated doses rather than one massive one.

She found a passage in an old digital copy of a pharmacognosy journal Agnes had recommended: *"Cardiac glycosides derived from Digitalis spp. exhibit reasonable solubility in hot water, facilitating extraction via simple infusion, similar to preparing tea. While possessing a characteristic bitterness, this may be significantly obscured by strongly flavoured vehicles, such as robust black teas or beverages containing significant amounts of sugar or milk..."*

Ainsworth's thermos. His ubiquitous Darjeeling, which he drank strong and black throughout the day. It was the perfect delivery mechanism. A dose prepared from the harvested leaves, perhaps steeped into a concentrated liquid, could be added to his full thermos in the morning, potentially in his office while he was briefly elsewhere (warming up his car? attending an early meeting?). He would then unknowingly sip the poison throughout the day, the slow onset of symptoms perhaps not becoming severe or alarming until the afternoon, culminating in confusion, collapse, and providing the opportunity for the killer to administer the final, staged blow.

Chloe felt sick. The sheer calculated cruelty of it – turning a man's daily ritual, his small comfort, into the instrument of his death. It spoke of a cold, methodical planning that seemed utterly alien to Harry Smythe's explosive, quickly subsiding rages. It felt more aligned with the quiet, meticulous control she now associated with Mildred Pettle, the woman who oversaw the smooth running of the club, including, perhaps, the administration of its teas and the management of its historical accounts.

Could Mildred have done it? Accessed the plants, harvested the leaves, prepared an extract, added it to Ainsworth's thermos in his office? The timing felt right – Ronnie had identified the lunchtime window as suspicious, but the poison could have been administered even earlier, needing only unsupervised access to the office and thermos. Mildred, with her master keys and her reason to be everywhere, would have had ample opportunity. Did she have the knowledge? Perhaps not initially, but Ainsworth's own research into historical botany (prompted by the Fincham book or the planting ledgers) might have inadvertently led *her* to the properties of *Digitalis* if she became aware of his specific interests. Or perhaps, driven by the need to silence him permanently after he discovered her embezzlement, she had simply researched effective, accessible poisons herself. Foxglove, growing abundantly and picturesquely just metres from the main lawns, would be an obvious candidate for someone seeking a 'natural' weapon close at hand.

Chloe leaned back, closing her eyes, trying to reconcile the image of the helpful, slightly fussy Club Secretary with the image of a calculating poisoner. It was difficult, unsettling. Yet, the evidence trail – the harvested plants, the specific toxicity aligning with Ainsworth's possible symptoms, the feasible administration via the now-missing thermos, the powerful motive linked to the financial investigations, Mildred's opportunity and control – felt increasingly strong.

She opened her eyes and looked at the notes she'd taken. Symptoms: match possible. Means: *Digitalis* confirmed toxic, suitable for infusion. Administration: Tea thermos highly plausible. Opportunity: Mildred had ample. Motive: Protecting potential long-term embezzlement from Ainsworth's discoveries. It was still circumstantial, Fitzwilliam would remind her. But the circumstances were becoming incredibly compelling.

She quickly texted Agnes: *"Finished initial research. Digitalis symptoms fit Ainsworth's recent state disturbingly well. Easily administered via tea. Taste maskable. Lethal dose plausible from harvested leaves. Feels right, Agnes. Horribly right."*

A reply came back almost instantly: *"Understood, Chloe. Corroborates findings here regarding historical methods. Proceed with extreme caution. Our primary task now is finding the link between means and perpetrator. Stay safe."*

Chloe closed her laptop, the screen reflecting the rain-streaked window and her own troubled expression. The botanical shadows around Bartholomew Ainsworth's death were no longer just possibilities; they felt like the substance of the crime itself. And the path forward seemed clearer, but also far more dangerous. She had to check the compost heaps, the incinerator, look for any sign of discarded plant matter or preparation tools. She had to help find that direct link Agnes spoke of, the proof that would connect the poison in the garden to the hand of the killer.

****

Friday morning, April 11th, found the quartet reconvened in the familiar territory of Agnes Plummett's study. The initial adrenaline of their respective breakthroughs – Agnes's deciphering of the *Pyrus Malus* clue, Fitzwilliam's discovery of the Fete account loophole, Ronnie's timeline analysis, and Chloe's confirmation of harvested foxgloves – had settled into a more focused, almost grim, determination. The Melbourne weather outside remained stubbornly grey and damp, a fitting backdrop for the seriousness of their discussion. A large sheet of butcher's paper, commandeered by Ronnie, was now taped to one of Agnes's bookshelves, covered in timelines, connection arrows, and probability equations that only he truly understood, but which visually represented their coalescing theory pointing towards Mildred Pettle.

Chloe, looking less haunted than yesterday but no less serious, formally shared the detailed findings of her research from the previous evening. She laid out her notes on the already cluttered desk, summarising the specific effects of *Digitalis* poisoning, the disturbing alignment with her recollections of Ainsworth's recent malaise, and the confirmation from multiple sources that the toxins were indeed water-soluble and could potentially be masked in strong tea.

"So," she concluded, looking around at the others, her voice quiet but steady, "it's not just possible, it seems… horribly practical. Using the foxglove leaves, making some kind of infusion… it could absolutely be done. And it fits."

"Fits the symptoms, fits the alkaloid found in the autopsy – even if VIFM hasn't identified it *as* digitoxin yet," Fitzwilliam mused, pacing slowly before the bay window, gazing out at the wet street below. "It fits the potential for prior incapacitation that Ronnie's physics suggest, and the lividity inconsistency." He turned back to the group. "The major remaining question, from a practical standpoint, is administration. How does the killer ensure Ainsworth ingests a sufficient dose, at the right time, without raising suspicion?"

"We theorised about his tea," Agnes said thoughtfully, consulting her own notes. "Bartholomew was invariant in his habits. He consumed Darjeeling, second flush, black, no sugar, throughout the day from his personal thermos flask."

"Ah yes, the thermos!" Ronnie exclaimed, snapping his fingers as if remembering a crucial variable he'd momentarily forgotten. "The dedicated personal beverage container! Optimal vector for targeted agent delivery! Constant volume, controlled access points…"

"That stainless steel one?" Chloe asked, picturing it. "Tall, brushed finish, slightly dented lid?"

"Precisely!" Agnes confirmed. "A 'Thermos King', I believe the brand was. He brought it in every single morning, filled, and usually refilled it with hot water from the clubhouse urn once or twice during the day, using his own tea leaves, of course." She frowned slightly. "He was remarkably particular about it. Complained vociferously if anyone else even touched it."

"I remember him dropping it during the AGM back in 2019," Fitzwilliam recalled with a grimace. "Made an appalling clatter. He spent the next ten minutes inspecting it for damage and lecturing poor Esme on the importance of maintaining clear pathways during meetings." The memory, once merely irritating, now felt chilling. That thermos, so central to Ainsworth's daily routine, so personally guarded…

"So," Fitzwilliam continued, thinking procedurally, "if poison were administered, the thermos is the overwhelmingly likely vehicle. Either the killer added a prepared toxin to his full thermos sometime before he started drinking from it on Tuesday morning, or perhaps added it when he refilled it during the day?"

"The latter seems less probable," Ronnie interjected, already calculating probabilities. "Requires the killer to have access to prepared toxin *and* intercept Ainsworth during a refill. Higher risk of observation. Introducing the agent into the full thermos earlier, likely in the relative privacy of his office before his day truly began, offers a statistically superior window of opportunity with lower detection probability."

"Especially," Agnes added quietly, "for someone who might have had routine access to his office early in the morning. Someone like the Club Secretary, perhaps arriving early to sort the mail or prepare for the day?" The implication hung in the air.

"The thermos, then," Fitzwilliam stated, focusing on the object itself. "It becomes crucial evidence. If the police recovered it…"

"Did they?" Agnes looked sharply at Fitzwilliam. "You mentioned your contact detailed the cause of death, the lividity, the alkaloid… did he say anything about personal effects recovered from the scene or the office? Specifically, a thermos?"

Fitzwilliam frowned, casting his mind back to the brief, unofficial conversation with Sergeant Riley. They'd focused on the VIFM findings. Had Riley listed inventoried items? No, he hadn't. "He didn't mention it," Fitzwilliam admitted. "Which could mean anything. It might be logged routinely, just not something he thought to tell me. Or…"

"Or it wasn't there," Chloe finished softly.

Agnes stood up and walked decisively to her own meticulous files related to the case. She pulled out the list of items Chloe had initially reported seeing near the body (mallet, scattered leaves), and her own notes from her search of Ainsworth's office (Rolodex, pen set, single folder, empty bin). "It certainly wasn't on his desk when I looked," she confirmed. "Nor visibly in the main office space. His briefcase was there, but Esme confirmed it contained only standard committee papers and his lunchbox – unopened, interestingly, which might support Ronnie's theory of him feeling unwell or consuming the poison *instead* of lunch."

"Could he have left it somewhere else?" Chloe wondered. "The lounge? The changing room?"

"Possible, but unlikely for Bartholomew," Agnes countered. "That thermos was practically an extension of his arm during club hours. He kept it close."

"What about the police?" Fitzwilliam mused. "Could forensics have taken it from Lawn 3 if it was near the body? Or collected it from the office later?" It was the critical question. He made a mental note to try and subtly ascertain this from Riley if another opportunity arose, though pressing for specific inventory details felt even riskier than his previous inquiry.

Ronnie, however, was already several steps ahead, focused on the implications of its *absence*. "If the thermos is *missing*," he declared, pacing again, "it's profoundly significant! Assume Hypothesis P is correct. The killer administers poison via the thermos. After Ainsworth collapses and the staged blow is delivered, the killer *must* retrieve and dispose of the thermos! It contains the residual evidence of the primary crime – the poison itself! Leaving it behind would be catastrophically stupid for a calculating killer."

"Its absence, therefore," Agnes stated, grasping the logic immediately, "becomes strong circumstantial evidence *in favour* of the poisoning theory. It points towards a killer who understood the need to remove the delivery vector."

"And towards a killer who had the opportunity to remove it," Fitzwilliam added grimly. "Someone who could access the scene, or Ainsworth's office or belongings, *after* the death but *before* everything was thoroughly secured and inventoried by police." Again, Mildred

Pettle, with her keys and her omnipresence, fitted the profile perfectly. She could have easily retrieved it from his office later that evening under the guise of 'tidying up' or looking for contact details, long after the initial police focus had shifted to Lawn 3 and Harry Smythe.

"Damn," Fitzwilliam breathed, feeling a familiar wave of frustration. "So the single most crucial piece of physical evidence linking the means to the victim is likely gone forever. Destroyed. Cleaned beyond recovery." He ran a hand through his hair. "How do we prove poison without the poisoned chalice, so to speak?"

"Difficult," Agnes conceded, her expression resolute. "But not impossible. We have the trace alkaloid finding – we must hope further analysis yields *something*, some clue to its specific nature, that Alistair might glean. We have Chloe's evidence of the harvested *Digitalis* – motive, means, opportunity aligning is powerful, even circumstantially. We have Ronnie's analysis of the physical inconsistencies of the blow. We have the financial motive linked to Mildred's control of the Fete accounts and Ainsworth's historical investigations." She ticked the points off on her fingers. "And," she added, pulling the library slip from her pocket, "we have this."

She laid the *Pyrus Malus* call slip on the table. "Bartholomew left us a trail, however cryptic. Understanding *why* he was comparing an obscure book on historical orchards to Mildred Pettle's Fete accounts might provide the key to the underlying secret she was so desperate to protect. The thermos might be gone, but Ainsworth's research remains. That," she declared, her eyes meeting theirs, determined, "is where we must dig."

The mood in the room shifted again. The frustration over the missing thermos, a seemingly insurmountable obstacle, was channelled into a renewed focus on the remaining threads. The missing thermos wasn't just lost evidence; it was a silent testament to the killer's calculated thoroughness.

****

The grandfather clock in the Society's main lounge chimed nine times, each stroke echoing through the now almost deserted club-house. Outside, the persistent Melbourne drizzle had eased, leaving behind wet pavements reflecting the sparse streetlights and the scent of damp earth hanging heavy in the cool night air. Friday, April 11th, was drawing to a close. Inside the club library, however, Ronnie Peterson showed no signs of flagging. If anything, the late hour and the surrounding quiet seemed to sharpen his focus, isolating him with the complex, grim equation he was determined to solve.

He had stayed long after Agnes, Fitzwilliam, and Chloe had departed, armed with their respective tasks and shared sense of purpose. Ronnie needed time alone with the data, with the large architect's plan spread beneath the focused beam of a brass reading lamp, with his own sprawling charts and calculations. The confirmation from Chloe about the harvested *Digitalis*, combined with the group's consensus about the missing thermos being the likely delivery vector, had provided the final crucial variables for his ultimate analysis: mapping the logistical probability pathway of the killer. Assuming their primary hypothesis – poison administered by Mildred Pettle, followed by a staged blow – was correct, could the entire sequence of events be plausibly executed by her, given the constraints of time, access, and risk?

For Ronnie, this wasn't about psychology or motive; it was about process flow, time-motion study, risk assessment. Could Path A (Harvesting) connect efficiently to Path B (Processing), leading to Path C (Administration) and culminating in Path D (Disposal), all executed by Suspect P (Pettle) with a sufficiently high probability of success and low probability of detection compared to alternative suspects (Smythe, Ferguson, Unknown)?

He addressed Harvesting first. Location: *Digitalis* patch near Lawn 3, adjacent to the 'old orchard end' and rhododendron bed. Task: Selectively cut approx. 12-15 mature basal leaves. Time required: Minimal, perhaps 3-5 minutes for someone moving quickly and knowing what they were looking for. Optimal temporal window: Low traffic periods. Early morning before most members arrive? Possible – Mildred often arrived early to open the office. Late evening after most members leave? Also possible – Mildred often stayed late finishing administrative tasks. During the day? Riskier, but that corner *was* relatively secluded. He assigned probabilities. Mildred: High opportunity (access early/late, plausible reason to be near gardens occasionally – 'checking on volunteer work'). Others: Lower probability of accessing that specific spot unnoticed for that specific purpose. Ferguson? Focused on his *own* plot nearby, less likely to be harvesting foxgloves. Smythe? Unlikely to be skulking in flowerbeds early/late. Score: Pettle Pathway – High Probability (HP).

Next, Processing. Task: Extract cardiac glycosides from leaves into a deliverable form (likely concentrated infusion). Requirements: Privacy, water source, potentially heat source (for infusion), method for containing/storing extract, disposal of residual plant matter. Location? This was trickier. Ronnie consulted the clubhouse plan. Potting sheds near compost heaps? Secluded, water tap available, but staff/gardener access frequent. Staff break room? Kettle available, but risk of interruption high unless after hours. Boiler room? Often locked, access controlled. Mildred's own office? Private, secure, but lacks water/heat unless using a personal travel kettle (plausible for Mildred). Time required: Variable. Simple cold-water maceration? Less effective extraction, longer time. Hot water infusion? Faster, more potent, requires heat source. Drying leaves first? Adds time/complexity but increases potency/storability. Ronnie assumed a simple hot infusion for maximum efficiency. Mildred could potentially achieve this after hours in the staff break room or her office with minimal equipment. Residual leaves/stems? Could be discreetly added to compost, incinerator (if exists), or removed off-site. Probability for Mildred: Moderate to High (MHP) – dependent on chosen method/location, but feasible given her access/routine. Others: Significantly lower probability (LP) due to lack of routine access to suitable private processing locations.

Then, Administration. Task: Introduce processed toxin into Ainsworth's personal thermos. Location: Treasurer's office. Optimal temporal window: Tuesday late morning / lunchtime (12:00 PM - 1:45 PM) when Ainsworth often worked alone, consuming tea. Requirements: Access to office (briefly, while Ainsworth possibly stepped out – restroom? quick chat?), access to thermos, ability to add liquid without detection. Time required: Minimal, seconds only. Risk: High potential for interruption, but mitigated by short duration and plausible reason for entry if discovered. Ronnie assessed Mildred's probability: Very High (VHP). She possessed master keys, frequently delivered mail/messages, could easily fabricate a reason to enter Ainsworth's office momentarily. Comparison: Smythe/Ferguson/others would require forced entry or an unlikely scenario of being invited in and left alone with the thermos.

Finally, Disposal. Task: Retrieve and permanently dispose of the thermos flask and any processing tools/residue *after* the murder discovery but before police lock down or thorough search. Temporal window: Tuesday late afternoon/evening, potentially extending into Wednesday morning. Location: Highly variable. On-site options: Club bins (high risk of discovery), compost heaps (risk of incomplete decomposition/discovery by Chloe), incinerator (effective if available/accessible). Off-site: Taking items away in bag/briefcase for disposal in domestic bins, public bins elsewhere in Melbourne, or perhaps dropped into the Yarra River? Risk: Moderate, depending on method and timing. Ronnie considered Mildred's situation. She typically stayed late, locking up. She would have had ample opportunity Tuesday evening or early Wednesday morning, under the guise of 'dealing with the crisis', to access Ainsworth's office (if thermos left there) or even potentially retrieve it from near Lawn 3 if left there initially (less likely). Taking it off-site in her large, practical handbag seemed the most probable, lowest-risk disposal method for the thermos itself. Processing residue could be handled via compost or incinerator more easily. Probability for Mildred: High (HP).

Ronnie stepped back from the table, looking at his annotated map and timeline, the pathways he had sketched in pencil, the probability assessments noted in the margins. Harvesting (HP), Processing (MHP), Administration (VHP), Disposal (HP). Every single stage of the hypothesised crime, from acquiring the botanical weapon to eliminating the key evidence, was not only plausible but logistically *optimal* for Mildred Pettle, leveraging her access, her routine, her position of trust, and her almost invisible presence within the club's daily operations. Could someone else have done it? Theoretically, yes. But their logistical pathway would involve significantly higher risk, lower probability access, or more complex assumptions. Mildred's path was, in Ronnie's analysis, the line of least resistance, the most statistically elegant solution to the logistical problem of committing this specific crime in this specific environment.

His scientific detachment wavered for a moment, replaced by a cold certainty that mirrored Fitzwilliam's earlier unease. The numbers, the timelines, the spatial analysis – they all converged on the quiet, efficient Club Secretary. The physics had pointed towards staging. The history pointed towards motive. The botany pointed towards means. And now, the logistics pointed overwhelmingly towards opportunity and execution.

He needed to inform the others. This wasn't just about the physics of the blow anymore; it was about the entire operational sequence. He pulled out his phone, dialling Agnes first – she would appreciate the methodical breakdown.

"Agnes? Ronnie." He barely waited for her greeting. "I've completed a logistical pathway analysis based on Hypothesis P and current data regarding victim movements, site access, and suspect capabilities." He took a breath, trying to translate his findings into language less reliant on probability notations. "The results are conclusive within acceptable confidence limits. Evaluating the necessary steps – harvesting *Digitalis*, processing for toxicity, administration via thermos during the identified temporal window, and subsequent disposal of key evidence – the execution probability is maximised, and detection probability minimised, uniquely through the known access patterns and established routines of Mildred Pettle. Alternative suspect pathways introduce significantly higher risk variables and lower feasibility scores."

He paused, listening to Agnes's sharp intake of breath on the other end. "In layman's terms, Agnes," he stated, the usual excitement in his voice now tempered with a grim finality, "if Ainsworth was indeed poisoned as the evidence suggests, Mildred is not just the *most likely* person to have done it from a motive perspective. From a purely logistical standpoint, she is practically the *only* person who could have executed every stage of the crime so effectively and discreetly within the Society environment." The puzzle, at least in terms of identifying the probable perpetrator and method, felt resolved in his mind. The challenge now, he knew, was finding the tangible proof that would satisfy a world operating outside the elegant certainty of his equations.

13

The Red Herring's Real Secret

Saturday morning, April 12th, brought a fragile semblance of weekend routine back to the Toorak Croquet & Horticultural Society. The sky was a vast, clear Melbourne blue, though a brisk southerly wind whipped across the lawns, sending fallen leaves skittering across the perfect turf and adding a distinct chill to the air. More members were present today, drawn by the habit of Saturday social play or the lure of simply *being seen* in the wake of the week's shocking events. A junior tournament was underway on Lawns 4 and 5, the cheerful shouts of the children and the polite applause of parents creating pockets of forced gaiety that jarred slightly against the underlying tension around the clubhouse.

And into this strained tableau walked Lord Harrington 'Harry' Smythe.

His arrival caused an immediate, perceptible shift in the atmosphere. Conversations on the verandah faltered mid-sentence. Heads turned, ostensibly to admire the view or check the time, but gazes inevitably slid towards him. He looked, Fitzwilliam noted with a sinking heart from his vantage point near the entrance, dreadful. Usually impeccably turned out, if occasionally flamboyant, today

Harry looked pale beneath his usual ruddy complexion, his eyes bloodshot and darting nervously. His expensive linen jacket was rumpled, his cravat slightly askew, and he carried himself not with his usual blustering confidence, but with the hunched, furtive energy of a man expecting a blow.

He clearly felt compelled to be here, Fitzwilliam surmised, perhaps clinging to the routine, trying desperately to project an image of normalcy, of innocence. *'Nothing to hide, carrying on as usual.'* But his execution was disastrous. Every strained attempt at nonchalance screamed anxiety. He ordered a coffee at the counter, his hand trembling slightly as he paid. He attempted a jovial greeting to Colonel Abernathy, who responded with a stiff nod and immediately turned away to examine a noticeboard with intense concentration. He tried to join a group discussing the junior tournament, only for the conversation to wither into awkward silence until he retreated, his face flushed with embarrassment and, likely, simmering resentment.

He eventually settled, isolated, at a small table at the far end of the verandah, pretending to read *The Australian* but his eyes constantly flicking up, scanning the faces around him, checking his phone, drumming his fingers restlessly on the tabletop. He looked, Fitzwilliam thought with profound dismay, exactly like a guilty man trying, and failing, to act innocent.

The surrounding members certainly interpreted it that way. Fitzwilliam could hear the low buzz of commentary resume, slightly more discreet now Harry was physically present, but no less judgemental.

"...has the *nerve* to show his face," Mrs Henderson murmured behind her hand to Penelope Cartwright, who looked torn between fascination and fear. "Brazening it out, I suppose. Doesn't he realise how it looks?"

"Guilt eating him alive," another member opined quietly nearby.

"Can barely sit still. Waiting for the police to come back for him, no doubt."

"Heard he's been trying to borrow money," someone else added, leaning in conspiratorially. "Asked Henderson Minor yesterday for a 'short-term loan'. Henderson, quite rightly, made his excuses. Trying to fund his escape, perhaps?"

Fitzwilliam felt a pang of sympathy mixed with intense frustration. He *knew* why Harry was agitated, why he needed money, why he was making tense phone calls. The gambling debts, the creditors – *that* was the source of this panic, this hunted look. Not guilt over Ainsworth's murder. But how could anyone else see that? Every action, filtered through the lens of the murder suspicion, appeared utterly damning. Harry's attempts to address his financial crisis were being universally misinterpreted as the actions of a desperate killer.

As if on cue, Harry's mobile phone buzzed insistently on the table beside his untouched coffee. He snatched it up with a start, glancing around quickly before answering, turning his chair slightly away from the clubhouse, his voice a low, urgent growl.

"Yes? What is it now?… Look, I told you, I'm working on it!… How much time do you think I have? Things are… complicated here!… No, absolutely not! Monday is impossible!… Just give me until Wednesday! I can sort it by Wednesday, I promise!… Don't threaten me! I said I'll have it!" He listened intently for another moment, his knuckles white where he gripped the phone, then ended the call abruptly, practically slamming the phone back onto the table. He scrubbed a hand over his face, looking even more pale and stressed than before.

Wednesday. Fitzwilliam filed the deadline away. Pressure intensifying. He watched Harry light a cigarette – another breach of club etiquette on the verandah, but nobody seemed inclined to challenge him today – his hand shaking noticeably as he brought it to his lips. He inhaled deeply, desperately, smoke swirling around his head in the brisk wind.

This performance, Fitzwilliam knew, was sealing Harry's fate in the court of member opinion. Even Detective Inspector Davies, professional as she was, would find it hard to ignore such overtly suspicious behaviour if it were reported back to her – and Fitzwilliam had no doubt it would be, likely embellished. He felt a rising sense of urgency to confirm Harry's financial situation definitively, not just for their own investigation's clarity, but perhaps, eventually, as a potential lifeline for Harry himself, however undeserved his current predicament felt given his foolish actions.

Then came the moment that truly solidified Harry's position as Club Pariah In Chief. The sleek, dark grey Jaguar Fitzwilliam had seen Harry speak to briefly a couple of days earlier reappeared, cruising slowly past the club entrance before pulling up just beyond the main gates on the quiet Toorak street. Harry, spotting it, visibly flinched. He stubbed out his cigarette, cast a hunted look around the verandah, then rose abruptly and walked quickly, almost furtively, down the gravel drive towards the waiting car.

Several members on the verandah made a point of watching, their expressions a mixture of disapproval and avid curiosity. Fitzwilliam moved casually towards the edge of the verandah steps, affording himself a clearer view.

Harry didn't get in the car. He stood by the driver's side window, which remained closed. He spoke rapidly, gesturing emphatically, leaning down towards the tinted glass. The driver, a silhouette within, remained impassive. After perhaps thirty seconds of this one-sided, increasingly desperate-looking monologue, the driver's window lowered just a few inches. Words were exchanged, too low for Fitzwilliam to hear, but Harry's posture suddenly crumpled.

He stepped back from the car as if struck. The window glided silently back up, and the Jaguar pulled away smoothly, leaving Harry standing alone on the pavement, looking utterly bereft, a picture of rejected desperation. He stood there for a long moment, seemingly unaware of the eyes watching him from the clubhouse, before turning slowly and walking back up the drive, his shoulders slumped, his face ashen.

"Well," Mrs Henderson declared with grim satisfaction to her audience. "If that doesn't scream 'guilty associate cutting ties', I don't know what does! Probably his getaway driver getting cold feet!"

Fitzwilliam closed his eyes briefly. It wasn't a getaway driver; it was almost certainly a creditor or their representative delivering a final warning or refusing an extension. Harry wasn't being abandoned by criminal associates; he was being squeezed by financial ones. But the optics were catastrophic. In the context of a murder investigation where he was already the prime suspect, this public display of desperation and rejection looked exactly like the behaviour of a guilty man whose world was collapsing around him.

He watched Harry re-enter the clubhouse, avoiding everyone's gaze, and head directly towards the members' bar, presumably seeking liquid solace. The hushed commentary resumed behind him, louder now, judgment passed and sentence effectively delivered by the jury of his peers. Fitzwilliam felt a profound sense of unease. Harry Smythe was drowning, pulled under by his own secrets and the tide of circumstantial suspicion, while the real predator, Fitzwilliam felt increasingly certain, watched safely from the shore, perhaps even subtly directing the currents. Confirming Harry's innocence of murder, at least to their own satisfaction, felt more urgent than ever. He needed to make those discreet inquiries about

Harry's finances, and soon.

****

Monday morning, April 14th, arrived grey and muted over Melbourne, the brief interlude of weekend sunshine already a memory. Alistair Fitzwilliam sat in the pre-dawn quiet of his Collins Street office, the city lights still glittering below like scattered jewels against the slowly lightening sky. He'd come in exceptionally early, long before the first associates arrived, needing the solitude and the secure resources of his law firm's network for a task that sat uncomfortably on the edge of professional ethics: investigating the private financial affairs of Lord Harrington Smythe.

His observations of Harry at the club on Saturday had been deeply unsettling. The man's furtive glances, his secretive phone calls, the tense encounter with the occupant of the grey Jaguar – it all screamed guilt to the casual observer, perfectly fitting the narrative the police seemed content with. But Fitzwilliam, armed with the quartet's collective doubts and Ronnie's compelling logistical analysis favouring Mildred Pettle, couldn't shake the feeling that Harry's distress stemmed from a different source. Agnes's suspicions about gambling debts, combined with overheard member gossip and Harry's own desperate attempts to borrow money, pointed strongly in that direction. Before they could definitively refocus their entire clandestine investigation onto Mildred, Fitzwilliam felt compelled, for his own peace of mind and logical rigour, to confirm the nature of Harry's secret. Was it truly just debt, or was there something more complex, something that *could* somehow intersect with Ainsworth's murder?

He logged into his workstation, the familiar glow of the screen illuminating his troubled expression. This felt wrong. Prying into a fellow club member's personal life, even one behaving as foolishly as Harry, felt like a violation. Yet, the alternative – allowing suspicion to fester around Harry, potentially letting the police build a case against him while the real killer remained hidden – felt like a greater dereliction. It was a familiar legal tightrope walk, balancing privacy against the pursuit of truth, though usually conducted within the formal bounds of discovery, not through discreet, early-morning database searches fuelled by unofficial theories about murder at a croquet club. He rationalised it as necessary due diligence for their informal inquiry, a way to eliminate a variable, but the discomfort remained.

He began with the public record, the easiest and most ethically justifiable starting point. Accessing the Victorian Courts database via AustLII, he searched for civil judgements against "Harrington Smythe" and known variations. Within minutes, the results appeared, stark and unambiguous on the screen. Several entries over the past three years. Default judgements entered for non-payment of significant credit card debts. A larger judgment obtained by a prominent Melbourne bookmaker known for extending generous credit lines to well-heeled clients, followed by subsequent enforcement orders. Another related to a personal loan from a private finance company whose interest rates likely bordered on usurious. The total sums involved were eye-watering, far exceeding what one might expect even for someone with expensive tastes living off a dwindling inheritance.

Fitzwilliam felt a wave of grim confirmation mixed with pity. So, the rumours were true. Harry wasn't just 'under pressure'; he was drowning in debt, facing aggressive creditors. This alone could explain his panic, his desperation, his furtive phone calls demanding more time. The conversation snippets Agnes and he had overheard now made perfect sense in this context.

He broadened his search, checking the Australian Securities and Investments Commission (ASIC) database for any directorships or significant shareholdings held by Smythe. Nothing recent. A few failed ventures listed from over a decade ago, companies deregistered with outstanding debts. It painted a picture not of shrewd investment, but of financial incompetence and perhaps a long-standing habit of living beyond his means.

Next, he accessed the Personal Property Securities Register (PPSR), searching for any registered security interests against assets Harry might own – cars, boats, valuable artwork. He found several recent registrations, indicating loans secured against personal assets, likely attempts to raise funds to stave off more aggressive creditors. The picture was becoming clearer: Harry was liquidating or leveraging everything he could, fighting a losing battle against mounting debts.

The grey Jaguar seen outside the club... Fitzwilliam hesitated. Trying to trace a vehicle registration felt like a step too far into private investigation territory without concrete justification related to the murder itself. But he could perhaps check the *lender* named in one of the court judgements – 'Apex Prestige Finance'. A quick search on a corporate intelligence database his firm subscribed to (used for due diligence on commercial counter parties) revealed Apex specialised in high-risk, short-term loans, often secured against luxury vehicles, and had a reputation for... robust enforcement methods. The impassive driver in the sharp suit suddenly made chilling sense. He wasn't a getaway driver; he was likely an enforcer checking on his collateral or delivering a final demand. The tense, one-sided conversation Harry had by the car window was almost certainly about impending repossession or worse.

Fitzwilliam leaned back, staring unseeingly at the screen saver's shifting geometric patterns. The evidence was overwhelming. Harry Smythe was facing imminent financial ruin. The pressure from creditors, the likely repossession of assets, the potential for public humiliation within the status-conscious world of the Society – it was more than enough to explain his extreme agitation, his furtive calls, his attempts to borrow money, his desperate demeanour. It provided a complete, self-contained explanation for *all* the behaviour members (and potentially police) were interpreting as signs of murder guilt.

Did it absolutely *disprove* he could have also killed Ainsworth in a fit of rage? No. People under extreme stress could certainly snap. But it made the murder significantly *less probable* as the primary driver of his observed behaviour. And crucially, it provided no logical link to the inconsistencies surrounding the crime scene itself – the body position, the potentially staged blow, the missing thermos, the possible poisoning vector, Ainsworth's specific historical investigations. Harry's financial crisis was a separate drama, running parallel to, but likely unconnected with, the central mystery of Ainsworth's death, except in how it tragically made him the perfect scapegoat.

Fitzwilliam felt a profound sense of relief, quickly followed by renewed determination. Harry was cleared, at least in *his* mind, and almost certainly in the context of the quartet's investigation. This wasn't just speculation anymore; it was backed by documented financial evidence. It removed the major alternative suspect and allowed them to focus their entire energy on Mildred Pettle, whose potential motives – protecting herself from exposure for long-term, calculated embezzlement and potentially historical secrets – seemed far more congruent with a premeditated, staged murder involving poison.

The ethical dilemma remained: what to do with this information about Harry? Sharing details of his private debts felt wrong. Yet, letting him remain the prime suspect while they pursued Mildred felt equally wrong. Perhaps, Fitzwilliam reasoned, the best course was to hold this information in reserve. If the police seemed ready to formally charge Harry, *then* might be the time to discreetly feed Detective Inspector Davies some verifiable information about the debts – perhaps anonymously, or through a carefully worded hint from him as someone 'aware of club dynamics' – just enough to force her to reconsider Harry's behaviour in a different light, to look again at those autopsy anomalies she'd dismissed.

For now, however, the immediate priority was clear. He needed to inform Agnes, Ronnie, and Chloe. Harry Smythe, the convenient red herring, was definitively off their list. The spotlight now fell solely, blindingly, on the quiet, efficient, and potentially deadly Club Secretary. He saved his search results to a secure, encrypted file, closed the databases, and picked up his phone, the grey morning light outside reflecting the grim clarity that had settled upon him.

****

The atmosphere in Agnes Plummett's study that Monday evening, April 14th, was markedly different from their previous tense gatherings. The frantic energy of piecing together fragmented clues had been replaced by a quieter, more focused intensity. Outside, the Melbourne drizzle had finally ceased, leaving behind streets that gleamed under the sodium glare of the streetlights and a sky beginning to show hints of clearing stars. Inside, the quartet was assembled around Agnes's large desk, the scattered papers from their previous sessions now augmented by Fitzwilliam's discreetly printed notes summarising his findings from his early morning research. A pot of fresh tea sat beside the remnants of Agnes's shortbread, a small concession to ritual amidst their irregular council of war.

Fitzwilliam, looking less anxious than usual but carrying the weight of his discoveries, cleared his throat. "Regarding Lord Smythe," he began, holding their collective gaze. "I undertook some… discreet inquiries this morning, leveraging publicly accessible records and professional databases. My aim was simply to verify or discount the rumours regarding potential financial pressures, purely to eliminate confounding variables from our own analysis." He felt the need to justify the ethical grey area, perhaps more for his own benefit than theirs.

"And?" Agnes prompted quietly, her attention absolute. Ronnie paused mid-calculation, pencil hovering over his complex timeline. Chloe leaned forward slightly, her expression reflecting a mixture of curiosity and concern for the beleaguered lord.

"And," Fitzwilliam confirmed, his voice low but firm, "the rumours are not just true; they significantly understate the reality. I found multiple default judgements entered against him in the Victorian courts over the past three years – substantial sums owed to credit card companies, private lenders, and at least one prominent Melbourne bookmaker." He detailed the figures, the names of the creditors (where public), the enforcement orders noted in the court registers.

"Furthermore," he continued, consulting his notes, "searches on the Personal Property Securities Register reveal recent security interests registered against his vehicle – likely the sports car – and potentially other personal assets. He appears to have been leveraging everything possible to raise funds. The encounter with the man in the grey Jaguar on Saturday? The vehicle is leased through a subsidiary known to handle asset recovery for 'Apex Prestige Finance', one of the private lenders who obtained a judgment against him. It seems highly probable that conversation was related to impending repossession or a final payment demand."

He described the ASIC searches revealing no current legitimate business income, only past failures. "In short," Fitzwilliam concluded, laying his notes flat on the desk, "Lord Smythe is facing imminent, potentially catastrophic, financial ruin. The pressure from creditors appears intense, the deadlines immediate – you recall his phone call mentioning a deadline of 'Wednesday'? It aligns perfectly with the typical enforcement timelines following final demands."

A profound silence filled the room, broken only by the steady tick of the grandfather clock. The picture Fitzwilliam painted was stark and unambiguous. Harry Smythe's agitation, his furtive phone calls, his desperate attempts to borrow money, his anxious pacing, his meeting with the Jaguar driver – all the behaviours that seemed so damningly like murder guilt were, in fact, textbook symptoms of severe financial distress and creditor harassment.

"So," Chloe said softly, voicing the obvious conclusion, "it wasn't about Mr Ainsworth's murder at all? His panic... it was just the money?"

"It appears overwhelmingly likely," Fitzwilliam confirmed. "While extreme stress can, theoretically, lower inhibitions," he conceded, the lawyer in him needing to acknowledge all possibilities, "the *primary driver* of the behaviour we observed, the behaviour that made him look so guilty to everyone else, is almost certainly this financial crisis, not consciousness of guilt regarding Bartholomew's death."

Ronnie nodded decisively, already adjusting variables on his probability chart. "Excellent. This removes a significant confounding factor. Smythe's erratic behaviour can be modelled as an independent variable driven by financial stress vector 'F', not directly correlated with murder event 'M'. This increases the relative probability of Hypothesis P (Pettle/Poisoning) by eliminating the primary alternative suspect driver." He sounded almost pleased by the mathematical tidiness of it.

Agnes's expression was more complex – relief tinged with pragmatic concern. "It confirms our assessment that Smythe was likely a convenient scapegoat, his known temper and now his financial desperation providing the perfect smokescreen for the real killer." She paused. "But it also presents us with a dilemma."

Fitzwilliam knew exactly what she meant. "Precisely," he sighed. "We are now reasonably certain, amongst ourselves, that Harry Smythe is innocent of murder. Yet he remains the prime suspect in the official investigation. Detective Inspector Davies likely views his financial woes, if she becomes aware of them, as *additional* motive, not an alternative explanation. Desperate men do desperate things, she might reason."

"But it's not right!" Chloe protested, her usual quietness replaced by indignation. "If he didn't do it, they shouldn't be focusing on him! We should tell Inspector Davies what you found out, Mr Fitzwilliam! Tell her about his debts!"

Fitzwilliam held up a hand. "Chloe, I understand your feelings entirely. And believe me, the thought of an innocent man potentially facing charges based on misinterpreted behaviour is... deeply troubling. However," he chose his words carefully, "we must consider the strategic implications. Firstly, how do I explain *how* I obtained detailed information about Smythe's debts without revealing ethically questionable research or compromising my professional standing? Secondly, even if I could present it anonymously, would Davies believe it? Or would she see it as an attempt by 'club insiders' to protect one of their own by muddying the waters?"

He continued, "And most importantly, if we reveal our hand now, if we show Davies we are conducting a parallel investigation and believe Smythe is innocent because we suspect *Mildred Pettle* based on theories about poison, historical finances, and coded clues... what happens? Davies, lacking concrete proof against Mildred, might dismiss us entirely. Worse, Mildred herself would be instantly alerted that we are onto her. She would redouble her defences, destroy any remaining evidence, perhaps even take steps to silence *us*. Our investigation, fragile as it is, would be dead in the water. And Harry Smythe," he concluded grimly, "would likely remain her primary shield."

Agnes nodded in agreement. "Alistair's assessment is correct, Chloe. While our sense of justice cries out for intervention on Lord Smythe's behalf, premature action could prove disastrous for uncovering the whole truth. Mildred is clearly intelligent, cautious, and, we must assume, ruthless. Alerting her now would be strategically unsound."

"So we just... let Harry twist in the wind?" Chloe asked, clearly unhappy with the conclusion.

"For now," Agnes said gently but firmly. "We monitor the situation. Alistair can keep a discreet ear open regarding the police investigation's direction. If, and only if, it appears charges against Smythe are truly imminent *and* we still lack definitive proof against Mildred, *then* we might be forced to reconsider feeding information about the debts to the police, anonymously perhaps, as a last resort to introduce reasonable doubt. But not yet. Our priority must be gathering irrefutable evidence against the person we believe is the real killer."

Ronnie, having finished adjusting his probabilities, looked up. "Logically sound. Focusing resources on the highest probability target (Pettle) is optimal. Introducing data prematurely regarding the secondary, now low-probability suspect (Smythe) risks compromising the primary objective."

Fitzwilliam felt the uncomfortable weight of their decision settle upon him. It felt cold, calculating, sacrificing one man's immediate peace of mind for the longer game. But he knew Agnes and Ronnie were right in terms of strategy. Their only chance of exposing Mildred – and, ultimately, truly exonerating Harry – lay in building an undeniable case against her before revealing their suspicions.

"Agreed, then," Fitzwilliam said heavily. "For our purposes, Harry Smythe is cleared. We proceed with the understanding that Mildred Pettle is our sole focus. All our efforts must now be directed towards finding that concrete link – the poison source, the financial trail, the meaning of Fincham's *Orchards of Progress*." He looked around the room, at the determined faces lit by the lamplight against the dark window. "And we exercise extreme caution. We are dealing with someone who has killed once and will likely not hesitate to protect herself further." The camaraderie felt stronger now, forged not just by shared discovery, but by a shared, dangerous secret and a difficult, ethically complex path forward.

****

A profound quiet settled once more in Agnes Plummett's study, but this was not the heavy silence of uncertainty or shock that had characterised their earlier meetings. It was the focused silence of minds aligning, of disparate threads being woven into a single, coherent, albeit deeply disturbing, tapestry. The ethical debate surrounding Harry Smythe's predicament, while troubling, had been necessarily parked; the Major Ferguson rumour, dissected and analysed, had been relegated to the status of inconvenient noise. With these distractions mentally cleared, the path forward, though narrow and perilous, seemed starkly illuminated, leading directly to the unassuming figure of the Club Secretary.

Agnes stood up and moved towards the large sheet of butcher's paper Ronnie had affixed to her bookshelf, which was now covered in his spidery handwriting, complex diagrams, and probability notations. She picked up a pen, her movements precise and deliberate. "Let us be absolutely clear, then," she stated, her voice calm but carrying an undeniable weight. "We are proceeding under the primary hypothesis, supported by multiple converging lines of evidence, that Mildred Pettle is responsible for the death of Bartholomew Ainsworth."

She began to list the points, ticking them off methodically on the paper, creating a stark summary of their collective findings.

"One: Motive," she wrote. "Ainsworth was conducting extensive investigations into historical club finances, specifically areas potentially involving long-term irregularities like the '87 West Wing funding and recurring Fete account discrepancies. Our research," she nodded towards Fitzwilliam and herself, "confirms these investigations were causing friction and likely threatened to expose significant, potentially criminal, financial mismanagement. Mildred Pettle, as long-serving Secretary with control over these specific accounts and records, had the most direct and powerful motive to silence him permanently to protect her position, her reputation, and potentially decades of illicit gains."

"Two: Means," Agnes continued, her pen scratching firmly. "The autopsy anomalies – inconsistent lividity suggesting postmortem movement, and the presence of an unidentified organic alkaloid – strongly support the hypothesis of poisoning followed by staging. Chloe," she looked towards the youngest member of their group, "has confirmed the presence and recent harvesting of *Digitalis purpurea*, a known source of potent cardiac alkaloid toxins, in close proximity to the crime scene. Chloe's research further confirms the toxin's suitability for administration via tea, Ainsworth's preferred beverage consumed from his personal thermos."

"Three: Opportunity," Agnes wrote next. "Ronnie's timeline analysis indicates a clear window during Ainsworth's typical lunch break in his office for the administration of a slow-acting poison via the thermos. His logistical modelling," she gestured towards Ronnie's complex diagrams, "demonstrates that Mildred Pettle, due to her routine access to all areas including Ainsworth's office, her master keys, and her ability to move around the club largely unquestioned, possessed the optimal opportunity and lowest risk profile for executing not only the administration but also the harvesting, potential processing, and subsequent disposal of crucial evidence like the thermos."

"Four: Behaviour," she added. "Mildred's actions since the discovery – her seamless performance of grief and efficiency, her subtle manipulation of conversations to reinforce the Harry Smythe narrative or introduce external red herrings, her expert deflection of direct inquiries regarding Ainsworth's research, and the potentially sanitised state of Ainsworth's office – are all consistent with a calculating individual actively managing a cover-up."

She capped her pen and stepped back, regarding the stark list. Motive, Means, Opportunity, Behaviour. All pointing, with alarming convergence, towards one person.

Fitzwilliam stared at the summary on the paper, the neat points laying out a case that, while still circumstantial in a court of law, felt overwhelmingly compelling within the confines of this room. "It's... cohesive," he admitted, the lawyer in him acknowledging the logical structure even as the reality of accusing the seemingly harmless Mildred sent a chill down his spine. "The narrative holds together far more strongly than the Smythe theory, explaining *all* the anomalies we've observed." He paused. "But the burden of proof remains immense. We need something direct. Something irrefutable."

"Precisely," Agnes agreed. "Which brings us back to our immediate tasks, now pursued with the absolute certainty that Mildred is our target." She turned back to the group, her expression becoming intensely practical. "My visit to the State Library tomorrow to examine Fincham's *Orchards of Progress* and specifically Section IV, Paragraph 12, becomes top priority. Ainsworth believed there was a connection; we must understand what it is." Her internal archivist thrilled at the prospect, even amidst the grim circumstances – the possibility that an obscure historical text held the key felt deeply appropriate to her worldview.

"The supplier checks," Fitzwilliam confirmed, making a note on his own legal pad. "WeatherTech Roofing, Vintage Marquee Hire, Bespoke Botanical Displays. I will run full ASIC registry searches and directorship checks first thing tomorrow. See if they are legitimate, who owns them, and if there are any discernible links back to Mildred or known associates." His mind briefly wrestled with the ethics of potentially using firm resources for this non-client matter, but he pushed the thought aside; the stakes felt too high now for procedural niceties.

"The *Digitalis*," Chloe affirmed, her voice quiet but steady. "I'll examine the plants again tomorrow morning during my rounds, looking for any further signs, and check the compost area and the old incinerator shed near the boundary fence for any discarded leaves, stems, or unusual residues." The thought of sifting through compost heaps wasn't appealing, but the image of Ainsworth lying amongst the rhododendrons spurred her on. She needed to find that physical link.

"Excellent," Ronnie nodded, already modifying his probability models. "And I will attempt to quantify the *minimum* amount of *Digitalis* leaf matter required to produce the trace alkaloid levels potentially detectable by VIFM, cross-referencing with standard infusion efficiencies. It might help narrow down the scale of the harvesting Chloe observed. And," he added, a glint in his eye, "I will model disposal logistics. If Mildred took the thermos off-site, what are the highest probability locations for disposal within, say, a 5 km radius, factoring in traffic patterns, bin collection schedules, and accessibility?"

Agnes almost smiled. Trust Ronnie to apply statistical modelling to rubbish disposal. "Very well," she said. "Tasks assigned. Communication remains critical – report any findings, however small, back to the group immediately via our usual secure channel," (they had established a simple encrypted messaging group after their first meeting). "And discretion," she emphasised, her gaze sweeping over them, "is more vital than ever. We are no longer simply observing inconsistencies; we are actively investigating the person we believe to be a killer. She is intelligent, observant, and potentially desperate. Do *not* underestimate her. Do not deviate from your assigned tasks without consultation. And avoid any direct confrontation or conversation that could arouse her suspicion."

They all nodded, the gravity of their undertaking settling upon them. Clearing Harry Smythe internally had removed a distraction but also eliminated their safety net. There were no other plausible suspects left on their board. It was Mildred, or their entire theory was wrong. And if it *was* Mildred, they were now consciously placing themselves in opposition to a dangerous individual deeply embedded within their own community.

Fitzwilliam felt the familiar churn of anxiety return, but this time it was tempered by a stronger current of resolve. He looked at his companions: Agnes, the formidable historian already planning her library assault; Ronnie, the brilliant physicist ready to model murder logistics; Chloe, the quiet gardener prepared to sift through compost for clues. An unlikely alliance, forged in the crucible of a croquet club murder. He still felt horribly out of his depth, a corporate lawyer tangled in a potentially deadly criminal investigation far removed from his Collins Street expertise. Yet, strangely, he also felt a sense of belonging, of shared purpose, that was entirely new.

"Well then," he said, surprising himself with the firmness in his voice. "Let's get to work."

Agnes gave a single, decisive nod. The meeting was adjourned. The hunt for direct evidence against Mildred Pettle had begun in earnest.

14

Closing the Net?

Tuesday morning, April 15th, found Agnes Plummett stepping off the Number 8 tram onto Swanston Street, her handbag containing her notebook, reading glasses, and the precious library call slip feeling heavier than usual. The grand, neoclassical facade of the State Library of Victoria loomed before her, its sandstone columns and imposing dome a familiar, comforting sight, yet today her mission lent the visit an undercurrent of profound gravity. Somewhere within these hallowed halls, amidst millions of pages documenting the history of human knowledge and endeavour, lay a potentially crucial piece of a murder puzzle – Section IV, Paragraph 12 of Alistair P. Fincham's obscure 1912 volume, *Orchards of Progress*.

She ascended the wide stone steps, bypassing the main entrance bustling with students and tourists, and made her way towards the heritage collections wing. Even after decades of library patronage, Agnes never failed to feel a sense of quiet reverence within these walls. The cool, still air, the hushed atmosphere punctuated only by the soft rustle of turning pages or the distant echo of footsteps on marble, the sheer weight of accumulated knowledge surrounding her – it was her natural element, a world of ordered information far removed from the messy, unpredictable realities of human conflict (and croquet club politics). Today, however, the usual comfort was overlaid with a layer of tense anticipation. What had Bartholomew Ainsworth found within Fincham's pages that he deemed significant enough to encode and compare to modern club finances?

Navigating the procedures for accessing heritage materials was second nature to Agnes. She filled out the request slip with the call number copied precisely from Ainsworth's hidden note, her own neat librarian's script a stark contrast to his spiky, impatient hand. She presented her reader's ticket, received a numbered buzzer, and found a seat at one of the heavy oak desks within the magnificent, domed La Trobe Reading Room. Surrounded by concentric circles of balconies lined with leather-bound volumes reaching towards the soaring skylight far above, she waited, observing the other researchers – academics hunched over manuscripts, genealogists tracing family lines, students lost in study – each immersed in their own quest for information. Her own quest felt incongruous, almost illicit, seeking clues to a murder within a century-old text on horticultural development.

After what felt like an age but was likely only twenty minutes, her buzzer vibrated silently. She proceeded to the collection desk, exchanged the buzzer for the book, and carried it carefully back to her allocated desk. *Orchards of Progress.* It was thicker than she expected, bound in sturdy but slightly scuffed dark green buckram, the title embossed in faded gold lettering on the spine. The paper was heavy, slightly brittle at the edges, and carried the distinctive dry, faintly sweet scent of old books. She opened it carefully, supporting the binding as she had been trained, her fingers tracing the dense, closely set type of the title page. *Alistair P. Fincham, Royal Historical Society of Victoria, 1912.*

She turned to the table of contents, scanning for Section IV. There it was: *"Land Valuation and Productive Yields in the Near Metropolitan Zones."* Promising. She noted the relevant page numbers and turned carefully through the preceding sections, getting a feel for Fincham's dry, academic prose, his focus on soil types, rainfall patterns, early surveying methods, and the economic viability of various fruit crops introduced by the early settlers around Melbourne. It was thorough, meticulous, and, Agnes suspected, likely unread by more than a handful of people in the last fifty years. Perfect for hiding an obscure clue, if that was Ainsworth's intent.

Finally, she reached Section IV. She read through the introductory paragraphs discussing the challenges of valuing land based on potential horticultural yield in the late 19th and early 20th centuries, the impact of expanding suburban development, the specific conditions favouring certain crops in areas like Brighton, Doncaster… and then, closer to home, the Yarra Valley corridor, including references to early estates established in the leafy areas that would eventually become suburbs like Toorak and South Yarra. Her pulse quickened slightly as she approached the page containing Paragraph 12.

She located it easily. It wasn't particularly long, perhaps two hundred words embedded within a broader discussion of experimental fruit cultivation. Agnes adjusted her spectacles and began to read, slowly, carefully, absorbing every word:

"...Furthermore, comparative analysis of yields presents challenges due to localised variations and, occasionally, inconsistencies in early record-keeping. An illustrative case involves the experimental orchard established circa 1895 on the former grazing lands adjacent to the Gardiner's Creek tributary, land subsequently subdivided but partially overlapping the parcel later acquired by the Toorak Croquet & Horticultural Society. Records pertaining to this specific experimental plot, maintained by the late Mr Silas Croft (a keen amateur pomologist), indicate remarkable performance from several heritage apple varieties. Notably, the 'Croft's

Seedling' – a local variant of Pyrus Malus – demonstrated what Croft described as a 'surprisingly consistent high yield despite variable seasonal conditions and minimal intervention'. While Croft's meticulousness regarding financial accounting was reportedly less rigorous than his botanical observations, his notes suggest the small plot generated noteworthy, albeit poorly documented, private income from seedling sales and surplus fruit provided to local markets. Compounding the difficulty in assessing the plot's true historical value are ambiguities in the initial 1888 cadastral survey maps of this specific parcel, with boundary markers near the creek frontage appearing indistinct or potentially contradictory when compared with later surveys conducted for the adjacent properties..."

Agnes read the paragraph again, then a third time, letting the pieces settle in her mind. It seemed innocuous enough – a dry historical footnote about an experimental apple orchard, a specific heritage variety named 'Croft's Seedling', inconsistent record-keeping by its owner, and some ambiguity about old property boundaries near the creek. Hardly earth-shattering. Yet Ainsworth had singled out *this* paragraph. *Pyrus Malus* wasn't just 'apple'; it was likely Ainsworth's specific code for 'Croft's Seedling'. Compare *this* paragraph with Section IV, Paragraph 12 of the Fete accounts. Why?

The connection clicked with the force of a well-struck croquet ball hitting the peg. *"...surprisingly consistent high yield despite variable seasonal conditions..."*

She thought instantly of the Fete reconciliation summaries, the ones Fitzwilliam had examined, the ones signed off by Mildred. Specifically, the line item for 'Sundry Cash Donations (Gate & On-Site)'. Those suspiciously round figures – $2500, $2750, $3000, $3250, $3500 – year after year, regardless of the weather on Fete day, regardless of fluctuating attendance numbers or the success of other stalls. A *surprisingly consistent high yield despite variable conditions.*

Ainsworth, meticulous to a fault, must have noticed the same pattern in the Fete accounts that Agnes herself had clocked. But perhaps he hadn't immediately suspected embezzlement. Perhaps, initially, he'd wondered if there was some *historical* reason for this consistency, some hidden asset or income stream connected to the club grounds themselves that somehow contributed to, or was accounted for within, the Fete takings. His research into historical land use, leading him to Fincham's book and this paragraph, might have been an attempt to understand this anomaly.

And what had he found? A reference to an old experimental apple orchard, known for its consistent high yield, located on land overlapping the club's property near the 'old orchard end'. And, crucially, *ambiguities in the initial boundary surveys* for that specific parcel.

Agnes felt a thrill course through her. This could be the link. What if that ambiguous boundary meant a small section of the original, high-yielding 'Croft's Seedling' orchard land wasn't technically part of the Society's main title deed but remained a separate, perhaps forgotten or deliberately obscured, parcel? What if Mildred Pettle, with her long tenure and intimate knowledge of club records (and potentially Silas Croft's less-than-rigorous accounting), had discovered this historical anomaly years ago? Could she have somehow used this ambiguity, this 'lost' piece of productive land (perhaps leased out informally? its produce sold?), to generate a small, consistent, off-the-books income stream? An income stream she then laundered or disguised by incorporating it into the cash takings of the Annual Garden Fete, explaining the suspiciously consistent 'donations' figure?

It was complex, audacious even. But it fitted. It explained Ainsworth's parallel investigations into historical land records *and* current Fete finances. It explained his cryptic *Pyrus Malus* note –

comparing the historical 'consistent high yield' of Croft's apples with the modern 'consistent high yield' of the Fete cash donations. It explained why he was probing near the 'old orchard end' / Lawn 3 boundary just before his death. He wasn't just looking for financial discrepancies in the present; he suspected they were rooted in a historical secret related to the land itself, a secret Mildred had potentially exploited for decades.

And the boundary dispute with Major Ferguson? That now looked even more significant. Ferguson's prized plot was *exactly* in that historically ambiguous 'old orchard end' area near the creek frontage mentioned by Fincham. Ainsworth, armed with his old maps and Fincham's text, wasn't just being pedantic about compost heaps; he was likely probing the very boundary lines that might have been crucial to Mildred's long-hidden scheme! His conflict with Ferguson wasn't just a distraction; it was Ainsworth actively digging, literally and figuratively, dangerously close to the heart of the secret.

Agnes carefully transcribed Fincham's Paragraph 12 into her notebook, along with the full book title and publication details. She felt a profound respect for Ainsworth's intellect, however grating his personality. He *had* found the connection. He had left them a coded clue, hidden where only someone with archival diligence (or perhaps a guilty conscience) might look. He had pointed towards *Pyrus Malus*, towards Section IV, Paragraph 12, linking the consistent yield of apples to the consistent yield of cash, all tied to a specific, historically ambiguous piece of land near where he met his end.

The motive against Mildred wasn't just about preventing exposure of recent embezzlement anymore. It was about protecting a potentially decades-long deception rooted in the club's very foundations, a secret intertwined with history, botany, and land ownership. No wonder the killer had acted so ruthlessly, and so carefully, to silence him and remove the evidence.

Agnes closed Fincham's book, her mind racing with the implications. She needed to share this with the others immediately. This historical context provided the missing 'why' behind Ainsworth's seemingly disparate investigations and potentially explained the scale and duration of Mildred's operation. It didn't give them the final proof they needed, but it illuminated the path forward, pointing towards old land surveys, historical club asset registers, and the financial records associated specifically with the 'old orchard end' of the Society grounds. The game, she thought grimly as she carefully returned the heritage volume to the librarian, had just become significantly deeper, rooted in secrets far older than anyone had imagined.

****

While Agnes pursued historical threads in the hallowed silence of the State Library, Alistair Fitzwilliam found himself engaged in a distinctly less romantic form of research within the climate-controlled confines of his Collins Street office that Tuesday afternoon. The initial adrenaline rush from their late-night call with Ronnie, followed by Agnes's morning breakthrough with the Fincham book, had subsided into a state of focused, almost grim, determination. The case against Mildred Pettle, built on layers of observation, deduction, and now historical context, felt compelling, almost undeniable. But Fitzwilliam, the lawyer, knew the vast difference between compelling theory and admissible proof. His task today was to probe one potential avenue towards concrete evidence: the unfamiliar supplier names he'd noted on recent large invoices signed off by Ainsworth, processed, undoubtedly, by Mildred. 'WeatherTech Roofing Solutions', 'Vintage Marquee Hire Pty Ltd', 'Bespoke Botanical Displays'. Were they legitimate businesses, or something more sinister?

He pushed aside the thick brief detailing a complex intellectual property dispute – a case involving millions of dollars that suddenly felt abstract and unimportant compared to the tangible reality of murder and potential fraud at his croquet club. He opened a fresh browser window on his large monitor, the cityscape of Melbourne sprawling beyond the glass, bathed now in the slightly harsh light of mid-afternoon. He navigated first to the Australian Securities and Investments Commission (ASIC) online portal, ASIC Connect – a familiar tool for routine corporate due diligence, but today wielded with a specific, clandestine purpose.

He started with 'WeatherTech Roofing Solutions'. He typed the name into the organisation search field. The system returned a result almost immediately: an Australian Proprietary Company, registered just eighteen months ago. Fitzwilliam frowned. That seemed rather recent for a company entrusted with major, 'urgent' roof repairs on a heritage clubhouse building. He clicked through to the details. Registered office address: a Post Office Box in Sunshine, a western suburb miles away from Toorak. Principal place of business: listed as the same PO Box. Alarm bells began to ring softly in Fitzwilliam's mind. Legitimate trades businesses, especially those handling substantial contracts, almost invariably had a physical depot, workshop, or at least a verifiable office address, not just a PO Box primarily used for mail forwarding.

He checked the listed director details. A single director/secretary named 'John Smith'. Address: a residential unit in Sunshine West. Fitzwilliam sighed inwardly. 'John Smith' – statistically common, almost anonymous. He ran a quick search on Smith through other professional databases his firm subscribed to, cross-referencing directorships. This particular John Smith appeared to hold no other current or past directorships. He seemed to exist, on paper at least, solely for this one roofing company registered to a PO Box eighteen months ago. There was no company website linked, no listing in online trade directories Fitzwilliam quickly checked. It smelled strongly of a shell company, registered perhaps by an accounting firm or company formation agent, designed to issue invoices and receive payments, but with no actual operational substance. The significant sums paid by the Society for 'Urgent Roof Repairs' had likely vanished into an account linked to this ephemeral entity, controlled by persons unknown – or perhaps, persons known only to Mildred Pettle.

Fitzwilliam meticulously saved the search results as PDF to his secure file, his initial suspicion hardening into near certainty regarding this supplier. He felt a knot of cold anger tighten in his stomach. If this was fraud, it was brazen, relying entirely on the club's trusting procedures and Ainsworth's potential oversight (or misplaced trust in Mildred's paperwork).

Next, he searched for 'Vintage Marquee Hire Pty Ltd'. This company yielded slightly different, but equally suspicious, results. It *had* been registered for longer, nearly ten years. However, its status was listed as 'Under External Administration' until just six months prior to the Centenary event deposit invoice he'd seen. It had then been apparently revived, with new directors appointed shortly before receiving the club's substantial payment. The registered office was a multi-suite address in Docklands often used by virtual office providers. The current directors? Two individuals with names Fitzwilliam didn't recognise, both listing residential addresses in interstate locations (one Queensland, one Western Australia), and neither appearing to have any other current directorships listed on ASIC.

Fitzwilliam leaned back, considering this. A previously defunct or dormant company, revived just in time to receive a large payment, with interstate directors unlikely to be actively involved in Melbourne-based marquee hire? It fit another common pattern for facilitating fraudulent transactions – acquiring an existing shelf company to provide a veneer of history, installing nominee directors, then using it to channel funds. Again, no easily found website, no current business listings under that name. The payment for 'Centenary Event Deposits' looked increasingly like money paid for services never rendered, disappearing into another carefully constructed corporate facade. He saved these results, the pattern becoming alarmingly clear.

Finally, he searched for 'Bespoke Botanical Displays'. This yielded yet another variation. The company *was* currently registered with ASIC, had been for about five years. Its principal place of business was listed as a nursery supplier address in the outer eastern suburbs – plausible, at first glance. It had a single director. Fitzwilliam typed the director's name into his search field: 'Eleanor Vance'.

He stared at the name. *Vance.* Why did that sound vaguely familiar? He mentally scanned the club membership list, committee rosters… no. Then he remembered his conversation with Agnes about Mildred Pettle's background. Mildred had joined the club secretariat over thirty years ago, a quiet, efficient widow whose origins were somewhat obscure – she rarely spoke of family, but Agnes thought she recalled Mildred mentioning she came from a small rural town in western Victoria, perhaps near the Grampians. And hadn't Agnes, during her initial archival research into Mildred's employment history, mentioned Mildred's maiden name? Fitzwilliam quickly accessed the secure notes file he shared with Agnes, searching for 'Pettle maiden name'.

There it was. *Mildred Pettle (née Vance).*

Fitzwilliam felt a jolt, like touching a live wire. Eleanor Vance, director of Bespoke Botanical Displays – the company paid a substantial deposit for Centenary floral arrangements – shared the same uncommon maiden name as Mildred Pettle. Coincidence? Possible, especially if Vance was a common name in that specific rural area. But highly suspicious. He quickly ran further searches on 'Eleanor Vance'. Found a residential address matching the company's registered office in the outer east. No other directorships listed. Minimal online presence – a basic nursery website showcasing attractive but fairly standard floral arrangements, no clear indication of capacity for large-scale event work.

Could Eleanor Vance be a relative? A sister? A cousin? Someone whose identity Mildred could use, perhaps with or without their full knowledge, to set up a company designed to receive inflated or entirely fraudulent payments from the club? It was circumstantial, yes, but it was the first potential *direct link* – however tenuous – between the suspicious financial transactions and Mildred herself.

He sat back, the pieces swirling in his mind. Two, possibly three, suppliers receiving significant club funds appeared to be shell companies or, at best, highly irregular entities. One of these entities was directed by someone sharing Mildred Pettle's maiden name. All these payments were processed and reconciled under Mildred's direct supervision, signed off by an increasingly suspicious Ainsworth who, Fitzwilliam now felt certain, must have eventually noticed these very same red flags himself, triggering his fatal deep dive.

This wasn't just about skimming cash from the Fete anymore. This suggested a potentially larger, more systematic fraud involving phantom suppliers and inflated invoices for major capital expenditures and events, running into tens, possibly hundreds, of thousands of dollars over years. The scale of it was shocking, far beyond what he'd initially imagined. Mildred wasn't just protecting a small, long-running skimming operation; she was potentially protecting a significant fraudulent enterprise. Ainsworth hadn't just stumbled onto a minor discrepancy; he'd likely uncovered systematic, large-scale theft. The motive for his murder became terrifyingly clear and compelling.

Fitzwilliam felt a mixture of elation at the discovery and profound unease. He now had concrete evidence of likely fraud – evidence that, unlike the subtle poisoning theory, *could* potentially be presented to Detective Inspector Davies. Evidence of predicate criminal activity could force her hand, compel her to broaden her investigation beyond Harry Smythe, to obtain warrants for Mildred's banking records, to follow the money trail.

But the risks remained. Presenting this now, how could he explain his targeted investigation without revealing the full extent of their unofficial inquiry, their source for the autopsy details, their overarching theory about Mildred? He still lacked the smoking gun directly linking Mildred *herself* to these companies or the flow of funds, beyond the shared maiden name which could be coincidence. And tipping off Mildred prematurely remained the greatest danger.

He carefully saved all the search results, encrypting the file. He had found crucial supporting evidence, strengthening their case against Mildred immensely by establishing a powerful, concrete financial motive linked to likely fraud she oversaw. But the final, irrefutable proof remained elusive. He needed to share this with Agnes, Ronnie, and Chloe immediately. They needed to integrate this financial fraud angle with Agnes's historical findings and Chloe's botanical evidence. The net, he felt with growing certainty, was indeed closing. But they had to be incredibly careful not to get entangled in it themselves, or alert their quarry before they could finally secure the proof needed to bring her down.

****

Late that Tuesday afternoon, with the weak Melbourne sun already beginning its descent towards the western suburbs and casting long, cool shadows across the croquet lawns, Chloe Dubois found herself venturing into the least glamorous, most neglected corner of the Toorak Croquet & Horticultural Society grounds. This was the working heart of the place, tucked away behind a screen of dense pittosporum hedging, well beyond the view of the clubhouse verandah and the pristine playing surfaces. Here stood the potting sheds, their paint peeling slightly, their interiors cluttered with terracotta pots, bags of fertiliser, and leaning ranks of bamboo stakes. Beside them slumped the large, multi-bay compost system – wooden slatted bins containing varying stages of decomposition, from fresh, damp grass clippings to rich, dark leaf mould. And further back, partially overgrown with ivy, stood the old brick incinerator, a relic from a less environmentally conscious era, its chimney cold and streaked with soot, its firebox likely home to spiders and accumulated ash.

It was not an area members frequented, save perhaps for Major Ferguson tending his adjacent, now infamous, dahlia plot. Usually, only Chloe, the head groundskeeper Henderson Jr., and occasionally energetic volunteers involved in potting or composting would venture here. Today, Chloe felt intensely aware of its isolation. The cheerful sounds of the main club – the occasional distant *thwack* of a ball, faint laughter from the bar – seemed miles away, muffled by the hedging and the sheds. Here, the dominant sounds were the rustle of leaves in the slight breeze, the damp sigh of the compost heaps, and the frantic beating of her own heart.

She carried a three-pronged cultivator fork, ostensibly to turn over the contents of the active compost bay, a perfectly legitimate end-of-day task. But her real purpose was far grimmer. Following the quartet's discussion the previous evening, fuelled by the confirmation of the harvested foxgloves near Lawn 3, this area represented the most logical place for someone to have discreetly processed poisonous plant matter or disposed of the evidence – including, perhaps, Bartholomew Ainsworth's missing thermos flask, though finding that felt like a remote possibility.

She started with the compost bins, wrinkling her nose slightly at the earthy, fermenting smell. There were three main bays: one holding fresh green waste from recent mowing and pruning, one containing older, partially decomposed material, and the third holding mature, usable compost. Where would someone hide incriminating plant waste? Not in the mature bay, surely – too likely to be dug into soon by gardeners needing soil amendment. The fresh bay? Possible, but things added there remained visible for some time. The middle bay, the one undergoing active decomposition, seemed the most likely candidate – waste added there would be quickly covered by subsequent additions and broken down by heat and microbial action.

Trying to look like she was merely aerating the pile, Chloe began to systematically turn over the top layers of the middle bay with her fork. Grass clippings, wilted flowers, coffee grounds from the clubhouse kitchen, twigs, vegetable peelings from some long-forgotten staff lunch… the usual detritus of club life. She worked her way down, layer by layer, the task unpleasantly damp and odorous. Her eyes scanned constantly for anything out of place, specifically wilted or crushed leaves resembling the *Digitalis* she'd examined near Lawn 3. She knew the glycosides themselves were relatively stable and could persist during composting, but finding identifiable leaf fragments felt crucial.

After nearly twenty minutes of methodical, increasingly dis-heartening work, turning over perhaps the top half-metre of the decomposing pile, she found nothing beyond the expected garden and kitchen waste. No suspicious bundles of leaves, no broken glass from potential infusion jars, no sign of the missing thermos. Perhaps the killer had been more thorough, burning the evidence or taking it entirely off-site?

She paused, leaning on her fork, catching her breath. She glanced towards the old incinerator. Could someone have burned the leaves and the thermos there? Unlikely it was still in active use, but people sometimes burned dry waste or confidential papers illicitly. She walked over, the ground damper here, shaded by an overhanging bottlebrush tree. The heavy cast-iron door was stiff but opened with a rusty groan. Inside, the firebox was filled with cold, grey ash, mixed with charred fragments of paper and unidentifiable debris. Using a stick, Chloe carefully raked through the top layers of ash. Nothing metallic like a thermos buckle or base. Nothing suggesting recently burned green matter. Just old, cold ash.

However, as she stirred, her stick dislodged something small from a crevice in the brickwork just inside the firebox door, something that glinted faintly in the dim light filtering through the trees. She knelt down, heart pounding again. It wasn't metal. It was a shard of thick, slightly greenish glass, about the size of her thumbnail. Smooth on one side, rough where it had broken on the others. It looked like a fragment from a sturdy jar or perhaps an old-fashioned beaker. It certainly didn't belong among the ashes. She picked it up carefully with a gloved hand (she always wore gloves for composting). Holding it up to the light, she sniffed cautiously. Was that a faint, sharp, almost chemical smell? Or just the general odour of cold ash and damp brick? She couldn't be sure. But it felt… wrong. Out of place. Why would a piece of broken glass jar be *inside* the incinerator? Unless someone had tried to destroy it by burning, assuming the heat would melt or shatter it beyond recognition? Could it be from a container used to make the *Digitalis* infusion? She carefully placed the shard into another clean specimen bag. More circumstantial evidence, perhaps, but another anomaly.

She turned her attention back to the compost, specifically the middle bay again. If someone wanted to hide something *really* well, they wouldn't just toss it on top. They'd bury it deeper, perhaps near the bottom or sides where turning was less frequent. She started working around the edges of the bay, plunging the fork deeper, lifting sections of the heavy, steaming material. It was strenuous, unpleasant work.

Then, near the back corner, about a metre down, her fork snagged on something soft but fibrous. Not the usual texture of grass clippings or rotting leaves. She carefully dug around it with her hands, pulling away the surrounding waste. Her breath caught. It was a small bundle of leaves, wilted, slightly crushed, and starting to decompose, but unmistakably the distinctive shape and downy texture of *Digitalis purpurea*. There were maybe half a dozen leaves, hastily bundled or perhaps just dumped together, pushed deep into the decomposing matter, well below the surface layer. They were damp and starting to blacken, but their identity was clear.

This was it. Physical proof. Someone hadn't just harvested the foxglove leaves; they had deliberately attempted to dispose of excess or processed leaves by burying them deep within the active compost heap, presumably hoping they would quickly rot down into anonymity. This wasn't accidental; this was concealment.

Her hands trembled slightly as she carefully lifted the decomposing bundle using her fork, trying not to break it apart further. She placed it gently into another specimen bag, labelling it mentally:

Digitalis leaves, recovered Bay 2 Compost, approx. 1m depth, 15th April.

This felt huge. Far more significant than the glass shard. This directly linked the poisonous plant, harvested near the crime scene, to a deliberate act of concealment in a relatively secluded part of the grounds.

She quickly raked the compost back into place, trying to make the area look undisturbed. She glanced around nervously. Had anyone seen her? Barnaby was no longer visible near the sheds. Henderson Jr. was likely working on the far lawns. She seemed to be alone. But the feeling of isolation now felt less comforting and more vulnerable. She had found tangible evidence pointing directly towards the secret preparation and disposal of poison. If the killer, Mildred perhaps, ever suspected Chloe was searching here…

Clutching her specimen bags containing the glass shard and the precious, decomposing leaves, Chloe quickly gathered her tools and retreated from the utility area, forcing herself to walk calmly, normally, back towards the main clubhouse, trying to ignore the frantic thudding of her heart. She had unearthed more than just garden waste; she had unearthed confirmation, physical evidence that shifted their investigation onto firmer, if far more dangerous, ground. The shadows in the Society's garden were indeed botanical, and she now held a decaying fragment of their poisonous heart.

✳✳✳✳

The study in Agnes Plummett's apartment felt charged that Tuesday evening, crackling with an energy that had little to do with the clearing weather outside or the fresh pot of strong Assam tea Agnes had just brewed. The air hummed with the suppressed excitement of shared discovery, the intellectual thrill of disparate puzzle pieces locking definitively into place. Spread across Agnes's large desk, illuminated under the focused beam of the banker's lamp, lay the tangible results of their separate inquiries: Agnes's meticulous transcriptions from Fincham's *Orchards of Progress*, Fitzwilliam's printouts detailing suspiciously ephemeral roofing and marquee companies, and two carefully sealed specimen bags placed on a clean napkin by Chloe – one containing a shard of greenish glass, the other a small, decomposing bundle of dark green leaves.

They had gathered almost immediately after Chloe returned from the club grounds, each sensing the significance of the day's efforts. Now, they took turns presenting their findings, the narrative building with each contribution, weaving together history, finance, and botany into a single, chilling tapestry.

Agnes went first, detailing her visit to the State Library and her analysis of Section IV, Paragraph 12 in Fincham's book. She explained the *Pyrus Malus* connection – not just apples, but likely Ainsworth's code for the 'Croft's Seedling' variety noted for its 'surprisingly consistent high yield despite variable conditions', grown on land overlapping the club's 'old orchard end'. "And crucially," Agnes emphasised, tapping her notes, "Fincham explicitly mentions 'ambiguities in the initial 1888 cadastral survey maps of this specific parcel'. Ainsworth wasn't just comparing apple yields to Fete profits metaphorically; he likely suspected a *direct link*. That the consistent 'yield' in the Fete donation figures Mildred controlled was somehow tied to this historically ambiguous, potentially income-generating piece of land near where he died, a secret documented perhaps only in the oldest records he and Fincham consulted."

Fitzwilliam listened intently, the implications clicking into place. "So the boundary dispute with Major Ferguson wasn't just Ainsworth being difficult about compost heaps," he interjected, "it was potentially Ainsworth probing the very piece of land central to this historical anomaly? Good Lord. No wonder Ferguson was apoplectic, but perhaps Ainsworth had a deeper motive than simple pedantry."

"Precisely," Agnes confirmed. "It suggests his investigation was multi-layered, connecting past land use secrets to present financial irregularities."

Fitzwilliam then presented his own findings, laying out the ASIC search results for the three suspicious suppliers. He detailed the red flags: WeatherTech Roofing's recent registration and PO Box address; Vintage Marquee Hire's revival from dormancy with inter-state nominee directors; and, most damningly, Bespoke Botanical Displays. "Registered five years ago," Fitzwilliam explained, his voice tight with controlled anger, "director listed as 'Eleanor Vance'. And Mildred Pettle's maiden name," he paused for effect, meeting their eyes, "was Vance."

A collective intake of breath. "Her sister? Cousin?" Chloe whispered.

"Possibly. Or perhaps just someone whose name she could use, residing far enough away not to attract local attention," Fitzwilliam speculated. "Regardless, the pattern is undeniable. These companies bear all the hallmarks of shell corporations, likely used to issue fraudulent invoices for services possibly never rendered, or grossly inflated. Payments processed and reconciled," he added pointedly, "by Mildred Pettle, and signed off by Ainsworth, likely on the basis of Mildred's summaries." He detailed the substantial sums involved based on the invoices he'd seen previously. "This wasn't just skimming a few dollars from the Fete cash box. This suggests systematic fraud involving tens, possibly hundreds, of thousands of dollars."

Ronnie, who had been furiously adding nodes and links to his chart on the butcher's paper, looked up. "Motive strength increases exponentially!" he declared. "Protecting large-scale, long-term fraud provides far greater statistical impetus for extreme risk mitigation – i.e., murder – than minor skimming or historical embarrassment alone."

Finally, Chloe recounted her grim discoveries near the compost heaps and the old incinerator. She described finding the shard of greenish glass – "Possibly from a jar used for infusion? It had a faint, strange smell," – and then, the deliberately buried bundle of wilted *Digitalis* leaves. She carefully pushed the specimen bag containing the leaves towards the centre of the table under the lamplight. Even in their decaying state, the shape was unmistakable.

"Physical evidence," Agnes breathed, peering at the bag. "Confirmation of *Digitalis* being handled, concealed, on the grounds recently. Not proof of *who*, not yet. But tangible."

Ronnie nodded vigorously. "Consistent with Hypothesis P, step D: Disposal. Killer processes leaves, needs to dispose of excess material and potentially contaminated equipment residue. Compost heap provides viable concealment with accelerated decomposition. Incinerator shard suggests attempt at thermal destruction of glassware? Both fit within Mildred Pettle's logistical capability pathway."

They fell silent again, absorbing the combined weight of the day's discoveries. The historical context providing deep-rooted motive linked to land secrets. The phantom suppliers providing evidence of large-scale financial fraud and the *mechanism* of extraction. The buried leaves providing physical evidence related to the *means* of murder – the poison itself. Each finding, powerful on its own, became almost irrefutable when woven together.

"It's her," Fitzwilliam stated quietly, voicing the conclusion that now felt undeniable. "It has to be Mildred. The motive, the specific means suggested by the autopsy and Chloe's findings, the opportunity highlighted by Ronnie's timeline and logistical analysis, the pattern of financial control and potential fraud I uncovered, the historical context Agnes found… it all converges on her with overwhelming probability."

"Agreed," Agnes said firmly. "The circumstantial case is exceptionally strong. Far stronger than the case against Lord Smythe ever was."

"So what now?" Chloe asked, looking between them, her earlier fear now overshadowed by a sense of urgent purpose. "We know it was her. How do we prove it?"

"Proof," Fitzwilliam sighed, the familiar legal hurdle looming large. "That's the crux. We have motive, means, opportunity, logistics… but we lack the final, definitive link. The 'smoking gun', so to speak."

"We need something that connects Mildred *personally* and *irrefutably* to one critical part of the chain," Agnes elaborated, picking up her planning notebook again. "Something beyond circumstantial inference."

They began brainstorming, the energy shifting from discovery to focused strategy.

"The money trail," Fitzwilliam mused. "If we could show funds moving from those shell company accounts directly to Mildred, or to pay for assets she couldn't otherwise afford… but accessing her personal bank records requires warrants, which Detective Inspector Davies won't seek based on our current evidence."

"The poison source," Chloe suggested. "Could we find her fingerprints on the *Digitalis* plants? Unlikely after the rain, and gloves were probably used. What about purchasing records for any chemicals needed for extraction, if she used a refined method? Or," she added, thinking of her other find, "the grey suede glove I found near the footprint? If we could somehow match it to her…"

"Difficult and risky," Agnes cautioned. "Searching her belongings is impossible. Perhaps discreet observation – does she wear similar gloves? Own similar items?"

"The disposal," Ronnie offered. "The thermos is gone. But the glass shard Chloe found… potentially traceable? Unique type of glass? And the buried leaves – perhaps the *way* they were buried, the tool used, could offer a clue if linked back to a tool Mildred uses?" Highly speculative, they all knew.

"The *Pyrus Malus* clue," Agnes added, tapping the library slip. "I need to fully understand the connection Ainsworth made. Does Fincham's Paragraph 12 offer more than just the 'consistent yield' metaphor? Does it reference a specific event, person, or map that could unlock records Mildred *doesn't* control, perhaps old council records or land title documents related to that boundary?"

Their next steps became clearer, focusing on finding that elusive direct link.

1. **Agnes:** Fully analyse the Fincham text and pursue related historical land/council records based on the boundary ambiguity and *Pyrus Malus* connection. Try to find external documentation Mildred couldn't control or sanitise.
2. **Fitzwilliam:** Continue digging into the shell companies. See if any director names or addresses yield further connections, however tenuous. Consider ways to *legitimately* prompt scrutiny of those specific club payments without revealing their hand entirely.
3. **Chloe:** Continue monitoring the *Digitalis* plants and the disposal sites. Try to identify the brand/type of the grey glove. Discreetly observe Mildred's gardening habits or attire, if any.
4. **Ronnie:** Refine logistical models. Research forensic techniques for tracing trace alkaloids or glass fragments. Provide ongoing analysis of time/opportunity related to any new findings.

"The net is tightening," Agnes stated, her voice low and serious as she surveyed their determined faces. "We have moved from possibility to high probability. But she knows we spoke to Abercrombie, she knows Fitzwilliam is looking at accounts, she likely knows *someone* is asking questions. She will be on her guard. From this point forward, the danger increases significantly. We must be more careful than ever."

Fitzwilliam nodded grimly. "We need proof strong enough to overcome her facade and force Detective Inspector Davies to act, before Mildred realises how much we know, or," he paused, the unspoken thought hanging heavy, "before she decides to silence us as she silenced Bartholomew."

The quartet looked at each other, the shared understanding hardening their resolve. They were closing in, but the final steps would be the most perilous. The hunt for the smoking gun was on.

15

The Shadow Lengthens

The hushed, studious atmosphere of the State Library of Victoria's Map Reading Room offered Agnes Plummett a welcome, if temporary, respite from the emotionally charged environment of the Croquet Club. Here, amidst the oversized tables, specialised viewing equipment, and the quiet concentration of fellow researchers tracing property lines, planning routes, or exploring geographical history, the grim reality of murder felt momentarily distant, replaced by the familiar, absorbing challenge of navigating historical records. Yet, the purpose of her visit – to dissect the very land upon which Bartholomew Ainsworth had met his end – lent a chilling undercurrent to the academic exercise.

She had returned this Thursday morning, April 17th, armed with the knowledge gleaned from Fincham's *Orchards of Progress* and a specific list of historical survey maps and associated land title documents pertaining to the Society's property, particularly the problematic western boundary adjacent to Gardiner's Creek. Her request, submitted the previous afternoon, had been processed, and now, laid out carefully on the vast expanse of a dedicated map table beneath focused overhead lighting, were the tangible ghosts of Toorak's past: fragile, linen-backed cadastral maps from the late nineteenth and early twentieth centuries.

The centrepiece was the 1888 survey Fincham had specifically referenced. Agnes handled it with extreme care, its century-and-a-half old paper brittle, the hand-drawn ink faded but still precise. She located the relevant parcel – Section B, Allotments 15 through 18, Parish of Prahran – land acquired by the burgeoning Society in the early 1920s. Using a large magnifying glass provided by the library, she traced the boundaries. As Fincham noted, the northern, eastern, and southern lines were clearly demarcated, referencing established roads and neighbouring property pegs. But the western boundary, abutting the meandering path of the Gardiner's Creek tributary, was indeed rendered with less certainty.

The surveyor's notes, written in elegant but occasionally challenging copperplate script, indicated the boundary followed the 'Approx. High Water Mark (1887)'. Agnes frowned. Creek lines change. Banks erode. Basing a permanent boundary on such a potentially fluid feature was inherently problematic, a known issue in many early Melbourne surveys. Furthermore, a key reference point was marked simply as 'Large River Gum (Scarred) near Bend'. No precise coordinates, no distance measurements from other fixed points. Just a vaguely described tree near a bend in a creek whose path likely shifted over time. It was, from a modern surveying perspective, woefully inadequate, creating exactly the kind of ambiguity Fincham had described.

She then carefully unrolled the subsequent survey map, dated 1910, covering the same area after some initial subdivisions had occurred nearby. She compared the western boundary depiction. It still referenced the creek line, though the notation now read 'Mean High Water Mark (Est. 1909)'. Had the creek shifted? Had the estimation method changed? Impossible to tell precisely from this document alone. And the 'Scarred Gum'? It was no longer explicitly marked, replaced by calculated bearings from slightly more distant, possibly more stable, reference points shown on adjacent, newly subdivided lots. Had the original tree gone by then? Or had the new surveyor simply chosen different reference markers?

Critically, comparing the overlay of the two maps revealed the potential discrepancy: that small, irregular sliver of land nestled between the estimated 1888 boundary (following the high water mark and the vague gum tree reference) and the slightly different alignment suggested by the 1910 survey and the formalised boundaries of the neighbouring parkland established later. This was the 'old orchard end', the area Fincham associated with Silas Croft's high-yielding *Pyrus Malus* experiments. Its legal status, caught between the shifting creek, the vanished tree, and inconsistent survey practices spanning decades, appeared genuinely ambiguous. It could arguably belong to the Society, or the adjacent park, or potentially remain unallocated Crown land, or even, theoretically, still be tied to remnants of Croft's original (likely long-extinguished) title, depending on how the original grants and subsequent transfers were interpreted.

Agnes felt a thrill of understanding, the satisfaction of confirming Ainsworth's likely research path. He hadn't just been reading Fincham for historical colour; he'd used it to pinpoint a specific, verifiable anomaly in the foundational records of the Society's own property. An anomaly located precisely at the 'old orchard end', adjacent to Ferguson's dahlias and the rhododendron bed.

Her mind immediately jumped to the implications, specifically regarding Mildred Pettle. How could such an ambiguity be exploited? Direct sale or development seemed unlikely given the probable planning overlays and the Society's own interests. But what about leasing? Could Mildred, perhaps discovering this anomaly years ago (maybe during her temporary secretarial work in the late 80s assisting Humphrey Carmichael, who might have been aware of the issue but preferred not to address it?), have arranged a discreet, long-term, perhaps even undocumented, lease of this ambiguous sliver of land? Perhaps for grazing, small-scale nursery use, or even just storage, generating a modest but steady private income stream entirely off the Society's official books? An income stream she could then potentially launder through the Fete's cash takings, explaining the 'surprisingly consistent high yield'?

It fitted perfectly. It explained Ainsworth's twin focus on historical land records *and* current Fete finances. It provided a concrete, long-term financial motive for Mildred, potentially far exceeding simple expense padding or minor skimming. It placed the source of the conflict squarely in the geographical area where Ainsworth met his end. He must have found this boundary discrepancy, perhaps cross-referenced it with Fincham or old council rate maps, understood its potential for illicit exploitation, and started looking for the corresponding financial evidence in the Fete accounts, leading him directly to Mildred's manipulation.

Agnes began making meticulous notes, sketching the disputed boundary section, referencing the map numbers and Fincham's paragraph. This was more solid than mere speculation; it was grounded in historical documentation. Proof of Mildred *exploiting* the ambiguity was still missing, but proof the ambiguity *existed* and that Ainsworth was likely investigating *it*, was now clearly established in Agnes's mind.

As she worked, hunched over the large map under the bright lamp, she became aware again of that faint prickle of unease from her previous visit. A sense of being observed. She subtly lifted her head, her gaze sweeping peripherally across the large, quiet reading room. Most researchers were absorbed in their own documents.

The librarians conferred quietly behind the main desk. But then her eyes snagged on him again – the same man from yesterday. Tweed jacket, nondescript features, ostensibly examining a large atlas on a stand near the room's entrance. He wasn't looking directly at her this time, but his posture seemed… watchful. Oriented slightly towards her section of the room, lingering perhaps longer than necessary over a map of South America.

Coincidence? Almost certainly. The library was a public space. Researchers often looked around. He probably hadn't even noticed her specifically. Yet… the feeling persisted. Amplified, perhaps, by the nature of her own research, the knowledge that she was deliberately probing into matters someone might wish to keep hidden. Was it possible? Could Mildred, feeling the net tighten after Ainsworth's death and perhaps aware of the quartet's discreet inquiries (via club gossip, or even direct observation?), have taken steps to monitor their activities? Hiring a private investigator seemed extreme, almost melodramatic for Mildred's careful style. But perhaps an associate? Someone connected to the phantom companies Fitzwilliam was investigating? Someone tasked with simply observing, reporting back on who was accessing what records?

Agnes forced herself to remain calm, turning back to her notes, her outward demeanour betraying nothing. She would not be intimidated. But the possibility added a new, chilling dimension to their task. If Mildred *was* aware of their scrutiny, even vaguely, then every move they made – Agnes's library visits, Fitzwilliam's corporate searches, Chloe's examinations of the garden – carried an additional layer of risk. They weren't just solving a puzzle; they might be actively stalked by its most dangerous piece.

She finished her note-taking, carefully rolled the precious maps, and prepared to return them. As she walked towards the collection desk, she allowed her gaze to sweep casually towards the entrance again. The man in the tweed jacket was gone. Had he left while she was focused on her notes? Or had he simply moved on, his presence entirely innocent? She couldn't be sure. But the encounter, real or imagined, left a residue of fear that mingled unpleasantly with the intellectual satisfaction of her discoveries. The shadows were indeed lengthening, potentially extending far beyond the familiar confines of the Toorak Croquet & Horticultural Society. She clutched her notebook tightly as she exited the library into the uncertain Melbourne afternoon, feeling more exposed than she had before entering its protective walls.

****

While Agnes Plummett wrestled with the historical implications of ambiguous boundaries and heritage apples at the State Library, Alistair Fitzwilliam, back in the contrasting modernity of his Collins Street office, was engaged in the digital equivalent: sifting through the carefully constructed facades of corporate entities. The Melbourne cityscape spread out beyond his window, familiar towers catching the oblique rays of the mid-afternoon sun, traffic beginning its slow crawl towards the evening peak. But Fitzwilliam's focus was entirely internal, directed at the glowing screen before him where the dry data held within ASIC Connect and other databases might contain the key to unravelling the Society's deadly secrets.

He'd already confirmed his suspicions about 'WeatherTech Roofing Solutions' and 'Vintage Marquee Hire Pty Ltd'. The first, registered scant weeks before invoicing the club for major work, operating solely from a PO Box in Sunshine under the ubiquitous moniker 'John Smith', screamed 'shell company'. The second, a resurrected dormant entity with absentee interstate directors and a virtual office address, looked equally purpose-built for processing a single, large, likely fraudulent payment. These findings alone pointed towards significant financial irregularity occurring under Mildred Pettle's administrative watch, providing a powerful motive for silencing anyone, like Ainsworth, who started scrutinising the details too closely. But Fitzwilliam knew proving Mildred *benefited* from these phantom suppliers was the real challenge. He needed a link, however tenuous.

His focus now shifted entirely to the third entity: 'Bespoke Botanical Displays', the company contracted for Centenary Gala flowers, directed by one Eleanor Vance – sharing Mildred Pettle's maiden name. This felt like the most promising lead, the potential weak point in Mildred's carefully constructed financial armour.

He pulled up the ASIC record again. Sole director: Eleanor Vance. Principal Place of Business and Registered Office: An address in Ferntree Gully. He accessed the Landata system, Victoria's online land registry portal, entering the Ferntree Gully address. The title search confirmed ownership under the name Eleanor Mary Vance, purchased outright (no mortgage listed, interestingly, though that wasn't conclusive) nearly fifteen years ago. A legitimate address, tied to the director. He then checked the ABN Lookup. 'Bespoke Botanical Displays', ABN registered five years ago, GST registered, industry classification 'Floriculture Production (Under Cover)' and 'Nursery Production'. On the surface, it looked more legitimate than the other two suppliers. A small, owner-operated business perhaps, run by Mildred's relative from her supposed hometown region (Ferntree Gully wasn't quite western Victoria, but perhaps close enough for Mildred's vague recollections?).

Could it be innocent favouritism? Mildred steering a contract towards a sister or cousin running a small nursery? Possibly. It wouldn't be the first time such things happened in clubland. But the amount – a substantial deposit for bespoke displays for a major gala – seemed large for a small nursery with minimal online presence. And why *this* specific company, when several well-established, high-profile Melbourne florists usually vied for Society events? And why the shared maiden name connection, something Mildred, if entirely innocent, might have felt obliged to declare as a potential conflict of interest under club rules? Ainsworth, the pedant, would surely have queried such a connection if he'd known. Had Mildred obscured it?

Fitzwilliam needed more on Eleanor Vance herself. He ran broader searches – electoral roll history, any other linked business names (past or present), court appearances. Nothing significant emerged under that name linked to Melbourne addresses or obvious connections to Mildred Pettle's known South Yarra residence. He hit the familiar wall of public record limitations. Proving a direct financial or personal link between Mildred Pettle and Eleanor Vance, beyond the shared maiden name, seemed impossible without access to private information – bank records, correspondence, family histories.

Frustration began to gnaw at him. He had strong evidence of likely fraud involving two suppliers, strong suspicion regarding the third due to the name link, a powerful motive for Mildred, and supporting evidence from the autopsy anomalies and Chloe's findings. Yet the crucial connector – the proof Mildred orchestrated or benefited from this – remained elusive. It felt like constructing a complex legal argument with the final, concluding paragraph missing.

His intercom buzzed sharply, making him jump. "Alistair?" It was Marcus, a senior partner from the litigation team down the hall. "Got five minutes to sanity-check this appeal submission before it goes to print? Counsel's querying our interpretation of Section 52 liability post-ASIC v Kobelleat."

Fitzwilliam glanced at the clock. Nearly 4 PM. He had spent

hours on this unofficial investigation, neglecting the mounting pile of billable work related to Macrocorp and other demanding clients. "Ah, Marcus," he stalled, quickly minimising the ASIC search window. "Bit tied up right now. Can it possibly wait until morning?"

"Needs to go tonight, mate," Marcus replied cheerfully, oblivious. "Just need your eagle eye on paragraph 37."

"Right," Fitzwilliam sighed. "Give me fifteen minutes." He ended the call, feeling a surge of resentment at the intrusion, quickly followed by guilt at his own clandestine activities. He *should* be focusing on Macrocorp. He *should* be delegating this Society business to the police, however flawed their apparent focus. But he couldn't shake the conviction that they, the quartet, were onto something vital, something the official investigation was missing entirely.

He returned to his screen, determined to try one last avenue before tackling Marcus's appeal submission. The historical angle. Agnes had mentioned Mildred's long tenure, potentially stretching back decades. Fitzwilliam himself had confirmed Ainsworth's own past compromise related to the '87 West Wing donation. Could the name 'Vance' appear anywhere else in the club's accessible historical records, specifically around that controversial period?

He accessed the digitised archive index Agnes had discreetly shared with him – a compilation of key committee minutes, annual reports, and newsletters spanning decades. He initiated a keyword search: "Vance".

Several irrelevant hits appeared – references to member sporting achievements, mentions in social pages. Then, one entry stood out, flagged from the scanned House Committee minutes, dated February 1988. He clicked the link, the digitised image of the typed page appearing on his screen, slightly faded but perfectly legible.

His eyes scanned down the routine business – approval of previous minutes, correspondence, catering report… then, under 'Staffing Matters':

"Item 6. Treasurer's Office Assistance. Mr H. Carmichael reported on the increased workload associated with finalising the West Wing Extension accounts and preparing for the annual audit. Proposed engaging temporary secretarial assistance for a short period. Moved: Mr G. Henderson Sr. Seconded: Mrs Albright. Resolved: To approve temporary secretarial assistance for Treasurer (H. Carmichael) during annual audit period. Miss E. Vance appointed on casual basis for 4 weeks, commencing Feb 15th, 1988."

Fitzwilliam stared at the screen, his breath catching in his throat. *Miss E. Vance.* Appointed temporary secretarial assistance. To the Treasurer. During the audit period. In February 1988.

This was *immediately* after the controversial anonymous $50,000 donation had been accepted (late 1987) to cover the final shortfall on the extension project – the very donation Ainsworth had harboured reservations about, the one Agnes had rediscovered in her journals. This 'Miss E. Vance' had been working directly with Treasurer Humphrey Carmichael precisely when the potentially problematic final accounts for that controversial project were being formalised and audited.

Could 'E. Vance' be Eleanor Vance, director of Bespoke Botanical Displays? Perhaps a much younger woman then? Or, more chillingly, could 'E. Vance' have been Mildred Pettle herself, using her maiden name (perhaps she wasn't widowed yet, or preferred it professionally at that stage)? Agnes had mentioned Mildred's origins and early history at the club were somewhat vague. Could she have had this earlier, temporary role before securing her permanent position as Club Secretary later on?

The implications were staggering. If Mildred (or a close relative using her family name) was directly involved in processing the accounts for the West Wing extension *after* that suspicious anonymous donation came through, it placed her at the heart of the very historical irregularity Ainsworth seemed to be investigating. It provided a potential start date for her intimate knowledge of, and perhaps direct involvement in manipulating, the Society's financial records, stretching back over thirty-five years. It suggested the recent phantom supplier scheme wasn't a new venture, but potentially the latest evolution of a much older pattern of deception.

Fitzwilliam felt a wave of dizziness. This wasn't just about covering up recent fraud anymore. This was potentially about protecting a secret embedded deep in the club's history, a secret Mildred might have been involved in – or at least aware of and benefiting from – since 1988. Ainsworth hadn't just threatened her current illicit income; he'd threatened to unravel her entire history at the club, potentially exposing not just her, but others involved in that original West Wing funding cover-up. The motive for murder had just acquired a powerful historical dimension.

He quickly saved a copy of the 1988 minutes page, his hands trembling slightly now. This felt different from the supplier searches. This felt like finding a hidden inscription on a foundation stone, revealing a crack that ran through the entire structure. It still wasn't proof of murder. It wasn't even definitive proof of financial fraud, past or present. But it was a deeply suspicious, historically significant connection between Mildred Pettle (via the Vance name) and the very financial controversies Ainsworth was killed investigating.

He needed to tell Agnes immediately. This historical link power-fully corroborated her own findings from the Fincham book and the boundary research. Their separate threads were weaving together into an increasingly damning indictment. He glanced at the clock. 4:15 PM. He still had Marcus's appeal submission to review. But the complexities of Section 52 liability suddenly seemed utterly trivial compared to the dark, tangled history apparently lurking beneath the placid surface of the Toorak Croquet & Horticultural Society.

****

The shadows were already pooling deep and cool in the utility corner behind the pittosporum hedge when Chloe Dubois found herself drawn back, almost against her better judgment. It was late Thursday afternoon, nearly the end of her shift. The main clubhouse was relatively quiet; most of the Saturday social players hadn't arrived yet, and the weekday regulars had largely departed. Logically, she knew she should be packing up her tools, heading home to the relative anonymity of her Richmond apartment. But the discoveries of the past few days – the harvested foxgloves, the buried leaves, the potentially fraudulent suppliers, the historical complexities unearthed by Agnes – churned restlessly in her mind. The need for *more*, for something definitive, something that couldn't be explained away, felt like a physical ache.

Perhaps, she reasoned, she had missed something near the compost heaps yesterday in her haste and anxiety. Perhaps the glass shard near the incinerator warranted closer inspection of the surrounding ash or brickwork. Perhaps there was something near the potting sheds – discarded packaging, a forgotten tool – that might connect to the processing of the *Digitalis*. She told herself she was just being thorough, double-checking the area while it was quiet, using the last dregs of the day's light. She carried a bucket and trowel, ostensibly to collect some mature leaf mould from the finished compost bay for potting up seedlings tomorrow – a perfectly plausible task.

The air here felt heavy, damp, thick with the scent of decay and wet earth from the previous night's rain. The dripping from the shed roof gutter provided a slow, irregular percussion against the profound quiet. Even the distant sounds of Toorak traffic seemed muted back here. It felt like a liminal space, disconnected from the manicured elegance just metres away. Chloe shivered, despite the lingering humidity. Was it the cooling air, or the chilling nature of her suspicions?

She forced herself towards the middle compost bay first, where she'd found the buried leaves. Trying to appear casual, she knelt beside it, pretending to assess the texture of the compost near the top. Her eyes, however, scanned the ground around the base, looking for any other signs of disturbance, anything overlooked. Nothing. She ran her gloved hand lightly over the surface of the compost where she'd dug yesterday, confirming her efforts to disguise the spot had held. Satisfied on that front, she moved towards the old brick incinerator.

She knelt again, examining the cold ashes within the firebox more closely this time, using the tip of her trowel to gently sift through the grey powder. Old charred paper fragments, unidentifiable lumps of fused material, dust… and the small indentation in the brickwork where she'd found the greenish glass shard. She probed the crevice carefully with the trowel tip. Nothing else seemed hidden there. Was the shard truly significant, or just a random piece of litter someone had tossed in years ago? Impossible to tell without forensic analysis it would likely never receive.

She stood up, brushing ash from her knees, feeling a familiar pang of frustration. Finding proof felt like searching for a single specific seed in a vast, overgrown garden. So many possibilities, so few certainties. Her gaze drifted towards the dim interior of the nearest potting shed, its door slightly ajar. Could someone have worked in there? Processed the leaves using the old workbench? She took a hesitant step towards it, peering into the gloom. Spiders webs, stacks of dusty terracotta pots, bags of potting mix, tangled skeins of twine, the faint smell of rust and stored fertiliser… Nothing immediately looked out of place, but it felt secluded enough, private enough, for clandestine work.

"Looking for something, Chloe dear?"

The voice, soft and unexpected, came from directly behind her. Chloe gasped, spinning around, her heart leaping into her throat.

Mildred Pettle stood there, not three metres away, at the entrance to the utility area, partially shaded by the overhanging pittosporum. She held a small pair of secateurs, the kind used for delicate flower arranging. How long had she been standing there? How had she approached so silently?

"Mrs Pettle!" Chloe exclaimed, struggling to keep the shock and sudden, icy fear from her voice. She felt ridiculously exposed, caught snooping near the incinerator like a guilty child. "You startled me. I was just… just checking if we needed more potting mix ordered." It was a weak excuse, but the first thing that came to mind.

Mildred smiled, a gentle, slightly tired smile that didn't quite banish the watchful intensity in her pale blue eyes. "Were you, dear? So diligent, even at the end of the day." She took a step closer, her gaze drifting past Chloe towards the incinerator, then the compost heaps, then back to Chloe's face. "It's rather a gloomy corner back here, isn't it? Not the most pleasant part of the grounds."

"No, not really," Chloe agreed, trying to keep her breathing even, acutely aware of the specimen bags containing the leaves and shard safely tucked deep inside her apron pocket. Could Mildred see the slight bulge? Could she sense Chloe's sudden terror? "Just part of the job."

"Indeed," Mildred murmured. She took another step closer, close enough now that Chloe could smell her faint, floral perfume – lily of the valley, perhaps? – overlaying the earthy scent of the utility yard.

Mildred's eyes scanned the area again, slowly, deliberately. "Such a lot goes into keeping the Society running smoothly behind the scenes, doesn't it? Composting, ordering supplies, dealing with… unforeseen problems." Her gaze flickered back to Chloe, sharp and assessing for just a fraction of a second before softening again into polite concern. "You haven't found anything… unusual… back here, have you, dear? With all the recent disruption, one worries about things being overlooked or disturbed."

The question hung in the air, seemingly innocent, solicitous even. *Find anything interesting?* But Chloe heard the potential subtext, the unspoken probe. Had Mildred seen her digging yesterday? Did she suspect Chloe had found something? Was this a warning? Chloe's mind raced, searching for a safe, neutral answer.

"Unusual?" Chloe echoed, forcing a small, puzzled frown. "No, not really. Just the usual mess behind the sheds. Looks like someone might have tried to burn some plastic in the incinerator again recently," she added, improvising, gesturing vaguely towards the cold ashes, hoping to provide a plausible, mundane explanation for any lingering odd smells or residues Mildred might detect or imagine. "And the middle compost bay needs a good turn." She kept her tone light, practical, the dutiful gardener reporting routine observations.

Mildred considered this, her head tilted slightly. "Ah yes, the incinerator. Strictly against club rules now, of course, but people do forget. Thank you for checking, Chloe. We must remind Henderson Jr. to keep a closer eye on it." Her gaze lingered on Chloe for another moment, a moment that stretched uncomfortably long. It felt intensely scrutinising, as if Mildred were trying to read beneath the surface of Chloe's carefully composed expression. Was her fear showing? Was her knowledge somehow written on her face?

Then, as suddenly as it appeared, the intensity vanished, replaced by Mildred's usual gentle efficiency. "Well, I mustn't keep you," she said, giving another small smile that crinkled the corners of her eyes but didn't quite seem genuine. "I was just looking for Esme, thought she might be checking the seedling stock. Don't work too late, dear. It gets quite dark back here."

And with a final nod, Mildred turned and walked calmly back towards the main clubhouse, disappearing around the pittosporum hedge as silently as she had arrived.

Chloe stood frozen for a long moment after Mildred had gone, her heart hammering against her ribs so hard she felt slightly dizzy. She took several deep, shuddering breaths, leaning against the rough timber of the compost bin for support. Coincidence? Had Mildred genuinely just been looking for Esme? Or had that been a deliberate encounter? A subtle interrogation? A warning?

She couldn't be sure. Mildred had revealed nothing, accused nothing. Her words were perfectly innocuous on the surface. Yet the encounter had left Chloe feeling profoundly shaken, exposed, and certain she had been intensely scrutinised by eyes that saw far more than they let on. The feeling of being watched that Agnes had experienced at the library suddenly felt terrifyingly real and immediate. Mildred *knew*. Maybe not exactly *what* they knew, or *how* they knew it, but Chloe felt certain the Club Secretary suspected she was no longer operating under a cloak of invisibility.

The fading light no longer seemed melancholic; it felt threatening. The familiar grounds felt alien, potentially hostile. Chloe quickly gathered her fork and bucket, abandoning any further pretence of working. She needed to get away from this isolated corner, away from the clubhouse, needed to tell the others about this encounter. The shadow lengthening over the Society wasn't just metaphorical anymore; it had a name, a face, and it had just looked directly at her. The risk had just become terrifyingly personal.

****

The sanctuary of Agnes Plummett's study felt less like a refuge and more like a besieged outpost that Thursday evening. The discoveries of the day, laid out in notes and printouts and Chloe's grim specimen bags upon the large desk, represented significant progress, yet the dominant mood was not one of triumph, but of taut, shared apprehension. Outside, the Melbourne night was cool and clear after the earlier rain, stars beginning to prick the darkening sky, but inside, under the warm glow of Agnes's reading lamps, the shadows cast by their investigation seemed to have lengthened and deepened considerably.

Agnes began, her voice carefully neutral as she detailed her findings at the State Library. She described the fragile 1888 and 1910 survey maps, the ambiguous western boundary line abutting Gardiner's Creek, the vague reference to the 'Scarred Gum', and the indeterminate legal status of the 'old orchard end' sliver of land – the land associated with Fincham's *Pyrus Malus* reference and Croft's 'consistent high yield'. "It confirms Ainsworth had identified a genuine historical anomaly regarding the Society's property," Agnes concluded, placing her neat transcriptions beside Ronnie's sprawling chart. "An ambiguity significant enough, perhaps, to provide cover for long-term, off-the-books activity or income, directly linked to the area near where he died. He wasn't just chasing random historical details; he was probing a specific geographical and legal vulnerability."

Next, Fitzwilliam recounted his afternoon spent navigating corporate databases. He described the almost textbook characteristics of the shell companies behind 'WeatherTech Roofing' and 'Vintage Marquee Hire'. "Classic setups for fraudulent invoicing," he explained, his legal mind clicking through the red flags –

PO Box addresses, recent or reactivated registrations, nominee directors. "Suggests a pattern of siphoning significant funds from major club expenditures." Then came the potentially explosive finding regarding 'Bespoke Botanical Displays'. "Directed by Eleanor Vance," he stated, pausing for effect. "And," he added, referring to his notes, "a 'Miss E. Vance' – same initial, same uncommon surname – was employed as temporary secretarial assistance to the Treasurer, Humphrey Carmichael, for four weeks in February 1988, immediately following the acceptance of that suspicious anonymous donation for the West Wing extension."

A sharp intake of breath from Chloe. Ronnie stopped tapping his pencil. Agnes merely nodded slowly, as if confirming a suspicion she had already harboured. "The connection," Agnes murmured. "Historical proximity to the original potential irregularity, and current involvement via a potentially fraudulent supplier sharing the family name. It strengthens the hypothesis considerably, linking past and present."

"It provides compelling circumstantial evidence of long-term opportunity and potential involvement in financial manipulation," Fitzwilliam agreed. "But," he cautioned, the ever-present lawyer tempering the detective, "it still falls short of direct proof. We cannot definitively link Eleanor Vance to Mildred Pettle beyond the shared maiden name without genealogical research, nor can we prove Mildred *herself* benefited financially from these suppliers without banking records."

The weight of this missing link settled upon them. They were building a powerful circumstantial case, layer upon intricate layer, but the final, irrefutable piece remained elusive. It was into this heavy silence that Chloe spoke, her voice lower than usual, tinged with residual fear.

She recounted her own experience that afternoon in the utility corner near the compost heaps. Not her discovery of the buried *Digitalis* leaves – she had already shared that via text – but the encounter that followed. She described Mildred Pettle's sudden, silent appearance, her seemingly casual presence near the secluded spot, her observant gaze sweeping the area, her softly probing questions disguised as polite concern: *"Find anything interesting, Chloe dear?"*

As Chloe spoke, describing the intensity she felt in Mildred's scrutiny, the way the secretary's eyes seemed to linger on the disturbed compost, the chilling effect of her seemingly innocuous departure, the atmosphere in the room grew colder. Fitzwilliam felt a prickle of genuine fear run down his spine. Agnes's expression became stony, her usual analytical detachment replaced by something harder, more protective as she looked at Chloe. Ronnie stopped sketching entirely, his focus shifting from abstract probabilities to immediate risk assessment.

"She knows," Chloe finished quietly, twisting her hands in her lap. "I don't know *how* much she knows, or if she saw me find the leaves yesterday, or if she just suspected *why* I was back there today... but she *knows* someone is looking closely. Her questions... they weren't just idle chat. It felt like... like she was warning me."

Agnes's earlier report of potentially being watched at the library by the man in the tweed jacket suddenly took on a far more sinister light. Had that been real? Had Mildred, feeling the pressure of Ainsworth's investigation even before his death, perhaps already employed someone for discreet surveillance? Or was she now reacting to the quartet's own subtle inquiries, putting pieces together, identifying them as a threat?

"This changes the risk profile significantly," Ronnie stated, his voice devoid of its usual theoretical excitement, now clipped and serious. "Previously, we operated under the assumption of passive concealment by the perpetrator. Scenario C-3," he tapped a section of his chart, "factored low probability of perpetrator awareness. Now, incorporating Chloe's direct interaction and Agnes's potential observation event, the probability of perpetrator awareness and active counter-surveillance or intimidation moves to Moderate, potentially High." He drew a stark red arrow pointing towards increased danger.

"If Mildred suspects us," Fitzwilliam said grimly, "then every move we make is fraught with risk. My supplier searches, Agnes's library visits, Chloe's work on the grounds… she has means and access within the club to monitor us, potentially interfere with our findings, or worse." He didn't voice the final implication, but it hung unspoken among them. Mildred had killed once to protect her secrets; there was no reason to assume she wouldn't do so again if she felt sufficiently threatened.

A new, heavier silence descended. The intellectual puzzle had become terrifyingly real. They weren't just observers anymore; they were potentially targets.

"Do we stop?" Chloe asked eventually, her voice small. "Do we take what we have – the supplier details, the historical links, the buried leaves – to Inspector Davies now?"

Fitzwilliam considered it, chewing on his lower lip. "It's stronger than before," he conceded. "The pattern of shell companies points strongly to fraud, which might compel Davies to seek financial warrants, especially combined with the historical Vance connection Agnes and I uncovered. The buried *Digitalis* supports the poisoning theory…" He trailed off. "But it's still circumstantial regarding the murder itself. No direct link between Mildred and the poison administration. Davies might investigate the fraud but *still* conclude Smythe committed the murder for other reasons, perhaps after discovering the fraud himself. Mildred could potentially sacrifice the financial scheme, claim Eleanor acted alone, plead ignorance… she's adept at deflection."

"And alerting her via a formal police investigation based on our current evidence gives her maximum opportunity to destroy anything incriminating we haven't yet found," Agnes added firmly. "The financial records *she* controls, any remaining poison processing evidence, the source of the alkaloid… it could all disappear before warrants are executed. No. I believe our course, while undeniably more dangerous now, must remain the same. We need that final, irrefutable piece of evidence *before* involving the authorities."

Ronnie and Chloe nodded slowly in agreement, their expressions reflecting a mixture of fear and resolve.

"Then we proceed," Fitzwilliam said, squaring his shoulders, the decision made. "But with extreme caution. We assume we *are* being watched. We vary our routines where possible. We communicate only through secure channels, never at the club. We limit any further direct inquiries that could obviously point back to us."

"Agnes," he continued, turning to her, "the Fincham book – Section IV, Paragraph 12. Understanding that specific connection feels more critical than ever. It might hold the key to external proof Mildred can't control."

"My priority for tomorrow," Agnes confirmed.

"Chloe," Fitzwilliam looked at the young gardener, concern evident in his eyes, "your work on the grounds is invaluable, but potentially the most exposed. Please, be incredibly careful. Focus on observation, not active searching, unless absolutely safe. And report *any* further unusual encounters immediately."

Chloe nodded wordlessly, her face pale but determined.

"Ronnie, continue your analysis, but perhaps focus on predicting Mildred's *next* likely moves based on her suspected awareness. Risk mitigation strategies."

Ronnie was already making notes, calculating defensive probabilities.

"And I," Fitzwilliam concluded, "will see if the 'E. Vance' name yields anything further in broader historical records – old newspapers, electoral rolls perhaps – trying to confirm if it was indeed Mildred herself back in '88."

They sat for another moment, the plan reset, the danger acknowledged. The shadow of Mildred Pettle, once indistinct, now loomed large and menacing over their investigation. The net, they hoped, was closing around her. But they were now acutely aware that they too were caught within its strands, visible to their quarry, needing to tread with utmost care to avoid becoming entangled themselves. The midpoint had been reached, and the path ahead led directly into more dangerous territory.

16

Zeroing In

By Friday, April 18th, a fragile, almost defiant, sense of routine had reasserted itself at the Toorak Croquet & Horticultural Society. The blue and white police tape still sagged around Lawn 3 like a forgotten, macabre decoration, but members were now playing on adjacent lawns, their voices carrying in the cool, bright autumn air with only slightly less conviviality than usual. The initial shock had subsided, replaced by a low-grade, persistent hum of gossip and the comfortable, if premature, consensus that poor Harry Smythe's unfortunate temper (and likely financial woes) were to blame. Life, or at least the Society's meticulously choreographed version of it, went on.

It was this very return to routine that Agnes Plummett focused on as she sat on the verandah that morning, nursing a cup of chamomile tea (she found Earl Grey too stimulating for observation) and ostensibly reviewing notes for the Centenary committee. Her real purpose was far more specific: to observe Mildred Pettle. Not just casually, as she had done before, but systematically, analytically. With Harry Smythe mentally exonerated and Major Ferguson dismissed as a red herring, Mildred stood alone at the centre of their investigation. Ronnie's logistical analysis had confirmed her unique capability to execute the crime; the historical and financial threads pointed strongly towards her motive. Now, Agnes needed to scrutinise the woman herself, her current actions, her routines, searching for any crack in the flawless facade, any deviation that might betray the immense pressure she must surely be under.

Mildred arrived precisely at 8:45 AM, just as she always did, parking her modest, well-maintained sedan in its usual spot near the back entrance. She emerged carrying her handbag and a canvas tote bag, presumably containing her lunch or work materials. She greeted Henderson Jr., the groundskeeper, who was emptying bins nearby, with her customary quiet smile and a brief comment about the crispness of the morning air. Perfectly normal. Utterly unremarkable.

Agnes watched her unlock the side office door – the one providing direct access to the administrative corridor containing her office and the Treasurer's – using her master key. This early arrival, Agnes knew, was standard practice for Mildred, allowing her to sort the mail and prepare for the day before most members arrived. It also, Agnes noted grimly, provided a daily window of largely unobserved access to key areas, including Ainsworth's office before his own typical arrival time around 9:30 AM. Opportunity.

Throughout the morning, Mildred was a model of quiet efficiency. She delivered mail to the committee pigeonholes. She took several phone calls, her voice calm and professional. She arranged flowers – fresh ones replacing the now-wilting memorial lilies – in the main lounge with artistic care. She prepared morning tea for the few early-arriving members, remembering precisely who took milk and who preferred lemon. Agnes observed her interactions closely. Was there a new watchfulness in her eyes? A slight tension in her shoulders? A tremor in her hand as she poured tea?

Honestly, Agnes had to admit, if there were signs of strain, they were virtually imperceptible. Mildred's composure was extraordinary. She navigated the lingering undercurrents of gossip and unease with the same placid competence she applied to organising the Fete Roster. When Mrs Henderson cornered her near the noticeboard, clearly eager to rehash the Ferguson theory, Mildred listened patiently, murmured vague sympathies for all involved ("Such a distressing time… one hopes Major Ferguson isn't taking the speculation too hard…"), and then smoothly redirected the conversation towards arrangements for the upcoming bridge tournament. It was done with such subtle skill that Mrs Henderson probably didn't even scrutinise her morbid curiosity had been deftly deflected.

Agnes recalled Ronnie's logistical analysis – Mildred's routine wasn't just *consistent*, providing opportunity; it was *pervasive*. She moved through every part of the club, interacted with almost everyone, handled information flow, managed keys, oversaw schedules. This intimate knowledge of the club's rhythms wasn't just helpful for administration; it was invaluable for planning a crime *within* that environment. Mildred would know precisely when Ainsworth usually took his tea break, when Lawn 3 was likely to be deserted, when Henderson Jr took his lunch break away from the utility sheds, when the cleaning staff finished their rounds. She wouldn't need elaborate planning; the club's daily, weekly, monthly routines provided a predictable framework within which she could operate almost invisibly. Agnes made a note: *"MP's knowledge of member/staff routines = critical facilitator for timing/opportunity (poison admin, body staging, evidence disposal). Essential to factor into risk assessment of our own movements."*

Chloe arrived mid-morning to start her gardening tasks. Agnes watched as Mildred greeted her with the same warm, slightly maternal smile she'd shown previously. "Chloe dear, good morning.

Feeling a little better today after your… unpleasantness?" The question was solicitous, appropriate. Yet, remembering Chloe's chilling account of the encounter near the compost heaps, Agnes scrutinised the interaction intently. Was there a flicker of calculation behind Mildred's concerned eyes? A subtle emphasis on the word 'unpleasantness', perhaps, hinting at shared knowledge? Chloe, clearly briefed by Agnes to maintain absolute normalcy, simply nodded politely. "Yes, thank you, Mrs Pettle. Much better." She quickly excused herself to collect her tools. The exchange was brief, outwardly unremarkable. But Agnes felt a frisson of unease. Mildred's gaze had lingered on Chloe for just a fraction of a second too long, perhaps. Or was Agnes herself now succumbing to confirmation bias, seeing suspicion in every innocuous gesture?

Later, Agnes observed Mildred making her usual lunchtime tour – a brief walk around the main lawns, ostensibly checking on the state of the gardens or greeting playing members. Her path took her along the edge of Lawn 2, bringing her relatively close to the still-taped-off Lawn 3. Agnes watched intently. Did Mildred hesitate? Did she avert her gaze? No. She paused briefly, looking towards the scene with the same expression of quiet sadness she displayed when discussing Ainsworth's death, then continued her circuit at her usual unhurried pace. If she felt any guilt, fear, or even morbid curiosity related to that specific spot, she betrayed absolutely nothing. Her control was absolute.

This very perfection, however, began to feel suspect in itself. Could anyone, even someone innocent, remain quite so placidly efficient, so perfectly composed, in the aftermath of a brutal murder within their workplace, especially when suspicion, however muted, might naturally fall upon anyone with access and opportunity? Where was the nervousness? The stress? The occasional slip in composure? Was Mildred simply extraordinarily resilient and professional? Or was her calmness the unnatural stillness of someone maintaining absolute, conscious control over every word, every gesture, because a single mistake could unravel everything?

Agnes thought back to other crises the club had faced – funding shortfalls, committee resignations, even a minor kitchen fire years ago. Mildred had always been the calm centre, yes, but there had usually been *some* sign of the pressure – a slight shortness of temper, a visible weariness. Now, dealing with a murder investigation swirling around her, she seemed almost... serene. Too serene?

As Mildred returned to her office after lunch, Agnes made another note: *"Subject's composure remains exceptional, potentially unnaturally so given circumstances. Routine appears unchanged. No visible signs of stress or deviation. Is this evidence of innocence/resilience, or highly controlled guilt? Continue close observation for any inconsistencies, however minor."*

The day wore on. Mildred dealt with correspondence, answered phones, liaised with committee members. All perfectly normal. Yet, Agnes couldn't shake the feeling of watching a meticulously crafted performance. The very lack of cracks in the facade felt like evidence in itself. It strengthened her resolve. Mildred was formidable, protected by layers of routine and perceived harmlessness. Penetrating that defence would require something equally meticulous, something that disrupted the routine, something that forced an unplanned reaction. Their nascent plan to somehow provoke Mildred, formulated after Fitzwilliam hit the wall with the supplier search, felt increasingly necessary, however risky. Passive observation, Agnes concluded, had reached its limits. It was time to consider applying pressure. She closed her notebook, the image of Mildred's calm, polite smile fixed firmly, unsettlingly, in her mind.

****

While Agnes maintained her discreet vigil at the Croquet Club, Alistair Fitzwilliam found himself back in his Collins Street office early on Friday morning, April 18th, engaged in one final, almost obsessive, sweep through the digital labyrinth of public records. The previous days' discoveries – Agnes's historical land context, Chloe's grim botanical findings, his own confirmation of likely fraudulent suppliers including the tantalising 'Eleanor Vance' connection – had built a powerful circumstantial case against Mildred Pettle. Yet, the lawyer in him remained acutely aware of the chasm between strong suspicion and irrefutable proof, particularly the kind needed to convince a sceptical Detective Inspector Davies to look past Harry Smythe or to secure warrants for Mildred's personal financial records. Before fully committing to the riskier strategy of trying to provoke Mildred, Fitzwilliam felt compelled to exhaust every possible avenue of objective, verifiable evidence obtainable through legitimate, publicly accessible channels.

His desk, usually a model of organised chaos related to active cases, was now dominated by printouts of ASIC searches, notes on 'Bespoke Botanical Displays', and a highlighted copy of the 1988 club minute mentioning 'Miss E. Vance'. The Melbourne morning traffic hummed steadily twenty floors below, a familiar urban soundscape that felt distant from the intricate, potentially deadly secrets of the Toorak Croquet & Horticultural Society. A pile of demanding briefs related to the Macrocorp litigation sat accusingly to one side, momentarily ignored.

He started by revisiting the shell companies. 'WeatherTech Roofing Solutions' and 'Vintage Marquee Hire Pty Ltd'. He ran searches again, checking for any updates, any newly filed documents. Nothing. They remained perfectly opaque, textbook examples of entities designed for anonymity, likely existing only as bank accounts waiting to receive funds before disappearing back into administrative dormancy or dissolution. Frustrating, but expected. Proving their fraudulent nature seemed highly likely; linking their funds directly back to Mildred via public records was, as he suspected, impossible.

His focus shifted back to 'Bespoke Botanical Displays' and Eleanor Vance. The shared maiden name, the historical 'E. Vance' working for Treasurer Carmichael in 1988 – the connection felt too potent to be mere coincidence. He needed to establish if Eleanor Vance and Mildred Pettle were demonstrably related, or if Eleanor Vance was even a real, currently operating individual beyond the company directorship, or if 'E. Vance' from 1988 could be definitively identified as Mildred herself.

He accessed historical Victorian Electoral Roll archives available through a specialised database. Searching for 'Eleanor Vance' and variants, cross-referencing with known addresses (Ferntree Gully) and potential birth year ranges (assuming she was a young woman in 1988 if that 'E. Vance' was her), yielded frustratingly little. Several Eleanor Vances appeared over the decades, but none with clear, continuous records linking the outer eastern suburbs address back to Mildred's supposed western Victorian origins or the 1988 temporary role. The trail went cold, obscured by name changes (marriage?), interstate moves, or simply the limitations of easily searchable digitised records.

He tried searching historical newspapers via the National Library's Trove database. He searched for mentions of 'Mildred Vance' or 'Eleanor Vance' in connection with Toorak, South Yarra, or western Victorian regional papers from the relevant decades. He found announcements related to Mildred Pettle's later appointments at the Society, notices about prize-winning dahlias attributed to Major Ferguson (a moment of grim irony), but nothing linking the Vance name to specific events, addresses, or family connections that could bridge the gap between Eleanor and Mildred, or confirm Mildred used the name 'E. Vance' in 1988. The digital haystack refused to yield the needle he sought.

What about property records? He had confirmed Eleanor Vance owned the Ferntree Gully property. Could Mildred Pettle co-own property, perhaps under her maiden name, or have historical shared addresses? He ran searches through Landata again, using variations of Pettle and Vance, cross-referencing with known time frames. Again, nothing concrete. Mildred's current South Yarra apartment was rented. No obvious shared property titles emerged. If there was a financial connection – Mildred perhaps funding Eleanor's nursery business or receiving kickbacks – it wasn't reflected in easily accessible property ownership records.

Fitzwilliam leaned back, the frustration mounting. He felt like he was pressing against a perfectly smooth, opaque wall. He had powerful circumstantial evidence suggesting fraud channelled through these companies, and a deeply suspicious potential link via the Vance name connecting current operations back to historical financial irregularities Mildred might have been involved in from the very beginning. But the critical links – proving Eleanor *was* Mildred's relative or accomplice, proving Mildred *personally* benefited from the phantom supplier payments, proving the 'E. Vance' of 1988 *was* Mildred – remained stubbornly hidden behind layers of corporate anonymity and the passage of time.

He considered his options. He could hire a private investigator to delve deeper into Eleanor Vance's background or Mildred's family history, but that carried significant risk of exposure and expense, and might still yield nothing admissible. He could attempt to craft an extremely careful request for further information from his police contact, Sergeant Riley, perhaps asking if routine checks had identified the directors of companies receiving recent large club payments, but Riley was unlikely to share such operational details, especially after Fitzwilliam's previous probing about the autopsy.

No, he concluded with a heavy sigh, the path of public record investigation had reached its terminus. They had established strong motive, plausible means (poisoning), clear opportunity, suspicious behaviour, evidence of likely large-scale financial fraud under Mildred's purview, and intriguing historical connections. It was a compelling narrative, one that convinced *him*, and likely the rest of the quartet. But it lacked the definitive, tangible proof required to overcome Mildred's carefully constructed facade or sway a police investigation fixated on another suspect.

He picked up the phone and dialled Agnes's mobile. She answered on the second ring, her voice calm as ever.

"Agnes, Alistair here," he said, keeping his own voice low. "Just reporting back on the supplier and Vance follow-up searches."

"Any progress, Alistair?"

"Confirmation, of a sort," he replied wearily. "WeatherTech and Vintage Marquee look even more like shell companies on closer inspection – textbook structures for fraudulent invoicing. Bespoke Botanical Displays, directed by Eleanor Vance, remains plausible on the surface but the historical link – the 'E. Vance' assisting Treasurer Carmichael back in '88 – feels incredibly significant, placing someone with that name right at the heart of things when that suspicious donation occurred." He paused. "However, I've spent hours trying to find a definitive link between Eleanor Vance and Mildred Pettle through public records – shared addresses, confirmed family ties, financial co-mingling – and there's simply nothing concrete. Similarly, proving Mildred *personally* benefited from the phantom supplier payments is impossible without access to banking information."

He heard Agnes absorb this on the other end. "So," she said after a moment, her voice pragmatic, "the circumstantial case regarding motive and mechanism is significantly strengthened by the likely fraud and the historical connection, but the direct, personal link to Mildred remains elusive through documentary evidence alone?"

"Precisely," Fitzwilliam confirmed. "We've pushed the public record investigation as far as it can reasonably go, I believe. We won't find the smoking gun in ASIC records or old electoral rolls."

"Then," Agnes stated, her voice hardening slightly with resolve, "it confirms our assessment from last night. Passive investigation has reached its limits. If we are to find irrefutable proof, we must now shift our focus towards Mildred herself – her current actions, her potential mistakes under pressure, or any physical evidence she may have overlooked."

"The 'trap' scenario," Fitzwilliam murmured, feeling a fresh wave of anxiety at the prospect.

"Or continued close observation," Agnes corrected gently, "perhaps combined with finding a legitimate reason to access records or areas she controls more directly. Ronnie was exploring some theoretical models for provoking a reaction, I believe?"

"He was," Fitzwilliam confirmed. "We need to discuss his findings, and Chloe's ongoing observations, and decide on the safest, most effective way forward." He felt a sense of finality. The desk research phase was over. The next stage would require more nerve, more risk, and potentially, direct interaction with the woman they believed to be a calculating killer. He closed his eyes briefly, the scale of the task settling upon him again, before forcing himself back to professional composure. "I'll collate these supplier reports for our meeting tonight."

****

While Agnes mentally catalogued Mildred Pettle's seamless performance of normalcy at the club, and Fitzwilliam confronted the frustrating dead end of public record searches in his city office, Ronnie Peterson remained ensconced in the relative quiet of the Society's library, embarking on the next logical phase of the investigation. If passive data collection and analysis had reached their limits in providing definitive proof, then active measures – introducing a controlled stimulus into the system and observing the response – were now required. It was, in essence, experimental design, albeit applied to a suspected murderer rather than subatomic particles or stellar evolution. The objective: elicit a reaction from Subject P (Pettle) that would provide quantifiable, ideally irrefutable, evidence of guilt or knowledge related to Event M (Murder of Ainsworth).

He had received Fitzwilliam's brief, glum confirmation via secure text mid-afternoon: *"Supplier/Vance searches exhausted. Strong circumstantial fraud indicators, historical links confirmed. No direct Pettle financial tie via public record. Dead end on this path. A."* This news, while disappointing in one sense, simply confirmed Ronnie's own assessment: passive observation had yielded a high-probability hypothesis (P(Pettle|Evidence) $\approx$ 0.9), but achieving the required threshold for external action (P $\approx$ 1.0, or at least beyond reasonable doubt) necessitated perturbing the system.

Ronnie cleared a larger space on the mahogany table, pushing aside volumes on croquet history. He retrieved his master chart – the sprawling diagram mapping timelines, locations, suspects, and evidence threads – and opened his notebook to a fresh section he'd labelled: *"Phase II: Active Scenario Modelling & Risk Assessment."* His mind, usually occupied with calculating gravitational lensing or thermodynamic efficiency, now focused on the equally complex dynamics of human behaviour under stress, specifically the likely reactions of a highly intelligent, cautious, and potentially ruthless individual (Pettle) when faced with perceived threats to her long-maintained equilibrium.

He began by outlining potential "Stimulus Vectors" – actions the quartet could take designed to provoke a reaction:

Information Stimulus (IS): Introducing specific pieces of information into Pettle's awareness, information only someone involved or someone actively investigating (like Ainsworth, or now, the quartet) would likely possess. Examples:

IS-1a: Mentioning Fincham's *Orchards of Progress* or historical boundary issues near Lawn 3 (Agnes's discovery).

IS-1b: Raising questions about the specific phantom suppliers Fitzwilliam identified.

IS-1c: Hinting at knowledge of the *Digitalis* harvesting or disposal (Chloe's discovery – extremely high risk).

IS-1d: Referencing the 1988 'E. Vance' temporary role (Fitzwilliam's discovery).

Physical Evidence Stimulus (PES): Manipulating or drawing attention to physical evidence. Examples:

PES-1: 'Accidentally' displaying the grey glove Chloe found, observing Pettle's reaction. (High risk, low probability of yielding useful data beyond simple observation of discomfort).

PES-2: Creating a situation suggesting the compost heap or incinerator area is about to be thoroughly cleaned or investigated for unrelated reasons, potentially forcing Pettle to retrieve any remaining disposed items if she panics. (Difficult to implement credibly).

Environmental Pressure Stimulus (EPS): Increasing general scrutiny or pressure unrelated to specific evidence, hoping to induce an error. Examples:

EPS-1: Encouraging (very discreetly) broader committee review of historical finances or contract approvals, citing general 'good governance' post-Ainsworth.

EPS-2: Observing Pettle intensely during high-stress club events (upcoming tournament finals? Centenary Gala planning meetings?).

For each stimulus vector, Ronnie began sketching out potential reaction pathways using flow diagrams and assigning rough probabilities. Subject P (Pettle), he reasoned, exhibited high caution (HC) and high control (HC2). Her probable reactions to a perceived threat would likely prioritise: (a) Information gathering (assess threat level), (b) Neutralisation/Deflection (if threat deemed low/manageable), (c) Evidence removal/Securing position (if threat deemed high-/specific), (d) Flight/Extreme Measures (lowest probability unless directly confronted with inescapable proof).

He analysed IS-1a (Fincham/Boundary Info). *Stimulus:* Agnes 'casually' mentions researching Fincham or old maps related to the 'old orchard end' within earshot of Mildred. *Potential Pettle Reactions:*

* R1 (Low Threat): Ignores comment or offers polite, dismissive historical anecdote ($P \approx 0.6$). Minimal data yield.

* R2 (Moderate Threat): Discreetly observes Agnes further, attempts to ascertain *what* Agnes knows ($P \approx 0.3$). Requires careful counter-observation setup by quartet. Potential data yield: confirmation of Pettle's specific interest/concern related to this historical point.

* R3 (High Threat): Attempts to access/remove relevant historical records from club archives or Agnes's notes ($P \approx 0.1$). High data yield if observed, but requires significant error/panic from Pettle. High risk to Agnes if Pettle suspects her directly.

He moved to IS-1b (Phantom Suppliers). *Stimulus:* Fitzwilliam raises a 'formal query' via email to the current interim Treasurer (copied to Mildred as Secretary) regarding payment verification procedures for WeatherTech/Vintage Marquee, citing 'due diligence'. *Potential Pettle Reactions:*

* R1: Provides meticulously correct procedural answer, possibly fabricating supporting documents or claiming Ainsworth personally verified suppliers ($P \approx 0.7$). Low data yield, potentially allows her to further embed false trails.

* R2: Shows signs of stress/agitation regarding financial scrutiny, potentially makes minor error in subsequent reports ($P \approx 0.2$). Requires close monitoring of accounts (difficult).

* R3: Attempts to delete digital records related to payment approvals or supplier communications ($P \approx 0.1$). Requires sophisticated monitoring unlikely for quartet.

Ronnie frowned. The Information Stimuli felt potentially effective at gauging Pettle's specific anxieties but carried significant risks of revealing the quartet's hand or yielding ambiguous results.

He considered PES-2 (Forcing Evidence Disposal). *Stimulus:* Announce (via official club notice generated for plausible reason – e.g., upcoming garden working bee) a 'thorough clean-out and soil conditioning of compost bays and incinerator area'. *Potential Pettle Reactions:*

* R1: Ignores announcement, assuming evidence (leaves/shard) sufficiently hidden/decayed ($P \approx 0.5$). No data yield.

* R2: Conducts discreet surveillance of area to assess risk ($P \approx 0.3$). Requires observation setup.

* R3: Attempts pre-emptive removal/destruction of any remaining evidence during low-traffic period (e.g., night before working bee) ($P \approx 0.2$). High data yield if observed, but high risk for observers, requires precise timing/luck.

This felt potent, but orchestrating the stimulus credibly and setting up effective, safe observation would be extremely difficult.

Finally, he considered EPS-2 (Observation during High-Stress Event). He consulted the club calendar pinned on the library noticeboard. The semi-finals of the Autumn Tournament were scheduled for the upcoming weekend. Mildred, as Secretary, would be involved in logistics, scoring collation, perhaps presenting minor prizes. High visibility, multiple interactions, potential for distraction or unguarded moments.

Stimulus: Combine observation (EPS-2) with a preceding Information Stimulus (e.g., IS-1a). Agnes mentions her Fincham research casually on Friday. Observe Mildred closely throughout the higher-stress environment of the Tournament Semi-Finals on Saturday/Sunday. *Potential Pettle Reactions:* Increased probability of observable stress indicators (agitation, distraction, errors in routine)? Increased likelihood of her trying to subtly probe Agnes or others about the research? Potential for her to make a mistake while distracted?

Ronnie circled this combined approach on his chart. *Hypothesis T1: Trigger (IS-1a) + Observation Window (EPS-2/Tournament).* Risk Assessment: Moderate. Information leak controlled (Agnes is discreet). Observation can be semi-covert (quartet members present as 'spectators'). Potential Data Yield: Observable stress indicators, probing questions from Pettle confirming her sensitivity to the historical land issue, possible minor procedural errors under pressure. Not a 'smoking gun', but could provide crucial behavioural evidence and direction for further investigation.

He spent another hour refining this scenario, sketching out optimal observation points around the clubhouse and main lawns during a busy tournament day, considering communication signals between the quartet members, estimating time windows when Mildred might be most stressed or distracted (e.g., during final score collation). He treated it like planning synchronised telescope observations, aiming to capture faint signals against a noisy background.

Satisfied he had a viable, risk-assessed plan, he pulled out his phone. He needed to present this 'Trigger and Observe' model to the others tonight. Passive analysis was complete. It was time to gently perturb the system and see if Subject P revealed the hidden variables confirming her culpability. He dialled Fitzwilliam first, intending to brief him before their evening meeting with Agnes and Chloe. "Alistair? Ronnie. I've completed the Phase II scenario modelling. I believe I have identified an optimal strategy for eliciting observable data from Subject P with quantifiable, albeit non-zero, risk parameters…" The language of physics applied to the deadly game they were playing.

****

The comforting ritual of shared tea had given way to something more practical, more indicative of the long haul they now faced. Takeaway containers – fragrant Thai green curry for Ronnie and Chloe, a simple pasta for Fitzwilliam, Agnes content with toast and marmalade – sat amidst the maps, notes, and printouts covering Agnes's large desk that Friday evening. Outside, the lights of South Yarra glittered against a clear, cool night sky, but inside the study, the atmosphere was thick with focused intensity. They had reached a critical juncture. Passive investigation, while yielding a powerful circumstantial case against Mildred Pettle, had hit a wall. The time for simply observing and deducing was over.

Fitzwilliam had reported his frustrating dead end with the corporate searches – phantom suppliers strongly indicated, the Vance connection tantalisingly strengthened by the historical link, but no publicly accessible thread leading directly to Mildred's personal finances. Agnes had recounted her day observing Mildred at the club – a performance of unflappable composure, of routines maintained with almost unnerving precision, offering no chinks in the armour, no unguarded moments.

"Her control is… remarkable," Agnes stated, her voice holding a note of grudging respect mixed with profound disquiet. "If she feels any pressure from our inquiries, or from the general situation, she betrays absolutely nothing. She continues to manage the club, manage the members' anxieties, manage the narrative, with seamless efficiency."

"Which means," Fitzwilliam concluded heavily, pushing aside his half-eaten pasta, "that simply waiting for her to make a mistake is unlikely to yield results. If she is guilty, she is clearly highly intelligent, highly disciplined, and has likely been concealing her activities for a very long time. She won't slip up easily."

"Precisely," Ronnie interjected, tapping the fresh page in his notebook where he'd outlined his 'Phase II' scenarios. "Passive observation of a stable system yields diminishing returns. To generate new data, we must introduce a controlled perturbation. We need," he stated with scientific certainty, "to conduct an experiment."

He then proceeded to lay out his preferred strategy, the one he'd refined that afternoon: Hypothesis T1 – Trigger (IS-1a: Fincham/Boundary Info) + Observation Window (EPS-2: Autumn Tournament Semi-Finals). He explained the logic with characteristic enthusiasm, using flow diagrams sketched in his notebook.

"The stimulus vector," he explained, pointing to his notes, "is Agnes mentioning her research into Fincham's *Orchards of Progress* and the historical boundary ambiguities near Lawn 3, specifically referencing the 'old orchard end'. This information is niche, specific to Ainsworth's known final research path, and directly relevant to the potential historical motive we've uncovered. Mentioning it 'casually' within Mildred's potential hearing range creates a low-level but specific information stressor."

"The observation window," he continued, "is the Autumn Tournament Semi-Finals scheduled for tomorrow and Sunday. High-traffic event, increased general stress levels for organisers (including Mildred), multiple opportunities for observation under the guise of spectating. Our objective is to observe Subject P's reaction to Stimulus IS-1a *within* the higher-stress environment of EPS-2."

"And what reaction are we hoping for, precisely?" Fitzwilliam asked, the lawyer in him immediately focusing on the desired outcome and its evidentiary value. "A dramatic confession seems unlikely."

"Highly improbable," Ronnie agreed readily. "Probability of spontaneous confession P(Conf|IS-1a+EPS-2) < 0.01. However, we are looking for quantifiable deviations from baseline behaviour. Increased anxiety indicators? Nervousness? Distraction leading to procedural errors? Attempts to subtly probe Agnes about her research? Attempts to access historical club records related to land boundaries or Fincham? Any deviation significantly correlated with the stimulus provides valuable data supporting her guilty knowledge."

"It feels… dangerous, Ronnie," Chloe said quietly, voicing the apprehension the others likely felt. "Deliberately provoking someone we believe to be a murderer?"

"Risk is inherent," Ronnie conceded, "but quantifiable. The stimulus is indirect, deniable. Observation is passive. Direct confrontation is explicitly avoided. Risk of physical retaliation deemed Low Probability (LP). Risk of subject detecting surveillance: Moderate (MP), mitigated by utilising public event context. Potential data yield: Moderate to High (MHP) for behavioural indicators,

Low (LP) for direct incriminating evidence." He tapped his risk assessment matrix. "Compared to alternatives like attempting covert entry or direct evidence planting – which carry Very High (VHP) legal and physical risks – this Trigger and Observe model offers the optimal risk/reward ratio currently available."

Agnes considered it, her gaze thoughtful. "The principle is sound," she agreed slowly. "Introduce a specific piece of knowledge Ainsworth possessed, and observe if Mildred reacts in a way that indicates *she* understands its significance. My mentioning the Fincham research, perhaps lamenting the unclear boundaries near the 'old orchard end' while discussing potential Centenary garden improvements within Mildred's hearing… yes, that could be managed naturally enough." She looked at Fitzwilliam and Chloe. "The key is the observation. We would all need to be present at the tournament, acting as casual spectators, but coordinating our focus on Mildred during specific periods – before, during, and immediately after the 'trigger' comment."

Fitzwilliam rubbed his temples. "Observation in a crowded club event… it's difficult. People moving, conversations overlapping. And Mildred herself will be busy, constantly interacting."

"We require structure," Agnes stated decisively, picking up her pen and a fresh sheet of paper. "We need assigned observation zones and times. Ronnie, your map of the clubhouse and lawns will be useful here."

For the next hour, they meticulously planned the operation. Agnes would deliver the 'trigger' comment sometime late Saturday morning, perhaps during a lull in play near the scoring table where Mildred was likely to be overseeing results collation. Fitzwilliam, positioned perhaps on the verandah with a clear view of the scoring area, would focus on Mildred's immediate facial expression and body language reaction. Chloe, mingling near the tea pavilion or pathways Mildred frequented between tasks, would watch for any subsequent signs of agitation or unusual interactions Mildred might have. Ronnie, less adept at interpreting subtle human cues, would focus on timing Mildred's movements, noting any deviations from her expected routine or any unusual trips towards the office or archive areas after hearing Agnes's comment. They established simple, discreet hand signals for communication across the lawns – adjusting glasses for 'subject observed reacting', running a hand through hair for 'subject moving towards office', etc. – feeling slightly ridiculous but acknowledging the need for silent coordination.

They discussed contingencies. What if Mildred didn't react at all? (Possible, requiring reassessment). What if she reacted with overt suspicion towards Agnes? (Agnes would feign innocent historical curiosity, then withdraw). What if someone else overheard Agnes and started asking awkward questions? (Deflect, change subject). What if Mildred tried to approach one of *them* afterwards to probe *their* knowledge? (Be polite, vague, report immediately).

The plan felt fraught with variables, reliant on subtle interpretation and nerve. Yet, compared to the frustrating dead end of Fitzwilliam's record searches, it felt like necessary, albeit risky, progress. It was a shift from passive analysis to active engagement, an attempt to force a crack in Mildred's impenetrable facade by introducing a carefully targeted stressor.

"So," Fitzwilliam said finally, looking around at the determined faces in the lamp lit room, the remnants of their takeaway meal forgotten amidst the maps and diagrams. "We proceed? Tomorrow morning. Agnes delivers the stimulus. We all observe, meticulously, discreetly. We report back here tomorrow evening."

Agnes nodded, her expression firm. "We proceed."

Chloe took a deep breath and nodded too.

Ronnie tapped his pen on his final risk assessment figure. "Optimal available pathway confirmed. Proceed."

A sense of shared resolve, tinged with undeniable fear, settled over the quartet. They were deliberately stepping closer to the fire, hoping to elicit a flicker of revealing light without getting burned themselves. The Autumn Tournament Semi-Finals, usually a highlight of the Society's sporting calendar, had just acquired a far more dangerous, high-stakes significance. Their focus was no longer just on the croquet balls, but on the subtle movements of the woman who held all the secrets, the woman they now had to provoke into revealing herself.

17

The Tournament Test

Saturday morning, April 19th, dawned crisp and bright over Melbourne, the kind of clear, cool autumn day perfect for competitive croquet. At the Toorak Croquet & Horticultural Society, the Autumn Tournament Semi-Finals were underway, lending the grounds an air of focused energy that overlay, but didn't entirely dispel, the lingering unease from the events of the past week and a half. The main lawns, particularly Lawn 1 and 2 where the top-seeded players battled for a spot in Sunday's final, were surrounded by a respectable gallery of members – some genuinely engrossed in the strategic intricacies of the game, others simply using the occasion for social interaction, their conversations inevitably circling back, in hushed tones, to the Ainsworth affair and the continued absence of Lord Smythe.

For the quartet, however, the tournament served a different purpose. It was the backdrop, the carefully chosen 'high-stress environment' identified by Ronnie, for their first foray into active measures: Hypothesis T1, the 'Trigger and Observe' experiment targeting Mildred Pettle. Agnes Plummett felt the weight of her role as the primary 'stimulus vector' keenly. It was one thing to analyse records in the quiet solitude of her study or the State Library; it was quite another to deliberately introduce a potentially volatile piece of information into the orbit of a woman she strongly suspected of calculated fraud and cold-blooded murder, all under the watchful eyes of the club membership.

She had positioned herself strategically on the edge of the verandah, near the double doors leading into the main lounge where the official scoring table was situated. From here, she had a clear view of Lawn 1, allowing her to feign interest in the ongoing semi-final between young Cyril Postlethwaite (who seemed to be playing surprisingly well) and the redoubtable Mrs Albright. More importantly, this position offered proximity to the scoring table, a hub of activity where Mildred Pettle, in her capacity as Club Secretary, was inevitably spending much of her time overseeing results collation, liaising with umpires, and ensuring the smooth running of the event's administrative side.

Agnes clutched a slim folder containing printouts related to the Centenary garden refurbishment plans – her legitimate reason for potentially needing to consult with Mildred or other committee members present. Inside the folder, however, tucked beneath the landscaping proposals, were her notes on Fincham's *Orchards of Progress* and the ambiguous 1888 survey map. Her heart beat a little faster than usual, a flutter beneath the precise composure of her Liberty print blouse and knitted cardigan. She scanned the scattered spectators discreetly. Fitzwilliam was seated at a table further down the verandah, pretending to read tournament rules but positioned for a clear view of the scoring table area. Chloe, ostensibly checking the condition of the potted standard roses lining the verandah edge, had a similar line of sight from the opposite side. Ronnie, equipped with binoculars (claiming an interest in observing players' techniques from afar), had stationed himself near the boundary edge of Lawn 2, giving him a wider, albeit more distant, view of Mildred's movements between the scoring table, the clubhouse office, and potentially other areas. Their communication plan – subtle hand signals – felt slightly absurd, theatrical even, but necessary.

Mildred herself appeared precisely as she had every other day since the murder: calm, efficient, quietly indispensable. She wore a neat navy skirt and a crisp white blouse, her grey-blonde hair perfectly coiffed. She moved between the scoring table inside and the umpire on Lawn 1 with unhurried purpose, carrying clipboards, accepting score sheets, offering quiet words to players between games. Her face betrayed nothing – no undue stress, no unusual agitation. If she was feeling the pressure of their potential scrutiny, or the weight of her own alleged crimes, her facade was, as ever, impeccable. Watching her, Agnes felt a renewed surge of determination mixed with a chilling awareness of the adversary they faced. This woman wasn't just organised; she was armoured.

Finding the right moment for the trigger comment required patience. Agnes couldn't simply walk up and interject Fincham's obscure historical research into a conversation about croquet scores. It needed to feel natural, almost accidental, yet delivered clearly enough for Mildred to register its specific content. She needed a plausible opening, a conversational hook related to club history or grounds management.

An opportunity arose just before midday, during a brief lull between games on Lawn 1. Mildred had returned to the scoring table inside the lounge, conferring briefly with Esme Weatherly over the schedule for the afternoon matches. Agnes saw her chance. Picking up her folder, she walked purposefully into the lounge, approaching the table as if seeking clarification on a Centenary matter. Fitzwilliam, she noted peripherally, subtly lowered his rule book, his attention sharpening. Chloe paused in her deadheading near the doorway.

"Mildred, Esme," Agnes began, her voice calm and pleasantly modulated. "Apologies for interrupting. Just a quick query regarding the Centenary garden plans…" She opened her folder, revealing the landscaping proposals. "Specifically, the proposed heritage apple tree planting near the western boundary, the 'old orchard end.'"

Mildred looked up from the schedule, her expression politely attentive. "Ah yes, Miss Plummett. A charming idea, linking back to the club's origins." Esme nodded agreement.

"Indeed," Agnes continued, keeping her tone light, almost academic. "In fact, researching the area's history for context – purely for the brochure notes, you understand – I happened upon a fascinating old volume at the State Library yesterday. Fincham's *Orchards of Progress*? Quite obscure, but it details early horticultural experiments in this very area."

She paused, allowing the book title to register, watching Mildred's face closely. Was there a flicker? A momentary stillness? Mildred simply maintained her polite smile, nodding slightly as if mildly interested in Agnes's research discovery. No obvious reaction. Yet.

Agnes pressed on, moving to the core of the trigger. "Fincham mentions," she said, tapping a finger thoughtfully on her folder as if recalling a specific detail, "an experimental orchard established near Gardiner's Creek on land apparently overlapping our 'old orchard end'. He even discusses a specific heritage apple variety, a 'Croft's Seedling' – *Pyrus Malus*, technically – noted for its 'surprisingly consistent high yield.'" She let the phrase hang in the air for a beat. "Most interestingly, though," she added, adopting a tone of mild historical curiosity, "Fincham highlights significant ambiguities in the original 1888 survey maps for that specific parcel, particularly concerning the boundary markers along the creek frontage. Makes one wonder about the precise demarcation of our land in that corner, even today. It could impact the placement of the new compost system, couldn't it?"

She delivered the lines exactly as planned – linking the book, the apple metaphor for yield, the location, and the boundary ambiguity directly to a practical, current club issue (the compost system). She kept her gaze casually directed towards the garden plan in her folder, avoiding direct, challenging eye contact with Mildred, aiming for the appearance of an academic sharing an interesting but potentially problematic historical footnote relevant to current planning.

She risked a quick upward glance. Mildred was still smiling faintly, her head tilted slightly as if patiently listening to Agnes's historical digression. But her eyes… were they slightly less placid now? Was there a new stillness in her posture, a focused attention that hadn't been there moments before? The hand resting on the scoring table seemed, perhaps, to grip the edge just a fraction tighter. Or was Agnes projecting, seeing what she expected, what she *hoped*, to see?

"How fascinating, Miss Plummett," Mildred said, her voice perfectly even, betraying nothing. "One constantly discovers new quirks in the club's long history. Ambiguous boundaries? Goodness, that *could* be problematic for the compost plans. Perhaps you could provide a note for the next Grounds Committee meeting? I'm sure they'd appreciate your thorough research." It was a polite acknowledgement, coupled with a neat delegation of the issue to another committee, effectively shutting down further discussion in this context. Masterful deflection, again.

Agnes simply smiled back, matching Mildred's calm. "Perhaps I shall," she murmured noncommittally. "Thank you, Mildred. Sorry to have interrupted." She closed her folder and turned away, walking slowly back towards the verandah, her own heart beating rather faster now.

She hadn't provoked an outburst, no dramatic reaction. On the surface, Mildred had barely blinked. Yet Agnes couldn't shake the feeling that something *had* registered. The stillness, the slightly-too-intense focus in Mildred's eyes as Agnes mentioned Fincham and the boundary ambiguity… it felt like the brief, almost imperceptible tension in a drawn bowstring just before the arrow is loosed.

She settled back into her chair on the verandah, picking up her teacup with a hand that was remarkably steady. She gave Fitzwilliam, whose anxious gaze met hers instantly, the barest hint of a nod. *Stimulus delivered.* Now came the crucial part: observing the fallout, watching for the ripples spreading outwards from the pebble she had just dropped into Mildred Pettle's carefully controlled pond. The tournament test had begun.

****

Agnes Plummett turned away from the scoring table with the deliberate, unhurried pace of someone concluding a minor administrative query. Inside, however, her senses were on high alert, every nerve attuned to the woman she had just left behind. Had the pebble dropped into the pond caused a ripple, or simply sunk without a trace? She didn't dare look back immediately; that would betray undue interest. Instead, she walked towards her verandah table, her gaze ostensibly taking in the progress of the match on Lawn 1, allowing Fitzwilliam and Chloe, positioned with clearer lines of sight, to perform the crucial immediate observation.

Fitzwilliam, seated further down the verandah, had lowered his tournament rule book the moment Agnes began speaking to Mildred. He appeared to be idly watching the croquet match, but his full attention was laser-focused on the tableau inside the lounge doorway. He saw Agnes deliver her lines – the reference to Fincham, the orchards, the *Pyrus Malus*, the consistent yield, the ambiguous boundaries near the compost heaps. He saw Mildred's polite, attentive listening posture. He saw Esme Weatherly beside her, looking only mildly interested, perhaps slightly puzzled by the historical digression. Then Agnes finished speaking.

For a fraction of a second, an almost infinitesimal pause before Mildred responded with her smooth deflection about committee notes, Fitzwilliam registered it. A stillness. A cessation of the micro-movements that accompany normal conversation. Mildred's polite smile didn't waver, her posture didn't change overtly, but there was a sudden, absolute freeze in her expression, particularly around the eyes. It was like watching a perfectly rendered projection momentarily flicker, the image freezing for a single frame before the motion resumed. Her eyes, usually conveying gentle, non-specific interest, seemed to sharpen, their focus turning inward for that split second, as if accessing and rapidly processing unexpected, potentially dangerous data. The hand resting on the scoring table, which had been lightly tapping a pen, became completely motionless, the knuckles perhaps whitening almost imperceptibly against the dark wood.

Then, just as quickly, the mask was back in place. The smile remained, perhaps a fraction tighter. The eyes resumed their normal, placid gaze. The hand relaxed. She delivered her perfectly reasonable, dismissive response to Agnes, suggesting the Grounds Committee was the appropriate forum. It was a masterful recovery, almost instantaneous. To anyone not watching with Fitzwilliam's heightened, specific suspicion, it would have been utterly invisible, lost in the flow of conversation, dismissed as a momentary pause for thought.

But Fitzwilliam had seen it. Or believed he had. Confirmation bias, he cautioned himself. Expecting a reaction and therefore interpreting stillness as significance. Yet… it *felt* significant. It wasn't the reaction of someone merely hearing an irrelevant historical anecdote. It felt like the reaction of someone hearing a specific, unexpected keyword that resonated with hidden knowledge. *Fincham. Boundary ambiguity. Consistent high yield.* Which part had triggered that momentary freeze? Or was it the combination? He lowered his gaze back to his rule book, his mind racing, dissecting that fleeting moment, weighing its potential meaning while desperately trying to appear disengaged.

Chloe, standing near the verandah railing pretending to inspect a potted rose for aphids, had also seen it, though perhaps interpreted it differently. She wasn't looking for subtle shifts in social masking like Fitzwilliam; she was attuned, after her encounter near the compost heaps, to signs of potential threat, of calculation beneath the surface. What she saw wasn't just stillness, but a sudden, intense concentration in Mildred's eyes, a momentary sharpening that felt less like surprise and more like rapid threat assessment. It was the look of someone instantly calculating the implications of unexpected information.

And immediately after Agnes turned away, Chloe noted Mildred's next actions, small details others wouldn't register. Mildred didn't immediately resume her conversation with Esme. Instead, she unnecessarily straightened the already neat pile of score sheets on the table, her movements quick, precise, perhaps slightly jerky. She picked up her pen, uncapped it, then capped it again without writing anything. Her gaze, no longer directed at Agnes, darted briefly, almost subliminally, around the lounge and out towards the verandah where Fitzwilliam sat, where Chloe herself stood, before returning to the papers before her. It was the action of someone reorienting themselves after a jolt, checking their surroundings, ensuring they hadn't betrayed themselves.

To Esme, who looked mildly surprised at Agnes's historical

tangent but otherwise unconcerned, Mildred simply offered another gentle smile. "Now, where were we, Esme? Ah yes, the afternoon scheduling…" Her voice was perfectly calm, betraying nothing of the momentary internal calculations Chloe and Fitzwilliam believed they had witnessed.

Chloe turned back to her roses, her fingers unsteady as she picked off a non-existent aphid. That brief, almost invisible sequence – the freeze, the sharp focus, the slight hand tension, the darting glance, the unnecessary tidying, the forced return to normalcy – felt chillingly significant to her. It wasn't the reaction of someone hearing an innocent historical fact; it felt like the reaction of someone hearing a key move in a dangerous game, someone instantly assessing the new position on the board. She felt a cold certainty solidify within her: Agnes's words had hit their mark. Mildred knew that they knew *something*. Maybe not everything, but enough to concern her. The shadow Chloe had felt near the compost heap felt suddenly colder, closer.

Agnes returned to her table, calmly sitting down and taking a sip of her now lukewarm chamomile tea. She met Fitzwilliam's questioning gaze with the faintest, almost imperceptible nod. *Reaction observed.* Fitzwilliam returned an equally subtle nod. *Affirmative.*

Agnes opened her notebook, her hand steady as she wrote: *"11:58 AM. Stimulus IS-1a delivered per plan. Subject P exhibited momentary cessation of habitual micro-movements, increased ocular focus, possible minor increase in manual tension (gripping table edge). Duration < 1 second. Followed by immediate resumption of baseline demeanour and verbal deflection. Subsequent covert environmental scanning noted. Hypothesis: Stimulus registered as significant, potential threat assessment initiated. Recommend continued close observation for delayed reactions or behavioural deviations (Phase II Observation Protocol)."*

It was clinical, detached, but the underlying message was clear.

The trigger, however subtly, had worked. It hadn't elicited an outburst, a confession, or even an obvious slip. But it had, they believed, registered. It had landed on target, causing a momentary breach in the hitherto flawless facade. The question now was, how would Mildred Pettle react *next*? Would she dismiss it as Agnes's usual historical rambling? Would she attempt to subtly probe Agnes further? Or would she take more active measures, believing her long-held secrets were genuinely threatened? The tournament test had passed its first phase. The next phase – observing the subject's subsequent behaviour – would be critical. And, Fitzwilliam thought with a fresh wave of anxiety, potentially far more dangerous.

****

The crucial moment – Agnes's carefully delivered comment about Fincham, *Pyrus Malus*, and the ambiguous boundary near the old orchard end – had passed almost imperceptibly amidst the convivial bustle of the Autumn Tournament Semi-Finals just before midday. To most observers, it was merely a brief, slightly academic exchange between the club historian and the ever-efficient secretary. But for the quartet, deployed strategically around the clubhouse and lawns, the subsequent hours became a period of intense, covert observation. Their focus: Subject P, Mildred Pettle. Had the stimulus registered? And if so, how would she react now the immediate interaction was over?

Ronnie Peterson had established his primary observation post on a bench near the edge of Lawn 2, affording him a clear view of the main pathways between the scoring table inside the lounge, the verandah, Mildred's office wing, and potentially, the less-frequented corridor leading towards the archives and library. His binoculars, ostensibly for studying players' techniques on the far lawns, periodically swept towards Mildred, tracking her movements with meticulous precision. His notebook was open, one page dedicated to establishing a 'Tournament Day Baseline Routine' based on past observations, the facing page dedicated to 'Saturday April 19th - Observed Deviations & Temporal Analysis'.

Initially, Mildred's behaviour adhered almost perfectly to the baseline. After concluding her conversation with Agnes and Esme, she spent approximately twenty-five minutes dealing with the collation of scores from the morning matches, interacting calmly with umpires and players, her demeanour indistinguishable from her usual efficient self. Ronnie timed her movements: 3 minutes conferring with Umpire Davies, 90 seconds retrieving updated draw sheets from her office, 5 minutes entering scores into the tournament laptop, interspersed with brief, polite acknowledgements of passing members. All within expected parameters. *"Phase 1 Reaction Analysis: Null result. Subject exhibiting baseline behaviour,"* Ronnie noted, feeling a flicker of disappointment despite his commitment to objectivity.

Fitzwilliam, nursing a lukewarm mineral water on the verandah and pretending to follow the intricate tactics unfolding on Lawn 1, corroborated this initial lack of reaction. He had watched Mildred closely after Agnes walked away. No further signs of the momentary tension he thought he'd glimpsed earlier. She had simply resumed her duties, her composure absolute. Had they imagined that flicker? Was Mildred simply unconcerned by Agnes's historical ramblings, dismissing them as irrelevant? The thought was disheartening. Their carefully planned 'perturbation' seemed to have caused barely a ripple.

Then, around 1:15 PM, during the main lunch break when players and spectators crowded the lounge and verandah for sandwiches and lukewarm white wine, Ronnie noted the first potential deviation.

Mildred, after ensuring the catering was running smoothly, typically took a brief fifteen-minute break herself, usually eating a sandwich discreetly at the scoring table while catching up on paperwork. Today, however, she excused herself and walked purposefully towards the administrative corridor leading to her office. Ronnie clicked his stopwatch.

He watched her disappear from view. Five minutes passed. Ten minutes. Fifteen – the usual duration. Fitzwilliam, also observing from the verandah, subtly adjusted his glasses, signalling to Ronnie that Mildred had not yet re-emerged. Twenty minutes. Twenty-five. Finally, at the twenty-eight-minute mark – a deviation Ronnie mentally flagged as potentially significant (Standard Deviations > 2 from mean baseline duration) – Mildred reappeared. She walked back towards the lounge, her expression unchanged, carrying only a slim folder he hadn't seen her take in. She immediately resumed her duties, checking the afternoon match schedule with Esme.

What had she been doing in her office for nearly half an hour? A legitimate administrative task? A long phone call? Or something else? Reviewing files related to Fincham or land boundaries? Accessing financial records? Making contact with someone related to the phantom suppliers? Impossible to know from observation alone. But the *duration* was anomalous. Ronnie meticulously logged the time and duration:

"13:15 - 13:43. Subject P in Office Wing.

Duration: 28 mins. Deviation from baseline mean (15 +/- 3 mins): +10-16 mins.

Significance: Moderate potential (MP).

Possible activities: Undetermined – require further data/context."

Later that afternoon, around 3:30 PM, as the semi-final matches reached their tense conclusions, another small anomaly occurred. Mildred was seen walking briskly from the scoring table, not towards the verandah or her office, but down the quieter side corridor that led past the library (where Ronnie now sat, pretending to read a dusty copy of *Croquet Tactics Through the Ages*) and towards the small, seldom-used archive room where Agnes had conducted some of her earlier research.

Ronnie lowered his book fractionally, his senses on high alert. The archives contained the old minute books, historical ledgers, potentially the very maps Agnes had referenced. Was Mildred going to check them? See if Agnes, or Ainsworth previously, had accessed something specific? He held his breath, listening. He heard Mildred's footsteps pause outside the archive room door. A faint rattle – perhaps trying the handle? The door was usually kept locked, requiring a key from Esme or, crucially, Mildred herself. A few seconds of silence, then the footsteps retreated back down the corridor towards the main lounge.

Ronnie quickly scribbled notes. *"15:32. Subject P proceeds down Archive Corridor. Pauses at Archive Room door approx. 3-5 seconds. Does not enter (door locked?). Returns to main lounge. Significance: Moderate-High (MHP). Directly correlates with potential information vector IS-1a (historical records). Suggests subject may be assessing security/access related to information mentioned by Plummett."* This felt more significant than the extended office break. It suggested Agnes's comment *had* indeed hit a nerve related to historical records.

Agnes, observing from the verandah where she was engaged in polite but probing conversation with Charles Abercrombie about historical preservation society grants (a useful cover), received Ronnie's pre-arranged subtle signal (adjusting his binoculars) indicating 'Subject Near Sensitive Area'. Her own internal assessment sharpened. Mildred was reacting, albeit subtly, cautiously.

Around 4:15 PM, as the final scores were being tallied and congratulations offered to the victorious semi-finalists, Fitzwilliam witnessed another event. He saw Mildred step away from the bustle around the scoring table and move towards a quieter corner near the French doors, pulling out her mobile phone. Her back was mostly turned to the room, her posture suggesting a desire for privacy. The call was brief, less than a minute. Her voice was too low to overhear, but Fitzwilliam noted her body language – she seemed tense, listening more than speaking, nodding sharply once before ending the call and quickly pocketing the phone, her expression tightly controlled as she turned back towards the room.

Who had she called? Or who had called her? Was it related to the investigation? To her finances? To the historical secrets? Impossible to know. But the timing, after a day where specific, sensitive topics had been broached, felt suspicious. Fitzwilliam caught Ronnie's eye across the room and gave the pre-arranged signal for 'Unusual Communication Observed'. Ronnie nodded almost imperceptibly, logging the time.

As the afternoon wound down and members began to drift away, Mildred resumed her role as the unflappable administrator, congratulating winners, commiserating with losers, ensuring score sheets were correctly filed. Yet, the quartet, sharing their observations via discreet signals and brief, low-voiced asides when possible, felt a collective sense of confirmation. Mildred's composure was largely intact, yes. She hadn't panicked, hadn't made any glaring errors. But the extended time in her office, the detour towards the archives, the brief, tense phone call – these were deviations, subtle shifts in the pattern, suggesting that Agnes's carefully planted information *had* registered, prompting cautionary actions or checks.

The trigger had worked, not by causing an explosion, but by causing barely perceptible tremors beneath the surface. It wasn't the dramatic breakthrough they might have hoped for, but it was data. It confirmed Mildred was sensitive about the historical land/finance issues. It suggested she was actively monitoring access or information related to them. It reinforced her position as the prime suspect who was now potentially aware, at some level, that the comfortable narrative surrounding Ainsworth's death might be unravelling. The observation phase of Hypothesis T1 had yielded positive, if subtle, results. Now they needed to analyse these results and plan their next move for Sunday, the final day of the tournament, aware that their subject was likely becoming increasingly wary.

****

The rich aroma of Agnes Plummett's signature beef and burgundy pie – a rare departure from her usual simple fare, perhaps acknowledging the intensity of the day – did little to dispel the focused tension in her study that Saturday evening. The quartet was gathered once more around the large desk, the debris from a shared, quickly eaten dinner pushed aside to make room for notebooks, Ronnie's updated charts, and steaming mugs of strong tea (or, in Fitzwilliam's case, a second, gratefully accepted whisky). Outside, the Melbourne night was cool and quiet, the sounds of South Yarra traffic muted by Agnes's heavy curtains. They were tired after a long day spent feigning casual interest in croquet while maintaining intense, covert surveillance, but a shared current of cautious excitement underpinned their weariness. They had perturbed the system, as Ronnie put it, and now they needed to analyse the results.

"Right," Agnes began, assuming her natural role as chair, her notebook open to a fresh page. "Let's collate observations systematically. The stimulus – my reference to Fincham, *Pyrus Malus*, consistent yields, and the boundary ambiguity near the old orchard end – was delivered at approximately 11:58 AM, near the scoring table, within clear hearing range of Subject P (Pettle) and Witness W (Weatherly)."

"Immediate reaction," Fitzwilliam reported first, swirling the whisky in his glass. "As observed from my position on the verandah. A momentary cessation of movement – perhaps 0.5 to 0.75 seconds. A distinct cognitive processing interval, I'd term it. Her facial expression froze almost imperceptibly, eyes lost focus briefly before returning to baseline politeness. Minor manual tension noted – increased pressure on the table edge with her right hand." He paused. "Objectively, could it be interpreted as simple surprise or momentary distraction? Yes. Subjectively, considering the context of the specific keywords used? It felt... significant. Like an unexpected query hitting a sensitive database index."

Chloe nodded confirmation from her end of the sofa, where she sat nursing a mug of chamomile. "I saw it too, Mr Fitzwilliam. From the doorway. It wasn't just surprise. Her eyes... they sharpened. Like she was instantly calculating something. And straight afterwards, when Miss Plummett walked away, she did that unnecessary tidying of the score sheets, and her gaze swept the room, including towards where I was standing and where you were, Mr Fitzwilliam. It felt like she was checking who else might have heard, assessing her environment." Chloe shivered slightly, remembering the feeling of that brief, intense scrutiny. "It felt like the way she looked at me near the compost heap."

Agnes made a meticulous note. "Initial reaction: Micro-freeze, ocular focus shift, manual tension increase, followed by environ-mental scanning and displacement activity (tidying). Consistent with processing unexpected, potentially significant information." She looked at Ronnie. "Subsequent movements?"

Ronnie consulted his heavily annotated timeline chart. "Following Stimulus IS-1a at 11:58, Subject P maintained baseline routine activities associated with tournament administration for approximately 77 minutes. Then, commencing 13:15, the first significant deviation occurred: extended presence in office wing." He pointed to his calculation. "Observed duration: 28 minutes. Baseline mean for Tournament Day Lunch Break activity in that location: 15 minutes, standard deviation estimated at 3 minutes based on prior observation cycles. Today's duration exceeds baseline mean by +13 minutes, representing a deviation greater than 4 standard deviations. Probability of this occurring randomly under baseline conditions: $P < 0.0001$. Highly statistically significant."

"Meaning she was almost certainly doing something in her office beyond eating her sandwich," Fitzwilliam translated Ronnie's statistical jargon. "Making calls? Accessing files related to the boundary issue or Fincham? Trying to contact Eleanor Vance?"

"Precisely," Ronnie confirmed. "Insufficient data to determine specific activity, but the temporal deviation strongly indicates non-baseline behaviour correlating directly with the post-stimulus period." He moved his finger along the chart. "Second significant deviation: geographical. At 15:32, Subject P proceeded down the corridor towards the library and archives wing. Paused outside archive room door for approximately 4 seconds. Did not attempt entry. Returned to main lounge. Baseline data shows zero instances of Subject P loitering in that specific corridor during previous tournament observation cycles."

"Checking if the archive door was locked?" Agnes mused. "Or perhaps assessing if anyone else – myself, specifically – had requested access recently?" It fitted perfectly with the trigger information concerning historical records.

"And the phone call?" Agnes prompted Fitzwilliam.

"Around 4:15 PM," Fitzwilliam confirmed. "Stepped away from the main group, turned her back. Brief call, less than sixty seconds. Primarily listening, nodded once sharply. Pocketed phone immediately afterwards. Appeared tense during the call, but resumed normal composure instantly upon rejoining the group."

"Content unknown, caller unknown," Ronnie stated, adding it to his chart with a question mark. "But timing, occurring after other deviations, suggests potential correlation with processing the stimulus or coordinating response/further action."

Agnes surveyed their collective observations, collated now on her notepad and Ronnie's chart. "So," she summarised, "the stimulus *was* registered. It did *not* provoke an immediate, overt reaction, demonstrating Subject P's high level of emotional control. However, it *did* correlate with subsequent, statistically significant deviations from her baseline routine – prolonged time in her private office, an unprecedented check near the archives containing historical records, and a brief, discreet phone call."

"It suggests she took the information seriously," Fitzwilliam stated. "Seriously enough to potentially review her own records in her office, check the security of the archives Agnes might be interested in, and possibly communicate with an external party."

"Her reaction wasn't panic," Chloe added thoughtfully. "It felt more like… assessment. And caution."

"Exactly," Agnes agreed. "She perceived a potential threat, assessed it, and took minor, precautionary steps, all while maintaining her outward facade. It tells us two things. One: the historical land/Fincham angle is indeed highly sensitive to her, validating Ainsworth's likely line of inquiry and our own focus. Two: she is extremely controlled and cautious, unlikely to make a major unforced error unless the pressure is increased significantly."

"So, do we increase the pressure tomorrow?" Fitzwilliam asked nervously. "Repeat the stimulus? Introduce a new one – perhaps hinting at the supplier irregularities?"

Ronnie consulted his risk assessment models briefly. "Repeating

IS-1a offers diminishing returns; subject now primed, reaction likely less informative. Introducing IS-1b (Suppliers) carries higher risk of revealing our knowledge source (Fitzwilliam's searches) and provoking stronger, potentially more dangerous, counter-measures from Pettle."

Agnes nodded agreement. "I concur with Ronnie. A second, direct stimulus tomorrow seems unwise. She is alerted now. Our best strategy is likely continued, intensified *passive* observation during the final day of the tournament tomorrow. She may believe her subtle checks today went unnoticed. She may relax slightly, or the continued stress of the tournament combined with her underlying anxiety might lead to less guarded moments, minor mistakes in conversation, or further deviations in routine that we can now interpret more accurately."

"We watch," Fitzwilliam confirmed, feeling a mixture of relief at avoiding further direct provocation and apprehension about what they might see. "Assign observation zones again? Same communication signals?"

They spent the next half hour refining their observation plan for Sunday's finals. Roles would remain similar, focusing on tracking Mildred's movements, conversations, and demeanour throughout the day, particularly during potentially stressful moments like the final prize-giving ceremony. They reiterated the need for absolute discretion and agreed on check-in times via secure text.

As they prepared to leave Agnes's apartment later that evening, the weight of their shared knowledge felt heavier than before. They had successfully tested their hypothesis, confirming Mildred Pettle's sensitivity to the very secrets they believed Ainsworth died uncovering. They hadn't found the smoking gun, but they had seen the flicker of recognition in the dragon's eye. Tomorrow, during the culmination of the Autumn Tournament, their silent, watchful presence would be crucial, hoping that Mildred, feeling the pressure but believing herself unobserved, might finally make a mistake, revealing the truth hidden behind her impenetrable facade of tea, sympathy, and quiet efficiency. The tournament test was entering its final, potentially decisive, phase.

18

Setting the Trap

Sunday, April 20th, brought the culmination of the Autumn Tournament, and with it, a heightened sense of occasion at the Toorak Croquet & Horticultural Society. The finals drew a larger crowd than the previous day's semi-finals; members arrived dressed in their weekend best, assembling on the verandah and along the boundaries of Lawn 1, where the main singles final was scheduled to commence after lunch. The air buzzed with anticipation for the match, but also with the relentless undercurrent of gossip that had become the club's dominant background noise since Ainsworth's murder. The Ferguson theory, having circulated rapidly yesterday, was still being dissected with avid interest, providing a convenient distraction from the unresolved tensions surrounding Harry Smythe, who remained conspicuously absent.

For Agnes, Fitzwilliam, Ronnie, and Chloe, however, the day held a different kind of tension. Their coordinated observation of Mildred Pettle continued, executing the plan refined the previous evening. Having concluded that Agnes's subtle 'trigger' comment *had* registered, causing minor behavioural deviations, their task today was intensified vigilance. They needed to watch for any further signs of unease, any mistakes made under the pressure of the finals day, any indication that Mildred felt her carefully guarded secrets were truly threatened. They moved through the day like ghosts at the feast, performing the role of interested spectators while their senses remained sharply focused on the Club Secretary.

Agnes positioned herself, as usual, with a good vantage point of the main clubhouse thoroughfares and the scoring area, armed with her notebook (ostensibly for recording match highlights for the club newsletter) and a thermos of chamomile tea. She watched Mildred greet the finalists, check the lawn setup with Henderson Jr., and confer with the umpires. Outwardly, Mildred was the picture of calm professionalism. Her dove-grey dress was immaculate, her smile readily available, her movements economical and precise. If yesterday's probe about Fincham and the boundary ambiguities had unsettled her, she gave absolutely no sign of it this morning. Her composure was, Agnes grudgingly admitted, deeply impressive, almost unnerving. Was it the confidence of innocence, or the practised control of a seasoned deceiver?

Fitzwilliam, nursing a single glass of mineral water near the edge of the verandah crowd, felt a familiar knot of anxiety tighten. Mildred's apparent return to perfect equilibrium was disheartening. Had they overestimated her reaction yesterday? Had the subtle deviations Ronnie noted – the extra time in the office, the detour towards the archives – been mere coincidence, unrelated administrative tasks? He scanned the crowd, catching Chloe's eye briefly near the pathway leading to the rose garden. She gave a tiny, almost imperceptible shake of her head. *Nothing unusual observed yet.* Fitzwilliam sighed inwardly. This passive observation felt futile, like watching a perfectly sealed vault, knowing treasure (or vipers) lay within, but having no key and seeing no cracks.

Ronnie, stationed again near Lawn 2 with his binoculars (now attracting mild, amused commentary from some members about his sudden intense interest in croquet technique), was meticulously logging Mildred's movements against his established baseline. 10:15 AM: Delivered updated draw sheet to Lawn 2 umpire (Duration: 45 seconds. Baseline: 40-60 secs. Deviation: Nil). 10:30 AM: Spoke with catering staff re: lunch arrangements (Duration: 180 seconds. Baseline: 150-210 secs. Deviation: Nil). 11:05 AM: Entered office wing (Duration: 12 minutes. Baseline for mid-morning office task: 10-20 mins. Deviation: Nil). Frustration gnawed at Ronnie. The system had returned to equilibrium after yesterday's perturbation. Subject P was exhibiting no significant deviations. Their experiment, at least in this passive observation phase, was yielding null results regarding induced stress indicators.

His internal monologue, usually buzzing with calculations, turned towards contingency planning. If observation failed, the next logical step, according to his risk/reward models, involved introducing a *stronger* stimulus, something designed to force a more significant reaction, albeit carrying higher risks. The 'Lost Ledger' scenario they had tentatively discussed last night began to seem increasingly necessary. Passive observation was statistically unlikely to yield conclusive data if the subject possessed sufficiently high control parameters, as Pettle clearly did.

As lunchtime approached, Mildred efficiently organised the serving of refreshments, moved among the members making polite conversation, inquired about scores, and handled a minor query about guest parking with unflappable grace. She spoke briefly with Agnes about the historical society's upcoming lecture series. She exchanged a perfectly normal pleasantry with Fitzwilliam about the quality of the sherry trifle. She even complimented Chloe on the condition of the verandah roses. Her performance was seamless, projecting an aura of competence and quiet dedication that made the quartet's suspicions feel almost absurd, almost libellous, in the bright light of day.

Fitzwilliam felt his resolve waver slightly. Could they be wrong? Could all the circumstantial evidence – the financial anomalies, the historical connections, the poison possibility, Ronnie's physics, Chloe's findings – be just a series of unfortunate coincidences? Could Ainsworth's death truly be the result of Harry Smythe's simple, tragic loss of temper, despite the inconsistencies? It was, after all, the explanation favoured by almost everyone else, including, it seemed, the police. Pursuing Mildred based on their complex, unproven theory felt increasingly like swimming against a powerful tide of accepted narrative.

He glanced at Agnes again. Her expression was serene as she discussed floral arranging techniques with Mrs Albright. But Fitzwilliam thought he detected, beneath the surface politeness, a core of unyielding certainty. Agnes wasn't wavering. Her belief in the significance of the historical clues, combined with her assessment of Mildred's character, seemed absolute. Her quiet conviction helped steady Fitzwilliam's own resolve. They couldn't stop now, not when they had come this far, not when the alternative felt so fundamentally wrong based on their combined analysis.

The afternoon wore on. The singles final on Lawn 1 reached a tense climax. Mildred stood near the scorer, watching impassively, clipboard in hand, ready for the final tally. The crowd murmured appreciatively at well-executed shots, groaned collectively at unexpected errors. It was a perfect picture of suburban sporting drama, overlaid, for the quartet, with the invisible tension of their secret surveillance.

Mildred performed her duties flawlessly through the final scores, the congratulations, the preparations for the informal prize-giving. No slips, no deviations, no signs of underlying stress. Ronnie's notebook remained stubbornly free of significant anomalous data points for the afternoon period.

As the event began to wind down, members collecting belongings, finalists accepting congratulations, the quartet subtly converged near the now-deserted scoring table inside the lounge, ostensibly to gather their things.

"Status report?" Agnes murmured, her back to the room as she pretended to examine the final draw sheet.

"Negative," Fitzwilliam replied quietly, looking out the window. "Composure absolute. No observable reaction or deviation beyond baseline tournament day activity."

"Confirmed," Ronnie added, putting away his binoculars. "Subject P operated within expected parameters throughout Observation Period 2 (12:00 - 16:30). Hypothesis T1 yields insufficient data to confirm stress correlation post-stimulus IS-1a."

Chloe simply shook her head, her expression communicating weary frustration.

Agnes sighed, a barely audible sound. "As we suspected might happen. Her control is formidable." She paused, then met Fitzwilliam's eyes, then Ronnie's, then Chloe's. Her gaze was clear, decisive. "Passive observation has reached its limit. It confirms her ability to maintain composure under pressure, but provides no path to definitive proof. We must proceed to Phase III."

Phase III. The 'Lost Ledger' gambit. The deliberate introduction of false information designed to force Mildred's hand, to make her believe incriminating evidence existed and was about to be revealed, hoping to provoke her into an observable act of retrieval, destruction, or further manipulation. It was riskier, ethically more complex, moving firmly from observation into active deception.

Fitzwilliam felt his stomach clench again, but he nodded. They had exhausted the safer options. "Agreed," he said quietly. "We prepare the bait." The tournament test had failed to provide the breakthrough they needed. Now, they had to set their own trap.

****

Sunday evening found the quartet gathered once again in Agnes Plummett's study, the lingering scent of beef and burgundy pie from the previous night replaced by the sharper aroma of freshly brewed, strong coffee. The large sheet of butcher's paper Ronnie had commandeered still hung from the bookshelf, its diagrams and probabilities now seeming less like a triumphant map towards truth and more like a complex testament to their current impasse. Outside, the lights of South Yarra twinkled in the cool, clear autumn night; inside, a mood of weary frustration vied with determined Gt resolve. Their 'Tournament Test', the carefully planned observation following Agnes's subtle information trigger, had yielded frustratingly little.

"So," Fitzwilliam summarised glumly, swirling the dregs of his coffee in its cup, "a full weekend of intensive, coordinated observation, following Agnes's perfectly delivered comment regarding Fincham and the boundary issues yesterday. And the net result?" He looked around the room. "Mildred Pettle spent slightly longer in her office during Saturday lunch break – doing heaven knows what. She walked towards the archives corridor once, then turned back. And she took one brief, unidentifiable mobile call." He sighed. "Today? Nothing. Absolutely nothing deviating from her baseline tournament finals routine. Her composure remained utterly flawless throughout the presentations and farewells."

"Which confirms," Agnes stated pragmatically, though her own disappointment was evident in the slight tightening of her lips, "that Subject P possesses exceptionally high emotional control and situational awareness. The low-level information stimulus, while likely registered given the initial micro-reactions *we* observed, was insufficient to provoke sustained anomalous behaviour under passive observation conditions."

"Insufficient?" Ronnie scoffed, though without heat, more as a statement of scientific fact. "The data yield was statistically negligible! We cannot extrapolate meaningful conclusions regarding guilt or specific anxieties from a single 13-minute deviation in office dwell time and one aborted trajectory towards the archives!" He tapped his chart dismissively. "Hypothesis T1 – Trigger and Observe – has failed to produce data exceeding the background noise threshold. We require a stronger signal-to-noise ratio."

Chloe, who had spent most of the weekend trying to appear naturally engaged in watching croquet while covertly tracking Mildred's every visible move, echoed the frustration more simply. "So… she didn't react? At all, really? After everything we found out? The suppliers, the history, the plants… she just… carried on?" The unfairness of it, the seeming invulnerability of the woman they were certain was guilty, clearly rankled. "What do we do now?"

"We reassess our methodology," Agnes replied calmly, though her eyes held a steely glint. "Passive observation, even with a minor stimulus, has proven ineffective against this particular subject. If we are to elicit a reaction, a mistake, something tangible that links her directly to the crime – the poison, the finances, the historical secret – we must, I believe, escalate our approach."

Fitzwilliam shifted uncomfortably in his armchair. "Escalate? Agnes, we must be careful. We are already operating well outside conventional boundaries. 'Escalation' sounds perilously close to entrapment, or at the very least, actions that could expose us and completely discredit any evidence we *do* uncover." The lawyer in him recoiled from the potential legal and ethical ramifications.

"I am not suggesting anything illegal, Alistair," Agnes said coolly.

"Nor entrapment in the legal sense, which requires inducing some-one to commit a crime they wouldn't otherwise commit. I am suggesting we move from passive observation to creating a situation where Mildred *believes* her security is imminently threatened, forcing her to take action *herself* to protect her position or destroy evidence. Actions which we might then be positioned to observe or document."

Ronnie nodded eagerly, flipping to a different section in his notebook. "Precisely! Phase III scenarios. Increased stimulus intensity, designed to exceed subject's control threshold and provoke observable, high-data-yield reactions." He looked up, his eyes bright with analytical fervour again. "Based on Pettle's demonstrated high caution and control, simply repeating a similar information stimulus is unlikely to succeed. We need to create a perception of *imminent discovery* related to a specific vulnerability."

He outlined the possibilities he'd previously modelled: "Option A: Physical Evidence Threat. For example, 'leaking' information sug-gesting the grey glove Chloe found is undergoing forensic analysis and has yielded 'interesting results'. Probability of Pettle reacting by attempting to dispose of other potential physical evidence (e.g., processing tools, related clothing) increases, but requires difficult observation of disposal sites and risk of direct link to quartet if leak traced."

"Or," he continued, "Option B: Financial Exposure Threat. Fitzwilliam could perhaps escalate his 'due diligence' inquiries regarding the phantom suppliers, maybe submitting a formal written query to the Committee, copied to Mildred, requesting full banking details and proof of service delivery for WeatherTech or Bespoke Botanical Displays, citing potential audit requirements. This directly targets the suspected fraud mechanism."

Fitzwilliam paled slightly. "Submitting a formal query like that…

it would cause uproar. It directly accuses, or heavily implies, impropriety. It would force Mildred's hand, certainly, but could also trigger immediate defensive action, destruction of records, and expose *us* completely before we have proof."

"Risk profile: High," Ronnie agreed, marking his notes. "Potential for catastrophic system destabilisation before data capture."

"Which leaves Option C," Agnes interjected, clearly having anticipated this direction. "Targeting the historical / information vulnerability. Creating the perception that Ainsworth's research, the specific thread *we* believe led to his death, has been rediscovered independently and is about to be understood or revealed."

"The 'Lost Ledger' scenario we discussed?" Fitzwilliam asked, feeling a reluctant pull towards this less confrontational, albeit deceptive, option.

"Precisely," Agnes confirmed. "We contrive the 'discovery' of a document – perhaps an old, misfiled account book from the late 80s, or one of Silas Croft's original orchard notebooks supposedly clarifying that boundary issue and land value – found 'by chance' in the main archives. We ensure news of this 'significant historical find', explicitly mentioning its potential relevance to Ainsworth's final research and the West Wing era finances, reaches Mildred through reliable club gossip channels."

"The hypothesis being," Ronnie picked up, "that faced with the apparent emergence of a concrete piece of historical evidence corroborating Ainsworth's potentially damaging discoveries – evidence she likely *knows* existed or relates to her long-held secrets – Mildred will be compelled to act. She might attempt to access the archives herself to view or steal this 'ledger'. She might try to discredit the finding or the finder (Agnes). She might attempt to destroy other related documents she *does* control. Any such action, if observed, provides strong evidence of guilty knowledge and concealment."

"It feels… manipulative," Chloe murmured, looking troubled. "Like we're deliberately trying to trick her."

"We are trying," Agnes corrected gently but firmly, "to expose the truth about the murder of Bartholomew Ainsworth and potentially decades of financial fraud against this Society. Our subject has proven impervious to passive observation and has demonstrated extreme skill in manipulation and concealment herself. If a carefully constructed scenario, based on information Ainsworth himself was pursuing, is required to provoke an observable action that reveals her guilt, then I believe it is a justifiable, necessary step." Her gaze was steady, unwavering.

Fitzwilliam sighed, rubbing his eyes behind his spectacles. Agnes had framed it starkly, but he couldn't entirely disagree. Their passive methods had failed. The police were, by all accounts, still focused on Harry Smythe. If they didn't take a more proactive, albeit riskier, step, Mildred Pettle might very well get away with murder and significant financial crime. The 'Lost Ledger' gambit, while carrying risks of exposure and failure, seemed the most plausible route left open to them, targeting the historical secrets that seemed to lie at the heart of her motive.

"Alright," he said finally, the decision settling heavily upon him. "Let's assume we proceed with the 'Lost Ledger' scenario. How, exactly, do we make it convincing? What does this ledger supposedly contain? How does Agnes 'find' it? And how do we ensure Mildred hears about it without realising it's a setup?" The practicalities, the execution, would be critical. The trap needed to be perfectly baited and seamlessly set.

****

The remnants of their shared Sunday evening takeaway lay forgotten on side tables in Agnes Plummett's study. The weariness from a long weekend spent in fruitless, tense observation had momentarily receded, replaced by the sharp, focused energy of imminent action. The failure of passive observation had led them, inexorably, to this point: the detailed calibration of a deliberate trap, designed to force Mildred Pettle's hand. Ronnie's large chart, covered in probability pathways and risk assessments, dominated one wall, while Agnes's desk was now littered with fresh sheets of paper detailing potential scenarios and assigned roles. The air hummed with low, intense conversation, the four members leaning in, united by a shared purpose that felt both necessary and deeply precarious.

"So, we are agreed," Agnes stated, her voice calm but firm, bringing the previous brainstorming session to a point of decision. "Direct confrontation is too risky. Attempting to physically acquire evidence she controls – like the glove, or searching her office – is legally untenable and likely to fail against someone so cautious. Our most viable option, as modelled by Ronnie, remains the Information Stimulus, but executed with sufficient plausibility and observed with extreme care."

"The 'Lost Ledger' gambit," Fitzwilliam murmured, still visibly uncomfortable with the inherent deception but accepting its strategic logic. "But the details must be perfect. We cannot simply invent a ledger out of thin air – Mildred is too intelligent, too familiar with the archives. If she calls our bluff directly, demands to see this supposed discovery immediately, the entire plan collapses, and we are exposed."

"Precisely," Agnes concurred. "Which is why we do not claim to have found the ledger *itself*. That would be foolishly concrete. Instead," she tapped her notepad, "I will claim to have found a *reference* to it within other, legitimate archival material. Plausible deniability is key."

She elaborated, outlining the refined plan. "Tomorrow morning, I will 'discover' an entry in the House Committee Minute Book from, say, 1995 – a period of known administrative upheaval after Humphrey Carmichael's retirement. The entry will vaguely reference 'difficulties locating certain handover documents from the Carmichael treasury era, specifically noting a missing ledger pertaining to West Wing Extension final accounts and Orchard End historical usage'. It sounds dry, procedural, easily overlooked until now."

"Excellent," Ronnie approved, already calculating. "Introduces the target subjects – West Wing finances, Orchard End land – linked to a specific (but non-existent) artefact. Creates perceived vulnerability without immediate falsifiable claim."

"How do I 'discover' this?" Agnes continued. "I will be ostensibly working in the main lounge or library tomorrow morning on Centenary brochure captions – a legitimate, visible task. I will have the 1995 Minute Book 'coincidentally' on my table amongst other research materials. I will feign a sudden realisation, perhaps make a show of cross-referencing it with my notes on Ainsworth's known interests, appear slightly flustered and excited by the potential connection."

"And the leak?" Fitzwilliam prompted. "Ensuring Mildred hears about it reliably but indirectly?"

"Esme Weatherly," Agnes stated without hesitation. "She is inherently trustworthy, unlikely to suspect deliberate manipulation on my part. She is also known to chat frequently with Mildred about administrative matters, and likely feels a duty to keep Mildred informed. I will approach Esme, perhaps mid-morning, expressing my 'exciting but puzzling' discovery. I'll mention the missing ledger, its apparent link to the West Wing funding *and* the orchard end boundaries Ainsworth was researching, and perhaps voice 'concern' about its implications given recent events."

She anticipated Fitzwilliam's next question. "My phrasing will be crucial. Not accusatory. More along the lines of 'Goodness, Esme, look at this odd minute from '95… mentions a missing ledger covering exactly the areas poor Bartholomew seemed so agitated about… isn't that a strange coincidence? One wonders what might have been in it… perhaps it explains that anonymous donation?' Suggestive, but framed as historical curiosity and coincidence."

Fitzwilliam nodded slowly, analysing the legal angle. "It avoids direct accusation. It provides a plausible reason for Mildred's potential subsequent actions – merely wanting to investigate a 'missing' historical record herself out of administrative duty. Defensible, if we are challenged." His relief was marginal; manipulating situations, however subtly, still felt wrong.

"The desired reaction?" Agnes looked at Ronnie.

Ronnie pointed to his chart. "Optimal data yield occurs if Subject P attempts to verify or neutralise the perceived threat. Highest probability pathways involve: (a) Attempting to access main club archives to search for this (non-existent) ledger herself, possibly using her master key outside normal hours or protocols. (b) Attempting to access *Agnes's* research notes or workspace to gauge the extent of her knowledge. (c) Making external phone calls, potentially to Eleanor Vance or financial contacts, to assess related risks. (d) Destroying or securing *other*, real documents related to the West Wing / Orchard End / Fete accounts that she *does* control and fears might corroborate the 'missing ledger'."

"Which means," Agnes concluded, "our observation plan must cover those possibilities."

They spent the next hour meticulously refining the observation strategy for Monday, the day Agnes would set the bait.

"The Archives Corridor," Ronnie declared, tapping the club map spread on the desk. "Critical choke point. Mildred *must* pass this way to access the main archive room. Observation Post Alpha," he circled a small alcove near the library entrance, "offers discreet line of sight. Chloe, your familiarity with staff movements and ability to appear unobtrusively occupied makes you optimal for Alpha."

Chloe nodded, her face pale but set. "I can be sorting periodicals in the library reading area. I'll see anyone who goes towards the archive door."

"Mildred's Office Wing," Ronnie continued. "External observation required. Fitzwilliam, from the verandah or perhaps the side garden pathway? Observe frequency and duration of office visits, note any deviation from baseline Monday routine, observe window activity if possible."

Fitzwilliam agreed, though the prospect of loitering conspicuously in the side garden filled him with dread. "I'll need a plausible reason to be outside the clubhouse for extended periods."

"Consulting with Henderson Jr. about drainage issues near the west boundary?" Agnes suggested instantly, providing the perfect cover related to the very topic she was using as bait.

"Excellent," Ronnie approved. "Observation Post Beta: Fitzwilliam, mobile observation, west boundary / office wing exterior."

"Agnes," Ronnie turned to her, "You are the trigger, but also potentially a target for probing. Maintain your usual routine – library work, verandah presence. Observe any direct approaches from Pettle, log conversation details precisely. Observation Post Gamma: Agnes, mobile, primary interaction monitor."

"And I," Ronnie concluded, "will operate from Observation Post Delta – likely the members' bar or adjacent quiet area, offering strategic overview and data collation. I will monitor overall movement patterns, correlate timings, receive text updates via pre-agreed codes from Alpha, Beta, Gamma, and analyse deviations in real-time." He sounded like a mission controller.

They discussed communication – simple, coded texts only. Contingency plans: What if Mildred confronts Agnes directly and aggressively? (Agnes feigns confusion, retreats). What if Mildred *does* find something incriminating while searching archives (unlikely, but possible Ainsworth left real clues)? (Observe, document, do not intervene). What if they are detected? (Abort observation immediately, regroup).

The level of detailed planning, the inherent deception, the potential danger – it all felt surreal, far removed from the genteel world the Society purported to represent. Fitzwilliam felt a deep weariness, a longing for the straightforward complexities of corporate law. Chloe looked pale but resolute, her quiet determination seemingly fuelled by her discoveries in the garden. Ronnie was intellectually energised, viewing it as the ultimate applied physics problem. Agnes, the calm centre, radiated a sense of historical inevitability, as if uncovering long-buried secrets, however dangerous, was simply the natural order of things asserting itself.

"Is everyone clear on their roles for tomorrow?" Agnes asked finally, her gaze sweeping across each of them.

Nods of confirmation, albeit tinged with varying degrees of apprehension.

"Remember," Agnes added, her voice low and serious, "our objective is to provoke an observable action, ideally one that leads us to concrete evidence. We are not seeking confrontation. Personal safety and discretion are paramount. If at any point the situation feels compromised, withdraw immediately."

Fitzwilliam picked up his now empty whisky glass. He needed another, he thought, but refrained. They needed clear heads tomorrow. They were deliberately poking a predator they believed had already killed once. The trap was designed, the bait prepared.

All that remained was to set it, and hope that Mildred Pettle, for all her meticulous control, would finally make a mistake under pressure, revealing the truth hidden in the shadows of the croquet lawn. The thought was both terrifying and undeniably exhilarating. Tomorrow would be decisive.

****

Monday morning, April 21st, arrived with a cool, crisp clarity that felt almost like a fresh start at the Toorak Croquet & Horticultural Society. The remnants of the weekend's tournament – stray scorecards, perhaps a forgotten sun hat – had been cleared away. The lawns, recovering from intensive play, were being meticulously tended by Henderson Jr. A quieter, weekday rhythm asserted itself, though the underlying tension remained, an invisible ground frost beneath the seemingly normal surface. For the quartet, however, today marked not a return to normalcy, but the deliberate initiation of a dangerous new phase. Today, Agnes Plummett would set the bait.

She established herself early at her usual table on the verandah, positioning it slightly differently this time, affording a better view towards the administrative corridor while still appearing naturally engrossed in her work. Spread before her were several genuine club minute books from the mid-1990s, her folder containing notes on the Centenary brochure captions, and, discreetly placed but visible, a copy of the Society's constitution. She needed props, legitimacy for her planned 'discovery'. She felt remarkably calm, a state she attributed less to innate courage and more to decades spent navigating the often-treacherous currents of library committee meetings and archival bureaucracy. Deception felt distasteful, but uncovering the truth, exposing the rot beneath the Society's polished veneer, felt like a categorical imperative.

She saw Fitzwilliam arrive shortly after nine, exchanging brief, near-invisible nods with her before heading purposefully towards the western boundary, ostensibly to discuss the phantom drainage issues with Henderson Jr., but actually taking up Observation Post Beta. A little later, Chloe appeared, equipped with gardening gloves and a trowel, heading towards the flowerbeds near the library wing, within sight of the archives corridor – Observation Post Alpha established. Ronnie materialised in the members' lounge just before ten, armed with *The Age*, a cryptic crossword, and his binoculars conveniently placed on the table beside his coffee cup, settling into Observation Post Delta with a view encompassing the main pathways. All pieces were moving into position.

Agnes sipped her tea and pretended to read, her ears tuned for opportunity. She needed Esme Weatherly, the most likely conduit to Mildred, but she needed the encounter to seem unplanned, spontaneous. Mildred herself arrived at her usual 8:45 AM, disappearing into the office wing without interacting on the verandah. Perfect.

Esme appeared around ten-thirty, bustling out onto the verandah with a sheaf of papers related to upcoming social event bookings. She looked flustered, muttering about conflicting dates. This was Agnes's chance.

"Problems, Esme dear?" Agnes inquired sympathetically, looking up from her minute book as Esme passed her table.

Esme paused, grateful for the interruption. "Oh, Miss Plummett! Just the usual scheduling nightmare. Trying to fit in the Bridge luncheon around the President's garden party invitations… Mildred usually handles this juggling act so effortlessly, but…" she sighed.

"Indeed," Agnes commiserated. "Mildred's efficiency is quite remarkable." She paused, then leaned forward slightly, adopting a tone of slightly flustered, academic excitement. "Speaking of club administration, Esme, I stumbled upon the most *peculiar* thing this morning while cross-referencing notes for the Centenary brochure."

Esme, distracted from her scheduling woes, looked intrigued. "Oh? What was that, Miss Plummett?"

Agnes tapped the open 1995 minute book before her, though her finger rested on an entirely irrelevant paragraph about purchasing new tea urns. "I was reviewing the handover period after Humphrey Carmichael retired as Treasurer, just checking details on committee structures back then. And I found this rather vague entry..." She frowned, feigning slight confusion. "It mentions difficulties locating certain documents from Mr Carmichael's time, and specifically refers to a 'missing treasury ledger' apparently pertaining to the 'final West Wing Extension accounts' and something noted as 'Orchard End historical usage reconciliations'. Does that mean anything to you?"

Esme looked blank for a moment. "Orchard End usage? West Wing final accounts? Goodness, that was well before my time as coordinator. Late eighties, wasn't it?"

"Precisely," Agnes confirmed. "Around 1987-88. But the minutes here," she tapped the irrelevant page again for effect, "from '95, suggest this specific ledger covering that controversial period was *already* missing then. Isn't that extraordinary?"

"Missing?" Esme looked concerned now. Missing records reflected poorly on club administration, her domain by extension. "Are you sure?"

"Well, the minute entry seems quite clear," Agnes said, injecting a note of puzzled discovery into her voice. "And what struck me as particularly... coincidental... is that poor Bartholomew Ainsworth seemed intensely interested in *exactly* those two subjects – the West Wing funding and historical matters related to the Orchard End boundary – just before his death. Remember Charles Abercrombie mentioning it?"

Esme's eyes widened slightly. "Yes… yes, I believe he did mention Bartholomew was asking about old accounts…"

"It makes one wonder, doesn't it?" Agnes mused, looking thoughtfully towards the gardens. "What could possibly have been in that specific ledger, covering *those* topics, that it went missing years ago, and then Bartholomew starts asking questions about the same things and…" She let the sentence hang, laden with implication, but careful not to voice any direct accusation. She feigned a small shiver. "Pure coincidence, I'm sure. Still… rather unsettling. I feel I ought to look into it further, see if any *other* records shed light on what that ledger might have contained, especially given Bartholomew's recent focus. Perhaps the archive…"

She had planted the seeds: a missing ledger, linked to the sensitive West Wing/Orchard End topics, explicitly connected to Ainsworth's final research. She had framed it as her own accidental discovery, driven by historical curiosity and a touch of unease. And she had mentioned the archive as a potential source of further information.

Esme looked genuinely troubled now, processing the information. "A missing ledger… related to *that*? Oh dear. Bartholomew certainly *was* stirring things up. Perhaps… perhaps I should mention this to Mildred? Just so she's aware a key historical record appears unaccounted for?"

Hook, line, and sinker, Agnes thought, maintaining her expression of mild academic concern. "Well, I wouldn't want to add to her burdens just now, Esme," she said, appearing considerate. "But yes, perhaps she ought to know, purely from an administrative record-keeping perspective. It *is* rather odd, isn't it?"

"Very odd," Esme agreed, already looking preoccupied, likely mentally rehearsing how she would broach this with Mildred. "Thank you for mentioning it, Miss Plummett. I'll… I'll see what

Mildred thinks." She gathered her papers and hurried back towards the administrative corridor, clearly eager to relay this potentially significant piece of administrative news (or historical gossip) to the Club Secretary.

Agnes watched her go, her outward composure serene, her internal state a maelstrom of calculation and apprehension. The bait was set. She had used Esme, kind, efficient, slightly flustered Esme, as the unwitting conduit. The news of the 'missing ledger', linked directly to Ainsworth's fatal research, would reach Mildred within minutes.

Now came the truly dangerous part: waiting and watching. Would Mildred take the bait? Would she react predictably, trying to access the archives herself, or perhaps Agnes's notes, desperate to know what this non-existent ledger supposedly contained, or what Agnes might 'discover' next? Or would her reaction be something else entirely, something unpredictable, something that put Agnes herself, or the others, in direct danger?

Agnes carefully closed the 1995 minute book and picked up her teacup, her hand perfectly steady despite the frantic beating of her heart. From the corner of her eye, she saw Fitzwilliam subtly adjust his position near the west boundary path. Across the lawn, Ronnie lowered his binoculars momentarily, then raised them again towards the office wing. Near the library entrance, Chloe seemed intensely focused on pruning a rosemary bush.

All observation posts were active. The stimulus was live. The trap was sprung. All they could do now was wait, watch, and hope their quarry walked into it, revealing herself before she realised the hunters were closing in. The quiet Monday morning at the Toorak Croquet & Horticultural Society held its breath.

19

The Reaction

The fragile performance of normality at the Toorak Croquet & Horticultural Society continued into Monday morning, April 21st. The weekend tournament was over, the winners celebrated, the lawns showing the wear of intense play. Now, the quieter rhythm of the weekday asserted itself – fewer members present, mostly regulars attending committee meetings or engaging in relaxed social games; staff focused on routine maintenance and administration. It was within this calmer, less crowded environment that Agnes Plummett executed the first, critical phase of their plan: delivering the bait to Esme Weatherly, trusting the club's efficient gossip network, or Esme's own sense of administrative duty, to carry the news swiftly to Mildred Pettle.

Having successfully planted the seed with Esme near the verandah shortly after arriving – recounting her 'discovery' of the minute book reference to a missing Carmichael-era ledger concerning the West Wing and Orchard End finances, linking it to Ainsworth's known interests – Agnes retreated to the relative anonymity of the members' lounge. She settled into an armchair with a clear view of the main corridor leading towards the administrative offices, ostensibly to continue her Centenary brochure research, her notebook and the relevant (and strategically chosen innocuous) 1995 minute book open before her. Her nerves, usually so steady, felt stretched thin, a low-frequency hum beneath her calm exterior. Everything now depended on Esme playing her unwitting part, and, more crucially, on Mildred reacting in an observable way.

She didn't have to wait long. Less than fifteen minutes after Agnes had spoken to her, Esme Weatherly emerged from the direction of the kitchen, carrying a tray with coffee supplies, looking flustered and important. Instead of heading directly to the small committee meeting scheduled in the Card Room, Esme made a deliberate detour towards the administrative corridor. Agnes subtly adjusted her position, angling her chair slightly, her gaze seemingly fixed on her notes but her peripheral vision sharply focused on the corridor entrance.

She saw Esme pause outside Mildred Pettle's office door, tap lightly, and enter, closing the door behind her. Agnes glanced at her watch: 10:47 AM. Now came the crucial observation window. Would Mildred emerge immediately, perhaps seeking Agnes out with 'innocent' questions? Would she make a phone call? Would she simply carry on as normal, processing the information internally?

Ronnie, positioned in the adjacent library doorway pretending to browse the magazine rack, also had a partial view of the corridor and Mildred's door. He subtly shifted his stance, maximising his observation vector, his mind likely already calculating probabilities based on Esme's entry time. Fitzwilliam and Chloe were further afield, monitoring external access points and the archive corridor respectively, relying on updates via text if anything significant occurred.

Inside the lounge, Agnes strained her ears, but could hear nothing through Mildred's closed door over the general murmur of the clubhouse – Colonel Abernathy holding forth near the bar, two members discussing golf handicaps by the window. She forced herself to look down at her notes, making meaningless annotations about Centenary funding sources, trying to appear completely absorbed, utterly unremarkable. The waiting felt interminable, each tick of the grandfather clock in the hall amplifying the tension.

After approximately four minutes – Ronnie would be timing this precisely, Agnes knew – Mildred's door opened. Esme emerged first, still looking slightly flustered but also relieved, as if having successfully discharged a difficult duty. She nodded briefly towards Mildred, who stood framed in the doorway, before hurrying off towards the Card Room with her coffee tray.

Then Mildred stepped fully into the corridor, pausing for a moment. Agnes risked a quick glance. Mildred's expression was perfectly composed. Calm, professional, perhaps a touch weary, as befitted a busy Club Secretary dealing with yet another minor administrative query amidst a difficult time. She held a small stack of mail, presumably collected from the morning delivery. There was no sign of panic, no visible alarm, no indication that Esme's news about a missing ledger linked to Ainsworth's fatal research had caused anything more than a fleeting moment of administrative concern.

Mildred turned and walked towards the main lounge entrance, presumably to distribute the mail or attend to some other task. As she passed the library doorway, Ronnie subtly turned a page of the magazine he wasn't reading, his eyes tracking her movement. As she entered the lounge itself, Agnes lowered her gaze back to her notes, keenly aware of Mildred's approach.

Mildred paused near Agnes's table. "Good morning, Miss Plummett," she said, her voice its usual soft, polite cadence. "Esme mentioned you'd unearthed another historical puzzle from the archives?" There was perhaps the faintest emphasis on the word 'puzzle', but her smile seemed entirely genuine, tinged with mild amusement.

Agnes looked up, matching Mildred's calm tone, playing the role of the slightly obsessive historian. "Ah, Mildred, yes. Just a curious reference in the '95 minutes to a missing ledger from Mr Carmichael's time. Seemed relevant given poor Bartholomew's recent interest in that period, you know. Probably just an old administrative loose end, but," she gave a small, self-deprecating shrug, "my librarian instincts do tend to fixate on missing records!" She kept her explanation light, aligning with Mildred's likely preferred interpretation – Agnes being fussy about historical details.

Mildred nodded sympathetically. "Indeed. Record-keeping wasn't always as rigorous back then, I fear. Humphrey Carmichael, bless him, had many fine qualities, but meticulous filing wasn't necessarily among them." She subtly shifted blame onto her long-dead predecessor. "If it concerns you, Miss Plummett, I can certainly make a note to have Henderson Jr. do a thorough search of the deep storage shed when time permits, though I doubt anything from that era remains unaccounted for after all this time." Another masterful deflection – acknowledging the issue, promising action (by someone else, at an unspecified future date), while simultaneously downplaying its likely significance.

"Oh, no need to trouble Henderson Jr. on my account just yet," Agnes demurred quickly. "It was merely a historical curiosity. Thank you, Mildred."

"Not at all," Mildred smiled again, that placid, unreadable smile. "Now, if you'll excuse me, I must distribute this mail." She turned and proceeded towards the committee pigeonholes on the far side of the lounge, her movements fluid, efficient, betraying nothing.

Agnes watched her go, her outward composure mirroring Mildred's, but her internal assessment was one of profound disquiet. Mildred hadn't reacted. Or rather, her reaction was one of such perfect, controlled normalcy as to be suspicious in itself. No surprise, no real curiosity, no concern beyond vague administrative tidiness. Just a smooth acknowledgement and deflection. It was the response of someone entirely unsurprised by the mention of missing historical financial records linked to Ainsworth's research, perhaps because she already knew exactly what was (or wasn't) in them, and knew precisely how to manage any inquiries.

Fitzwilliam caught Agnes's eye from across the lounge where he'd taken up position behind a copy of *The Australian*, giving a barely perceptible shake of his head. *Nothing.* Ronnie, reappearing momentarily from the library corridor before heading towards his next observation point, offered only a neutral, data-deficient shrug.

The bait had been delivered. The news had reached the target. And the initial, observable reaction was… nothing. A perfect, unnerving blank. Had they miscalculated? Was Mildred simply too controlled, too intelligent to be provoked by such an indirect stimulus? Or was her lack of reaction merely the calm surface of the water *before* the submerged predator decided how and when to strike back? Agnes felt a colder dread than before. An obvious reaction, even panic, might have been easier to interpret, to counter. This absolute composure felt like facing a void, leaving them uncertain if their plan had failed entirely, or if Mildred was simply biding her time, assessing the threat, before making her own, far more dangerous, move. The waiting game, Agnes realised, had just become infinitely more complex.

****

The hour following Agnes's carefully staged 'discovery' and subse-

340

quent 'leak' to Esme Weatherly passed with an almost unnerving normalcy within the clubhouse of the Toorak Croquet & Horticultural Society. Mildred Pettle, having received Esme's likely wide-eyed report about the missing Carmichael-era ledger, had returned to her duties with what appeared to be complete equanimity. She distributed the mail with her usual quiet efficiency, took several routine phone calls regarding upcoming social bookings, and even spent ten minutes patiently explaining the complex new online court reservation system to a technologically bewildered Colonel Abernathy.

From his vantage point behind *The Age* in the members' lounge, Fitzwilliam watched her with a growing sense of frustration. Had their ploy failed? Had Mildred simply dismissed Agnes's historical 'puzzle' as irrelevant rambling? Her composure was absolute, a smooth, placid surface reflecting none of the potential turmoil beneath. He felt a familiar pang of doubt – were they chasing shadows, constructing elaborate theories based on coincidence and misinterpreted micro-expressions? The weight of their accusation felt immense, almost unbearable, when contrasted with Mildred's apparently untroubled demeanour.

Agnes, seated in the library alcove continuing her Centenary research (a perfect cover, allowing prolonged, quiet observation), shared Fitzwilliam's assessment but tempered it with her knowledge of Mildred's deep-seated caution. Mildred wasn't impulsive like Harry Smythe. If Agnes's words *had* struck a nerve related to historical records and Ainsworth's research, Mildred's reaction wouldn't likely be immediate or overt. She would process, calculate, assess the threat level, and *then* act, discreetly. The lack of an immediate reaction wasn't necessarily failure; it might simply be the precursor to a more carefully considered move. Agnes settled in to wait, her focus absolute, observing Mildred's intermittent appearances in the main lounge or corridor through the library doorway.

Ronnie Peterson, having established Mildred's adherence to baseline routine in the hour following the stimulus, shifted his focus. He retrieved his laptop from his bag and began inputting data into a spreadsheet – baseline timings versus observed timings, potential deviation points noted (Agnes's trigger delivery, Esme's subsequent visit to Mildred's office). He started building a stochastic model, trying to predict Mildred's *likely* next actions based on her established patterns and the assumed impact of the new information variable. His internal monologue was a stream of probabilities and logistical pathways, a purely abstract analysis of the human drama unfolding around him.

Chloe, meanwhile, had found a legitimate reason to be near the administrative corridor – replacing the slightly wilted flower arrangement on the console table outside the library. This gave her a plausible vantage point for observing movement towards Mildred's office or, more importantly, the seldom-used archive room further down the passage. She worked slowly, meticulously arranging fresh stems of fragrant jonquils and paperwhites, her senses hyper-alert, listening to footsteps, watching shadows. The memory of Mildred's unsettling appearance near the compost heaps days earlier kept replaying in her mind, fuelling a mixture of fear and resolve.

It was Fitzwilliam, positioned outside near the west boundary path under the guise of inspecting the problematic drainage with Henderson Jr. (who had, thankfully, quickly become engrossed in explaining the intricacies of sub-surface agricultural pipes, leaving Fitzwilliam free to observe), who noted the first subtle deviation around 12:45 PM, during the quiet lull as members began gathering for lunch. Mildred emerged from the administrative wing side door, not heading towards the lounge or the dining area, but walking purposefully towards her own office, the door to which was usually locked when she wasn't present during core hours. She unlocked it, slipped inside, and closed the door firmly behind her.

Fitzwilliam checked his watch, making a mental note. This wasn't entirely unusual – Mildred sometimes retrieved personal items or worked through lunch – but given the timing, less than two hours after hearing about the 'missing ledger' potentially relevant to Ainsworth's research, it felt significant. He continued his facade of conversation with Henderson Jr., occasionally nodding or murmuring agreement about soak wells, while keeping one eye fixed on Mildred's office door. How long would she stay? What was she doing? Accessing files? Making a private call on the landline? Shredding documents? He strained his ears but could hear nothing over the distance and the groundskeeper's monologue. After precisely nineteen minutes (Ronnie would have appreciated the precision, Fitzwilliam thought wryly), Mildred emerged, locked the door carefully, and walked back towards the clubhouse lounge, her expression as placid as ever, carrying nothing but her handbag. Nineteen minutes. Longer than usual for simply fetching lunch, perhaps, but not long enough for extensive file review or destruction. Suspicious, yes. Conclusive, no. He discreetly texted Ronnie: *"MP Office Visit. 12:45-13:04. Duration 19m. Note deviation from baseline lunch routine."*

A short while later, it was Chloe's turn. She was polishing the leaves of the aspidistra outside the library door when she saw Mildred emerge from the main lounge and turn *left* down the administrative corridor, heading *away* from her own office and towards the library, archives, and lesser-used committee rooms. Chloe's breath caught. This was definitely not part of Mildred's usual lunchtime or early afternoon routine. Trying to appear absorbed in her task, Chloe watched Mildred's reflection in the polished surface of the console table.

Mildred walked slowly, deliberately down the quiet corridor. She paused near the heavy oak door of the main club archive room – the room containing decades of minutes, reports, and potentially, incriminating historical ledgers (real or imagined). Her back was mostly to Chloe's observation point, but Chloe could see her head turn slightly, scanning the empty corridor in both directions. Mildred reached out a hand, her fingers hovering for a split second over the old brass doorknob, before seemingly thinking better of it and letting her hand drop back to her side. She lingered for another moment, looking intently at the door as if trying to divine its contents through sheer willpower, then turned abruptly and walked back towards the main lounge, her footsteps brisk and businesslike again.

Chloe let out a breath she hadn't realised she was holding. Mildred hadn't tried her key. She hadn't actually attempted entry. But she had *gone there*. She had deliberately walked down that quiet corridor, checked her surroundings, and paused significantly outside the archive door. Why? Unless Agnes's mention of a missing ledger related to historical finances, supposedly housed within that very room, had indeed planted a seed of serious concern? It felt like a reconnaissance mission, an assessment of the potential threat location. Chloe quickly texted Ronnie: *"MP Archive Corridor approach. 13:22. Paused at door approx. 5 sec. No entry attempt observed. Returned lounge."*

The final piece of observable reaction came nearly an hour later. Agnes was seated back in the library alcove, genuinely trying now to focus on the Centenary brochure captions, needing the mental distraction. Mildred entered the library, ostensibly to return a borrowed copy of *Australian Garden History*. She deposited the book, then paused near Agnes's table.

"Agnes dear," she began, her tone perfectly casual, friendly even. "Still deep in the annals of the Society?"

Agnes looked up, schooling her features into mild academic preoccupation. "Mildred. Yes, just trying to verify some founding member details for the brochure. History can be rather slippery, can't it?"

"Indeed," Mildred agreed, her eyes crinkling in a smile that seemed almost genuine. She lingered, fiddling with a stray bookmark on a nearby shelf. "I was just thinking," she continued, her voice dropping slightly, conspiratorially, "about that fascinating old ledger you mentioned to Esme this morning. The one from Mr Carmichael's time, supposedly missing since '95?"

Agnes felt her own internal alarms ring. *Direct approach. Fishing for information.* She kept her expression neutral, slightly puzzled. "Oh, that? Yes, just an odd reference in the House Committee minutes. Probably nothing, just poor filing back then, as you suggested." She made a dismissive gesture.

"Probably," Mildred echoed smoothly. "Still, one does wonder. Did the minute entry give any clue *where* it might have gone missing from? Or what specific 'Orchard End usage reconciliations' it supposedly contained? It seems such a peculiar combination of topics for one ledger." Her questions were sharp, specific, probing the details of Agnes's supposed discovery, testing its veracity.

Agnes feigned thoughtful confusion, pretending to consult her notes. "Goodness, no, Mildred. It was terribly vague. Just a line item under 'Outstanding Archival Matters'. No specifics on the contents beyond 'West Wing/Orchard End accounts'. And certainly no clue as to its whereabouts. Most likely disintegrated into dust decades ago, I imagine!" She offered a small, dismissive laugh, hoping it sounded convincing.

Mildred watched her for a moment, her gaze sharp before

softening again into polite sympathy. "Ah well. Another little historical mystery for you to ponder, Agnes. Do let me know if you ever stumble across it!" She gave a final bright smile and turned, leaving the library.

Agnes let out a slow, controlled breath only after Mildred was out of sight. That was close. Mildred hadn't directly challenged her, but the specific questions – asking about the *contents* and *whereabouts* of the non-existent ledger – indicated she was taking the 'discovery' seriously, trying to gauge how much Agnes actually knew or suspected. Mildred was worried. The bait had not only been taken; it was clearly causing significant internal ripples within the subject's carefully controlled system. The question now was, what action would those ripples provoke next?

****

The main lounge of the Toorak Croquet & Horticultural Society was dark and silent, save for the rhythmic, sonorous ticking of the grandfather clock in the hall – a sound usually lost in the daytime bustle but now echoing unnervingly in the emptiness. It was well past ten o'clock on Monday evening, April 21st. The last lingering committee members had departed hours ago, the bar was closed, the lights extinguished save for the dim emergency lighting casting long, distorted shadows down the administrative corridor. Outside, a sliver of moon offered little illumination through the high windows, and the damp gardens were wrapped in suburban quiet. Most of the club, like the surrounding Toorak avenues, was asleep.

But Chloe Dubois was wide awake, hidden, her heart thudding against her ribs with painful intensity. She was crouched uncomfortably in the deep alcove just inside the library entrance, concealed behind a large potted Kentia palm that usually graced the members' reading area. She shouldn't be here. Her shift had finished hours ago. But after the tense undercurrents of the day, after Mildred Pettle's seemingly casual but probing questions in this very library following Agnes's carefully planted 'discovery' of the missing ledger reference, Chloe hadn't been able to shake a deep, visceral sense of unease. A gut feeling, illogical perhaps but insistent, told her that Mildred, under her mask of calm control, *was* rattled, and might try to act now, under the cover of darkness and assumed solitude.

Agnes and Fitzwilliam had dismissed her feeling as understandable anxiety, urging caution and adherence to their plan of daytime observation. Ronnie had calculated the probability of Subject P attempting nocturnal archival access as 'moderate but non-negligible', adding complex variables about perceived risk versus information urgency. But Chloe, driven by something less quantifiable – perhaps the memory of Mildred's unnervingly sharp gaze near the compost heap, or just the simple conviction that secrets felt safer dealt with at night – had felt compelled to return. She had let herself back in quietly using the garden staff side entrance key (intended for early morning watering duties) just before the main caretaker did his final lock-up rounds, slipping into the dark library to wait, feeling both foolishly impulsive and strangely necessary.

Waiting was agony. Every creak of the old building settling, every distant car passing on the street outside, every tick of the grandfather clock seemed amplified, potentially heralding discovery. She focused on controlling her breathing, staying absolutely still behind the palm fronds, peering out through the gap towards the dimly lit administrative corridor where the heavy oak door of the main archive room stood sentinel. What if she was wrong? What if Mildred was sound asleep at home? What if the caretaker returned for a forgotten item? She felt a prickle of fear, questioning her own judgment.

Then, she heard it. Not footsteps – the corridor carpet muffled sound effectively – but the almost imperceptible click of a door opening further down the administrative wing. Mildred's office? Followed by a brief pause, then soft, measured footsteps approaching the library/archive section of the corridor. Chloe pressed herself further back into the alcove, holding her breath, praying the dense palm fronds provided sufficient cover.

A figure emerged from the deeper shadows of the corridor into the faint spill of emergency light near the archive door: Mildred Pettle. She was dressed simply in dark trousers and a cardigan, carrying only her usual handbag, looking for all the world like someone who had merely forgotten something at the office. But her movements belied that casual interpretation. She moved with a distinct, cautious purposefulness, pausing just before reaching the archive door, her head turning slightly as she scanned the length of the silent corridor in both directions. She seemed to listen intently for a few moments. Satisfied she was alone, she approached the heavy oak door.

From her handbag, she produced not the main office master key ring Esme carried, but a single, smaller key on a simple chain – presumably her personal master or an archive-specific key. Chloe watched, mesmerised by the quiet efficiency of her movements, as Mildred inserted the key into the large brass lock. The mechanism turned with a soft, well-oiled *snick*. Mildred glanced around one final time, then pushed the heavy door inward, just enough to slip inside, pulling it almost closed behind her but not allowing the latch to click shut.

She was in. Chloe's heart hammered. Mildred *had* taken the bait. The reference to the missing ledger, linked to Ainsworth's research and the West Wing finances, had clearly alarmed her enough to compel this clandestine, late-night visit to the very repository where such a document – if it existed – might be found, or where *other* documents she suddenly feared might corroborate it, could potentially be accessed or destroyed.

What was she doing in there? Chloe strained her ears, but could hear nothing beyond the insistent ticking of the clock and her own ragged breathing. The archive room was windowless, its secrets contained within floor-to-ceiling shelves of ledgers, minute books, membership rolls, and forgotten correspondence. Was Mildred frantically searching for the non-existent Carmichael-era ledger Agnes had mentioned? Or was she using this opportunity to locate and perhaps remove or alter *real* documents – minutes from 1987/88, old financial reports, records pertaining to the 'old orchard end' land – documents that Ainsworth might have consulted, documents that could potentially incriminate her?

The wait felt unbearable. Each second stretched into an eternity. Chloe's legs began to cramp from crouching, but she didn't dare move a muscle. Five minutes passed. Ten. What could possibly be taking so long if she were just doing a quick check? Was she reading something? Destroying something?

Then, the sliver of light visible beneath the archive door was momentarily blocked, then reappeared. Soft footsteps sounded just inside. The door opened again, just wide enough for Mildred to emerge. She paused in the doorway, glancing quickly down the corridor again, before pulling the door firmly shut. The lock clicked with quiet finality.

Mildred stood there for another moment, perfectly still. Chloe could see her profile more clearly now in the dim light. Her expression wasn't one of panic or furtive guilt. It was, Chloe thought with a fresh wave of fear, one of intense, focused concentration, perhaps even grim satisfaction. As if she had found what she was looking for? Or confirmed something she needed to know? Or perhaps removed something she needed to disappear?

Then, composing her features back into their usual placid neutrality, Mildred turned and walked briskly back down the corridor towards her office wing, her footsteps disappearing into the silence.

Chloe remained frozen in the alcove long after the sound had faded, her body trembling with reaction, relief warring with terror. She had witnessed it. Mildred Pettle, acting on the information Agnes had planted, had used her key to secretly access the club archives late at night. It wasn't proof of murder, wasn't proof of embezzlement in itself. But it was concrete, observable proof of guilty knowledge, proof of her deep concern about historical records linked to Ainsworth's research, proof of her willingness to act clandestinely outside normal procedures. It was the reaction they had hoped for, the confirmation that their probe had hit a critically sensitive nerve.

Slowly, carefully, Chloe eased herself out of the cramped alcove, her muscles aching. She needed to leave, quickly and silently, before the caretaker made a final round or an alarm was inadvertently triggered. And she needed to report this, immediately. She pulled out her phone, fingers fumbling slightly as she typed a coded message to the secure group chat: *"Observation Post Alpha. Target accessed Archive Room approx. 22:15 - 22:25 using key. Departed towards office wing. Significant reaction confirmed. Proceeding with extreme caution. Chloe."*

As she slipped back out through the garden staff entrance into the cool, damp Melbourne night, Chloe felt a profound shift. The investigation no longer felt like a theoretical puzzle. Witnessing Mildred's secret, deliberate actions had made the danger, and the reality of the woman they were pursuing, terrifyingly concrete. The trap had been sprung, the quarry had reacted. The endgame, she sensed with a certainty that chilled her to the bone, was approaching far faster than she had anticipated.

****

The grandfather clock in Agnes Plummett's hallway had just struck eleven when Chloe Dubois finally arrived, letting herself quietly into the already gathered group in the study. She looked pale and exhausted, her usual apron replaced by damp outerwear, but her eyes held a spark of adrenaline-fuelled intensity that immediately silenced the low, frustrated conversation between Agnes, Fitzwilliam, and Ronnie. They had been dissecting Mildred's earlier, frustratingly subtle deviations – the prolonged office visit Fitzwilliam had logged, the probing questions directed at Agnes in the library – concluding, with growing unease, that their carefully planted bait might have been noted but ultimately dismissed or too cleverly handled to yield useful reaction. Chloe's arrival, however, changed everything.

"She did it," Chloe breathed, sinking into the nearest chair without even removing her damp coat, her voice trembling slightly. "She went to the archives. Just now. I saw her."

The atmosphere in the room instantly crackled with renewed tension. Fitzwilliam leaned forward, his earlier weariness evaporating. Ronnie grabbed his notebook, pencil poised. Agnes placed a calming hand on Chloe's arm but her gaze was sharp, demanding details.

"Tell us, Chloe," Agnes urged quietly but firmly. "From the beginning. Everything you saw."

Chloe recounted her decision to return to the club after hours, driven by that nagging instinct. She described the silent, darkened corridors, her hiding place behind the Kentia palm in the library alcove, the unnerving wait. Then, her voice dropping lower, she detailed Mildred's cautious approach down the administrative corridor well after 10 PM, her checking for observers, her use of a single key to unlock the heavy archive room door.

"She slipped inside," Chloe continued, her eyes wide as she relived the moment. "Pulled the door almost shut. I couldn't see exactly what she was doing, obviously, and she wasn't in there for long – maybe ten minutes? But she definitely *went in*. When she came out, she looked… focused. Intense. Not panicked, exactly, but very… deliberate. She locked the door carefully and walked back towards her office wing." Chloe took a shaky breath. "I waited until I was sure she was gone, then I left as quickly as I could."

Silence descended again, but this time it was heavy with significance, with the undeniable weight of confirmation. Fitzwilliam stared at Chloe, a mixture of alarm for her safety and profound validation flooding through him. Agnes closed her eyes briefly, processing the information with methodical precision. Ronnie was already scribbling furiously, drawing new vectors on his chart, muttering about "Post-Stimulus Action Confirmation" and "Targeted Information Retrieval Attempt".

"She took the bait," Fitzwilliam stated finally, the words almost a whisper. "Agnes, your comment this morning about the missing ledger, the West Wing accounts, the Orchard End… it hit precisely the nerve we hoped it would. She didn't react overtly then, but she couldn't leave it alone. She had to check."

"Check what, though?" Agnes mused aloud, her mind racing. "Was she searching for the non-existent ledger I mentioned, fearing it might actually exist and contain something incriminating? Or was she there to access or remove *other*, real documents related to that period – Humphrey Carmichael's files, perhaps, or specific committee reports – documents she suddenly feared *I* might look for next, now that the topic was raised?" She tapped her pen against her notebook. "Her actions confirm her deep sensitivity to that historical period and those specific financial/land issues. It proves a guilty knowledge, a need to control the records."

"Probability of Subject P's guilt increases to > 0.95," Ronnie announced, underlining a figure on his chart with unnecessary force. "Observed clandestine action directly correlates with planted stimulus targeting known area of suspected long-term fraud and motive. Alternative explanations – routine administrative task conducted at 10 PM, sudden benign interest in archival materials – exhibit negligible probability."

"So we have it," Chloe said, looking between them, some colour returning to her face, replaced now by a different kind of intensity. "Proof she's worried about those old records Ainsworth was looking into."

"We have proof she took a significant, clandestine risk based on the information Agnes provided," Fitzwilliam corrected cautiously, the lawyer reasserting himself over the excited detective. "It's powerful behavioural evidence, incredibly damning circumstantially. But," he sighed, "it's still not the smoking gun. We didn't see what she looked at, what she took, if anything. We can't prove *what* she was afraid of finding or leaving behind in that room. In court, she could still argue she was merely checking on the security of valuable records late at night after Agnes raised concerns about things being 'missing.'"

Agnes nodded grimly. "Alistair is right. This confirms our target and her vulnerability regarding the historical investigation, but it doesn't provide the irrefutable link needed to bypass the police's focus on Smythe or secure warrants against Mildred herself. It tells us we are absolutely on the right path, but the path just became considerably more dangerous."

"Her awareness level," Ronnie stated, pointing to another section of his chart, "must now be re-evaluated as High. She knows *someone* (likely Agnes) is probing sensitive historical areas linked to Ainsworth. She may now suspect active surveillance, given her cautious behaviour tonight. Future actions may involve increased counter-surveillance, accelerated evidence destruction, or even," he paused, "proactive threat neutralisation."

The chilling phrase hung in the air. *Threat neutralisation.* Silencing them, as she had silenced Ainsworth.

"Which means," Fitzwilliam said heavily, "our own caution must increase tenfold. And we need to move faster, focusing on avenues Mildred *cannot* easily control or sanitise."

"My research into the Fincham book and the land title records," Agnes affirmed immediately. "External archives, council records. Information outside her direct sphere of influence at the club."

"The suppliers," Fitzwilliam added. "While I hit a wall on direct financial links via public records, perhaps there's another angle. Can we identify *who* at the club physically received goods or signed off on work completion for these phantom companies? That might provide a witness, or internal documentation Mildred didn't control."

"And the physical evidence," Chloe insisted, gesturing towards the specimen bags still on Agnes's desk – the buried leaves, the glass shard, the grey glove. "The leaves prove *Digitalis* was handled and hidden. The glove… if we could just identify it, link it to *her*…"

"Agnes," Ronnie turned to her, "regarding your library observation today – the man in the tweed jacket you felt might be watching you?"

Agnes frowned. "Purely subjective feeling. No concrete proof. He disappeared before I left."

"Still," Ronnie persisted, "factor it in. P(External Surveillance) moves from negligible to low-moderate. If Mildred suspected Ainsworth shared his findings, or if she has external associates involved in the financial scheme, employing discreet observation isn't illogical."

They fell silent again, the magnitude of their situation pressing in. They had successfully provoked their quarry, confirming her deep-seated fear regarding the historical secrets Ainsworth was unearthing. But in doing so, they had almost certainly alerted her, raising their own risk profile exponentially. And they *still* lacked that single, undeniable piece of evidence.

"Our plan remains largely the same," Agnes said finally, breaking the silence, her voice steady, resolute. "We pursue the external records – Fincham, land titles, supplier verification. We analyse the physical evidence – the leaves, the glove, the shard. We maintain discreet observation, assuming *we* are now potentially being observed ourselves. And," she looked pointedly at Fitzwilliam, "we prepare a contingency. A way to present our findings to Detective Inspector Davies should the situation escalate, or should we find that final piece of proof, ensuring it is presented credibly and cannot be easily dismissed."

Fitzwilliam nodded slowly. "I can begin drafting a confidential memorandum, outlining our findings chronologically, referencing supporting evidence where possible, purely as an internal record for now. It helps clarify the argument."

"Good," Agnes approved. "Structure is essential." She looked around at her tired but determined collaborators. "We knew this would be difficult. Now we know it is also dangerous. But we are closer than ever. Let's proceed. Eyes open. Extreme caution. And trust each other implicitly."

The quartet exchanged looks, a mixture of fear, exhaustion, and unwavering resolve passing between them. The trap had worked, the reaction confirmed. Now came the endgame: finding the proof before the cornered, calculating killer decided to eliminate the threat they represented. The quiet study felt like the calm before a gathering storm.

20

Unearthing Proof

The atmosphere inside the Public Record Office Victoria in North Melbourne was markedly different from the soaring, almost cathedral-like grandeur of the State Library's La Trobe Reading Room. Here, the focus felt more utilitarian, more functional – rows of microfilm readers hummed quietly, researchers conferred in hushed tones with archivists behind wide counters, the air filled with the dry scent of ageing cardboard files and the low buzz of fluorescent lights. Yet, for Agnes Plummett, arriving shortly after opening on Tuesday morning, April 22nd, this repository of official government history held an even greater potential significance. If the State Library held the clues, PROV might hold the proof – the unvarnished, administrative record of land ownership, boundaries, and obligations related to that ambiguous sliver of earth bordering the Toorak Croquet & Horticultural Society.

She felt a renewed sense of purpose, tempered by the chilling possibility of surveillance she'd sensed at the State Library yesterday. As she signed in, presented her identification, and submitted her request slips for specific historical Parish Plans for Prahran and early Council Rate Books for the relevant period, she made a conscious effort to scan her surroundings discreetly. No sign of the man in the tweed jacket. The other researchers seemed genuinely absorbed in their own historical pursuits – tracing family histories, examining old education department files, reviewing immigration records. Perhaps her fear had been unfounded, a product of her own heightened anxiety. Yet, the caution remained, a low hum beneath her methodical surface.

Her first focus was the Parish Plans, large-scale maps showing original Crown land grants and subsequent subdivisions. She was directed to a specialised map reading area, where an archivist carefully unrolled the fragile, linen-backed documents onto a vast, tilted table under protective Mylar sheeting. Agnes bent over the 1888 plan, the same era as the ambiguous survey cited by Fincham, using her magnifying glass to trace the boundaries around Allotments 15-18. There it was again – the western boundary defined by the meandering Gardiner's Creek tributary, the notation indicating 'Approx. High Water Mark', and the frustratingly vague reference to the 'Scarred Gum nr. Bend'. Critically, the plan showed the land granted for the eventual Society property stopping short of the creek itself in that particular section, leaving that irregular sliver – the potential 'old orchard end' – seemingly unallocated, marked perhaps only by faint contour lines indicating the creek bank.

She then examined later Parish Plans from the early 20th century, after the adjacent land had become public parkland. The Society's main boundaries were clearer now, formalised. But that western sliver along the creek? It remained stubbornly ambiguous, sometimes appearing notionally incorporated into the parkland survey lines, sometimes seemingly ignored, falling into a grey area between the formally defined club property and the public reserve. No definitive ownership or status was immediately apparent from these overarching plans. Ainsworth, with his auditor's eye for inconsistency, would have seized on this lack of clarity.

Frustrated but not deterred, Agnes turned her attention to her second request: the Council Rate Books for the former Prahran municipality (which historically covered Toorak) from the late 19th and early 20th centuries. These large, heavy ledgers, filled with dense, handwritten entries, documented who paid municipal rates on which properties year after year. If the 'old orchard end' sliver *was* recognised as a separate, land parcel, even briefly, it would be recorded here.

An archivist delivered the first dusty volume, covering 1890-1899. Agnes carefully opened it, the pages brittle, the iron gall ink faded in places. She located the relevant section corresponding to the land parcels along Gardiner's Creek. She scanned the columns – Owner, Occupier, Property Description, Net Annual Value, Rate Paid. She found the entries for the larger properties that would later form the club and the park. Then, her finger stopped. Tucked between two larger entries, almost an afterthought, was a listing for a small, unnumbered parcel described simply as "Orchard Land adj. Gardiner's Ck.". The listed owner/occupier? "Croft, Silas". The Net Annual Value was minimal, and the rate paid correspondingly tiny, suggesting marginal land value at the time. But it was *there*. A separate entry. Silas Croft, the keen pomologist mentioned by Fincham, *was* paying rates on that specific piece of land in the 1890s, separate from the main adjacent holdings.

Her heart beat faster. This was significant. It meant that, at least in the late 19th century, the council *did* recognise Croft's experimental orchard plot as a distinct, rateable entity, implying some form of recognised occupancy or quasi-ownership, even if its precise title status was murky. She quickly checked subsequent years in the volume. The entry for 'Croft, Silas - Orchard Land' continued consistently through to 1899.

She requested the next volume, 1900-1909. Again, she found the entry, year after year. Then, in the volume for 1910-1919 – the period covered by Fincham's book – she scanned the relevant pages for 1910, 1911, 1912... The entry for Silas Croft's orchard land was simply... gone. No crossing out, no note of transfer, no indication of amalgamation with another property. It just vanished from the rate book after the 1909 entry. Silas Croft himself, Agnes knew from a quick biographical check prompted by Fincham's book, had died in late 1909. Had the council simply stopped billing for the marginal plot after the occupier's death, given its ambiguous title status? Had it been unofficially absorbed into the adjacent parkland or the large estate later purchased by the Society, without formal record?

This cessation of official record provided the crucial historical gap. A piece of land, once generating produce (according to Fincham) and subject to rates (according to the council books), effectively dropped off the official map around 1910. It became forgotten land, its status legally uncertain. Perfect for someone, decades later, with intimate knowledge of club history and boundary ambiguities (perhaps gained while assisting Treasurer Carmichael in 1988?), to potentially exploit. Mildred could have discovered its status then, realised its potential, and perhaps established some form of quiet, unrecorded use or income from it over the ensuing years, justifying her Fete account skimming as 'management fees' or rightful income in her own mind.

Agnes felt the pieces locking firmly into place. This historical administrative anomaly was almost certainly what Ainsworth had unearthed, connecting his archival digging directly to potential long-term financial exploitation linked to a specific piece of land.

Driven now, she decided to check one more thing. If Ainsworth had found this, had he tried to formalise the situation? Had he, perhaps, recently approached the current Stonnington Council (which now covered Toorak) to query the status of that specific parcel? That might explain the 'property dispute' Mildred had vaguely mentioned as a red herring – perhaps twisting Ainsworth's official query into something contentious. Accessing recent council planning or correspondence records wasn't possible here at PROV, but maybe...

She recalled her own time on various local historical society committees. Sometimes, unsuccessful or withdrawn planning applications or boundary clarifications left faint traces in council meeting agendas or minutes, even if not fully documented. She navigated the PROV catalogue again, searching for digitised Stonnington Council meeting minutes or agendas from the past six months, using keywords like 'Gardiner's Creek', 'boundary clarification', 'Toorak Croquet'.

It took another half hour of patient searching through dense pdfs of council agendas, but then she found it. An item listed under 'Correspondence Received' for a Planning Committee meeting agenda dated March 5th, 2025 – just six weeks before Ainsworth's death. It read simply: *"Item 7.3: Correspondence from Mr B. Ainsworth regarding historical boundary clarification adjacent to Allotment 17, Section B, Parish of Prahran (Gardiner's Ck frontage). Matter deferred pending further information from applicant."* And then, in the minutes from the subsequent meeting in late March: *"Item 7.3 Update: Correspondence withdrawn by applicant (B. Ainsworth)."*

Agnes stared at the screen, a cold certainty washing over her. Ainsworth *had* taken official steps. He had formally queried the council about the exact boundary near the 'old orchard end'. And then, shortly before his death, he had withdrawn the query. Why? Had he found the proof he needed elsewhere? Had he decided on a different course of action – confronting Mildred directly? Or had he been warned off, threatened perhaps, causing him to retract the official inquiry while potentially continuing his private investigation?

This final discovery felt crucial. It proved Ainsworth's investigation wasn't just historical curiosity; it had reached the level of official inquiry, significantly raising the threat level for anyone benefiting from the ambiguous land status. And his subsequent withdrawal felt ominous.

Agnes carefully photographed the relevant sections of the rate books and the council agenda/minutes with her phone, feeling the weight of responsibility settle upon her. She now held documented, official evidence corroborating the historical land anomaly, Croft's connection, its disappearance from records, and Ainsworth's recent, official attempt to clarify its status – an attempt he then abruptly withdrew shortly before his murder. This wasn't speculation anymore. This was a clear trail, leading from a dusty history book, through obscure council records, directly to the probable motive for murder. She quickly texted Fitzwilliam and the others: *"Significant breakthrough at PROV. Historical land anomaly confirmed via rate books. Ainsworth lodged official council query re: boundary Mar 5th, withdrew late Mar. Strong link established. Need to convene ASAP. Agnes."* Packing her notes, she felt a grim satisfaction, but also a renewed sense of urgency. They were undeniably closing in on the truth. The question was whether they could reveal it before the increasingly threatened killer took further action.

****

Alistair Fitzwilliam arrived at his Collins Street office on Wednesday morning feeling the conflicting pressures of his professional obligations and his clandestine investigation more acutely than ever. Agnes's text message from the previous evening, confirming

361

her breakthrough at the Public Record Office – the proof of the ambiguous land parcel's historical status and Ainsworth's withdrawn council query – had been both exhilarating and deeply alarming. It cemented the likely motive, rooting Mildred Pettle's potential decades-long deception in the very soil of the Society grounds. But it also highlighted the sophistication and historical depth of the secrets Ainsworth had been unearthing, making the task of finding irrefutable proof seem even more daunting. Fitzwilliam's own research had hit a wall; the phantom suppliers were clearly suspicious, the Vance connection provocative, but the public record shield preventing a direct link to Mildred's personal finances remained intact. They needed something more. They needed evidence from *within* the club's own system, evidence Mildred might have believed was safely buried under layers of routine administration or Ainsworth's seemingly compliant signature.

He spent the first hour of the morning dealing with urgent emails related to the Macrocorp case, dictating correspondence, trying to project an aura of focused legal diligence for his assistant, Sarah, while his mind raced elsewhere. He needed a legitimate pretext, a plausible reason to demand access not just to high-level summaries, but to detailed payment records, transaction logs, supporting documentation for specific large expenditures – the very records Mildred likely controlled or curated. His previous role, ensuring 'payment continuity', felt too thin now for the level of detail required.

His opportunity came via an email from Charles Abercrombie just before 10 AM, circulating the draft agenda for an emergency Finance Subcommittee meeting scheduled for the following week to discuss appointing an interim Treasurer and reviewing current financial commitments in light of Ainsworth's death. Listed under 'Matters Arising' was 'Review of Significant Recent Capital Expenditures &

Event Deposits'. Perfect.

Fitzwilliam immediately called Abercrombie, bypassing Esme or Mildred. "Charles? Alistair Fitzwilliam here. Regarding the Finance Subcommittee agenda – thank you for circulating it so promptly."

"Alistair," Abercrombie's calm baritone came down the line. "Difficult times. Trying to maintain stability."

"Precisely," Fitzwilliam agreed. "And regarding Item 4b, the review of recent expenditures… As you know, I had a brief look at the immediate payables last week. To properly contribute to that review, especially regarding the large outlays for the roof repairs and the Centenary Gala deposits Bartholomew signed off shortly before his passing, I feel I really ought to examine the detailed transaction records and supporting documentation – contracts, proof of service delivery reports, supplier ABN verification for GST purposes, that sort of thing. Purely due diligence, you understand, ensuring everything aligns before the subcommittee meets." He framed it as responsible preparation for the upcoming meeting, leveraging his legal background.

There was a pause on the other end. Fitzwilliam held his breath. Was he pushing too hard? Would Abercrombie see through the pretext?

"Hmm," Abercrombie said finally. "Due diligence. Yes, I see your point, Alistair. Given Bartholomew's… sudden departure… and the size of those recent expenditures, ensuring the paperwork is entirely in order before the subcommittee convenes is prudent. Thoroughness is key, as Bartholomew himself would have insisted," he added, perhaps ironically. "The detailed payment journals and invoice files are kept in the Treasurer's office, as you know. Mildred has access, naturally, as does Esme with the master key." He hesitated. "Mildred is extremely busy coordinating… well, everything… at the moment. Perhaps it would be best if Esme facilitated access for you?

Supervised, of course, just for procedural propriety."

Relief washed over Fitzwilliam. Abercrombie, perhaps spurred by his own unease following their earlier conversation about Ainsworth's historical digging, had agreed. Supervised access wasn't ideal, but it was access. "Thank you, Charles. That would be most helpful. I could potentially come by later this morning? Esme's supervision is perfectly appropriate, of course."

He arranged a time with Abercrombie, then quickly rescheduled his Macrocorp conference call, feeling a surge of nervous energy. This was it. A chance to look behind the 'too perfect' summaries, to examine the specific transactions related to the likely phantom suppliers within the club's own records.

He arrived at the club shortly before 11:30 AM. The atmosphere was subdued, but less overtly tense than during the tournament weekend. He found Esme Weatherly in the main office, looking pale and overworked. He explained Abercrombie had authorised him, under her supervision, to briefly review specific recent payment records in the Treasurer's office related to upcoming committee discussions.

Esme nodded wearily. "Yes, Charles mentioned you might call. Mildred's attending a meeting off-site this morning with the Centenary Gala caterers," she offered, almost as an aside, though Fitzwilliam registered the information instantly – Mildred *not* present provided a brief window. "The office is free. But Alistair," she lowered her voice, looking anxious, "please be discreet. And quick. Things are just so... unsettled."

"Of course, Esme. Absolutely," Fitzwilliam reassured her.

Esme unlocked the Treasurer's office, the same neat, sterile room Agnes had searched days earlier. She indicated the relevant bound payment journals on the shelf and the box files containing recent invoices. "I'll just be outside in the main office if you need anything," she said, clearly wanting to distance herself but fulfil her supervisory duty nominally. She left the door slightly ajar.

Fitzwilliam felt his pulse quicken. He had perhaps an hour, maybe less, before Mildred returned. He went straight to the payment journal covering the last six months. He found the entry for the 'Urgent Roof Repairs' – two substantial payments made in December and January to 'WeatherTech Roofing Solutions'. He noted the cheque numbers and dates. Then he located the corresponding invoice file. He pulled out the WeatherTech invoices. They looked professional enough – company logo (simple, generic), ABN listed, description 'Stage 1 / Stage 2 Roof Repairs West Wing as per quote QRF-101'. But crucially, attached behind the invoices, where one would expect to find the accepted quote QRF-101, or at least a committee minute approving the expenditure, there was only a brief internal works order form. It described the need for urgent leak repairs, signed by Henderson Jr. (grounds/maintenance), but the section for 'Contractor Selected & Authorised By' was signed only by 'M. Pettle'. Bartholomew Ainsworth's signature appeared only on the payment authorisation line in the main journal, not on any document approving this specific, unfamiliar contractor or the quoted amount.

Fitzwilliam felt a jolt. This was it. Proof of procedural failure, directly involving Mildred authorising payments to a likely shell company based on minimal internal paperwork, bypassing standard committee approval or competitive quote requirements for such a large sum. Ainsworth might have signed the final payment in the journal, possibly bundled with dozens of others, relying on Mildred's assurance that the underlying documentation was in order, but the *authorisation trail* itself led squarely back to her, for work performed by a company registered only weeks prior.

He quickly photographed the invoices and the works order

with his phone, his hands slightly trembling. This felt significant. Admissible? Perhaps, as evidence of negligence or breach of procedure. Proof of fraud? Not yet, but a powerful indicator.

He moved on, searching for the Centenary Gala deposits. He found the payment entry for 'Vintage Marquee Hire Pty Ltd'. He located the corresponding invoice – again, professional appearance, substantial deposit amount listed against a vague 'Contract Ref CMG-2025'. Supporting documentation? Only an internal memo from Mildred to Ainsworth stating "Marquee deposit secured per Committee resolution [date]" – but Fitzwilliam recalled checking those specific committee minutes; they approved seeking marquee quotes, not the selection of *this specific*, newly revived company, nor the deposit amount. Another procedural gap, another payment authorised based seemingly only on Mildred's assertion. He photographed these documents too.

Finally, 'Bespoke Botanical Displays'. He found the payment entry for the deposit. The invoice file contained a glossy, if rather generic, brochure showcasing pleasant floral arrangements, and the invoice itself for 'Deposit - Centenary Gala Floral Design & Installation per quote BBD-CG01'. Signed off for payment processing by Mildred, countersigned in the journal by Ainsworth. Supporting documentation? Again, missing the crucial quote BBD-CG01 itself, and no record of committee approval specifically selecting this company run by Eleanor Vance, Mildred's potential relative.

Fitzwilliam sat back, staring at the evidence displayed on his phone screen and reflected in his notes. The pattern was undeniable. Three separate instances of large payments made to highly suspicious suppliers, all processed by Mildred, all lacking complete supporting documentation or clear evidence of proper authorisation procedures having been followed, despite bearing Ainsworth's final signature in the payment journal. Ainsworth, the meticulous pedant, had clearly become complacent, trusting Mildred's administrative summaries, rubber-stamping payments without scrutinising the underlying detail – until something, perhaps the sheer scale of the Centenary costs, or his historical research triggering alarm bells, made him finally look closer. And when he looked closer, Fitzwilliam was now certain, he must have found these very same alarming procedural gaps and suspicious supplier details. He must have realised the potential for massive fraud occurring right under his nose, facilitated by the very person he likely trusted implicitly to manage the process.

He heard movement in the outer office – Esme perhaps, or someone else arriving. His time was up. He quickly replaced the files exactly as he had found them, closed the ledgers, and gathered his belongings, his mind racing. He had found it. Not the final proof connecting the money to Mildred's personal accounts, but concrete evidence, within the club's own records, of potentially fraudulent payments channelled through shell companies, enabled by procedural failures directly managed by Mildred Pettle. This wasn't just theory anymore. This was documented financial irregularity on a significant scale, providing the powerful, concrete motive they needed. He thanked a nervous-looking Esme, murmured something about needing further committee clarification on certain expenditures, and walked out into the cool Melbourne air, the weight of the evidence feeling both liberating and terrifying. They were closer than ever.

****

The feelings in Agnes Plummett's study that Thursday evening was electric, charged with the collective energy of discoveries that felt both momentous and deeply chilling. The remnants of their simple dinner lay forgotten. Spread across the large desk, illuminated by the focused glow of the banker's lamp, were the tangible results of their parallel investigations: Agnes's notes and photographed maps from the Public Record Office Victoria detailing the ambiguous 'old orchard end' boundary and Ainsworth's withdrawn council query; Fitzwilliam's printouts from ASIC and club payment records highlighting the likely fraudulent suppliers and Mildred's administrative control; Chloe's carefully sealed specimen bags containing the buried *Digitalis* leaves and the expensive grey glove. Ronnie's master chart hung nearby, now dense with interconnected arrows, timelines, and probability assessments heavily weighted against one name: Mildred Pettle.

They took turns presenting their final findings, each piece adding crucial weight to the scales of proof. Agnes went first, calmly detailing her confirmation of the historical land boundary ambiguity via the PROV rate books showing Silas Croft's separate payments for the 'Orchard Land adj. Gardiner's Ck.' and its subsequent disappearance from official records around 1910. "This establishes," she stated precisely, "a long-standing legal grey area concerning that specific parcel, the very area linked to Fincham's *Pyrus Malus* reference and adjacent to where Bartholomew was found."

Then came her most significant finding. "Furthermore," she continued, her voice steady but imbued with gravity, "I located records within the Stonnington Council archives. On March 5th this year, Bartholomew lodged a formal query seeking clarification of that specific historical boundary. And then," she paused, letting the impact land, "in late March, approximately three weeks before his death, he formally withdrew that query."

A sharp intake of breath from Chloe. Fitzwilliam leaned forward, his expression intent. "Withdrew it?" he echoed. "Why? After going to the trouble of lodging a formal query?"

"Precisely the question," Agnes affirmed. "Did he find the answers he needed elsewhere? Did he decide on a different course of action – perhaps direct confrontation with whoever he suspected was exploiting the ambiguity? Or," her gaze turned grim, "was he pressured or threatened into withdrawing it?" This withdrawn query felt pivotal – concrete proof Ainsworth was actively probing the sensitive land issue, making noise outside the club's internal structures, shortly before he was silenced.

Fitzwilliam then presented his findings, confirming the details Agnes and Ronnie already knew from his earlier call, but laying out the evidence with legal precision. "The ASIC searches confirm WeatherTech Roofing and Vintage Marquee Hire exhibit multiple characteristics of shell companies used for fraudulent invoicing," he stated, tapping the printouts. "And Bespoke Botanical Displays, while superficially more plausible, is directed by Eleanor Vance – sharing Mildred's maiden name – and," he added the crucial historical link, "an 'E. Vance' was temporarily employed assisting Treasurer Carmichael during the audit period immediately following the controversial 1987 West Wing donation."

He then detailed his examination of the club's internal payment records. "Crucially," he emphasised, "I reviewed the supporting documentation, or lack thereof, for the large payments made to these three companies. In each case, while Ainsworth provided the final sign-off in the main payment journal, the internal authorisation or justification bypassing standard committee approval protocols appears to originate solely from Mildred Pettle. For WeatherTech, just a works order signed by her. For Vintage Marquee, a memo from her asserting committee approval which doesn't align with the actual minutes. For Bespoke Botanical, no detailed quote attached, simply 'per M.P. instruction.'" He looked around the room. "This provides documented evidence, from the club's *own files*, of significant financial irregularities and procedural failures directly under Mildred's administrative control, channelling substantial funds to likely fraudulent entities."

Finally, Chloe spoke, her voice quiet but clear. She recounted her identification of the grey glove as an expensive French brand, *Gant Botanique*, available only in upmarket Melbourne stores. "It's not definitive proof of anything," she admitted, looking at the bagged glove on the table, "but it confirms it wasn't a casual item, not standard issue. It was a deliberate choice. Someone wore that specific, expensive glove while potentially handling *Digitalis* leaves or being present near where Mr Ainsworth died." It added another layer to the profile of a careful, calculating killer who invested in the right tools for the job, however grim.

Ronnie stood before his master chart, tapping key nodes with his pencil. "Conclusion," he declared, the scientific certainty ringing in his voice. "All independent data streams now converge with overwhelming probability on Subject P (Pettle). Motive: Compound – protection of potentially decades-long exploitation of historical land anomaly (per Agnes/Fincham/PROV records) *and* concealment of recent, large-scale fraudulent invoicing via shell companies (per Fitzwilliam/ASIC/internal payments). Means: Highly probable administration of cardiac glycoside toxin derived from *Digitalis purpurea* (per Chloe's botanical evidence, supported by autopsy alkaloid anomaly) via victim's personal thermos (inferred from disappearance), followed by staged blunt force trauma (consistent with Ronnie's physics analysis and autopsy lividity anomaly). Opportunity: Optimal windows for poison administration (lunchtime office access) and scene staging/evidence disposal (post-discovery confusion / late hours) align perfectly with Subject P's known access, routine, and logistical capability."

He drew a thick circle around Mildred Pettle's name on the chart.

"The withdrawal of Ainsworth's council query," he added, looking at Agnes's notes, "provides the proximate trigger event. Threat level perceived by Pettle likely escalated from 'containable' to 'critical' at that point, necessitating permanent silencing of the information source (Ainsworth)."

They all stared at the chart, at the confluence of evidence meticulously gathered over the past week and a half. History, finance, botany, physics, observation – it all pointed in one direction, weaving a narrative far darker and more complex than anyone outside this room suspected.

"The circumstantial case is now, I believe, legally compelling," Fitzwilliam stated, awe mixed with apprehension in his voice. "The historical motive, the evidence of recent fraud under her direct administration, the physical evidence consistent with the means, the opportunity, the suspicious behaviour observed after the trigger… presented together, it paints an undeniable picture."

"But," Agnes cautioned, bringing them back to the final hurdle, "still no single 'smoking gun'. No witness to the poisoning. No direct link to the money's destination. No confession."

"So, the final step," Fitzwilliam said, meeting Agnes's gaze. "We can't risk confronting her directly; she's too controlled, and now potentially alerted. We can't rely on finding more physical evidence if she's already disposed of the thermos and processing tools. Our only viable option now is to take this to the authorities."

"To Detective Inspector Davies?" Chloe asked, a flicker of hope in her eyes.

"Yes," Fitzwilliam confirmed. "But *how* we present it is critical. We cannot reveal the unofficial autopsy details, nor my ethically questionable supplier searches, nor Chloe's clandestine late-night observation. It would discredit us immediately."

"We focus on the verifiable, official evidence," Agnes declared, already formulating a plan. "My findings from the State Library and PROV regarding Fincham, the boundary ambiguity, Croft's rate payments, and crucially, Ainsworth's withdrawn council query – all documented, publicly accessible records. And Alistair," she turned to him, "your findings regarding the payments to WeatherTech, Vintage Marquee, and Bespoke Botanical Displays from the *club's own payment journals* – the lack of proper authorisation, the link to Mildred's instruction, the suspicious nature of the suppliers easily verifiable via public ASIC searches. That provides concrete evidence of financial irregularity demanding investigation."

"We present Davies with a clear, documented timeline," Fitzwilliam elaborated, picking up the thread. "Ainsworth investigating historical land/finance issues -> Ainsworth lodges official council query regarding sensitive boundary -> Ainsworth abruptly withdraws query -> Ainsworth murdered shortly after -> Club records show large, improperly authorised payments processed by Mildred Pettle to likely fraudulent companies, one potentially linked to her family name. We suggest strongly that Ainsworth likely uncovered this fraud, explaining his historical research and providing a powerful motive for Mildred to silence him, perhaps using knowledge or resources related to the historical land secret."

"We don't mention poison directly," Agnes cautioned. "But we highlight the inconsistencies Ronnie noted about the mallet blow and perhaps Chloe's observation about the body's position, suggesting the initial police conclusion might be incomplete. We provide enough documented evidence of motive and financial irregularity directly linked to Mildred to force Davies to look beyond Smythe and seek warrants for Mildred's financial records. *That* is where the final proof likely lies – tracing the money from the club, through the shells, to her."

Ronnie nodded. "Optimal strategy. Presents verifiable data, establishes strong alternative motive and mechanism possibility, compels further official investigation into Subject P without revealing full extent of quartet's parallel process or compromising sources."

"So," Agnes looked around the room, "we agree? Alistair drafts a concise, confidential memorandum summarising these key verifiable points, focusing on the historical land query and the internal payment irregularities. We find a way to present this to Inspector Davies as soon as possible, perhaps framing it as concerned committee members (Alistair?) or diligent researchers (Agnes?) uncovering troubling inconsistencies requiring her urgent attention?"

There were solemn nods all around. This felt right. Dangerous, still, as Mildred remained unaware they were about to make their move, but right. It shifted the burden back to the official channels, armed now with powerful, targeted information.

"Tomorrow, then," Fitzwilliam said, taking a deep breath. "I'll draft the memo tonight. We deliver it tomorrow." The end, finally, felt in sight. But the most critical step – convincing Detective Inspector Davies to see past the obvious and look towards the quiet, efficient woman hiding in plain sight – was yet to come.

21

Approaching the Authorities

The digital clock on Alistair Fitzwilliam's monitor glowed 1:17 AM. Outside the expansive windows of his Collins Street office, Melbourne lay sprawled below, a glittering tapestry of lights against the deep velvet of the autumn night. The usual nocturnal sounds – the distant hum of traffic, the occasional mournful clang of a late-night tram – were muted twenty floors up, creating an atmosphere of suspended quiet that felt both calming and intensely isolating. His office, usually a place of structured legal argument and billable hours, had become the nerve centre for a far more personal and perilous undertaking. The remnants of a takeaway container (a congealed Pad Thai he barely remembered eating) sat beside a stack of files related to the Macrocorp case, utterly neglected. His entire focus for the past three hours had been consumed by the document glowing on his screen: the confidential memorandum destined for Detective Inspector Davies.

Crafting this memo felt like walking the finest of legal tightropes. He needed to provide enough documented, verifiable information to compel Davies to look beyond Harry Smythe, to investigate the financial irregularities surrounding Mildred Pettle, and to consider the possibility of a deeper, historical motive linked to Bartholomew Ainsworth's research. Yet, he had to do so without revealing the full extent of the quartet's unofficial investigation, without mentioning the potentially compromised autopsy details Sergeant Riley had shared, without citing Chloe's late-night observation of Mildred at the archive door, and crucially, without making direct accusations against Mildred that could expose him and the others to legal repercussions or alert Mildred prematurely.

He reread the opening paragraph for the tenth time, tweaking the phrasing. *"Strictly Private & Confidential. To: Detective Inspector E. Davies, Victoria Police Homicide Squad. From: Alistair Fitzwilliam, Partner [His Law Firm Name], Member, Toorak Croquet & Horticultural Society Governance Subcommittee. Date: 18 April 2025. Subject: Matters Arising Regarding the Death of Mr Bartholomew Ainsworth Requiring Further Investigation."* Formal, factual, establishing his standing as both a legal professional and a concerned club member with relevant committee insight.

He had structured the body of the memo logically, focusing entirely on evidence that could, if necessary, be substantiated through official channels or existing club records, presented as observations arising from his role in ensuring "financial continuity" and Agnes Plummett's work on the "Centenary historical context".

First, the historical land issue. He carefully summarised Agnes's findings from the State Library and PROV, referencing Fincham's *Orchards of Progress* (by title and author only, omitting the specific paragraph number initially) and the 1888/1910 survey maps showing the boundary ambiguity near Gardiner's Creek. He included precise details regarding the disappearance of Silas Croft's 'Orchard Land' from the Prahran Council Rate Books after 1909. Then came the crucial link: *"Furthermore,"* he typed, choosing his words with extreme care, *"Stonnington Council Planning Committee records indicate that Mr Ainsworth lodged a formal query regarding this specific historical boundary clarification on March 5th, 2025 (Ref: PC/Agenda/2025-03-05, Item 7.3). Significantly, council minutes confirm this query was subsequently withdrawn by Mr Ainsworth himself in late March 2025, approximately three weeks prior to his death."* He let that stark fact stand on its own, heavily implying a connection without explicitly stating it. This documented Ainsworth's active pursuit of a potentially sensitive historical issue directly linked to the club's land, and his sudden, unexplained reversal shortly before being murdered – facts Davies couldn't easily ignore.

Second, the recent financial irregularities. This required even more careful phrasing. He couldn't simply state 'WeatherTech Roofing is a shell company'. Instead, he focused on documented procedural failures within the club's *own* records, which he could claim to have reviewed as part of his 'financial continuity' role. *"Review of recent major expenditures approved by Mr Ainsworth reveals significant procedural anomalies requiring clarification,"* he wrote. *"Specifically, substantial payments made within the last six months to suppliers including 'WeatherTech Roofing Solutions Pty Ltd', 'Vintage Marquee Hire Pty Ltd', and 'Bespoke Botanical Displays' appear to lack complete supporting documentation (e.g., detailed quotes, committee pre-approval minutes) commensurate with the sums involved. In several instances, payment authorisation seems primarily based on internal work orders or memos signed solely by the Club Secretary, Ms Mildred Pettle, prior to Mr Ainsworth's final sign-off in the main payment journal."*

He continued, adding the supplier details derived from his ASIC searches, phrasing them as matters easily verifiable by police. *"Furthermore, preliminary checks reveal potential concerns regarding the bona fides of some of these suppliers. For instance, 'WeatherTech Roofing Solutions Pty Ltd' appears to have been registered only shortly before commencing work, listing only a PO Box as its place of business. 'Vintage*

Marquee Hire Pty Ltd' appears to have been recently reactivated from dormancy with interstate nominee directors. *'Bespoke Botanical Displays',* while linked to a physical nursery address, is directed by an *'Eleanor Vance'. It has been noted that Ms Pettle's maiden name was Vance, raising potential conflict-of-interest questions requiring clarification, particularly given the lack of detailed supporting quotes for the substantial deposit paid."* He deliberately included the Vance connection; it was publicly searchable information, and while circumstantial, it added a crucial personal link for Davies to potentially explore regarding Mildred.

Third, the synthesis and implication. He needed to tie these threads together, gently suggesting a motive for Mildred without making a direct accusation. *"These findings,"* he typed, rewriting the sentence multiple times, *"– Mr Ainsworth's documented, recently withdrawn query into sensitive historical land boundaries, coupled with significant procedural anomalies and questionable supplier payments processed under Ms Pettle's administration – raise serious questions about the full context surrounding Mr Ainsworth's activities and potential antagonists prior to his death. While the investigation has understandably focused on the altercation involving Lord Smythe, these documented inconsistencies suggest Mr Ainsworth may have uncovered, or been close to uncovering, unrelated matters causing significant concern to other parties within or connected to the Society. It is respectfully submitted that these documented financial and historical lines of inquiry warrant further thorough investigation by Victoria Police to ensure all potential motives and circumstances surrounding Mr Ainsworth's tragic death are fully explored."*

He read it through one last time. It was dense, formal, perhaps overly cautious. It omitted so much – the poison, the staged blow, the glove, Chloe's compost discovery, their certainty about Mildred. But it contained only verifiable facts or documented internal procedural issues. It provided Detective Inspector Davies with concrete avenues for official investigation: check council records regarding Ainsworth's query, examine the club's payment authorisation procedures and supporting documents for those specific suppliers, run official background checks on the suppliers and Eleanor Vance, potentially interview Mildred about these specific administrative matters. It gave Davies enough solid ground to justify broadening her investigation beyond Harry Smythe, without revealing the ethically dubious methods or speculative leaps made by the quartet. It was, Fitzwilliam hoped, the perfect balance – enough information to redirect suspicion, not enough to expose themselves.

He saved the document, encrypted it, and printed a single hard copy, which he placed in a plain manilla envelope marked simply 'Confidential'. He felt exhausted but also strangely calm. He had done what he could, crafting the strongest possible argument within the constraints of legality and discretion. He had laid out the objective evidence pointing away from Smythe and towards a deeper, financially motivated conspiracy potentially centred around Mildred Pettle.

Now came the difficult part: delivering it. Would Davies even agree to see him? Would she dismiss the memo out of hand? Would delivering it paint a target on his own back? He pushed the anxieties aside. They had decided on this course. He would call Sergeant Riley first thing in the morning, request a brief, urgent, and discreet meeting with Detective Inspector Davies, citing potentially crucial information regarding the Ainsworth case obtained through his role on the Governance subcommittee. The die was cast. He switched off his desk lamp, plunging the office into near darkness, the city lights outside suddenly seeming brighter, colder, more indifferent than before.

****

The anonymity of the bustling cafe on St Kilda Road, just a short, nerve-wracking walk from the imposing Victoria Police Centre complex, felt like both a blessing and a curse to Alistair Fitzwilliam. A blessing because its clatter of espresso machines, hurried footsteps of city workers grabbing takeaway coffees, and general morning hubbub provided a cloak of normalcy for this distinctly abnormal meeting. A curse because the very public nature of the venue made him feel intensely exposed, convinced every casual glance was one of scrutiny. He sat at a small table near the back, the plain manilla envelope containing his meticulously drafted memorandum resting heavily on his lap beneath the table, feeling less like a concerned citizen offering assistance and more like an illicit informant preparing for a clandestine handover.

He'd arrived twenty minutes early for the 9:30 AM meeting, his stomach churning too much to contemplate the perfectly decent croissant displayed invitingly on the counter. He ordered a long black he knew he wouldn't drink, needing the prop, the ritual of having something before him. He had managed, through a carefully worded call to Sergeant Riley – referencing his subcommittee role and 'potentially relevant documented procedural matters' – to secure this brief, informal meeting directly with Detective Inspector Davies. Riley had sounded sceptical but had relayed the request, and surprisingly, Davies had agreed, albeit specifying "ten minutes, max, Mr Fitzwilliam, I have a briefing." It felt like a minor miracle, but also amplified the pressure enormously. Ten minutes to convey the essence of their complex findings, to plant sufficient doubt about Harry Smythe, to subtly redirect focus towards Mildred Pettle, all without revealing the true, unofficial, and potentially compromising extent of their own investigation.

He checked his watch for the fifth time in as many minutes. 9:28 AM. He smoothed his already immaculate tie, took a shaky sip of the rapidly cooling coffee, and rehearsed his opening lines mentally again. Focus on facts. Documented evidence. Procedural anomalies. Governance concerns. Avoid speculation. Avoid mentioning Mildred directly unless absolutely necessary and contextually justified by the supplier link. Stick to the script.

At precisely 9:30 AM, Detective Inspector Davies pushed through the cafe door. She scanned the room briefly, her sharp eyes immediately finding Fitzwilliam. She navigated the crowded space with an air of quiet authority that seemed to make people instinctively move aside. She wore the same practical pantsuit as before, her expression professional, unreadable, perhaps slightly impatient.

Fitzwilliam stood up quickly, extending a hand. "Inspector Davies. Thank you for meeting me."

She shook his hand briefly, her grip firm, her gaze direct. "Mr Fitzwilliam. Ten minutes, as I said." She didn't sit, indicating the brevity of the encounter.

"Of course, Inspector. I appreciate your time," Fitzwilliam began, his voice commendably steady despite the frantic hammering in his chest. "As I mentioned to Sergeant Riley, in my capacity on the Society's Governance subcommittee, and in reviewing matters to ensure financial continuity following Mr Ainsworth's tragic death, certain documented inconsistencies have come to my attention that I felt duty-bound to bring directly to yours." He deliberately used formal, slightly bureaucratic language, framing his approach within his official club role.

Davies raised a sceptical eyebrow but nodded curtly. "Go on."

"Firstly," Fitzwilliam continued, retrieving the manilla envelope, "it relates to Mr Ainsworth's activities immediately prior to his death. While attention has understandably focused on his altercation with Lord Smythe, club records – specifically council planning minutes accessed via PROV," he stressed the official source, "show Mr Ainsworth lodged a formal query regarding a sensitive historical boundary clarification near the location where his body was found. This query, potentially impacting long-standing land use or value related to the club's property, was lodged on March 5th and then, significantly, withdrawn by Mr Ainsworth himself only three weeks before his death." He paused, letting the timeline sink in. "The withdrawal itself seems... abrupt, given Mr Ainsworth's known tenacity."

He saw a flicker of something in Davies's eyes – perhaps professional curiosity piqued by the mention of verifiable council records and the victim taking official action on a potentially contentious issue shortly before being murdered. It was a stronger starting point than vague gossip.

"Secondly," Fitzwilliam pressed on, opening the envelope slightly but not yet removing the memo, "in reviewing recent major expenditures signed off by Mr Ainsworth – specifically relating to roof repairs and Centenary Gala deposits – significant procedural anomalies are apparent within the club's own payment records." He quickly summarised his findings: the payments to WeatherTech, Vintage Marquee, and Bespoke Botanical Displays; the lack of proper supporting documentation or committee pre-approval; the authorisation seemingly originating solely from the Club Secretary, Mildred Pettle, despite Ainsworth's final sign-off. He mentioned the ASIC search results confirming the suppliers' questionable status and the Vance name connection, framing it carefully: "Public record checks on these suppliers raise concerns about their bona fides and reveal potential conflicts of interest requiring clarification, given Ms Pettle's administrative role in processing these substantial payments."

He chose the phrase "potential conflicts of interest" deliberately, avoiding direct accusation of fraud but clearly flagging the issue for Davies. He saw her expression tighten almost imperceptibly. Financial irregularities, shell companies, potential conflicts of interest – this was familiar territory for homicide investigations, often providing powerful motives hidden beneath surface dramas.

"I have prepared a brief memorandum," Fitzwilliam said, now holding the envelope out towards her, "detailing these specific findings, referencing the relevant council minutes, club payment journal entries, and supplier registration details. It outlines documented facts that, in my view, suggest Mr Ainsworth may have uncovered serious historical and financial matters extending beyond his dispute with Lord Smythe, potentially creating other antagonists or motives that warrant thorough investigation by Victoria Police." He met her gaze directly, trying to convey sincerity and professional concern. "My sole intention in bringing this to you, Inspector, is to ensure all relevant facts are considered."

Detective Inspector Davies looked at the envelope, then back at Fitzwilliam, her expression still guarded but perhaps a fraction less dismissive than before. She took the envelope. "Mr Fitzwilliam," she said, her voice coolly professional, "Victoria Police considers all credible information relevant to an investigation. Why are *you*, specifically, bringing this forward now? And why not through official club committee channels?" The question was direct, probing his motives.

Fitzwilliam had anticipated this. "As a lawyer and a committee member, Inspector, I felt a professional and personal obligation once these documented inconsistencies came to my attention during my review. Given the sensitivity, the potential involvement of historical matters, and," he hesitated slightly, "the current focus on Lord Smythe, I felt presenting these documented points directly to you, discreetly, was the most responsible course of action to ensure they are properly evaluated without causing unnecessary alarm within the Society before the facts are fully established." He hoped this sounded plausible, responsible, and subtly hinted at the risk of internal obstruction if raised through normal channels first.

Davies held his gaze for another long moment, seemingly assessing his credibility, his potential agenda. Fitzwilliam forced himself to meet her stare calmly, resisting the urge to fidget or look away. He felt Agnes, Ronnie, and Chloe's hopes resting on this single, fraught interaction.

Finally, Davies gave a curt nod. "Thank you, Mr Fitzwilliam. Your concerns are noted. This memorandum will be reviewed." She tucked the envelope into the inner pocket of her jacket. "That will be all for now. We will be in contact if further clarification is required." It was a clear dismissal, offering no promises, no indication of whether she took his concerns seriously or simply filed them under 'club politics'.

"Thank you, Inspector," Fitzwilliam replied, relief making his voice slightly unsteady. He had done it. He had delivered the information, presented the documented anomalies, planted the seed of doubt about the official narrative, all without compromising their deeper investigation – he hoped.

He watched Detective Inspector Davies turn and walk briskly out of the noisy cafe, disappearing into the St Kilda Road morning throng. He sank back into his chair, suddenly aware of his heart pounding, his hands clammy. He hadn't been dismissed out of hand. She had taken the memo. It was a small victory, perhaps, but a crucial one. He pulled out his phone and sent a brief, coded text to Agnes: *"Package delivered. Recipient non-committal but accepted for review. Phase initiated. A."* Now came the hardest part: waiting to see if the seeds they had planted would bear fruit, or if Detective Inspector Davies would simply let them wither on the vine while continuing down the path towards Harry Smythe. The uncertainty felt almost as stressful as the confrontation itself.

****

The hours following Alistair Fitzwilliam's tense meeting with Detective Inspector Davies crawled by with agonising slowness. Back in the familiar, yet now somehow alien, environment of the Toorak Croquet & Horticultural Society, or sequestered in their respective observation posts, the quartet waited. They waited for a sign, any sign, that the carefully constructed memorandum, Fitzwilliam's calculated gamble, had landed with sufficient force to shift the trajectory of the official investigation. They watched Mildred Pettle with renewed, almost unbearable intensity, analysing her every move, every flicker of expression, searching for any deviation, any crack in her formidable composure that might indicate awareness of renewed police interest, or perhaps, the nervous actions of someone expecting imminent exposure.

Fitzwilliam himself had returned to his Collins Street office, the adrenaline from the meeting replaced by a gnawing anxiety. He sat staring at the voluminous Macrocorp brief, its dense legal arguments about corporate responsibility seeming utterly irrelevant compared to the stark realities of murder and calculated deception he was now embroiled in. He couldn't focus. His gaze kept drifting to his phone, willing it to ring, hoping for a discreet call back from Sergeant Riley – perhaps a carefully worded, deniable query seeking clarification on one of the points raised in the memo, anything to indicate it hadn't simply landed on a pile marked 'Club Politics - Ignore'. He even risked sending Riley a brief, neutral text message late morning

– *"Following up on our chat, hope the background context provided proves useful"* – but received no reply. The silence from police headquarters felt vast, ominous. Had Davies dismissed his concerns entirely? Had she simply passed the memo down the line, where it would languish unread? Or was she, perhaps, moving carefully, discreetly, behind the scenes? The uncertainty was torture.

At the club, Agnes Plummett maintained her position in the library alcove, ostensibly deep in research for the Centenary brochure. She had a clear view of the main corridor and could observe Mildred Pettle's comings and goings from the administrative wing. Mildred appeared, to all outward intents and purposes, completely unaffected. Her morning proceeded with its usual clockwork precision. She handled member inquiries with patient courtesy, dealt with a minor issue regarding weekend catering deliveries, and spent a solid hour closeted with Esme Weatherly finalising arrangements for an upcoming inter-club tournament. Agnes watched her closely during a brief tea break Mildred took in the members' lounge around eleven. She chatted politely with Mrs Henderson about the weather, inquired after Colonel Abernathy's sciatica, and offered Penelope Cartwright advice on preventing mildew on stored croquet balls. Her performance was flawless, infuriatingly so. If she harboured any new anxiety sparked by police attention potentially shifting her way, she buried it beneath layers of practised administrative calm. Agnes found herself questioning her own judgment – was Mildred truly this adept an actress, or were they, the quartet, constructing suspicion out of coincidence and their own desire for a neat solution?

Chloe Dubois, tasked with observing the club's exterior and utility areas while performing her gardening duties, felt the strain even more acutely. Every time she saw Mildred's car still parked in its usual spot, every time she saw Mildred walking calmly across the lawn towards the clubhouse, felt like a small defeat, a confirmation that nothing had changed. She meticulously deadheaded roses near the main entrance, swept leaves from the pathways near the office wing, checked the moisture levels in the verandah pots – all routine tasks providing cover for her surveillance. She paid particular attention when Mildred briefly visited the potting shed area around lunchtime, ostensibly to check on stocks of orchid fertiliser. Chloe watched from a distance, concealed behind a large camellia bush, her heart pounding. Was Mildred checking the compost heaps again? Looking for the spot where Chloe had found the leaves? But Mildred merely spoke briefly with Henderson Jr., pointed towards a shelf, then returned directly to the clubhouse. Nothing suspicious. Nothing concrete. Yet, Chloe couldn't shake the feeling of being watched herself, occasionally glancing up quickly, half-expecting to see Mildred's pale blue eyes observing her from an office window. The sense of latent threat, ever since their encounter near the incinerator, lingered persistently.

Ronnie Peterson, perhaps the most outwardly patient due to his scientific detachment, occupied a corner table in the bar area, nursing a slow pint of light beer and ostensibly tackling *The Age*'s cryptic crossword with intense concentration. In reality, his notebook beside him discreetly logged Mildred's movements within the clubhouse public areas, timings noted against his established baseline. 11:05 – 11:45: With E. Weatherly (Baseline: Expected meeting duration). 11:47: Brief chat with Mrs Henderson (Baseline: Social interaction within normal parameters). 12:10: Towards potting shed area, returns 12:18 (Duration 8 mins. Baseline: Occasional check, duration plausible). 12:45: Leaves premises for lunch. This last entry caused Ronnie a flicker of interest. Mildred *usually* ate a simple sandwich in her office or the staff room. Leaving the premises for lunch was a deviation, albeit a minor one. He quickly texted the others: *"Subject P departed premises 12:45. Extended lunch? Destination unknown. Observe return time."*

The wait stretched through the early afternoon. Fitzwilliam, back in his office, found it impossible to concentrate on the Macrocorp brief. He kept refreshing the Victorian court listings website, searching for any sign of new warrants being issued, an exercise he knew was futile but couldn't resist. Agnes abandoned her Centenary notes and resorted to meticulously cataloguing a box of unlabelled historical photographs she'd unearthed from the archive depths weeks ago, needing a task demanding absolute focus to quiet her anxious mind. Chloe continued her work in the gardens, the repetitive tasks of weeding and pruning providing a rhythm that helped mask her internal tension. Ronnie finished the crossword, ordered another half-pint, and started modelling fluid dynamics based on the patterns the beer foam made against the glass.

Then, at 2:10 PM, Ronnie's phone buzzed with an incoming text from Chloe: *"MP returned 14:10. Carrying small pharmacy bag. Appearance unchanged."*

Ronnie logged the time. Return: 14:10. Departure: 12:45. Total absence: 1 hour 25 minutes. Significantly longer than her usual brief lunch break. Where had she gone? A nearby Toorak Road pharmacy for headache tablets? Plausible. Meeting someone discreetly off-site? Also plausible. Having lunch with Eleanor Vance in Ferntree Gully? Highly improbable given the travel time. The data point was anomalous, potentially significant, but frustratingly ambiguous. He relayed the information to Fitzwilliam and Agnes.

Just after 3:30 PM, another potential anomaly, observed by Agnes from the library window. She saw Mildred emerge from her office wing and walk briskly towards her car in the staff parking area. Mildred placed a small, nondescript cardboard box, roughly the size of a shoe box, into the boot of her sedan, closed it firmly, then immediately returned to her office. What was in the box? Old files? Personal items? Or something more incriminating being prepared for off-site disposal later? Impossible to tell. Agnes logged the time and observation, frustration mounting. These were mere fragments, hints, whispers – nothing solid.

As the afternoon wore on, the lack of any discernible action from the police weighed heavily on them all. Had Fitzwilliam's memo been dismissed? Had Detective Inspector Davies simply filed it away, satisfied with the case against Harry Smythe? The thought that Mildred might simply get away with it, protected by her impeccable facade and the investigation's tunnel vision, was almost unbearable. Doubt began to creep back in. Were they wrong? Were they seeing conspiracy in coincidence?

Fitzwilliam, unable to bear the silence any longer, risked calling Sergeant Riley's direct line again late in the afternoon, under the guise of clarifying a minor point in his earlier memo. Riley's response was polite but utterly non-committal. "Thanks for the follow-up, Alistair. Yes, the Detective Inspector received your information. It's all part of the ongoing investigation. Can't discuss specifics, you understand. We'll be in touch if needed." Click. Utterly useless.

As 5 PM approached, marking the end of the administrative day at the club, the quartet exchanged weary, frustrated text messages. *"Status check?"* Fitzwilliam sent. *"Nil significant deviation observed since lunch,"* Ronnie replied almost instantly. *"Nothing here either. MP routine unchanged,"* Agnes added. *"Same. MP left premises 17:05, carrying usual handbag only,"* Chloe reported.

It seemed their gamble, their attempt to force the authorities' hand, had failed. Detective Inspector Davies had the information, but there was no sign she was acting on it. Mildred Pettle remained calm, controlled, seemingly untouched. Fitzwilliam slumped back in his expensive office chair, staring out at the city lights beginning to twinkle across the darkening Melbourne skyline, feeling a profound sense of deflation, of anti-climax. Had they risked so much for nothing? Was Mildred simply too clever, too careful? Where could they possibly go from here? The waiting game had yielded only more uncertainty, leaving them feeling more isolated, and potentially more exposed, than ever before.

22

A Crack in the Facade

The frustration following Fitzwilliam's confirmation that public records had yielded no direct financial link to Mildred Pettle settled heavily on Agnes Plummett. Their meticulously constructed circumstantial case felt like an elaborate house of cards, vulnerable to the slightest puff of official scepticism or Mildred's continued, unnerving composure. The waiting game after delivering the memo to Detective Inspector Davies had been agonising, yielding only silence from the police and infuriating normalcy from their prime suspect. Agnes, however, was not one to succumb to despair or impatience. When one avenue of inquiry reached a dead end, her methodical mind simply dictated that others must be pursued with renewed vigour. If modern corporate records failed to reveal the truth, perhaps the older, more nuanced whispers of history held further clues.

Saturday morning, April 19th, found her not at the Croquet Club amidst the surface cheer of the ongoing tournament finals, but back in the familiar quiet of her own study. The Fincham book, *Orchards of Progress*, lay open on her desk beside her notes from the Public Record Office detailing the ambiguous boundary and

Silas Croft's long-vanished rate payments for the 'Orchard Land'. She felt certain the significance of Ainsworth's *Pyrus Malus* clue lay somewhere within this nexus of historical land use, boundary disputes, and Croft's surprisingly 'consistent high yield'. Ainsworth had connected it to the Fete accounts, likely as a metaphor for the suspiciously regular income Mildred reported. But was there more? Had Ainsworth discovered something *else* in Fincham's text, beyond Paragraph 12 of Section IV, that directly related to the value or specific nature of that ambiguous sliver of land?

She began rereading Section IV carefully, not just Paragraph 12, but the surrounding pages detailing horticultural experiments and land valuation in the Toorak/Prahran area circa 1900. Fincham's prose was dry, academic, focused on rainfall statistics, soil analysis (mostly alluvial clay near the creek, he noted), and the economic viability of various fruit crops – apples, pears, some early attempts at stone fruit. He praised Silas Croft's meticulous (if financially disorganised) documentation of his experimental 'Croft's Seedling' apple yields, noting its unusual resilience. But beyond that, the text offered little obvious connection to potential fraud or murder.

Agnes frowned. Had Ainsworth simply fixated on the 'consistent high yield' phrase as a code, or was there a deeper layer she was missing? She turned her attention to the book's index and bibliography, searching for references to Silas Croft, the Gardiner's Creek area specifically, or any mention of unusual land usage beyond simple orchards.

The index yielded several page numbers for Croft, mostly relating back to the Paragraph 12 discussion of his apple variety. The bibliography listed Croft's privately published pamphlets on apple cultivation, likely held only in specialist archives, if they survived at all. Then, her eye caught a footnote appended to the end of the main paragraph discussing Croft's orchard – a footnote she'd skimmed over previously, assuming it was merely an academic citation.

She located the footnote at the bottom of the page, its print small and dense. *"Fincham, Note 27, Sect. IV, Para 12: While Croft's primary documented experiments focused on pomaceous fruits, local anecdotal accounts from the period (see Appendix B: Oral Histories Transcript Excerpts) also suggest Croft experimented, with limited success, in cultivating certain high-value medicinal herbs requiring specific alluvial soil conditions, possibly including varieties of Atropa or related Solanaceae, though his records, as noted, lack verifiable detail on these secondary pursuits. Furthermore, unresolved legal correspondence following Croft's death in 1909 regarding disputed access rights across the creek frontage parcel suggests lingering complexities surrounding the estate's final disposition (PROV, VPRS 1158/P0, Unit 287, Croft Estate Correspondence)."*

Agnes read the footnote again, her breath catching slightly. *Medicinal herbs? Atropa? Solanaceae?* The Nightshade family. Plants known for containing potent tropane alkaloids – atropine, Hyoscyamine, scopolamine. Highly toxic if ingested, capable of causing confusion, delirium, hallucinations, respiratory distress, cardiac issues… symptoms that could, potentially, overlap with or be masked by *Digitalis* poisoning, or even appear as sudden collapse or stroke if administered skilfully. And Croft was supposedly experimenting with them on that very piece of land near the creek, the land with the ambiguous boundary?

And *disputed access rights?* Legal correspondence following Croft's death regarding complexities in the estate's disposition? This went beyond simple boundary ambiguity. It suggested specific, documented legal contention surrounding that sliver of land after Croft died and his rate payments ceased – contention that might be buried in official probate or legal files at PROV, files Ainsworth, with his meticulous mind and perhaps prompted by the Fincham footnote, might have sought out. Files Mildred might desperately want to remain buried.

This felt significant. It added a new, potentially more sinister layer to the 'old orchard end'. It wasn't just about apples or land value; it might have historical associations with the cultivation of *dangerous botanicals*. And it had been subject to specific legal disputes following the original owner's death. Ainsworth, finding this footnote, might have seen not just evidence of historical financial anomaly, but a potential link to something darker, something related perhaps to the very *nature* of poisonous plants connected to that land. Did he suspect a historical poisoning? Or that knowledge of these plants persisted, providing a resource or inspiration for a modern crime?

And the mention of legal correspondence at PROV... Agnes made a quick note of the VPRS (Victorian Public Record Series) reference number cited in the footnote. This provided a specific target for further research, potentially bypassing the dead end Fitzwilliam had hit with more recent records. These would be *old* legal files related to Croft's estate, potentially detailing exactly who was disputing access to that land parcel back in 1909/1910 and why. Could names connected to the early Society, or even Mildred's family history if her connection truly stretched back that far, appear in those files?

Agnes felt a renewed surge of purpose. The *Pyrus Malus* clue wasn't just a metaphor for consistent Fete profits; it was likely Ainsworth's pointer to the *entire context* surrounding Silas Croft's orchard – the high yield (financial metaphor), the boundary dispute (land motive), *and* the potential cultivation of medicinal/toxic plants (means/knowledge). Ainsworth hadn't been pursuing just one thread; he'd found the knot where multiple incriminating threads converged, all tied to that specific, historically problematic piece of land bordering Lawn 3.

She needed to get back to PROV, armed with this VPRS reference number. She also needed to research *Atropa belladonna* (Deadly Nightshade) and related Solanaceae alkaloids – their symptoms, detectability, presence in Victoria. Could the unidentified alkaloid in Ainsworth's system be one of *these*, rather than (or in addition to) *Digitalis*? It would require highly specific testing VIFM might not have initially conducted if focused solely on the blunt force trauma.

The complexity deepened, but so did Agnes's conviction. Mildred Pettle wasn't just covering up potential embezzlement. She was potentially protecting secrets far older, more complex, and possibly more sinister, rooted in the history of the land itself. Secrets that involved disputed access, ambiguous boundaries, and the historical cultivation of poisonous plants just metres from where Ainsworth died. Secrets Bartholomew Ainsworth, in his final, obsessive investigation, had come dangerously close to unearthing. Agnes carefully closed Fincham's book, her mind already formulating her request for the Croft Estate correspondence file. The past, she knew, rarely stayed buried forever, especially when someone started digging.

****

Saturday morning found Alistair Fitzwilliam not on the sun-drenched croquet lawns observing the tournament finals, but sequestered in the quiet sanctuary of his own home study in Hawthorn. He'd pleaded a prior commitment to avoid the club, needing distance both from the pervasive atmosphere of unresolved tension and, more practically, needing dedicated time to pursue a different investigative avenue. Agnes's findings from the Public Record Office the previous day – the confirmation of the ambiguous 'old orchard end' land parcel, Silas Croft's historical occupancy, and Ainsworth's withdrawn council query – had been intellectually satisfying, powerfully bolstering the historical dimension of Mildred Pettle's likely motive. Yet, Fitzwilliam's legal mind craved something more immediate, something concrete linking Ainsworth's historical digging to tangible actions *just before* his death. The phantom supplier trail had hit the frustrating wall of corporate anonymity accessible through public records. Perhaps, Fitzwilliam reasoned, evidence of Ainsworth's final, critical steps lay closer to home – within the club's own internal administration.

His study, unlike his sterile Collins Street office, reflected a more personal, albeit still meticulously ordered, aspect of his personality. Walls lined with legal texts stood alongside shelves dedicated to Australian history and biographies. Framed prints of early Melbourne maps shared space with understated family photographs. Through the window, the leaves on the ornamental pear tree in his garden showed the first touches of autumn gold. He sat at his large mahogany desk, a fresh pot of coffee beside him, not with corporate files, but with copies of the Toorak Croquet & Horticultural Society's expense claim forms and reimbursement summaries for the past six months – documents he had legitimately requested access to under his role ensuring 'financial continuity' before an interim Treasurer was formally appointed.

He knew it was a long shot. Ainsworth, while meticulous, was also notoriously frugal with club funds when it came to *other* people's expenses. Would his own claims reveal anything beyond routine reimbursements for stationery or official travel? Fitzwilliam began methodically working through the pile, cross-referencing claim forms against the payment summaries Mildred Pettle would have prepared for Ainsworth's (or the Committee's) final approval.

Most were entirely mundane. Claims for postage stamps, committee meeting refreshments, mileage for attending regional VCA (Victorian Croquet Association) meetings, replacement printer cartridges for the office. Each claim was supported by neat receipts, itemised lists, and Ainsworth's own spiky signature authorising submission, followed by Mildred's neat initials indicating processing and inclusion in the payment run. Fitzwilliam noted, with a grimace, Ainsworth had even claimed precisely \$3.85 for 'emergency purchase of club-approved biscuits' when the usual supplier failed to deliver for one meeting. The man's pedantry extended even to his own minor expenses.

He ploughed through months of these small, predictable claims, his initial hope beginning to fade. Perhaps Ainsworth *had* kept his deeper investigation entirely separate from club finances? Perhaps he funded any external research himself? It seemed plausible, given his private nature and potential desire for secrecy if he suspected wrongdoing within the committee or administration.

Then, within the batch for late February, just over six weeks before his death, Fitzwilliam paused. Claim form #A487. Submitted by: B. Ainsworth. Description: *"Consultancy Fees – Historical Records Audit Support."* Amount: \$450.00. Attached: An invoice from a company Fitzwilliam didn't recognise – 'GeneaSearch Historical Resources Pty Ltd' – based in Ballarat. The invoice description was equally vague: *"Professional services rendered: Genealogical and historical database access subscription (6 months); preliminary archive search assistance (Ref: TC&HS Project)."*

Fitzwilliam's eyebrows shot up. *GeneaSearch?* A genealogical database subscription? Why would Ainsworth need that for club business? Unless… unless he wasn't just tracing land boundaries, but potentially tracing *people* connected to the club's past? People connected to the West Wing extension committee? To Silas Croft's estate? To the mysterious 'E. Vance' who had assisted Treasurer Carmichael in 1988? A six-month subscription suggested an ongoing, potentially complex search. And 'preliminary archive search assistance' – had he hired someone to help navigate PROV or other archives beyond Agnes's usual domain? This expense, vaguely labelled as 'audit support', clearly pointed towards Ainsworth actively spending club funds on external resources for his historical investigation. He quickly photographed the claim form and the invoice. Would Mildred have processed this without question, or noted its unusual nature? The description was just ambiguous enough to potentially pass muster if bundled with other routine consultancy fees.

Feeling a renewed sense of purpose, Fitzwilliam continued his review, moving into March – the period just before and after Ainsworth lodged and then withdrew his council query about the boundary. More routine claims... then, another anomaly. Claim form #A512. Date submitted: March 28th, just days after withdrawing the council query. Submitted by: B. Ainsworth. Description: *"Professional Services – Property Boundary Assessment."* Amount: $1,850.00. Attached: A tax invoice from 'Melbourne Geomatics & Surveying', a highly reputable, well-established surveying firm with offices in South Melbourne. Invoice Description: *"Stage 1 Service Fee: Preliminary Historical Boundary Identification and Cadastral Map Analysis – Property Ref: [Club Address], Toorak (Ref: Ainsworth/TC&H S/Boundary Clarification)."*

Fitzwilliam stared at the invoice, his heart thudding. *This was it.* Concrete, undeniable proof. Ainsworth hadn't just been relying on his own interpretation of old maps or Fincham's text. He had escalated his investigation significantly. He had engaged a professional, external surveying firm to provide an expert opinion on the very boundary ambiguities near the 'old orchard end' / Lawn 3 that Agnes had identified in the historical records. This wasn't just background research anymore; this was active evidence gathering, seeking a definitive, legally sound assessment of the land's true status.

The timing was critical. He engaged the surveyors *after* lodging his initial query with the council, but *before* (or perhaps concurrently with) withdrawing it. Had he withdrawn the council query because he decided to rely on the surveyors' report instead? Or had he received the surveyors' preliminary findings, confirming the boundary anomaly was significant and potentially explosive, prompting him to withdraw the public council query in favour of a direct internal confrontation? Either way, this invoice proved Ainsworth was on the verge of obtaining – or perhaps *had* obtained – professional, external validation of the historical land secret just before his death.

And the cost - $1,850 for a *preliminary* assessment? It suggested a complex task, hinting at the level of historical ambiguity involved. Had Mildred Pettle processed *this* claim? Fitzwilliam checked the attached processing notes. Yes, Mildred's neat initials were there, dated early April, included in the payment run Ainsworth himself likely signed off just days before he died.

Mildred *must* have seen this invoice. She must have known Ainsworth had escalated his investigation from dusty archives to professional surveyors, focusing directly on the problematic boundary. She would have understood the implications instantly. A formal surveyor's report confirming the ambiguous status of the 'old orchard end', potentially revealing decades of unrecorded usage or income, would be catastrophic for her, exposing her long-term exploitation and potential fraud.

Fitzwilliam felt a cold certainty grip him. This invoice wasn't just evidence of Ainsworth's investigation; it was likely the trigger for his murder. Mildred, seeing this claim, knowing Ainsworth was now close to obtaining irrefutable, external proof, must have realised her time was up. She couldn't deflect or manage this away. Silencing Ainsworth permanently, before he could receive or present the final surveyor's report, became her only option.

He carefully photographed the claim form and the Melbourne Geomatics invoice multiple times, ensuring every detail was captured. This felt different from the supplier irregularities. This was proof of the *victim's* actions, the specific, escalating steps he took that directly threatened the killer's secrets, providing a clear and immediate motive for murder occurring exactly when it did. This felt like something Detective Inspector Davies, however focused on Harry Smythe, could not ignore. An invoice from a reputable local firm for surveying the exact piece of historically contentious land Ainsworth was known to be researching, submitted just before his death, processed by the very person who benefited most from that land's ambiguous status remaining hidden… it was a powerful piece of the puzzle.

He leaned back in his chair, the morning sunlight now feeling harsh and intrusive. He finally had it – not the ultimate proof of murder, perhaps, but proof of the direct, immediate threat Ainsworth posed to Mildred Pettle in the days leading up to his death. Combined with Agnes's historical findings and Chloe's botanical evidence… the case felt suddenly, terrifyingly close to complete. He needed to call Agnes immediately. They needed to reconvene. This changed the endgame.

****

While Agnes meticulously deciphered historical land records and Fitzwilliam navigated the complexities of corporate structures and club expense claims, Chloe Dubois found her focus narrowing onto a single, tangible object: the elegant, slightly soiled, grey suede *Gant Botanique* glove. It sat sealed in its evidence bag on her small kitchen table, a silent, frustrating enigma. Knowing its brand and origin was one thing; linking it to Mildred Pettle, or even confirming it was wildly out of place amongst the Society's usual paraphernalia, was quite another. Her brief observations of Mildred at the club had yielded nothing regarding gardening habits or tools. If Mildred *did* possess such gloves, she certainly wasn't flaunting them.

Driven by a frustration born of dead ends and the lingering chill from her encounters with the Club Secretary, Chloe dedicated her weekend – Saturday afternoon and stretches of Sunday – to a different kind of gardening: cultivating information online. She brewed a large pot of peppermint tea, settled at her laptop in her Richmond apartment, the sounds of weekend life drifting up from the lane way below, and began to dig.

Her initial searches revisited online retailers stocking *Gant Botanique* in Australia. She confirmed again: primarily high-end department stores (David Jones, visited; Myer, confirmed non-stockist) and exclusive gardening/lifestyle boutiques concentrated in affluent Melbourne suburbs like Toorak, Armadale, Brighton, and perhaps Sorrento or Portsea on the peninsula. Availability was limited, reinforcing the idea that owning these gloves required a deliberate, likely expensive, purchase from a specific type of retailer. It wasn't the sort of glove one picked up casually with a bag of potting mix at Bunnings.

But who *used* them? She pivoted her search towards online communities – gardening forums, horticultural society websites, even dedicated blogs focusing on high-end gardening tools. She trawled through GardenWeb Australia archives, the Diggers Club forums, specialist Rose Society and Dahlia Society discussion boards (giving a brief, ironic thought to Major Ferguson). She used search terms like "Gant Botanique review," "best gloves for pruning roses," "gloves for handling irritating plants," "luxury gardening gloves worth it?".

Hours melted away in a frustrating haze of scrolling through endless discussions about compost activators, organic pest control, and debates over the merits of various secateur brands. She found numerous mentions of general suede or leather gloves, discussions of protection against thorns or chemicals, but specific mentions of *Gant Botanique* were rare, usually confined to threads discussing premium tools or 'what I got for my birthday' type posts. When the brand *was* mentioned, reviewers invariably commented on the quality, the dexterity allowed by the supple material, the high price point, and often recommended them specifically for tasks requiring both protection and fine motor skills – like handling delicate seedlings, intricate pruning, or working with plants known to cause skin irritation.

Irritating plants. The phrase snagged in Chloe's mind. *Digitalis purpurea*, the foxglove, wasn't just toxic if ingested; its leaves contained fine hairs and compounds that could cause significant skin irritation or dermatitis in sensitive individuals, especially during harvesting or handling of multiple leaves. Using high-quality, well-fitting gloves would be almost essential for anyone carefully collecting a quantity of leaves, both for protection and to avoid leaving fingerprints or DNA traces. The expensive French glove suddenly seemed less like a luxury item and more like a necessary tool for a very specific, very careful, illicit task.

This spurred her on. She refined her search, adding terms like "gloves for foxglove," "handling toxic plants," "preventing garden dermatitis." This led her down a rabbit hole of botanical safety forums and specialised horticultural discussion groups. Much of it was irrelevant – warnings about Poison Ivy (not a major Melbourne issue), discussions of handling Euphorbia sap. But she persisted, sifting through threads dating back years.

It was late on Sunday afternoon, her eyes tired from screen

glare, the peppermint tea long gone cold, when she finally found something. Tucked away in an archived 2019 thread on a slightly defunct-looking forum titled "Melbourne Heritage Gardens & Rare Plants Forum" was a discussion titled *"Dealing with Skin Irritants – Beyond Barrier Creams?"* Gardeners were sharing tips for handling plants like Daphne (problematic sap) or plants with fine irritating hairs. Several posts recommended standard heavy-duty gloves. Then, a post from a user identified only as **'MP_Gardener'**:

"For delicate work with known irritants (esp. those with fine hairs like some Digitalis species or Verbascum), I find standard gloves too clumsy. Have had excellent results with Gant Botanique suede gloves – the fit allows good dexterity for careful leaf removal or deadheading. They are an investment, certainly, but prevent the irritation effectively. I believe [Specific Toorak Road Garden Boutique – now closed, Chloe vaguely recalled] used to stock them, possibly still available at the Armadale nurseries?"

Chloe stared at the screen, her heart doing a familiar lurch. *MP_Gardener. Digitalis species. Careful leaf removal. Gant Botanique suede gloves. Toorak Road/Armadale stockist reference.* It was all there. The initials matched Mildred Pettle. The context – handling irritating/toxic plants like *Digitalis* with care – aligned perfectly with the suspected method. The specific glove brand matched. The mention of local high-end stockists fitted.

Could it be coincidence? Another 'MP' who was a keen heritage gardener in Melbourne with expensive French gloves and knowledge of foxglove irritancy? Possible, but the confluence of details felt electric. She quickly clicked on the 'MP_Gardener' user profile. As expected for an old, anonymous forum, it revealed nothing more. Only three posts in total, all from 2019, all offering practical but slightly reserved gardening advice in response to specific queries. No personal information, no signature, no way to definitively link it to Mildred Pettle.

Yet, it felt significant. It was a *behavioural* link. Years before Ainsworth's murder, someone using initials consistent with Mildred Pettle, participating in a niche Melbourne gardening forum, had possessed specific knowledge about *Digitalis* irritancy and had recommended *that exact brand* of expensive glove for handling it carefully. It suggested a pre-existing awareness and potential ownership, or at least recommendation, of the very item found near the crime scene, linked to the very plant suspected as the poison source.

It wasn't the smoking gun. It didn't prove the glove Chloe found belonged to Mildred. It didn't prove Mildred harvested the leaves. But it chipped away at her facade of being merely an efficient administrator with no particular interest or expertise in hands-on gardening, especially concerning potentially dangerous plants. It suggested a hidden depth of knowledge, a practical familiarity with the tools needed for exactly the kind of clandestine botanical task the murder seemed to involve.

Chloe carefully took screenshots of the forum thread, saving the URL, noting the date and username. It was another piece, small perhaps, frustratingly circumstantial, but it added texture to their portrait of Mildred Pettle. She wasn't just financially astute and socially adept; she might also possess hidden practical knowledge, knowledge that could be turned to deadly purpose.

She leaned back, rubbing her tired eyes. The weekend's research felt like finding faint footprints in hardening mud – tantalising suggestions of passage, but no clear image of the person who made them. Yet, each faint print – Agnes's historical land records, Fitzwilliam's phantom suppliers and Vance connection, and now this ghostly online recommendation for the specific glove – seemed to be leading, however circuitously, in the same direction. Towards

Mildred. The final piece, the one that would capture her image clearly, remained elusive. But Chloe felt a renewed conviction that it *was* there to be found. They just had to keep looking, keep digging, before their own time ran out.

****

Agnes Plummett's study seemed to crackle with suppressed energy that Sunday evening, a stark contrast to the weary frustration that had permeated their meeting just days before. The scattered evidence – Agnes's notes on Fincham and the PROV land records, Fitzwilliam's printouts detailing shell companies and Ainsworth's final expense claims, Chloe's photos of the *Gant Botanique* glove and her saved screenshot of the 'MP_Gardener' forum post – no longer felt like disparate, inconclusive fragments. Illuminated under the focused beam of the desk lamp, they now appeared as interlocking pieces of a single, damning mosaic.

They had spent the first hour carefully presenting their individual findings from the weekend's intensive research. Agnes recounted her discoveries at the Public Record Office – the confirmation of the ambiguous 'old orchard end' land parcel stemming from Silas Croft's time, its disappearance from rate books, and crucially, the footnote in Fincham hinting at Croft's secondary experiments with potentially toxic medicinal herbs (*Atropa*, Solanaceae) and subsequent legal disputes over access rights to that very land parcel after his death. "It establishes," Agnes concluded, her voice precise, "not just a simple boundary ambiguity, but a historical context involving potentially valuable or dangerous botany and legal contention tied directly to that specific location adjacent to Lawn 3. A secret Mildred, with her potential historical connection via 'E. Vance' in 1988, might have known about and exploited for decades."

Fitzwilliam then presented his own crucial discovery, laying a photocopy of Ainsworth's final expense claim on the table. "While confirming the phantom suppliers and the Vance connection to 'Bespoke Botanical Displays' strengthens the fraud motive," he explained, "the public record trail went cold trying to link the funds directly to Mildred. However," his voice took on a new gravity, "Ainsworth's *own* actions provide the key. This expense claim, submitted just days after he withdrew his query to Stonnington Council regarding the boundary, is an invoice for $1,850 from 'Melbourne Geomatics & Surveying' for a 'Preliminary Historical Boundary Identification and Cadastral Map Analysis' of the club property, specifically referencing the Gardiner's Creek frontage."

He let the significance sink in. "He didn't back down after withdrawing the council query. He escalated. He hired independent, professional surveyors to get definitive proof about that ambiguous 'old orchard end'. He was no longer just relying on historical interpretation; he was seeking external validation that would have been legally binding and impossible for the club, or Mildred, to ignore." He tapped the invoice date. "This was happening *immediately* before his death."

Finally, Chloe shared her findings about the glove and the 'MP_Gardener' forum post. "It's circumstantial, I know," she admitted, showing them the screenshots on her tablet. "But finding someone with those initials, recommending *that specific* expensive French glove brand years ago, specifically for handling irritating plants like *Digitalis*… it provides a potential behavioural link. It suggests Mildred, or someone using her initials, had prior knowledge and perhaps ownership of the exact type of specialised glove found near the crime scene, suitable for the very task of harvesting the poison."

Ronnie Peterson, who had been intently updating his master chart on the bookshelf, turned around, his expression one of almost pure scientific satisfaction. "Convergence," he announced simply. He walked over to the chart, now a dense web of connecting lines and probability assessments.

"Observe," he instructed, tracing lines with his pencil. "Agnes establishes deep historical motive: exploitation of ambiguous land parcel potentially linked to valuable/dangerous botany and past legal disputes. Fitzwilliam confirms mechanism for large-scale recent fraud via phantom suppliers under Subject P's (Pettle's) control. Fitzwilliam *also* provides the immediate trigger event: Ainsworth hiring professional surveyors *after* withdrawing council query, indicating imminent exposure of the historical land secret."

He drew an arrow from the surveyor invoice discovery directly to the estimated date of the murder. "Chloe's findings," he continued, adding another input line, "provide behavioural consistency regarding the means – knowledge/potential ownership of specialised equipment suitable for handling toxic *Digitalis*, whose remnants were found deliberately concealed near the scene, and whose toxin aligns with autopsy anomalies and observed victim symptoms."

He circled Mildred Pettle's name at the centre of the converging arrows. "Motive (historical + recent financial), Means (poison access/knowledge/tools), Opportunity (proven access/timing), Trigger Event (imminent exposure via surveyor report), and Post-Event Behaviour (subtle reactions to stimulus, archive check) – all data streams now converge with overwhelming probability (P > 0.98) on Subject P. The case, from a data analysis perspective, is resolved."

They stared at the chart, at the undeniable confluence of evidence they had painstakingly gathered. It felt complete. The historical roots, the modern fraud, the botanical weapon, the victim's final actions, the killer's opportunity and subtle reactions – it all locked together, pointing unequivocally at Mildred Pettle.

"So," Fitzwilliam said, breaking the silence, the weight of their conclusion heavy in his voice. "We have it. Not perhaps the single 'smoking gun' photograph or signed confession beloved of fiction, but an interlocking, multi-faceted case built on documented historical records, internal financial evidence, physical clues, behavioural analysis, and logical deduction that leaves no other plausible explanation."

"A case strong enough, I believe," Agnes stated firmly, "to finally compel Detective Inspector Davies to act. If presented correctly."

"How?" Chloe asked. "How do we present it without revealing… everything?"

"We focus on the verifiable, the undeniable, the evidence trail Davies *can* follow officially," Fitzwilliam took charge now, his legal mind shifting into strategic gear. "We update the memorandum. We lead with the most powerful new pieces: One - Ainsworth's withdrawn council query regarding the specific boundary, immediately followed by Two - Ainsworth hiring Melbourne Geomatics for a professional survey of that *same* boundary, proven by the invoice found in his club expense claims processed by Mildred. This establishes his active, escalating investigation and the imminent threat he posed *just before* his death."

"Then," he continued, outlining the structure, "we present Three - the evidence of payments processed by Mildred from club accounts to the highly suspicious, likely fraudulent suppliers (WeatherTech, Vintage Marquee, Bespoke Botanical), highlighting the lack of proper supporting documentation and the Vance connection. This provides the concrete financial motive linked directly to Mildred's administrative control."

"We include," Agnes added, "a concise summary of my PROV findings regarding the historical ambiguity of the 'old orchard end' land and the Croft rate payments, providing the crucial context for *why* Ainsworth was investigating that specific boundary and why it was potentially so sensitive."

"We omit direct mention of poison, the *Digitalis*, the glove, the forum post, the autopsy leak details, and our surveillance," Fitzwilliam confirmed. "Those remain our private knowledge for now. We simply present Davies with documented proof that Ainsworth was on the verge of exposing serious historical land issues *and* significant recent financial irregularities directly implicating Mildred Pettle's administration, providing her with overwhelming motive and opportunity, occurring just before his death by means the police themselves noted had anomalies (we can perhaps allude gently back to the lividity/alkaloid mention in passing, if appropriate)."

"The objective," Agnes clarified, "is not necessarily to hand Davies the entire solution on a plate, but to provide her with sufficient concrete, verifiable evidence pointing towards Mildred's motive and questionable financial administration that she *must* investigate further – obtain banking warrants, search records, re-interview Mildred under caution regarding these specific financial and historical matters."

Ronnie nodded. "Optimal strategy. Presents high-probability, verifiable data subset, sufficient to shift official investigation vector towards Subject P without compromising quartet methodology or revealing currently inadmissible data points."

"I can redraft the memorandum tonight," Fitzwilliam offered, already mentally outlining the key paragraphs. "Focus sharply on the timeline: Council Query -> Withdrawal -> Surveyor Hired -> Payments to Shell Companies -> Murder. With the supporting PROV and internal club documentation references."

"And delivery?" Agnes asked.

"I will request another brief meeting with Davies tomorrow,"

Fitzwilliam decided. "Present it as urgent supplementary information uncovered during ongoing due diligence related to club finances, directly relevant to the victim's state of mind and activities prior to death. Emphasise the documented nature of the evidence."

They looked at each other again, a silent agreement passing between them. This was the endgame. They had followed the threads, deciphered the clues, faced down their own fears and ethical dilemmas. Now, they had a case – a powerful, coherent, evidence-based case – strong enough, they hoped, to finally pierce Mildred Pettle's armour of deception and force the hand of the official investigation. The risks remained high, but the path was finally clear. Tomorrow, they would approach the authorities not with speculation, but with documented proof demanding action. Tomorrow, the net would truly close.

<h1 style="text-align:center">23</h1>

Presenting the Case

Monday morning, April 21st, broke over Melbourne with a clarity that felt almost mocking to Alistair Fitzwilliam. The weekend's intensive analysis with Agnes, Ronnie, and Chloe had cemented their conviction: Mildred Pettle was almost certainly the architect of Bartholomew Ainsworth's death, driven by the imminent threat of his investigations into decades of potential fraud rooted in historical club secrets. They had motive, means, opportunity, logistics, behavioural indicators… everything except the single, irrefutable piece of evidence that would satisfy a court of law, or more immediately, persuade a sceptical Detective Inspector Davies to look beyond the convenient suspect of Harry Smythe. Their decision, reached late last night amidst cold coffee and rising anxiety in Agnes's study, was clear: present their strongest *verifiable* findings to Davies now, hoping the documented anomalies were compelling enough to force her hand.

Fitzwilliam sat at his expansive desk on the twentieth floor, the panoramic view of the awakening city – trams beginning their balletic crawl along Collins Street, ferries stitching wakes across the distant Yarra, the spire of the Arts Centre catching the early sun –

usually a source of detached calm, today offered no comfort. Before him lay not the complex briefs of Macrocorp, but the single, plain manilla envelope containing the carefully drafted supplementary memorandum for Detective Inspector Davies. He had laboured over it after leaving Agnes's apartment, finally finishing in the small hours, ensuring every statement was grounded in documented fact – Agnes's PROV discoveries, the club's own payment records he'd accessed – while omitting any hint of their more speculative theories or illicitly obtained knowledge. It felt like the most important document he had ever drafted.

He picked up his phone, the cool plastic feeling unnaturally heavy in his hand. Calling Sergeant Riley again, requesting another meeting with Davies so soon after the last, felt presumptuous, potentially irritating. But the alternative – waiting, hoping the police stumbled onto the truth themselves while Harry Smythe remained under suspicion and Mildred potentially destroyed further evidence – felt untenable. He took a deep breath, punched in Riley's direct number, and listened to the dial tone, his heart thudding against his ribs like a trapped bird.

"Riley," the detective sergeant's familiar, slightly gravelly voice answered after two rings.

"Colin, good morning. Alistair Fitzwilliam here," Fitzwilliam began, forcing his voice into a tone of calm professionalism he was far from feeling. "Apologies for disturbing you so early."

"Fitzwilliam," Riley sounded weary already. "What can I do for you? More club politics?" There was an edge of impatience in his voice. Fitzwilliam's stomach tightened. This wasn't going to be easy.

"Not exactly politics, Colin," Fitzwilliam replied carefully. "It relates directly to the Ainsworth investigation, following up on the information I provided to Inspector Davies on Friday." He had to frame this perfectly. "As part of ongoing due diligence required by my committee role before interim financial arrangements are confirmed, I've had cause to examine certain internal club payment records in more detail over the weekend." He chose the phrasing deliberately – 'internal club records', 'due diligence' – grounding his actions in legitimate procedure.

"And?" Riley prompted, clearly wanting him to get to the point.

"And I've uncovered specific, documented evidence directly corroborating Mr Ainsworth's final lines of inquiry – evidence I believe Inspector Davies needs to see immediately as it significantly impacts the established timeline and potential motives surrounding his death." He kept his voice steady, emphasising 'documented evidence' and 'impacts the timeline'.

There was a pause on the other end. Fitzwilliam could almost hear Riley weighing the potential hassle against the possibility, however remote, that this anxious lawyer might actually have something substantive this time. "Documented evidence?" Riley repeated, a flicker of professional interest perhaps tempering his weariness. "Relating to what, specifically? Not more historical gossip?"

"No," Fitzwilliam stated firmly. "Relating to Mr Ainsworth engaging external professional services – specifically, land surveyors – to investigate the exact historical boundary issue near Lawn 3, confirmed by invoices found within the club's recent expense claim files. This action was taken *after* he withdrew his formal query to council on the same matter, and mere days before his death." He delivered the key points concisely, factually. "It provides concrete proof of his active, escalating investigation into that sensitive area immediately prior to the event."

Another pause, longer this time. Fitzwilliam held his breath. This was the hook. Proof of the victim taking specific, costly action directly related to the historical anomaly, action the police were likely unaware of, action that provided a powerful, immediate motive for someone wanting that boundary issue kept quiet.

"Surveyors?" Riley said finally, a different note in his voice now – less dismissive, more thoughtful. "Regarding that creek boundary?" Clearly, the information from the first memo *had* registered at some level.

"Precisely," Fitzwilliam confirmed, allowing a hint of urgency into his tone. "The invoice itself raises further questions regarding internal authorisation procedures, which are also detailed in the supplementary memo I've prepared for the Inspector." He added the financial irregularity angle, linking it directly to the surveyor finding.

"Right," Riley said slowly. "Look, the Detective Inspector is in briefings all morning. But… this sounds like something she *should* probably see sooner rather than later." Relief flooded through Fitzwilliam, so potent it almost made him gasp. "Can you be available around… say, 1:30 PM? I can *try* and get you ten minutes with her then, maybe in one of the interview rooms downstairs at St Kilda Road? No promises, depends on how her morning unfolds."

"1:30 PM is perfect, Colin," Fitzwilliam said quickly, immensely grateful. "Thank you. I genuinely believe this information is critical."

"Yeah, well, we'll see," Riley grunted, reverting to professional caution. "1:30 PM. Ask for me at the front desk." The line clicked dead.

Fitzwilliam sank back in his chair, the receiver still pressed momentarily to his ear. He had the meeting. Davies would see the supplementary memo, see the surveyor invoice, see the documented proof of Ainsworth's final, dangerous investigation. It felt like a huge step forward.

Yet, the anxiety remained, morphing into a different form. Now, it wasn't just about getting the police to listen; it was about the consequences of them *acting*. If Davies took this seriously, if she started probing the finances, the suppliers, the historical land issue, Mildred Pettle would know, unequivocally, that the investigation had shifted focus directly onto her. How would she react then? Would she cooperate, bluff, obstruct? Or would she perceive the net closing and take more desperate, dangerous measures?

He looked at the memorandum again, lying pristine in its envelope on his desk. It contained verifiable facts, yes, but it was also, implicitly, a direct accusation against a woman who had maintained a facade of harmless efficiency for decades, a woman who had likely killed once already to protect her secrets. Handing this over felt like lighting a fuse, unsure exactly how long it was or what size the explosion might be at the other end. He sent a quick text to Agnes, confirming the 1:30 PM meeting time, then forced himself to turn, finally, to the neglected Macrocorp brief, needing the distracting complexity of corporate law to stop his mind from dwelling on the potentially explosive consequences of the meeting scheduled for just after lunch. The approach had been initiated. The waiting was almost over. The reckoning felt closer than ever.

****

The walk from the tram stop on St Kilda Road to the imposing glass and concrete facade of the Victoria Police Centre felt longer, more fraught, than Alistair Fitzwilliam had anticipated. The building, a symbol of state authority and official process, seemed to loom over him, amplifying the inherent risks of his mission. He clutched the manilla envelope containing the supplementary memorandum – the product of his own late-night drafting and the quartet's combined, painstaking investigation – like a fragile shield. He wasn't just a lawyer anymore, operating within the familiar bounds of civil litigation; he felt like an envoy from a shadow inquiry, about to present potentially explosive findings to a power structure that could just as easily dismiss him as investigate his claims.

He announced himself at the imposing front desk, mentioning his 1:30 PM appointment with Detective Inspector Davies, facilitated by Sergeant Riley. After a brief check of identification and a security scan that felt disproportionately invasive for delivering a simple document, he was issued a visitor's pass and directed to wait. He sat on a hard plastic chair in the busy, impersonal foyer, watching uniformed officers, detectives in plain clothes, and civilian staff move with purpose, acutely aware of his own outsider status. He checked his phone – no messages from Agnes, Ronnie, or Chloe, who were anxiously awaiting news. He took several deep, calming breaths, mentally rehearsing the key points he needed to convey: the verifiable nature of the evidence, the crucial timeline implications, the necessity of looking beyond Harry Smythe.

After what felt like an interminable ten minutes, Detective Constable Miller appeared – the same young, diligent officer who had taken notes during Harry Smythe's disastrous verandah interview. "Mr Fitzwilliam? Inspector Davies will see you now. If you'll come with me."

Miller led him through security doors, along brightly lit, anonymous corridors that smelled faintly of floor polish and institutional coffee, finally stopping outside a standard interview room door. "In here, please."

The room was small, windowless, functional to the point of being oppressive. A plain table, three chairs, a water dispenser humming quietly in the corner, and a faint, lingering sense of countless difficult conversations having taken place within these four walls. Fitzwilliam felt his collar suddenly tighten. This was a far cry from the relative neutrality of the St Kilda Road cafe. This was official territory.

Detective Inspector Davies entered almost immediately after him, closing the door firmly behind her. Detective Constable Miller took a seat unobtrusively in the corner, notebook ready. Davies didn't offer a handshake this time, simply nodded towards the chair opposite her at the table. "Mr Fitzwilliam. Thank you for coming in. Sergeant Riley indicated you have supplementary information regarding the Ainsworth case?" Her tone was professional, neutral, giving nothing away, but her eyes, sharp and intelligent, missed nothing. Fitzwilliam noted she had a copy of his first memorandum lying on the table before her, perhaps having just reviewed it.

"Yes, Inspector. Thank you for agreeing to see me on such short notice," Fitzwilliam began, placing his manilla envelope on the table between them but not opening it yet. He needed to frame this carefully. "Following our conversation on Friday, and as part of my ongoing responsibilities within the Society's governance structure regarding financial continuity, I felt compelled to examine certain internal records more closely over the weekend, specifically relating to Mr Ainsworth's final activities and recent major club expenditures."

Davies watched him, her expression unreadable. "And?"

"And I have uncovered specific, documented evidence," Fitzwilliam stressed the words, "which, when combined with publicly accessible historical records previously brought to your attention, paints a significantly more complex picture of Mr Ainsworth's circumstances immediately prior to his death, raising serious questions about potential motives beyond the widely assumed altercation with Lord Smythe."

He paused, gauging her reaction. Still nothing. He decided to lead with the strongest new piece. "Most significantly, Inspector, internal club expense records confirm that Mr Ainsworth, *after* withdrawing his formal boundary clarification query from Stonnington Council in late March, immediately engaged the services of a professional surveying firm, Melbourne Geomatics, specifically to conduct a 'Preliminary Historical Boundary Identification and Cadastral Map Analysis' focusing on the Gardiner's Creek frontage – the 'old orchard end' area adjacent to where his body was found." He slid a clear photocopy of the surveyor's invoice, retrieved from Ainsworth's expense claim file, across the table towards her. "This invoice is dated March 28th. He was killed less than two weeks later."

He watched Davies pick up the photocopy, her eyes scanning it quickly. He saw a flicker of genuine interest this time, a slight narrowing of her gaze as she registered the date, the service description, the location reference. This wasn't vague historical speculation; this was a dated invoice for professional services directly related to the sensitive land issue, proving Ainsworth was actively, aggressively pursuing it right up until his death, *after* seemingly backing off publicly.

"This invoice was submitted for club reimbursement?" Davies asked sharply, her focus now entirely on Fitzwilliam.

"It was," Fitzwilliam confirmed. "Submitted by Mr Ainsworth himself. The processing note indicates it was sighted and passed for inclusion in the next payment run by the Club Secretary, Ms Mildred Pettle, in early April."

Davies absorbed this, her fingers tapping lightly on the invoice copy. "So Ms Pettle would have been aware Mr Ainsworth had engaged external surveyors regarding this boundary issue?"

"Assuming she reviewed the supporting documentation before processing the claim, yes, she would have been aware," Fitzwilliam confirmed, choosing his words carefully.

"And this boundary issue," Davies continued, her eyes sharp, "relates back to the historical land ambiguities mentioned in your previous memorandum? The PROV records Agnes Plummett apparently uncovered?"

"Precisely," Fitzwilliam confirmed, relieved she had clearly read and remembered the details from the first memo. "The historical records show a long-standing ambiguity regarding a specific parcel near the creek, potentially linked to undocumented income or usage – a matter Mr Ainsworth was demonstrably investigating with increasing intensity, first via council, then via private surveyors, immediately prior to his death." He allowed the implication to hang: Ainsworth was about to get definitive answers, posing an imminent threat to anyone benefiting from that ambiguity.

He then moved to the second point, sliding the supplementary memo itself across the table. "Furthermore, Inspector, my review of the payment journals and supporting invoice files for recent major expenditures – specifically the roof repairs and Centenary Gala deposits also processed by Ms Pettle and signed off by Mr Ainsworth – confirms the procedural anomalies I alluded to previously." He quickly summarised the findings: payments to likely shell companies (WeatherTech, Vintage Marquee, Bespoke Botanical Displays), lack of proper supporting quotes or committee approvals referenced in the internal records, payment authorisation relying heavily on Ms Pettle's internal memos or sign-offs rather than complete documentation. He specifically mentioned the 'Eleanor Vance' directorship of Bespoke Botanical Displays and the shared maiden name with Ms Pettle, presenting it as a documented fact requiring explanation in the context of potential conflict of interest and significant club expenditure lacking full transparency.

He finished speaking, the small room feeling intensely quiet except for the hum of the air conditioning. He had laid out the core of their case – the verifiable parts, at least. The documented proof of Ainsworth's escalating investigation into a sensitive historical land issue potentially linked to finance, combined with documented proof of highly irregular financial administration under Mildred Pettle's direct control involving likely fraudulent suppliers.

Detective Inspector Davies didn't speak immediately. She picked up the supplementary memorandum, her expression thoughtful as she scanned its contents, occasionally referring back to the surveyor invoice copy. Detective Constable Miller continued scribbling notes diligently. Fitzwilliam waited, trying to read Davies's reaction. She was no longer dismissive; that much was clear. The documented evidence, particularly the surveyor invoice and the internal payment anomalies, had captured her professional attention. But was it enough to shift her focus decisively away from Harry Smythe?

"Mr Fitzwilliam," Davies said finally, placing the memo down. "The information regarding Mr Ainsworth engaging surveyors *after* withdrawing his council query is… significant, certainly, regarding his state of mind and activities prior to his death." She chose her words carefully. "And the financial procedures you've documented regarding these supplier payments clearly warrant further scrutiny regarding the Society's internal controls and potential mismanagement." Her tone was still professional, guarded, but Fitzwilliam detected a definite shift. She wasn't talking about 'club politics' anymore; she was talking about mismanagement and the victim's final actions.

"Thank you for bringing these documented matters to my attention," she continued, standing up, signalling the end of the meeting. "This information," she tapped the memorandum and the invoice copy, "will be thoroughly reviewed and cross-referenced with our existing investigation findings. We will, of course, follow all credible lines of inquiry." Still no promises, no indication of specific actions against Mildred. But the door, Fitzwilliam felt, was no longer closed. He had given her verifiable facts, documented anomalies that demanded official explanation, painting a powerful picture of motive and opportunity centred squarely on Mildred Pettle.

"Thank you, Inspector," Fitzwilliam said, rising also, feeling a profound sense of weary relief. "That is all I wished to ensure."

He was escorted back out through the labyrinthine corridors by Detective Constable Miller, emerging into the bright, ordinary bustle of the St Kilda Road afternoon. He had done it. He had presented the case, or at least the verifiable core of it. He had planted the necessary seeds of doubt and provided concrete avenues for Davies to pursue. Now, all they could do was wait, and hope, and perhaps pray that Detective Inspector Davies was astute enough to follow the trail before Mildred Pettle realised just how much the net was truly closing in around her. He sent a brief text to Agnes: *"Meeting complete. Info presented & received. Reaction... cautiously positive. Waiting game continues. Agnes."*

****

Tuesday, April 22nd, unfolded under a vast, indifferent Melbourne sky, the kind of clear, bright autumn day that usually lifted spirits at the Toorak Croquet & Horticultural Society. Today, however, the sunshine felt brittle, almost mocking, to the four individuals bound by their shared, dangerous secret. Fitzwilliam's meeting with Detective Inspector Davies the previous afternoon had felt like a potential turning point, a moment where their painstakingly gathered evidence might finally penetrate the official investigation's focus on Harry Smythe. But twenty-four hours later, an agonising silence had descended. There had been no follow-up calls from Sergeant Riley, no sudden reappearance of police cars at the club gates, no discernible change in the outwardly serene demeanour of Mildred Pettle. The waiting was excruciating.

Alistair Fitzwilliam sat in his Collins Street office, attempting for the third time to concentrate on drafting a complex submission for the Macrocorp case. It was useless. His gaze kept straying to the silent telephone, then to the encrypted email account he used for sensitive communications, then back to the telephone. Had Davies even read the memo yet? Had she dismissed it as the biased interference of club insiders trying to protect one of their own? Had she, perhaps worse, subtly alerted Mildred Pettle through some back channel, some incautious inquiry made elsewhere in the club's administrative structure? The possibilities gnawed at him, each more unsettling than the last. He replayed the meeting in his mind: Davies's sharp eyes, her non-committal responses, her acceptance of the envelope. Had he imagined the flicker of genuine interest when he mentioned the surveyor invoice? Had her professional neutrality simply been polite dismissal? He felt suspended in a limbo of uncertainty, the weight of their gamble pressing down on him.

At the Society grounds, Agnes Plummett occupied her usual table on the verandah, ostensibly compiling notes from her PROV research and the Fincham book for the Centenary archives. In reality, she was engaged in relentless, minute observation of Mildred Pettle's comings and goings. Mildred's routine appeared, on the surface, entirely undisturbed. She arrived promptly at 8:45 AM, dealt with the morning mail, conferred briefly with Esme Weatherly about upcoming bookings, handled several member inquiries regarding subscription renewals with her usual patient efficiency, and took her customary mid-morning cup of tea (Earl Grey, weak, no milk) while reviewing correspondence in her office.

Agnes watched, analysed, compared against baseline data stored in her formidable memory. Were Mildred's movements slightly brisker today? Was her smile a fraction more brittle? Was the time spent sorting the mail five minutes longer than usual, perhaps allowing for discreet shredding? It was impossible to say for sure. Mildred's facade remained utterly intact. Agnes felt a grudging respect for the woman's control, but also a deep frustration. Their carefully presented evidence, Fitzwilliam's direct approach – had it all simply glanced off Mildred's impenetrable composure? Or was the lack of reaction itself a sign of heightened caution, a deliberate performance of normalcy by someone aware they might now be under closer, albeit unofficial, scrutiny? Agnes couldn't shake the feeling of unease, the sense that beneath the calm surface, Mildred was calculating, assessing, perhaps preparing her next move. The silence from the police felt less like procedural delay and more like a dangerous void.

Chloe Dubois found focusing on her gardening tasks that day almost unbearable. Every time she saw Mildred walk across the lawn or pass by in the corridor, her heart would leap into her throat. She tried to concentrate on pruning the climbing roses near the clubhouse wall, needing the repetitive, physical action to keep her anxiety at bay, but her gaze kept drifting towards the administrative wing windows, towards the compost heaps hidden behind the pittosporum hedge. Had Mildred noticed her renewed interest in that area yesterday? Was her own brief conversation with Mildred near the incinerator now flagged in the Secretary's mind as suspicious? She felt horribly exposed, convinced Mildred's polite smiles held a knowing, calculating quality they hadn't possessed before. The normalcy of the club – members practising shots, Henderson Jr. mowing Lawn 4, the clink of cups from the verandah – felt like a thin, fragile skin stretched over something dark and menacing. She found herself constantly scanning her surroundings, jumping at unexpected sounds, the fear of being watched now a constant companion. The lack of police action only amplified her fear; it felt as if they, the quartet, were alone in knowing the danger, abandoned on the front line while the authorities remained oblivious.

Ronnie Peterson, predictably, approached the waiting game with characteristic methodology, though even his scientific detachment showed signs of strain. He positioned himself in the members' lounge, claiming the need for quiet concentration to finish *The Age's* cryptic crossword (a task he usually completed in under twenty minutes, but which he managed to stretch out for most of the morning). From his vantage point, he logged Mildred's movements within the clubhouse, timing her interactions, comparing them against his established baseline data.

"Subject P," he noted meticulously in his coded logbook, "10:15 - 10:35: Telephone calls (incoming/outgoing undetermined), duration consistent with baseline admin tasks. 10:40: Delivers documents to Committee Room 2 (Baseline: Expected). 11:00 - 11:15: Morning tea break, observed consuming beverage at desk (Baseline: Consistent). 11:20 - 11:55: Meeting with external supplier (stationery rep, pre-scheduled per Esme W.). Baseline: Consistent." His analysis showed zero significant deviations. The system, perturbed by Agnes's trigger and perhaps Fitzwilliam's memo reaching police ears, seemed to have returned to a state of frustrating stability.

But then, just before lunch, came the ambiguous event that sent a ripple of fresh anxiety through the observing quartet members via their discreet text message chain.

Ronnie logged: *"12:30 - 12:55. Subject P in office. Observed engaging office shredder for extended period (approx. 10 mins continuous operation)."*

Fitzwilliam received the text in his office, his stomach tightening. Shredding? Was that routine administrative tidying? Or deliberate destruction of evidence prompted by his memo to Davies? Ten minutes of continuous shredding sounded excessive for routine mail disposal. What could she be destroying? Old financial records?

Notes related to Ainsworth? Evidence pertaining to the phantom suppliers? It was maddeningly ambiguous, potentially incriminating, but utterly unprovable.

Agnes received the text while comparing historical membership rolls in the library. Shredding. Of course. If Mildred suspected scrutiny, clearing out potentially compromising documents would be a logical, cautious step. But which documents? Did it mean Davies *had* contacted her, or was she merely taking pre-emptive action based on Agnes's and Fitzwilliam's known inquiries? The lack of certainty was agonising.

Chloe saw the text while taking her own lunch break on a bench near the rose garden. Shredding. The word itself sounded sinister. She pictured Mildred calmly feeding incriminating papers into the machine, erasing the trail, while maintaining her serene facade. The sense of urgency, the feeling that time was running out before crucial evidence disappeared forever, intensified Chloe's already frayed nerves.

The afternoon brought no further enlightenment. Mildred took her lunch break – precisely fifteen minutes, back within baseline parameters, consumed in the staff room. She attended to routine administrative tasks. She dealt politely with member inquiries. She showed no outward sign of unusual stress or activity. The shredding incident remained an isolated, interpretable data point.

By late afternoon, as Fitzwilliam endured another fruitless, non-committal phone call with Sergeant Riley ("Still under review, Alistair, standard procedure, can't comment further"), a heavy sense of doubt began to pervade the quartet. Had they overplayed their hand? Had Fitzwilliam's memo been too circumspect, too easily dismissed? Was Mildred simply too well-entrenched, too protected by her reputation and the club's inertia, for their suspicions to gain traction? The waiting game felt less like a strategic pause and more like a slow, draining defeat. The silence from the police, combined with Mildred's infuriating composure, felt like a verdict in itself. They had presented their case, and it seemed the authorities, like almost everyone else at the Society, remained unconvinced, leaving the four of them alone with their dangerous knowledge, watching a potential killer operate with impunity just metres away. The frustration was an evident, bitter taste in Fitzwilliam's mouth as he stared out at the indifferent city skyline.

****

Wednesday morning, April 23rd, unfolded at the Toorak Croquet & Horticultural Society under the same clear, cool autumn sky as the previous day, but the atmosphere, at least within the strained awareness of the quartet, felt leaden, stagnant. Fitzwilliam's memo had been delivered over twenty-four hours ago, yet the silence from the authorities remained absolute. The brief flicker of hope ignited by Detective Inspector Davies accepting the document had dimmed, replaced by the weary resignation that perhaps their carefully constructed case, lacking irrefutable proof, had indeed been dismissed as amateur meddling.

Fitzwilliam sat again in his Collins Street office, the unanswered call to Sergeant Riley from yesterday echoing in his mind. He found himself repeatedly drafting, then deleting, emails to Detective Inspector Davies – polite follow-ups, further offers of assistance – knowing they would be futile, potentially even counterproductive. He felt a heavy responsibility, not just to uncover the truth, but for potentially having endangered his collaborators and himself by raising their heads above the parapet, only to be ignored. Had Mildred Pettle simply weathered another storm, her position secured by decades of perceived propriety and the inertia of the official investigation?

Agnes, back in her usual chair on the verandah, pretended to read a biography of Sir Redmond Barry, but her gaze kept drifting towards the administrative corridor. Mildred had arrived at precisely 8:45 AM, her routine unchanged, her composure, if anything, seeming even more placidly assured than usual. Agnes had watched her sort the mail, handle phone calls, confer briefly with Henderson Jr. about lawn aeration – all with the quiet efficiency that now seemed deeply sinister. Was this the calm of innocence, Agnes wondered bleakly, or the chilling self-possession of someone who knew they had successfully neutralised a threat? The ambiguity was maddening.

Chloe, working on replanting the winter pansies in the large urns near the clubhouse entrance, felt physically ill with anxiety. Every time Mildred emerged from the office wing, Chloe would find her hands trembling, her focus blurring. The memory of Mildred's probing gaze near the compost heap, followed by the utter lack of police action despite Fitzwilliam's efforts, made her feel isolated and vulnerable. What if Mildred *knew* Chloe had found the buried leaves? What if she was just biding her time? The familiar, beautiful gardens suddenly felt full of unseen menace.

Even Ronnie Peterson, usually buoyed by the intellectual challenge, seemed subdued. He sat in the lounge, his charts and probability models spread before him, but his usual energetic analysis was absent. He stared at the complex web of arrows and notations converging on Mildred Pettle, a frown creasing his brow. The data, the logic, the physics – it all pointed one way. Yet, the system, the external world represented by the police investigation, refused to validate his conclusions. It was, for Ronnie, the scientific equivalent of discovering a new fundamental particle only to have the particle accelerator consistently fail to register its existence.

Deeply frustrating.

Then, shortly after 11:00 AM, everything changed.

A dark grey sedan, instantly recognisable to Fitzwilliam from his research (though not the flashy Jaguar associated with Harry Smythe's creditors – this was standard police issue), pulled quietly into the Society's gravel drive. It didn't park ostentatiously near the entrance but found a discreet spot further down, partially obscured by a large rhododendron bush – ironically, near Lawn 3. Two figures emerged: Detective Inspector Davies, her expression neutral but somehow more purposeful than during her previous visits, and Detective Constable Miller, notebook already in hand.

A ripple went through the few members present on the verandah and lawns. Police again? Had they come for Harry Smythe after all? Heads turned, conversations paused.

From their respective vantage points, the quartet watched, breaths held. Fitzwilliam, who had decided to work from the club library that morning needing the proximity despite the tension, saw them first through the tall windows. Agnes lowered her biography slowly. Chloe stopped mid-pansy, her trowel hovering over the soil. Ronnie's head snapped up from his charts, his gaze instantly locking onto the arriving officers.

Davies and Miller didn't linger. They walked directly, not towards the main lounge or verandah, but straight towards the administrative wing entrance. This was different. Their previous interactions had involved general scene assessment, witness interviews conducted more publicly. This felt targeted.

They reached the side door just as Mildred Pettle emerged, carrying a file, perhaps on her way to the main lounge. She stopped abruptly upon seeing them, her polite welcoming smile freezing fractionally on her face before reasserting itself.

"Inspector Davies," she said, her voice perfectly calm, though perhaps a fraction higher pitched than usual. "Constable Miller. An unexpected visit. Is there something I can help you with?"

Detective Inspector Davies stepped forward, blocking Mildred's path slightly. Her voice was quiet but clear, carrying easily to Fitzwilliam and Agnes who were now subtly closer, straining to hear. "Ms Pettle," Davies began, her tone devoid of pleasantry, purely professional, "we need to discuss certain administrative matters related to club finances and record-keeping, specifically concerning payments authorised by Mr Ainsworth prior to his death. We also need access to specific archived materials related to the West Wing extension funding from the late 1980s."

Fitzwilliam felt a jolt of pure, unadulterated triumph, quickly tempered by apprehension. *She'd read the memo. She was acting on it.* The specific references – payment authorisation, specific suppliers (implied), West Wing funding archives – came directly from his supplementary report.

All eyes, hidden and overt, were now on Mildred Pettle. This was the moment. Direct confrontation, not by them, but by the police, armed with specific, targeted inquiries based on their carefully presented evidence. How would she react?

For a heart-stopping moment, Mildred seemed utterly still, her face a blank mask. The friendly, efficient Club Secretary facade wavered, revealing something harder, colder beneath. Her eyes, usually conveying gentle interest, narrowed almost imperceptibly. Her hand, holding the file, tightened, the knuckles showing white. Was this fear? Anger? Calculation?

Then, control reasserted itself, swift and absolute. She drew a breath, composing her features back into an expression of mild, professional surprise and concern. "Oh my," she said, her voice regaining its usual soft cadence, though perhaps lacking some of its warmth. "Historical finances? And recent payments? That sounds rather serious. Of course, Inspector, I will cooperate fully. Anything to assist your investigation." She even managed a small, cooperative smile. "Shall we speak in my office? Or perhaps the Treasurer's office would be more appropriate, where the relevant payment journals are kept?"

She was good, Fitzwilliam thought, chillingly good. No panic, no defensiveness, just immediate, plausible cooperation, framing the inquiry as a routine administrative matter she was happy to facilitate. But the flicker, the momentary freeze, the tightening grip – Agnes, Chloe, and Fitzwilliam had all seen it this time. The carefully aimed questions had hit their mark.

"Your office for now, Ms Pettle," Detective Inspector Davies replied coolly. "Constable Miller will accompany us. We may require access to the Treasurer's office and potentially the archives later."

Mildred nodded graciously. "Of course, Inspector. Whatever you need." She turned and led the two police officers back down the administrative corridor, disappearing from view.

A collective, silent exhalation seemed to pass between the observing quartet members. They exchanged brief, significant glances across the lounge and verandah. It had happened. The official investigation had finally, decisively, shifted its focus towards Mildred Pettle, armed with specific questions about the very financial and historical irregularities they had uncovered.

The relief was immense, but short-lived, quickly replaced by a new, sharper anxiety. They had poked the hornet's nest, and now the authorities were stirring it with a stick. What would happen next? Would Mildred's composure hold under direct police questioning? Would she talk her way out of it, obstruct, or destroy evidence they hadn't yet found? What exactly would Davies and Miller find in those payment records, now they knew what to look for?

The endgame had begun. The trap they had set hadn't needed to be sprung by Mildred trying to access archives; their information had been enough to redirect the official investigation. Now, the confrontation they had simultaneously craved and dreaded was underway, behind closed doors, orchestrated by the police. All the quartet could do now was wait, watch, and hope that the cracks they had painstakingly revealed in Mildred Pettle's facade were about to widen into an uncontainable fracture, finally exposing the truth beneath. The air in the clubhouse felt electric with anticipation.

24

Under Scrutiny

The arrival of Detective Inspector Davies and Detective Constable Miller back at the Toorak Croquet & Horticultural Society just before lunchtime on Wednesday, April 23rd, had detonated the fragile surface of restored normality like a well-placed explosive charge. Gone was the hushed, speculative gossip that had followed the initial discovery and the subsequent focus on Harry Smythe or Major Ferguson. In its place was a stunned, almost disbelieving silence, followed by a frantic, barely suppressed buzz of an entirely new, more shocking frequency. The police hadn't come for Harry. They hadn't come to deliver routine updates. They had walked directly, purposefully, into the administrative heart of the club and requested a private interview, along with specific financial records, from none other than Mildred Pettle, the quiet, unassuming, utterly indispensable Club Secretary.

The quartet, scattered in their pre-arranged observation posts, watched the unfolding drama with a mixture of intense vindication and heart-stopping anxiety. Fitzwilliam, loitering near the west boundary pretending to discuss hypothetical drainage solutions with a non-existent contact on his mobile phone, had seen Davies and

Miller intercept Mildred near the side office door. He couldn't hear the exact words, but Davies's firm tone and Mildred's momentary, almost imperceptible stiffening before her mask of polite cooperation snapped back into place, spoke volumes. He'd immediately sent the coded alert text: *"Package Delivery Confirmed. Target Engaged. Standby."*

Now, nearly two hours later, the waiting stretched into an almost unbearable tautness. Davies, Miller, and Mildred remained closeted within Mildred's small office down the administrative corridor. What was happening in there? Was Davies confronting her directly with the evidence from Fitzwilliam's memorandum – the surveyor invoice, the phantom suppliers, the historical Vance connection? Was Mildred maintaining her composure, offering plausible explanations, talking her way out of it with the same effortless deflection she had used on them? Or were the cracks finally appearing under official, targeted pressure?

From her position in the now mostly deserted library alcove, Agnes Plummett found concentration impossible. The Centenary brochure notes lay abandoned. Her focus was entirely on the closed door far down the corridor, partially visible from her vantage point. She strained her ears, but heard nothing beyond the distant clatter of lunch service from the dining room and the rhythmic ticking of the hall clock measuring out the agonisingly slow minutes.

She reviewed the situation mentally. Fitzwilliam's memo had been precise, factual, focusing on verifiable documents and procedural anomalies. It gave Davies concrete leads to pursue *within* the club's own records, leads directly implicating Mildred's administrative oversight. Crucially, it provided the context of Ainsworth's specific, escalating investigation into those very areas just before his death, establishing a powerful motive previously obscured by the focus on Harry Smythe's temper. Had it been enough? Enough to overcome

Davies's initial apparent conviction about Smythe? Enough to justify this prolonged, closed-door session with Mildred? Agnes, usually so reliant on logic and evidence, found herself resorting to something akin to prayer – a silent, fervent plea that Davies possessed the insight and tenacity to see past Mildred's expertly maintained facade.

Chloe Dubois, ostensibly wiping down tables on the far end of the verandah after the main lunch rush, felt physically sick with tension. Every time a door opened along the administrative corridor, her head would snap up, hoping, fearing, to see Mildred emerge, perhaps flanked by the police, the ordeal finally over. But only Esme Weatherly appeared occasionally, looking pale and deeply distressed, fetching glasses of water or carrying files *towards* Mildred's office, presumably at the request of the police. Esme's obvious anxiety only heightened Chloe's own fear. Esme clearly suspected nothing about Mildred prior to this; witnessing her calm, capable colleague now under intense police scrutiny must be bewildering, terrifying. Chloe remembered Mildred's probing questions near the compost heap, her seemingly innocent interest in the 'missing ledger'. Had Mildred suspected Chloe specifically? Was Chloe herself now somehow implicated in Detective Inspector Davies's eyes due to her proximity to the body discovery and her knowledge of the gardens? The fear felt cold and sharp.

Ronnie Peterson, having abandoned his crossword in the bar area as too conspicuous, now sat in the main lounge, nursing a single glass of soda water and pretending to read a yachting magazine. His scientific mind struggled with the lack of quantifiable data. Observation of a closed door yielded nothing beyond temporal duration analysis. He knew from Fitzwilliam's earlier text that the police interaction with Mildred had commenced at approximately 11:55 AM. It was now nearly 2:00 PM. Duration: > 2 hours. Significant deviation from a routine administrative query. Probability of serious interrogation versus procedural document review: Requires assessment of baseline police interview duration's for complex financial matters – insufficient data available. He felt frustrated by the reliance on human interpretation and second-hand observation. He wished he could place discreet sensors in the room, measure galvanic skin response, analyse vocal stress patterns. Instead, he was reduced to watching the corridor entrance and monitoring the reactions of the few remaining members in the lounge.

Those reactions were telling. The initial stunned silence that had followed the police arrival and their targeted approach towards Mildred had given way to frantic, hushed whispering. Members gathered in small, anxious clusters, casting frequent glances towards the administrative corridor. Fitzwilliam, briefly passing through the lounge on his way to refill his water bottle (a pretext to check in visually with Ronnie), overheard snippets:

"…Mildred? But that's impossible! She practically *runs* this place!" "…always thought there was something… *too* perfect about her, you know? Never a hair out of place…" "…financial records? What could Bartholomew have possibly found? Mildred's accounts are always immaculate…" "…perhaps she just assisted him with something, and the police need clarification?" (This offered hopefully, by someone clearly unwilling to contemplate the alternative). "…remember that fuss about the West Wing funding years ago? My late husband was on the committee then, always said Humphrey Carmichael wasn't quite sharp enough with the figures…" (This from an elderly member, unknowingly echoing Agnes's research).

The narrative was shifting, Fitzwilliam realised. The comfortable certainty surrounding Harry Smythe's guilt was fracturing, replaced by confusion, disbelief, and the dawning, uncomfortable possibility that the betrayal might have come not from an obvious outburst, but from the quiet, trusted centre of their own administration. The seeds of doubt, carefully planted by the quartet and now watered by direct police action, were beginning to germinate in the fertile ground of club gossip.

Just after 2:15 PM, the door to Mildred's office finally opened. Detective Constable Miller emerged first, carrying a slim document folio. He didn't look towards the lounge, just waited by the door. Then Detective Inspector Davies appeared, her expression as unreadable as ever, though perhaps, Fitzwilliam thought optimistically, tinged with a new seriousness. Finally, Mildred Pettle stepped out.

Every eye in the vicinity, including those of Agnes, Fitzwilliam, Ronnie, and Chloe (who had happened to be polishing brass near the lounge entrance), immediately fixed upon her. She looked... pale. Definitely paler than usual. Her customary serene composure seemed strained, brittle. Her hands were clasped tightly in front of her, her knuckles white. She avoided looking directly at anyone in the lounge, her gaze fixed somewhere straight ahead as she walked beside Detective Inspector Davies towards the main entrance. She wasn't handcuffed, wasn't under arrest – not yet, anyway. Davies paused at the entrance, spoke briefly to Mildred again – too low for anyone to overhear – then Davies and Miller exited the clubhouse, got into their sedan, and drove away.

Mildred stood alone near the entrance for a long moment, her back to the room. She seemed to take a deep, shuddering breath, her shoulders slumping almost imperceptibly before straightening again with visible effort. Then, she turned, forcing a weak, brittle smile onto her face, nodded vaguely towards the stunned onlookers in the lounge, and walked quickly, almost fleeing, back down the administrative corridor towards her office, closing the door firmly behind her.

The lounge erupted in a cacophony of whispers. The quartet exchanged brief, significant glances. Mildred wasn't arrested. But she was clearly shaken. The police had spent over two hours with her, focusing on finances and historical records. They had left without her, yes, but the investigation had undeniably, irrevocably shifted. The facade had cracked. The question now was, what would Mildred Pettle do next, knowing she was well and truly under scrutiny?

****

Thursday morning, April 24th, arrived crisp and clear at the Toorak Croquet & Horticultural Society, the bright autumn sunlight glinting off the dew-laden lawns. Yet, the idyllic scene felt fundamentally altered. Yesterday afternoon's departure of Detective Inspector Davies and Detective Constable Miller, after their prolonged session in Mildred Pettle's office and their specific requests for financial and historical records, had sent shock waves through the club's membership far more potent than the initial news of Ainsworth's death or the subsequent focus on Harry Smythe or Major Ferguson. This felt different. This felt like an internal betrayal, an attack on the very administrative heart of the Society, and the shift in atmosphere was chilling.

The previously dominant narrative – Harry's temper, Ferguson's dahlias – had evaporated almost overnight, replaced by bewildered, hushed conversations centred entirely on Mildred. *Mildred?* The name itself seemed incongruous whispered in connection with police interviews and financial scrutiny. Mildred, the calm centre, the ever-present helper, the keeper of keys and schedules and endless cups of tea. It seemed unthinkable, yet the police's targeted interest was undeniable.

Agnes Plummett, seated on the verandah with the *Times Literary Supplement* open but unread before her, observed the change with grim satisfaction. Members arriving for their usual Thursday morning roll-up game greeted each other not with cheerful inquiries about form or handicaps, but with low murmurs and significant glances towards the administrative corridor. Groups clustered near the noticeboard, ostensibly reading fixture lists but actually exchanging theories in hushed tones.

"…couldn't believe it when Esme told me," Mrs Henderson was saying, her voice heavy with shocked importance, to a small circle near the entrance. "The police were with her for *hours*! Asking about accounts, old files… What could poor Bartholomew possibly have found?" Her earlier certainty about Harry Smythe or Major Ferguson was conveniently forgotten, replaced now by fascinated horror directed at this new, far more unsettling possibility.

"Mildred always seemed so… reliable," offered Penelope Cartwright hesitantly.

"Still waters run deep," Colonel Abernathy pronounced darkly, clearly adapting his previous aphorism to the new target. "Always said there was something… overly controlled about her. Still waters, indeed."

Agnes allowed herself a small, internal sigh. The fickle nature of rumour, the swiftness with which suspicion could be redirected. While validation for their own investigation was welcome, the intensity of the gossip now directed at Mildred also carried risks. It might make Mildred even more guarded, more desperate.

The object of this intense speculation arrived at her usual time, 8:45 AM. Mildred Pettle emerged from her modest sedan, dressed impeccably as always, this time in a navy skirt suit with a pale blue blouse. From Agnes's vantage point, she watched Mildred walk towards the side office door. Did she seem paler than usual? Were those dark circles beneath her eyes, masked by carefully applied concealer? Was her usual calm stride perhaps a fraction too rigid, too deliberate? Agnes squinted, trying to discern subtle signs of strain beneath the habitual mask of composure.

Mildred paused at the door, fumbling slightly with her keys – a minuscule action, perhaps meaningless, perhaps indicative of inner turmoil disrupting practised routine. She glanced briefly, almost furtively, towards the main clubhouse verandah before quickly unlocking the door and disappearing inside. Agnes made a meticulous note:

"08:46. Subject P arrival. Appearance: Controlled, possibly strained (minor pallor? TBC). Action: Brief hesitation/fumble with keys at office door.

Significance: Potential low-level anxiety indicator (LI) or simple clumsiness (P=0.5?). Requires further observation."

Throughout the morning, Mildred attempted to maintain her normal routine, but the strain was subtly apparent, at least to those watching as closely as the quartet. Fitzwilliam, present again under the necessary pretext of conferring with the interim finance committee chair (a role Abercrombie had reluctantly assumed), observed her from the lounge. Her smiles seemed slightly more fixed, her interactions with members briefer, more purely functional than usual. When Colonel Abernathy tried to engage her in conversation about the police visit, Mildred politely but firmly cut him off, stating she had fully cooperated with the Inspector's inquiries regarding routine administrative matters and couldn't possibly comment further on an ongoing investigation. The deflection was smooth, but lacked her usual warmth, carrying instead a brittle edge.

Chloe, while working on replanting annuals in the beds flanking the main entrance, saw Mildred emerge mid-morning and walk towards her car. She wasn't carrying anything unusual, just her handbag. She sat in the driver's seat for nearly ten minutes, not starting the engine, just sitting, staring straight ahead, her hands gripping the steering wheel. Then, apparently composing herself, she got out and walked briskly back inside. What had she been contemplating? Flight? Or simply steeling herself for the remainder of the day under the weight of suspicion? Chloe quickly relayed the observation via text. *"MP sat in car approx 10 mins (10:35-10:45). No departure. Appeared stressed?"*

Ronnie, analysing yesterday's observation data in the library, received the texts from Fitzwilliam and Chloe. *"Subject P exhibiting increased stress indicators post-police interaction,"* he noted. *"Reduced social interaction duration, increased solitary/non-task-oriented intervals (office visit yesterday, car pause today), potential psychomotor agitation (key fumble). Consistent with Hypothesis P awareness/anxiety phase."* He began modelling potential next actions based on increased stress parameters: likelihood of evidence disposal attempt increases, probability of direct confrontation/flight remains low but non-zero.

The atmosphere at lunchtime was thick with unspoken tension. Mildred took her usual brief break, eating alone in the staff room this time, rather than at her desk or joining any members. Several members who usually sought her out for administrative queries seemed to avoid her, conferring instead with a visibly overwhelmed Esme Weatherly. Esme herself looked wretched, casting worried glances towards Mildred whenever she thought no one was watching, clearly caught between loyalty, duty, and the appalling possibility that her long-time colleague was involved in something terrible.

Agnes observed it all, feeling a cold sense of inevitability. The seeds of doubt about Mildred, sown by their intervention and watered by the police's targeted visit, were taking root throughout the club. The protective shield of Mildred's harmless reputation was fracturing. People were looking at her differently, questioning decades of quiet efficiency, reinterpreting past interactions through this new, sinister lens.

Late in the afternoon, Detective Inspector Davies and Detective Constable Miller returned. This time, their arrival caused less overt shock but a deeper, more focused wave of apprehension. They didn't approach Mildred directly. Instead, they conferred briefly with Esme, then Detective Constable Miller was seen carrying several labelled evidence bags and what looked like a secure hard drive case *out* of the administrative wing and loading them into their car. Had they executed a search warrant? Seized computers? Financial records? Document files related to the West Wing or suppliers?

Mildred remained in her office during this activity, the door closed. When the police finally departed again, Miller carrying the evidence, Davies pausing only to give Esme a brief, unreadable instruction, Mildred did not immediately emerge.

The quartet exchanged urgent, coded texts. *"Police departed 16:55 carrying evidence bags/case from admin wing."* *"Confirm subject P remained in office throughout."* *"Reaction?"* *"Unobserved directly. Awaiting subject emergence."*

They waited, the tension almost unbearable now. This felt decisive. The police had acted, secured potential evidence directly related to the financial and historical matters Fitzwilliam's memo highlighted. The net wasn't just closing anymore; it felt like it had been physically cast.

Finally, nearly twenty minutes after the police left, Mildred Pettle emerged from her office. She walked directly towards the main entrance, ignoring the few remaining members who fell silent, watching her pass. Her face was pale but composed, her expression utterly unreadable, her back ramrod straight. She didn't look left or right. She walked out of the clubhouse, got into her car, and drove away without a backward glance.

Agnes, Fitzwilliam, Ronnie, and Chloe watched her go, a shared understanding passing between them. This was it. The police had the internal evidence. Mildred knew she was the primary target. The facade, however expertly maintained, surely couldn't hold much longer. But what would she do now? Confess? Flee? Or, cornered and desperate, would she attempt something even more drastic? The sense of impending resolution was laced with a chilling, undeniable thread of danger. The final act was about to begin.

25

The Endgame Commences

Thursday, April 24th, dawned over Melbourne with a deceptive tranquillity that did little to soothe the frayed nerves of the four individuals who now carried the weight of the Ainsworth investigation almost entirely on their shoulders. The previous afternoon's events at the Toorak Croquet & Horticultural Society – the purposeful arrival of Detective Inspector Davies and Detective Constable Miller, their prolonged session within Mildred Pettle's office, and their departure bearing evidence bags and secure cases – had felt like a seismic shift, a validation of the quartet's painstaking work. Yet, the subsequent twenty-four hours had brought only a profound, unnerving silence.

Alistair Fitzwilliam sat in his Collins Street office, the stunning view of Port Phillip Bay in the distance utterly failing to capture his attention. The memorandum, the product of so much careful thought and ethical wrestling, had been delivered. The crucial evidence – Ainsworth's hiring of surveyors, the phantom supplier payments authorised under Mildred's administration – was now officially in police hands. Logically, Fitzwilliam knew, investigations took time. Documents needed analysis, correlations required

442

verification, warrants might need to be sought based on the findings. But the silence felt deafening. He found himself checking his phone every few minutes, scanning emails for any communication, however oblique, from Sergeant Riley or Detective Inspector Davies. Nothing.

He attempted to distract himself with the complexities of the Macrocorp litigation, dictating stern letters regarding discovery deadlines, reviewing expert reports on market volatility. But his focus continually drifted back to Toorak. What was happening *inside* those seized document folios and hard drive cases? Had the police forensic accountants immediately spotted the anomalies he and Agnes had identified? Had they cross-referenced the supplier names with ASIC records? Had they questioned Mildred about the missing authorisations, the Vance connection, the historical land issues? He longed for information, for confirmation that the official gears were finally grinding in the right direction, but he knew contacting Riley again so soon would be counterproductive, marking him as overly invested, potentially suspicious himself. The waiting, combined with the lack of control, was a unique form of torture for his precise, legalistic mind. He felt suspended in limbo, having lit the fuse but unable to see if the charge had ignited or fizzled out.

Agnes Plummett, similarly restless, found herself unable to concentrate on her usual archival pursuits at the club library. The atmosphere within the Society was thick with suppressed speculation. Mildred Pettle had arrived that morning at her usual time, her appearance, Agnes noted with clinical precision, impeccably composed. If yesterday's lengthy session with the police had rattled her, she showed no outward sign. She greeted members with her customary quiet politeness, dealt with correspondence, and attended the morning committee meeting (a pre-scheduled one regarding Centenary Gala logistics) with seemingly unwavering focus.

Agnes observed her across the polished mahogany table during the meeting. Mildred's contributions were concise, relevant, helpful as always. She deflected one or two awkward, indirectly probing questions from other committee members (who had clearly heard rumours about yesterday's police visit) with practised ease, framing the police interest as mere 'procedural follow-up' related to Ainsworth's treasury role. Yet, Agnes detected something subtly different beneath the surface. A heightened alertness in Mildred's gaze as she scanned the room. A slight rigidity in her posture. A tendency to keep her hands clasped tightly in her lap when not actively taking notes. Were these signs of immense stress being ruthlessly controlled? Or was Agnes merely projecting her own certainty onto ambiguous micro-expressions? The uncertainty was maddening. If Mildred could maintain this flawless facade even after the police seized her records, what hope did the quartet have of ever truly breaking through her defences without definitive, irrefutable proof? Agnes found herself mentally reviewing the Fincham footnote again, wondering if the key lay buried even deeper in the past than they had yet explored.

At the opposite end of the club grounds, Chloe Dubois felt the tension like a physical weight. Working near the main entrance, planting winter viola seedlings in the large terracotta pots, she found herself constantly glancing towards the administrative wing, towards Mildred Pettle's office window, half-expecting to see police cars return, half-fearing some other, less official, consequence of the shifting investigation. Mildred's calm arrival that morning had been almost more unnerving than seeing her look panicked. It felt unnatural, defiant. Chloe remembered the cold calculation she thought she'd glimpsed in Mildred's eyes near the compost heap, the subtle probing questions in the library. This woman, she felt certain, was capable of anything to protect herself. Chloe kept her head down, focusing on the rhythm of planting, the feel of the cool soil, trying to appear small, insignificant, just the gardener, hoping desperately that Mildred's attention was now entirely consumed by the police, not by those she might perceive as peripheral threats. Every unexpected footstep on the gravel path behind her made her jump. The waiting, the not knowing if or when the police would act, felt like standing braced for a storm that refused to break.

Ronnie Peterson, meanwhile, dealt with the uncertainty through data analysis, albeit of a speculative kind. He sat in the members' lounge, a complicated diagram taking shape in his notebook. Having concluded passive observation was yielding insufficient data, and acknowledging the police now possessed the key internal records, he turned his attention to modelling *Mildred's* likely next moves.

"Scenario Analysis: Subject P post-interrogation/evidence seizure," he wrote. *"Assumption: Subject P understands police focus has shifted to financial/historical matters under her purview. Objective: Maintain facade, assess threat level, neutralise remaining evidence/risk."* He listed potential actions with estimated probabilities:

- *Action P1: Maintain Normal Routine (High Probability - HP):* Continue duties flawlessly to project innocence/control. (Current observed behaviour).

- *Action P2: Discreet Evidence Destruction (Moderate Probability - MP):* Destroy personal financial records, any remaining items related to poison processing/disposal (e.g., glove?), potentially wipe personal devices. (Difficult to observe directly).

- *Action P3: Secure/Move Assets (Low-Moderate Probability - LMP):* Attempt to move embezzled funds if accessible, anticipating potential account freezes. (Requires banking access – police action imminent?).

- *Action P4: Flight Preparation (Low Probability - LP):* Make arrangements to disappear if police net closes further (booking travel, accessing cash). (Potentially observable – long lunch yesterday? Packing box in car yesterday?).

- *Action P5: Threat Neutralisation (Low Probability - LP, but High Impact):* Attempt to discredit/intimidate/silence members of Quartet perceived as driving the investigation. (Highest risk factor for quartet).

He stared at the list. Maintaining normal routine seemed the most likely immediate strategy for someone as controlled as Mildred. But Actions P2 and P4, evidence destruction and flight preparation, couldn't be discounted, especially if she felt the police were truly closing in based on the records they seized. The ambiguity of her actions yesterday afternoon – the shredding, the long lunch, the box in the car – could potentially fit within P2 or P4. And P5... Ronnie felt an uncharacteristic shiver. While logically low probability, the potential impact was catastrophic.

He found himself wishing, more than ever, for direct data streams – access to Mildred's phone records, her bank accounts, even covert audio surveillance. Without them, they were operating blind, relying on interpreting subtle behaviours and waiting for the official investigation to lumber forward. The silence from the police wasn't just frustrating; it felt dangerous, leaving Mildred in play, aware but unrestrained, potentially preparing her next move while they waited helplessly. He sent a text to the group: *"Analysis suggests Subject P likely maintaining baseline facade while potentially initiating low-observability countermeasures (P2/P4). Recommend extreme vigilance from all observation posts. Probability of police inaction causing increased risk to quartet = Non-negligible."* The scientific detachment couldn't entirely mask the underlying warning. The waiting game wasn't just passive; it was potentially allowing their quarry time to escape, or worse, to turn the tables.

****

The silence from the official investigation stretched through Thursday, April 24th, becoming less like a strategic pause and more like an unnerving void. At the Toorak Croquet & Horticultural Society, an air of forced normality prevailed, brittle and easily shattered. Members practised their shots, Henderson Jr. dutifully mowed the lawns furthest from Lawn 3, and the administrative machinery, now lacking its central cog, sputtered along under the increasingly frayed supervision of Esme Weatherly. Mildred Pettle had not arrived for work that morning.

Agnes Plummett, working diligently in her study – having decided against returning to the club's tense atmosphere while awaiting news – found her concentration repeatedly fractured by anxiety. She attempted to immerse herself in the complexities of Silas Croft's estate correspondence, searching the microfilm records she'd ordered from PROV after her initial visit, looking for names or details that might connect to the club's early finances or Mildred's family history. The archaic legal phrasing and faded copperplate script usually provided a welcome intellectual challenge, but today her mind kept replaying possibilities: Had Detective Inspector Davies dismissed Fitzwilliam's memo? Had Mildred successfully bluffed her way through the police interview? Was Mildred, even now, calmly shredding the last vestiges of incriminating evidence in her own home? Or worse?

Fitzwilliam reported similar frustration from his Collins Street office via their secure messaging app: *"Still nil from Riley/Davies. Attempted follow-up call regarding 'procedural clarification' – politely stonewalled. Assume memo is buried or being slowly processed. Main-*

taining observation of financial news feeds for any related anomalies (unlikely). A."

Ronnie, characteristically, channelled his frustration into complex modelling: "*Re-calibrating Subject P action probabilities post-non-response from authorities,*" his message read. "*Increased likelihood of P2 (Evidence Destruction) and P4 (Flight Preparation) if subject perceives investigation stall as temporary lull before escalation. Reduced probability of immediate P5 (Threat Neutralisation against quartet) while official focus remains ambiguous. Recommend continued high vigilance.*" Cold comfort.

Chloe texted from the club shortly after lunchtime: "*MP definitely not here. Esme looks ready to cry. Rumours starting among staff/few members present. Saying she might be ill? Or quit? No one seems to know anything. Still feels tense. C.*"

Agnes stared at Chloe's message, a cold knot tightening in her stomach. Uncharacteristic absence was one thing. Utter unreachability, especially given Mildred's meticulous nature regarding club duties, was another entirely. Mildred wouldn't simply fail to appear without arranging cover or notifying Esme or the Club President, unless… unless she was unable, or unwilling, to do so. The possibilities – flight, concealment, incapacitation (self-inflicted or otherwise) – felt suddenly, terrifyingly real.

Her train of thought was interrupted by the shrill ringing of her landline telephone – a sound increasingly rare in the age of mobiles, usually heralding either a nuisance call or someone who knew her preference for traditional communication. She picked up the receiver. "Agnes Plummett speaking."

"Miss Plummett! Agnes! Oh, thank goodness!" The voice on the other end was instantly recognisable, though distorted by panic – Esme Weatherly. "I didn't know who else to call! I tried Mr Fitzwilliam's office, but his assistant said he was in conference!"

"Esme? Calm down, my dear," Agnes said soothingly, though her own pulse had quickened. "What is the matter?"

"It's Mildred!" Esme sounded close to tears. "She still hasn't come in! She didn't call, didn't leave a message! Her mobile just goes straight to voicemail – has done since yesterday evening, I tried calling her about the tournament accounts! Her home phone just rings out! And Agnes," her voice rose in pitch, "the payroll submission! It was due to the bank by midday today for staff payments tomorrow! Mildred *always* handles it two days prior, meticulously! I checked her desk, the files are there, partially completed, but not signed off, not submitted! The staff won't get paid on time! And the caterers for the President's Luncheon this weekend – she was meant to confirm final numbers yesterday, they just called me asking where the confirmation is! It's unheard of! She would *never* just… disappear like this! Not Mildred!"

Agnes listened intently, her mind racing, filtering the practical administrative chaos Esme described through the lens of their investigation. Missing payroll deadlines, unconfirmed bookings, unreachable phones… this wasn't just an employee having an off day. This was a complete, uncharacteristic dereliction of duty by a woman renowned for her obsessive efficiency. And it followed directly on the heels of a multi-hour interview with homicide detectives regarding financial irregularities surrounding a murder victim.

"Did she seem unwell yesterday, Esme?" Agnes asked calmly, keeping her voice even, needing facts, not just panic. "After the police left?"

"Well," Esme hesitated, clearly trying to recall accurately through her distress. "She seemed… strained. Yes, definitely strained. Very pale. Quiet. But," she added quickly, perhaps defensively, "who wouldn't be, after being questioned by police for hours? She left promptly at five, just said 'Good evening', nothing else. Didn't mention feeling ill or having plans…"

"And her office? Did you notice if anything seemed unusual this morning when you realised she wasn't in?" Agnes probed gently.

"Unusual? Not really… it was tidy, as always. Perhaps… perhaps *too* tidy?" Esme sounded uncertain. "Like yesterday afternoon… I noticed her shredder bin looked quite full when I took some papers in for her to sign just before the police arrived back then. But Mildred is always shredding confidential documents, it's part of her job…" Esme trailed off, the implication perhaps dawning on her.

Excessive shredding, Agnes noted mentally. *Consistent with Ronnie's Action P2: Evidence Destruction.*

"Esme," Agnes said, making her voice firm but kind. "This is clearly very unusual and concerning. Have you informed the Club President?"

"Yes, just now," Esme sniffed. "He's equally bewildered. Said he'd try calling her home again later. Suggested she might just have a terrible migraine, perhaps?"

A convenient, benign explanation. But Agnes knew, with chilling certainty, it was likely far more than that. Mildred Pettle, cornered by the police investigation focusing on the very financial and historical secrets she had guarded for potentially decades, had vanished.

"Listen carefully, Esme," Agnes instructed, taking charge. "Document everything Mildred failed to complete – the payroll, the bookings, any other critical tasks. Note the exact time you last saw her yesterday and first realised she was missing today. Provide this information to the President. He may need to consider filing a missing person report if she cannot be contacted soon, given her role and responsibilities." She avoided mentioning their own suspicions, framing it purely as administrative concern.

"A missing person report?" Esme sounded horrified. "Oh, surely not… Mildred?"

"It's merely a precaution, Esme, if she remains unreachable," Agnes soothed. "Hopefully, there is a simple explanation. Now, I must go, but please keep me informed if you hear anything."

She ended the call, her hand trembling slightly now the immediate need for calm reassurance was over. Mildred was gone. Not just absent – vanished. Unreachable. After shredding documents yesterday. After the police seized records and questioned her for hours. The conclusion felt inescapable.

Flight. Action P4. Ronnie's models had predicted it as a possibility if the threat level became critical. Had Fitzwilliam's memo, combined with the police interview, been the final catalyst? Had Mildred decided her position was untenable, her exposure imminent, and chosen escape over facing the consequences? Or was it something worse? Had she gone somewhere to destroy further evidence – perhaps related to the Fincham book, the land parcel, or even the thermos – before disappearing? Or, a colder thought still, had her disappearance been… involuntary? Had associates connected to the phantom suppliers or the historical secrets decided *she* was now a liability?

No, Agnes decided, flight seemed most probable for someone as controlled and self-preserving as Mildred appeared to be. She had likely calculated the odds, realised the net *was* closing thanks to Ainsworth's research and now the police's renewed focus, and initiated her escape plan.

Which meant they had to act. Now. Immediately. Informing the police was no longer a strategic debate; it was an operational necessity. Mildred Pettle wasn't just a suspect in a historical crime anymore; she was potentially an absconding perpetrator in an active homicide investigation, possibly taking crucial evidence with her.

Agnes grabbed her phone, her fingers flying across the screen as she typed an urgent message to the secure group chat for Fitzwilliam, Ronnie, and Chloe:

"URGENT. Confirmed MP missing from club duties today. Unreachable since yesterday evening post-police interview per Esme W (highly distressed). Payroll missed etc. Assume Action P4 (Flight Risk) activated. Police MUST be notified potential flight risk immediately. Convene my place NOW to coordinate call. Agnes."

The endgame wasn't just commencing; it had suddenly accelerated into a desperate race against time.

****

The urgency in Agnes Plummett's text message – *"URGENT. MP failed to report to club today. Unreachable. Esme frantic. Assume flight risk activated. Convene my place ASAP."* – had sliced through the lingering fatigue and simmering frustration felt by Fitzwilliam, Ronnie, and Chloe. Within forty minutes, all four were gathered once more in Agnes's South Yarra study, the remnants of their individual days shed hastily at the door, replaced by a shared, tension that vibrated in the quiet room. The previous day's meticulous police questioning of Mildred, followed by the seizure of records, had clearly triggered a decisive reaction. The waiting game wasn't just over; the board itself felt like it had been violently upended.

Agnes stood by her desk, recounting her earlier phone conversation with a distraught Esme Weatherly, her voice calm but clipped with gravity. She detailed Mildred's unprecedented absence, the unanswered calls to her mobile and home, the critical missed deadlines – particularly the payroll submission due midday, a task Mildred, the epitome of administrative diligence, would *never* normally neglect. "Esme confirmed Mildred left the club at her usual time yesterday evening, around 5 PM, seeming strained but otherwise composed after the police departed," Agnes relayed. "She mentioned no illness, no planned absence. She has simply… vanished."

"Flight," Ronnie stated immediately, already modifying his probability charts spread across the desk. "Action P4 execution confirmed. Triggered by perceived critical threat level following police interrogation and evidence seizure. Optimal strategy for subject seeking to evade imminent legal consequences and preserve illicitly acquired assets, assuming means for relocation were pre-prepared."

"She shredded documents extensively the day before the police came back," Fitzwilliam recalled, rubbing his temples. "She put a box in her car. She took that unusually long lunch break – perhaps accessing funds? Making arrangements?" The ambiguous actions they had observed now snapped into sharp, alarming focus, retrospectively appearing as clear preparation for disappearance. He felt a surge of self-recrimination – should they have anticipated this more strongly? Warned the police sooner?

"We can't blame ourselves for her actions, Alistair," Agnes said firmly, sensing his distress. "We provided the police with verifiable information. Their decision regarding surveillance or immediate detention was theirs alone. Our concern now must be the consequences of her disappearance."

"If she flees the country," Fitzwilliam stated bleakly, "extradition can be complex, lengthy, sometimes impossible depending on the destination and the strength of the evidence presented. And crucial evidence – personal financial records connecting her to the shell companies, any remaining items related to the poison preparation or the thermos – likely disappears with her." Justice, which had felt tantalisingly close yesterday afternoon, seemed suddenly to be slipping through their fingers.

"So what do we do?" Chloe asked, her voice tight with anxiety. She looked pale, clearly shaken by this turn of events. "Can we just… let her go?" The thought of Mildred escaping, leaving Harry Smythe under suspicion and Ainsworth's murder effectively unsolved, felt intolerable. "What about Esme? The staff who won't get paid? What if Mildred… hurts someone else?"

"No," Fitzwilliam declared, his usual caution overridden by a sudden, fierce sense of responsibility. "We cannot simply do nothing. Chloe is right. Mildred Pettle isn't just a suspected embezzler anymore; she's the prime suspect in a homicide investigation, she has demonstrably fled under suspicious circumstances immediately following police intervention *that we initiated*, and she could potentially pose an ongoing risk. We have an ethical, arguably even a civic, duty to inform the police immediately of her disappearance and the strong likelihood that she is attempting to abscond."

Agnes nodded curtly, her expression resolute. "I agree. The strategic concerns about revealing our hand are now outweighed by the immediate risk of the primary suspect escaping justice entirely. Detective Inspector Davies *must* be informed that Mildred's disappearance coincides precisely with the police's focused inquiries into the financial and historical matters we highlighted."

"But how?" Fitzwilliam paced the small study, running a hand through his hair. "We still face the same dilemma. If I call Riley or Davies and say, 'Mildred Pettle has fled because we believe she murdered Ainsworth based on our secret investigation and the clues you dismissed' – they'll focus as much on *us* and our methods as on finding Mildred. We need to frame it carefully."

He stopped pacing, thinking aloud, the lawyer in him automatically constructing the safest argument. "We leverage Esme Weatherly's report. Esme, as acting administrator in Mildred's absence, has legitimate cause for extreme concern. The payroll failure *is* a critical disruption. Mildred *is* uncharacteristically unreachable *immediately following* police questioning at the club regarding financial matters pertinent to the Ainsworth case. *Those are the objective facts we present."*

"We frame the call," he continued, looking at the others, "not as vigilantes reporting their suspect has bolted, but as concerned club representatives relaying urgent, factual information about the inexplicable disappearance of a key figure, highlighting the *timing* relative to the police visit and the potential implications for the ongoing investigation – specifically, flight risk."

"Focus on 'uncharacteristic behaviour', 'dereliction of critical duties', 'unreachable since police interview', 'potential flight risk impacting investigation'," Agnes summarised, approving the strategy. "It provides Davies with the necessary justification to issue an alert, check airports, ports, border crossings, monitor financial activity, perhaps even secure a warrant for her home address now, without us needing to explicitly state our full conclusions or methods."

"Probability of police action based on 'Flight Risk Notification from Concerned Official Source' significantly higher than 'Speculative Murder Accusation from Amateur Group'," Ronnie confirmed, scribbling furiously. "Optimal communication strategy."

"Right," Fitzwilliam took a deep breath, feeling the weight shift onto his shoulders again. As the group's lawyer and previous police contact, making this call fell naturally to him. "I'll call Sergeant Riley first. Try to get put through to Davies directly if possible. I need to be very careful with the phrasing."

He picked up his mobile phone, his hand surprisingly steady now that a clear course of action was decided. The others watched him intently. Agnes stood straight, her expression composed but alert. Ronnie paused his calculations, observing with scientific curiosity. Chloe chewed nervously on her lower lip.

Fitzwilliam found Riley's number in his contacts and pressed dial, putting the phone on speaker so the others could hear, though he gestured for absolute silence. It rang once, twice, three times…

"Riley," the familiar gruff voice answered.

"Sergeant Riley, Alistair Fitzwilliam again," Fitzwilliam began, keeping his voice calm, professional, betraying none of the frantic urgency churning inside him. "Apologies for calling again so soon, but I have urgent information directly relevant to the Ainsworth investigation that Inspector Davies needs to be aware of immediately."

There was a weary sigh on the other end. "Fitzwilliam, as I said…"

"This isn't speculation, Sergeant," Fitzwilliam interrupted firmly but respectfully. "It's a factual report regarding the current status of a key individual interviewed by Inspector Davies at the Society yesterday – Ms Mildred Pettle."

That got Riley's attention. "Pettle? What about her?"

"She failed to report for duty at the club this morning," Fitzwilliam stated clearly. "She is completely unreachable – mobile phone off or disconnected, home phone unanswered. This is entirely uncharacteristic. Furthermore, she has failed to complete critical, time-sensitive duties, including the submission of the staff payroll due today, causing significant operational issues." He paused, letting the facts sink in. "Given this occurred *immediately* following her interview with Inspector Davies and the examination of certain club records yesterday, there is considerable concern among senior members," (a slight exaggeration, but justifiable, he thought), "that Ms Pettle may represent a significant flight risk relevant to your ongoing investigation."

Silence on the line again, but this time it felt different. Not dismissive weariness, but focused attention. Fitzwilliam could almost hear the gears turning in Riley's mind, connecting the dots: Police interview focusing on finance/history -> Subject immediately disappears -> Potential flight by key person of interest.

"Unreachable since yesterday evening?" Riley asked sharply.

"Correct," Fitzwilliam confirmed. "Last seen leaving the club premises around 5 PM yesterday. Has not responded to any calls or messages since."

"Right," Riley said curtly, his tone now all business. "Stay where you are, Fitzwilliam. Don't talk to anyone else about this. I need to brief the Detective Inspector immediately. This is… highly relevant. We'll be in touch." The line clicked dead.

Fitzwilliam slowly lowered the phone, looking at the others in the quiet study. A shared look of intense relief, mingled with profound apprehension, passed between them. They had done it. They had reported Mildred's disappearance, framed it as a potential flight risk linked to the police's own actions, and Riley had clearly understood the gravity. The official machinery was now, finally, fully engaged and pointed squarely at Mildred Pettle. The endgame wasn't just commencing; it was accelerating towards an unknown, potentially dangerous climax. All they could do now was wait, and hope the police found Mildred before she disappeared completely, or before she decided to tie up any other loose ends – potentially including themselves.

26

Flight and Pursuit

The immediate aftermath of Fitzwilliam's call to Sergeant Riley, reporting Mildred Pettle's disappearance and probable flight, plunged the quartet back into a state of acute, almost unbearable suspense, yet qualitatively different from their previous waiting games. Before, they had been waiting for a reaction, for a sign that their theories held weight, for confirmation from an indifferent officialdom. Now, they had triggered direct police action. The system was engaged, the hunt ostensibly underway. But the silence that followed Fitzwilliam's call felt, if anything, heavier, fraught with the unknown consequences of their intervention. Had Mildred already slipped away? Were the police moving quickly enough? Had they, by alerting the authorities, inadvertently pushed Mildred into a more desperate, perhaps more dangerous, course of action?

They remained gathered in Agnes Plummett's study late into Thursday night, April 24th, the adrenaline from their decision warring with profound exhaustion. The remnants of their earlier planning session – Ronnie's charts, Agnes's notes, Fitzwilliam's draft memo copies – lay scattered across the desk like the aftermath of a strategic battle. Agnes had brewed more tea, strong and black this time, while Fitzwilliam poured himself another, larger measure of whisky, necessity now overriding his usual moderation. Chloe sat huddled in an armchair, nursing a mug of lukewarm water, her eyes wide and tracing the patterns on the Persian rug, while Ronnie paced restlessly, inputting variables into a new model on his laptop labelled "Subject P Evasion Scenarios & Capture Probability."

Every ring of Agnes's landline, every buzz of a mobile phone, made them jump. Fitzwilliam checked his email constantly, hoping for some follow-up from Riley or Davies, however unlikely. Agnes tried to focus on organising her research notes, her hands moving with practised neatness, but her gaze kept drifting towards the clock. Chloe stared out the window at the dark, quiet South Yarra street, imagining Mildred driving through the night, disappearing into the anonymity of the sprawling city or the vastness of the country beyond.

"What do they actually *do*?" Chloe asked eventually, her voice small in the quiet room, breaking a long silence. "When they think someone's... fled?"

Fitzwilliam sighed, swirling the whisky in his glass. "Standard procedure, assuming they take the flight risk seriously, which Riley's tone suggested they now do... they'll issue an internal alert first. Check her known addresses – her home, obviously. Notify border control – airports, ports – flag her passport, if they know the details. They might track her vehicle via traffic cameras if they have the registration and sufficient grounds. Check recent financial activity – large cash withdrawals, credit card usage – though that likely requires warrants, which Davies might not have had time to secure yet, unless our information was deemed urgent enough." He paused. "They'll check known associates, family... though Mildred seems to have few, according to Agnes's research."

"Eleanor Vance," Agnes murmured thoughtfully. "The director

of Bespoke Botanical Displays, living in Ferntree Gully. If she *is* a relative, Mildred might head there."

"A possibility," Fitzwilliam conceded. "Though potentially too obvious? And accessing Vance's property also requires probable cause, warrants..." He trailed off, frustrated again by the legal constraints hampering swift action compared to Mildred's likely head start.

"Optimal escape vector depends on available resources and destination," Ronnie interjected, looking up from his screen. "Assuming Subject P pre-planned," (which her earlier shredding and potential cash access suggested), "she likely established a destination and travel method offering lowest probability of interception. Private vehicle offers initial anonymity but limited range and high visibility on major routes via traffic monitoring. Train or bus – requires navigating public hubs with potential CCTV. Air travel – passport flag renders international flight highly improbable unless using false documents (low probability without evidence of prior preparation). Domestic air possible initially, but passenger manifests are checked."

He tapped his screen. "Based on typical middle-aged female suspect profiles with moderate but not unlimited financial resources likely derived from long-term embezzlement, the highest probability initial vectors involve either: (a) Private vehicle travel towards regional Victoria or interstate via secondary routes, potentially aiming for cash-based anonymity in a smaller town, or (b) Short-term concealment within the Melbourne metropolitan area, perhaps utilising pre-arranged accommodation or relying on an unknown associate, while planning next move."

"So she could be anywhere," Chloe whispered, looking even paler. "Or still nearby." The thought was chilling.

They stayed late, fuelled by caffeine, anxiety, and a shared sense of responsibility, turning over possibilities, analysing fragments of information, waiting for news that didn't come. Eventually, close to 2 AM, sheer exhaustion forced a temporary adjournment. Fitzwilliam and Ronnie departed for their respective homes, promising immediate contact if anything changed. Chloe, clearly too unnerved to face her own apartment alone, accepted Agnes's offer of the spare room.

Sleep, however, proved elusive for all of them. Fitzwilliam lay awake staring at his ceiling, mentally rehearsing conversations with Detective Inspector Davies, composing legal arguments in his head. Agnes sat up in bed reading – not Fincham this time, but a well-worn collection of Sherlock Holmes stories, finding a strange comfort in Holmes's fictional certainties amidst their own very real, very messy investigation. Chloe tossed and turned in the guest room, startled by every creak of the old building, half-expecting Mildred Pettle's face to appear at the window. Ronnie, likely, was already back at his laptop, refining escape probability models based on estimated departure times and fuel tank capacities.

Friday morning, April 25th, brought no relief. The police silence continued. Fitzwilliam, back in his office, made another cautious call to Sergeant Riley around 10 AM. "Just checking in, Colin," he kept his tone light, "following up on the information provided last night regarding Ms Pettle's absence. Any developments the club should be aware of for operational reasons?"

Riley's response was brief, professional, and utterly non-committal. "Matter is under active investigation, Alistair. Can't provide operational details. If we require further assistance from you or the Society, we will be in touch directly." Click. Stonewalled again.

The quartet exchanged frustrated texts throughout the morning. *"Still nil from Riley."*

"MP car not in usual spot. Henderson Jr says she didn't show. Esme

frantic."

"Local news feeds checked - no reports related to MP or club yet."
"Probability of successful evasion increasing with elapsed time..."

The waiting felt corrosive, breeding doubt and second-guessing. Had they done the right thing? Had their intervention merely given Mildred warning, allowing her to slip away more effectively? Was Detective Inspector Davies taking this seriously at all, or were they back to being ignored while the official focus remained elsewhere, perhaps quietly building a flawed case against Harry Smythe based on the original autopsy finding? The lack of feedback, of visible action, was almost worse than outright dismissal. It left them suspended in a state of high anxiety, powerless observers once again, knowing a killer was likely on the move, potentially taking crucial evidence, and perhaps justice itself, further out of reach with every passing hour. The endgame had commenced, but its direction felt terrifyingly unclear.

****

Friday, April 25th, unfolded with excruciating slowness for the quartet. The knowledge that Mildred Pettle was officially missing, that the police had been alerted to her potential flight risk, and that the wheels of official investigation were presumably turning, did little to alleviate their gnawing anxiety. If anything, the lack of immediate news – no reported sightings, no dramatic arrest, just continued silence from Sergeant Riley and Detective Inspector Davies – only amplified the tension. They were caught in a frustrating limbo: having provided the crucial impetus for police action, they were now relegated to the sidelines, excluded from the official hunt, left to speculate and analyse with only fragments of information.

Agnes Plummett, finding the atmosphere at the club unbearable (a mixture of morbid curiosity directed at anyone associated with Ainsworth, and now, fearful speculation about Mildred), had retreated to her South Yarra study. The PROV documents and Fincham analysis felt momentarily exhausted. Her focus now shifted, with methodical determination, towards Mildred Pettle herself. Who *was* the woman behind the mask of quiet efficiency? Where might she run? Using online databases – historical electoral rolls accessible via library subscriptions, digitised newspaper archives on Trove, genealogical websites – Agnes began searching for traces of Mildred Vance before she became Mildred Pettle, looking for connections beyond Toorak. She focused on the western Victorian region Mildred had vaguely alluded to as her origin. Hours yielded little. The Vance name appeared occasionally, but establishing definitive links to *Mildred's* family, or identifying close relatives still living who might offer shelter, proved difficult without more specific biographical data. Then, pursuing the 'Eleanor Vance' connection, she broadened her search nationally, then internationally. A hit, finally, on a digitised New Zealand electoral roll from the early 1990s: an 'Eleanor Mary Vance' listed at an address in Christchurch for a two-year period, with an occupation listed simply as 'Administrator'. Was it the same Eleanor Vance, director of Bespoke Botanical Displays? Impossible to confirm. But if Mildred *did* have a close relative, perhaps a sister, who had lived overseas, could New Zealand be a potential destination? It felt tenuous, a whisper of a possibility across the Tasman, but Agnes meticulously noted the details. It was *something*. A potential direction Mildred *might* consider if truly desperate and seeking distant anonymity.

In his Collins Street office, Alistair Fitzwilliam found himself similarly hamstrung, yet driven. He couldn't ethically probe further into Harry Smythe's now-confirmed debts. He couldn't directly access Mildred Pettle's personal finances. But he *could* monitor the periphery, using his legal knowledge and networks. He spent an hour reviewing recent Victorian court bulletins and gazettes online, searching for any newly issued warrants or freezing orders related to Mildred Pettle or the shell companies he'd identified. Nothing yet – such actions often took time, requiring detailed affidavits presented to a magistrate. He then made a discreet, carefully worded call to a contact at a major Melbourne bank's internal fraud division – someone he knew professionally from past corporate litigation. Framing it as a hypothetical query regarding 'unusual transaction patterns potentially linked to incorporated associations', he tried to gauge how quickly accounts might be flagged or frozen if police requested information based on suspected large-scale embezzlement connected to a homicide investigation. The answer was frustratingly vague: "Depends entirely on the specifics of the police request and the evidence provided, Alistair. Could be hours, could be days." No help there. His final avenue was a brief check with his original police contact, Sergeant Riley, again under the guise of procedural follow-up. This time, Riley's response, while still guarded, held a sliver more information. "Can confirm warrants related to certain financial accounts associated with the investigation *have* now been sought and granted, Fitzwilliam," Riley stated gruffly. "Can't discuss specifics. Ball is rolling. Let us do our jobs." Fitzwilliam hung up, a grim satisfaction mixing with his anxiety. *Warrants granted.* That was significant. The police *were* now officially probing Mildred's finances, likely tracing the payments from the club to the phantom suppliers and beyond. The money trail, the most likely source of irrefutable proof, was finally being pursued.

Ronnie Peterson, working from his home study surrounded by whiteboards covered in equations, approached the problem from a different angle: escape logistics. Assuming Mildred had fled in her own car (a modest but reliable late-model sedan, details obtained from club parking records), what were her options? He researched the car's approximate fuel tank capacity and average highway fuel consumption. "Maximum theoretical range on full tank," he calculated, "approximately 650-700 kilometres." He brought up online maps of Victoria and surrounding states. "Departure time estimated post-17:00 Thursday. Elapsed time ~18 hours by Friday lunchtime." He began drawing arcs radiating from Melbourne. 700km covered major Victorian regional centres – Ballarat, Bendigo, Geelong, Sale, Mildura – and pushed well into South Australia towards Adelaide, or across the border into New South Wales past Canberra.

"However," he reasoned aloud, pacing his study, "Subject P exhibits high caution. Likely avoids major freeways with heavy tolling and camera surveillance (Hume, Princes East/West link sections). Secondary routes increase travel time, decrease efficiency." He started modelling routes using less direct highways – the Calder towards Bendigo/Mildura, Western Highway towards Adelaide but perhaps diverting via Grampians (Mildred's supposed origin area?), Princes Highway East towards Gippsland, potentially aiming for the NSW South Coast. He factored in estimated driving times, likely need for refuelling (cash payment probable to avoid card trace?). "Conclusion," he typed into a message for the group, "Subject likely still within Victoria or immediate border regions (SE South Australia, Southern NSW) if travelling continuously by own vehicle via secondary routes. Unless," he added a critical variable, "vehicle was swapped, or alternative transport (train, pre-booked flight under different name?) utilised immediately post-departure. Probability of latter options currently assessed as low-moderate without further data." His analysis provided constraints, boundaries, but no definitive location. Mildred was a variable within a large, complex equation, still frustratingly unresolved.

Chloe, meanwhile, spent another tense morning at the club. Mildred's absence was the sole topic of conversation among the few staff present and the handful of members who arrived for quiet practice. Esme Weatherly looked close to tears, fielding constant phone calls and trying desperately to manage the administrative chaos Mildred had left behind – particularly the failed payroll submission. Chloe tried to focus on her gardening tasks, weeding the rose beds with fierce concentration, but found herself constantly scanning the car park, the pathways, half-expecting Mildred to reappear, or the police to return with more dramatic news. She felt useless, unable to contribute to the remote tracking Agnes, Fitzwilliam, and Ronnie were attempting. Her skills lay in observation, in the tangible world of soil and plants. She thought again about the grey glove. Could she trace its purchase locally? Maybe visit the Armadale nursery Mildred's online persona 'MP_Gardener' had mentioned years ago? It felt like a thin lead, a desperate measure, but better than just waiting, feeling helpless.

As the afternoon wore on, the lack of news continued to fray their nerves. Fitzwilliam's confirmation that financial warrants *had* been issued was the only solid piece of progress. It meant Detective Inspector Davies was now officially pursuing the money trail, the path most likely to lead to incontrovertible proof against Mildred. But where *was* Mildred? Had she anticipated the warrants, emptied accounts, and fled beyond reach? Or was she hidden somewhere closer, planning her next move, perhaps aware that four determined, albeit amateur, investigators had been instrumental in directing the police towards her carefully constructed web of deceit? The waiting felt dangerous, pregnant with unspoken possibilities. The net was closing, Fitzwilliam's source had confirmed, but the quarry was still at large.

****

The tense vigil stretched into Friday afternoon, April 25th. For the quartet, scattered between Agnes's study, Fitzwilliam's office, and Chloe keeping a low profile after her morning stint at the club, the continued silence from the authorities felt increasingly ominous. Had Detective Inspector Davies been unable to secure the warrants? Had Mildred's lawyers intervened? Or worse, had Mildred simply vanished so completely that the police had no trail to follow? Doubt, cold and insidious, began to mingle with their anxiety. Every passing hour seemed to diminish the impact of the evidence Fitzwilliam had delivered, leaving them feeling exposed and potentially responsible for provoking a killer into successful flight.

Fitzwilliam found himself staring blankly at the Melbourne skyline through his office window, the Macrocorp file utterly forgotten. He refreshed the major news websites – *The Age*, the *Herald Sun*, ABC News Melbourne – searching for any hint of police activity, any mention of the Toorak Croquet Club that went beyond the initial discovery. Nothing. The city hummed along, oblivious to the hidden drama playing out, oblivious to the fact that a woman suspected of calculated murder and decades of fraud might be slipping through the cracks. He felt a profound sense of helplessness, a frustration with the slow, opaque grinding of the official justice system compared to the rapid, terrifying pace their own investigation seemed to have acquired.

Agnes, back in her study, had turned from researching Mildred's potential family connections (yielding only frustrating dead ends) to methodically re-reading her own journals from the past few weeks, searching for any overlooked detail, any nuance in Mildred's behaviour prior to the murder that might offer a clue to her current state of mind or potential destination. Had there been hints of unusual travel plans? Mentions of specific locations outside Melbourne? References to skills or resources that might facilitate an escape? It was meticulous, painstaking work, driven more by a need for activity than by any real expectation of a sudden breakthrough. The waiting was intolerable; structured research, even if retrospective, felt marginally more productive.

Ronnie, similarly needing to channel his restless energy, was running complex simulations on his laptop. Inputting Mildred's estimated age, likely financial resources (based on Fitzwilliam's fraud estimates), known vehicle type, and time elapsed since her disappearance, he modelled probability distributions for her current location across southeastern Australia. The results were discouragingly broad – vast swathes of Victoria, southern New South Wales, and eastern South Australia all fell within plausible range, especially if she had swapped vehicles or was utilising secondary roads. *"Conclusion: Current data insufficient for statistically meaningful location prediction,"* he texted glumly to the group chat. *"Probability of successful evasion increases linearly with time (t). Urgent need for new data input."*

It was mid-afternoon when the first potential break occurred, ironically through the very mainstream news Fitzwilliam had been fruitlessly monitoring. An alert popped up on *The Age*'s website: *"Police Operation Underway in Malvern East."* The brief report mentioned detectives executing a search warrant at a residential apartment building, believed to be linked to an ongoing major investigation. No names were mentioned, no connection to the Croquet Club explicitly stated. But Malvern East… wasn't that where Mildred lived? Fitzwilliam's heart leaped. He quickly cross-referenced the street name mentioned in the brief report with the address details he had previously noted for Mildred Pettle. A match.

He immediately messaged the others: *"News Alert: Police executing search warrant Malvern East apartment block - street matches MP address. No names released. Possible action based on our info? F."*

The replies came back instantly. *"Confirming street address matches MP residence. Monitor closely. A." "High probability correlation! P(Search|Our Memo) » Baseline! R." "Oh thank goodness! Are they getting her? C."*

The news sent a jolt of adrenaline through their anxious waiting. It wasn't confirmation of an arrest, but it was definitive police action, targeted directly at Mildred's home. Davies *had* taken Fitzwilliam's memo seriously. The warrants *had* likely been granted, possibly based on the financial irregularities providing probable cause to search for evidence of fraud, which could in turn uncover evidence related to the murder or her flight.

But the relief was short-lived, almost immediately replaced by new anxieties. What would they find? Would Mildred be there? Or would they merely find an empty apartment, confirming her escape but providing few clues as to her destination? And what evidence might remain? Had she shredded everything incriminating? Wiped computers? Emptied accounts?

As if summoned by the intensity of their shared focus, Agnes's landline rang, the shrill sound making her jump. Caller ID showed the main number for the Croquet Club. With a sense of foreboding, Agnes answered. "Agnes Plummett."

"Agnes! It's Esme!" The coordinator's voice was high-pitched, frantic, breathless. "Agnes, you won't believe it! The police! They were *here*! Well, not *here* here, but at Mildred's apartment block! Mrs Henderson's cousin lives in the same building, saw everything! Police cars, detectives going inside with evidence bags… they were there for hours apparently! They searched her apartment! Everyone at the club is talking about it – someone saw it on the afternoon news website!"

"Calm down, Esme," Agnes said, keeping her own voice level despite her racing pulse. "Did they say… did they find Mildred?"

"No! That's the thing!" Esme wailed. "Apparently, according to Mrs Henderson's cousin who spoke to a neighbour who spoke to the building manager… the apartment was empty! Like she'd just… vanished! But," Esme lowered her voice conspiratorially, "they say the police took away boxes! Computer equipment! Files! They were definitely looking for something specific!"

Empty apartment. Evidence seized. Agnes processed the information rapidly. Confirmation of flight. Confirmation the police were now actively seeking evidence related to Mildred's affairs, likely spurred by Fitzwilliam's memo detailing the financial and historical angles. This was significant progress.

"Esme, this is clearly very upsetting," Agnes said soothingly. "But try not to jump to conclusions. There could be many reasons Mildred is currently unreachable and why the police might need to secure documents from her home in her absence, purely as part of their investigation into Mr Ainsworth's death and the club's affairs." She offered plausible, calming explanations, while her mind raced with the real implications. "The best thing now is to cooperate fully with the police if they ask further questions, and focus on keeping the club running as smoothly as possible."

She managed to end the call after several more minutes of calming Esme's near-hysteria, promising to speak with the Club President herself later. Immediately, she relayed the key information to the quartet via their secure chat: *"Confirmed via Esme (source: member gossip via neighbour at MP bldg): Police executed search warrant MP apartment this afternoon. Apartment empty. Evidence (computers, files) reportedly seized. MP definitely fled home base. Police actively pursuing evidence trail now. A."*

The news landed amongst them like a thunderclap. Relief that the police were finally, demonstrably, acting on their information. Vindication that their suspicions about Mildred were clearly shared now by the authorities to the extent of securing search warrants. But overlaid with a sharp, cold fear. Mildred Pettle was officially on the run, her home searched, her potential crimes related to finance and historical secrets now under direct police scrutiny. A woman like Mildred, so meticulous, so controlling, now cornered, desperate, whereabouts unknown… what was she capable of now? Where would she go? And had she left any final, parting message for the four people who had helped unravel her carefully constructed world? The endgame wasn't just commencing; it felt like it was accelerating towards a dangerous, unpredictable climax.

****

The news that police had searched Mildred Pettle's empty Malvern East apartment settled over the quartet gathered in Agnes's study like confirmation of a dreaded diagnosis. Relief mingled uneasily with heightened tension. Relief, because it proved Detective Inspector Davies *had* acted decisively on Fitzwilliam's information, securing warrants and confirming Mildred's flight from her known residence. Tension, because Mildred was now officially a fugitive, her location unknown, her potential for desperate action significantly increased. The atmosphere in the room, thick with speculation about what evidence the police might have seized from the apartment, crackled with unspoken anxiety. Where was she? What was her plan? And had they, by flushing her out, inadvertently increased the danger to themselves or others?

Ronnie was already hunched over his laptop, inputting 'Home Base

Compromised' into his evasion models. "Probability distribution shifts significantly," he muttered, mostly to himself, adjusting parameters. "Subject P now lacks secure refuge. Increases likelihood of utilising secondary contacts (Eleanor Vance?), relying on cash reserves, potentially making errors under pressure due to lack of established routine. Capture probability increases, assuming continuous pursuit resources are allocated."

"Assuming they *can* find her," Fitzwilliam countered grimly. He paced restlessly before the bookshelves, the legal implications of a suspect absconding weighing heavily. "If she planned this properly – cash withdrawn beforehand, perhaps a change of vehicle, avoiding main roads, discarding her phone… she could disappear for quite some time, especially if she has funds stashed away from the embezzlement." He shuddered at the thought of the complex, potentially international, legal processes involved if she truly vanished.

"The warrants included her financial accounts, Alistair," Agnes reminded him calmly, though her own hands were tightly clasped in her lap. "Fitzwilliam's contact confirmed that. Police will be tracking any electronic transactions, large withdrawals, credit card usage. That provides a powerful tracing mechanism, provided she hasn't already converted everything to untraceable cash or assets."

"Which she might have," Fitzwilliam countered. "The shredding, the long lunch break before she disappeared… consistent with accessing funds, destroying personal financial records."

Chloe, who had been silently watching the others, voiced the fear lingering beneath their strategic analysis. "Do you think… do you think she might try to… contact any of us? Or come back here?" The thought of Mildred, cornered and desperate, appearing suddenly at the club or one of their homes sent a visible shiver through her.

Before Agnes could offer reassurance, Fitzwilliam's mobile phone rang, shrill and demanding in the tense quiet. All heads snapped towards him. He glanced at the caller ID, his eyes widening slightly. "It's Riley," he said, his voice hushed. He quickly tapped 'accept' and put the call on speakerphone, nodding for silence from the others.

"Fitzwilliam," Sergeant Riley's gruff voice sounded, devoid of its earlier weariness, replaced now with a distinct note of urgency, perhaps even grudging respect.

"Sergeant," Fitzwilliam replied, keeping his own voice level. "Any developments?"

"Developments, yes," Riley confirmed curtly. "Just confirming, as per your information provided yesterday, Ms Pettle was not located at her residence during the execution of search warrants this afternoon. Evidence consistent with recent departure and potential document destruction was secured from the premises, including computer equipment."

The quartet exchanged glances. Confirmation.

"Furthermore," Riley continued, "the financial warrants you mentioned proved… fruitful. Immediate flags were placed on her accounts. We can confirm a significant cash withdrawal – several thousand dollars – made from an ATM in Armadale two days ago," (matching Mildred's long lunch break, Fitzwilliam realised with a jolt), "and more importantly, a credit card transaction occurred less than three hours ago."

"Where?" Fitzwilliam asked, leaning closer to the phone, the others holding their breath.

"Fuel purchase. Small service station on the Western Highway, just outside Ballarat," Riley stated. "Card belonged to Pettle. Transaction confirmed via CCTV showing a woman matching her description driving her vehicle – the grey sedan."

Ballarat. Heading west. Towards the Grampians, her supposed origin? Or further, towards South Australia? Ronnie immediately began tracing the route on his laptop map, calculating distances, potential destinations.

"That's… significant progress, Sergeant," Fitzwilliam said carefully.

"It gives us a clear direction of travel, yes," Riley agreed. "Units in that region have been alerted, vehicle registration flagged. We also executed a check on the Ferntree Gully address linked to 'Bespoke Botanical Displays' and Eleanor Vance earlier today – neighbours confirm Ms Vance departed unexpectedly yesterday, apparently for an 'extended holiday'. Curioser and curioser." Riley's tone suggested the Vance connection from Fitzwilliam's memo was now being taken very seriously indeed.

He paused, then added, almost as an aside, but Fitzwilliam sensed its importance. "Your supplementary memo regarding the victim engaging surveyors… that was timely, Mr Fitzwilliam. Provided crucial context regarding Ainsworth's state of mind and immediate activities that significantly… refocused our timeline analysis around motive." It was as close to an admission that Fitzwilliam's intervention had changed the investigation's course as he was likely to get.

"Just glad the information was helpful," Fitzwilliam replied neutrally.

"One final thing," Riley said, his voice sharpening slightly again. "Your colleague, Ms Plummett, mentioned Ainsworth was potentially investigating historical matters related to the 'old orchard end' of the club grounds, possibly linked to ambiguities in early surveys and someone named Silas Croft?"

Agnes nodded silently beside Fitzwilliam. "Yes, that's correct, Sergeant," Fitzwilliam confirmed carefully. "Based on archival research."

"Did Ms Plummett's research, or any other club records, happen to mention the name of the solicitor or legal firm handling Croft's estate or any related access disputes back around 1910?" Riley asked. "Might give us another historical avenue to check regarding property title transfers, if related litigation occurred."

Agnes quickly consulted her notes from her PROV research. "Yes," she said clearly, leaning towards Fitzwilliam's phone. "Fincham's footnote referenced correspondence held at PROV. While I haven't accessed the full correspondence file itself yet, the catalogue entry indicated the primary legal firm involved appeared to be 'Blake & Riggall' – a very old Melbourne firm." (*Using a real historical firm name adds plausibility*).

"Blake & Riggall," Riley repeated, presumably noting it down. "Right. Got it. Okay, Fitzwilliam, thanks for your cooperation. We're actively pursuing the current leads. Advise you and your... associates... to stay well clear. Let us handle it from here." The implicit warning was clear.

"Understood completely, Sergeant. Thank you for the update," Fitzwilliam replied. The line clicked dead.

He placed the phone back on the table, looking around at the others. The relief in the room was immense, almost dizzying. The police weren't just listening; they were actively pursuing Mildred, armed with financial warrants, tracking her movements, investigating the historical angles. They had a direction – heading west from Ballarat. They knew Eleanor Vance had also disappeared, suggesting complicity or coercion. The net, thrown wide thanks to their intervention, was now being drawn tight by official hands.

"They're closing in," Chloe breathed, a shaky smile finally touching her lips.

"Probability of successful apprehension within 24-48 hours now exceeds 0.8," Ronnie declared, updating his models with satisfaction.

"Let's hope they reach her before she reaches the South Australian border, or worse," Fitzwilliam murmured, the lawyer in him still considering potential jurisdictional complications.

Agnes nodded, closing her notebook with an air of finality. "We have done all we can, I believe. We provided the necessary information, pointed the investigation in the correct direction. Now," she stated, her gaze meeting each of theirs in turn, "as Sergeant Riley advised, we wait. And we trust the authorities to conclude this matter."

A fragile sense of hope filled the room, warmer and brighter than the lamplight against the dark windows. They had navigated the treacherous path of amateur investigation, faced down their own fears and ethical dilemmas, and successfully redirected the course of justice. The final act – the capture, the confession, the full unravelling of Mildred Pettle's secrets – was now in motion, playing out somewhere on the highways west of Melbourne, leaving the quartet as anxious, but now finally hopeful, spectators awaiting the denouement.

27

The Walls Close In

Saturday morning, April 26th, dawned bright and deceptively peaceful over Melbourne. A typical crisp autumn day invited residents out into the sunshine, perhaps for a stroll along the Yarra, brunch in a bustling cafe, or indeed, a leisurely game of croquet at one of the city's many clubs. But for the four individuals connected by the dark secrets of the Toorak Croquet & Horticultural Society, the bright morning offered no respite, only a heightened sense of agonising anticipation. Sergeant Riley's call the previous evening had confirmed their greatest hopes and fears: Mildred Pettle was officially a fugitive, the police were actively pursuing her based on financial tracking and sightings placing her near Halls Gap in the Grampians, and the endgame had truly begun. Now, all they could do was wait.

Agnes Plummett sat in her South Yarra study, the PROV research notes and Fincham analysis neatly filed away for the moment. Instead, she found herself drawn to her extensive collection of Victorian regional histories and topographical maps. She located the section covering the Grampians National Park (Gariwerd) and the surrounding townships – Halls Gap, Stawell, Horsham. She studied the intricate contour lines depicting rugged sandstone ranges, deep valleys, dense forests. A vast, challenging terrain. Beautiful, certainly, but also potentially treacherous, offering countless places for someone desperate to hide, or to simply disappear – accidentally or otherwise.

Her mind sifted through what little she knew, or suspected, about Mildred's past. The vague references to a childhood in 'western Victoria'. The 'Vance' connection, possibly linking back to that region. Had Mildred chosen the Grampians as her destination because she knew the area? Possessed some forgotten family connection, a remote property, a place to lie low? Or was it simply a desperate, random flight towards perceived wilderness and anonymity? Agnes traced potential routes on the map, considering secondary roads, old logging tracks. Her methodical mind, usually finding comfort in structure and research, felt frustrated by the lack of data, the reliance on speculation. Knowing Mildred was *somewhere* within that rugged landscape felt profoundly unsettling. The image of the calm, controlled Club Secretary navigating that wild terrain seemed jarringly incongruous, hinting at depths of desperation and perhaps hidden resilience they hadn't yet factored in. She found herself hoping, strangely, for a swift, uneventful capture, preventing any further tragedy – for Mildred herself, or anyone who might cross her path.

Alistair Fitzwilliam found himself utterly incapable of relaxing into the weekend routine at his Hawthorn home. He had attempted to read the Saturday edition of *The Age*, but the articles on federal politics and international affairs seemed remote, meaningless. His attention snagged only on the briefest mention buried deep in the state news section: *"Police maintain increased presence in Grampians region related to ongoing investigation. Public advised minor traffic delays possible on approach roads to Halls Gap. Authorities assure no immediate threat to public safety.*" Vague. Non-specific. Offering no clue as to whether they were closing in or still searching blindly.

He abandoned the newspaper and resorted to pacing his study, wrestling with his thoughts. He felt a grim sense of vindication that Detective Inspector Davies *had* acted on his information, that the financial warrants and pursuit were underway. Their amateur investigation had successfully redirected the official one. Yet, the potential consequences weighed heavily. What had the police found in Mildred's apartment? In the seized club records? In her bank accounts? Would it be enough? What if Mildred talked her way out of it again? What if she evaded capture? What if, cornered, she became violent? And what about their own position? Riley's grudging acknowledgement was one thing, but if the full extent of their methods – the autopsy leak, the library surveillance fears (however unfounded), Chloe's late-night observation, the deliberate 'Lost Ledger' trap (which thankfully hadn't been needed) – ever came to light, the professional and potentially legal repercussions for himself could be severe. He had crossed lines, encouraged others to cross lines, all in pursuit of a truth the system seemed determined to ignore. Had the ends justified the means? He hoped, desperately, that the imminent capture of Mildred Pettle would provide that justification. The waiting, the uncertainty, was almost worse than the initial investigation itself.

In her Richmond apartment, Chloe Dubois tried to distract herself by sketching. She picked up her charcoal sticks, opened her large pad, but found herself drawing not the usual cityscape or botanical studies, but fragmented images from the past two weeks: the unnatural angle of Ainsworth's shoe beneath the rhododendron, the gleam of the antique mallet on the grass, the decaying *Digitalis* leaves in the compost, Mildred Pettle's pale blue eyes watching her near the incinerator. She shuddered, pushing the pad away. The memories felt too raw, too close. She checked the secure group chat on her phone for the tenth time that morning. Only anxious 'Anything?' messages from Fitzwilliam and Ronnie, met by Agnes's calm 'Nil further updates'. Chloe walked over to her windowsill, fussing with her collection of potted succulents, needing the simple, tactile connection to something living, something predictable. She felt utterly helpless, a small cog in a large, dangerous machine set in motion, waiting for news from afar that would determine the outcome. The relief of knowing Mildred wasn't nearby was overshadowed by the fear of what a cornered Mildred might do, and the simple, aching desire for it all to be *over*.

Ronnie Peterson, naturally, approached the waiting period as a data analysis problem under conditions of extreme information scarcity. He sat in his home study, the whiteboards now covered in branching diagrams labelled 'Subject P Evasion/Capture Probabilities'. Having modelled the likely travel range, he now focused on variables affecting capture likelihood in the Grampians region. Terrain complexity (high). Availability of shelter/resources (moderate if sticking near towns, low if truly remote). Subject P's potential survival/navigation skills (unknown, assumed low). Law enforcement resource allocation (high, given homicide context + flight risk). Public awareness/assistance (currently low, police keeping details vague).

He cross-referenced recent weather reports for the Grampians – cool nights, possibility of showers – factors that could hinder both the fugitive and the searchers. He calculated heat loss estimations, dehydration curves. It was grimly fascinating, reducing human desperation to a set of differential equations. "Probability of unassisted survival > 72 hours in remote Grampians terrain, assuming minimal preparation = P < 0.1," he typed into the chat, perhaps unnecessarily. "Probability of capture via police cordon/search operation within

48 hours > 0.75, assuming subject remains within designated search radius." The numbers offered a cold sort of comfort, suggesting capture was likely, but the wide error bars and unknown variables still left room for significant doubt. He found himself frustrated by the lack of real-time data – GPS tracking, thermal imaging feeds – the kind of inputs that would make his models truly predictive. Waiting for anecdotal news reports felt scientifically primitive.

And so the morning passed, measured out in anxious text messages, fruitless web searches, and the slow ticking of clocks in studies and apartments across Melbourne. The city went about its Saturday rituals, unaware of the silent, high-stakes drama unfolding miles away in the rugged ranges to the west, unaware of the four individuals waiting with bated breath for news that would signal the end of a deadly game played out behind the respectable facade of their suburban croquet club. The silence from the police wasn't just a lack of information; it was a vacuum, pulling their anxieties into sharp focus, amplifying every doubt, every fear, as they waited for the walls to finally, definitively, close in.

****

The tense vigil stretched agonisingly through Saturday morning and into the early afternoon. For the quartet, each passing hour without news felt like a victory for Mildred Pettle, increasing the likelihood she had slipped through the nascent police net or found a secure hiding place beyond their reach. Fitzwilliam's attempts to glean further information from Sergeant Riley were met with polite but firm silence. News websites offered only frustratingly vague reports of an 'ongoing police operation' in western Victoria, devoid of specifics. The lack of concrete development frayed their already strained nerves, leaving them suspended in a shared state of anxious impotence.

Fitzwilliam was in his Hawthorn study, ostensibly sorting through personal paperwork but actually scrolling endlessly through the ABC News Melbourne website, hitting refresh every few minutes, when the push notification finally arrived just after 2:30 PM. The sharp alert chime made him jump, spilling lukewarm coffee across a bank statement. He fumbled for his phone, his heart suddenly pounding.

ABC News Alert: *"Abandoned Vehicle Linked to Toorak Homicide Investigation Found Near Grampians National Park. Police Search Intensifies."*

He clicked the link immediately, his eyes scanning the brief article with desperate intensity.

"Victoria Police have confirmed a vehicle belonging to a person of interest in the ongoing investigation into the death of Toorak Croquet Club treasurer Bartholomew Ainsworth has been located abandoned on a minor road near the southern edge of the Grampians National Park (Gariwerd). The vehicle, a late-model grey sedan registered to missing Club Secretary Mildred Pettle, 59, was found empty by a local resident earlier today. Police sources indicate Ms Pettle has been missing since Wednesday evening following questioning by homicide detectives. An extensive ground search involving local police, SES volunteers, and supported by the Police Air Wing is now underway in the rugged bushland area adjacent to where the vehicle was discovered. Police are appealing for information but currently believe Ms Pettle may still be within the park or immediate surrounds..."

Found. Abandoned. Grampians National Park. The words hammered in Fitzwilliam's mind. She hadn't simply vanished. She hadn't driven interstate or boarded a plane (or at least, not easily). She had driven west, towards the rugged wilderness of the Grampians, and abandoned her car. Why? Was she trying to disappear on foot? Did she know the park well enough to survive or hide? Or was this an act of desperation, a final dead end?

His hands trembled slightly as he immediately forwarded the news link to the quartet's secure group chat, adding only:

"CONFIRMED. *Car found Grampians. Search underway. A.*"

In her South Yarra study, Agnes Plummett saw the message pop up on her tablet, where she had been meticulously re-examining the 1910 survey map, searching for any nuance she might have missed. She read Fitzwilliam's text, then quickly clicked the news link he'd sent. *Grampians. Abandoned vehicle. Extensive ground search.* Her initial reaction was a wave of profound relief – Mildred hadn't simply vanished beyond trace; the police had a concrete location, a focus for their pursuit. But relief was immediately followed by cold dread. The Grampians were vast, wild, potentially dangerous terrain, especially for someone unprepared, someone potentially desperate. This wasn't just a flight risk anymore; it carried the grim possibility of a tragic, solitary end, accidental or otherwise – an ending that might bury the full truth along with Mildred herself. She thought of the rugged sandstone cliffs, the dense bushland depicted in photographs – a far cry from the manicured lawns of Toorak. What was Mildred thinking? Did she have a specific destination within that wilderness, perhaps linked to her obscure past or the historical secrets Agnes had been researching? Or was it simply a place to lose oneself, literally and finally?

Ronnie Peterson received the text while inputting atmospheric pressure data into a completely unrelated astrophysics simulation in his home study. He immediately switched screens, bringing up detailed topographical maps of the Grampians National Park, cross-referencing the area mentioned in the news report ('southern edge', 'minor road') with his previous escape vector models. *"Abandoning primary transport vector significantly alters probability distribution,"* he muttered, already calculating new variables. *"Subject now pedes-*

trian. Search area geometrically complex but geographically constrained. Factors: Terrain difficulty (high), vegetation density (variable), water sources (limited?), night temperatures (lowering), subject preparedness (assumed low). Increases capture probability over time but introduces high risk of exposure/hypothermia for subject. Optimal strategy for subject: seek immediate shelter (cave, disused structure?) or follow watercourse. Optimal strategy for searchers: thermal imaging via Air Wing, ground teams focusing on tracks/watercourses/known shelters." His mind processed it as a complex search-and-rescue problem, overlaid with the grim context of a homicide investigation. The human element – Mildred's fear, her desperation – remained largely outside his equations, yet the numbers pointed towards a rapidly narrowing window for her survival or continued evasion.

Chloe Dubois was in her Richmond apartment, sketching the *Digitalis* flower from memory, trying to capture its elegant but sinister beauty, when Fitzwilliam's text arrived. She read the news alert with a gasp, her hand freezing above the page. The car found. Abandoned. Near the Grampians. The image that flashed into her mind wasn't of police cordons or search teams, but of Mildred Pettle, alone, perhaps lost, in the vast, imposing landscape of the national park – a place Chloe knew from hiking trips for its breathtaking views but also its sudden weather changes and challenging trails. She felt a confusing mix of emotions: relief that Mildred was seemingly cornered, fear of what might happen next, and an unexpected, unwelcome pang of empathy for the desperate situation Mildred must now be in, regardless of her guilt. Had Mildred driven there seeking refuge in a place she knew from childhood? Or was it simply the end of the road, a place to make a final, perhaps fatal, stand against the closing walls? The image of the neatly dressed, efficient Club Secretary lost in the rugged bushland felt deeply incongruous, deeply disturbing.

The quartet's text chat quickly became a flurry of reactions and analysis.

Agnes: "Grampians location potentially significant if linked to W. Victorian origin claims. Known hiking area - did MP have outdoor experience? Seems unlikely based on observed persona."

Ronnie: "Vehicle abandonment suggests shift to low-observability tactics (foot travel) or potential resource depletion (fuel/funds). Search complexity increases, but containment probability also rises. Critical window now."

Chloe: "It's huge park, easy get lost even if know area. Weather can turn fast. Hope police find her safely, whatever happens next."

Fitzwilliam: "Police action confirms they consider her primary target now. Abandoning car = strong consciousness of guilt evidence. Question is: hiding, lost, or planning something else? Need update on search progress."

They were united in their assessment: this was a major development. Mildred was geographically contained, her primary means of escape neutralised. The police search, now focused and intensified, seemed likely to yield results soon. But the uncertainty remained agonising. Was she armed? Was she capable of violence if cornered? Would she be found alive? The image of the polite, efficient Club Secretary, the suspected poisoner and long-term embezzler, now potentially a desperate fugitive somewhere in the vast wilderness of the Grampians, was a stark and terrifying culmination of their investigation. They could do nothing now but watch the news feeds, wait for Fitzwilliam's phone to ring again, and hope for a swift, safe resolution to the chase they themselves had set in motion. The walls were closing in, geographically at least. The question was what would happen when they finally met.

****

Saturday evening descended upon Melbourne, painting the sky in bruised hues of purple and orange before fading to an inky, star-pricked canvas. In Agnes Plummett's South Yarra study, however, the beauty of the clear autumn night went largely unnoticed. The four individuals who had become unlikely co-investigators were gathered once more, drawn together by the unbearable suspense following the news that Mildred Pettle's abandoned car had been found, triggering an intensive police search in the rugged expanse of the Grampians National Park. The waiting, which had been agonising before, was now amplified to an almost physical pressure. They knew the police were closing in, but the final act remained hidden, playing out miles away in the dark, imposing wilderness.

Agnes had made soup – a simple, nourishing pumpkin soup – and insisted they all eat something, though appetites were minimal. They sat mostly in the study, the remnants of the simple meal on trays pushed aside, the large desk still bearing the charts and notes that represented their journey towards this precipice. The atmosphere was thick with unspoken questions and anxieties. Fitzwilliam paced intermittently between the window overlooking the quiet street and his armchair, occasionally checking his phone for news alerts with a compulsive frequency. Chloe sat curled on the sofa, sketching absently in her notebook – not flowers this time, but jagged lines and abstract shapes that seemed to mirror the tension coiling inside her. Ronnie had his laptop open, displaying topographical maps of the Halls Gap region alongside complex probability charts, his fingers occasionally tapping commands, analysing search patterns or perhaps weather data impacting visibility for the Police Air Wing's thermal imaging cameras. Agnes herself sat upright in her usual chair, a volume of poetry open on her lap, though her gaze was distant, contemplative.

"Maximum effective range for pedestrian evasion in unfamiliar rugged terrain decreases exponentially after nightfall," Ronnie announced suddenly, breaking a long silence, his tone purely informational. "Assuming Subject P lacks significant bush craft skills and preparedness – food, water, appropriate clothing, navigation tools – the probability of accidental self-incapacitation via fall or exposure increases significantly as overnight temperatures drop. Grampians low forecast tonight: 4 degrees Celsius."

The clinical assessment hung in the air, stark and chilling. Mildred, the meticulous administrator, the potential poisoner, facing hypothermia or a broken ankle alone in the dark bushland. Fitzwilliam shuddered visibly. "Let's hope the police find her before that happens, Ronnie," he murmured, rubbing his arms as if feeling the cold himself. "Whatever she's done, a protracted search ending tragically doesn't serve anyone."

"Indeed," Agnes agreed quietly. "One hopes for a resolution, however difficult, not merely an ending." She found herself thinking, strangely, of Silas Croft and his ambiguous orchard land. Had he met some misfortune out there near the creek, leaving his affairs, and the land's status, unresolved for Mildred to later exploit? History felt uncomfortably close tonight.

Chloe looked up from her sketching. "Do you think... do you think she *wanted* them to find the car? Like she's leading them somewhere specific within the park?"

It was a possibility none of them had explicitly voiced. "A deliberate false trail?" Fitzwilliam considered it. "Possible, I suppose. Divert the main search while she heads elsewhere? But abandoning her primary transport seems an extreme gamble unless she had another vehicle or assistance arranged."

"Probability of pre-arranged secondary transport vector currently assessed as low," Ronnie stated, consulting his models. "Requires accomplice network (Eleanor Vance? Others?) and complex logistical coordination Pettle likely couldn't arrange reliably post-initial flight. Abandonment more consistent with panic, mechanical failure, or deliberate transition to foot travel for evasion in difficult terrain she *believes* offers concealment advantage."

"Perhaps she *does* know the area," Agnes mused, returning to her earlier thought. "If her family connection to western Victoria is genuine… people develop an affinity for, a knowledge of, their local landscapes, even rugged ones like the Grampians." She remembered Mildred once mentioning, during a discussion about club excursions, that she found densely forested areas 'restorative'. Had it been a clue, hidden in plain sight?

They lapsed back into silence, each lost in their own cycle of speculation and anxiety. Fitzwilliam found himself mentally reviewing the evidence again, constructing the arguments he might need to make if called upon by the police or, heaven forbid, during legal proceedings. He focused on the surveyor invoice – Ainsworth's clear, final act of investigation. That felt solid, undeniable. Combined with the internal payment anomalies… yes, it was strong. But would it be enough to secure a conviction for *murder*, especially if Mildred maintained her composure, offered alternative explanations, denied everything? The burden of proof remained daunting.

Agnes turned pages in her poetry book, but her mind was on Mildred, trying to reconcile the image of the calm, efficient secretary with the desperate fugitive potentially hiding out in the cold, dark Grampians. What drove such long-term deception? Greed? Fear? A sense of entitlement rooted in that historical land ambiguity? Or something darker still? She thought of the *Digitalis*, the buried leaves, the calculated cruelty of the poisoning. That spoke not just of desperation, but of a profound coldness, a capacity for ruthless action that was hard to fathom behind Mildred's gentle facade.

Ronnie continued his analysis, now seemingly modelling potential search grid efficiencies for the police and SES teams based on terrain difficulty and estimated subject travel speed. He murmured about optimal spiral patterns versus parallel sweeps, apparently finding intellectual solace in the geometry of the hunt, detached from the human stakes involved.

Chloe closed her sketchbook. The abstract lines felt meaningless. She thought instead of the glove – the soft grey suede, the neat stitching. An expensive, careful choice. Had Mildred worn it while harvesting the leaves? Had she worn it while striking the final blow? Had she disposed of its partner somewhere just as carefully as she had buried the leaves? The small, tangible object felt like a key, if only they could find the lock it fit. She felt a surge of frustration at their helplessness, reduced now to waiting for news like passive spectators after weeks of intense, risky investigation.

Fitzwilliam checked the online news sites again. Nothing new. Just recycled versions of the afternoon report: "Police Search Continues for Missing Woman Linked to Toorak Death." He switched to the television, turning the volume down low, flicking through the late-night news channels. Mostly state politics, international affairs, a local sports scandal. Then, a brief update on the ABC: footage, likely from earlier in the day, showed police vehicles gathered near a roadblock on a scenic Grampians road, uniformed officers conferring, an SES volunteer adjusting ropes. The reporter spoke gravely about the difficult terrain and the ongoing search for a 'person of interest' related to a Melbourne homicide investigation, confirming a vehicle had been found nearby. No new details, but the visual confirmation of the extensive police operation brought the reality home more forcefully.

They watched the brief report in silence. Seeing the rugged landscape, the serious faces of the police, the coordinated effort involved in the search, somehow amplified the tension in Agnes's quiet study. Mildred Pettle was out there, somewhere in that vast darkness, and the forces of the state were methodically closing in.

"They'll find her," Fitzwilliam said eventually, more to reassure himself than the others. "With that level of resources deployed, in a contained area… it's only a matter of time."

"Unless she…" Chloe began, then stopped, unable to voice the darker possibility.

"Let us hope for a swift and safe resolution, for everyone involved," Agnes said quietly, closing her poetry book. "All we can do now is wait."

The waiting stretched on, measured by the ticking clock, the occasional sigh, the clink of a teacup, the low murmur of the television newsreader discussing tomorrow's weather forecast for regional Victoria. The climax was imminent, they could all feel it. Somewhere out there, in the cold shadows of the Grampians, the final act of this long, dark drama was reaching its conclusion. And all they could do was wait for the curtain to fall.

****

The hours following the news of Mildred's abandoned car bled into one another, marked only by the relentless ticking of Agnes's grandfather clock and the periodic, fruitless checking of phones and news websites. Saturday evening deepened into night outside the windows of Agnes's study. The initial adrenaline rush had faded, leaving behind a heavy residue of fatigue and gnawing suspense. They had gathered together at Agnes's apartment – Fitzwilliam driving over from Hawthorn, Chloe taking a tram from Richmond, Ronnie arriving with his laptop brimming with updated probability models – needing the shared space, the quiet solidarity, as the unseen police operation reached its climax miles away in the Grampians.

Agnes had made more soup, Fitzwilliam had produced a bottle of surprisingly decent Cabernet Sauvignon he'd had stashed in his briefcase for emergencies (a category this situation undoubtedly qualified for), and Chloe had arranged some biscuits artfully on a plate. They went through the motions of eating and drinking, but mostly they waited, conversation sporadic, punctuated by long, tense silences. They rehashed the evidence, revisited Ronnie's logistical analysis, speculated on what Mildred might have taken from her apartment or the club archives, wondered about the contents of the evidence bags the police had seized. But it was all circling the same unbearable point of uncertainty: Had they found her yet?

Ronnie occasionally murmured updates from his laptop – "Thermal imaging conditions optimal due to temperature drop," "Search grid contraction suggests focus on south-eastern park boundary near Mount Abrupt," – but these were inferences, not facts. Fitzwilliam's phone remained stubbornly silent; Sergeant Riley clearly had no intention of providing a running commentary.

By midnight, exhaustion was profound. Chloe had curled up in an armchair, drifting in and out of a restless sleep. Ronnie's relentless calculations had finally slowed, his screen displaying complex search pattern simulations that seemed more like an academic exercise now than active tracking. Agnes sat upright, rereading a passage in Fincham, though her gaze seemed distant. Fitzwilliam stared out at the dark, quiet street, the city lights reflecting on the wet pavement left by an earlier shower, feeling the immense weight of the past weeks threatening to crush him. Had they done enough? Had their intervention truly helped, or merely complicated matters, potentially endangering themselves and others? The silence felt accusatory.

It was just after 1:30 AM on what was now technically Sunday morning when Fitzwilliam's mobile phone, lying face up on the desk, suddenly vibrated, its screen illuminating the darkened room with a sharp, intrusive light. The caller ID displayed Sergeant Riley's number.

Every trace of fatigue vanished instantly, replaced by a jolt of pure adrenaline. The others were immediately awake, alert, their eyes fixed on Fitzwilliam as he snatched up the phone, his hand surprisingly steady.

"Fitzwilliam," he answered, his voice slightly hoarse.

"Alistair," Riley's voice came back, rough with tiredness but carrying an unmistakable note of finality. "Just letting you know. We got her."

Fitzwilliam closed his eyes for a fraction of a second, an almost overwhelming wave of relief washing over him. "You… you found her? Is she… is everyone alright?"

"Located her about an hour ago," Riley confirmed. "Holed up in a disused shearer's hut off a remote track deep in the southern Grampians, not far from where the vehicle was dumped. Looks like she knew the area, or got lucky finding shelter." There was a pause. "Apprehended without significant incident. She put up no physical resistance. Bit incoherent initially, suffering from exposure by the look of it, but otherwise unharmed. She's in custody, en route back to Melbourne now under escort."

In custody. The words resonated in the quiet study. It was over. The chase, at least.

"That's… that's excellent news, Sergeant," Fitzwilliam managed, acutely aware of Agnes, Ronnie, and Chloe watching him, hanging on every word. "A credit to your team's efforts in difficult terrain."

"We had good intel," Riley said, and Fitzwilliam detected the faintest hint of grudging acknowledgement. "Your supplementary information regarding the financial accounts and that surveyor invoice… it proved critical in obtaining the necessary warrants quickly and confirming Ms Pettle as the primary person of interest when she absconded. Expedited things significantly." It wasn't exactly praise, but it was validation. Their efforts had mattered, had directly contributed to this outcome.

"Was there… anything found with her?" Fitzwilliam ventured carefully, thinking of the missing thermos, historical documents, perhaps even poison residue.

"Can't discuss specifics of evidence recovered at this stage, Fitzwilliam, you know that," Riley replied curtly, the professional wall back in place. "Suffice to say, the investigation is proceeding. The Detective Inspector will likely want formal statements from yourself and Ms Plummett, possibly others, in the coming days regarding the information you provided. We'll be in touch to arrange times."

"Of course," Fitzwilliam agreed readily. "We'll cooperate fully."

"One last thing," Riley said, his tone shifting slightly again, perhaps curiosity overcoming protocol. "That historical angle Ms Plummett raised… the Croft estate, the boundary, the solicitors Blake & Riggall. We ran a check. Turns out Blake & Riggall *did* handle probate for Silas Croft back in 1909-1910. And their archived files – which we may now have cause to access – potentially contain correspondence regarding disputed access or ownership claims related to that specific creek-side parcel mentioned in the PROV records." It was a confirmation that Agnes's historical thread was indeed substantial, potentially holding keys to the original motive or Mildred's long-term exploitation.

"Fascinating," Fitzwilliam murmured, glancing at Agnes, who nodded almost imperceptibly, her expression intense.

"Right," Riley concluded, sounding utterly exhausted now. "That's all for now. As I said, stay well clear, let us handle the formal process.

And Fitzwilliam?"

"Yes, Sergeant?"

"Good work," Riley said gruffly, before the line went dead.

Fitzwilliam slowly lowered the phone, the silence in the room amplifying the impact of the news. He looked up, meeting the wide, expectant eyes of Agnes, Ronnie, and Chloe.

"They have her," he announced, his voice thick with exhaustion and overwhelming relief. "Apprehended about an hour ago. In a hut near the Grampians. She's in custody."

The tension in the room snapped, releasing like a physical force. Chloe let out a choked sob, burying her face in her hands, tears finally flowing freely – tears of relief, fear, sheer exhaustion. Ronnie slumped back against his chair, running a hand through his already dishevelled hair, a rare, unguarded expression of profound weariness crossing his features before he murmured, "Capture probability resolved to 1.0. System stable." Fitzwilliam himself felt suddenly, incredibly tired, the adrenaline draining away, leaving behind the bone-deep ache of weeks of anxiety and suppressed fear.

Agnes alone seemed relatively composed, though Fitzwilliam saw the faint tremor in her hands as she reached, almost automatically, for the teapot. She poured four cups of now-cold tea, a strangely grounding ritual amidst the emotional aftermath. "Well," she said quietly, handing Fitzwilliam a cup. "It seems Bartholomew Ainsworth's accounts, both financial and historical, can finally be rendered."

They sat there for a long time in the pre-dawn quiet of the study, the city lights beginning to pale outside. They didn't talk much. There would be time later for analysis, for formal statements, for dealing with the inevitable fallout at the club. For now, there was only the immense, shared relief of survival, the quiet satisfaction of having pursued the truth against the odds, and the profound weariness that comes at the end of a long, dark, and dangerous journey. Mildred Pettle was caught. The immediate threat was over. The walls had finally closed in.

28

Accounts Rendered

The call from Detective Inspector Davies's office came late on Monday morning, April 28th. Fitzwilliam took it in his Collins Street office, the familiar cityscape outside momentarily invisible as his entire focus narrowed onto the clipped, professional voice on the other end. Detective Inspector Davies requested his presence, along with Miss Agnes Plummett's, for a follow-up discussion regarding the Ainsworth case at two o'clock that afternoon. She didn't offer a location, simply stated she would meet them *at* Miss Plummett's apartment in South Yarra – a significant deviation from standard police procedure that spoke volumes about the unusual nature of their involvement and, perhaps, Davies's grudging acknowledgement of it.

Fitzwilliam immediately contacted Agnes, then Ronnie and Chloe, relaying the request. A sense of combined anticipation and trepidation hummed through their brief phone calls. This was it. The official debrief. Confirmation, hopefully, of Mildred Pettle's culpability and the validation of their own perilous investigation.

At precisely two o'clock, Detective Inspector Davies and Detective Constable Miller arrived at Agnes's apartment building. Agnes admitted them herself, leading them into the same comfortable living room that had served as the quartet's unofficial headquarters for the past two weeks. Fitzwilliam was already there, seated stiffly in an armchair, clutching a slim legal pad. Ronnie and Chloe had offered to wait discreetly in Agnes's kitchen, respecting the formality of the occasion but remaining on hand if needed.

Detective Inspector Davies surveyed the room – the overflowing bookshelves, the antique desk now clear save for a vase of chrysanthemums, the faint scent of beeswax – her expression revealing nothing. Detective Constable Miller took a seat near the door, notebook ready. Davies accepted Agnes's offer of tea ("Just black, thank you, Ms Plummett") before settling into the armchair opposite Fitzwilliam.

"Thank you both for making yourselves available," Davies began, her tone formal but lacking the slight edge of scepticism Fitzwilliam had detected in their previous encounters. "As you are aware, following information received regarding her unexpected absence and potential flight risk, Mildred Pettle was located and apprehended by Victoria Police units in the Grampians National Park region early on Sunday morning."

Agnes and Fitzwilliam nodded mutely, waiting.

"She was found alone," Davies continued, "in a state of some distress but physically unharmed, taking shelter in a disused forestry hut near where her vehicle was abandoned. She offered no physical resistance upon apprehension and was subsequently transported back to Melbourne and formally interviewed yesterday." Davies paused, taking a sip of the tea Agnes had placed before her. Fitzwilliam noted her hand was perfectly steady.

"Based on that interview," Davies went on, meeting Fitzwilliam's gaze directly, then Agnes's, "and corroborated by evidence secured from Ms Pettle's residence, analysis of financial records obtained under warrant, and further review of materials seized from the Toorak Croquet & Horticultural Society, Mildred Pettle has now been formally charged with the murder of Bartholomew Ainsworth."

The air seemed to leave Fitzwilliam's lungs in a rush. *Charged.* It was official. He felt Agnes's hand briefly touch his arm, a small gesture of shared relief and validation.

"Furthermore," Davies continued, her voice crisp, "evidence uncovered strongly supports additional charges relating to multiple counts of obtaining financial advantage by deception – specifically, systematic embezzlement from the Society over a significant period, potentially decades, through the manipulation of accounts and likely involving the use of fraudulent supplier invoices."

Fitzwilliam nodded slowly, absorbing the confirmation. Their theories, pieced together from fragments of history, anomalous numbers, and careful observation, had been proven correct in their entirety.

"The motive," Davies stated, confirming their deductions, "appears directly linked to Mr Ainsworth's final investigations. Evidence seized, including fragmented documents retrieved from Ms Pettle's shredder and data recovered from her computer hard drive, confirms Mr Ainsworth had recently confronted her, or was about to confront her, regarding both historical financial discrepancies linked to the 'West Wing extension' era and significant irregularities in recent payments to specific suppliers – namely," she consulted her notes briefly, "'WeatherTech Roofing', 'Vintage Marquee Hire', and 'Bespoke Botanical Displays'."

"Ms Pettle appears to have become aware, likely through Mr Ainsworth's direct questioning or his engagement of external surveyors," – here Davies glanced pointedly at Fitzwilliam – "that her long-standing activities were on the verge of exposure. Facing professional ruin, disgrace within the community she had meticulously cultivated, and inevitable criminal prosecution, she took pre-emptive action."

Agnes leaned forward slightly. "And the method, Inspector? Was it… as we suspected?"

Davies hesitated, clearly bound by the constraints of discussing details of an ongoing prosecution. "The final VIFM report is pending," she said carefully. "However, preliminary analysis of exhibits recovered from Ms Pettle's residence and vehicle indicates the presence of processed plant matter containing significant concentrations of cardiac glycosides, consistent with *Digitalis purpurea*. Residue analysis is underway on items believed to be associated with preparation." She didn't mention the thermos directly, likely because it hadn't been recovered or its status was still evidentiary, but the implication was clear. "While the official cause of death remains attributed to blunt force trauma pending the final report, the evidence strongly suggests prior incapacitation through poisoning was the primary mechanism, with the subsequent head injury likely inflicted post-collapse to simulate death during an altercation and mask the toxicological evidence."

Ronnie would be vindicated, Fitzwilliam thought. Hypothesis P confirmed by official analysis.

"The historical dimension," Agnes probed gently, "the land boundary issue near Lawn 3?"

"That appears to be the foundational element," Davies acknowledged, surprising Fitzwilliam with her candour. "Our preliminary review of the files you highlighted, Ms Plummett, including the PROV records and early council documents related to Silas Croft's orchard and the subsequent ambiguous surveys, suggests a longstanding anomaly that Ms Pettle likely discovered decades ago — possibly during her temporary role assisting Treasurer Carmichael in 1988, as suggested by the minute Mr Fitzwilliam located. It appears she may have exploited this ambiguity, perhaps generating undisclosed income or using it as leverage or justification for her subsequent, more extensive embezzlement via the Fete accounts and later, the phantom suppliers. Mr Ainsworth's decision to formally query that boundary with the council, and then hire surveyors, represented a direct threat to exposing the entire edifice she had constructed over thirty years."

It was a stunning confirmation, tying together every thread they had painstakingly uncovered. Agnes nodded slowly, her expression grave but satisfied.

"Your contributions," Davies said, turning back to Fitzwilliam, her tone remaining professional but losing some of its earlier frostiness, "specifically the supplementary memorandum detailing the surveyor invoice and the internal payment anomalies linked to Ms Pettle's administration, were… instrumental. They provided the necessary verifiable evidence to broaden the investigation beyond the initial, obvious suspect and secure the warrants that ultimately uncovered the financial evidence underpinning the motive." She offered a curt, almost imperceptible nod. "The information was timely and accurately presented."

Fitzwilliam felt a flush of profound relief and professional pride, quickly suppressed. "We merely wished to ensure all relevant facts were available to you, Inspector," he murmured.

"Quite," Davies replied drily. She gathered her notes. "Ms Pettle is remanded in custody. The legal process will now take its course. Formal statements will still be required from both of you, detailing your knowledge of Ainsworth's research, the club's financial procedures, and the specific documents you reviewed. Detective Constable Miller will be in contact to arrange suitable times." She stood up. "Thank you again for your assistance. We trust we can rely on your continued discretion regarding the specifics of this case pending trial."

"Of course, Inspector," Agnes and Fitzwilliam replied in unison.

Davies nodded once more, then she and Miller departed, leaving a sense of quiet deflation in the room after the intensity of the confirmation.

Fitzwilliam let out a long, slow breath he hadn't realised he'd been holding. "Well," he said, looking at Agnes, a shaky smile touching his lips. "It seems... we were right."

Agnes returned the smile, a rare warmth reaching her eyes. "Indeed, Alistair. It appears the accounts, both historical and financial, have finally been rendered." The long, complex, dangerous investigation was essentially over. Justice, it seemed, was finally being served, thanks in no small part to their own unlikely, tenacious pursuit of the truth.

****

The departure of Detective Inspector Davies and Detective Constable Miller left a profound silence in Agnes Plummett's study, a silence that felt heavier, denser, than any that had come before. The air, moments earlier charged with the formal tension of the police debrief, now seemed thick with the grim reality of confirmed murder, calculated fraud, and decades of meticulously maintained deception. Mildred Pettle, the quiet, efficient hub around which the Society revolved, was formally charged. Their suspicions, painstakingly pieced together from disparate clues, were validated. Justice, it seemed, was finally on its inevitable course.

Ronnie Peterson and Chloe Dubois emerged quietly from the kitchen, where they had waited with excruciating patience, their faces etched with anticipation. Fitzwilliam, looking utterly drained but with a lawyer's grim satisfaction replacing his usual anxiety, met their questioning gazes.

"She's been charged," he stated simply, the words falling into the quiet room with immense weight. "Murder. Embezzlement likely to follow based on the financial evidence seized."

Chloe let out a shaky breath, sinking onto the arm of the sofa. Ronnie nodded slowly, a single, sharp affirmation, as if confirming a final data point.

Agnes, ever practical, moved to replenish the teapot, the familiar ritual a small anchor in the emotional swell. "Inspector Davies confirmed much of what we deduced," she reported, relaying the key points as she measured out fresh Assam leaves. "The primary cause of death, while officially still pending the final VIFM report, is strongly indicated to be poisoning, likely via the *Digitalis* Chloe identified, administered sometime before the physical altercation was staged. The head injury appears secondary. They found," she paused, her voice carefully neutral, "materials consistent with cardiac glycoside extraction at Ms Pettle's residence."

"The foxgloves," Chloe whispered, staring down at her hands, perhaps imagining Mildred carefully harvesting the leaves she herself tended.

"Precisely," Ronnie confirmed, stepping towards his large chart, vindicated. He picked up a marker. "Hypothesis P validated. The sequence becomes clear." He began sketching on a clean section of the paper, explaining not just to the others, but seemingly organising the final data points for himself.

"Step 1: Preparation. Subject P (Pettle) identifies need for subject V's (Victim Ainsworth) permanent neutralisation due to imminent exposure threat (Surveyor engagement, historical/financial probes). Selects Means: *Digitalis purpurea*, readily available on site, toxicity potentially mis-attributed or masked by secondary trauma. Harvests leaves discreetly," he nodded towards Chloe, "as confirmed by physical evidence. Processes leaves – likely simple hot water infusion method, concentrating glycosides, minimal equipment required beyond basic heating element (kettle?) and container (glass jar?). Police finding processing evidence confirms this stage."

He drew an arrow. "Step 2: Administration. Vector: Victim's personal thermos flask. Optimal window identified: Tuesday late morning/lunch break (approx. 12:00-13:45), victim routinely consumes tea alone in office. Subject P requires brief, plausible access to office/thermos. Given her role and master key access, probability VHP (Very High). Introduces concentrated *Digitalis* infusion into thermos containing Darjeeling tea – strong flavour potentially masks bitterness."

Chloe shuddered visibly. "His own tea..."

Ronnie continued, focused on the mechanics. "Step 3: Incubation & Onset. Victim consumes contaminated tea over next 1-2 hours. Glycosides absorbed. Slow onset of symptoms: nausea, potential visual disturbance, confusion, cardiac arrhythmia begins – consistent with Chloe's recollection of victim seeming 'unwell'/'irritable' and potentially explaining his unusual movement towards the secluded rhododendron bed post-argument with Smythe (seeking quiet? feeling faint? disoriented?)."

"Step 4: Incapacitation & Staging. Victim collapses near Lawn 3 due to cardiac event/severe symptoms (approx. 15:15-15:45). Subject P, likely monitoring victim or discovering him shortly after collapse, approaches incapacitated (or possibly already deceased) victim. Crucial decision point: ensure termination and create misdirection. Retrieves pre-stashed weapon (Smythe's antique mallet, previously removed from potentially unsecured locker) or uses it opportunistically if nearby. Delivers single, calculated blow to posterior cranium."

Fitzwilliam winced. "Calculated... even after he was down?"

"Logically consistent with maximising misdirection," Ronnie stated clinically. "Creates obvious alternative COD, focuses attention on blunt force trauma, away from subtle toxicology. Also consistent with *my* analysis of impact force/angle – easier to deliver specific blow to stationary, prone target than during dynamic altercation. Explains relative tidiness of scene."

Agnes nodded grimly. "Consistent with historical poisoning cases where a secondary method is used to obscure the primary cause."

"Step 5: Scene Arrangement & Departure," Ronnie continued, drawing another arrow. "Subject P potentially adjusts body position slightly to better fit 'fall after blow' narrative (explaining lividity inconsistencies noted by VIFM). Leaves mallet near body, ensuring discovery implicates Smythe. Departs scene discreetly before Chloe's arrival (~17:15)."

"Step 6: Evidence Disposal," Ronnie concluded the sequence. "Crucial phase. Occurs likely post-discovery but pre-police lock down, or later under cover of darkness/routine duties. Primary target: Thermos flask (contains direct toxicological evidence). Secondary: Any processing equipment (jar fragments?), residual plant matter (buried leaves found by Chloe). Method: Off-site disposal for thermos (highest probability). On-site concealment for plant matter (compost) and potentially heat-treated items (incinerator shard). Subject P's routine access and late/early presence facilitate this."

He put down the marker, surveying the completed sequence. "The entire operation demonstrates significant premeditation, meticulous planning, knowledge of victim routine, exploitation of environmental resources (*Digitalis*), manipulation of circumstance (Smythe's argument/temper), and controlled execution, including post-event evidence sanitisation. Profile inconsistent with impulsive rage; highly consistent with calculated elimination of perceived critical threat."

The four companions stared at the stark flowchart, the cold, logical breakdown of Mildred Pettle's crime laid bare. Hearing it articulated so clearly, step-by-step, grounded now in the confirmation from Detective Inspector Davies, was profoundly chilling. The image of Mildred calmly harvesting leaves, carefully brewing poison, adding it to Ainsworth's familiar thermos, watching him sicken, delivering a brutal final blow, then meticulously cleaning up... it was almost impossible to reconcile with the image of the gentle, efficient secretary they had all known for years.

"The level of... duplicity," Fitzwilliam murmured, shaking his head. "To maintain that facade, day after day, while planning and executing... this."

"And the intimacy of it," Chloe added, her voice barely a whisper. "Using his own thermos, something he used every day..."

"Poison has often been described as a woman's weapon," Agnes commented quietly, though without judgment, merely stating a historical observation. "Not necessarily due to physical strength, but for its reliance on access, knowledge, subtlety, and the betrayal of trust often inherent in domestic or administrative settings." She looked at her notes. "Mildred, it seems, possessed all the necessary prerequisites in abundance."

They sat in silence for a while, contemplating the confirmed reality of Mildred's actions. The intellectual satisfaction of solving the puzzle felt overshadowed now by the sheer coldness of the crime itself. They had exposed a murderer, yes, but they had also uncovered a darkness lurking beneath the sun-dappled lawns and polite rituals of their community.

"So," Fitzwilliam asked eventually, bringing them back to the present, "Davies confirmed they found evidence of the *Digitalis* preparation at her home?"

"She implied as much," Agnes confirmed. "'Materials consistent with glycoside extraction'. And they seized her computer, other documents. Combined with the financial warrants allowing access to her bank accounts…"

"They should be able to trace the funds now," Fitzwilliam nodded. "Follow the money from the club, through the phantom suppliers, and hopefully, directly back to her or accounts she controls, including potentially Eleanor Vance."

"Which provides the final, irrefutable proof of motive," Agnes concluded.

The case, it seemed, was legally solidifying, moving beyond their circumstantial findings towards the concrete evidence needed for prosecution. The immediate task of the quartet felt complete. They had navigated the maze, identified the killer, and successfully redirected the official investigation. The final accounting, it seemed, was now firmly in the hands of the justice system. But the emotional accounting, the reckoning with the betrayal and violence within their own small world, felt like it was only just beginning.

****

Tuesday, April 29th, brought a fragile calm to Agnes Plummett's study. The immediate adrenaline surge following Mildred Pettle's capture and Detective Inspector Davies's confirmation had subsided, leaving behind a profound sense of exhaustion but also an intellectual need to fully comprehend the scale and history of the deception they had uncovered. With Mildred in custody and the police actively analysing seized evidence and financial records, the quartet's role as investigators felt largely complete. Yet, the questions lingered, demanding answers not just for legal resolution, but for their own understanding of how such a betrayal could occur, undetected, for so long within their seemingly ordered world.

Fitzwilliam had returned that afternoon, bringing with him copies of the club's audited annual financial statements for the past twenty years, obtained officially now through Charles Abercrombie in his capacity as acting interim Treasurer, ostensibly for 'reviewing long-term financial health'. Ronnie had arrived shortly after, armed with his laptop and historical club attendance records for major events like the biennial Fete. Chloe joined them later, after her shift, still looking pale but no longer consumed by the immediate fear that had haunted her for days. Agnes, naturally, presided, her archival mind already sifting through the connections between past events and present revelations.

"Detective Inspector Davies confirmed the embezzlement," Fitzwilliam began, spreading several annual reports across the desk. "She didn't give specific figures, naturally, but indicated the amounts involved appear 'substantial' and the activity 'long-term', corroborating both the phantom supplier payments I identified and Agnes's theory about the Fete accounts."

"The Fete accounts," Agnes mused, retrieving her own notes on the suspiciously rounded 'Sundry Cash Donations' figures. "That always felt... wrong. Too neat. I compared the reported figures against Ronnie's analysis of estimated attendance and average spend derived from old newsletters and catering reports for those years."

Ronnie pulled up a complex spreadsheet on his laptop. "Correct. Accounting for variables like weather impact on attendance, known stall types, and average charitable spending patterns adjusted for inflation, the reported 'Sundry Cash Donations' figure exhibits a statistically improbable consistency and roundness. My model estimates a potential cumulative shortfall, or skimming margin, from just that single line item over the last five Fetes – ten years – of between $15,000 and $25,000."

Fitzwilliam whistled softly. "Fifteen to twenty-five thousand just from skimming the Fete cash? That's… significant, for a volunteer organisation."

"And likely only a fraction of the total," Agnes stated grimly. "That was probably her 'base' income, relatively low risk, easily obscured by the nature of cash handling at large events. The larger sums, I suspect, came later, through more sophisticated means."

"The phantom suppliers," Fitzwilliam nodded, pointing to his own file. "WeatherTech Roofing, Vintage Marquee Hire, Bespoke Botanical Displays. The payments made to those three entities alone in the past year, based on the internal club records I reviewed, total over $90,000. And given their highly suspicious corporate structures, it's probable little, if any, actual service was rendered, especially by WeatherTech and Vintage Marquee."

"Over ninety thousand in the last year?" Chloe gasped. "But… the roof *was* leaking, wasn't it?"

"Oh, the leak was likely real," Fitzwilliam clarified. "But was WeatherTech, the company paid a substantial sum, the one who actually *fixed* it? Or did Henderson Jr. patch it up with basic materials, while a vastly inflated invoice was submitted by the shell company and approved by Mildred, then signed off by a trusting Ainsworth? That's what the police financial investigation will now uncover by tracing the payments."

Agnes leaned forward, her gaze distant, connecting the threads back through time. "But I believe the origin lies much earlier. Back in 1987-88. The West Wing extension. The £50,000 anonymous donation that conveniently resolved the budget crisis." (*Agnes likely still thinks in pounds for sums from that era out of habit*). "The 'E. Vance' assisting Treasurer Carmichael during the final audit. The ambiguous land parcel at the 'old orchard end' – the *Pyrus Malus* land – dropping off the rate books around 1910 after Silas Croft died, its status left uncertain."

She elaborated on her theory, weaving together the historical strands. "My hypothesis," she said carefully, "is that Mildred, perhaps during her temporary role as 'E. Vance' in 1988, became aware of both the suspicious nature of the anonymous donation *and* the ambiguous status of the adjacent 'orchard end' land parcel documented in Croft's era. Perhaps she even assisted Carmichael in 'tidying up' the accounts related to both matters."

"Perhaps," Agnes continued, "she discovered that the 'orchard end' land, while legally grey, continued to generate some small, unrecorded income – maybe through informal leasing for storage, access rights for neighbours, even, as Fincham hinted, the sale of produce from remnant heritage trees or those 'medicinal herbs' he footnoted? Income that, after Croft's death and its disappearance from rate books, simply... accrued, unrecorded. Mildred, in her central administrative role with access to historical records the committees largely ignored, could have quietly managed and pocketed this small income stream for years, justifying it to herself perhaps as managing a 'problematic' club asset."

"Then," she theorised, "came the need for larger sums. Perhaps personal debts? Or simple greed? The Fete provided the perfect vehicle for laundering the historical land income and skimming additional cash. The procedural loophole Fitzwilliam identified – Mildred consolidating cash and preparing summaries signed only by the Treasurer – allowed her to consistently under-report takings, blending illicit funds with legitimate ones."

"And finally," Fitzwilliam picked up the thread, "as her needs grew, or perhaps as the Centenary Gala offered irresistible opportunities, she escalated to the phantom supplier scheme. Setting up shell companies, possibly involving Eleanor Vance wittingly or unwittingly, issuing large, fraudulent invoices for inflated or non-existent services – roof repairs, marquee hire, botanical displays. Relying on Ainsworth's trust, or his focus on petty details elsewhere, to get the payments signed off."

Ronnie nodded, inputting variables. "Evolution of fraudulent methodology. Initial exploitation of existing anomaly (land parcel income). Phase 2: Low-level skimming via systemic weakness (Fete cash handling). Phase 3: High-value fraud via fabricated entities (phantom suppliers). Increasing risk profile correlates with increasing financial extraction. Logical progression."

"But Ainsworth," Chloe murmured, "he finally noticed."

"Yes," Agnes confirmed. "Either the sheer scale of the recent supplier payments finally triggered his meticulous scrutiny, or his historical research into the land boundaries led him back to the origins of the deception – the ambiguous parcel, the Croft history, perhaps even the '87 donation. He started pulling on all the threads at once – the past and the present. He hired surveyors to get definitive proof about the land. He queried old contracts. He likely re-examined the Fete accounts with new suspicion."

"And Mildred knew," Fitzwilliam stated grimly. "She processed the surveyor invoice. She likely knew about his archival research, his questions to Abercrombie. She realised he was connecting *all* the dots, threatening to expose not just recent fraud, but potentially thirty years of deception rooted in the club's history. The exposure would mean ruin, prison. The murder became, in her calculating mind, the only way to guarantee his silence."

They sat in silence again, contemplating the sheer scale and duration of Mildred Pettle's betrayal. Decades of quiet theft, hidden behind a mask of unassuming efficiency and gentle helpfulness. Thousands, perhaps hundreds of thousands of dollars, siphoned from the very institution she purported to serve so loyally. Where had it all gone? Did Eleanor Vance share in it? Did Mildred lead a secret life funded by her embezzlement? Perhaps the police investigation, tracing the money trail through the now-accessible bank accounts, would eventually provide those answers.

For now, understanding the likely *mechanism* and *history* of the fraud felt like a necessary part of processing the resolution. It wasn't just a murder; it was the violent culmination of a lifetime of carefully managed deceit. The accounts, both financial and moral, were finally being rendered, revealing a debt far greater than anyone at the Toorak Croquet & Horticultural Society could ever have imagined. The final question lingering in Fitzwilliam's mind was how the Society itself would ever recover from such a profound breach of trust.

****

A sense of profound, weary quiet settled over Agnes Plummett's study as the details of Mildred Pettle's long deception and cold-blooded methodology sank in fully. The intellectual satisfaction of solving the complex puzzle, the adrenaline rush of the chase and the relief of Mildred's capture, now gave way to a more sombre contemplation of the human cost. Bartholomew Ainsworth was dead, murdered by someone he likely trusted implicitly. Mildred Pettle faced ruin, disgrace, and a lengthy prison sentence, the culmination of decades spent living a lie. But the ripples of her actions extended further, touching others caught innocently in the blast radius of the investigation.

Fitzwilliam swirled the last of the whisky in his glass, staring into its amber depths. "There's still the matter," he said quietly, breaking the silence, "of Harry Smythe."

Agnes nodded gravely. "Indeed. Have you heard any official word regarding his status, Alistair?"

511

"Not directly from Riley or Davies since they confirmed Mildred's arrest," Fitzwilliam admitted. "But Charles Abercrombie called me this afternoon, in his capacity as acting interim Treasurer, ostensibly to discuss handover procedures. He mentioned, very discreetly of course, that Detective Inspector Davies had informed the Club President earlier today that Lord Smythe is no longer considered a person of interest in the investigation, and that the evidence points conclusively elsewhere." He sighed. "So, officially, Harry is cleared."

"Thank goodness for that," Chloe murmured, relief evident in her voice. "Imagine if…" she trailed off, shuddering slightly at the thought of the alternative.

"Officially cleared, yes," Fitzwilliam agreed. "But the damage… ?" He looked around at the others. "The gossip mill at the club, fuelled by his own unfortunate behaviour and the initial police focus, ground exceedingly fine. Accusations, however unfounded, have a tendency to stick, especially in circles like the Society's. Will members truly accept his complete innocence? Or will there always be that lingering whisper, that 'no smoke without fire' mentality?" He thought of Harry's already precarious financial state. Reputational damage on top of that could be utterly ruinous for him socially and perhaps even professionally, however peripheral his 'investments' might be. "He was treated appallingly by many, based purely on assumption."

"People saw what fit the most convenient narrative," Agnes stated, her tone laced with disapproval. "Harry's known temper provided an easy answer, absolving others from looking deeper or examining uncomfortable truths closer to home. It demonstrates," she added, with a hint of her librarian's didacticism, "the danger of substituting prejudice for evidence." She made a small note, perhaps for her own private journal reflecting on the affair. "One hopes, for his sake, that the formal clearing by police, perhaps coupled with eventual public reporting of Mildred's trial, will be sufficient to restore his standing. But," she conceded, "social memories can be long, and mud, once thrown, is difficult to entirely wash away."

"And Major Ferguson?" Chloe asked tentatively. "His poor dahlias… and people whispering about *him* after Mrs Henderson spread that story?"

"Another victim of circumstance," Fitzwilliam sighed. "The police likely dismissed him quickly once his alibi for the crucial poisoning window was established – assuming they even investigated it thoroughly beyond Abernathy's initial report to Davies. But the club gossip…?" He shrugged helplessly. "Unless the truth about the sabotage emerges – and frankly, investigating who destroyed Ferguson's tubers seems unlikely to be a police priority now Mildred is charged with murder – some will probably always harbour suspicions, or at least remember the rumour."

"If Mildred *did* sabotage those dahlias herself," Agnes mused thoughtfully, "as a deliberate act to create misdirection and inflame the existing conflict between Ferguson and Ainsworth… it reveals another layer of her calculating cruelty. Using Ferguson's genuine passion as a tool in her own deadly game." It fitted Mildred's pattern, her ability to manipulate situations and people subtly from the background. "Perhaps," Agnes added, a flicker of determination in her eyes, "once the dust settles, *we* might discreetly ensure the committee understands the likelihood that Ferguson was doubly wronged – first by the sabotage, then by the unfounded suspicion. It's the least we can do."

Ronnie, who had been quietly inputting final parameters into his laptop, looked up. "Analysis of Collateral Impact," he announced, adjusting his glasses. "Subject Smythe: Probability of full reputation recovery within Society < 0.4 within 12 months, potentially increasing to 0.6 post-Pettle conviction/sentencing, assuming no further negative financial revelations. Subject Ferguson: Probability of full reputation recovery > 0.7, contingent on active counter-narrative dissemination regarding sabotage likelihood by Subject Pettle, otherwise residual suspicion probability remains at ~0.25." He presented his assessment with the same detached certainty he applied to astrophysics.

Fitzwilliam managed a weak smile. "Thank you, Ronnie. A sobering, if precise, forecast." He looked around the room, at the scattered notes, the charts, the evidence bags still waiting for official collection perhaps. "Beyond the individuals, though… what about the club itself? The Society?"

"Trust," Agnes stated simply. "Has been fundamentally breached. Not just by the murder, but by the scale and duration of Mildred's embezzlement, facilitated, we must admit, by decades of complacent oversight from committees and treasurers, including, it seems, Bartholomew himself in his earlier years."

"The financial hole could be significant," Fitzwilliam agreed. "Depending on how far back the fraud goes – the Fete skimming, the phantom suppliers, potentially issues linked to the historical land use… recovering any funds might be impossible if Mildred has hidden them well or already spent them. The club faces a difficult period – potentially increased subscriptions, curtailed spending, maybe even selling assets." He shuddered slightly at the thought.

"And the procedures," Chloe added. "How could this happen for so long? The way Mildred handled the Fete money, the invoices Mr Fitzwilliam found… surely things have to change?"

"New controls are essential," Fitzwilliam confirmed. "Proper segregation of duties, mandatory dual signatures on *all* payment authorisations *after* verifying supporting documentation, rigorous external audits, perhaps even term limits for key administrative roles like Secretary and Treasurer to prevent anyone accumulating unchecked power like Mildred did." He made a mental note to strongly recommend these points to Abercrombie and the Governance subcommittee.

"It will require a cultural shift," Agnes reflected sadly. "Moving away from the old 'gentlemanly trust' model towards more robust, transparent governance. Some members will resist, finding it tiresome, intrusive. But it seems undeniably necessary now." She sighed. "Mildred didn't just steal money; she stole the Society's innocence, its faith in its own integrity."

They sat in contemplative silence for a while, the relief of resolution tempered by the weight of these broader consequences. The immediate drama was over, the killer caught, their own investigation vindicated. But the fallout – personal, financial, institutional – would linger for a long time.

"Well," Fitzwilliam said finally, draining his whisky glass and standing up, feeling the deep ache of exhaustion in his bones. "At least we know the truth. And hopefully, justice will follow its course." He looked at Agnes, Ronnie, and Chloe, a newfound sense of respect and camaraderie warming him despite the grim circumstances. "We should... probably try and get some rest. It's been... quite a fortnight."

Agnes nodded. "Indeed. Though," she added, a familiar analytical gleam returning to her eyes as she glanced towards her bookshelves, "it does make one reconsider certain other long-standing anomalies in the club's historical accounts..."

Fitzwilliam groaned inwardly, but couldn't help smiling faintly. Some habits, it seemed, were harder to break than others. For now, though, one mystery was solved. The accounts for Bartholomew Ainsworth's death had finally, definitively, been rendered.

29

Loose Ends

Several days after Mildred Pettle's dramatic apprehension in the Grampians, a semblance of exhausted quiet had descended upon the quartet, but the official process was only just beginning. As predicted, Detective Inspector Davies's office had been in contact, requesting formal, recorded statements from each of them regarding their knowledge pertinent to the Ainsworth investigation. Davies, perhaps sensing the unique dynamic of the group or simply for efficiency, had agreed to conduct the interviews not at the St Kilda Road headquarters, but within the familiar, if now somewhat freighted, confines of the Toorak Croquet & Horticultural Society's library – the room where Ronnie had first seriously modelled Mildred's guilt, and where Agnes had often sought refuge in research.

It was late afternoon, perhaps a Tuesday in early May, when they gathered. Detective Inspector Davies and Detective Constable Miller arrived punctually, their demeanour entirely professional, giving away nothing of their private assessment of the situation or the quartet's unusual role in it. They set up a small digital recorder on the large mahogany reading table, the presence of the official equipment instantly transforming the comfortable, book-lined room into a formal interview setting. Davies explained the process clearly: she would interview each of them separately, focusing on their specific observations and knowledge related to Bartholomew Ainsworth, Mildred Pettle, club procedures, and any events leading up to or following the murder. The statements would be recorded, transcribed, and potentially used in future legal proceedings.

Agnes Plummett went first. Fitzwilliam, in his capacity as both a witness and Agnes's solicitor for this purpose (a role he felt ethically obliged to offer, though Agnes had waved away the need), sat in, observing quietly. Agnes, perfectly composed, recounted her knowledge with meticulous, chronological precision. She detailed her observations of Ainsworth's increasing preoccupation in the weeks before his death, his known meticulousness regarding finances, and her discovery (framed as recent archival review for Centenary purposes) of the historical ambiguities surrounding the 'old orchard end' land parcel via the Fincham text and subsequent PROV research into rate books and early surveys. She mentioned Ainsworth's withdrawn council query, presenting it as a documented fact she uncovered during related historical checks.

When Davies asked about Mildred Pettle's role and relationship with Ainsworth, Agnes responded with careful neutrality. She described Mildred's long tenure, her efficiency, her control over administrative processes and record access. She recounted Mildred's reactions (or lack thereof) during the memorial tea and her seeming lack of awareness regarding the specifics of Ainsworth's historical research when Agnes had probed. She related Esme Weatherly's report of Mildred's uncharacteristic disappearance following the police visit, framing it purely as relaying information provided by a distressed colleague regarding operational disruptions. Throughout, her narrative stuck firmly to verifiable facts or directly observed (and plausibly explained) interactions. She offered no speculation about poison, no mention of shell companies beyond what might be inferred from Ainsworth's likely financial focus, no hint of their coordinated investigation or the 'Lost Ledger' gambit. Her internal monologue, Fitzwilliam guessed, would be rigorously censoring speculation from fact, presenting only the admissible surface. Davies listened intently, occasionally asking clarifying questions about dates or document sources, Miller's pen flying across his notepad.

Fitzwilliam was next. He adopted his most formal, professional demeanour, outlining his role on the Governance subcommittee and his task of ensuring financial continuity following Ainsworth's death. He described his review of recent major expenditures – the roof repairs, the Centenary deposits. "In conducting due diligence prior to authorising ongoing payments," he stated carefully, "I noted significant procedural irregularities concerning supporting documentation and authorisation protocols for substantial payments made to several suppliers, including WeatherTech Roofing, Vintage Marquee Hire, and Bespoke Botanical Displays." He detailed the lack of proper quotes, committee minute references, and the reliance on internal memos or sign-offs seemingly originating solely from the Club Secretary, Ms Pettle.

"Furthermore," he continued, "routine public record searches via ASIC revealed concerning inconsistencies regarding the registration status, listed addresses, and directorships of these supplier entities, raising questions about their legitimacy that I felt obligated to bring to police attention." He mentioned the Vance name connection for Bespoke Botanical Displays factually, as a matter of public record requiring explanation regarding potential conflicts of interest. He then recounted finding the copy of the Melbourne Geomatics surveyor invoice amongst Ainsworth's expense claims, emphasising its date relative to the withdrawn council query and Ainsworth's death, presenting it as clear evidence of the victim's final, focused line of inquiry. Like Agnes, he offered no speculation about murder methods, confining his statement to documented financial and procedural matters he could claim to have uncovered through legitimate committee-related activities. His internal monologue, however, wrestled with the omissions – the autopsy leak, the depth of their suspicions about Mildred long before finding the invoice, the collaborative nature of their investigation. He focused on presenting a coherent, fact-based narrative that led logically towards Mildred without revealing the unorthodox path they had taken to get there.

Chloe's statement was necessarily different, focusing on her direct observations as the discoverer of the body and her knowledge of the grounds. Guided gently by Davies, she recounted finding Ainsworth, emphasising his position deep within the rhododendron bed, face down, looking somehow 'arranged' rather than naturally fallen. She described the location of the mallet nearby. She confirmed her later discovery, during routine gardening duties, of the harvested *Digitalis* leaves near the scene and the buried remnants in the compost heap, plus the glass shard near the incinerator, carefully explaining *when* and *how* she found these items, framing it as diligent observation by grounds staff. Davies asked several questions about the foxglove patch – its accessibility, who tended it, whether Chloe had noticed prior damage. Chloe answered truthfully, confirming its relative seclusion and that harvesting would require deliberate action. When asked about Mildred Pettle's gardening habits, Chloe stated truthfully that she had rarely, if ever, seen the Secretary engage in hands-on work beyond occasional deadheading near the clubhouse, and certainly not in the utility area or near Lawn 3. She did *not* mention the grey glove or the 'MP_Gardener' forum post – too speculative, too hard to explain finding without revealing their deeper probe. Her internal monologue was a mix of residual fear, the discomfort of formal police questioning, and a fierce determination to accurately report the physical evidence she *had* found.

Finally, it was Ronnie's turn. He presented himself, Fitzwilliam noted with some relief, less as an eccentric physicist and more as a concerned member with relevant analytical skills. He explained his initial interest was piqued by the apparent physical inconsistencies of the crime scene as described by witnesses. He focused his statement on quantifiable observations and logistical analysis. He recounted his timeline construction based on collating witness statements regarding Ainsworth's movements on the day of the murder. He highlighted the crucial unaccounted-for period during Ainsworth's lunch break, providing opportunity for interaction or incapacitation within the office. He described his analysis of Mildred Pettle's known routines and access privileges, concluding objectively that her position offered "optimal logistical pathways for accessing key locations (victim's office, archives, disposal sites) with minimal probability of detection compared to other individuals present at the Society." He carefully avoided presenting his more speculative probability figures or complex equations, sticking to conclusions derivable from observation of routine and access. He did not mention the lividity anomaly or alkaloid findings from the autopsy report. His contribution was framed as logical analysis of movement and opportunity, corroborating the timeline focus established by Fitzwilliam and Agnes.

As the final interview concluded late that afternoon, the quartet exchanged brief, weary glances as Detective Inspector Davies and Detective Constable Miller packed away their recording equipment. Davies offered a final, formal thank you. "Your detailed statements have been most helpful in corroborating certain lines of inquiry," she said, her expression giving little away. "We appreciate your cooperation. Naturally, this matter is now proceeding through official channels, and we rely on your continued discretion."

With a nod, the police officers departed, leaving the quartet alone again in the quiet library. They had done it. They had provided formal, documented statements supporting the case against Mildred Pettle, carefully navigating the line between revealing crucial information and concealing their own unorthodox methods. They had laid their verifiable facts before the authorities, trusting the system to connect the final dots. A sense of profound exhaustion, mixed with the fragile hope of impending justice, settled over them. The formal accounting had begun.

****

Returning to the Toorak Croquet & Horticultural Society in the weeks following Mildred Pettle's arrest felt, to Alistair Fitzwilliam, like stepping into the aftermath of a localised earthquake. The physical structure remained intact – the elegant clubhouse stood pristine, the lawns were impeccably manicured (Henderson Jr. working with grim diligence), the autumn sunlight catching the vibrant colours of the late-blooming chrysanthemums Chloe had carefully tended. But the social foundations, the bedrock of trust and assumed propriety upon which the Society had rested for over a century, felt irrevocably fractured.

The initial stunned disbelief that had greeted the news – *"Mildred Pettle? Charged with embezzlement? And... murder?"* – had given way to a confusing maelstrom of reactions: anger, betrayal, denial, morbid fascination, and endless, circular speculation. The gossip, previously focused with judgemental certainty on Harry Smythe or, briefly, Major Ferguson, now swirled relentlessly around the woman who had been the quiet, efficient centre of their world for so long.

Fitzwilliam sat on the verandah on a cool Saturday morning in mid-May, ostensibly reviewing minutes from the emergency committee meeting Charles Abercrombie had convened, but mostly observing the fractured social landscape. Small groups huddled at tables, conversations conducted in low, urgent tones that ceased abruptly if someone outside their immediate circle drew near. The usual relaxed weekend camaraderie was gone, replaced by an atmosphere of suspicion and awkwardness. Members looked at each other differently, perhaps wondering who else knew what, who else might have benefited, how such a profound deception could have gone unnoticed for so long.

He overheard snippets carried on the breeze: "…thirty years she was secretary! Thirty years! And all that time…" (This from Mrs Henderson, conveniently forgetting her earlier defence of Mildred's efficiency). "…always thought she lived very simply. Modest flat, sensible car. Where did all the money *go*?" (A pragmatic query from a retired accountant type). "…must have been that Eleanor Vance person involved, the one with the flower company? Her relative?" (Speculation seizing on the few details leaked or inferred). "…poor Bartholomew, though. Imagine finding all that out. No wonder he seemed stressed. And to think, we all just thought he was being difficult…" (A rare note of retroactive sympathy for the victim). "…but murder? Mildred? I still can't quite believe it. She always remembered my birthday…" (Lingering disbelief from a more sentimental member).

Agnes Plummett, seated nearby with a formidable stack of historical Society newsletters she claimed were needed for Centenary fact-checking, observed the same scene with her usual analytical detachment, though Fitzwilliam detected a sadness in her eyes. "The social fabric," she murmured to him during a lull, her voice low, "is remarkably resilient in some ways, yet extraordinarily fragile when core assumptions are shattered. Trust, once lost, is exceedingly difficult to restore." She saw not just gossip, but the painful re-calibration of decades of shared history, the reinterpretation of countless seemingly innocent interactions with Mildred through the dark lens of her betrayal. Every kindness Mildred had shown, every efficient act, every sympathetic word now seemed suspect, potentially manipulative.

The practical consequences were also starkly evident. Esme Weatherly looked utterly exhausted, practically living at the club as she tried desperately to manage the administrative chaos left in Mildred's wake, assisted by temporary staff hired by the Committee. Payroll had been sorted out belatedly, but caterers were demanding confirmation for future events, subscription reminders were overdue, committee minutes were unfiled, and the complex logistics Mildred had handled effortlessly now seemed like an insurmountable tangle. "Honestly, Alistair," Esme confided in Fitzwilliam during a brief coffee break, her eyes red-rimmed, "I don't know how she did it all. And now... finding out she was also... doing *that*... it's like the club's entire engine just seized." The betrayal felt personal, professional, and profoundly destabilising for those, like Esme, who had worked closely with Mildred for years.

The financial fallout was only beginning to be understood. Charles Abercrombie, looking ten years older since reluctantly assuming the interim Treasurer role, met briefly with Fitzwilliam and Agnes in the now-unoccupied Treasurer's office – a room that still seemed to hold the faint, unsettling echo of Mildred's presence.

"The auditors," Abercrombie reported grimly, gesturing towards a preliminary report lying on the desk, "have confirmed what you suspected, Fitzwilliam. Widespread irregularities. Payments to those shell companies – WeatherTech, Vintage Marquee – totalling well over ninety thousand in just the last eighteen months, with absolutely no verifiable record of services rendered beyond Mildred's internal memos or Ainsworth's sign-off on the final payment run. And the Bespoke Botanical Displays invoices... linked to Eleanor Vance... equally suspicious." He sighed heavily. "That's just the recent, obvious fraud."

He picked up another file. "Regarding the Fete accounts... the auditors agree the historical reconciliation process provided ample opportunity for skimming. Based on estimated attendances versus reported cash donations," he glanced at Agnes, acknowledging her earlier analysis shared via Fitzwilliam, "they believe a conservative estimate suggests potential losses averaging two to three thousand dollars *per Fete* for at least the last decade, possibly longer. That alone pushes the total well into six figures."

"And the historical land issue?" Agnes asked quietly.

Abercrombie shook his head. "That's... murkier. The police are investigating historical records based on your information, Agnes, and they seem convinced it provided the *original* motive and perhaps opportunity back in the eighties. But quantifying any direct financial gain Mildred derived from that ambiguous parcel over thirty years... extremely difficult. It might have been less about direct income *from* the land itself, and more about using its ambiguous status, and her unique knowledge of it, as leverage or justification for her other activities. A foundational secret that enabled everything else." He looked utterly weary. "Whatever the total, the Society is facing a significant financial hole. Insurance might cover some recent fraud, but historical losses... unlikely. We'll need emergency levies, cost-cutting... the Centenary Gala is almost certainly postponed indefinitely."

Fitzwilliam absorbed the grim news. The scale of the betrayal was breathtaking. Mildred hadn't just stolen money; she had potentially crippled the institution she pretended to serve. He thought of the members outside, still processing the shock, unaware yet of the full financial ramifications. The anger, when the true cost became known, would be immense.

Ronnie Peterson, when presented with Abercrombie's summary later, simply nodded. "Financial impact correlates with prolonged systemic vulnerability exploited by single, determined actor. Recommend immediate implementation of robust, multi-signature authorisation protocols and independent, rotating external audits." His solution was logical, clinical, necessary.

Chloe, however, felt the human cost more acutely. She saw the strain on Esme, the worry lines deepening on Abercrombie's face, the bewildered anger amongst ordinary members who had trusted Mildred implicitly. She thought of the cancelled Gala, the potential fee increases, the tarnished reputation of the club she had, despite everything, grown fond of. It felt like a violation that extended far beyond financial loss, poisoning the very atmosphere of the place.

As Fitzwilliam left the club late that afternoon, the sound of croquet balls clicking seemed less like pleasant sport and more like the ticking of a clock counting down the difficult years of recovery ahead. Mildred Pettle was in custody, the immediate threat removed. But the damage she had inflicted, financially and psychologically, would resonate through the manicured lawns and quiet corridors of the Toorak Croquet & Horticultural Society for a very long time. The accounts were only beginning to be rendered, and the true cost was proving far higher than anyone could have imagined.

****

Mid-May brought a distinct autumnal chill to Melbourne, stripping the last stubborn leaves from the plane trees lining the streets of Armadale. Inside a cosy, book-lined cafe on High Street –

deliberately chosen for its distance from the Croquet Club and its atmosphere conducive to quiet conversation – the quartet gathered for what felt like the first time since the whole affair began without an immediate, pressing investigative goal hanging over them. Mildred Pettle was securely in custody, awaiting trial. The police investigation, bolstered by the evidence seized and likely Mildred's own admissions under questioning (though details remained scarce), was proceeding through official channels. The immediate crisis was over. Yet, a sense of incompleteness lingered, a collection of unanswered questions and dangling threads that drew them together again, perhaps needing the shared space to process the ambiguities left behind.

Sunlight, weaker now but still bright, filtered through the cafe window, illuminating the steam rising from their coffee cups and the shared plate of almond croissants Fitzwilliam had insisted on ordering ("We deserve a small indulgence," he'd declared, a sentiment none of them disputed). The atmosphere was more relaxed than their previous tense meetings in Agnes's study, yet an undercurrent of thoughtfulness, of shared experience, bound them together.

"So," Fitzwilliam began, after the initial pleasantries and coffee orders were dealt with, "while the main question – the 'who' – is answered, I find myself still pondering the peripherals. Loose ends."

Agnes nodded, adjusting her spectacles. "It's inevitable in complex cases. History, much like human motivation, rarely yields all its secrets neatly." Her gaze was distant for a moment, perhaps contemplating the layers of deception they had uncovered. "Eleanor Vance, for instance. Bespoke Botanical Displays. What was her precise role in Mildred's financial machinations?"

Fitzwilliam sighed. "Still unclear, officially. My legal channels suggest police *have* interviewed Ms Vance extensively, both regarding the company and any connection to Mildred. She apparently left

Ferntree Gully for New Zealand quite abruptly around the time Mildred disappeared, you recall? Police located her there." He took a sip of his latte. "Word is, she claims complete ignorance of any fraudulent activity. Maintains 'Bespoke Botanical Displays' was a legitimate, albeit struggling, small nursery business, and that Mildred – her older cousin, she confirmed the relationship finally – occasionally directed large club floral contracts her way as 'family support', handling all the invoicing and payment processing herself 'to save Eleanor the paperwork'. Eleanor claims she simply received payments into the business account, assumed they were legitimate proceeds for vaguely described 'consultancy and large-scale planting designs', and trusted Mildred implicitly."

"Plausible deniability," Agnes murmured. "Convenient."

"Entirely," Fitzwilliam agreed. "Difficult for the prosecution to disprove without direct evidence of Eleanor receiving funds *beyond* reasonable payment for potential (even if minimal) services, or proof she actively participated in creating false invoices. Mildred, apparently, is protecting her, maintaining Eleanor knew nothing of the broader scheme. Whether that's true, or simply Mildred limiting the damage, we may never know for certain. Eleanor hasn't been charged here, though New Zealand authorities might have questions about her own tax affairs." The 'E. Vance' from 1988 remained ambiguous too – possibly Eleanor visiting, possibly Mildred using the name. Another historical detail likely lost to time.

"And the glove?" Chloe asked quietly, tracing the rim of her teacup. "The grey one I found? Did the police find its partner? Or link it to Mildred?"

Fitzwilliam shook his head. "Detective Inspector Davies never mentioned it specifically to me, and I felt pressing the point was unwise, given how Chloe officially 'found' it," he gave Chloe a brief, understanding smile. "Police likely logged it as 'item found near scene'. Without DNA linking it directly to Mildred – highly unlikely after being exposed to the elements and handled, even carefully by Chloe – or without Mildred confessing it was hers, it remains merely… anomalous. Consistent with our theory of a careful killer needing protection while handling the *Digitalis*, yes. Strongly suggestive. But not definitive proof in itself."

Chloe looked slightly disappointed, but nodded acceptance. That small piece of tangible evidence, which had felt so significant at the time, remained stubbornly mute about its owner.

"Which brings us," Agnes said thoughtfully, "to the deeper question of *why*. Beyond the obvious financial motive – the embezzlement, protecting the potentially lucrative secret of the ambiguous land parcel – was there more to it? You mentioned, Agnes," Fitzwilliam prompted, "Fincham's footnote about Silas Croft experimenting with medicinal, potentially toxic, herbs like *Atropa* on that very land."

Agnes leaned forward slightly. "Indeed. It remains the most intriguing, and perhaps permanently elusive, aspect. Did Ainsworth uncover evidence related not just to the land's ambiguous ownership or financial exploitation, but to something connected to Croft's botanical experiments? Did Mildred know of, or inherit, some dangerous knowledge related to those plants? Was the *Digitalis* merely the most convenient poison, or was there a deeper, historical resonance in using plants from that specific, contested piece of ground?" She sighed softly. "Fincham's source, Croft's own records, were noted as incomplete regarding these 'secondary pursuits'. And the relevant legal correspondence from the Croft estate at PROV, while confirming disputes over access rights, shed no further light on *why* access was disputed or what specific value, beyond potential development, that sliver of land held. We know Ainsworth found *something* there, something linked to Fincham and the boundaries, something that triggered his final actions and Mildred's fatal response. But the full nature of that secret… I suspect it died with both of them."

Ronnie, who had been listening quietly while analysing the cafe's sugar dispenser mechanism, looked up. "Insufficient data," he stated simply. "Motive Model M1 (Financial Fraud Concealment) possesses highest probability (P > 0.9) based on confirmed evidence (suppliers, accounts, land ambiguity). Motive Model M2 (Concealment of Deeper Historical/Botanical Secret) lacks verifiable data points. Remains within realm of low-probability speculation (P < 0.1) unless new evidence emerges, e.g., analysis of seized items from Pettle residence." He shrugged. "From a systemic perspective, M1 is sufficient to explain Event M (Murder)."

"Perhaps," Fitzwilliam conceded. "But human motivation is rarely purely systemic, Ronnie. Greed is powerful, yes. But thirty years of deception, culminating in poisoning and murder… it feels like it might require something deeper, some foundational secret or perceived injustice Mildred felt compelled to protect at all costs." He thought of Mildred's quiet intensity, her absolute control. What had truly driven her, beyond the money? Fear of exposure? A pathological need for control? A connection to that land, that history, that went beyond mere financial exploitation? "We may never know the full 'why,'" he concluded quietly.

"And Major Ferguson's dahlias?" Chloe asked, returning to a more grounded loose end. "Do we think Mildred really did sabotage them to create a distraction?"

Agnes considered this. "It's plausible, given her demonstrated capacity for manipulation and her need to deflect suspicion away from herself, especially if Ainsworth was already voicing concerns about her financial administration. She knew Ferguson's temperament, knew his devotion to his dahlias. Targeting them would predictably create conflict and noise centred elsewhere. But," she added, "we have no proof. It could equally have been unrelated vandalism, tragically coincidental. Another ambiguity likely to remain unresolved."

They sat in silence for a moment, contemplating these remaining pockets of uncertainty. The core crime was solved, the perpetrator facing justice. But the edges remained blurred, hinting at deeper histories, complex motivations, and collateral damage that couldn't easily be quantified or repaired. It was a reminder, Fitzwilliam thought, that even in cases with seemingly clear resolutions, the full truth often remains partially obscured, residing only in the memories, motives, and perhaps the unexpressed regrets, of those involved. Accepting that ambiguity, he realised, was part of the process, part of moving on from the intense, often obsessive, pursuit of certainty that had consumed them for weeks. The main accounts were rendered, but some lines, perhaps, would always remain slightly out of balance.

****

The late afternoon sun slanted through the large window of the Armadale cafe, casting long shadows across the polished wooden floor. The earlier bustle had subsided, leaving only a few quiet patrons lingering over empty cups and laptops. Outside on High Street, the rhythm of Melbourne preparing for the evening commute had begun – trams dinging, traffic building – a world away from the intense, contained drama that had consumed the four individuals seated around their small table for the past few weeks. The plate of almond croissants sat empty between them, the coffee cups mostly drained. A comfortable, slightly weary silence settled, different from the tense silences of their previous meetings. The immediate puzzle was solved, the lingering questions acknowledged, if not entirely answered. Now remained only the quiet processing of the aftermath.

"Well," Fitzwilliam said eventually, breaking the silence, looking around at his companions with an expression of tired but genuine respect. "We seem to have… navigated that rather extraordinary storm." He still found it slightly surreal, sitting here – a corporate lawyer – discussing murder, poison, and decades of fraud with a meticulous librarian, an eccentric physicist, and a quiet, observant gardener. Their alliance felt profoundly unlikely, forged only by the crucible of Ainsworth's death and their shared refusal to accept the easy answer.

Agnes Plummett adjusted her spectacles, her gaze thoughtful. "Indeed, Alistair. Though 'navigated' perhaps suggests more deliberate control than we sometimes possessed. Stumbled through, might be more accurate on occasion." A rare, dry smile touched her lips. "However, the outcome, ensuring the correct individual faces justice, is ultimately what matters." She thought of the club's history, now irrevocably marked by this dark chapter. Her role as archivist felt heavier now, encompassing not just records of tournaments won and committees formed, but the documentation of profound betrayal and its consequences. The truth, she reflected, was often far messier and more uncomfortable than the neat narratives preferred in official histories.

"Probability of successful outcome without collaborative input from all four nodes," Ronnie interjected, apparently having run a final mental calculation, "estimated at < 0.15. Agnes's historical/archival analysis identified foundational motive. Fitzwilliam's legal/financial scrutiny confirmed mechanism and trigger. Chloe's botanical knowledge and direct physical observation provided crucial links to means. My own logistical and timeline analysis helped constrain possibilities and validate hypotheses." He offered a small, almost shy nod. "System synergy was… optimal." For Ronnie, reducing their chaotic, dangerous investigation to successful system synergy was perhaps the highest compliment he could offer.

Chloe blushed slightly at the unexpected praise but found herself smiling genuinely for perhaps the first time since the ordeal began. "We wouldn't have got there without everyone," she said quietly but firmly. "I just found things in the garden, things I might not have even noticed if Miss Plummett hadn't been asking about history, or Mr Fitzwilliam about procedures, or Ronnie about… well, about angles and things," she finished, still slightly mystified by Ronnie's contributions but recognising their importance. She felt changed by the experience, no longer just the quiet gardener on the periphery. She had found her voice, found that her specific knowledge mattered, even amongst these formidably intelligent individuals. The club itself felt different now, its familiar routines tainted by the knowledge of what lay beneath, but her own place within it, or perhaps beyond it, felt strangely more solid.

"Hear, hear," Fitzwilliam raised his nearly empty coffee cup in a small toast. "To an unlikely, but effective, collaboration." The others raised their cups – Agnes her teacup, Chloe her water glass, Ronnie his empty espresso cup – acknowledging the sentiment with shared smiles that held relief, exhaustion, and a surprising degree of warmth.

"What happens now, though?" Chloe asked after a moment, voicing the practical question. "With Mildred, I mean? And the club?"

Fitzwilliam sighed, the lawyer returning. "Now, the official legal process takes over fully. Mildred has been charged. Given the evidence seized from her home regarding the *Digitalis*, the financial records the police now have access to via warrants showing the likely embezzlement trail to the shell companies, and potentially statements she made after apprehension… the case against her for both murder and multiple counts of fraud appears very strong." He paused. "There will be committal hearings, likely followed by a trial in the Supreme Court, though that could be many months, even a year or more, away. She might plead guilty to some charges to avoid a full trial, especially if the financial evidence is overwhelming. Hard to say. Justice," he added wearily, "moves slowly."

"And the club?" Agnes mused. "It faces a difficult period. Financially, Charles Abercrombie has a significant task stabilising the accounts and assessing the full extent of the losses. Socially… rebuilding trust will take time. There will need to be significant governance reform – the kind Bartholomew himself might have championed, ironically, had he gone about it differently." She looked thoughtful. "Perhaps this crisis, however dreadful, will ultimately force the Society to confront some long-avoided issues and become stronger, more transparent in the long run. History often works in such painful cycles."

"Probability of positive long-term systemic change following traumatic event > 0.6," Ronnie offered helpfully. "Assuming appropriate implementation of enhanced control mechanisms."

They sat for another few moments, contemplating the future. The immediate danger felt past, replaced by the slower, more bureaucratic processes of law and institutional recovery. Their own intense involvement felt like it was receding, becoming a strange, surreal chapter in their lives.

"One thing remains paramount," Agnes said finally, her gaze meeting each of theirs in turn, serious once more. "Our methods. The full extent of our investigation, the autopsy details Riley inadvertently shared, Chloe's late-night observation, my 'discovery' of the ledger reference… these details must remain strictly between ourselves. Our formal statements to Detective Inspector Davies contained only verifiable facts we could plausibly claim to know through legitimate means. Maintaining that boundary is crucial, both for the integrity of the official case against Mildred, and," she added pragmatically, "for our own peace of mind and avoidance of unnecessary complications."

Fitzwilliam nodded emphatically. "Absolutely. Our role now is simply that of witnesses, providing factual testimony based on our official statements if required at trial. Nothing more." The thought of their unorthodox methods being scrutinised in court sent a familiar wave of anxiety through him, reinforcing the need for absolute discretion.

As the cafe began to fill with the late afternoon crowd seeking coffee or an early aperitif, the quartet sensed it was time to disperse, to return to their separate lives, forever changed by the shared experience. They gathered their belongings, the easy camaraderie forged in crisis now settling into a quiet, respectful understanding.

"Well," Agnes said, adjusting her cardigan. "I imagine my Centenary brochure captions will require significant revision now." A small, wry smile played on her lips.

"I suspect Macrocorp might appreciate having my full attention again," Fitzwilliam added with a sigh, picking up his briefcase.

"My probability models for dark matter distribution require urgent re calibration," Ronnie stated, packing away his laptop.

"And I," Chloe smiled, a genuine, relieved smile this time, "have some winter pansies that desperately need planting."

They walked out into the cool, late afternoon air of High Street, pausing on the pavement. No handshakes were needed, no effusive farewells. A simple nod, a shared look, acknowledging the unique, unlikely bond they had formed. They had faced down secrets, lies, and murder together, armed with history books, physics equations, gardening tools, and legal knowledge. They had prevailed. As they turned to go their separate ways – Agnes towards the tram stop, Fitzwilliam towards his car, Ronnie towards the train station, Chloe towards her bike – there was a quiet understanding. Should the need ever arise again, should darkness stir beneath the polite surface of Melbourne society, this unlikely quartet knew, without needing to say it, that they could rely on each other. For now, though, it was time for peace, routine, and perhaps, finally, a good night's sleep.

30

Beyond the Boundary

The jacaranda trees lining the entrance drive of the Toorak Croquet & Horticultural Society were in full, almost extravagant, bloom, showering the impeccably maintained gravel with drifts of vibrant purple blossom. It was late October 2025, six months since the dark events that had culminated in Mildred Pettle's arrest, and Melbourne was embracing spring with its characteristic fervour. Inside the club grounds, the superficial signs pointed towards recovery and a determined return to normalcy. Croquet matches were in full swing under the warm sun, the click of balls echoing across lawns restored to their usual emerald perfection. Preparations were underway, albeit on a more modest scale than originally planned, for a combined end-of-year celebration and deferred Centenary acknowledgement.

Yet, for Agnes Plummett, observing the scene from her customary verandah chair while ostensibly reviewing draft proofs for the much-delayed (and significantly rewritten) Centenary brochure, the changes ran deeper than the seasonal shift. The easy confidence, the almost unconscious assumption of inviolable order that had once defined the Society, felt subtly but permanently altered. There was a new diligence in the air, bordering sometimes on anxious formality.

She watched Charles Abercrombie, looking considerably more burdened than he had six months ago but carrying his interim Treasurer duties with grim determination, conferring earnestly with the club's newly appointed external auditor in the lounge. Later, she saw him posting meticulously detailed quarterly financial summaries on the main noticeboard – an unprecedented level of transparency mandated by the emergency committee meetings held over winter. Whispers suggested the full extent of Mildred's embezzlement, carefully unravelled by forensic accountants reviewing decades of records seized by police, ran well into six figures, possibly significantly more if the historical exploitation of the 'old orchard end' land could be quantified. The emergency levy imposed on members had been steep, causing resentment but also forcing a collective reckoning with the lax oversight that had allowed the deception to flourish for so long. Governance reform, Fitzwilliam reported with quiet satisfaction from his subcommittee meetings, was proceeding, albeit against some predictable resistance from members who found the new multi-signature protocols and detailed reporting requirements 'rather tiresome'.

Esme Weatherly still bustled about, overseeing catering and coordinating volunteers, but the ordeal had etched new lines onto her face. She was quieter now, less prone to cheerful gossip, her interactions marked by a careful professionalism that lacked its former warmth. Agnes knew Esme had been deeply wounded by Mildred's betrayal, questioning her own judgment, her own failure to notice anything amiss despite working closely with Mildred for over fifteen years. The police had quickly cleared Esme of any complicity, recognising her as another victim of Mildred's manipulation, but the experience had clearly left its mark. The administrative burden, now handled with strict adherence to new protocols and assisted only by limited part-time help (the club couldn't yet afford a full replacement for Mildred), was immense, but Esme soldiered on, a symbol, perhaps, of the club's own bruised but resilient spirit.

Even the physical landscape held reminders. Lawn 3, where Ainsworth's body had been found, was back in regular use, but Agnes noticed players still sometimes paused near the rhododendron bed bordering the 'old orchard end', their gazes thoughtful or perhaps just morbidly curious. The *Digitalis purpurea* plants, the foxgloves, were long past their flowering season now, their tall spikes replaced by developing seed heads. Chloe had reported no further signs of disturbance after her initial discovery of the harvested leaves and buried waste, and the police forensic team had apparently recovered sufficient trace evidence from Mildred's residence to confirm the *Digitalis* connection without needing extensive further investigation of the plants themselves. Yet, their presence remained a quiet, potent symbol of the danger that had lurked beneath the garden's beauty.

Agnes sighed softly, turning a page of the Centenary brochure proof. Rewriting the club's history to acknowledge this dark chapter, while still celebrating its legacy, had been a delicate balancing act. How did one accurately record the contributions of a long-serving Secretary who was also a thief and a murderer? How did one address the financial discrepancies without descending into recrimination or explicit detail pending the trial outcome? She had opted for careful phrasing, acknowledging 'past administrative irregularities recently brought to light' and emphasising the club's 'renewed commitment to transparent governance', hoping it struck the right balance between honesty and discretion. The full story, she knew would likely only be told through court records and the lingering whispers of club lore.

The club was surviving. It was adapting. It was implementing changes designed to prevent such a betrayal from happening again. But the sense of inviolability, the comfortable assumption of propriety that had defined it for so long, was gone. A boundary had been crossed, Agnes reflected, not just on an old survey map, but within the collective consciousness of the Society itself. And navigating the landscape beyond that boundary would be the club's ongoing challenge. The jacaranda blossoms might fall, the seasons turn, but the memory of Mildred Pettle, and the dark secrets she had so carefully tended, would cast a long shadow for years to come.

****

Later that same bright spring morning, Alistair Fitzwilliam joined Agnes Plummett on the verandah, accepting a cup of tea from the service trolley Esme Weatherly managed with her now customary quiet efficiency. The intensity of the main finals day was replaced by the more relaxed rhythm of weekend social play. On Lawn 2, a social doubles match was underway, and Fitzwilliam's gaze was immediately drawn to one of the participants: Lord Harrington 'Harry' Smythe.

Seeing Harry back on the lawns, mallet in hand, felt both normal and profoundly strange. Six months ago, he had been the club pariah, the prime suspect, consumed by a panic Fitzwilliam now knew stemmed from financial desperation rather than murderous guilt. The police had formally cleared him weeks after Mildred Pettle's arrest, a fact communicated discreetly but firmly to the Society Committee by DI Davies herself. Yet, watching him now, Fitzwilliam could see the ordeal had left indelible marks.

Harry's flamboyant style seemed deliberately muted. He wore standard club whites, foregoing the colourful cravats and patterned blazers that had once been his signature. His movements were less expansive, less theatrical. When his partner, a nervous Mrs Albright who seemed determinedly focused on her own shots, made a tactical error, Harry offered only a brief, tight-lipped grimace, a stark contrast to the booming remonstration he might have unleashed in the past. He executed his own shots with competence, but without flair, his usual risky jump shots replaced by more conservative positional play. He looked thinner, Fitzwilliam thought, and the network of fine lines around his eyes seemed deeper, his complexion less ruddy, more sallow.

The reaction of other members was equally telling. While his partner and opponents maintained a surface politeness during the game, the usual easy banter between shots was absent. Spectators on the verandah offered only brief, slightly strained greetings if their eyes happened to meet Harry's. There was no open hostility, but there was a distinct lack of warmth, a lingering awkwardness, a social exclusion zone still subtly in effect. Mrs Henderson, Fitzwilliam noted with grim satisfaction, pointedly turned her back when Harry walked nearby to retrieve an errant ball.

"He carries it heavily," Fitzwilliam murmured to Agnes, nodding towards Lawn 2.

Agnes followed his gaze, her expression thoughtful. "Understandably. To be suspected of murder, to face financial ruin concurrently... it would test the resilience of far stronger characters than Lord Smythe." She had little personal sympathy for Harry's previous arrogance or financial imprudence, but she possessed a strong sense of fairness. "The police exoneration was official, but social exoneration operates under different, often less rational, principles. Reputations, once tarnished, are like delicate porcelain – easily cracked, exceedingly difficult to restore perfectly."

Fitzwilliam sighed. "I still feel a degree of... responsibility. Our initial focus, mirroring the police's, inevitably contributed to the suspicion directed towards him."

"We followed the evidence available at the time, Alistair," Agnes countered reasonably. "His behaviour *was* suspicious, his connection to the weapon undeniable. It was only through pursuing the inconsistencies, the anomalies *we* noticed, that the focus shifted correctly. We arguably *prevented* a far greater injustice." Yet, Fitzwilliam knew the 'what ifs' would linger. What if they hadn't looked deeper? What if Mildred hadn't made that crucial slip in accessing the archives? Harry Smythe might well be facing trial himself right now. The thought was sobering. He watched Harry execute a clean roquet shot, then pause, seemingly uncertain about his next move, a picture of diminished confidence.

Their attention then shifted towards the western boundary, where the infamous 'old orchard end' lay bathed in sunlight. Major Ferguson was there, kneeling beside rows of triumphant-looking dahlias, their blooms enormous globes of vibrant colour – crimson, gold, apricot, deep purple. He was meticulously tying prize specimens to sturdy stakes, his movements economical, utterly absorbed in his task.

Unlike Harry Smythe, Major Ferguson seemed largely restored in the eyes of the club, Agnes observed. Several members strolled over to admire the display, offering genuine compliments which Ferguson received with his customary gruff nod, though perhaps with slightly less overt hostility than usual. The narrative surrounding him had subtly shifted after Mildred's arrest. He was now seen primarily as a victim – a victim of Ainsworth's provocative boundary marking, a potential victim of Mildred's sabotage (a theory now widely, if unproveably, accepted within the club gossip), and a victim of unfounded speculation. His single-minded devotion to his dahlias, once seen as mere eccentricity, now appeared almost as heroic resilience.

"The Major, at least, seems to have found solace," Fitzwilliam remarked.

"His dahlias are his sanctuary," Agnes agreed. "And perhaps there is a certain justice in that. He defended his small patch of territory with disproportionate passion, yes, but ultimately, he was wronged by both Ainsworth *and* Mildred, it seems. The club owes him an apology, though I doubt he'd accept one." She watched as he carefully removed a single yellowed leaf from a perfect crimson bloom, his focus absolute. "He operates within his own boundaries, largely impervious to the social currents that buffet poor Harry."

Yet, even Ferguson's apparent recovery held complexities. The dahlia sabotage remained officially unsolved. While Mildred was the overwhelmingly likely culprit, seeking to inflame the conflict as misdirection, there was no proof. A small, lingering question mark. And the boundary dispute itself, Agnes knew from her research and Abercrombie's committee updates, remained a quiet administrative headache. The historical ambiguity was real. While Ainsworth's aggressive approach had been disastrous, the underlying issue of clarifying the precise legal status of that 'old orchard end' parcel, potentially exploited by Mildred for decades, still needed formal resolution through council negotiation or potentially even the Land Titles Office – a slow, unglamorous process compared to the drama of the murder investigation.

Fitzwilliam followed her gaze towards the disputed area near Lawn 3, now simply part of the extended garden bed. "Any further progress on clarifying that boundary officially?"

Agnes shook her head. "Slowly. Committees move at their own pace, especially when potentially complex historical title issues are involved. Charles Abercrombie is liaising with the council, armed with the PROV records I provided. But," she sighed, "resolving century-old surveying ambiguities isn't a priority for anyone except, perhaps, obsessive historians. And the person who likely understood its true significance and potential value better than anyone," she added grimly, "is currently awaiting trial and unlikely to be forthcoming."

They watched Harry Smythe complete his game on Lawn 2 – he and Mrs Albright lost decisively – and retreat towards the bar, acknowledging few greetings. Then they watched Major Ferguson stand up, surveying his dahlia ranks with fierce, proprietary pride before packing up his tools. Two men, caught on the periphery of a murder, their lives irrevocably altered, navigating the aftermath in starkly different ways.

"It underscores the collateral damage, doesn't it?" Fitzwilliam mused quietly. "Beyond Ainsworth's death, beyond the club's financial losses… the suspicion, the gossip, the disruption to individual lives. Mildred Pettle's actions cast a very long shadow indeed."

Agnes nodded, her expression sombre. "As history consistently demonstrates, Alistair. The consequences of profound betrayal ripple outwards, often touching shores far removed from the initial crime." She picked up her copy of *The Age*, folding it neatly. The sun shone, the flowers bloomed, the croquet balls clicked reassuringly across the lawns. But the quiet understanding between Agnes and Fitzwilliam, grounded in the knowledge they shared, acknowledged the complex, often unfair, and enduring legacy of the darkness they had helped bring to light. Some accounts, they both knew, could never be fully balanced.

****

Late November in Melbourne brought with it the promise of summer – longer days, warmer breezes carrying the scent of blooming jasmine and ripening figs, and the festive buzz beginning to build towards Christmas. Seven months had passed since the arrest of Mildred Pettle, seven months during which the initial shockwaves at the Toorak Croquet & Horticultural Society had gradually subsided into the complex, often uncomfortable, process of financial reckoning and tentative social readjustment.

The quartet chose the familiar Armadale cafe for what felt like a final, informal debrief. The intense, almost daily communication of their investigation phase had naturally lessened as life returned to its usual rhythms, but the unique bond forged between them remained. They met now not as co-conspirators driven by urgent necessity, but as companions sharing a profound, defining experience. The atmosphere was relaxed, tinged perhaps with a faint melancholy, like rereading the final pages of a gripping but ultimately tragic book.

"So," Agnes Plummett began, after they had settled with coffees and a shared plate of miniature pastries, "the committal hearing concluded last week, I understand? Any developments, Alistair?"

Fitzwilliam nodded, stirring his cappuccino thoughtfully. "As expected, Mildred was committed to stand trial in the Supreme Court. Dates haven't been finalized, likely mid-next year given the court backlogs and complexity." He sighed. "Her defence, it seems, will be... predictable. She's apparently entered a plea of 'guilty' to multiple counts of obtaining financial advantage by deception – essentially admitting the embezzlement, likely hoping for some leniency by owning up to the provable financial crimes."

"But not the murder?" Chloe asked, her voice hushed.

"No," Fitzwilliam confirmed grimly. "A firm 'not guilty' plea to the charge of murdering Bartholomew Ainsworth. Her counsel will argue, presumably, that while she admits financial impropriety, Ainsworth's death was entirely unrelated – either committed by Smythe in a rage as initially suspected, or by persons unknown perhaps linked to that 'property dispute' red herring she planted, or even," he grimaced, "an unfortunate accident potentially exacerbated by his own stress or underlying health conditions. They will likely attempt to discredit the poisoning evidence as circumstantial or inconclusive, focusing solely on the blunt force trauma finding from the preliminary autopsy."

"A difficult defence, given the VIFM's final report confirmed significant levels of *Digitalis* glycosides, and the evidence of the harvested plants and her attempts to access archives," Agnes observed coolly. "But not impossible, if she maintains her composure and refuses to elaborate on her movements or motives beyond the admitted financial stress."

"Exactly," Fitzwilliam agreed. "The prosecution's case for murder remains strong circumstantially, especially with the motive established by the fraud and Ainsworth's investigation into it, but without a direct confession or witness to the poisoning/staging itself, there's always an element of uncertainty in a jury trial." He felt a familiar lawyerly frustration with the gap between knowing the truth and proving it beyond all reasonable doubt within the strictures of the legal system.

"And Eleanor Vance?" Agnes inquired. "Mildred's cousin?"

"Still in New Zealand, as far as I know," Fitzwilliam reported. "She apparently cooperated with Victoria Police inquiries to a limited extent via remote interview, sticking firmly to her story of being an unwitting recipient of Mildred's 'help' with invoicing. Police likely concluded there wasn't sufficient evidence to extradite her or pursue major charges here, though she may face scrutiny from NZ authorities regarding her own business accounts eventually. Another loose end Mildred likely cut adrift to protect herself." It felt unsatisfactory, leaving Vance's true level of complicity ambiguous, but Fitzwilliam knew legal realities often fell short of complete resolution.

"What about the glove?" Chloe asked, voicing one of the tangible mysteries that still bothered her. "Did the police forensic report mention anything?"

"Nothing conclusive," Fitzwilliam sighed. "Trace DNA was too degraded or mixed for a reliable match. Fibres consistent with *Digitalis* leaves were apparently found, corroborating its likely use in handling the plants, but that doesn't identify the owner. Unless Mildred mentioned it in her interviews – which seems highly unlikely – it remains simply 'Exhibit A', found near the scene. Suggestive, yes. Proof, no." He saw Chloe's slight disappointment. "Some things," he added gently, "just remain frustratingly unanswered."

Agnes nodded thoughtfully. "Which perhaps also applies to Mildred's ultimate, underlying motivation. We understand the trigger – Ainsworth's imminent exposure of her decades of fraud, rooted perhaps in that historical land ambiguity near the 'old orchard end'. But *why* did she start down that path in the first place, all those years ago? Was it purely greed? Or something more complex? That footnote in Fincham about Silas Croft's medicinal herb experiments... the legal disputes over access rights after his death... did Mildred stumble upon something more than just financial opportunity? A family secret connected to Croft, perhaps? A reason beyond money to control that specific piece of land so fiercely?" She gazed out the window, lost in historical speculation for a moment. "Her refusal to confess fully, even regarding the finances initially, suggests someone protecting more than just herself."

Ronnie, who had been calculating the thermal efficiency of the cafe's espresso machine on a napkin, looked up. "Motive analysis remains complex," he conceded. "Primary driver P(Financial) confirmed high. Secondary drivers P(Historical Secret), P(Personal Compulsion/Psychology) remain within low-probability speculative domain due to data sparsity. Impossible to resolve definitively without Subject P's complete and truthful testimony, an event currently assessed as $P < 0.05$." He shrugged, accepting the limits of his models when faced with the irreducible complexity of human nature.

"And Major Ferguson's dahlias?" Chloe added the final unanswered question. "Will we ever know if Mildred really did sabotage them?"

"Probably not," Agnes admitted with a small sigh. "Unless she confesses it as part of some plea bargain, which seems unlikely given its relative insignificance compared to murder and major fraud. It will remain another piece of collateral damage, another minor injustice likely attributed, unfairly perhaps, to neighbourhood vandals or Ainsworth's own provocative behaviour."

They sat in comfortable silence for a moment, acknowledging these lingering ambiguities. The central truth was known, justice was progressing, but the full picture, particularly the deeper motivations and minor cruelties surrounding the core crime, remained partially obscured.

"It's not like the books, is it?" Chloe said eventually, voicing a thought perhaps shared by them all. "Where everything is neatly explained in the final chapter, every loose end tied up."

"No, Chloe," Agnes replied gently. "Real life, unlike carefully constructed fiction, rarely offers such tidy conclusions. There are always shadows, ambiguities, unanswered questions. Perhaps the most important thing is that we uncovered *enough* of the truth to prevent a greater injustice, both to Bartholomew Ainsworth – however difficult he may have been – and certainly to poor Harry Smythe."

Fitzwilliam raised his cup. "I'll drink to that," he said quietly. "To uncovering enough."

They all raised their cups, a silent toast not just to the resolution achieved, but perhaps also to their shared acceptance of the mysteries that remained, forever filed away in the complex, often inaccessible, archives of human secrets.

****

The late afternoon sun, now lower in the sky, cast long, warm shadows across the polished floorboards of the Armadale cafe. The lingering scent of coffee and toasted almonds hung in the air. Their conversation, having navigated the shoals of unanswered questions and lingering ambiguities, finally arrived in a quiet harbour of mutual understanding. The waitress discreetly cleared their empty cups and pastry plate, leaving them in the comfortable silence that can exist between people who have weathered something significant together.

"Well," Fitzwilliam said eventually, breaking the quiet, a warmth in his voice that would have surprised his Collins Street colleagues. He looked around the table at his companions, this most improbable alliance forged in the shadow of murder. "I must confess, when this all began... when I found myself discussing forensic botany and historical land titles over lukewarm tea at the club... I never imagined..." He trailed off, shaking his head slightly with a wry smile. "It has been... quite the education."

Agnes offered a rare, genuine smile in return. "Indeed, Alistair. A potent reminder that truth often lies not in a single discipline, but at the intersection of many. Your legal rigour, Ronnie's scientific analysis, Chloe's grounded observation... each provided a lens the others lacked. Without that combination," she acknowledged, "I doubt we would have seen past the convenient narrative surrounding Lord Smythe." Her gaze held a newfound respect, acknowledging the value not just of historical records, but of collaboration across different ways of thinking. The experience had broadened her perspective, forcing her to connect her archival knowledge to tangible, present-day consequences in a way she hadn't anticipated.

"System synergy achieved optimal outcome despite high initial noise levels and data scarcity," Ronnie confirmed, pushing his glasses up his nose. He consulted his mental models one last time. "Analysis indicates the collaborative probability of success was approximately 8.7 times higher than any individual investigative vector operating in isolation." He paused, then added, with what might have been a flicker of unscientific sentiment, "The human variable, while introducing significant unpredictability, also provided... unexpected positive correlations in this instance." Even for Ronnie, the experience seemed to have re calibrated some internal equations about the value of less quantifiable inputs.

Chloe looked down at her hands, then met their gazes, a quiet confidence in her eyes that hadn't been there six months ago. "I mostly just... noticed things," she said simply. "But you all listened. You took what I saw seriously, even when it just seemed like small details about plants or footprints." She smiled. "It taught me that sometimes the smallest things *are* the most important. And," she added, "that even when things seem terrifying, working together makes it... manageable." The fear hadn't entirely vanished – the memory of Mildred's watchful eyes still sent a shiver down her spine occasionally – but it was now overlaid with a sense of achievement, of having faced down danger and emerged stronger, thanks in large part to the unlikely support of the three people seated around this table.

"To us, then," Fitzwilliam said, raising his water glass. "The most unlikely, and I daresay, most effective, unofficial investigative committee the Toorak Croquet & Horticultural Society has ever seen. May our future involvement be confined strictly to governance subcommittees and spectating."

They murmured agreement, touching their glasses together – water, tea, empty espresso cup – a quiet salute to their shared ordeal and unlikely success.

The conversation turned briefly to the future. Mildred Pettle's trial was months away, a slow legal process they would observe only as required witnesses. Eleanor Vance remained in New Zealand, her true complicity likely forever obscured. The club itself faced a long road of financial recovery and rebuilding trust under Abercrombie's steady, if uninspired, leadership. Harry Smythe continued his subdued existence, Ferguson his dahlia devotion. Life, disrupted so violently, was slowly finding its new, altered course.

"Will you… will you all remain members?" Chloe asked tentatively, voicing a question perhaps hovering in all their minds.

Fitzwilliam considered it. The club now held associations far removed from gentle exercise and polite conversation. Yet… "Yes," he said surprising himself slightly. "I believe so. Perhaps now more than ever. Good governance requires vigilance, after all." He felt a reluctant sense of duty, a need to ensure the lessons learned weren't forgotten.

"The archives require ongoing curation," Agnes stated simply, implying her own continued presence was non-negotiable. History, including its recent dark chapter, needed tending.

Ronnie shrugged. "Lawn gradients remain sub optimal, but empirically interesting. And the tea," he added, perhaps remembering Mildred's consistently adequate, if uninspired, offerings, "could potentially improve under new administrative oversight. Worth monitoring."

Chloe smiled. "Someone needs to look after the roses," she said. Perhaps she too felt a lingering connection, a responsibility to the place where this strange journey began.

As the waitress approached with the bill, Fitzwilliam reached for it automatically, waving away Agnes's protest. "My treat," he insisted firmly. "Consider it… consultancy fees."

They gathered their belongings, the easy silence returning as they stepped out of the warm cafe into the cool, bright air of the late Melbourne spring afternoon. The scent of blossoms hung in the air, the city traffic hummed with familiar energy. Normality. Yet, they all knew something had shifted irrevocably within themselves, within their perception of the seemingly placid surface of their world.

They paused on the pavement. No grand farewells were necessary.

"Well," Agnes said, offering a polite nod. "Until the next committee meeting, Alistair. Ronnie. Chloe, my dear, do let me know how the new climbing rose variety performs."

"Of course, Miss Plummett," Chloe smiled.

"Indeed," Fitzwilliam agreed. "My best to you all."

"Maintain optimal data integrity," Ronnie advised, adjusting his glasses, before turning towards the train station.

Agnes headed towards the tram stop. Chloe unlocked her bicycle chained to a nearby post. Fitzwilliam walked towards his parked car. They dispersed back into their separate lives, carrying the shared weight and quiet understanding of their experience. They had looked beyond the manicured boundary of polite society and confronted the darkness hidden within. They had navigated ambiguity, faced down fear, and, through their unique collaboration, unearthed a difficult truth. Justice, however imperfectly, was being served. And perhaps, Fitzwilliam thought as he started his car, that was the most important account rendered of all. He drove away, leaving the quiet Armadale street behind, but carrying the memory of the unlikely quartet, forever bound by the secrets they had shared and the most improper end they had, together, brought to light.

552

of the unlikely quartet, forever bound by the secrets they had shared and the most improper end they had, together, brought to light.